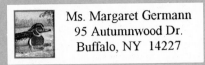

David William Ross

EYE of the HAWK

SIMON & SCHUSTER

New York   London   Toronto   Sydney   Tokyo   Singapore

SIMON & SCHUSTER
Simon & Schuster Building
Rockefeller Center
1230 Avenue of the Americas
New York, NY 10020

SIMON & SCHUSTER and colophon are registered trademarks
of Simon & Schuster Inc.

Designed by Karolina Harris
Manufactured in the United States of America

1   3   5   7   9   10   8   6   4   2

Library of Congress Cataloging-in-Publication Data
Ross, David William, date
Eye of the hawk / David William Ross.
p.   cm.
1. Texas—History—1846-1950—Fiction. I. Title.
PS3568.084318E94   1992
813'.54—dc20   92-3567
CIP

ISBN: 0-671-75513-7

To Helena

and a love more faithful than the sun

Contents

Many hope to avoid their destiny
like fieldmice darting in
unsuspected moments from cover,
belatedly discovering fate is
an Argus-eyed hawk.

—ANON

Part One

Medina County, Texas

November 1841

1

Had she not been watching heat lightning flashing along the horizon behind the low hills marking the course of the creek, she never would have seen them. But she knew at once they were Comanches. She knew by the effortless way they sat their ponies and the terrible horned headgear she could see outlined against the fading sky. Their dusky figures were coming forward slowly, revealing they knew she was alone with only Inez and the baby, the menfolk all away.

Her first thought was for her child, Jason. Just one year old and now fast asleep. "Inez!" She had to struggle to keep herself from screaming. The young Mexican girl came quickly from the small kitchen bay off the main room, her dark startled eyes acknowledging she had heard the terror in Isabelle's voice. "Quick, take Jason. Hide him in the well pit under the hut. Keep that blanket around him. Inez, please! Hurry!"

Inez rolled the baby in the blanket and slipped out the narrow kitchen doorway, latching it firmly behind her. The night seemed full of eyes as she scampered the hundred feet to the adobe hut she shared with Carlos. There was a half-dug well pit in the corner of their only room. She put the sleeping baby into it softly and pulled the thick straw ticking over. Breathlessly she turned to rush back to the house. As she started to run across the coarse earth, lifting her skirts to free her legs, a hand suddenly came out of the near darkness to grab the thickly braided lock of dark hair that ran down her slender, graceful back. A vicious jerk pulled her off her feet and she found herself lying on the still-warm earth staring up at the garishly painted faces of two Comanche braves. Slowly they knelt and pressed her back upon the ground, their rough hands pulling at her skirts and probing her slim body.

Isabelle ignored the rifle hanging by the door, realizing at once it was worse than useless. Even if she could manage it she could kill only one, and then surely the others would put them all to excruciating deaths. For a moment she wondered if she could bribe them, giving them Seth's remaining horses still in the corral, but her heart froze as she realized they knew the horses were already theirs. She had heard what Comanches did to white women taken alive, and the thought of killing herself swept through her mind. But there was Jason. And where was Inez? A heavy gun stock slammed against the barred door several times before a hatchet slowly started chopping at the wooden frame that held the door. Each stroke seemed louder than the last, until finally the frame split and the door, groaning on its makeshift hinges, sagged open.

Still clutching their weapons, they pushed into the house, the dung that dressed their matted hair assaulting her nostrils. She stood there frozen as they sullenly circled her, striking her table and cupboard with their hatchets, smashing her heirloom mirror as they went by. Their faces were covered with red and white dabs of buffalo grease, their breaths heavy and foul as spoiled meat. One, the tallest, who seemed to be the leader, took the rifle from the wall and grunted at its long, polished barrel. Another opened the drawers where the kitchen utensils were kept and slowly stuck her three long bone-handled knives into the carving board; a third started pulling clothes from their single cedar chest. Two small oil lamps threw their jumping shadows against the plank walls as one broke the hasp on a little trunk where mementos from the East and their small amounts of money were kept. He turned the trunk over and emptied it. Everything fragile was smashed, but little attention was paid to the thin roll of money.

Then they started muttering to each other and she felt a dryness in her mouth as she knew they were turning to her. The leader's eyes were already fixed on her bright blond hair tied into a neat bun with a strip of black ribbon. He put his hand up and grabbed her hair, then with a quick movement of his knife he cut the ribbon loose and her hair fell out in a long golden spray. Now his hand, still holding the knife, twisted itself into her hair and forced her head back while his other hand grabbed at her open blouse and ripped it down to her waist. She started to scream as she felt hands on her breasts, but one of them struck her temple with the handle of his hatchet and she fell back stunned. She could feel them cutting through and pulling off her clothes and within moments they had her naked and spread out on the floor. She felt the weight of the tall one on her body and knew he was forcing himself into her while the others were kneeling down, grasping at her flaxen hair and grunting lustily as they waited their turn. She caught sight of one of them holding her large bone-handled carving knife, hinting what would follow her rape. Feeling an unbearable pain as the second one raping her started pressing something hard and sharp against her quivering stomach, she heard an ungodly shriek somewhere in the night. Only then did she mercifully faint.

Brandy knew something was wrong. Even from a distance he could see that the shaggy painted ponies in the yard had the rough-cut look of wild mustangs; they were not the taller, smoother stock with Kentucky blood bred so carefully by Seth. "Lordy, lordy," he mumbled to himself as he pressed his mount into a cluster of trees and dismounted to run to the top of the rise. "Injuns! God A'mighty!" Flattening himself to the ground, he could see only one staying with the horses, but there were five empty mounts. The smooth but firm features on his mulatto face sunk deeper into the grass as he realized they were Comanches. He carried only the pistol with the single charge, and he would have to get a lot closer to make sure even that one counted. He was no match for that many. Then his eye caught movement crossing the yard. It was Inez. She was running back to the house. Suddenly she stopped and seemed to fall, but as he lifted his head he could see that two figures had pulled her down and were pressing her to the ground. There was still enough light, even without the flashes of lightning, to see that they had started ripping off her clothes, were pressing her legs apart, beginning to rape her. Now he would have to go down. There was no other way. Seth had left for San Antonio to join the ranging company forming there—as if that man hadn't had enough of fighting—and Carlos was delivering horses to the militia at Porcupine Creek. He himself had just ridden the eight miles to the neighboring MacFee ranch, which kept a milk cow, to fetch some fresh milk for little Jason. He found himself shaking as he faced the thought of torture and death, but he had seen the bodies of women after Comanches were through with them and the thought of Isabelle and Inez with their bellies and breasts slit open, their scalps torn from their heads and their features mutilated beyond recognition made him hurry to his feet. He would ride down and attack the two in the yard. He avoided thinking about the other three that must be in the house. A man had to die somehow, and he, son of a slave woman and a crude Creole overseer, could think of no better way to meet Lord Jesus than defending folks who had given him his freedom and treated him as one of their own.

At his horse again, he unstrapped the skin container of milk that hung from the saddle horn and ran his mount up to the rise. Here he could see Inez still pinned to the ground with one of the thick forms steadily pumping over her. He placed one foot into the stirrup and raised himself up in the saddle, but at that moment his eye caught something that made him rein in suddenly and slip slowly back again to earth.

Beyond the house was a knoll that rose before the woods that ran back to the creek. In a flash of lightning he saw that the knoll was covered with silent mounted figures that even in the poor light he knew were not whites, and when a multitude of turbans and head-bands began to appear against the skyline he knew they were not Mexicans. They had already quietly started making their way down to surround the house. His breath stopped as he realized there were as many as thirty or more. He could readily see their movements from his vantage point on the rise, but he knew the Comanche sentinel holding the horses could not. Stunned by the sight, he could not take his eyes off that lone Comanche as they closed in. Surely he must see them, surely he must shout an alarm. But no, the Comanche seemed to be listening to sounds rising from the house, his eyes fixed on the open door. He sat there statuelike, not seeing the figures coming behind him until a lariat snaked out of the near darkness and fell about his neck. Then he let loose a spine-chilling shriek as it yanked him with its death grip from his horse.

The Mexicans who enjoyed an illicit traffic with him along the border called him Joachim, but his Apache name was Snake. He was a large man with almost sad eyes, but his body was blocky and firm and his strength prodigious. He sat with his band of Mescaleros, along with a few Jicarrilas and Lipans who were among the last of those decimated tribes. They had come from Chihuahua, from their hidden camp in the Sierra Madre, and they had come to kill Comanches. They would not have come for their long-smoldering revenge alone; Snake had taught them to do it for a profit. No white man could ever understand the enmity that existed between these two native peoples. A ferocious war of no quarter that had exterminated whole bands and even tribes had dragged through a bloody century. Multitudes of Apaches had died or fled their homelands forever. The Comanches, with their awesome horsemanship and their thirst for war, had proved invincible, and when joined by the fierce, some said blood-crazed, Kiowas, they ruled over thousands of miles of country that only the courageous Utes or Osages dared in rare moments to tread upon.

But Snake, watching from his mountains, had learned something about Comanches that appealed to his sinister talents. The Comanches had a long tradition of raiding deep into Mexico, sometimes hundreds of miles, where resistance to their savage, predatory attacks was weak or nonexistent. There they would collect booty and captives, the latter to be killed, enslaved or ransomed by the civil authorities in New Mexico. But on their return, once across the Rio Grande, they would split up into small parties, each going off with its share of booty and captives to make winter camp.

These small parties Snake had learned to ambush, keeping the booty and earning some pesos sending the captives into peonage through money-hungry authorities in Chihuahua. This was dangerous work, but two things made Snake's success possible. The first and clearly the most significant was the arrogance of the Comanches. They did not believe an enemy, particularly one so decisively beaten and craven in defeat, would dare enter their hunting range. Second, Snake had the wisdom and tenacity to wait until he had these small parties outnumbered six or seven to one. He came to Texas to murder and loot, not gamble.

He had been watching this particular party for some time now. There had been eleven braves when he first picked up their trail, more fighting men—particularly when they were Comanches—than he chose to take on. But luck had been with him. They had stopped and made camp, and the following day six of the braves had left to raid a Texas ranch, leaving only five to guard their women, children, captives and booty.

His followers urged him to attack the camp at once, but Snake was too cunning for that. Clearly, with their numbers, they could easily take the camp, but on their return the six Comanches would spend no time crying over the carnage they would find. Two would start tracking the Mescaleros, and the others would ride for help. Snake had great respect for Comanche endurance and knew they would never rest until he and his band were cornered and slaughtered. No, he cautioned his tribesmen, better to follow and kill these six first, then return and demolish the camp. That way there would be no survivors. Word would not get to the main Comanche camps for weeks, if not months—far too late in the season to start a pursuit. Next year was a long time away in the life of a Plains Indian. Besides, tracks weathered and died like the sagebrush.

The vehemence of the quick, savage struggle that followed the scream made Brandy's horse rear up wildly and try to bolt. The Comanches instinctively made for their mounts, but the Mescaleros were ready for them, overpowering the two in the yard and wounding the first two that raced from the house through the sagging door. The unequal numbers quickly ended the grisly slaughter. Three Comanche bodies were dismembered, and the two already mortally wounded, though still conscious, had their clothes and loincloths stripped off and firebrands held to their armpits and crotch. One groaned almost internally as death numbed the pain and then made it pointless. The other, the leader, tried to push the brand away with his hand until the smell of burning flesh filled the air. Then it was his turn to die as a loud hissing sound rose from a wide gash that yawned across half his outstretched throat.

Suddenly there was silence. Brandy was already bounding down the slope to find Inez struggling to her feet, her face smeared with dirt and streaks of colored grease, her dress in tatters revealing her small breasts. He went to her, putting his arm about her, and together they moved toward the house.

The blood-crazed Mescaleros had seen them and were watching as they approached, the frantic tension of the battle having not yet settled even with the death of the Comanches. Snake was standing before the open door, his eyes fixed on Isabelle's bare legs, which could be seen lying across the room. As Inez neared the doorway, she stopped uncertainly. Apaches could be as dangerous as Comanches, and they were notorious thieves. Behind her, Brandy pushed her into the house, allowing her time to cover Isabelle's nakedness before he followed. Together they lifted Isabelle onto the bed, finding her conscious now but her hands gripping their arms like iron tongs as she gasped, "Jason! Jason!"

"He safe. He safe," Inez half sobbed.

She told Brandy where the child was, and he ran quickly to fetch him. When he returned, the dark-frowning Snake was already inside the house with three of his followers. The rest he had ordered to stay outside and search the stables and corrals.

Brandy watched Isabelle, who, in spite of the shock that drained her face, cried with relief as she hugged Jason. Yet secretly his mind was on Snake and this horde of Apaches still wielding their bloody hatchets. He was the only protecting male left on the ranch, and he knew their mortal danger was far from over. He didn't like the way Snake kept looking at Inez and wished she'd take a moment away from Isabelle to cover her own breasts. If Carlos had been there, their jeopardy would have been doubled. Carlos was not only insanely jealous but dangerously, even stupidly, quick-tempered. What a blow it would be for him to hear that Inez had been raped by Comanche braves.

In spite of what he might hear, Brandy found himself wanting Snake to start speaking. He wanted to judge the Indian's intent. But Snake was busy thinking what he could safely do now that the first part of his plan had so quickly succeeded. There were possibilities here he had not counted on. That Mexican girl with her firm young breasts would bring a high price in distant locales, but this suspicious-looking black, who clearly lacked the defeated, submissive look of a slave, bothered him. Of course it was within his power to kill them all, but his mind balked at killing Texans. They were not like Mexicans, poor *mestizos* who could be robbed, their women ravished, their children carried off as slaves. Nothing came of it unless someone rich or powerful was affected. But in Texas a farmer had only to miss a colicky cow and within hours a hastily formed militia, or, worse still, the new ranging companies that even the Comanches were learning to avoid, would be scouring the country with only one sentence for any and all Indians encountered. The many bloody depredations of the Comanches had made "redskin" synonymous with rape and murder in the Texan mind. No, too much mischief here might even help their old enemies become aware of their presence.

His eyes had been quietly searching the room, and finally they fell on the rifle that now leaned against the broken table. "Take gun," he grunted.

Brandy had been following Snake's gaze and, being nearer the gun, had turned casually and picked it up. "Dis gun belong soldier man." It was the only rifle left on the ranch, Seth and Carlos having taken the other two. Brandy had earlier noticed the little roll of money still lying on the floor; now with his toe he kicked it toward Snake. "You take money. Better'n gun."

Snake knew something about paper money. He picked it up and almost smiled as he thumbed through it. Suddenly some of his Mescaleros were at the door, telling him excitedly that they had found eight handsome-looking horses in the corral. This was real wealth by Indian standards. Snake nodded to them and turned to Brandy. "Take horses."

Brandy drew in his breath and held it only with effort. These were the horses he, Seth and Isabelle had sweated and suffered to bring from faraway Kentucky and Tennessee. This was the stock they had sold their every earthly possession for. These fast, highbred horses held in their loins the future of the ranch. It was the breeding stock upon which all their dreams depended. To lose them meant going back. To lose them meant giving up years of labor and sacrifice.

"I's sorry, sir, dem horses not for sale." Brandy's voice was strained and unnatural, making Inez and even Isabelle look up at him.

Snake spat meaningfully on the floor. "Not buy! Take!"

Brandy could feel perspiration running down his chest and back. He wondered how long he could keep from shaking. "Dem horses belong to soldier man," he half croaked. "He be fightin' mad if he come home and dey gone."

Snake waited for Brandy's words to sink in. Then, smacking himself on the chest, he half roared, "Me, Snake, Apache war chief. Me come save soldier man's women from Comanches. Soldier man give Snake big present. Horses big present."

Brandy could see that the braves around Snake were muttering to one another and taking a firmer grip on their weapons. From behind he could hear Isabelle and Inez weeping and urging him to give them the horses, but Brandy sensed that something was wrong. Snake could simply take the horses if he wanted them. They were helpless to stop him, but here he was wanting them as a gift, as pay for killing the Comanches. Something was staying his hand.

Brandy had spent the first twenty years of life as a slave groaning and sweating in the cotton fields of eastern Mississippi, watching overseers with blacksnake whips and clubs threatening Negroes who worked too slowly or dallied too long in the shade. But badly beaten and often injured Negroes couldn't work at all, so there was a widespread tendency to frighten slaves with fierce threats which, unless things grew unusually ugly, were never carried out. Quick-witted Negroes soon began to recognize the tone and inflection of these crude bluffs, which experience taught them with a little caution could be ignored. But this was knowledge they knew the overseer must never suspect. Now when Snake looked darkly at him, then at the two women and the baby, saying gruffly, "Maybe all want die," Brandy sensed these menacing words were a bluff.

What he did now he could never have thought out. He simply followed his instincts. Somehow in the long-sustained tension his fear of death had almost vanished. He was still holding the rifle, and quietly he raised it till its muzzle was only a foot or two from Snake's muscular stomach. He pulled the hammer back and let it click into place as he spoke. "Me, I's bin ready to die for quite a spell now—is you?"

Snake's eyes fell to the muzzle of the rifle, and the silence in the room became complete as every breath stopped. After long moments, Snake crossed his arms before him and looked at the armed braves around him. Then, with great effort, he laughed. Brandy lightened his hold on the rifle. He knew he had won. "So, you want kill Snake, huh?" said the Indian. The words squeaked forth like a defiant question, but Brandy wasn't fooled. *Never let the overseer suspect you know he's bluffing.* Snake, he knew, could not be allowed to lose too much face before these braves.

"No, sir," replied Brandy with pointed respect. He was feeling a distant surge of confidence. "Snake big chief. Big friend. We give present. Two horses. When herd get bigger we send plenty mo'. Soldiers comin' soon. We tell folks Snake good friend, save us from Comanches."

Snake stared back at him guardedly but with respect. This black man was nobody's fool; his firm build, broad shoulders and dark but almost Caucasian features were poised in a resolute stance. The Apache was sure that had he not just a few moments before subtly signaled his retreat, he would have had his stomach blown out. That was not Snake's way. They already had six horses belonging to the Comanches. He would take the money and the two horses and the comforting thought that the Texans would not be trailing them. He would never admit to gratitude, even to himself, but he was sly enough to know that this strange black man had made it possible for him to extricate himself from a stupid and dangerous trap. Now with relief he saw his braves still awaiting his commands. Besides, there was still that Comanche camp with its women, captives and booty to be taken. That's what they had come for. "Ay-yee!" he shouted to his mounting warriors, who, thinking he had shown strong medicine, were shouting back. The camp and its spoils would be theirs by dawn.

It was after midnight when Brandy, finishing his frantic trips for help, got back to the ranch. By then there was a sizable fire in the yard and half a dozen lamps were visible through the windows of the house. As he dismounted, he noticed that a lone light was glowing in the dark interior of the hut.

When the Apaches left, everyone at the ranch had to deal with a draining emotional release that left them shaking, but all of them knew there were things that had to be done. Brandy hurriedly fetched in the milk for the now crying and hungry Jason, left the loaded pistol and rifle where they would be handy for Isabelle and Inez, and quickly rode at a gallop to the MacFees'. The MacFees' grown sons, Scott and Tyler, upon hearing his words, saddled up and left immediately. Old man MacFee, his wife, Sara, and their daughter, Carrie, left a few minutes later in their wagon. Brandy rode on nine more miles to the Salingers'. Here he was given a fresh horse, and the Salinger boys promised to get word upriver to the Sawyers and the Bonhams before they headed for Seth's ranch. Bessie Salinger and her younger sister, Kate, set out bravely with only a small hand pistol in a one-horse rig. The dark of night meant nothing on the frontier; a neighbor in trouble meant a community in crisis. No one knew who would be in desperate need next.

The longest trip for the hard-riding Brandy was to Doc Michalrath's, who lived almost thirty miles from Seth Redmond's ranch. The old doctor was in bed already, but he and his son, Jed, heated Brandy some coffee while they tended to Phoebe, the doctor's spinster sister who was doing poorly. But while the old woman could not leave her bed, she fretted at them for wasting time with her and urged them on their way. The three of them mounted as lightning started flashing again across the heavens, and for the first time Brandy thought he could hear thunder in the distance.

When Doc Michalrath finally arrived to dismount stiffly and enter the house, everyone but old Mrs. MacFee and Bessie Salinger, who was the same age as Isabelle and her closest friend, quickly left. Isabelle was propped up in bed. The women had cleaned her up and fixed her hair. She had a small bruise over her left temple but otherwise seemed unhurt until the doctor examined her stomach and found two wide cuts about an inch and a half apart. They looked painful enough, but he knew at once they were not serious. He cleaned them with alcohol and decided they would heal faster if left alone. The doctor knew she had been raped, but he also knew that raped women were sometimes shamed into silence about the horrors they had endured. Fortunately, he had met Isabelle several times before and reckoned her to be a strong and sensible girl.

"Was there any blood?"

"A little," she replied evenly.

"Do you have any pain?"

"Not as much as before."

Doc Michalrath looked at his watch. He guessed that whatever sperm had survived the tender washing was well beyond reach by now, and since she was not visibly bleeding, the inner membrane could not have been seriously torn. Thanks to Jehovah the rape had been interrupted by the Apache attack. He had seen the bodies of more than one woman raped by Comanches, then tortured, killed and dismembered. In his heart he shared the Texas frontier conviction that Comanches were vermin who should be hunted down and exterminated. Old Sam Houston was too goddamned easy on Indians for his taste. Maybe this new president, Lamar, would carry out his campaign promise to abolish them from Texas soil.

Knowing there was nothing more he could do, and recommending that Isabelle get some rest, he went outside to view the Comanches' bodies. The MacFee and Salinger boys, at Isaac Sawyer's direction, were working at burying them behind the barn. In a way he was also looking for the Mexican girl Brandy said had been "hurt" by the marauding Indians, but at the moment she was nowhere in sight. He caught Brandy coming from the stable carrying two long-handled shovels.

"Where's that Mex gal you mentioned?"

Brandy caught the rude inflection in his voice, but it was well known that Doc's eldest son, Bret, had been captured with Fannin at Goliad by Mexicans under Urrea and had been executed along with hundreds of others in an outrageous and never-to-be-forgiven violation of the surrender terms. Doc Michalrath's attitude toward Mexicans was not significantly different from his attitude toward Comanches.

Brandy turned and found he could still see the single light glowing in the hut. He knew that Inez would have gone there when the Texans started arriving. She and Carlos were aware of the hostility that still hung like an evil presence along the border.

"Ah'll fetch her," said Brandy quietly, putting down his shovels and heading for the hut.

Brandy found her standing beside a single large candle, partially concealing two basins of water she must have brought from the house. One, he knew, was used for carrying hot water from the house stove. She had changed from the ragged torn dress to a simple black frock and had carefully cleaned her face, revealing a cheek and a side of her neck that was badly scraped. As she turned to him, he noticed she was holding her left arm strangely; it must have been wrenched by the Comanches.

"Dat doctor, he here," he said gently, knowing she would be nervous and withdrawn with so many armed Texans about.

"Not need doctor," she replied hurriedly.

He looked at the dark, frightened eyes that stared across at him like flickering points in the candlelight. "Missy Inez, you bin hurt. Best you see dat doctor."

"Inez not hurt. Just this," she pointed to her face and then brought her right hand around to gently hold her left arm. "Maybe this a little bit—but not bad. Inez not hurt. No worry."

Brandy noticed that the water in both basins was discolored, but only a bunched rag lying partially in the darkness showed any signs of blood. He drew a deep breath. He knew Inez was upset, shaken and understandably scared, but he wanted her to get whatever help the doctor could give her.

"Missy Inez, I see'd wat dem Injuns did to you, just like they did to Missum Isabelle. I's up yonder on de hill. Dey catch you here in de yard."

She came closer to him, her eyes fixed strangely on his. "You make mistake!"

Brandy gestured to her helplessly. "Missy Inez, a man see wat he see."

Her eyes were locked on his in desperation. "You tell this to others?"

"Just dat doctor man. I tell him you hurt, dat's all."

Inez came even closer to him. Smelling her freshly washed hair, he realized she had never been so close. "Brandy, you like Inez?"

Brandy took a half step backward. "Missy Inez . . ." No words to match his sudden confusion would form.

Inez looked up at him, her eyes now openly despairing and pleading. "Brandy tells this to no one." She took his hand and held it to her breast. "Brandy does this for Inez."

He withdrew his hand and held her away by placing his hands on her shoulders. "What fo' I should do that?"

She gave a strange choking sound and collapsed in a seizure of sobbing on his chest. "Carlos! *Madre de dios!* He must not know!"

Carlos? Brandy was beginning to understand. In the few hours he had been away, Inez had had time to think ahead and grasp what her being raped by savages would mean to the madly possessive and almost hysterically jealous Carlos. As the thought settled in his mind, Brandy became sure Carlos would rather see her dead than think of her body being used by lewd, brutish men. He could feel her quivering under his grasp.

"You do this for Inez," she breathed against his ear.

"Yas'm, Missy Inez, I do it."

Then, sighing in troubled relief, she turned around slowly, bent down and blew the candle out.

Outside Doc Michalrath was standing over a dead Comanche, holding a metal belt buckle in his hands. It was a large silver one obviously taken from some dead Mexican. It had two sharp-edged metal blades shaped like angels' wings reaching out from its shiny surface. Doc was measuring the distance between the two sharp wings with his pipestem. "Yup," he drawled. "That's what cut her." He paused and kicked the body beneath him. "And this is the bastard that was a'top of her when it happened."

Scott MacFee came up to place a rope around the dead Indian's neck. They were dragging them beyond the stables where his brother, Tyler, and the Salinger boys had dug a deep hole. Isaac Sawyer, trying to see if anything was left to identify the band, found a long Comanche lance that he stuck in the ground before the house. "We need more protection," he said grimly, knowing this was a sentiment almost too obvious to express. "If Seth had a mite of sense, he wouldn't be gallivanting off leaving womenfolk to their lonesome."

"He's gone to join up with Bartlet's outfit," Doc muttered, watching Brandy come up. "We need more ranging companies patrolling the Nueces." Michalrath noticed Brandy was hesitating strangely as he approached.

The black man came to a stop a few feet away and kept his eyes on the ground as he spoke. "Missy Inez say she not hurt, only little scratch. She say she gotta sleep now."

The doctor stared at him curiously for a moment, then shrugged. "Well, Mex gals don't usually fuss much 'bout rough handling. Heard tell some even cotton to it."

Brandy said nothing. He was looking at the little hut that stood now in darkness, unable to forget Inez reaching up as he laid her on the straw ticking and kissing him as she murmured, "Brandy good to Inez. Inez not forget."

He shook his head as he turned away to the stables, the sound of women talking and starting breakfast in the kitchen fading away behind him.

2

Seth Redmond rode into San Antonio moments before the rain came. Cold winds springing up from the northwest struck the massive clouds banked above the settlement and the rain came down in gray diagonal sheets, turning the deeply rutted dirt streets into quagmires of red mud.

The gusting wind tugged at his wide-brimmed hat as he hunched his shoulders under a heavy buckskin jacket that reached well below the belt of his coarsely patched jeans, the legs of which were tightly tucked into high boots with mule-eared straps. He was tall, his close-cropped hair a light coppery brown. He was clean-shaven and had a determined jaw and firm mouth. His eyes were a deep blue that people tended to remember, and about the cleft in his chin lay a faint crimson glow that deepened as it rose to spread over the high points of his cheeks, betraying his years of fighting the southwestern sun and wind. He was remarkably well mounted and carried a heavy pistol and a long-barreled rifle that caused many Mexicans, huddled under arches or in doorways beneath their wide sombreros, to spit and mutter *"Diablo Tejano"* as he passed.

The rough two-day journey from his ranch had been a troubled and worrisome one for Seth, whose mind was on Isabelle and Jason and the ranch he had been struggling for years to make prosper. It had been a hard decision to leave her alone with only Brandy and the Mexican, Carlos, a step he had finally been forced to take, knowing that the marauding bands of Comanches coming more and more often into the Nueces country had to be dealt with. His mind told him there was only one way this menace could be ended. Conditions now were as bad as they had been in '39, when the ranging companies had taken the field to threaten the southern Comanches with extinction. Regrettably, the fledgling government of Texas had lacked the funds to keep its ranging companies on station, and the Indians were now back on the attack. Seth had ridden with the ranging companies in those days and was convinced that their tactics were the only way the Comanche threat could be removed. It was this conviction that had brought him to San Antonio. No rancher or farmer, or even a local militia hastily formed, could hope to prevail over those fierce and even arrogant warriors, whose every energy was devoted to war and whose horsemanship could not be equaled. Every season fresh graves could be found alongside the charred remains of adobe-caulked pine cabins, where grim-faced men and devastated women buried the hideous remnants of scalped and scorched bodies that had once been their loved ones. Some, dispirited, had given up the land they had fought for to return east. Others—stubborn ones like Seth, whose pride precluded backing off from a race of brutal savages—hung on but had to live with the horrors they knew were being inflicted daily on their neighbors. It was a rare man on the southwest Texas frontier who did not harbor a growing outrage at the endless reports of murder, rape, torture and particularly abductions. When children were carried off, families were kept in agony about their fates for years. The constant terror had leached away all emotions on the frontier but one. The blood of the helpless victims soaking into the Texas soil had brought forth its own deadly fruit, for now a deep racial and ethnic hatred of the Comanches had risen to sinister proportions in the Anglo-Texan mind.

This emotion was finding naked expression in the ranging companies, or Texas Rangers, as the eastern newspapers, aware of their growing reputation, had dubbed them. For almost a week now experienced Indian fighters, many from the ravaged frontier itself, had been riding in to volunteer. Others could join too, but unless a man had visible mastery of his horse and gun, he was quietly but firmly discouraged. Amateurs could be a menace in this grueling and exacting warfare. Among the Rangers there was no semblance of military protocol or even insignias of rank. Officers were elected by the men themselves with the understanding that this was hazardous work and blood was going to be spilt. Men's lives would depend upon their companions' coolness under fire and indifference to the rigors of the trail.

Ranger leaders were pragmatic, realistic men. They realized the futility of tracking war parties after lightning raids; war parties could keep splitting up till the pursuers found themselves following a single track, and any attempt to defend hundreds of miles of open frontier was ridiculous in view of their numbers. No, experience had taught them to take the field in late fall, as they were doing now, and move into Indian country with their Lipan Apache scouts, who needed no urging to help bring down their ancient enemies. Stealthily but tirelessly they would hunt down the usually complacent Comanche winter camps, capture or stampede the Indian horse herd, then attack with a combination of surprise, deadly efficient shooting and an indifference to age and sex, which in most cases meant massacre of all the camp's inhabitants.

These were not tactics widely advertised in the East, where Indian peace policies enjoyed an intellectual and even a political respectability. Such policies were always conceived far from the carnage. The border had spawned a breed of men brutalized by the sight of male companions left to die with tongue and genitals cut off or female relatives, both young and old, impaled on sharp stakes, their humiliation ended only by agonizing death. There were grieving husbands and fathers who reveled in such work and were not above giving wounded Comanches some of their own inhumanity before dispatching them. Given to violence and often stirred by the fanaticism of frontier religions, such men regarded Comanches as demented beasts and their extinction the moral duty of all God-fearing males. They thought of it not as war between men of different cultures or colors, but as war between men and dangerous, degenerate animals. They wasted no time on parleys or negotiated surrenders. They neither wanted nor had the means to deal with prisoners. They took none. These were men who rode forth with iron resolve and the slaying hands of crusaders. Evil was to be purged from the earth. They were the instruments of God.

Seth Redmond was one such man.

Seth was glad to see Will Bartlet standing under a narrow, rickety thatched roof running along the side of the plaza where the Rangers were gathering. At first glance, Bartlet appeared to be a man few people would challenge, but he had a firm faith in law and order and his craggy, sun-darkened face only hinted at his talents as a field captain and his gifts for handling men.

He was talking now with a white-suited Mexican whom Seth recognized as Julio, a local republican who had sided with Texas in the rebellion and now raised sturdy draft mules south of town. It looked to Seth as he came under the overhead and out of the rain that Julio was excited and pleading for something that Bartlet was mulling over, frowning with indecision. The rain and the murmurings of Rangers standing about drowned out their words until he was standing beside them.

"Without the mules I am ruined! *Arruinado!* Señor Bartlet, you are the law here, yes? You must help Julio!"

Bartlet gave Seth a nod of greeting as he came up, and Julio, like all members of his class a man of manners, bowed slightly to him. "Glad to see you, Seth," began Bartlet, but his mind was still on the excited Julio. "Appears there's a sight of bandits in town. They stole Julio's mules. He wants them back. Wants us to get them for him. What do you think?"

"My business is with Comanches," replied Seth, offering Julio an expression he hoped looked apologetic. "When do you figure to leave, Will?"

Bartlet pursed his lips and stared out at the plaza. The rain was lessening and the Rangers were beginning to leave their cover and saunter toward the enclave where Bartlet stood. "You know, Seth, our mandate is to preserve law and order," he drawled quietly. "Seems we ought to do something. This is Texas soil even if the town is mostly Mex. Any goddamned outlaws on the loose are our responsibility."

Seth looked at him steadily for a moment, a wisp of irritation far back in his blue eyes. A second elapsed before he forced an internal adjustment to take place and the Rangers' code to prevail. "What d'you want me to do, Will?"

Bartlet grunted and nodded almost imperceptibly, his way of showing gratitude. "Take a couple of the boys and get him his mules back."

Seth started to look around at the gathering crowd of Rangers moving toward them, but two standing near, having heard their conversation, spoke first. "We'll trail along." Bartlet nodded at them, satisfied.

Julio's face registered shock. "Señor, three men only! In the name of Jesus, there are thirty . . . maybe forty of them!"

Bartlet smiled patiently at the Mexican. "Don't get to frettin', Julio, we'll get your mules back. Next time you better keep a closer eye on them."

Seth looked at the Rangers who would be joining him. One was Tanner, whom he recognized from San Jacinto, a slim but incredibly fast gunman who had left three road agents dead in an all-night gun fight along the Guadalupe. The other proved to be Tanner's younger cousin, Cole Purdy, who smiled readily but carried his gun strangely low for a harmless ranch hand. Seth gave them the normal Ranger greeting of "Howdy" and turned back to Julio. "Where are these buzzards?"

Julio was still expressing grave concern for the discrepancy in numbers. He had expected Bartlet to send the whole Ranger company or at least half of the fifty or sixty men. Three seemed ridiculous, if not suicidal. "Señor, I beg you, take more *compadres*. They are down by the river in a cantina, the Casa Colorada, a very dangerous place. Estavez is a very dangerous man."

Seth looked to where his horse was hitched. "Let's git going," he snapped to Tanner and Purdy. Then, turning to Bartlet, he said, "Believe we'd best git out yonder afore the weather breaks. Even Apaches can't track if we get snow." He knew Bartlet was well aware of this, but he also knew Bartlet would hear the deep worry and annoyance in his voice. Will Bartlet did. When it came to his Rangers he heard everything, no matter how obliquely expressed. That was what made him a leader.

Not more than an hour after Seth, Tanner, Purdy and Julio had left, Jed Michalrath spurred his lathered horse into the plaza and, seeing Bartlet in the center of a crowd of men, raced toward him. The group made way for him as he rode up. "Seth Redmond!" he called out.

Will Bartlet came closer to him, his eyes on Jed's drained and exhausted face. "What's the trouble, son?"

Jed swallowed hard. "Comanches hit his ranch day 'fore yesterday."

Bartlet's dark face grew slightly pale. "His wife . . . Isabelle . . . is she . . . she dead?" Bartlet was beside Jed now, reaching up to hold his arm. "What happened, son?"

"Pa says Seth ought to be gettin' back."

Bartlet's voice remained even, but he did not release Jed's arm as he repeated his question. "What happened?"

Jed covered part of his face with one hand. "Mrs. Isabelle . . . well, Pa says them red devils likely hurt her some."

Bartlet released him and stepped back to curse under his breath. He had read the oblique message in Jed's words too.

On the face of it, three Texans riding unconcerned along streets where hostile Mexicans thronged and dangerous conspiracies were known to exist might well have amazed a foreigner. But these Texans had something more than the Colt pistols they were making famous to strengthen their hand. Buck Travis, Commander at the Alamo, with his red hair and soldierly rhetoric, had started it on the walls of the old mission, where two thousand Mexicans had died in a bloody battle to the death with fewer than a hundred and eighty Texans who neither asked for nor wanted any quarter. This was quickly followed by chilling firsthand accounts from San Jacinto of enraged Texans charging at Mexican soldiers and smashing in their heads with rifle butts, stabbing them to death with hunting knives or strangling them with their bare hands as they followed them into the water. These and a thousand minor conflicts had convinced most Mexicans that these domineering, pugnacious people from beyond the Rio Grande, with their self-confident way of handling guns, their touchy pride of heritage and most of all their indifference to death whenever their courage was questioned, were best left alone. For some they had even become objects of terror. Women, their faces partly covered by rebozos, watched them pass, gasping, *"Los tejanos sangrientos"*—the bloody Texans—while crossing themselves and hurrying their children away.

Seth, to avoid the deep-holed and even dangerous mud banks along the river, decided they would hitch their horses in front of an abandoned stable and walk along the narrow footpath that Julio indicated led to the Casa Colorada. Julio, still trying to persuade them to wait for reinforcements, dismounted reluctantly and walked last. Seth led the way, all but deaf to Julio's endless cautions. But his mind was rankled by thoughts of Isabelle and Jason alone on that ranch, and he was fighting a growing irritation that events had caused him to be wasting time here. Tanner and Purdy, other than stopping occasionally to swear and pry loose the mud that incessantly clogged their boot heels, said nothing.

The Casa Colorada looked like an old warehouse, which it might well have been. There were three or four steps up to a round, cheaply constructed porch backed by a wide opening that revealed a long bar and a wide, poorly lit room filled to its back wall with tables. The bar was crowded, but the place was unnaturally quiet and Seth noticed that there was no traffic in or out.

Seth took only a few moments to discuss his intentions with Tanner and Purdy, after which they nodded agreeably and the three of them started up the mud-splotched steps. Julio stayed behind.

Yoquito Estavez could have passed for a *mestizo*, but there wasn't a drop of Spanish blood in his veins. Like most of his followers, he was pure *indio*. He was from the province of Zacatecas, and while he spoke only Spanish, his name was not Estavez. That name he had taken from a *ranchero* he had worked for and then murdered before he and his growing band of bandits had drifted north to the Rio Bravo country. Here they had discovered that the border offered opportunities for pillage and extortion unmatched anywhere in the south. The Texas rebellion was officially over, but neither side could afford to patrol the river. Mexico's interminable revolutions kept its armies pinned to the capital, while Texas, whose first president, Sam Houston, wanted and needed peace, lacked funds and could mount only an untrained army of recruits. In consequence, the river valley and its environs had become one of the most lawless and dangerous areas in the ever-perilous Southwest.

Yoquito, his only real name, and his band did well south of the river, collecting tribute from small communities wishing to avoid murder and rape. North of the river they sometimes fared even better. Posing as partisans, they would appear in beleaguered Mexican communities and demand money, food and horses to help the national cause. Those reluctant to contribute would be warned that a lack of patriotism constituted treason during war and the central government would extract harsh punishment when it returned. Some Mexican communities knew they were being outrageously plundered, but unlike the U.S. and Texas governments, the volatile Mexican governments, not without substantial reason, were skeptical of their people's loyalties and did not allow their citizenry to bear arms. What guns were available were usually found in the hands of bandits.

As extravagant as he was with his loot and as wantonly as he abused his power, Yoquito was becoming progressively wealthier. Still, he had two brutal habits which he had been warned would sooner or later lead to trouble. When not satisfied with what a small isolated community could raise to meet his demands, he would callously kidnap the *alcalde* or a rich merchant and a member of his family. These he would hold for ransom. If the ransom was not paid by a certain date, the family member would be delivered with his or her throat cut and a second date, usually a close one, would be set. Missing the second date meant the *alcalde*'s or merchant's life. Not surprisingly, he was usually promptly paid.

The other and potentially more dangerous habit was his way of procuring females. Unlike his sullen countrymen, he was a big, unkempt, boisterous man with a gargantuan appetite for food and liquor, matched only by his lust for sex. Among the poor peones of Mexico any woman or young girl that caught his fancy, unless she had powerful male protectors, was accosted on the spot or, if that proved impractical, abducted to be raped later, usually during his nightly bouts with wine. His lieutenants had warned him that these practices would one day lead to determined vigilante pursuit, especially if attempted north of the border—advice Yoquito might have taken had he not experienced a turbulent emotion he did not understand and had he not seen Elena María López with her father walking in the central plaza of rustic Laredo. Elena's family were crîollos, pure-blooded Spaniards born in Mexico, a status which, while lacking the Castilian patina of the old conquistador families, still put her at the top of Mexico's very conscious caste society. Yoquito, being an *indio*, was at the very bottom. Yoquito was spellbound by her beauty. Never had he seen such delicate white skin or such feminine grace. At the sight of her, impetuously and in the grip of an anger too deep for awareness, he decided that no matter the price or even the peril, this was one female he had to have. But Yoquito, in his arousal, reckoned without her father. Señor López was a prominent and even influential man who controlled vast stretches of land along the river and was even an officer in the Tamaulipas cavalry. He knew the brash, lecherous-looking Yoquito Estavez for what he was, and while he had no powers of arrest, he bravely ordered the brigand out of town and warned him not to return. Yoquito was not discouraged. He had the López house watched day and night, knowing Elena would have to venture forth sooner or later and under circumstances that would fit his intent. His design was to abduct her and carry her off to Coahuila, to a favorite well-concealed haunt on the Rio Salado, one he had prepared as a sanctuary for himself in past years. There he would enjoy deflowering and then debauching this jewel from a class that had looked upon him since his birth as just another clod of dirt. Spain, while doing nothing for its subjects' enlightenment or welfare, was responsible for three centuries of genocide, exploitation and serfdom, suppressing a people whose temperament had produced sun priests who had demanded endless human sacrifices, and warriors who had created rock-hewn deities to be worshiped and emulated. They were now to discover they had also suppressed a Tarascan savagery that slumbered but never died.

But Yoquito once more had reckoned without Señor López. Don López hired many men, among them *vaqueros* whose own mottled history provided a familiarity with bandit methods and mentality. They soon smelled out Yoquito's spies and recommended that the whole gang be run down and executed. López gave this serious thought, but it would mean taking the bulk of his men in a chase that could end up deep in the *despoblado,* the cacti-studded desert of northern Mexico, far away from his family and property when other, even larger, bands were known to be raiding on the river.

In desperation, he hit upon a solution that promised to solve his dilemma. Elena must disappear. His mind settled on sending her north to a presently estranged cousin, who with his political convictions had sided with Texas in its rebellion. This had caused a temporary bitterness between them, but in Mexican culture family was the real bond. Besides, his cousin was not a soldier but a highly successful businessman in San Antonio who was well liked by the Texans themselves. His cousin's name was Julio.

A few days later, shortly after nightfall, Elena María López, accompanied by two mounted and heavily armed *vaqueros,* slipped out of quiet Laredo and, making their way across the river, started the long, exhausting trip to San Antonio.

But this time Don López reckoned without Yoquito Estavez. Being of devious mind himself, he had considered this possibility of escape for his quarry, a consideration that, along with watching the house, had caused him to send men to watch the river crossings, particularly at night. So when the stunning Elena López reached Julio's small mule-raising farm on the outskirts of San Antonio and fell into the arms of her adoring and delighted kinsman, Yoquito's band was riding hard only an hour or two behind her.

But Yoquito was beginning to have problems, ones he had been made aware of long before but in his rising heat and dark desire for Elena had failed to properly weigh. For some time his men had been anxiously noticing that they were getting dangerously close to San Antonio, a large town full of slow-talking but fast-shooting Texans, some of whom might know about their lengthening list of crimes. This was not the relatively safe and easy booty they followed Yoquito for. As they approached Julio's farm, his lieutenants, Pepe and Juan, abruptly brought the issue to a head.

"Yoquito," said Pepe, reigning in to turn impatiently to his boss. "I think this women, she make you *loco*. What you figure to do? Shoot your way into that house?"

"First we just talk," said Yoquito, his voice determined and rough with command.

"Talk?" repeated Juan, betraying a long-suppressed exasperation. "What you going to talk about? The weather? They will not give you the girl. Our only chance was to catch them before they got here. Now our horses are exhausted. Shooting will only bring the *gringos*. If they come now, we are finished."

There was wisdom in what he said, but Yoquito had not lost his faith in terror. Before he hailed the house, he had it surrounded by more than thirty of his men, all brandishing loaded and cocked rifles. "We wish to see the señorita," he called out in his rumbling bass voice. "We wish only to talk with her."

Julio, his two sons, their two hired hands and the two *vaqueros* who had escorted Elena cautiously poked rifle barrels through the windows. "What do you want to talk about?" Julio answered, his fear for Elena tightening his voice.

"It is a personal matter," responded Yoquito. "It will be very bad if we must come get her."

Julio looked about him. Giving them Elena was out of the question, but fighting their numbers was asking for death for himself and his sons. Julio abhorred violence, but he was a man of principle. He knew he must fight. Besides, the sound of gunfire this close to town might bring help. Not wanting to start the shooting, he hesitated until his own sons were looking at him, embarrassed by his silence. "Shoot the big-talking bastard," said his oldest, Ricardo.

Julio took a deep breath and cried out, "The señorita will not come out. If you try to come in, we will shoot. Go away before the Texas soldiers come. This is not a border town. We have law and order here."

"Ha!" roared Yoquito. "You are brave men, eh? Maybe if we start a little fire you and the señorita come out for a little talk, eh? It is not good for the health to stay in a burning house, eh, amigo?"

Julio swallowed hard. "She's not coming out!"

Pepe was by Yoquito's side, pulling his arm. "You cannot start a fire. It will bring half the town here. Yoquito, use your head. We are not in the Sierra Madre. Let's get out of here. We will find her again."

Yoquito looked around him stubbornly. He had to make the people in that house talk, make them understand he was a man to be feared, a man who got or took what he wanted. He pulled back and started to ride around the house. In the distance he saw two corrals full of mules. Upon closer inspection, he could see they were high-quality animals, representing a lot of wealth. He turned to Juan. "Have some men round up these mules. Take them a few miles further south. Keep them there. I think this foolish man might like to talk about what is happening to his fine mules."

Pepe looked at him sourly. "What we going to do while the señor grieves about his mules? The men are restless. It is no good."

"Of course they are restless," laughed Yoquito harshly, slapping him on the back. "They are restless because they are thirsty. We go now to the cantina, everybody gets wine or tequila, pretty soon they not restless anymore."

Pepe looked at him for a moment before turning away, but Yoquito was tiring of this constant eying from his lieutenants. "Not you, Pepe," he called after him. "No tequila for you. You take two men and watch the house. If anyone leaves, follow them. I want to know what they are going to do without their mules. Miguel says he knows San Antonio. He says the Casa Colorada is the safest place for us to drink. I will be there. If something happens, come *pronto. Comprende?*"

Watching him leave, Pepe took out a thin cigar and, swearing to himself, lit it slowly.

Julio had watched them running off his mules. He knew that losing his entire selling stock meant financial ruin. It was only when he had settled down that he remembered the big craggy-faced Texan, Señor Bartlet, mentioning that a company of Rangers was mustering in town that day. It seemed like a godsend, and immediately he prepared to slip out of the house and go for help. His only doubts were about

Elena. Should he mention her? She was, after all, a Mexican citizen and a member of a family that had fought hard against Texas in its fight for independence. He decided it might raise complications. Besides, the only really lawless act he could point to was his stolen mules, but without them he knew he would have trouble helping himself, let alone Elena.

Only minutes before Seth and his fellow Rangers reached the Casa Colorada, Pepe hurried in through a rear portal he had been told to use, a feature that gave the cantina its popularity with patrons whose occupations required quick exits.

Yoquito watched him scurrying up, his homely face wrinkled with alarm. "Yoquito!" he began, still fighting for breath. "That man, he go to *los rinches*, the Rangers. They come here *pronto!*" A noisy shuffling broke out as men pushed themselves back from tables or slammed glasses down on the bar. One patron not a member of Yoquito's gang, whose face was badly scarred, had been standing between the tables throwing knives into a target behind the bar. He hesitated till the minor uproar subsided as Yoquito in irritation signaled for silence. Then he threw another knife. Yoquito gave him a dark look and turned to Pepe. "How many come?"

"Only three, but *caramba*, there is fifty or sixty in the plaza. Yoquito, we must go!"

Yoquito's little eyes looked out through the wide entrance, rubbing his chin while he speculated on Pepe's words. "Only three, eh? They not coming to fight. They come only for the mules."

Juan spit derisively. "Give them the fucking mules. You want to die here?"

Yoquito screwed his face up in a way those around him knew was a grim warning of his mounting anger. "Juan, you afraid, maybe? Maybe Yoquito needs men who don't piss the pants like women when a few *rinches* come."

Pepe could already see the Rangers coming along the footpath leading to the cantina. "Yoquito, Juan is right. We are too far from the border to risk trouble. These crazy *tejanos* hang you for stealing animals. You know our horses need feed and rest. We cannot run far. Give them the mules. Say it is big mistake. You meant only to borrow them."

Yoquito, now seeing the Rangers coming himself, pushed Pepe

away. "I will do the talking, *estúpido*. You think Yoquito is not very wise, eh? You will see." He turned abruptly to a tall man standing a few feet away. "Miguel, take a few men, go out the back way, get those mules back to that fool's farm. Don't come back here, wait for us below."

The silent knife thrower suddenly threw another flashing blade into the target, and Yoquito turned to look at him again. "Everybody quiet!" he shouted. "Yoquito Estavez will show you how to deal with the *gringos*."

Seth came into the cavernlike bar looking over the strange, silent groupings of swarthy armed men standing about. He straightened his gun belt with one hand as he pointedly raised his voice.

"Estavez?"

A big paunchy man with a broad, almost flat face smiled in his direction. *"Buenas tardes, señor.* You wish something?"

Seth started moving toward him. "You Estavez?"

"Sí."

Tanner moved around to be on Seth's right side, while Purdy slowed down to cover his left.

Seth came to within a foot of the bandit's face. "There's a man named Julio who says you've rustled his mules."

Before Yoquito could answer, another knife swept through the air and sank into the target. Seth turned and saw a slim, badly scarred but broad-shouldered Mexican holding a bunch of throwing knives in his hand. He seemed oblivious to the tense confrontation taking place only twenty or thirty feet away. The man was standing to Seth's rear, and it bothered him. He could see the other's body bending slightly forward again, ready to throw another knife.

"Mister, put those pig-stickers up for a spell. We got business here. You can play with them all you want when we leave."

The knife thrower did not even look at him, but carefully set his eye on the target and deliberately threw another knife.

Tanner spun around like a wounded puma. "Y'all don't hear too well, do you?" The twang in his voice sounded curiously menacing.

The man looked at Tanner for a brief instant, then calmly took another knife blade between his thumb and forefinger. But now, as he raised his arm, Tanner's gun was out and flashing, shooting the knife out of his hand. There was a hushed moment when the knife hurler looked at his empty hand and his strange, cruelly scarred face began to register rage. In a swift movement he aimed another knife at Tanner which would surely have gone home had not Tanner's second shot taken him in the shoulder and spun him around, leaving him sprawled out over one of the tables. By now Seth and Purdy had their guns out, not knowing what this crazy exchange was all about. It could well be a signal for every outlaw in the place to open fire. They had no way of knowing that this odd, mute Mexican with his quiver of knives was not a member of Yoquito's gang.

But Yoquito, suddenly sensing that an accidental outburst would bring on fifty or sixty Rangers much like these quick-triggered three, was pounding the bar and thundering almost in panic, "*Señores! Señores! Por favor!* No shooting!" He swung around to his men in a burst of agitation. "Pepe, Juan, Santos, take that bastard with the knives and throw him out! If he makes more trouble, kill him!"

Seth was still standing before him, holding his left hand over the hammer of his Colt. He watched Yoquito's lieutenants grabbing the wounded man and said, slowly and coldly, "Tell them to just throw him out. If there's any killing to be done, we'll do it." Secretly he was glad Tanner had not killed the man, but he knew Tanner and probably Purdy were deadly hands with guns, men who did not think of themselves as lawless but stayed alive in this primitive land by never doubting that survival lay in shooting first. As the air settled, Seth's eyes focused on Yoquito again. "Well, what about those mules?"

"Señor, this poor man is mistaken. No one steals his mules, only to see if they ride or carry packs well. I am poor trader from San Quita, but my men no think they can work well with mules. Besides, dese mules cost too much money, eh? We leave them back on the farm. *Muy bien!* No problem."

Seth knew he was not talking to any trader from San Quita, a place he had never heard of, but his orders were to get the mules back. Something in Estavez' eyes told him they were back. This strange but dangerous-looking outlaw was clever enough to know he had overplayed his hand. The unexpected appearance of the Rangers had shocked him out of whatever devilry he was up to.

He turned to Purdy, who was closest to the door. "Tell Julio to get back to his farm. Tell him his mules are supposed to be there. If they're not, tell him to send a priest. We got some hombres here that might be wanting last rites."

Yoquito tried to smile good-naturedly, but there was no mistaking the intensity in this Ranger's face. Seth was angry beyond reasoning that he had been sent there at all. He wanted to get that Ranger company moving out beyond his ranch, and the thoughts of Isabelle and Jason alone in that threatened countryside kept haunting him.

He turned back to Yoquito. When he spoke, his voice had a disquieting tone that carried its own message. "Listen, Señor Estavez. The next time you decide to 'borrow' something in Texas, you're going to find out all we got to lend is a rope. Now clear out of here and don't show your face in San Antonio again. If this sounds like a warning—consider yourself lucky. The law hereabouts doesn't mention warnings."

With that he turned and, motioning Tanner and Purdy to follow him, stomped out of the cantina.

Yoquito watched him go, a sly smile working around the corners of his mouth. "You see, *compadres,* it is not a thing of great difficulty."

"Maybe, just maybe," said Pepe cautiously. "Even so, *vámonos.*"

"Yes, we go. But not too far. Yoquito Estavez has come for something. He does not go home without it."

His companions looked at him again and then away to the disappearing figures of the three Texans, many secretly glad the big Ranger with the coppery brown hair and strange blue eyes had not heard Yoquito's remarks.

But no words of Estavez would have mattered to Seth, who was holding his breath at the sight of Will Bartlet and Jed Michalrath coming toward him on the footpath. One look at Jed's face and a sharp pain slipped around his heart. The boy's stumbling words struck him like hammer blows that shattered his reasoning. He heard only two things. One, Isabelle and Jason were still alive and, two, he must hurry back. Will Bartlet watched him go, shaking his head. That look of dread displaced by helpless fury that had swept Seth's face wrenched his mind back to that moment on the Pedernales when he and Nat Twilly had returned to find their families slaughtered. No one had been left alive except old Randal, Nat's father-in-law, who had crawled into the brush to die. The desecrated bodies of their women, Will's wife and two daughters and the Twilly girls, already covered and pecked at by vultures, some too gorged to fly, were impossible to look at. Nat could only sit and stare at the head of his son, who, old Randal said with his dying breath, had tried to slip away the night before for help but had been caught by the Comanches.

They had placed his head on a stake where it would be seen by the terrified defenders at dawn. The women had fought until their ammunition ran out and then endured these final scenes of horror. Bartlet could still see Nat Twilly, his great leonine head turning from his son's hideous impalement and looking in hatred toward the horizon where the heavy tracks of unshod ponies had disappeared, crying out in the rustic tongue of the Cumberland hills, "If'n yer gonna fight thatta way—we'll fight thatta ways!"

For over a year Nat, alone and deranged, had haunted the Panhandle, living only to stalk Comanches—be they man, woman or child. Regarded by all as a madman, Nat was no longer accepted in civilized communities. His person was covered with filth and dried blood. Witnesses said he ate the game he shot raw. But no Indian he caught, whatever their age or sex—and a belt of twisted scalps, putrid from lack of proper drying, wrapped around his waist attested to their number—died an easy death. Stakes holding empty skulls marked many a lonely stretch above the Red River, till one day Nat's joined theirs in the only ending such hatred allowed.

3

Seth had trouble keeping Sam, his spirited chestnut stallion, to a safe pace. His first frantic urge was to press that powerful animal for all the speed it was capable of. But his knowledge of horses, which had been his life's work, warned him that an hour or two at that grueling gait and his well-trained and willing mount, strong as it was, would founder. He forced himself to rein in and use his experience with horseflesh to judge how fast Sam could carry him home without being crippled by the effort.

To keep his thoughts away from his raided ranch—for he was slowly beginning to grasp what Jed's excited mumblings were hinting at—he forced himself to think back to more secure days, back to his father's farm in the rolling hills of North Carolina. There his solemn, hardworking family had raised draft and farm horses. There he had fallen in love with his angelic fourteen-year-old second cousin, Isabelle, with her waist-length golden hair and her adoring eyes. There he had first felt that hint of physical passion that even her first child-like embraces left a man's blood pulsing, knowing it would one day mount as her body filled out and she flowered into womanhood. Marriages between first and second cousins was a long-standing tradition in the South, and many girls of thirteen or fourteen were already betrothed if not actually married. But much as he had wanted Isabelle—and she secretly him—Seth had not been ready. Reluctantly he had worked with his two younger brothers, raising his father's draft and farm horses—heavy breeds with Clydesdale and Percheron blood—and seeing to the fodder and grain to be hauled in as feed. But his heart had been with the smaller Chickasaw quarter horses, with their sudden starting speed and their ability to respond instantly to the slightest touch of a man's heel. They were far more exciting, if less profitable, for a young man of his edgy and uncertain temperament.

Every Sunday after church he had found moments to be alone with Isabelle, and after their kissing sessions, which grew more intense as their physical need for each other slowly dissolved all previously set moral boundaries, he had found himself increasingly restless. The long workweek on the horse farm under his father's exacting and humorless supervision was drudging labor, filled by endless and repetitious chores. He kept feeling an anger that surfaced as an irate moodiness, made worse each time some carefree adventuresome farmhand rode by heading west and talking about the dazzling opportunities on the new Texas frontier.

Then without warning an incident had taken place that had changed his life and marked young Seth Redmond in the minds of others as a man to be reckoned with and perhaps one who could not be measured in normal terms.

For some time a band of local toughs had been raiding the camps of the Cherokees living peacefully back in the foothills, taking the helpless Indians' livestock and sometimes their lives. They knew the white man's law would do little to protect a tribe whose valuable and often cultivated land was wanted and whose presence was not. When the Cherokees, deprived of their means of livelihood and hearing rumors that they were to be forcibly resettled in the Oklahoma Territory, had begun to hide deeper in the mountains, the gang, missing this easy, convenient, unscrupulous source of revenue, had decided the Redmond horse farm was one of the few spots that offered a suitable substitute for their enterprise.

It had been a fatal miscalculation.

When Seth and his brothers had ridden in to find their father badly wounded and dying and fifteen of their best breeding stock run off, they had sent their eleven-year-old sister for the county sheriff and taken off after their property.

They had left their mother, dazed and incoherent with grief. "All your pa wanted to do was talk, and they kept a-shootin' him," she had said over and over again. Their father had been a hardworking, honest but rigidly pious man who read from the Bible before every evening meal and whose sons were never allowed to touch liquor or miss church. But Seth and his father's notion of righteousness had differed, and there had been serious arguments and long periods of silence between them. But now his strange blue eyes gazed upon his father's unconscious and dying body for long moments before he took his rifle from the wall. Signaling his brothers to do the same, he embraced his mother and turned to go. At twenty-one Seth was the oldest, and his brothers, lacking his determined manner, followed him without comment.

In the lonely, sparsely traveled backcountry it was not hard to follow five men herding fifteen head of heavy horses. Soon they found themselves riding into Jerkins' Corner, which was not much more than a wide spot in the road named after Jerkins' Bar and General Store. Rolly Jerkins was a man of uncertain reputation and peculiar cronies. He was the type bred in back communities where the law was lax and trouble with one's neighbors unpopular. Here in Jerkins' squalid bar they found the gang drinking each other's health and assuming that their reputation would discourage any manure-shoveling farmers from trying to recover their property. It was an error they were not destined to repeat. Seth, cocking his rifle as he entered the bar, quietly reminded his two younger brothers that trying to talk to this sin-ridden scum was what had gotten their father killed.

The gang leader was a darkly bearded, barrel-chested ex-blacksmith whom Seth knew only by reputation and who went by the name of Bull. This sinister-looking, heavily muscled ruffian was a well-known sadist who reportedly had beaten more than one man to death. He was also wanted near Asheville, from which he had disappeared when two prostitutes, last seen in his diggings, were found savagely beaten and stamped to death. He was a man all decent and respectable people in the county steered away from. Now when he saw Seth and his brothers coming into the bar, rifles at the ready, he flung away the glass he was holding and dug for his pistol. According to Rolly Jerkins, who was watching from his private corner table, which he used to partially cover his enormous paunch, Bull's pistol never cleared leather before Seth's rifle bullet hammered him against the bar, sending bottles and glasses flying in all directions. His brothers, following his example, fired before the roar of Seth's gun died down, and suddenly there were three lawless horse thieves slumping to the floor while the remaining two had their hands high in the air, pleading with the brothers, who had already pulled out their handguns, to let them surrender.

Seth walked forward slowly, matter-of-factly disarmed the remaining two and ordered them outside. Meanwhile, Rolly Jerkins, pale behind his table, was beginning to shake, not knowing how much these Redmond boys knew about his own role in the horse theft.

Outside a crowd was already gathering. The Redmonds soon discovered that their horses were being held in a pen at the other end of Jerkins' Corner's only street. Seth sent his brothers to recover them while he watched the crowd press closer to the surrendered outlaws. An experienced eye might have recognized this as a sign of trouble. Word was spreading, and people were arriving from all directions. Young boys could be seen racing out to nearby farms to bring their family's menfolk on the run. Seth's brothers finally came riding back driving some stock but reported that three valuable mares were still missing. Seth, having reloaded his rifle, turned it on the two prisoners. "I'm only asking once! Where are they?"

The prisoners were pale and visibly quaking, not only because of Seth, but because the ominously mounting crowd now contained vengeful faces, some they recognized as victims of their crimes, who were now shouting to the Redmond boys to finish the job. One of the trembling men, his eyes fixed desperately on Seth, said, "Bull, he swapped those three to Jerkins. It was pay for letting us hole up in his cabin on Big Piney for a spell. He even threw in some victuals."

With singularly bad judgment, Rolly Jerkins picked that moment to make his appearance outside his barroom door, his rotund body bathed in sweat. He had taken off his belt to show everyone he was unarmed, but what he really wanted was to make it known that these three youths had opened fire without giving Bull's gang a fair chance to draw. He wheeled his huge bulk into a stance of defiance before Seth. "You didn't give those fellows ary a chance, did you?" His shrill, nervous voice rose, piercing the air like a scalded pig's squeal. Because of the noise, Rolly had not heard the frightened prisoner revealing his own complicity in dealing with Bull for the stolen horses.

Seth swung his loaded rifle around and jammed it as hard as he could into Rolly's immense gut. "They got the same chance they gave my pa!" Seth's face was only inches from Rolly's. He cocked the rifle. Rolly's eyes popped out like a speared frog, his shaking hands gripping desperately at the pain that seized his pierced stomach. "The same chance I'm giving you, fat man. Where's those stolen horses?"

Rolly realized that death was already inches inside his gut. This madman before him was more than ready to blow him apart. Instead of offering support, the crowd was clearly as threatening a menace as this blue-eyed killer. "Kerby," he breathed, fighting for breath, naming his barkeep. "Kerby running them over to your place," he managed to wheeze in a scratchy whisper. "Fer certain they should be there afore sundown."

Seth did not release the pressure on the gun. "Sundown," he said grimly. Rolly backed off to keep the gun barrel in his gut from making him sick. "Yeah, sundown," he wheezed.

Seth looked long and hard at Jerkins, then at the bar and general store. There was no give in his voice. "Sundown, or you and this whole shebang won't be seeing sunup."

Seth motioned to his brothers to start the twelve recovered horses on their way, but the two surrendered outlaws reacted to this motion to depart with instant alarm. "You ain't leaving us here, are you? Remember, we're your prisoners. By rights you got to turn us over to a sheriff!"

"Ain't got one handy," said Seth, not even looking at the man. The crowd now contained people who had been robbed by these men, flint-faced farmers whose hands were callused from wresting a living from the rocky soil, here and there a woman who had been molested when caught alone or whose purse or few trinkets had been snatched away from her. Most serious of all were the grim-faced, bullwhip-armed teamsters, who had more than once discovered goods stolen from their wagons for sale in Jerkins' store.

"We want the law!" cried one of the cringing prisoners, noticing that somehow Rolly had disappeared. "Don't let that fat bastard get away—he's done more than we ever did!"

Seth wanted to leave, but his brothers pressed him to stop and say something. They recognized some of their distant neighbors, many of whom belonged to their church. Like most townships in that part of the state, it was an almost inbred community. Seth, reluctantly giving in, turned around resignedly. "Just this," he said, and the crowd, impressed with the determination and bearing of the young man, listened. "I'm only a man like the rest of you. I ain't no judge or lawman or anything like that, but it seems to me if you live outside the law like these buzzards, you got no business expecting to be protected by it. My sister has gone to fetch Sheriff Cleary. I reckon he'll be along sooner or later. Now our father is a-dyin' and we got to get home. All we came for is our stock, which everyone here knows has been raised up on our farm." With that they rode away.

Behind them they left a mob whose emotions were approaching

the flash point. A teamster, who moments before had been standing obscurely in the crowd, suddenly shouted, "We don't need no sheriffs to tell us what to do. We got some real handy laws around here good enough for these bastards!" Coarse shouts of encouragement rose from all sides. He turned to a young man standing next to him. "Clem, there's a parcel of rope in the wagon—reckon you'd best fetch it!"

A few hours later Sheriff Cleary, with Kate Redmond riding at his side, rode into Jerkins' Corner and noticed that only a handful of people were standing about, most with their backs to him, mumbling conspiratorially to one another. He could see three bodies covered with sheets lying in front of Jerkins' bar and in the distance at the other end of the single street a big sycamore tree. From it two bodies were turning to and fro in the wind. Cleary did not know the whole story, but he soon pieced it together. "Seth Redmond!" he half whispered in amazement. "Well, I'll be goddamned!" he said to himself, not wanting the eleven-year-old girl to hear him swear.

Seth decided he would have to travel all night if he wanted to be home by the morrow, but that meant stopping to rest Sam and let him graze for an hour or two. He lit no fires but rolled himself in his blanket and tried to catch a few moments of sleep, something his anxious mind told him was impossible. It was far easier to keep his thoughts on the happenings that had brought him to this raw, primitive and now maybe sorrow-laden land, far easier to think about how his neighbors had changed after the Jerkins' Corner incident, how when the tempers had cooled and the hysteria had vanished folks had begun to look at him strangely as though he himself had infested them with primitive urgings and weighted their conscience with a riotous and lawless act. Even church became an ordeal of half whispers and averted eyes until he told his brothers to go alone. With his father gone, he began to see Isabelle in the evenings, for she, making no secret of her feelings for him, held her beautiful head high whenever his name was mentioned and openly acknowledged her love for him. His determined and seemingly uncompromising nature stirred some feminine need in the depth of her, and she proved it every night by lying ever more yielding in his arms.

But Seth was being consumed from within by a burning anger at the life around him and could not bring himself to marriage if it meant staying in that valley. His eyes said as much, and with his temperament, even Isabelle knew action of some sort was not very far off.

Though his mother had grown increasingly depressed and withdrawn since his father's death, his brothers began to prove they could carry on the farm with the help of a single hired hand, an arrangement Seth waited to see work before he took Isabelle in his arms and told her he was leaving. He looked into her troubled eyes and assured her over and over again that he was leaving only the valley, not her, for he would be back and he would bring with him their future and all the elemental blessings the young and in-love yearn for. Isabelle sobbed against his chest and made it evident with the rising heat of her kisses that she wanted their love consummated that night, that for her it would mean that in the deep recesses of their spirits and flesh they now belonged to each other, were already married in the sight of God.

Seth had often thought about it, for it was a night no man could expect life to repeat. Isabelle, with her persistent need for a confirmation of their love, had squirmed for long moments beneath him in delicious pain before she began a hushed screaming as endless waves of ecstasy pulsed through her open, quivering body. After, they had simply held each other tenderly as she slowly descended to weep and sigh in relief. The exhaustion of this first tryst had put both of them to sleep, but they had awakened to make love over and over again, sometimes violently, sometimes with only a drowsy peaceful murmuring, until shafts of sunlight whispered that the world with its cares and its painful separation was again at hand.

In Tennessee Seth's future had suddenly come into focus. He had spotted a horse he was told came down from Kentucky, and he had known at once that this "Thoroughbred," with its striking mixture of Arabian and Barbary blood, and perhaps a little Turk, would be part of the existence he had visualized for himself since childhood.

And it was in Texas that he had met Sam Houston. On the banks of the Trinity he had discovered that this big, strange, passionate man of destiny also loved horses. It was Houston who had told him Texas needed a strong and enduring supply of horseflesh if it was ever to win and hold fast its freedom. Texas had already declared its independence from Mexico, but the Mexican cavalry of experienced, well-mounted horsemen was chopping Texan foot soldiers to pieces whenever they met. Later they would discover that the mounted Comanches and Kiowas were also too skilled as riders, their mustangs too rugged and maneuverable, to be easily overcome by their own standard farm breeds and the average pioneer's level of horsemanship. Slowly but inexorably Seth's destiny had unfolded before him.

Like so many others, he had fought for Texas at San Jacinto, that bloody birthplace of Texas freedom, and had received his grant of land. Knowing that married men received more land than single ones, he had signed in both his and Isabelle's name. But he had discovered that his grant, almost fifty miles west of San Antonio, was in hostile country. He had soon met a young surveyor named Jack Hays who had told him, in quiet subdued tones that didn't match his renowned fighting ability, about their "Indian problem."

He had written to Isabelle to tell her about the country and the intoxicating spell of space that left a man hushed upon viewing it. Sometimes he had written about the free, fenceless plains and the visions he had of vast herds of horses and cattle that would one day be theirs. Not wanting to frighten or discourage her, he had said very little about the ominous Comanche threat, except that he had joined a ranging group led by a mild-mannered, slightly built young man named Jack Hays. Best of all, he would soon be coming home to marry her.

That night he crossed the swift-flowing Medina River and pushed on toward the Hondo Valley.

Before dawn he found himself thinking back on but finding it hard to remember the exciting moments of his long-awaited return to the farm in North Carolina. He had been away for nearly three years, years he had slowly discovered were needed to prepare for a future that at times seemed to slip away before him like an elusive dream. Much of this long sojourn had been spent with the Rangers in a spartan existence of cold camps and endless stalking of bloody-handed warriors in all kinds of weather. But morale was high and the men firmly believed in their purpose and fearlessly saw to its execution. Daily they viewed what the Comanches did to their hapless victims, and nothing could diminish the Rangers' appetite for slaugh-

ter whenever they caught the Indians off guard. Not surprisingly, by
the second year it was clear that the Rangers were speaking a language the Comanches understood. The southern Comanches, at least,
stopped raiding and the frontier finally experienced a sustained period of peace. That was when Seth returned to find his Isabelle blossomed into the deep sensuous woman the warmth of her girlish
embraces had always promised.

Though they were married as soon as possible, and though their
intense lovemaking satisfied some of the deep hungers Seth felt, it
was clear that the confines and dull daily cycle of his father's farm
were irritants that kept him anxious to leave, to get to the freedom
of that spacious vibrant country and the beginnings of the ranch he
had dreamed about for so long.

He resolved to take with him an outstanding herd of horses. They
were to be the seeds of their future and, he hoped, of their fortune.
They sold everything they could, and Seth bequeathed his share of
the farm to his brothers for four strong draft horses and what cash
they could raise. Money would be needed to buy the Kentucky stock
he had seen in Tennessee, though he was taking with him six of the
best Chickasaw quarter horses his brothers had continued to raise in
his absence. Even so, when he looked at the heavy wagon loaded with
things he and Isabelle felt they would never find in Texas, he realized
that the wagon and the horse herd were more than the two of them
could safely handle. He knew something about those trails crossing
Texas. They were not to be confused with the turnpikes or post roads
of the East.

While wrestling with this problem he discovered Brandy, a runaway slave Sheriff Cleary was renting out for a dollar a day—"to pay
for his grub till we find out where he's from," said Cleary. But Brandy
wasn't telling anyone where he was from, and as time went by, no
wanted sheets fitting his description came through the mail. Seth had
hired him on two occasions and had noticed how well he understood
and handled horses. He approached Isabelle with the idea of buying
Brandy, but she made it clear she wanted no slaves. "A horrid business, that slavery," she said and flounced away. But Seth bought him
anyway, getting Cleary to shorten the number of months he was
legally supposed to wait before putting an unidentified runaway slave
back on the market. Cleary, although he never mentioned it, always
felt he owed Seth a favor. He had never fancied taking on Bull's gang
or even Rolly Jerkins by himself, though it was fast becoming his

duty. Seth had unwittingly saved him the trouble. One favor deserved another.

Seth talked to Brandy as they made their way back to the farm. "How'd you like to be free?" Seth began.

"Ah'd like that real much, sir," responded Brandy guardedly.

"How'd you like to go to Texas?" continued Seth.

"Texas? Where dat?" Brandy asked puzzled.

"A mighty long ways from here!"

Brandy smiled in spite of himself. "Cain't be far enough for dis nigger."

Seth explained what he had in mind and Brandy was so intensely relieved he took a fit of laughing. Not only was he free, but if what this strange but impressive man said was true, he was going where no overseer would ever find him again.

They had been on their way for well over a month before Isabelle realized she was pregnant. At first Seth thought they would wait in Tennessee until the baby came, for he was having more trouble than he thought in getting the quality horses he wanted. But Isabelle insisted they go on. She wanted her baby born in Texas. But as her condition grew more delicate, they were forced to move more slowly, and as the rough trail stretched out before them, the wisdom of bringing Brandy along became apparent. It made it possible for Seth to drive the wagon while Isabelle lay on the bedding within. Brandy, cheerful and seemingly always in good spirits, handled the sizable horse herd with ease, built fires, fetched water and even helped with the cooking. Many of the things they had packed before leaving they had had to sell in Tennessee, partly because they needed more money to buy the high-spirited horses they wanted and partly because while going through the mountains, even the stout draft horses were beginning to stumble, convincing Seth that the wagon was simply too heavy.

Slowly they moved on through northern Louisiana and into Texas. The long waits at the many river crossings were the worst, but they got as far as Gonzales before an old doctor and his wife took Isabelle into their home. After an all-night vigil, Jason was born.

In barely a week Isabelle was ready to move on. They passed through San Antonio and made their way west to the valley of the Hondo. Moving north through it now, Seth was reminded of his first sight of his land, and of his surprise at finding a Mexican named Carlos living on it in a little adobe shack with an extremely slim, pretty girl he was visibly in love with and very possessive of. At first he had seemed sulky and resentful, but on seeing the horses and hearing Seth was going to build a ranch there, he had brightened up and offered his services as a *vaquero*, a ranch hand, an offer Seth accepted. Although he didn't like or even trust Carlos, he was secretly hoping the girl could be a help to Isabelle, who now had a baby to contend with.

Though the land looked deserted, in the years he had been away he had collected a surprising number of neighbors. In western Texas neighbors were folks who lived within fifteen miles of one's spread. On their second day, five families sent their menfolk to help the Redmonds erect a house. The MacFees, the Salingers, the Bonhams and young Jed Michalrath all showed up. Bessie Salinger, with her pretty, pert face and trim, energetic body, and old Mrs. MacFee brought enough food to feed them all.

About a hundred feet from the adobe hut they found the foundation of a fair-sized house that had been burnt to the ground. At first it appeared to be the work of Indians, but Carlos quickly told them that it had belonged to an *hidalgo*, who had claimed he owned this land but had decided to move south when Texas declared its independence. This *hidalgo* had also been determined to leave nothing behind for the *gringos*. They discovered a well under the rubble and quickly, after cleaning it out, began to build a house that started with the kitchen. Ten days later, a plank-and-adobe domicile had been erected.

It was a memorable day.

But it was another three weeks before Seth, Brandy and Carlos finished the stable and adjoining corrals and dug a sizable well to water the stock. Inside the stable a half loft was built for Brandy, who with Isabelle's help made it a comfortable and even cozy roost to live in. Finally, to please Carlos and Inez, another smaller well was started in the hut. It seemed they had carved their home out of the wilderness and their trials were behind them. But now, as dawn started blushing along the eastern horizon and he could make out the sharp peaks of the hills to the west, Seth's heart began to pound—for his ranch and his Isabelle, with her golden hair and soft supple body, and all that he had striven for would soon be in sight.

4

Isabelle rose before dawn. Her sleepless night had been spent crying over the dread she felt at the thought of Seth's seeing her body and having to hear from her own lips what had been done to her. At the first light of day she was standing before a large piece of the broken mirror and wincing at her nude body, with its grotesque black-and-blue marks where her breasts and legs had been held tightly as the Indians pinned her to the floor. In revulsion she saw again, starting high in her pubic hairs, the two broad red welts where the skin had been scraped away. They were already beginning to swell as Doc Michalrath had said they would before turning dark and scabbing over. Fighting back her tears, she dressed her long blond hair and between bouts of anguish tried on her few worn dresses, none of which had the power to make her seem fresh or youthful. Inez had told her not to worry, Seth loved her and a man who loves a woman does not stop loving her easily. Inez had even pointed warily at Carlos, her eyes holding a peculiar light, but Isabelle had been too full of herself to think of Inez or Carlos or even Brandy, who had seemed disturbed and distressed after Carlos had returned the previous day. She had lost herself in tending to Jason, who, gratefully, was now asleep. Outside the partially repaired door the Comanche lance that Isaac Sawyer had stuck there still sat unnoticed except by Isabelle, who had asked Brandy to remove it. But Brandy, worried and fretful, had forgotten.

When the sun finally rose above the horizon and the land was bathed in its early-morning light, Isabelle went to stand beneath the cottonwood tree Seth had left standing before their home, saying one day he wanted to build a shady place beneath it for visitors to rest. She was praying quietly as she stood there, for somehow she already felt his presence in the valley. She was praying that he would go on cherishing her and desiring her as he had since she was a child, but that jagged piece of mirror said her body was no longer desirable, and the fear that he would one day see this lay like a dreadful darkness down the corridor of her life.

Seth rode over the last rocky rise and saw her figure in the distance, the early rays of the sun setting off the gold in her hair, her white dress making her appear like a tiny angel heralding the dawn.

He pressed Sam to a gallop and, finally reaching her, bounded down from the saddle to take her in a powerful embrace that took her breath away and brought tears gushing from her eyes as the torrent of pain that arose when he pressed her bruised body against his hard frame mingled with rapture at being back in his arms.

For long moments they didn't speak. It seemed enough just to cling to each other, holding to a kiss that had to endure until some deep, sensual contact between them was restored. When finally he drew back to look at her, he was stilled by her dark, sunken eyes and the faint new lines along her bruised forehead.

Holding to each other, they turned and walked slowly to the house. Although everything that could be quickly repaired or restored had been done the day before, the place was still a shambles. They found it difficult to talk. He could only mutter "I'm sorry" a number of times without being able to go on. She, not knowing how to respond or where to start, put on her kettle and, taking him by the hand, led him to the small room behind the kitchen where Jason slept. They looked at the baby for a few moments. Then, not wanting to awaken him, they went back to the broken table that had been propped up with rough rails of wood brought up from the stable.

Now here for the first time the dreadful consequences of her ordeal appeared. Moving behind her, he ran his hands gently around her waist, then up to cup her breasts, a warm, affectionate gesture of his she had always loved, and one that often started their lovemaking, but now she had to grab his hands and hold them away. Her breasts were far too sore to touch, let alone fondle.

It was a sobering moment, and Seth, not knowing what to do, sat down heavily at the table while she, quickly brushing away a tear, shakily prepared two cups of coffee and placed them on the table. They sat across from each other, waiting. Neither touched the coffee, and a dead stillness lay over them till finally he looked at her till she met his eyes and said in a half whisper, "All right, Isabelle. Tell me. I want to know. Tell me what they did to you."

The day before, Carlos had come racing into the ranch yard, his dark, mustachioed face looking strained and deeply lined with the angry turmoil he had felt since meeting the Salinger boys on his way back from Porcupine Creek and hearing about the raid. They knew nothing about Inez except they reckoned she was all right. It was just like those *gringos* to half order him back to the ranch, where they said Isabelle—there was no mention of Inez—needed him.

Dismounting, he ran into the hut and enfolded Inez in his arms, kissing her bruised face and plying her with questions upon half-answered questions as his hands moved over her body. It was some time before she could quiet him down, but as he grew more calm, his questioning grew more probing and precise. What had they done to her? She told him they had seized her and threw her to the ground, her scraped face and bruised body spoke for themselves. She said hesitantly that they had been planning to rape her, but when the Apache attack came they had released her and she had escaped into the hut. Brandy, she repeated over and over again, had seen it all from the rise. Carlos pulled her dress up to look at her legs and, seeing they were bruised, ran his hands further up around her pubic area. Though she was still internally sore, she managed a little nervous laugh and pecked his cheek with a kiss before she pressed him away and determinedly pulled her dress down again, saying, "Carlos, not in the daylight, please. You want to shame me?"

Settling on the straw ticking, they talked some more, she keeping his mind from the Comanches by telling him about the big Apache named Snake and Brandy's handling of him. He watched her intently as she spoke until finally he rose, his eyes restlessly sweeping the interior of the hut. His gaze seemed to be trying to find something to fix on as he said, "All right. Tonight then. We wait. But Carlos needs love badly, you hear, Inez?" She let him kiss her again but then pushed him away and watched with relief as he left.

Carlos took his horse to the stable and found Brandy repairing a halter and some saddle straps. Brandy didn't look up. "So, you big brave man. Comanches no hurt you, eh?" said Carlos caustically.

Brandy kept his back to him. "You wasn't here, so don't be makin' smart talk 'bout bein' brave." He noticed the mount Carlos had ridden. "Rub dat horse down before you feed him. He's soakin' wet." He had never liked Carlos, but he was well aware of why the Mexican was there and what Inez wanted him to say.

Carlos, ignoring Brandy's rebuff, backed the roan into a stall and picked up a towel. He whistled for a moment, then said, his tone striving to be casual, "They no get Inez, eh?"

Though he wasn't facing him, Brandy dropped his eyes. "No, she got away."

"You see this?"

"I see her 'scape into de hut when dem Apaches attack."

Carlos' face seemed to relax. "But they get Isabelle good, eh? They give her plenty loving, eh?"

Brandy looked at him in contempt. "And dey pay for it. Dey all lyin' in a big hole back o' dis stable."

Carlos concentrated on his rubbing. "Seth, he come back?"

"Reckon," said Brandy. "And reckon you better get to work. Dey's plenty to do 'round here."

Carlos spat and walked out of the stable. Though Seth had left Brandy in charge, Carlos didn't relish niggers telling him what to do. Besides, something about the look of that brooding dark man bothered him.

Later Carlos went to the house to give Isabelle the money he had gotten for the horses at Porcupine Creek. She seemed too distracted to talk about selling stock or anything else. She shoved the money between two jars on the shelf as their chest had been broken. He saw the bruise on her temple and thought of how it must have been for her when the Comanches had stripped and raped her right in that room. In some way the thought of it excited him. Tonight it should be especially good with Inez. His young, beautiful Inez. He bit his lip with tension. Those Comanches had felt her legs and probably her breasts, but they had not penetrated her. Even the thought of how close that tragedy had come to him made him feel limp and sick all over.

◆   ◆   ◆

Covering her face with her hands as she tried to retain control, Isabelle struggled through the terrible scenes of her attack, breaking down time after time as Seth moved beside her to comfort her. She strove bravely to tell him everything she could put together in words. How they had struck her, stripped off her clothes, forced her to lie naked on the floor, raped her and somehow left two painful cuts on her lower stomach. She found it easier to talk about the miraculous appearance of the Apaches, but by then Seth was helping her over to the bed and lying down beside her, holding her tenderly and trying to get her to rest. But try as she would, she could not stop weeping, and only Jason's crying when he finally awoke seemed to help retain her control.

Seth aided her with the baby, but for some reason he wanted to get out of the house, away from that room. Somehow he sensed he could still hear her screaming as those filthy brutes forced themselves into this beautiful girl he had loved all his life. The full shock and impact had not really hit him yet as he walked in a half daze toward the stable, not noticing Inez watching him while she nursed her own secret misery within the adobe hut.

He found Brandy in the stable rubbing down the big chestnut, Sam, and preparing to feed him some grain. Brandy knew it had been a rough and hurried trip back from San Antonio, but he always admired the care with which Seth handled his horses.

"Good to see you back," he said, not surprised when Seth didn't answer.

Seth's eyes were glazed over like a man whose emotions refused expression. He walked around the stable as though he were slightly drunk, though Brandy knew he rarely touched liquor. Finally, gazing out the cutaway door that faced the pasture to the north, he said, "Where's Carlos?"

"He done gone to git dem strays dat keep driftin' over to duh creek. Sometimes when the water is low dey cross over an' we lose 'em."

Seth kept staring at the range to the north where the hills began to mount as they approached the valley of the Guadalupe. He noticed there were two Kentucky blooded horses missing, but he had no will to ask why. Somehow his whole life there seemed pointless now. The future seemed empty and his will to go on was drained. Already he felt that Isabelle was not the same woman he had left but a few days before. Something indefinable had gone out of her, but he was incapable of measuring what it was.

He was brought back to the moment by Brandy calling to him that someone was coming. After listening for a few seconds, he heard the hoofbeats that told him a rider was approaching the ranch from the south. Brandy followed him to the stable door, where they could see that it was Isaac Sawyer coming up on his big sorrel. As Seth went forward to meet him, Brandy remained at the stable door, but he hesitated there only a moment while he peeked at the adobe hut and wondered how it was with Inez, whom he had heard pleading in excited Spanish with Carlos the night before. He walked back, trying to keep his mind on his two sick colts. Carlos had been in a particularly ugly mood that morning. Maybe there was trouble in the wind; maybe it was blowing his way.

Isaac Sawyer had come with some things his wife felt Isabelle could use now that much of her kitchenware was smashed. There was a china pot with some old but serviceable cups and a medium-sized mirror with a yellow flower painted in one corner. "Says she has an extra chest of drawers too, if Isabelle has a mind to use it."

Seth thanked him, but the gifts only reminded him of the loss of the many precious pieces carried all the way from North Carolina. Isaac, sensing the strain Seth was under and noticing that Isabelle had not come out to greet him, dismounted quietly to advise Seth that some of the neighbors had been talking and had decided to take a day or two to come over to repair the damage to both the house and its furnishings. Isaac, in spite of his gruff appearance, was a sensitive man and understood the Redmonds' momentary need for privacy and a withdrawal from any eyes but their own. But he was also a seasoned veteran of the frontier, having been a civilian scout in the northern territories before coming to Texas. He knew tragedies had to be endured, life had to go on, neighbors had to let the stricken know they were not alone. On the frontier, human friendship and support had to be there always. It was what made the uncertainty and harshness of that life endurable. "We'll wait till you're ready for us," he said, preparing to mount again. Then his eye caught the Comanche lance still stuck into the ground before the door. "Meant to mention to you, they probably weren't Wasps or Southern Comanches that hit you. There's an old Arapaho scalp wrapped around the shaft of that lance. Means they're probably from the north, likely above the Red. They've been feuding with the Arapahos up there for quite a spell." He pulled himself into the saddle. "Wouldn't leave it lying about if I were you. You never can tell."

Seth nodded and Isaac rode off. Seth rubbed his hands through his hair. Somehow his mind still seemed a blank. For a moment he looked at the knoll that rose before the house and the hills around them. The sun was up now and beginning to throw out a little heat. He decided he would go back into the house and carry Jason out. For a moment he stared at the lance. He would burn it or just break it up and bury it later. But his senses were registering strangely that morning, and it was not until the following day that he got around to removing the lance. By then it was too late.

Inez sat watching Carlos finishing the jars of wine he had brought back from Porcupine Creek. She had spent part of the afternoon sitting in a tub of warm water carried laboriously from the house in pitchers, but it had done little to ease the pains over and inside her body. She dreaded the coming of night, and now as they sat in the growing darkness she wondered if she could maintain her pretense once Carlos started making love to her. She hardly remembered the pain of losing her virginity. When bandits had killed her parents, Carlos had taken her to live with him at the age of thirteen. The local priest had wanted to marry them, but there was so much danger and fighting in Coahuila that Carlos and his brothers, all experienced *vaqueros*, had decided to go north into the then relatively peaceful New Mexico and try their hand at cattle raising.

Even at her young age, she knew Carlos was in love with her, and as she developed into a woman, although his lovemaking became more and more intense, he was always gentle with her. Even when he was making passionate love to different parts of her body, she knew she could always restrain him with only a few hushed words. Now at eighteen she was no simple little peasant girl, but a woman who had a deep, instinctive wisdom about men. It was evident that Carlos was insanely jealous of her. Living in close quarters with his brothers, who did not have women of their own, Inez had found keeping their hands off her legs and budding breasts a mounting and finally impossible task. The inevitable day came when one of them, returning early to their little ranch house, caught her coming nude from her bath. More out of panic than anything else, she had scratched his face as he forced her onto the bed and started to ravish her. Carlos had burst into the room, knife in hand, and only Inez' screaming and blocking him with her nude body had kept him from killing his own brother.

But there was no living as a family after that. Carlos and she had traveled east into Texas, where he could search for work in known cattle country. Still, it was a difficult and even dangerous journey. Fortunately, they had come across a Mexican *ranchero* who was abandoning his land and heading south. He was an *hidalgo* and had no desire to live under a Texas flag once Texas had declared its independence. Carlos had been attracted to the spot when he saw the ranch house going up in flames. The *ranchero* had told him he was not leaving his house for the *gringos* to use, but if Carlos was interested, the half-built adobe hut sitting hearby was his. He and Inez had moved in and had been there only a short while when Seth arrived and found them.

Now he discouraged her from lighting a lamp in the dark hut and moved over to the bed to put his arm around her. She decided to brace herself and see if he could be quickly and easily satisfied that evening. Maybe the wine would make him sleepy, keeping his desire down. But she was wrong. He soon had her breasts out and his mouth over her nipples, which pained her some but would be nothing compared to what she now sensed was coming when he settled between her legs. Usually he was patient and warmed her up with his foreplay, but now, though he went through some hurried efforts to excite her, it seemed only to increase her discomfort and pain. She was not a big girl. She had slim hips, and the Comanches, when they grabbed her, had frightened her so that her body had frozen up. Yet they had been strong, muscular men and had forced their way into her, abusing her internal membranes as they rose to their savage climax.

As Carlos pressed forward to enter her, she couldn't contain a little shriek of pain that caused him to draw back and look at her. He put his hand down there, and she had to endure his probing between her legs as tears of anguish filled the corners of her eyes, mercifully hidden by the dark. Then something seemed to seize him, and he grabbed her and entered her abruptly, displaying a strange kind of desperation as he pressed her down and held her beneath him on the bed. She managed to bite her lip and keep from gasping as she waited for his orgasm, and when it came, she strove to move her body in partial response. But then he slowly rolled off her and his hand came up to hold her chin, keeping her eyes level with his. "What is wrong? You don't make love. You only pretend."

"My legs!" she cried in a muted scream. "Don't you understand? They are so sore. Very sore."

He looked at her for a long moment, the darkness concealing his expression. Then he left the bed and, muttering under his breath, moved about the room. She heard him finishing his wine. When he returned, it was some moments before she realized he was holding something in his hand, something he finally pressed against her side. It was his knife. "You lie to Carlos, eh?"

"*Nunca*, never," she said, her breath catching in her throat.

He looked at her in the dark, breathing heavily in and out. Then slowly he ran his hands over her body, even turning her over and groping her buttocks. Deeply frightened, for she knew he was seething with suspicion, even if slightly drunk. She was still alert enough to wince openly when he touched her legs or her bruised side, and then hold still, keeping her breath even, while his fingers explored her vagina. After an incredibly long time, he put the knife down on the floor and sat up in the bed. She noticed he had an erection again but was grateful he was making no move to force it into her. What he needed and wanted, she knew, was some form of total intimacy with her, something she had never given to another. She was right; he did want something, something he had been desiring from her for years, something a prostitute had once done to him when he was young, and he had never forgotten it. Pulling her up and kissing her deeply, he pressed her head down between his legs and she realized it was with her mouth that she must satisfy this bitter, possessive and now, isolated as she was, even dangerous man and bring this terrible night to a close.

For Seth and Isabelle, their first night together brought a sense of clawing despair. Before bed she had kept herself carefully covered, putting on a long, heavy nightgown that rose to her neck, and although he asked to see her body, particularly the open red scars, she could only sink beneath the covers and hold herself closer as she shook her head in wretched denial. Something told her that she must wait until her body repaired itself, until the discoloration faded and the scars healed over. If he saw her nude now, the nauseating sight might stay in his mind forever.

There was no thought of lovemaking. Both tried in increasingly fitful starts to escape into sleep, but both also began to sense and then fear another presence in their bed, a cold, strange presence. It had no corporeal form, but it hung between them, refusing to dissolve. They never discussed it then or later, but that night they both felt its ugly seed quicken in the darkness. Something indefinable had changed.

However, there was another presence around that night, one which, had they been aware of it, would have ended all thoughts of rest until dawn. This shadowy figure's face was painted black, and three dried scalps hung like a necklace about his chest. He was from the Kotsoteka, the "Buffalo-Eaters," a band of northern Comanches, and he was the half-mad son of the Comanche chief who had led the attack upon the Redmond ranch. He already had a reputation, even among his own particularly warlike people, as a violent, aggressive warrior and a great slayer of enemies. His name was Blood Hawk, and his dark, lusterless eyes gave no hint in this darkness of the cold fury behind them.

He had been traveling with his own smaller band only two sleeps behind his father on their return from Mexico, and he had come that morning upon his father's camp to find it massacred. The five dead warriors had clearly been killed defending the camp, but the young women had been raped, then mutilated and slaughtered. The few old ones, men and women alike, along with the children had been tortured to death. All the captives and loot were gone, taken by a large party that had gone south.

The nature of the torture, they knew, ruled out the whites, but Blood Hawk and his companions were well aware they had plenty of Indian enemies, many with old and unforgotten scores to settle. They decided that two of them would pursue these attackers till they could be identified. Then the great winter Comanche Council would decide their fate.

But Blood Hawk, an excellent tracker, set about finding the bodies of his father and the five other warriors that were still missing. It was not long before he picked up the hoofprints of his father's favorite war pony. Apparently his father and some of his braves were getting in one last raid against the hated *tejanos* on their way home. He followed their tracks until he saw he was approaching a small ranch house. Then he dismounted to slip into the brush and wait for darkness.

Even in the rising moonlight, he could see a Comanche lance standing upright in the ground before the house. By staying close to the earth and moving only when the racing clouds above obscured the moon, he was soon beside it, removing it as soundlessly as the high wind that moved the clouds. Once he had it in his hands, he realized only too well what had happened. It belonged to his father's half brother, who always carried it with him, and it was still decorated with a war trophy, which meant it would never have been left behind if any of the warriors had survived. On his way there he had already found the tracks of the large party that had wiped out the camp. Somehow at this ranch his father and his warriors had been overwhelmed and killed by this sizable party and their bodies probably, in the white man's way, buried in a hole in the ground. Who these people at the ranch were he did not know, nor did he care. They had played some part in his father's death, and that was enough.

It was a Comanche warrior's duty to take vengeance on those who killed his kinsmen, particularly his father, but as Blood Hawk stood motionless on this strange night and looked at the house, the adobe shack and the stable, he realized from his early watching that all three were occupied and he was dangerously outnumbered. Besides, he wanted to destroy this entire ranch and all in it. He decided he could wait. In his burning mind and in the gruesome leanings of his imagination, these *tejanos* were already as good as dead. The Comanches had wiped out far larger and far better fortified ranches than this. He promised himself that with his own hands he would put all those taken prisoner to slow, agonizing deaths.

As he moved about like a wraith in the darkness, he spied the good-looking horses in the corrals, but taking them would only put these whites on his trail, and he had recently learned there were Rangers up on the Colorado, scouring country he had yet to pass. No Comanche needed to be told that the Rangers, once they got on a Comanche's trail, required more than strong medicine to be scared off. No, he could wait. It would be something to make secret medicine about and lust over during the coming winter. A bloody revenge was something a Comanche liked to think about and enjoy, and a warrior such as he, seeking to be a chief, needed trophies and the scalps of annihilated enemies to dance with around the campfire in celebrations that always marked their homecoming.

He ripped the Arapaho scalp from the lance. It was a war trophy and could never be allowed to fall into enemy hands. Arrogantly he wanted these *tejanos* to know that he, Blood Hawk, a Comanche, had walked boldly through their camp, had marked them for death, and would be back for his revenge with the new grass in the spring. It would give them something to think about, to smoke over during the long winter.

Returning to the house, he stealthily laid the iron point of the lance lightly against the door, setting it so that as the door opened, the lance would fall in point first. Then, taking a hard look around, he stared up at the skies and muttered a silent oath of revenge. It was an oath that in Comanche custom only death could release him from. It decreed that he must return and bring death to these craven enemies who had taken his father's life.

Anxious to end a sleepless night that was adding to rather than reducing her fatigue, Isabelle rose in the false dawn to try distracting herself by cleaning her kitchen. Scraps of food, which had to be buried to keep from attracting coyotes, wolves or those hateful buzzards, lay in an iron bucket she emptied frequently to avoid an onslaught of flies. Now, lifting it quietly, she started for the new trench that had been opened at the side of the house. Though her mind was moving as in a trance, she noticed that the door opened almost too quickly, and suddenly she caught a glimpse of something long and dark swinging down to land with a strange, muffled sound at her feet. She had to bend over to discern its shape, but as she did, she began a shrill screaming that brought Seth, desperately clawing himself awake, from the bed. In the darkness they stood together, holding each other, not knowing what the appearance of the lance meant. They only knew that some unknown hand had approached in the darkness and placed it against their door. What it symbolized they couldn't guess. Isabelle had no need to guess. She knew what that lance was doing there, what it meant. It was there to keep alive in her the only thing this whole terrible country had ever held for her—fear!

5

For the next few weeks Seth buried himself in his ranch work, forcing his distraught, brooding mind to do the many things that needed to be done, finding it easier to work out on the range than feeling hemmed in around the stable and corrals, looking at the house and entering it to face Isabelle again. He and Brandy extended the wings of their horse trap and searched to the west for herds of wild horses to drive into it. Seth had developed great respect for the stamina, maneuverability and toughness of these sturdy mustangs that served the far-traveling Indians so well. They were much like his Chickasaw quarter horses, although he reluctantly admitted they did better when both were on wild forage than the homebreds that were accustomed to grain in their feed. Once in a while they trapped a prime stallion, which they roped with considerable difficulty and brought in to breed, but usually they ended up with mares, colts and some culls. Seth kept only the mares with the best lines, and sometimes there were none fit to breed. By now all his suitable mares were being turned out with the Kentucky stallions, which were grazed in small, separately fenced pastures close to the stable. Brandy watched Seth riding out each dawn, staring into the far horizons like a man forcing his mind away from the painful thoughts hanging in the shadows of his ranch.

Isabelle, slowly recovering from the trauma that had marred her mind and body, found no escape from the endless toil this isolated frontier demanded. Food, while plentiful, came only with labor. Their scratch garden provided small amounts of corn, beans, squash and even yams, but both women had to spade and hoe the hard ground, carry water from the creek, particularly in dry spells, and haul manure from the stable to nourish the thin soil. Quantities of salt pork were fetched from the Bonhams, who kept hogs, but the long-horned cattle Seth slaughtered had to be butchered, salted and hung on the rough-hewn racks in the squat pine smokehouse. Mud, which plagued every foot-slogging Texas settler, became Isabelle's infuriating and ubiquitous enemy. It entered everywhere, slowly drying to a fine dust that crept into every crevice, seam of cloth and dish in the house. Soap had to be constantly made, a process involving long, exhausting hours. Even with Seth's and Brandy's help, it was a task that left Isabelle and Inez spent. Lye had to be leached from barrels of wood ash, then boiled for long periods in animal fat and grease. The yellow clumps of soap produced cleansed but coarsened the skin as the women took turns rubbing and churning the hot tubs of homespun or linsey-woolsey clothing. Almost every need had to be filled by hand. There were lanterns, but oil was forever running low and had to be fetched from San Antonio. If candles could suffice, the lanterns were rarely lit. Yet the candles wasted away as readily as the soap. The primitive candle molds borrowed from the Salingers helped, but the tallow had to be boiled, mixed with beeswax and carefully poured around finely twisted wicks of cotton. Such chores, along with Isabelle's unending tasks of cooking, baking and caring for Jason, burdened her days, but she forced herself to find a grim blessing in this drudgery. Aching fatigue kept her from lying awake at night by Seth's side, grappling with a mind choked with anger at this hellish land that had not only savaged her body but turned the deep urging of her flesh, which made her a woman, into something ugly. Night after night she closed her eyes, secretly hating it with a bitterness that beggared words

On the morning Seth found the lance fallen across their threshold, he left the still-shaken Isabelle to show it to Brandy, whom he found up at dawn. Scratching his head, Brandy had been studying some moccasin tracks he had found along the small holding corral, which was a high-railed extension of the barn. Brandy had thought the horses had been unusually restless during the night, but in his sleepy state he had suspected the cause might be a wolf whose scent had hit them as it slunk about looking for the sick colts that lay locked in the stable. But the thought of a wolf put him in mind of something. "What we needs here, Seth, is a dog," he said, "and no puppy, neither. We needs a big dog who can take care of hisself and bark when dey's trouble comin'."

Seth immediately saw the wisdom of this suggestion and was irritated that he himself had not thought of it sooner. A barking or, better still, attacking dog, even if killed, would have made it impossible for an Indian to skulk about his ranch in the dark. He vowed he would search the surrounding country for a suitable dog as soon as possible.

Strangely enough, only the morose Carlos realized what the lance really meant. "They come back," he said. He grimaced and spat, continuing gravely, "They think we killed those ones." He pointed with his chin toward the rear of the stable where the Comanche bodies were buried. "Now they come back for revenge."

Seth looked at him steadily for a moment. "Come back? When? It's mighty late in the season to be raiding."

Carlos shrugged his shoulders. "Comanches no got clocks, calendars, just good memories. When they ready, they come. Maybe not till summer. Maybe not till next year. But they will come."

Seth thought about it but finally decided that this chilling warning did not change things much. The threat of Comanche attack had been there from the beginning. That was why he had made his desperate decision to join the Rangers, a thought that began to run through his mind more and more often now. His earlier despondency slowly churned into an anger that on occasion boiled up into visible fury. The monstrous impact of what these savages had done to his young wife, how they had corrupted the softness of her loins with their foul flesh, was beginning to hit him, and each day he became more bitter, resentful and enraged. Isabelle suffered from this most of all. But there was no stemming this new tide of hate that was rising and roiling about his mind. His only recourse seemed to be to exhaust himself during the day so that sleep claimed him at night like a drug. Isabelle noticed how quickly he stretched out on the bed as soon as it was dark, his breathing almost at once assuming the heavy, faintly whistling rhythm of sleep. In the beginning she watched him in a painful quandary, thankful her own exhaustion brought on sleep to avoid the nagging dread that their spontaneous and sensuous lovemaking might be lost to them forever.

◆ ◆ ◆

Since Seth and Brandy had started working together across the Hondo it had become more and more common for them not to see Carlos, who was riding herd on their cattle miles away. Usually they would meet only in the late evening, when the horses came in to be cared for. Curiously, on a few days they failed to see him at all. Seth wondered about this, but he was always far too tired to give it much thought. But Brandy, who managed a few words with Inez every evening, began to hint that maybe Seth had something to think about. It was a long ride to a smelly shack on the main east-west trail to the south, a shack surrounded by a messy yard of broken jugs and bottles, but Carlos seemed to be making it. Two renegade Mexicans and one yellow-toothed, unwashed Texan had set up a shop to sell wine and other more powerful spirits they had stolen from warehouses in San Antonio. Anyone coming down the trail could stock up on cheap liquor if he had cash or jewelry in gold or silver settings. These gentlemen had shown little interest in bartering for meat or foodstuffs. At first Carlos would simply bring home a bottle or two of wine, but they would be empty by dawn. But then, more and more often he began coming home drunk, yet so late at night that only Inez was aware of it. His lovemaking had remained rough, but it had fallen off, and often he did nothing but slump on the bed and sleep off his stupor. For a while she almost welcomed this, but then he began waking up at night or early in the morning and seizing her, his language suddenly vicious. He would accuse her of lying to him, cheating on him, even with his own brothers. Always she had to quiet him and satisfy him with her mouth, but little by little she realized her doing this had changed her in his eyes. There was a coarseness in his touch now. He no longer treasured her as he once had, she could feel it. Then finally one frightening night he struck her, and as she lay sobbing on the bed, he took his knife and cut off her beautifully braided hair. Seeing that his cold eyes had become strangely wild, she shrank away from him in mute panic, only to find herself frozen with fear as he followed and stood over her, forcing her head up and pressing his knife against her cheek. When he left that day, she knew she had to tell someone. She could not face another night alone with him.

Her first thought was to turn to Isabelle, but Isabelle was already near the breaking point with her own miserable plight. Inez could sense it. Isabelle's eyes were always on the verge of tears, and her

voice would often suddenly grow unsteady and in strained moments
even completely die away.

That left only Brandy, for she could not bring herself to approach
the seemingly angry and lately forbidding-looking Seth.

In the darkness that evening, Brandy listened to her as he rubbed
his face in exasperation. What could he do? He decided the one thing
he could do, should do and to avoid any further risk for Inez—who
was hugging him in her need for another's strength—had better do,
was to tell Seth. The following morning, when he discovered Carlos
had shown up only to change his vomit-soiled clothes and leave again,
he told Seth. Seth unhesitatingly turned on his heel and approached
the hut.

Calling out to Inez for permission to enter, he watched her come
to the door and for the first time noticed that the dark plait of hair
that always flowed down her back was gone. His long training in
being courteous to women unconsciously softened his tone, but his
questioning was blunt.

"You say he struck you?"

"Yes, señor, he did."

"And he's been drinking?"

Inez took him inside and showed him two empty bottles and a jar.
He lifted them to his nose for a moment, then put them down and
turned to Brandy. "Where is he?"

"He suppose to be on dat south range mendin' fences, but he could
be workin' dem hills lookin' for strays."

Seth went directly to his horse. "I'll find him," he said abruptly.
Then, turning to Brandy, he lowered his voice. "If he comes back
here, don't let him leave, and don't let him get alone with Inez."

"Yas, sir," said Brandy, feeling better already. He went back to the
stable, and there, in a strange excitement, he strapped on his single
shot pistol.

By following Carlos' tracks, which were easy to spot in that almost
virgin country, in less than half an hour Seth knew he was riding
east into the low hills. He had suspected all along he would be headed
there, if only to get closer to that shack he'd heard about that sold
those cheap stolen spirits. An hour later he saw the Mexican dismounted and drinking from a small stream, one that worked its way
eastward toward the Medina.

Carlos' shock and surprise at seeing him was apparent, but Seth was in no mood for delicate talk. "What the hell are you doing over here?"

Carlos swallowed hard for a second, then got his breath. "Señor, I don't understand. What are you doing here?"

"Looking for a varmint that can't hold his cheap liquor and beats and knife-whips his woman."

Carlos' face clouded over. "Inez, she tell you this!"

"Nobody needed to be told. A man has only to look at her to see how she's been treated."

"Señor, you are mistaken."

"No, you're the one who is mistaken if you think you can work for me and take a knife to a helpless girl. Get the hell back to the ranch and be there when I get back! I've got more to say." With that he rode off.

Seth, pausing to rest Sam, had sensibly decided after coming this far east that he would ride the additional seven or eight miles south and visit the Salingers. He knew they kept dogs, and it had never left his mind that his ranch needed one.

The girls, Bessie and Kate, were out visiting, but the boys, Rick and Prentiss, were glad to see him. They were younger than Seth and, having heard of his exciting years with Jack Hays and the Rangers, admired him. He saw several mongrel dogs leaping about and barking but almost forgot to discuss them when he heard Prentiss had just returned from San Antonio with word of Will Bartlet and his ranging company. Apparently there had been a fierce running battle up on the Colorado and some Rangers had returned wounded. Bartlet had sent word that he could use any available experienced men.

Prentiss, being the older of the boys, had gotten his father, Adam, to agree to let him ride north and join Bartlet. Adam, who had been a great fighter and hunter in his day but had lately been suffering from rheumatism and old shoulder and leg wounds, was soon pouring coffee from their big iron pot. "One way or t'other, we got to gun those red heathens down," he was saying as he poured. "Leave 'em for the crows afore this country will be fit to live in. That fella we got for president, Lamar, he's got the hang of it. Exterminate them like the vermin they are."

Seth nodded in grim agreement, but his thoughts had already traveled to Bartlet on the Colorado. "When you figure on leaving, Prent?"

"Soon as we finish that smokehouse yonder. Shouldn't be but a few days."

Seth looked at him as though the remark had put him to deep thinking, but suddenly one of the dogs was scratching at the screen door and he was reminded of why he had come. He turned to old Adam. "Adam, I'd like to buy one of your dogs."

Adam smiled. "You've done heard about Lizzie's litter too, eh?"

"Lizzie's litter?"

"Yep. Ole Lizz threw a litter of pups here some weeks back, and by golly, three different outfits have been after 'em."

"What's so special about her litter?" asked Seth, who had never given much mind to dogs.

Adam laughed. "Wal, a fella up on Squaw Creek had a mean-looking critter he claimed was half wolfhound. Don't know if such was the truth, but it was sure big enough. We ran ole Lizzie up there when she was in heat, and for the promise of two pups we now got five."

As Adam talked, Seth remembered that Lizz was a big yellow bitch that could run down jackrabbits in spite of her size. He figured one of her pups with some wolfhound blood in its veins would do just fine. "How much you charging?"

Adam laughed again. "No money needed, you know that, Seth. But we'd be mighty obliged if we could send over our young mare for one of your Kentucky studs."

Now Seth had to smile. Money didn't count for much on the frontier. There were things men who had to fight this lonely land for a living found more important. High among them was a good horse. Over some more coffee and friendly joshing they made a deal, Rick offering to bring the mare and a pup over in a few days.

As he prepared to leave, Seth stood and faced old Adam. "Didn't happen to hear about some varmints selling booze up on the trail, did you?"

"Dang right I did," answered Adam. "What's more, I'm just waitin' for a few handy guns to run 'em off! With Injuns on the loose, that much liquor settin' about could be dangerous."

Seth looked out to where Sam was nibbling some growth at the edge of the yard. "I was planning to visit them on my way back— maybe give them a mite of warning."

Adam threw up his hands. "No, Seth. Don't head there alone. There's three of them."

"I could tag along," said Prent, rising.

"No need to, Prent," said Seth, turning to go.

"That's where you're wrong," bawled Adam, pounding the table and shifting away from it to come to his feet. "Never give scum like that the odds. I've had to live by my gun most of my life, and I'm still alive because I always figured that being brave business was nothing but damned foolishness." He turned to his younger son. "Rick, get me my horse."

Nothing Seth could say would dissuade them, and they finally left with Adam holding his reins and saddle horn in one hand and a smooth-bore shotgun in the other. Only poor Rick was left behind, wondering why it was that the two years' difference between him and his brother made Prent a man and him still a boy.

An hour later they reined up a hundred feet from the shack to find four horses hitched before it. Either there was a customer inside or there was one more in this gang than they had figured. It turned out to be the latter. A squat bald-headed man confronted them as they stepped single file through the open door. "Howdy, gents," he said, his very stance making him the center of authority in an incredibly dirty and cluttered room that passed for a store. There were bottles, jugs, half-open crates and cloth-bound casks lying everywhere. A tall, toothy Texan was sprawled in one corner, and two Mexicans were coming out from behind a blanket that hung across a doorway separating the store area from a second room beyond. The bald man, seeing the newcomers eyeing his wares and exchanging glances with one another, continued to talk. "Looks to me like you fellows got yourselves a powerful dry and are coming for the fixin's." He rubbed his hands like a man ready to conduct business. "Am I right?"

"No, you're wrong," said Seth, moving slowly between two large casks and stopping directly before him. "There's no room around here for the likes of you and whatever you're fixing to do with this mess of liquor. Smells as bad as you do, and we're here to tell you you'd best put it back in your wagon and move on."

The bald man's expression darkened as he turned to look back at his companions. A jerk of his head brought the toothy Texan to his feet. His eyes ran over the three of them but settled on Seth. "This is a free country, partner. We ain't figuring on movin' anywhere."

Seth noticed one of the Mexicans had slipped behind a crate he had been idly resting on a moment before. He dropped his hand to his gun belt, hearing Adam and Prent shifting to new positions behind him. "Better do some more figuring, mister. This is the only visit we got time for."

There was a moment of silence as the air in the crowded room became charged with imminent violence. Every man in the room was armed. There was no law here to intervene. Both sides knew that in the unbending code of this land they were at a point of no retreat.

The bald man's voice rose, a little tighter now. "How was you figuring to make us move on?"

"Like this, maybe!" exclaimed Adam as he fired his shotgun at an array of bottles stacked along shelves running into a corner of the room. A shower of glass and colored fluid came out to spray a third of the floor space, and the cloying odor of cheap wine and *aguardiente* rose to meet the smell of burnt powder in the stale air.

The noise and shock of this action took most of them by surprise, but Seth had not taken his eyes off the Mexican who had slid behind his crate. Now he saw the barrel of a rifle coming up as its muzzle dipped, and he knew that once it was level it would fire. He managed to draw and shoot just in time, hitting the Mexican in the forehead and driving him back through the hanging blanket into the room beyond.

Immediately the bald man's hands were in the air and he was shouting desperately to both sides to hold their fire. He had been a thief and a smuggler all his life, but like most thieves he didn't believe in dying over right and wrong, and surely not over the morality of property rights. He was not against killing. It was often profitable. But he liked his victims unsuspecting or defenseless, not standing a few feet away with cocked guns in their hands. "We didn't come here to make trouble!" he shouted. "We was only settin' up an honest-to-God legitimate business!"

Adam was slowly and deliberately reloading his shotgun. He stared at the other with scorn. "How legitimate was the way you come by this liquor?"

"We don't have to discuss any of our business dealings with you," replied the other defensively. The bald man knew the deadly threat was over. It did not concern him that he had lost; he was secretly glad the Mexican and not this intense blue-eyed stranger before him had been shot. That could have brought real trouble. But he was too savvy to abandon his expressions of indignation or to show any signs of relief.

"Nobody's asking you to discuss your business," said Seth, looking at the blanket now hanging crookedly and knowing a Mexican was lying dead behind it. "Just move this rotten swill somewhere else *pronto*, and move it where we ain't likely to find it again!"

Prentiss looked a little pale as they turned to go, but Adam backed away holding his shotgun at the ready, facing the others till Prentiss and Seth were out the door.

"What about this poor helper of mine?" cried bald-head, his voice aggrieved. "You gents killed him! What am I supposed to do with him?"

"Maybe take a good look at him!" shouted Adam as he exited. "That way you'll know what you're likely to look like if we have to come back."

A cold wind with a smell of snow in it was whipping around Seth as he approached the ranch at dusk. With his long knowledge of this weather, he sensed that a blue norther would be on them by dawn. Sam put his head into the wind and showed he was eager to get to the stable by finishing their last mile on the run. At the ranch, Seth dismounted, slapped Sam on the flank and watched him trot down to the stable where Brandy would be waiting.

As he entered the house, Isabelle, her hair freshly done up with a satiny green ribbon and her white skin gleaming, greeted him with new eagerness. He felt the added pressure in her kisses, and something in the way she came into his arms told him she was ready to be hugged again and have her body touched. Taking her by the shoulders, he held her away from him to look at her slightly teary but smiling face. She was still very beautiful, and for a moment he felt aroused, but a disturbance outside reminded him that he had left the problem of Carlos to be dealt with when he returned.

A hurried glance out the door assured him that the noise was only Brandy herding the skittish mares and colts into the stable and holding pen, where there was some cover. Brandy liked to shout at the fractious ones who balked at the narrow pen gate, but he too must have sensed a storm coming. There was no sign of Carlos or Inez.

Isabelle had set out their two borrowed plates and had dinner ready. Realizing he hadn't eaten since breakfast, Seth opened his sleeves, washed up at the kitchen pump and joined her at the table. Although there was a lantern already burning, he noticed she had put two small candles on the table, and their flickering light served to soften both their faces, carrying a hint of their earlier and happier life together.

"You've been away all day," she said hesitantly, not wanting her words to sound accusing.

"Had a mite of visiting to do," he answered, his tone dismissing the day's importance, his eyes holding to the food he was gathering on his plate. "Seen Inez or Carlos around today?"

"No. Hardly at all. Is something wrong?"

He looked up. "Got reason to believe there might be?"

"Oh, no. Just that they've been in that hut all day. Why isn't he working? He looks terrible."

Deciding she'd have to know sooner or later, Seth told her about Carlos' treatment of Inez. Isabelle looked troubled. "Why hasn't that girl said something?"

"Probably reckoned you had worries enough. She's a plucky gal."

Isabelle bit her lip for a moment. "My God. What are you planning to do?"

"Warn him."

"Will that be enough? Oh, poor Inez." Isabelle pressed a hand to her lace neckline. "I'd hate to see anything happen to her. Wherever is he getting those spirits?"

"Where he won't be getting them any longer."

She put down the fork she was about to lift to her mouth. "He won't be what?"

He told her about his visit to the liquor shack with the Salingers. He did not mention the dead Mexican. She studied him thoughtfully as he spoke and smiled only when he mentioned they were getting a dog. "I hope this puppy and Jason get along," she added in mock concern. "He's into everything now, you know, and with no other children around, it will be nice for him to have a pet to play with."

After dinner Seth pulled on his heavy jacket and headed for the stable. Every man on that frontier went armed when leaving his ranch grounds, but it was common practice to put the heavy gun belts aside while working around the ranch itself. Fighting equipment was bulky and could get in a busy man's way. Seth smiled to see Brandy standing in the stable with his single shot pistol strapped on.

Brandy saw the smile. "Sumpin' funny, Seth?"

"See you're wearing your shooting iron."

Brandy's eyes blinked. "Didn't you say I's to keep an eye to dat Carlos?"

Seth looked at him again with only the faintest trace of a smile left. "Didn't figure you'd need a gun to handle the likes of him."

Brandy was silent for a few moments while Seth carefully looked over the horses in the stable. Finally Seth agreed that the right ones had been brought in. He squatted down to study the two sick colts but could tell at once from their newly clear eyes and quick movements that Brandy was bringing them back to health as fast as possible. They'd be out and romping about in a day or two. He decided that the horses in the holding pen, which the wind would have crowding around the lee side of the barn that made up part of the stable, should be put on grain if the storm struck. He'd always felt it increased their resistance to disease.

That done, he turned again to Brandy. Nodding toward the hut, he half muttered, "Well, what's been happening with those two today?"

"Mighty little," said Brandy. "They ain't hardly come out of dat hut."

Seth walked to the stable door and stood looking through the darkness at the small adobe hut. There was one solitary candle burning in its interior, indicating they were still up. He decided he had better settle this business before this stormy night began.

Not being told to stay behind, Brandy walked along with Seth, and when Inez pulled back the light thatched door, he entered with him.

Carlos was lying on the ticking, apparently half asleep, but Inez, after letting them in, stood back against the wall where she could hardly be seen in the dim light.

"Get up!" said Seth, sensing that Carlos knew he was there.

Carlos sat up on the bed slowly, his hands rubbing his face like a man shaking off sleep. "You want something, señor?"

Seth pulled him to his feet. "You know damn good and well I want something. I want you to tell me you're going to behave like a man and treat this girl right!"

Carlos grunted and his lips closed in a thin bitter line. "Inez is my woman—she not your business."

"Anytime I see a woman mistreated, I make it my business."

Carlos looked down sullenly, his eyes beady and resentful. At the foot of his bed lay his knife, but he made no attempt to reach for it.

Seth looked around and made out Inez standing against the wall. "I want you both to hear this," he said, his voice filled with something

more than anger. "Carlos—I catch you with liquor around here again
and you're riding out. If I ever hear you've raised a hand to Inez again,
you'll be riding out with something more than *'adios'* to remember
me by. I want you to stay here for the next few days and finish digging
this well, and you'd best keep in mind if it wasn't for Inez you wouldn't
be drawing pay here at all. Now, if you've got anything to say, say
it. I want this business settled!"

Carlos grimaced and kicked his foot against the bed. "Carlos is
vaquero, not well digger."

"The well is for you and Inez," answered Seth, "and if you're not
digging by tomorrow, you'll be camping out by sundown."

"Inez is my woman. If I go, she goes," said Carlos doggedly.

"That's up to her," said Seth, his eyes seeking her slim form in the
dim light.

The three men stood in silence for a moment, awaiting the most
significant response of all. But Inez lowered her eyes in the darkness
and clasped her hands before her without a word.

In bed that night Isabelle lay closer to Seth than she had for a long
while. He put his arm about her, but it lacked the tension by which
she had always sensed his male arousal. He was either overtired or
preoccupied, and she knew her first shy attempt at rekindling their
intimacy had failed. The bruises on her body had cleared up consid-
erably, and much of the soreness was gone. She wanted him to slip
his hand under her nightgown, but he seemed unaware of her read-
iness, her vulnerability, her muted desire. Instinct warned her it
would be dangerous to press him for more affection now. It would
only betray if not confirm her fears. He was holding her in a comfortable embrace and one hand had moved up to rest against the side
of her breast. It was enough. She understood that Seth was grappling
with something apart from her, something that seemed to have replaced the rage that for a time had simmered behind his every word
and deed.

"What shall we name the puppy?" Her question rose as she turned
her cheek to touch his.

He smiled in the darkness and shook her gently. "You know you're
better at naming things than I am. You'll think of something. Just
make sure it's a manly name, better still, a fighting name."

"What if it's a female?"

"It won't be—I saw to that."

She turned so that her lips touched his face and kissed him lightly. "What are you thinking about, Seth?"

After a long moment he replied in a voice low enough to be a whisper. "Will Bartlet."

Her head fell back. "You've heard from him?"

"Prent Salinger did. There was a fracas up on the Colorado. They tried to trap a large band of Comanches and I guess some Kiowas. Something went wrong. Couple of Rangers were wounded."

"Oh, heavens! Will this never stop!"

"Not till we stop it."

She did not want to think about Comanches. She wanted them torn out of her memory. But now she knew what was hanging like a shroud over her husband's mind. "Seth, please, you're not—"

"Prent said Will needs every experienced man that can reach him. By rights I should have been there."

Isabelle wanted to scream *"By rights you should have been here!"* But she knew that would only bring the whole horrifying experience back to mind. Instead she said, "Seth, maybe we should give up this ranch, at least till the country is safe, and move back east. I can't stand being here alone anymore, and I'm terrified of something happening to Jason." She could feel his body stiffen as she talked, but there was too much emotion behind her thoughts to conceal them. "I can't imagine what I'll do if you leave again."

"I haven't said I'm leaving."

Now she moved her body until it lay partly over his and clung to him childlike. They lay together in silence while the wind rose outside and gusted through the great cottonwood in front of the house. Isabelle finally took his free hand in hers. "Seth, tell me you're not going." Her voice was strained as she squeezed his hand, making her plea more intense.

He pulled her closer still, but it was a while before he answered. "Isabelle, we can't go back. It's taken too much . . . too many years to get us here. This is our home. We've sacrificed everything for it. We'll never be safe as long as those murdering savages are allowed to ride free. We can't deal with them alone. The Rangers are our only hope."

"But you've done your share. There must be others to take your place."

He shook his head. It was not something he could ever explain, but backing off was impossible. When he spoke, his voice had the timbre of deep conviction. "Isabelle, every man in this range who could make it has gone north. Prent Salinger is fixing to go. I know a heap of those Ranger fellows. They're mostly folks like us, only wanting to rid this land of heathen swine so they and their families can live in peace. But it's not a job a man leaves to his neighbor. You've got to understand, the Rangers have their own way of seeing things. No man can take another man's place in a fight."

She choked back a rising sob and hugged him helplessly, burying her face in his chest, trying to think of words that would make him feel her desperation. He hugged her back, but it was a response she knew was meant to comfort her, to transfer to her his strength and resolve. Oh, God, she thought to herself, the loneliness and grief she had known since coming to this damn bitter tract of earth. Was God himself out here? Did he know of her hideous fears? Would he grant her strength to go on? Would he spare and protect this man she had suffered so for? Would he keep Seth loving her? For hours she lay clutching him, listening to the storm as it mounted outside.

Sometime during the night he slept, but Isabelle lay until dawn listening to the plank roof overhead groaning as the furious wind swept over it and howled into the trees that covered the knoll beyond.

6

Will Bartlet peered through the thin light of dawn until he made out the small dark mounds with heavy skins thrown over them. The storm was finally over, and only occasional streaks of snow or icy slush could be seen or felt underfoot. The wind had died down, leaving the air raw and damp and the sky overcast and nearly as dark as the land. His Apache scouts had signaled where the small camp lay snug in the protective bend of a creek that dug its way through a deep ravine running between the jagged hills.

When the storm struck, they were forced to abandon their hot but dangerous pursuit of a large band they had failed to trap on the Colorado. But Bartlet, like many Ranger captains, had developed an uncanny insight into the Comanche mind. They were a people of habit, custom and superstition, and their behavior could be fatally predictable. With a norther blowing in and the game disappearing, he sensed they would break up into small groups and hole up under cover until the storm blew itself out. Knowing his company was too large for any coordinated effort while the storm lasted, he split it into three separate search parties in an attempt to ferret out the smaller campsites. Late the night before, his strategy had borne fruit. One of his Apache scouts had smelled smoke as the storm lessened and the wind started shifting about, and now they had a small encampment surrounded and the horse herd spotted and ready to be stampeded. From the size of the herd, they reckoned there were fifteen or twenty warriors and surely some squaws with their offspring in the camp, but Bartlet was confident his eighteen Rangers and their scouts could surprise them and get the job done.

Although earlier in the week Ranger rifles and marksmanship had kept the Indians at bay, the fight on the Colorado had gone badly. Four Rangers had been wounded, two seriously, and had to be taken back. Bartlet had miscalculated and suddenly found himself seriously outnumbered and almost outmaneuvered. Very shortly, he planned to move up between the Red and the Canadian, where all signs indicated the really large winter camps were to be found. He needed more Rangers and had sent word back with the wounded, asking any ex-Rangers who could to meet him on the Pedernales. He found himself hoping Seth Redmond would be one of these.

He watched now as the silent camp below lay in the dawn, unaware that death, like a serpent, was coiling about it. He could not see his Rangers, but he knew they were closing in. To a man they understood the task before them. Any "red nigger" coughing up his life's blood on the bone-strewn Texas plains today was one less to worry about tomorrow.

Moving forward, he could see two dark figures in motion about the center of the campsite. They would be squaws up starting the breakfast fires. It would be only moments before they spotted the Rangers. He brought up his rifle, knowing the alarm would bring braves tumbling out already armed. Once they realized they were trapped, they would fight to the death.

It was a noise from the direction of the horse herd that touched it off. A young Comanche night guard, attempting to give a warning cry, died when a pistol shot, sounding like a small branch snapping, pierced the dank air. Immediately two squaws let out screams and the deeper voices of the braves rose like distant thunder before they were drowned out by the Rangers' first volley. Both squaws were down, and other figures could be seen doubling over or crumpling to the ground. The braves began stumbling out from under cover as the Rangers moved into the camp, pistols in hand. It was vicious, frantic, animalistic and grotesque, but it was suddenly over. The Rangers looked around and found nothing left to shoot at but heaps of bodies sprawled awkwardly in the cold dawn. Their onslaught had been complete. Not a man, woman or child survived. Two Rangers had suffered knife wounds and one had an arrow through his sleeve, but none seemed to be seriously concerned.

The Rangers stood around in a restive silence as Bartlet reminded them to reload their guns. A few of them bent over to work a souvenir necklace or medicine bag from a brave's body, but most of them seemed to want to move on. That much death that quickly made even hardened men uneasy. Bartlet himself wanted to get away from there. The deafening noise might have alerted other camps. The lesson learned on the Colorado was not wasted on him.

As they made their way back to the horses, the men found themselves studying the low-lying ridges, which had suddenly acquired an ominous look. A few of the men spoke briefly to one another, but none bothered to look back at the campsite where the Apache scouts were still grimly scurrying about, blood dripping from the curved scalping knives in their hands.

Snug in his half loft, Brandy shook his head slowly and smiled to himself as he reached up to rap his knuckles against the heavy beam running above his head. He had just had a tremendous revelation. Outside the storm roared, but Brandy, with a small iron stove he had found rusting on the trail from San Antonio, kept his roost in the stable at least as comfortable as Isabelle and Seth's house, and far more so than Inez and Carlos' hut.

Brandy had lain awake half the night thinking of Seth's words when he had arrived the evening before. At first the comment had annoyed Brandy, especially coming from Seth, but the more he thought about it the more he realized what it implied. *Didn't figure you'd need a gun to handle the likes of him.* Seth was not paying him a compliment. Brandy had heard compliments aplenty, such as Isaac Sawyer saying, when he heard how Brandy had stood up to the big Apache, Snake, "Boy, you sure showed a surprising bit of pluck," or Doc Michalrath's exclaiming while looking elsewhere, "Glad you didn't let 'em buffalo you, boy." Their words were all right, but the tone wasn't very far from "Boy, good to know you ain't no thieving nigger" or "Boy, you sure enough show proper respect." Seth had gone unarmed into the Mexican's hut and pulled him out of bed for a tongue-lashing. Seth was saying he figured Brandy could do the same. Seth was saying Brandy as a man was his equal.

Brandy got up and lit his lamp to look at himself in the jagged piece of mirror Isabelle had given him from her smashed heirloom. His mother had been a Negro slave, but his father was a Creole overseer, and his features, though dark, were not thick and his hair, while black, was curly, not kinky. In fact, with his tall, muscular body and ready smile, many women catching a fleeting glimpse of him would have thought him handsome. But Brandy had a drawback common to those of his origins. He had been raised as a slave, and the marks of servility were still on him. He had been taught by fear of the lash to bow out of other folks' way, not to talk back and never to think himself free to shape his own destiny. The biggest influence of his youth had been a slave named Napi. Brandy had never spoken to the man and had only seen him being hanged and his body soaked in turpentine and burned. But he had heard about Napi, as had all the slaves, for Napi was a daring rebel Negro who had led an ill-fated local uprising. He had gotten his name from the whites, who had made cruel jokes about him thinking himself Napoleon. Yet Napi had smiled his scorn at them as he went to his death. Napi had carried himself like a man who expected and accepted his fate. Napi had died and his body had been destroyed, but Brandy knew now that the rebel had said with his bearing that the spirit that moved his bid for freedom was every man's heritage and unlike flesh consumed by fire was indestructible.

Brandy looked back in the mirror, his mind grappling with his new understanding of his boss. Seth had simply smiled when he heard about Brandy's deadly showdown with Snake. At first it had bothered Brandy and made him wonder, but now he knew it was only what Seth expected from a real man defending helpless women. It's what he would have expected from Seth! Brandy put out the lamp and got back into bed. The next morning as he dressed he glanced at the old pistol he had been carrying since Seth had told him to keep an eye on Carlos. "Cain't imagine what made ole Brandy think he needed a gun to handle the likes of him."

The storm loomed over the Redmond ranch for two days, howling and driving the temperature down until frost began to form on the water in the pails. Inez brought blankets from the main house and wrapped them around her with Carlos' old belt to keep warm. Carlos managed to fend off the chill by digging his well, but the soil could not be moved outside and he swore as he saw it pile up beside the door and spread across the room. It would mean another job when it was finally moved under the stable for fill. Inez watched him mutely for hours, for he had ceased to talk to her and sat with her only when she brought hot food from Isabelle's stove, a chore she went through the storm twice during the day to carry out.

When Seth and Brandy had left, there had been a long period of silence between them, but sometime during the night he had turned to her in the darkness and sunk his fingers into her frail shoulder. "*Puta!* Slut! You no longer Carlos' woman, eh? You like the *gringos* better, eh? Maybe they want you to make love with your mouth, eh? I know. You think I'm a fool? Someday I'll take my knife to you, woman, and whores with black pock marks on their faces will be prettier than Inez."

Now she lay in the dark trembling. She was only a poor mestiza and lived in a world where every woman needed a man to help fend off poverty and keep her from becoming a helpless target for other men. From childhood on she had known she would not be safe until some good man fell in love with her. Carlos surely had, but having been orphaned when little more than a child, she had had scant choice and in any case had been too young to judge. In her innocence and gratitude, she had overlooked much that might have warned off an attentive mother or older girl. But Inez had been blessed with great native intelligence. She had seen men and women caught up in primitive emotions in the rawest settings and instinctively knew what havoc and near-madness lay beneath the passions that flared between the sexes. A man whose pride and masculinity were threatened was a dangerous man, particularly when the woman he considered his allowed her body to be used by others.

For the first time she realized that Carlos, with his knife and his threats, was a weak man. A strong man, deciding she no longer pleased him, would have found himself another woman. But another woman couldn't help Carlos. He needed another child. Throughout the night she thought about her wretched days with him, how he was so possessive of her body even though she never flirted with others or resisted his embrace. She lay looking into the darkness, thinking about Seth and Isabelle. Seth was a strong man. He knew his woman had been raped and yet he was there, holding her tenderly, making her know he understood, lending her his strength. But Carlos' mind was churning with demons of suspicion. He lived in a hell of his own fury that he was intent on making her share. Should she have told him in the beginning she was raped? Might he have learned to live with the loathsome truth? But in her deepening wisdom she knew now in the end it would have been the same. The rape would have been an outrage not for her but for him. It would have been not her agony and humiliation but his. She remembered how it had been with his brothers, for when he talked of them now, it was never their fault but hers. She had allowed them to come close. She had had no business being nude, even though she thought she was alone. Her lip trembled, and she bit into it to hold it still. Never had she been so deeply frightened or felt so alone. What chance would she have if Seth left? It was only then that her eyes opened in the darkness and she saw for a moment the kindly, almost affectionate expression with which Brandy had always greeted her since she had turned to him on the night of the attack.

Isabelle watched the storm dying out with a growing dread, knowing it would bring the frightening issue to a head. For two days she and Seth had moved about each other awkwardly—talking about or playing with Jason, or in the evenings just sitting before the stone fireplace watching the pine faggots and cottonwood limbs burn, she trying to make conversation by asking how the livestock would weather the winter and he, his eyes fixed on the flames, his thoughts seeming far distant, replying, "Reckon we'll know come spring." She felt helpless.

The day after the storm faded away she watched the youthful Rick Salinger arrive with a young mare and a gangling black-and-yellow puppy that wobbled about the floor and then sat down to look at Jason. The baby was crawling toward it, bubbling excitedly and reaching out to touch the puppy's fur. The little dog sniffed at his tiny hand and then gave its little black tail one solitary wag.

Isabelle was on her knees helping them get acquainted, but her ears were nervously straining to catch the words being exchanged between Seth and Rick outside her door. Seth was looking the young mare over as he talked.

"When's Prent figuring on leaving?"

"Tomorrow, I reckon." Rick's answer sounded reluctant, as though he felt life was unfair for a youngster who was practically an honest-to-God man.

Seth finished examining the mare and nodded his head in apparent approval. Then he turned to the boy, his voice rising in quick, clipped tones. "Tell Prent to meet me 'bout noon at the Medina crossing. I'll be going along."

"Golly gee," said Rick aloud, his eyes opening as though it was all painfully clear. The world was unjust, and others, particularly Prent, were getting to hog all the fun and excitement. Seth was a local hero. Prent was going to go hunting redskins with a hero!

Beyond the door Isabelle put her head down to hide her tears. The sound of Seth's voice had left her numb. There was an undeniable change coming over Seth. She could feel it in his sudden retreat into silence, in the quick, unexpected way he glanced off into the distance as though hearing an alarm that rang for him alone.

That evening she tried to mask her foreboding as they sat about making up names for the puppy. Isabelle could not bring herself to care what they named the dog, but she roused herself enough to say his black spots made Pepper a fitting name. But Seth waved it off as he did King and Prince, saying this was a rough-and-ready fighting dog, not some royal fop. It was Brandy coming by and hearing the discussion that settled the issue. "If that dog is a-gonna smell out trouble for us, why don't yuh just call him Scout?" Scout it was, and the puppy, as though aware its identity had been established, began sniffing its way around the house.

In bed that night Seth finally told her he was leaving. For a moment she thought he was going to make love to her, for he held her warmly and his hands started searching her body, his kisses becoming deep and lasting. But as the moment of passion swelled, suddenly a strange hesitancy overtook him, blunting the edge of his desire. Unaccountably the intensity of their embrace began slackening, even as they continued to cling to each other, their feelings growing confused, disturbed, both realizing that as true lovers this moment should have climbed to a climax, making them one—both knowing it had failed.

Wanting but unable to fight a feeling of lost meaning, they settled back in the darkness, sensing it better to say nothing, wanting to believe it was a matter to be healed by time. But Isabelle's womanly instincts were at last grasping the fringes of truth. In these moments that had come between them, she had sensed the maelstrom of wrath he had been concealing with his silence, the suppressed rage consuming him, crippling his emotions, truncating any response to her intimacy or love. She knew now why he had to go and destroy Comanches: because they had raped and ravished her, because they had fouled and defiled her mysteries as a woman, because they had taken with brutality what he had made precious and even sacred with his lifetime of love. She wished their ugly existence swept from his mind, for those who had raped her were dead and rotting in the ground, but she was aware now of some primitive streak in Seth's perplexing nature, and she had come to know from hearing neighboring men talk that there were crimes in a man's mind for which there had to be a bloody atonement, a blind, indiscriminate but cleansing punishment.

It was an agonizing, pain-filled night. She lay there in the grip of emotions she only vaguely understood while Seth, though remaining silent, stayed close and did not sleep. An hour or two before dawn they began to talk once more, slowly finding each other again. They had loved each other too long and too completely not to find comfort in each other's nearness. Nothing was said about the hurtful outcome of their attempt to make love, but Seth began to whisper, his voice husky and unnaturally strained by his own emotions, that he loved her, that his going was something he had to do, that he would be back when the fighting was over to start life anew, that they would be happy again. She believed him. In an outpouring of tears she kissed him and held him close, for as desperately as she wanted him physically, she knew now as she stared into the darkness that she could endure this anguished life only as long as she held his love.

Brandy saddled up Sam, the big chestnut, one more time and led him to the house. Brandy was wagging his head with secret frustration as he went over the hurried instructions he had been given. Carlos was to check how much the storm had caused the cattle to drift. After working the strays back to pasture, he was to finish the well. That done, he was to keep him mending fences and extending the water trough running alongside the holding pen and stable. There was little said about the horses; Brandy already knew their breeding plans, but the news that Rick Salinger would be back in a day or two with two rifles and a six-gun Adam was lending them was climaxed with Seth's curt remark: "Reckon you better start teaching these women to shoot. Not likely there'll be any trouble till I get back, but it's best we get used to the notion that folks who want land around here are going to have to fight for it."

Brandy wondered if Seth would ever get enough of fighting. He thought of all the directions trouble could come from, and something told him that before Seth returned—if he ever did—old Brandy would know more about trouble than was fitting for any runaway nigger to conjure up.

What he said when he faced Seth, though, was as firm and as confident as he could make it. After all, it was already understood he could run this ranch as well as any man.

❖   ❖   ❖

Inez watched Seth riding off with her hands over her breasts and her tongue slowly tripping over her lower lip. She knew he would be gone for some time, leaving Isabelle and Jason alone in the house, and she wondered if Isabelle would allow her to move into the house and sleep away from Carlos. No longer able to drink, he had become quiet and even withdrawn, but she knew from his looks that he wanted her body again, and every night the issue drew closer. Now with Seth gone it would only be a matter of time before she awoke with his hands on her. She picked out the best of her worn frocks and set it aside. After she had talked to Isabelle, she thought she might walk down to the stable and visit Brandy.

Two days later, Isabelle sat with Jason on her lap, looking at the bright blond curls he had gotten from her and the deep blue eyes he had gotten from his father. He was a beautiful child and just beginning to have a personality. She was thinking of that morning in Tennessee when she had awakened feeling nauseous, with a strong acid taste that had stayed in her mouth for hours. Seth had immediately worried, for there was talk of cholera about, and he had insisted she go at once to the old country doctor whom the local people had recommended. The doctor turned out to be a curt but kindly old man who, after examining her and asking her a few questions, had simply smiled, patted her on the arm and told her she was pregnant. That was a joyous moment, and the nausea she had continued to feel in the morning no longer bothered her. But now it was already well over a month since her rape and the flow of blood had not come. At first she thought that the emotional throes of her horrifying experience had interrupted her normal cycle, and then, although expecting it and keeping some cotton batting handy, she was happy it had not appeared while she waited for Seth's love. But suddenly she wanted to scream with fright as she re-counted the days, the weeks; the red blood she, in some dark corner of her mind, had been silently praying for had not come. An unnameable dread seized her as she grasped Jason and held the startled baby to her, for this morning she had awoken with severe nausea and a strong acid taste that had stayed in her mouth for hours.

Part Two

CRY
of the
WAR EAGLE

February 1842

7

A raw, gusty wind greeted them on the Pedernales. They hadn't gone through San Antonio but had ridden northeast for two days until they struck the river some twenty-five miles west of its confluence with the Colorado. They found the Ranger camp in the small loop of the river, the very spot Seth remembered their using in '39. Prentiss was amazed at its barrenness. There was no cover. The men had been sleeping in the open, and the few fires he could see were low and at best keeping warm a pot of coffee. He spotted the carcasses of two deer hanging from a limb back from the river. It was the only food in sight. Down by the water, where thick clumps of dead grass stretched for hundreds of feet, the horses were either hobbled or milling about inside a rope corral.

Because Seth had taken the precaution of approaching the camp in the open, where Ranger sentinels could easily see them, Prentiss was not surprised they rode in unchallenged. Some of the Rangers waved briefly at Seth. There was no shout of greeting. Rangers in Indian country learned to avoid making noise, and when Seth dismounted to shake hands with a tall, bearded man whose craggy face could not quite conceal a smile of satisfaction at their arrival, Prent glanced around him and knew he was sure enough in the midst of men who held the bloodstained salvation of Texas in their hands.

That evening they ate charred venison and drank hot coffee while Seth heard that sixteen other ex-Rangers had shown up. Bartlet was going to move in the morning, allowing he had enough men now to work his way north and at least make a strike at any camps he found along the Red. Their Apache scouts had reported heavy signs across the Colorado, and Bartlet had decided to cross the river and work along the east bank as they angled their way northward. Seth said nothing when he heard they had already wiped out a small bunch of Comanches, nor did he mention Isabelle or the raid on his ranch. Will Bartlet didn't need to be told that if Isabelle had survived the raid unscathed Seth would have made a point of it. He studied the newly etched lines that lent even more prominence to Seth's hard blue eyes and said nothing. However, he did look quizzically at Prent and particularly at his horse. Jack Hays had lived by the adage that a Ranger was only as good as his horse. Fortunately Prent had come on a sturdy bay and when Seth introduced him he was careful to say, "This is Adam Salinger's son."

Bartlet grunted in agreement. He had known the old gunfighter well and knew him to be a formidable but sensible man. This son might be hewn from the same stuff, but Bartlet had seen too many greenhorns facing fire for the first time to take things for granted. "Keep him close to you till he gets the hang of it," he said to Seth as he shook Prent's hand just long enough to make him feel welcome. Then his eyes settled on Seth. "As you probably figured, we'll be leaving come sunup and Berry is going to take the point." Berry was a quiet, dark Texan whom some said carried Cherokee blood. Once he found a trail, he had never been known to lose it. Bartlet cleared his throat. "Going to keep some of the boys riding back a ways. This is rough country and the redskins know we're here. Figure you might take over and see we don't straggle too much. Stay close enough so we can hear your shots if you smell trouble. Fire twice, count to five and fire twice more."

Seth nodded.

The following morning he found he had six men including Prent in his rear patrol. Tanner and Purdy, whom he hadn't seen since the Casa Colorada, also turned up, both just nodding at him, making no mention of the desperate hurry with which he had left San Antonio. Seth kept his group only a mile or two behind the main party, but he kept looking back. He knew Berry was on the point and their Apache scouts on their flanks. If there was a threat in this dangerous terrain, it was likely to come from the rear.

The day was tense, but nothing untoward happened. Late in the afternoon, following a growing suspicion, he pulled his men into an outcropping of rock and dismounted, telling them to stay put while he climbed to the top terrace of the rocks. A half hour went by before he saw a quick flash of metal near a low-lying ridge they had crossed earlier. There, then, was his answer. They were being followed.

When Bartlet was told, he spat in disgust, realizing there would be no surprising any camps as long as the Comanches knew their whereabouts. That night in a council of war that included Seth, Berry and two well-seasoned Rangers, one of whom could speak passable Comanche and the other whose familiarity with sign language helped Bartlet direct their Apache scouts, it was decided they had to lose the horsemen trailing them, a difficult feat and one that could be accomplished only at night. Bartlet, realizing that to wait would only increase the risk of failure, passed the word that they had two hours to rest, get their last meal of charred meat and hot coffee and be ready to move. Prent Salinger, exhausted from the long tension-ridden day and more than ready to roll up in his blanket, looked at Seth as though more explanation were due. But Seth just turned away. "Be ready, Ranger," he muttered. Prent, rising slowly to fold back his blanket, smiled in spite of himself. By God, he was a Ranger now, and that had to be explanation enough for everything.

Fortunately, and perhaps critically for the white frontier, the Comanches, those warlike nomads aggressively defending their hunting grounds against others, put their faith in magic rather than reason. Blind to the realities of numbers and firepower, they continued to rely upon the occult powers of incantations and medicines and failed to learn from the Rangers as the Rangers so readily learned from them. The Comanches' favorite strategy for losing pursuers was known to every Ranger, so Bartlet's orders, though brief and brusquely given, were immediately understood. When darkness had fallen they started moving along the river, staying in shallow water until they reached the first ford. There they started breaking up. In every group there were Rangers who knew the country and knew where they were headed. By continual splitting there were at least ten groups by midnight, with seven or eight men in each. It was a maneuver most easily carried out at night, as Indians did not cotton to fighting in the dark. By two hours before dawn they had split again and by circling or working back over rocky surfaces had left so many trails that the Comanches would have been running into each other attempting to follow them all. They had traveled only fifteen miles as the crow flies, but before dawn they were all settled in a shallow depression between the hills, their horses picketed along a tiny brook that trickled through the depression.

Bartlet had already sent the Apache scouts out to discover if any large hostile parties were about, but Seth was scanning the sky and quietly sniffing the air. Comanches were creatures of habit, and though hardy and used to a rigorous existence, they still liked a few vital creature comforts. The weather was deteriorating again, and it was not their way to stay out on the windswept plains, matching wits with a well-armed enemy who clearly wanted to escape them.

The Apache scouts were soon back making the sign for no enemies in sight. Bartlet gave permission to start a few fires; the temperature was dropping and eastward a gray sheath was replacing the wan pink sky of morning. The smell of coffee soon permeated the air and the horses along the picket line began to shudder and stamp their hooves as the rising wind whined lightly above the depression and began to dip into the camp with a new and ever-sharpening edge. Bartlet reckoned that if conditions got much worse than the last storm they might have to seek cover themselves—but not for long. Bad weather was their single but indispensable ally. It immobilized the enemy, it enabled the Rangers, who were unencumbered by women and children, the sick or the aged, to attack on their own terms.

Bartlet stared at the sky over his tin cup of steaming coffee, listening to Seth advising him to move northward along the Colorado and delay any crossing of the river till they got beyond the San Saba. Seth figured they'd pick up some heavy trails heading north toward the Red between the San Saba and the Concho.

Will Bartlet pursed his lips as he weighed Seth's words. He had thought to cross the river here and head north until he reached the Brazos, then sweep the many creeks feeding the Red from the south. But Seth could be right; there could easily be plenty of Comanches closer to home. Not a man for quick decisions, he waited till Seth finished his brief comments. Then he nodded his head in mute appreciation and murmured, "Mebbe so."

Isabelle had been so upset she no longer trusted her own senses in their recording of events. On the day Bessie Salinger was to arrive she searched half the morning for the money Carlos had brought back for the horses they'd sold, and which she thought she had stuck between two jars on her shelf. Quite possibly she might never have thought of it for months; money had begun to play so little part in their lives. Almost all transactions in this raw, unsettled land were made on credit or barter, and unless one traveled to San Antonio there was no place money could be spent. But now, after frantically thinking about it for two sleepless nights, she had decided she must see Dr. Michalrath. She had sent Brandy with a note to Bessie Salinger, explaining her need to see the doctor and asking Bessie to come up with her one-horse rig and travel with her on the daylong trip the visit would require.

Brandy returned saying that Missy Salinger had read the note and told him to say she would come on the morrow and stay the night so they could get an early start the following morning. Isabelle realized they would be traveling at least part of the way over the main trail that stretched from San Antonio to the Hondo. She remembered that along that trail there were often traders who carried sundry household articles and sometimes spices or even bolts of cloth in their wagons. But such merchant-traders were always transients and dealt only in cash. Knowing this, she decided to take along part of their money to buy something for Bessie and perhaps Phoebe Michalrath, the doctor's ill sister, to repay them for their help. But after stripping the shelves and even looking into the broken chest—where she knew, for she had been into it a dozen times, the money could not be—she finally resigned herself to the fact that it was gone. Could Seth have taken it? No, he would have less need of it than she. Besides, Seth would surely have told her. With some shock she realized that with everything else tormenting their minds the money for the horses had never been mentioned. Even when Snake's taking of their small cache from the chest had come up, the potential disasters looming over those dreadful moments had dwarfed it in importance. Seth had probably discussed the sale with Carlos, that was his way, but she couldn't be sure. However, the thought of Carlos prompted her to think the Mexican might remember where she had put the tightly folded bills, for she recalled his bringing them on that day she was so distraught, the day after the raid, and there was a chance he would remember what she had done with them.

Later she walked to the stable to tell Brandy she'd like Carlos to stop by the house that evening when he returned.

◆ ◆ ◆

Almost squealing as she stepped down from her rig, Bessie Salinger hugged Isabelle warmly, for it was a great treat in that lonely country to have someone your own age and sex to talk to, to share secrets with, maybe even dreams. It was a world few men knew about but young women facing the same stage of life, and having developed a sisterly love, reach a harmony of understanding that sometimes makes them grow euphoric when they have a chance to be together for a moment, away from the testy if unspoken rivalry that makes up the world of men.

This time, however, as soon as they were alone in the house, Isabelle broke down in tears and sobbed in Bessie's arms. In a seizure of agony and relief she poured out her paralyzing fears and wept uncontrollably as she told Bessie how frantic she was and how desperately, even prayerfully, she hoped Dr. Michalrath could help her. Bessie, visibly recovering from the initial shock, took her firmly by the arms and settled her on the bed, holding her comfortingly as she quieted her down. "Isabelle, Isabelle, could it . . . could it not be Seth's?"

"I don't know . . . I'm just afraid."

Bessie shook her head as though she were striving to gather her thoughts. "Now, as I remember, Seth had just left for San Antonio. Did you . . . did you and Seth . . . did anything happen just before he left?"

"Oh, dear." Isabelle put her head down. "I can't think. I don't honestly remember. Seth was so worried about leaving. I'm not sure."

Bessie kissed her and slapped her own knee lightly in an effort to move Isabelle to a lighter mood. "Isabelle, Ma always told me it was foolish to worry about milk that hasn't been spilt. You must stop torturing yourself this way. Lord knows you've suffered enough." She took a deep breath and hugged Isabelle again, saying with energy, "I do believe I could use a cup of tea."

The two women talked most of the day and, apart from playing with and feeding Jason, a pleasure Bessie insisted on hogging, they did not see another soul. It was only when Isabelle mentioned that Inez was having trouble with Carlos that her growing anxiety over leaving Jason behind on the morrow surfaced. Bessie sighed in mock exasperation. "It's plain to see why you're as pale as a banshee dipped in flour. You worry about everything." She juggled Jason on her knee, murmuring and kissing him. "Tell you what. We'll bundle him up and take him with us. He'll be good company for Aunt Bessie. He and I can get acquainted while you're visiting with old Michalrath." Isabelle felt a stir of warmth. Though her voice seemed feeble beside Bessie's exuberance, she no longer felt lost and alone.

In the evening they built a fire and talked on until Bessie finally remarked that they would have to make a very early start in the morning and had best get to bed. Isabelle, somewhat more settled but still deeply exhausted, finally fell asleep next to her dear, comforting friend, not realizing until the next morning that Carlos had failed to come by the house as she had asked. Nor did Brandy show up to explain.

Seth's leaving had been the clinching factor in Carlos' decision to put an end to his shameful lot. Inez was his. These *gringos* had no right to deny him his woman. In Mexico such a thing was unheard of. How he treated her was his affair. He had put up with this unmanly disgrace long enough. Riding through the hills alone, he mulled over how he would make his stand, how he would show them he was *vaquero* enough to take what was his. After all, he had only this overbearing nigger to deal with now, and though well muscled, the irritating ex-slave was no longer even carrying a gun. At the peak of his seething anger he swore viciously that they had even fixed it so he could no longer have his cheap wine.

Then suddenly the picture changed. The day before Seth left he had spotted a rider leading a pack horse and coming up from the main trail in what was meant to seem a random search. But as he drew closer he recognized the squat Mexican who had worked at the liquor lode Seth and the Salingers had forcibly closed down. After more than the usual elaborate Mexican greeting, the man informed him that though the bulk of their liquor had been moved fifty miles to the southeast, below San Antonio, this courier was on hand with adequate supplies for appreciative customers. Carlos was secretly squirming with joy until he learned this service was not available to those who bought only one bottle of wine. To make this arduous and risky effort worthwhile, the squat hairy one explained, purchases would have to be at least twenty bottles and paid for in full. Carlos pulled back and frowned. Were not his days bedeviled by ill luck! Still, after more words and a peek at the appealing wares, Carlos agreed to meet him again the following day.

Carlos had never had any money to speak of. In fact, the only time he had ever handled any sizable amount was when he had taken the Redmond horses up for sale. Now on his way home, after viewing the shiny red bottles, his need for a drink began to mount. His fury at his many humiliations increased until the tension in his face resembled pain. More and more often the distracted way Isabelle had stuck the money he had given her for the horses between her jars began to slip along the edges of his mind.

Brandy watched Isabelle walking away from the stable, muttering to himself, "Lordy, lordy, what's troubling you, Missum Isabelle?" She had spoken to him in a voice near breaking, and it was clear she had been crying, for her eyes were slightly swollen and her hands kept lifting and holding a kerchief to her mouth. He did not think Seth's leaving a few days ago could have caused all that. He knew she was making the long trip to see Dr. Michalrath on the morrow. What was that all about? Now she was asking to see Carlos. What was that about? Brandy waited until she was back in the house before he returned to spreading hay in the main corrals where the once-plentiful grass had been grazed away.

In the early afternoon he had seen Bessie Salinger arriving. He hoped Missy Salinger would put Isabelle in a better mood.

Late that afternoon, hearing nothing from the house, he knocked on the door of the adobe hut and immediately sensed that Inez must have been watching him come from the stable, for the door opened at his knock and she was standing there motioning him in.

They had already talked obliquely about her anxieties concerning Carlos, and Brandy, feeling if not completely understanding her fright, had assured her he would keep an ear out for trouble. They arranged to have her leave a small candle in the one window facing the stable if she felt a threat brewing. Inez had at first shaken her head at this, knowing that if trouble came it would surely come when all her candles were out. But they could think of nothing else.

Now he told her that if Carlos arrived at the hut before he came to the stable she was to tell him Isabelle wanted to see him. Inez nodded. "You have talked to the señora?"

"Yeah, and she sure don't look too good."

"She is very troubled, no?"

"I 'magine so."

They were very close together. Inez was looking up at him, and he had a queasy feeling that she wanted him to reach out and hold her, a physical way perhaps of making her feel protected. His hands rose toward her for a moment, but his courage failed him. He was not sure what she really wanted, and he ended by taking an awkward step backward. Seeing this, she smiled at him shyly, but then came forward boldly to hug him, and feeling the pressure of her arms around him he reached down and kissed her cheek. Both breathed out together, relieved that this first step toward intimacy had been taken.

Brandy was back long after dark, for Carlos did not come in and was nowhere to be found. Inez was glad to see him, for her intuition told her this absence was a bad sign.

"Could it be he just up and left?" asked Brandy, remembering Carlos had taken one of their best-bred horses that morning.

Inez looked around her and replied with an edge of alarm in her voice. "No, he will be back." There were too many things in that hut Carlos would never part with, such as his faded dress jacket with its two silver buttons and his second knife.

"Reckon somethin' must be keepin' him."

Inez lifted a hand to her throat, her expression tense and uneasy. "You will tell this to the señora?"

"No, let her be. There ain't nothin' she can do."

"We wait, eh?"

Brandy nodded. Somehow he couldn't keep himself from wondering what Seth would do.

It was long after midnight when Brandy heard the low thudding of horses' hooves moving slowly with rough uneven steps across the yard. The horse whinnied constantly, which told Brandy it was nervous and possibly wanting to bolt. Before he was out of the stable he was sure he had heard the clink of glass, and halfway across the yard he heard the door of the hut close.

The horse, which had been left standing, tried to shy when Brandy came up, but he spoke to it and stroked its muzzle until it quieted down. The smell of wine coming from the horse's mane and withers was overpowering. A sack tied before the saddle was brimming with long, thin bottles that continued to clink at every motion of the horse's body.

Brandy, well aware of what had happened, started for the hut. He saw a candle flame up only to be immediately snuffed out. Inez's voice reached him next. "Carlos, no!" Her words rose in the frantic whine of a frightened animal about to feel the teeth of its predator. As Brandy reached the door of the hut he could hear something tearing, and the labored grunts of someone struggling, but coming into the hut he could see only the thrashing movements of two figures on the bed. He grabbed the one on top and pulled it to the floor. He knew he had hold of Carlos, but then Inez was gasping as though a grip on her throat had just been released, "Watch out! His knife!"

Brandy bent over the clawing figure at his feet. It reeked of wine, but it was crouching and coming up. He could not see the knife, but he straightened up and delivered a solid kick that drove the figure back against the wall. "Git us a light!" he shouted to Inez, but now he could make out the dark figure climbing up against the adobe wall. He reached out and found an arm. He did not know if it held the knife or not, but he twisted it behind the other's back until he heard a whimper of pain. Then he smashed at the other's head with his fist and the figure slumped to the floor again. With a tinge of disgust Brandy realized he was dealing with a drunken man and that more violence was ridiculous. As he stopped, looking down at the collapsed figure on the floor, the light of a candle began to filter through the room. He turned to find Inez with a candle in one hand and Carlos' knife in the other. She was nude, Carlos having torn off her sleeping shift.

Brandy reached down and pulled Carlos up onto the bed, where he lay in a drunken stupor. In spite of the frantic scene that had taken place, Brandy knew there had not been enough noise to reach Isabelle or the Salinger girl sleeping on the other side of the house. After thinking a moment, he blew the candle in Inez' hand out and, taking a blanket from the bed, wrapped it around her. He kept her folded in his arms, feeling his rising erection pressing against her bare stomach as she returned his embrace with pressure of her own. As though in a long-held but mute understanding they grasped each other's hands as they left the hut and made their way in mounting tension to the stable. There, lying on his bed and opening her legs, Inez let Brandy make love to her, her deep need for human contact and her new sense of her worth as a woman bringing her breath up in a series of tremulous sighs. In all the many lonely years she had shared Carlos' bed she had never known orgasms as deep and lasting as those that rose from her loins to ripple through her body over and over again that night.

Rousing himself from a euphoria of sleep and gently rocking Inez awake, Brandy had Bessie's horse and rig waiting at the house before dawn. The two women were ready with Jason in a large basket surrounded by food and toys. They stood finishing their coffee as Brandy placed the basket and Seth's old rifle behind the narrow seat. He noticed that Bessie's pistol was hanging in a leather strap from her shoulder.

"Brandy, did you plain forget I wanted to see Carlos last night?" asked Isabelle, her voice strained and nervous as she appeared to be having trouble swallowing her coffee.

Brandy knew this was the wrong moment to burden Isabelle with the awkward problem of Carlos. "No, missum, it's just dat Carlos, he got in mighty late last night and I had to send him out not a moment ago. Some of the brood mares done broke out of dat far pasture."

Isabelle looked at Bessie, trying to cover her irritation which was made all the worse by her brooding worries. "Oh, mercy, I did so hope he would remember where I put that money."

"Isabelle, stop fretting. Money doesn't fly. You'll find it sooner or later." Bessie's voice sounded curt but reassuring. "I think we'd best be on our way. Weather looks fair enough, but it might not hold. This time of year one can never tell."

The women rode off and Brandy watched them go, his worry about what was troubling Isabelle replaced by worry about what he had just heard. Although he had told Inez to return to the hut and wait until Carlos awakened, he knew now he had to speak to her again. "Seems dey ain't no end to trouble," he said to himself.

Inez had slipped back into the hut to find Carlos still sprawled on the bed snoring and occasionally groaning in the manner of vaguely conscious drunks. She stood in the lingering shadows, quietly bathing herself and holding her small breasts that still tingled from Brandy's fondling and nuzzling that she had at first enjoyed and then encouraged. In the little mirror she kept above the washbasin she saw her slim olive face suffused with what seemed an internal smile. In some deep sensual way she felt fulfilled and even enjoyed a rare kind of peace. She knew now that ever since she had seen Brandy pointing that rifle at Snake while she and Isabelle sat frozen with fright, something had been happening between them, and she recalled with more and more understanding how she had always noticed Seth treating Brandy with a measure of respect he did not show Carlos.

She was startled and surprised to hear pebbles striking the thatched door, but she peeked out to see Brandy motioning her to join him. With an anxious glance at Carlos, whose loud but uneven breathing was warning her he was slowly sobering up and his eyes would soon be blinking open, she slipped out and ran to Brandy's side.

At noon the two women pulled into the Michalrath yard and young Jed came out to take their rig. Dr. Michalrath and Phoebe greeted them warmly, but the doctor's heavyset face was soon looking at Isabelle quizzically. He had seen enough people with trouble on their minds to know when one was sitting in his parlor.

"What can I do for you ladies?" he said after they had for the moment refused Phoebe's offer of tea and biscuits.

Isabelle's lips were drawn tightly together. "I'd like to talk to you, Doctor, if I may."

Michalrath knew she meant alone. He gestured to an adjoining room where he treated his patients. "Of course. Let's step in here." With the door closed behind them, Isabelle marshaled enough strength to tell him her terrible anxieties and what lay behind them. He listened, his expression revealing, as he heard the symptoms and their timing, that her concerns were not likely misplaced.

When she finished he grunted like a man deciding to look closer at a problem with little doubt as to what he would find. "Well, let's have a look, you never can tell."

Isabelle was too frightened to be shy. She reached under her dress and slipped her underwear off, then she sat up on the table and pulled her skirt and petticoats up to her hips. The doctor looked at her shapely legs in the way old men have of quietly admiring what once would have excited them and then matter-of-factly started to examine her.

He did not take long. He probed her gently and asked a question or two about her breasts. Then he stepped over to the washbowl, washed his hands quickly and came back drying them slowly. She did not need to be told. The doctor looked at her with eyes that had seen many hard truths faced, far harder than this one, but he said kindly enough, "Isabelle, I'm afraid you're pregnant."

Idiotically she gasped, "What's going to happen?"

He cleared his throat, realizing from her remark what a strain she was under. "You're going to have a baby, my dear."

Isabelle reached out to take his arm. "Dr. Michalrath, can't we do something? I just can't have this baby."

Michalrath took her hands in his. He knew what she was urging, but he was a doctor who'd seen the dangers in that kind of surgery. Two cases he had witnessed in his youth, one a girl who bled to death and the other a young woman who died of blood poisoning. His first responsibility was to the lives of his patients. "Isabelle, you don't know yet who the father is. It could be Seth."

"I can't risk that."

Michalrath sighed. "Isabelle, whatever Seth wants, he wants you alive. If you go home and take care of yourself, the worst that can happen is you'll have a baby. Then you can decide what to do. Mind me now and stay away from any drugs. The Mexicans have something they think brings on miscarriages, but it's nothing but pure poison. Seth and Jason need you. Don't turn this spell of bad luck into a godawful tragedy."

Isabelle was having trouble making her mind work. She wanted Michalrath to do something about her pregnancy. She wanted someone to tell her this was nothing but an ugly dream that would be gone tomorrow. She wanted some way to be sure it was Seth's seed, and Seth's seed alone, alive in her. But the doctor's words contained the cruel realities that bored into her brain. After a time she said "When . . . when will we know . . . about . . . about the father, I mean?"

"When the child is born."

Isabelle turned away and bent over to slip her underwear on again. As she straightened her skirt she thought of Seth and the fragile state of their love when he had left. At that moment she wished she were dead.

Brandy sat looking at the rumpled bills and the handful of silver Inez had taken from Carlos' pockets. He knew it had to be Isabelle's money. He had already taken the wine and stored it on the high beams of the stable, the same beams that had run just above their lovemaking. At least now he had little trouble deciding what Seth would do about the theft. He had heard what happened to the thieving thugs who had stolen Redmond horses in North Carolina. Beyond that, he had heard Seth telling Carlos that the next time he caught him drinking he was going to run him off, not to mention what was promised if he was caught threatening Inez again. But Brandy was becoming troubled by other thoughts, thoughts that began to temper his night of love with Inez. Would Isabelle and particularly Seth feel the same way about him knowing he had taken the lonely, frightened Inez, another man's woman, into his bed? And what of that dark taboo he had heard since he was a child, that Negroes must fornicate only with Negroes? He didn't know. But with Carlos gone he knew his own masculine drives, released by Inez' lithe passionate body, would be impossible to hide. The long night of wild, exciting but increasingly tender lovemaking had left them clinging together, knowing but strangely frightened of voicing their illicit love. He kicked at the barrel that stood upright holding the money and wondered if he ever really had been the man Seth thought him to be. Maybe he was something else, something less, something with no claim to pride or honor like Seth. Other worries began to move unbidden into his mind. Could he really run this sprawling ranch by himself? Could a single rider handle the horses and cattle and stay close enough to the house to offer Isabelle and Inez any protection? As he waited for Carlos to appear he began to think he had better hold off doing anything until Isabelle returned. The problem that had taken her to Dr. Michalrath in distress might somehow affect whatever decision had to be made.

When Carlos finally appeared, it was with Inez holding him by the hand and pulling him toward the stable. Brandy decided to leave the money on the barrelhead where Inez had placed it and let Carlos see for himself what waited to be explained.

The sight of Carlos' face coming closer made Brandy's eyes flick open a trifle wider. The Mexican's pupils were glazed over and the whole left side of his face was badly bruised; a string of hardened blood that had trickled from the corner of his mouth was still there. Even from six feet away Brandy caught the sickening odor of his breath.

Carlos stood looking for a full minute at the money before his hands ran slowly over his pockets. Finding them flat, he slumped forward in a mute resentment that brought ugly contours to his swollen face.

"Where did dis money come from?" asked Brandy, watching the other closely.

"I find it. What you think?"

"Where did you find it?"

"Over on the main trail, lots of cattle drift that way since storm."

Brandy grunted in mock agreement. "And where did you git dat mess of wine?"

"Wine?" Carlos stopped and looked around him as though he were gathering hazy and scattered thoughts, grasping for the first time what had transpired during his drunk. *"Carajo!* You take the wine?"

"Yeah, you know Seth don't hold with no liquor on his ranch."

"Give Carlos back his wine—he will go."

"Where you figure to be going?"

"Is my business. I take my woman. We go."

Inez, who all her life had backed away and sought the shadows when Carlos talked to others, now took a step forward. "Inez is no more your woman."

Carlos turned to her, a feral quality tightening his face. "What you mean, woman? You are mine! You come with me!"

Inez rose up until she was almost on her toes as she faced him, her eyes cold and steady, her mouth unbelievably firm. "You steal from these people who give us home and food to eat and you call Inez your woman! You come drunk in the night with your knife and rape me just like *loco* savage!" She brought her hands up to her face, making her glare seem more intense. "You beat Inez and force her to make love like whore and still you say she is your woman." She took another step toward him. "I spit on you! If you touch me again, I will kill you!"

Carlos staggered back a step, but he was clawing for the knife that wasn't there. He finally steadied himself, even as he choked and sputtered on his fury and frustration. "I go," he finally blurted. But then, throwing the ground at Inez' feet an openly threatening look, he spat. "Remember, one day I come back."

"You ain't goin' anywheres," said Brandy, quietly gathering up the money. "Leastways not till Missum Isabelle gits here."

That afternoon young Jed Michalrath came into the parlor where Isabelle and Bessie were finishing the tea and warm bread Phoebe had finally managed to serve with fruit preserves. Jason was asleep. "Wind is picking up and blowing cold," he said. "There's mean weather making up to the west."

Dr. Michalrath excused himself and stepped out onto the porch.

He saw a gray curtain of clouds that seemed to be forming from nowhere moving on a chill wind toward them. He came back patting a loose strand of hair back into place. "Best you figure on staying over tonight, ladies, you don't want to be caught out in the cold and wet with a baby this time of year."

"Oh, dear, I should be getting back," said Isabelle, her breath seeming almost too weak to carry her words. Bessie squeezed her hand warmly and went to the window to see for herself. She knew they could not get back until well after dark. If a storm broke they could cover Jason with a slicker, but they themselves would be drenched and frozen, and God alone knew what condition the trails would be in. It was common for visitors from any distance to stay overnight this time of year. Heavy rains made the best trails treacherous and sometimes impassable, and cover for stranded travelers was almost impossible to find in this empty, brooding land.

A little more than an hour later, rain mixed with sleet began a light roaring as the wind drove it against the windows and the Michalraths' steepled roof. Then Bessie and Isabelle agreed to stay the night if Phoebe would only get to her bed and allow Bessie to prepare dinner.

Brandy pumped water into the narrow trough for the horses and scratched his head, knowing he had to keep Carlos and Inez apart. He sent her to the house, telling her to stay there until Isabelle arrived and busy herself with any tasks she could find. Carlos he marched back to the hut. For all his suppressed fury, the Mexican immediately headed for the bed, sprawling on it and groaning as he buried his eyes in the single pillow, trying to shut out the still-nauseous torment that was the aftermath of too much wine.

But Brandy wasn't about to allow this wretch, trembling with helpless fury and likely becoming increasingly dangerous, to spend the morning nursing himself back to a clear head and steady hand. He kicked the other's foot and ordered him back to his feet. Pointing to the pile of dirt still lying across the wall to the right of the door, he said, "Git yourself a shovel and doan put it down till you move this mess o' dirt under duh stable. If dey's any trouble dey's room under dat stable for more'n dirt."

Carlos cringed, his painful face a signal he was on the verge of vomiting. When Brandy warned him that Isabelle, after hearing of his crime, might want him taken to San Antonio and turned over to the law, he forced himself to move. Only a drugged idiot would risk being a convicted Mexican in a Texas jail.

During the afternoon Brandy noticed the sky turning gray and the wind from the west growing brisk and coming in gusts that smelled of damp and frost. He began to wonder and then worry about Isabelle and Bessie. By evening, though, with the storm roaring and sleet whipping across the yard, he concluded that the women had decided to stay at Michalrath's overnight. It was the sensible thing to do, and he had always thought Bessie Salinger had more sense than most men.

With the storm coming on, Carlos, on the verge of collapse, pleaded that he had to stop work. Brandy, seeing that almost all the dirt had been moved, let him go and watched him crumbling onto the bed and almost immediately starting to snore. He knew the strenuous day's work, on top of his excesses of the night before, would leave Carlos in an exhausted sleep until morning. Putting aside the pitchfork with which he had been moving hay, he headed for the house.

As he entered, Inez, childishly overjoyed at seeing him, rushed into his arms, but he held her away for a few moments and looked at her, his forehead thinly lined with worry. "Not here," he said, glancing about and noticing that everything seemed clean and tidy. Her joyous expression slowly changed to one of puzzled doubt, faintly tinged with fear. He knew what she was thinking and managed a half smile as he said, "When it's real dark put on somethin' to keep you dry and come down to de stable."

Her expression lightened a bit. "Carlos?"

"He's sleepin' like he dead."

Squeezing her arms to let her know his feelings for her were still alive, he backed out the door and disappeared.

The dark couldn't come quickly enough for Inez. By continually watching the stable, wrapped in a slicker and holding the kitchen door ajar, she finally saw a lantern come to life in the wide doors between the corrals. Moments later it flickered out. They hadn't agreed upon any signal, but Inez knew it was Brandy telling her to come.

She came into the stable breathless from her little run, her slicker dripping with freezing rain. Brandy was waiting to help her climb up to his loft. They left the damp slicker over one of the stalls, and she was glad to feel his little stove throwing out its amazing heat. They sat on the bed as Brandy kissed her and hugged her, but she knew, as she had come ready and anxious to abandon herself in his arms, that something was astir in his mind and holding him back.

"Brandy, you think of something, yes?"

"Yeah. Got a mite of thinkin' to do."

"You will speak of it to me?"

Brandy shifted himself around before he answered, "Guess so. Reckon we better talk some." He took her in his arms and pulled her closer. "Inez, we gotta tell Missum Isabelle."

"The señora?"

Brandy nodded.

Inez looked at him in the dark. "Why we tell her?"

" 'Cause it's what we gotta do."

Inez was silent for a moment. "She will not like us together?"

"Ah dunno."

Inez raised herself on the bed until her head was level with his, then she took him by the shoulders, "What you gonna tell her?"

Brandy took a moment to gather his thoughts, for that afternoon his mind had been rambling through the many ways he could approach Isabelle. None seemed right now or even easy. After a moment he said, "Jus' the truth, Ah reckon."

They were both silent for several minutes before Inez murmured, her voice almost dying away, "What if she not like us together?"

Brandy put his head down and shook it. His heart was not in his words, but he knew they were right nonetheless. "You know Brandy, he a free man now. If Missum don't want us together, reckon we just gotta try our luck somewhere else."

With that she breathed out in relief, smiled and kissed him. In her heart she was praying Seth and Isabelle wouldn't want to lose him any more than she did, for even though she was an illiterate *mestiza* Inez would have surprised many with the realities she had come to grips with. She knew secretly, in spite of their blustering and brave talk, that her people were no match for the cruel, murderous mounted Comanches that had ravaged and decimated their villages for ages. She knew, in spite of their smoldering resentment, that her countrymen north of the Rio Grande lived on the sufferance and indeed the protection of the Anglo Texans who actually hunted the savages down and destroyed them without comment or quarter. She knew her friendship with Isabelle was more to be cherished in this threatening land than any community of frightened impoverished Mexicans. Truly, she did not want to leave the pretty, gentle señora. But for Brandy leaving could be far worse. As an ex-slave, he would find life difficult and even dangerous without Seth and Isabelle, who had not only befriended him but given him a place in their lives. Even the gun-backed Texas laws offered little comfort to ex-slaves. The shadow of the Southern color barrier was still strong in Texas. Yet here he was willing to sacrifice what might well be his salvation for her. She could have wept in vexation. All her adult life she had lived only for the spiteful, selfish and growingly sadistic Carlos. Now she had a man who said he would live only for her. In her aching breast she was grateful and her gratitude deepened the responses of her body as they clung together in the full fervor that seizes the heart in erupting love.

The next morning broke crisp and clear, and Brandy knew Isabelle would be returning that day. He sent Inez to the house long before dawn and was not surprised to find Carlos up and watching as soon as the sun's rays began to lighten the cool blue sky. There was the smell of wet mesquite, scrub pine and hackberry in the air, and somewhere he could hear birds chirping as they fed toward the creek.

Carlos wanted to know if he could go to the house for breakfast, but Brandy, suspecting he was only beginning to wonder where Inez had spent the night, walked him up to the kitchen window and called to Inez to hand him out some coffee. It was followed by slices of bread covered with strips of beef cooked in bacon fat. He took only coffee himself, not wanting to enter the house and ignite a spark in Carlos' suspicious mind. When through, he walked Carlos back to the hut and pointed to the remaining dirt and unfinished well. Carlos knew he was in for another day of exhausting toil. He winced as he turned to Brandy. "Is very hard work. I not work for nothing."

"You'll git paid," said Brandy, knowing Isabelle would pay even a thief what he rightfully earned. "What you deserve is somethin' else."

Brandy hurried back to his stable and put the last two eggs brought from MacFee's farm on his stove. He reckoned Isabelle and Bessie would be arriving in the early afternoon, and he decided he had better finish his chores so he'd be free to talk to Isabelle when they came. This thing with Carlos could be mighty messy and take a bit of time, and he was afraid the issue of Inez could not be brushed over with only a word or two either.

◆ ◆ ◆

It was far too early for the women to be returning, and somehow the hoofbeats coming up the trail in midmorning seemed wrong for a horse pulling a rig, so he was hardly surprised when he emerged from the stable to find Rick Salinger dismounting and pulling two rifles from a duffel hanging from his saddle. With an air of importance Rick placed the heavy guns beside the door. The youngster looked almost comical with the thin bone-handled gun in his holster and a blue metal businesslike Colt stuck into his waist. "Hiya, Brandy!" he shouted, his face breaking into a smile when he saw the other man coming toward him. "Pa sent me over with some shootin' irons. Ole Satan himself likely knows we got us a house full of 'em."

Brandy was glad to see him. The Salingers were good people, always smiling and helpful, always, like old Adam, seeming a match for whatever troubles faced them. He remembered Seth telling him Isabelle and Inez had to learn to load and shoot, and he looked hard at the guns, wondering how they would handle the recoil of those heavy rifles. Young Rick might have looked foolish laden with guns, but he was no amateur when it came to using them. Brandy was amazed at his marksmanship. With the rifles he made a small triangle on a distant stump and, throwing a piece of clay into the air, hit it twice with the Colt six-gun before it hit the ground. The shooting brought Carlos out to watch from the hut and Inez to stand in the doorway half smiling as Brandy tried out the guns. He failed to duplicate any of Rick's feats.

But young as he was, Rick had the Salingers' generosity of spirit. "Shucks, Brandy, 'tain't nothin' to it. I mess with these guns all the time. Pa always said when I could shoot the eye out of a squirrel I'd be a man, but by jimmity when I finally did it he just shook his head and told me I got the wrong eye."

Laughing at himself, Rick went down to the stable to see his family's mare and follow Brandy around. He lent a hand with every chore taken on and seemed to enjoy it.

That afternoon when Isabelle and Bessie arrived, Rick and Brandy had finished lunch and were working on saddle straps as the rig pulled into the yard. Rick went quickly to hug his sister, while Brandy, having told Inez to go down to the stable when the women came, emptied the rig and carried the rifle and basket, with Jason crying and trying to pull himself up, into the house. It was a while before the women settled down after their long trip. They looked stiff and tired, and Brandy noticed that Isabelle still looked nervous and distressed. He had hoped she would rest and relax a little before facing the unpleasant business of Carlos, but it was not to be. Turning toward him suddenly, she asked, "Is Carlos here?"

"Yes'm," he responded.

"Good. I'm still hoping he can remember where I put that money."

Brandy tried hard not to sound alarming. "He remembered," he said slowly, taking the remaining bills and silver from his pocket and laying them on the table. "He remembered where you put it all right, and dere's what's left of it."

Isabelle gasped and put her hand to her throat. Bessie came over to stand beside her, and both of them stared at Brandy in visible shock. "Are you telling us he stole it?" asked Bessie, recovering first.

As calmly as he could, Brandy told them what had happened and what he had done about it. He explained to Isabelle his decision to wait until she returned before treating with Carlos. After all, it wasn't his ranch. There was a lot of work waiting to be done, and with Seth gone they were already shorthanded.

The women listened to him, stunned at his words. When he finished, Bessie again was the first to recover. "I say, worry about finding strays and such later. Send that thieving rascal on his way! A man who steals will do worse. I couldn't sleep with that treacherous Mexican on my land."

Isabelle rubbed her forehead, looking more upset than ever. Clearly trying to hold herself together, she questioned Brandy over and over again about the way Carlos had come in drunk, about the wine and where he had managed to get it, about whether they could handle the ranch without him. It was hours before any decisions were made. But Carlos had to go, Bessie would hear of nothing else. Isabelle, finding it hard not to weep from irritation, finally agreed. Seth would surely have demanded it. Brandy also nodded, but he was having trouble separating sending Carlos off from his desire to have Inez to himself. He knew it wasn't true, but in retrospect others might think that his agreeing to send Carlos packing was not all that innocent. But Bessie, with typical Salinger optimism, was already looking ahead. "Mercy, it just seems to me the Lord works in his own way. Rick here is fifteen and Pa has been looking for a way to help him grow up where he can't get in any trouble. Working for you would suit him just fine. He can ride, rope and shoot as well as any man."

Rick, who had retired to the corner of the room during the long discussion, lifted his head, trying to suppress a sudden eruption of smiles. He managed to keep still, but the thought of getting away from home, of becoming a man and earning real wages, made him want to jump up and shout. But he just said, "Gee, Sis, do you think Pa would really let me?"

"He will when I sit him down and clear the cobwebs out of his brain," retorted Bessie.

Rick clapped his hands. He knew old Adam was sometimes putty in the hands of his plucky daughter. It had been that way since their mother had died. Kate, his younger sister, was, like him, still in awe of their salty, commanding father.

Brandy had a feeling that with the energy and willingness of young Rick, who would surely learn fast, he could keep the ranch in reasonably good running order. It would be a big improvement over the sulky, ill-tempered, wine-sloshing Carlos. He heard Isabelle counting out two months' pay for Carlos and Bessie telling her it was a sin to reward thievery that way. The women bickered mildly for a moment till one month's pay, twenty dollars, was settled on. Isabelle gave it to Brandy, telling him to see that Carlos was gone before dark. Brandy, secretly relieved that no more had been said, was almost out the door when Isabelle appeared to remember something. "Oh, yes," she added. "What about Inez?"

Brandy tried to make his voice sound casual but failed. "Inez? Oh, she not goin' wid him."

There was an awkward moment as the women exchanged glances. Isabelle settled onto the bed and looked at Brandy in an odd way. But all she said as Bessie gazed at her in silence was "I see."

With Brandy gone and Rick sent out to get better acquainted with the ranch, Bessie put water on for tea and smiled gently at Isabelle.

"My, my, my, there have been some changes here."

"Brandy and Inez?" Isabelle whispered even though the two of them were alone. "I can't believe it."

"Why not? With that Carlos beating her and threatening her with Lord knows what . . . should have gotten shut of him ages ago."

Isabelle put her head down and grasped her hands between her knees. "I wonder what Seth . . . what the men around here will say."

Bessie laughed. "Men! Ha! They probably won't care a fig except for those that might have fancied her for themselves. She's a pretty thing."

"Bessie!" exclaimed Isabelle, taken aback.

"Oh, don't get to acting shocked. You've always had Seth and haven't seen much of the men around here, but I have. They come a-courtin' all the time."

Isabelle's head lifted quickly in a surge of unexpected interest. "My goodness! Have any proposed?"

Bessie began to wet the tea. "Oh, yes, Andy Sawyer. Every month with the full moon I have to listen to his plans for marrying me, plans for taking me to a spread he dreams about and says he has his eye on, plans for a flock of children. He's even got names picked out."

"Well?"

"Oh, no. Heaven forbid! He's as dull as dry corn. Pa would never forgive me if I took up with him." She filled the cups arranged on the table. "No, I'm waiting for that Todd Bonham to settle down. Right now he's as wild as a rutting longhorn mounting a cactus bush in the dark."

"You think he has plans for you?"

"No," laughed Bessie. "No plans, but he's got itchy hands. Don't let him catch you alone with the sun down!"

In spite of herself, Isabelle couldn't resist sharing Bessie's infectious laughter. "I can't believe the neighbors won't say something," she said finally, her mind going back to Brandy and Inez.

"Of course they will," rejoined Bessie. "That's what God made neighbors for. They keep pecking at you so as you'll have a good excuse to peck back." She got up from the table and rubbed the end of her nose in an almost perfect imitation of old Joss Bonham getting ready to speak. "Pshaw! 'Tain't like that nigger was takin' up with a white woman." Her mimicry was so perfect that Isabelle laughed till she shook. What a blessing this girl is, she thought.

"What do you think I should do?" she asked helplessly.

Bessie took a sip of her tea and looked thoughtfully at her dear friend. "Well, Isabelle, I would speak to Inez. After all, it's really her life. She can't be blamed for what Carlos did. And besides, considering what might happen, I believe you're likely to need her."

Isabelle nodded. "But Brandy—"

"Brandy's like any other man, Isabelle. He needs a woman. There are none here for him. If Inez wants him—and he sure is the best-looking Negro I've ever seen—then she won't be a temptation for other men. Isabelle, it's time you realized everybody can't have the love story you've had with Seth since childhood. Some of us have to settle for less. It seems to me it's sinful and opening the door to sin when young men and women can't find somebody or something to love."

Isabelle looked at her long and searchingly, realizing what a source of strength Bessie was, before she said in gratitude, "I do believe you're right, Bessie."

A hundred and thirty miles to the north, Will Bartlet was calling another council of war. That morning they had picked up a broad trail crossing the Colorado just east of the Concho. It was what they were looking for, and Bartlet wanted to be sure his Rangers followed up this promising sign without being detected or surprised.

Berry, their point man, his thin, dark face expressionless, reported that the trail could hardly be lost since the party that had made it was almost a village, containing women, children, even dogs, and heavily laden travois. There seemed little likelihood it was a trap, but he had a long-standing suspicion of tracks that were too easy to follow.

"If they're packing meat and lodgepoles more'n likely they're headed for one of their main camps," mused Bartlet. "Reckon we'll keep the scouts well out in front. No point in hanging too close. They're not trying to cover their tracks, and we don't want them stumbling onto ours."

"Up here they get a mite cocky," said Seth, his eyes following the trail that rolled away and disappeared in the low hills to the northwest. "Better keep an eye out for other trails running into this one. Wherever this bunch is going, they ain't likely to be heading there alone."

"Right," said Bartlet, spitting juice from the tobacco he always took to chewing when action approached and tension mounted. "Just remember, if we get separated, no shootin', shoutin' or lightin' up after sundown." He didn't need to say this and he knew it, but somehow he felt better knowing it had been said. Working themselves into a column, the Rangers moved toward the hills under a leaden sky, every man knowing that another struggle for the right to live in this angry land was about to begin.

• • •

Far beyond Seth's sight and along the banks of the fast-flowing
Wichita a Comanche camp of faded red and yellow tipis lay in a half-
mile-long, ragged line. There was little activity in the campsite during
the day. The horse herd was being watched by young boys who kept
them downstream where there were long patches of dried grass and
mesquite that had once been over a foot high. Lying throughout this
valley, cut eons ago by the stream, were groves of willows and cot-
tonwoods, which provided wood and some shelter for this winter
encampment. Occasionally a distant drum sounded as a medicine
man chanted and stroked the air with magic signs meant to cure a
feverish child. From the opposite bank squaws could be seen going
from one tipi to another, visiting or getting together for the dull work
of curing and dressing skins. In a few shelters old men sat alone,
intent on the exacting job of making arrows or ornaments that some
shaman would invest with spirit power. The warriors, used to the
harsh life of raiding and guerrilla war, enjoyed this spell of leisure.
They slept or casually hunted small game or just sat together and
smoked. It was still many days before the two most prominent chiefs
would leave for the main Comanche council on the Red. There would
be a big dance and feast before they left. At the moment there was
plenty of buffalo meat, as the smell of smoking pots and the sight of
buzzards hovering over bones and scraps heaped about the camp
attested. From time to time rangy dogs and even coyotes ran up to
scatter the carrion birds and tear at the putrefied meat.

Blood Hawk sat morosely in his barren skin shelter. The horses he
had taken to Black Moccasin for the hand of his daughter that morning had been refused. That rebuff was not the first; now three well-
respected warriors had turned him down as son-in-law. It was not
fair. If his own father had lived, they would have accepted him. His
father would have spoken for him or had other important relatives
step forth. His father would have added more horses to his gift and
spared him the humiliation of another refusal. Alone and unaware
that he was being watched, he screamed and pounded the earth with
his fist. Spittle trickled from his mouth. He swore he would make
powerful medicine against the *tejanos* who had killed his father and
uncle, and looking at the Arapaho scalp wrapped around his bow, he
wondered who among the young warriors would join him. Only
faintly did he realize he was no longer looked upon as a leader, nor

did he grasp that with his father's death several young men who had journeyed to Mexico with him were now quietly shunning him. Had it been the Indian way, Black Moccasin and other seasoned warriors could have told him his problem, but it was one the primitive mind recoiled from in superstitious dread. Blood Hawk was going insane. At first his fits of fury had seemed no different from battle frenzy. But since coming into camp his sudden strident screams in the night, and his recent, unaccounted-for attacks on tree trunks as though they were people, had alarmed the other fighting men, who depended upon stealth and crafty subterfuges for their victories in war. They did not reject him totally, for they believed that insanity was brought on by powerful spirits. A man so possessed was dangerous to mistreat. But Comanche chiefs and warrior leaders had little time for such an obvious liability in combat, and their daughters were not available for one so unlikely to amass the honors that came with prowess in battle, the sole Comanche route to power and wealth.

Blood Hawk, increasingly bewildered by events, understood none of this. In his deranged and distorted world he was still a great warrior, still going to lead a war party and massacre the ranch where he had found the lance, still going to have a nubile Comanche maiden for a wife. His people already knew he was a great slayer of enemies. Had they not seen him open the bodies and drink the blood of many captives? Was that not how he had won his great name? Had they not watched him cut the heart out of the brave Osage chief, killed in a raid against them, and eat it roasted by the victory fire? Yes, soon they would dance the returning warrior's dance with him. He had only to bring back the scalps of those faraway *tejanos*, and the faces of the war chiefs Buffalo Tongue and Ice would turn toward him again. Rising, he hit the earth several times with his bow and laughed. Tonight he would make medicine, strong medicine. He would smoke with the spirits that lived on the dark side of the moon. Quickly he covered his head with a blanket to hear the words that would call forth their power. Then, pounding the earth with his bow, he chanted the words over and over again. In the distance a flock of crows began setting up a ruckus over a freshly dressed carcass. Blood Hawk came out from under his blanket and nodded. It was his answer. Even the treacherous ones hiding in the tree trunks could not stop him now.

8

Bessie Salinger was right. There was only some sly chuckling and shoulder-shrugging when word spread that Brandy had taken Carlos' place with Inez in the hut. No one seemed to notice Rick Salinger, smiling over the first privacy he'd ever known, moving into the cozy stable loft. There was prejudice on the frontier, but it lacked acrimony. The Comanche threat and the bitter rivalry between white and red for the land drew off all the hatred and animosity the harried settlers could generate.

Fortunately for the hard-pressed ranchers, the short southwestern winter was abating. Two months after Seth left, the cold, raw days were becoming fewer, and Isabelle had started bringing Jason out to sit with her in the faintly warming sun or holding him as he tried his first steps around her chair. With the housework done, Inez came to take over the child, for Isabelle was beginning to swell with her pregnancy and seemed to tire more quickly with each passing day. She needed afternoon naps, but dreaded them. She often awoke with a start, realizing that Seth was still unaware of her pregnancy and its possibly shocking origin. A draining mental and physical fatigue had become part of her existence.

Yet there were events that gave the women new urgings to talk, and one that quietly but inevitably drew them closer together. Inez, unlike Isabelle, had never been pregnant and did not recognize its earliest signs. In all the years Inez had slept with Carlos it never occurred to her that her failure to conceive might be his fault rather than the disfavor of God.

Now, in the few months since she had begun making love to Brandy, her breasts had started tingling and she felt a new and strange gravity in her body. Isabelle had little trouble understanding what lay behind these symptoms, and when Inez candidly reported missing her menses, she advised her of her state.

To everyone's amusement, Brandy was overjoyed and with a seriousness that bordered on the comic set about restraining what Inez could do. Isabelle, pleading her condition, had long since stopped practicing with the guns. She hated firearms and only went near them because Seth had wanted it so. After her first hits on the targets she had refused to touch the rifles again. Inez could hardly have been a greater contrast. At first the recoil of the heavy Kentucky guns had bruised her slim shoulder, but she had learned to cushion the shock with a subtle twist of her body and in time became a remarkable shot. Rick praised her openly and encouraged her in his excited, boyish way, but Brandy kept his pride in her to himself while he secretly worked hard to match her skill. Now he saw in her pregnancy a reasonable excuse to cut down her use of the guns. "You doan wanna scare dat baby wid so much noise," he counseled earnestly. "Mebbe pretty soon he doan wanna come out."

Inez smiled. She looked at Brandy's smoothly cut dark features, wondering what her baby with its mixture of blood would look like. She did not know. She was only sure it would be beautiful.

Isaac Sawyer rode by to tell them old Sam Houston had been elected president again and was already yelling about the young republic's immense and growing debt. His first act was to repeal Lamar's costly if effective measures to expel all hostile Indians from Texas territory. This was more than just disquieting news. Houston, who had once lived with the Cherokees and had been accused of "coddling" Indians, had returned to power on the votes of the heavily populated and largely pacified east Texas, where there lived planters and farmers far removed from the mortal menace that still hung over the west. At the talk of disbanding the Rangers, some families began to think of sending their children and even their womenfolk back east for safety, while others gathered together to help fortify one another's homes. There was much daily Bible reading. But all knew that the season of fear was once again poised just beyond the horizon. When the grass turned green and rose again to fill the soft rolling swales, the hated Comanches would be back.

◆ ◆ ◆

It had taken nearly two weeks for Bartlet's hard-riding force to track down, spy out and plan their attack on the growing Comanche camp. For days they had had to hide, as their scouts detected one group after another approaching the stream. In the end they lived through three days of wet, freezing weather that brought intermittent snow before Bartlet decided they could wait no longer. In spite of the Indians' characteristic laxness when deep in their own country, Comanche hunters were now moving further and further from their camp site and in all directions. Sooner or later they must hit upon the maneuvering Texans.

Bartlet's final war council, coming after so much caution, was attended by all the Rangers and typically brief. Berry and the Apache scouts would stampede the horse herd. Bartlet would attack the main camp with two thirds of his men, Seth Redmond would cross the stream with the remaining third and set up an ambush for the escaping Indians. There was little doubt the Comanches would retreat in that direction as the gullies along the opposite bank offered the only cover in sight.

In the frosty false dawn, with patches of freezing mist drifting like specters across the land, the Rangers slipped or half crawled to their positions. Bartlet stood watching a tall, dusky figure coming to relieve himself at the edge of camp. He might have been the warrior destined to give the alarm, but Bartlet raised his heavy rifle and its sharp report lifted the figure from its feet and shattered the damp silence. A fusillade rang out and was immediately mixed with screams and war cries as the Rangers, their guns erupting streaks of orange, swept into the camp. His men were firing as fast as they could, but Bartlet kept urging them forward. He saw at once that the braves were rushing out, lances and bows at the ready, but instead of fleeing many were backing off toward the center of the camp. His combat savvy told him this meant trouble.

The village was bigger than they had reckoned, and a ragged resistance was suddenly, if clumsily, forming. Though attacking alongside his men, Bartlet, like a gambler whose life hung on every card, kept weighing the violently shifting odds. Suddenly he realized what was happening and, sensing their peril, scooped up a fallen war hatchet and started hacking his way into the mass of screaming bodies, whose uproar now was grotesque with squaws and young ones screeching in terror. Instinctively he knew that the chaos created by the attack would soon have to lessen, leaving a crisis only moments away.

The Comanches, though being steadily cut down, were no longer milling about in wild confusion, but slowly swarming toward the village center, fighting with a growing frenzy. The Rangers, grimly engaged in their ritual of efficient slaughter, were ignoring the growing force before them and advancing with the cold ferocity of gladiators intent on leaving the arena an abattoir. The din made speech pointless.

The pitch of battle kept rising until its savagery challenged sanity. In this Armageddon there were no impersonal deaths delivered by gun or cannon fire from afar. The fighting was now everywhere hand to hand. Death was a face flushed with hate and distorted with rage; death's knotted and callused hands dug into throats and tore at exposed flesh; men looked into one another's eyes, and the slain spewed their blood upon the slayers.

Swearing violently and blindly ignoring the many arrows that grazed his body, Bartlet literally shot and chopped his way to the center of the camp. There, beside an immense drum, a large warrior was roaring, his nude body painted black and red with magic signs used in a medicine dance the night before. He was shouting to the gathering braves to carry the battle to their attackers. He was counting on their numbers and trying to make the fight too costly to continue. But Bartlet unhesitatingly raised the war hatchet until all about him could see it, then slashed into the huge warrior's throat, driving him to the ground, his gruesomely painted head sagging back at a crazy angle from his body. Bartlet would later learn that he had slain their great war chief Buffalo Tongue, but for the moment he knew only that the vital panic he was counting on had at last begun.

With shrieking squaws and young ones beginning to escape across the cold, swiftly moving waist-high water, Seth, who had watched the struggle from the opposite shore with spiraling concern, suddenly nudged Prent, who was lying pale beside him, and glanced back at the long line of Rangers kneeling behind their screen of scrub pines and now coming to the ready. The whole camp had started to stampede across the water, but Seth, his pulse roaring, grimly waited until throngs of half-dressed and wildly gesticulating figures were gathered on his side before he gave his command to fire. The opening volley caused carnage and death almost beyond belief. Countless figures still in the water simply disappeared as the current began sweeping the dead and dying downstream. Women and children maddened with fear started scrambling toward the gullies, but the warriors, realizing they were in a trap, yelled for those behind them to hurry, while the few still able to fight came straight into the Rangers' guns.

Such mayhem could not last. Rangers on both banks of the stream were now pouring deadly fire into the swirling mass of Indians, many of whom had started paddling downstream to where they could pull themselves ashore beyond the range of Texan guns. There, Ice, their one remaining war chief, was waving his weapons and forcing some semblance of order. With great effort he set up a temporary line of defense, hoping to allow the women and children a few minutes' head start in escaping toward their nearest camp on the Red. Ice knew his village was facing extinction, and he brutally silenced the frenzied keening of the squaws as he commanded them to get away from the stream where the bodies of their dead continued to float by. His painted face was a mask of wrath, but in his heart he was fighting a fear of the devil gods he had heard rode with these *tejanos*. He pounded the earth with a lance he had desperately snatched from the water. Would there ever be a medicine strong enough to stop them?

With the Comanches withdrawing downstream in confusion, stumbling over one another as they fled for their lives, Seth's Rangers sallied out to pick off the stubborn few still firing sporadically from the grassy banks or nearby shallows. Except for this handful of warriors, who had decided to stand and die, bravely singing their death songs, it was more massacre than fight. Many of the braves, having sprung from their sleeping robes, were naked, their bodies painted in garish colors, their hair greased and tied with thin strips of rabbit skin. Seth moved to the bank and shot half the face off one who collapsed before him, the legs splaying open to reveal hideously diseased genitals, a badly swollen scrotum and a penis covered with sores. Seth turned away in revulsion as a nauseating image of Isabelle's nude body being forced down and raped flashed through his mind. Then, as though struck by some insane seizure, he swung back and emptied his gun into the already dead body and smashed its skull with his rifle butt. The Rangers about him glanced at him questioningly for a moment, then moved mutely on. A Texan with unspeakable memories awaiting a day of reckoning with these hated Comanches was hardly new.

Before long the Rangers had swept both banks and were coming up in numbers to the last gully, which was filled with squaws and young ones. The men halted, hesitantly starting to reload their weapons, many staring expectantly at Seth. Suddenly Bartlet, having ordered the tipis in the main camp put to the torch, came up. "Well, what the hell are yuh waitin' for?" he half shouted, seeing that they were holding back from the gully.

The issue of women and children was one that rankled in the minds of many Rangers. White bureaucrats in Houston tended to regard them as civilians even though experience said they were anything but. Rangers had been killed by squaws seizing their fallen braves' lances or bows, and adolescent boys were notorious for concealing knives that ended up in their captors' stomachs. There was also the bitter knowledge that squaws provided the most fiendish tortures for white captives and were particularly demonic with the bodies of *tejanos*. Pretending it was abandoned, many a warrior or young squaw would skulk within a tipi until a Ranger entered so they could take one more *tejano*'s life before giving up their own. That was why their tipis had to be torched.

Ever since Bartlet had lost his wife and two daughters on the San Saba in '39, his sentiments had been well known. His nod to Seth was unnecessary. Seth was already directing the Rangers to surround the gully. Some did, mouthing the brutal frontier rationale "Nits make lice." Others hung back, finding that such work jarred too heavily against their Christian upbringing. Prent Salinger was one of these.

Seth signaled the Rangers still with him to crawl up to the rim of the gully as he started to lower the muzzle of his rifle into the depression. There he saw more than a dozen squaws and a flock of young ones huddled around a few wounded braves. One squaw looked up to meet his eyes and screamed as he pulled the trigger. She collapsed over a brave's body and a multitude of guns roared from the rim of the gully until nothing more moved in the mass of human flesh heaped below.

If'n yer gonna fight thatta way—we'll fight thatta ways!

Later Bartlet sat recording figures he would have to submit on his return to San Antonio. Nine Rangers were dead or clearly dying, twelve more were too wounded to go any further and would have to be helped back. Many, including himself, had flesh injuries but were still able to serve. On a second count of the enemy they came up with the bodies of eighty-eight braves. No one knew how many had disappeared in the stream. There was no attempt to count squaws or children. By tacit understanding these figures were never recorded.

The two men walking the streets of San Antonio did not draw much attention as they stopped beside the fountain of the San Miguel mission to gaze at a mournful string of Rangers coming into town. Many of the men were wounded, and all were coated with trail dust and clearly exhausted from the long ride that had started by the banks of the bloody Wichita. One of the men stopping to gaze in spite of the blustery weather was dressed in a white cotton suit and wore a light brown sombrero with a loose chin strap. He was Jules Ferdinando Spinada, the mule merchant, better known to the citizenry of San Antonio as Julio. His companion was his eldest son, Ricardo, who was dressed like a plain *vaquero*, though his vest buttons had the look of tarnished silver and his sombrero was adorned with the small orange tassels that had just become fashionable with young men. Unlike others of his age and family standing, Ricardo wore a heavy, smooth-handled pistol that lay so far back on his body it was almost out of sight, sitting over the rear pocket of his jeans.

Removing his light sombrero, the anxious-faced Julio took a step forward to address the Rangers now passing by. *"Buenos días, amigos.* Señor Bartlet, he is coming back, yes?"

The nearest Ranger glanced at him without interest. The man was busy trying to turn and flex a heavily bandaged forearm, putting it to a painful test that clearly dominated his mind. "Nope," he finally replied, wincing. "Only us uns as got shot is a-comin' back."

Julio's face tightened. "Señor Bartlet, he does not come?"

"Reckon not. Not for a spell." The Ranger was moving off.

Young Ricardo, proud of his fluent English, shouted after him, "Sir, is Captain Bartlet all right?"

The Ranger looked back, noticing that the young Mexican spoke without an accent. "Reckon he is. Last time I saw, he was cutting sign up toward the Red." The Ranger moved on, still trying to work movement into his arm.

Julio looked down, shaking his head in disappointment. "Is bad, I think. Very bad."

Ricardo stood watching the Rangers move across the broad plaza toward a large adobe building built between the local stable and a cantina with a red door. It was a building often used by the Texans as a makeshift hotel or hospital. His eyes followed the wounded men and grew somber with respect. "You know, Father, those *rinches* are brave men. Maybe I should be one of them."

Julio grunted, calling quietly on his patron saint. "We no got troubles enough here, eh?" He was looking around the sparsely populated streets forlornly, his mind only remotely on his words. "Now Julio has a *loco* son who wants to go with the *rinches* . . . wants to look for trouble."

Ricardo shifted uneasily. "Papa, stop worrying about that stinking bandit. If he comes by one more time, I will shoot him."

Julio turned to his son with a flash of irritation that quickly dissolved into concern. "Ricardo, stop talking like that. You are going to get yourself killed. This Estavez is dangerous. He has many men."

"Not any more."

"What you mean?"

Ricardo smiled. "His men, papa, are not very happy here. Two of them got themselves shot trying to steal from us Texans. Little Chico at the Cadiz Cantina, the one with a cousin working at the Colorada, tells me they've gone south. It's much safer for *los cochinos* across the border. The great *bandido* Yoquito Estavez is now alone."

Julio studied his son's face with sobering interest. "This is true?"

"Papa. Ricardo does not lie. Stop worrying."

But Ricardo did not know what his distraught father was really worrying about. If Julio was nothing else, he was a man of the world. The presence of the stunning Elena María López in his home had brought problems far beyond the mere responsibility of protecting her. The disturbing truth was that Julio was secretly and seriously worried about his handsome son. Ricardo, though almost a year younger than Elena, was now clearly helplessly in love with her and insisted on being along to protect her whenever she ventured out. Julio knew his powerful cousin, Señor López, would never forgive any physical affection between them, but given their ages and temperaments he knew this relationship was fraught with danger. Unquestionably there were suitors of power and distinction awaiting Elena's hand in Mexico. Such long-considered arrangements by powerful families were not to be toyed with, and any shadow on the purity of their daughter would profoundly affect the López family's prestige and honor.

Fortunately Elena gave no evidence of responding to Ricardo or any of the seemingly mesmerized males in his household who found reason to pause in passing to view her tantalizing eyes and devastating figure every day. Julio's own desires kept him well aware that she was young, sensuously beautiful and perhaps spirited enough to risk a mild flirtation to relieve the boredom of her conventlike existence. But the young were blind to the spiraling power of passion, and one never knew where such a dalliance could lead. Since his wife had long since passed away, he had hired a widow to chaperone Elena, which only relieved his anxieties when she slipped off to church or made her infrequent trips with Ricardo and other armed *vaqueros* to market. But there was one thing he could do little about. He knew Ricardo desperately wanted Elena to think of him as a man and not a boy; Ricardo wanted to do something that would show Elena he could protect her even when her powerful father couldn't. Julio had watched him practicing with his pistol, carrying it strangely at his back like some *gringo* gunslinger.

Once, when Yoquito Estavez seemed to have disappeared, Julio had immediately started talking about Elena returning home. She was more than ready to go, and had it not been for continual reports of heavy fighting around Laredo, her plans to leave would already have been far advanced. But clearly Ricardo did not want her to go, not until he could find this bandit king and rid her life of him. He had practiced his draw from behind his waist, learning to turn sideways for a better stance and a smaller target. He cleverly avoided his father's worried stares and told no one of his plans.

His father did not need to be told of his plans. His father already knew them. He also knew that Estavez was a cunning and experienced killer and his daring, courageous son only a young man in love.

Madre de dios. He prayed silently that his own plans would work out first. If only Señor Bartlet or even that big blue-eyed Ranger who had gone with him to the Casa Colorada would come back.

But there was big trouble up on the Red. Even though they had joined up with another Ranger troop, led by old Hoyt Ingersohl, they were in deep peril. Reaching the valley of the Red, they soon encountered enormous numbers of redskins, not only in a main camp but in several smaller camps strung out along the river, making it easy to reinforce one another. These bands had already been alerted by refugees from the Wichita, and their warriors, mounted and roaring their battle chants in the pale salmon-colored dawn, were out in war regalia, covering surrounding hilltops to greet the unsuspecting Rangers.

The heavy skirmishing that came in uneven bursts that day raised Bartlet's suspicions. Several braves, their faces painted black, dashed within range of the Rangers' guns in a show of bravery or attempts to avenge relatives killed on the Wichita. The Rangers, refusing these taunts and firing their guns sparingly, wounded a few, but if this strange maneuvering revealed little, word that their Apache scouts were talking of deserting told volumes. Bartlet immediately called a council of war. These hardened, grim-faced old Rangers were experienced men. Coming together, Bartlet and Ingersohl exchanged meaningful glances. Something was wrong. This growing mass of warriors was clearly fighting a holding action. Bartlet vigorously argued that they should withdraw immediately, but Ingersohl's men, having come up the Brazos and missed the fight on the Wichita, were reluctant to retreat without seeing some action or at least gaining some knowledge as to why so many Indians were gathered here.

Berry put an end to such speculation by getting back at sundown from a scout across the river to tell them the Comanche camp was being heavily reinforced from the north. Fresh tracks running down from the Canadian were everywhere. At this Bartlet, in spite of the darkness, again demanded they move out at once. It was only after half an hour of tense discussion that he reluctantly agreed with Ingersohl, and even Seth, that the Indians' aversion to taking heavy losses made rifle fire their best bet for survival, and it was least effective in the dark. Besides, in spite of all the alarming signs, it still ran against the Rangers' grain—and strategy—to run away from Indians. That night, as they mulled over their decision, they could hear drums all along the river and see the loom of huge fires spiriting across the night skies as far as the eye could see. Every Ranger looking on and carefully cleaning his gun knew that night could not be wasted.

Seth was sent out to find a better position to defend. He was particularly concerned about the horses; they had been hard used for some time now and looked it. The Indian ponies would be far fresher. It took a couple of hours to find a pair of hillocks with a little stream flowing between them. There was some dense forage in that miniature valley, and even in the dark he could see the hillocks would be easy to defend.

Just before dawn the Rangers arrived and were hurriedly reinforc-

ing the redoubt the two hillocks formed, most of them quietly wondering if there would be time for coffee before the Indians struck.

There wasn't.

Ice had sat at the council fire in morbid silence. He had listened
to two Kiowa war chiefs talking of their victories in the north and
what the battle strategy should be here against these hated *tejanos*.
Secretly he was angry and bitter. He was waiting for Black Wolf,
their main Comanche chief, to speak. Comanches did not need Kiowas
to tell them how to fight, and he had no desire to speak himself. He
knew he was sitting under a cloud of disapproval. Even though he
had brought the remnants of his people back from their bloody encounter on the Wichita, in the eyes of his once-large tribal following
his medicine had failed. He had lost not only warriors but many old
and weak ones as well. That Buffalo Tongue's beheading had led to
the village's panic was never mentioned, even in whispers, for the
superstitious Comanches shunned talk of the dead.

Finally the Kiowa chiefs had finished their boastful oratory and
Black Wolf, allowing a few moments of respectful silence to pass,
came to his feet. He was taller than the average Comanche, and his
deep bronze skin seemed to shine beneath its streaks of white paint.
His voice was loud and had great resonance. It carried beyond the
big lodge in which he spoke, and outside many people crowded
around to hear their famous chief's words.

"For many suns the *tejanos* have come to take our land and kill our
people," he thundered. "We have scalped many of them and left their
lodges in flames, but still they come. Many times their great chief
has sent us presents to get us to sit for their peace talks, but in their
hearts they want us buried with our fathers. The Comanches and
their brothers the Kiowas are great warriors, and they are not afraid.
Even now, when the *tejanos* send their heavily armed killer-men to
strike our winter camps, we are ready for them. Even now, when they
hope to surprise us as they have so many times before, we are ready
with surprises of our own. The traders you have seen in our camps
have brought us heavy guns that shoot far and have medicine parts
that give them the eye of an eagle. Our Kiowa brothers are right. If
none of these *tejanos* get back to their own country alive they will
not come here again." He paused for a long moment, looking up to
where the wisps of smoke disappeared and the bone white lodgepoles

joined against the dark night sky. "Tonight they have gone to the Little Coyote hills and are preparing a strong place to fight in the white man's way. Hear me, my brothers: we have signs the spirits are with us, for they have chosen those hills in the darkness. Let every warrior prepare himself for victory, for our enemies will have their first surprise at dawn."

Ice stood outside the council lodge, running his hands through his ancient bear-claw necklace, a sacred piece of finery he had always felt brought him strength. For some reason his mind could not release the image of the big, craggy-faced *tejano* who had fought his way with war hatchet and pistol toward Buffalo Tongue's powerful and commanding presence and killed him. Like all born warriors, Ice admired bravery, even in a foe. But for him this *tejano* carried some evil spirit, and he had decided this *tejano* must die. Their own scouts had not been idle, and he knew that the whites who had attacked him on the Wichita were the ones nearby in the Coyote hills. He knew that big *tejano* would be there. He knew Black Wolf's plans for killing them all, but he wanted to be sure. He knew these *tejanos* his people called the "killer ones" did not die easily.

He approached a group of young, excited warriors, some of whom still nodded to him in respect. In the darkness he held his hand over his heart as he spoke. "Hear me, young men. We go soon into battle. Ice's heart tells him there is a *tejano* he must kill. I will ride toward him with death in my weapons, but he is a great warrior. He has killed many. If I cannot kill him, I want a warrior to ride with me and kill him while he brings me my death." He held the necklace out. The youths knew it carried strong *puja*, medicine. "Who does this thing will earn this ancient and sacred necklace to wear in the victory dances which our people will look upon and honor."

The eager eyes of the young warriors blazed in the darkness, each silently vowing the necklace would be his by morning. No one seemed to notice the strange-looking warrior standing in the rear, his eyes ablaze with something beyond eagerness, his face caught up in a vacant smile. He drifted away, looking queerly at the dark, stunted forms of the surrounding tree trunks. His name was Blood Hawk.

9

The thick mist that carpeted the ground before dawn had the Rangers peering in all directions when the loud report of a heavy gun split the air and the dying whinny of a horse told them that someone was firing into their mounts picketed in the ravine. Seth, Bartlet and Ingersohl had been moving about checking the men's defensive positions when the shot rang out, but within minutes they were down beside the horse that lay in agony with its hindquarters shattered by a heavy slug.

"What in the hell was that—a cannon?" asked Ingersohl, coming up breathlessly.

"No, but a damned heavy gun," replied Bartlet, looking about in angry, anxious confusion. "Where in Christ's name did it come from?"

Seth knew when he saw the position of the dying animal that the bullet had to have come from the west, and his eyes started working to penetrate the thick gray mist until they finally perceived the faintest outline of something that caused a cold shiver to start at the back of his neck and ripple down the skin over his spine. A thin column of rock that stuck up like a pipe stem was emerging through the rising mist, and he saw at once that its elevation gave it command of the hillocks and the tiny valley running between them. It had been invisible in the clouded night, but someone was up in that slender steeple of rock with a heavy gun. The horses would have to be taken beyond the low ridge to the east, or they would all be killed.

Another slug smashed into a nearby boulder and sprayed them with slivers of rock. The horses around them reared up, and a stream of blood appeared on Ingersohl's face.

"We got to get rid of that goddamned gun!" shouted Bartlet. But his voice was lost in a chorus of war cries as they found themselves surrounded by a sea of armed warriors, some of whom were firing guns in the air and throwing taunts at the Rangers, who were now bracing themselves behind the hurried defenses. The captains knew these defenses would never be enough. Unless they could find some way to protect their horses, they were all going to die.

At first they fired back at the thin rock column, but it soon proved pointless. Whoever was up there had a gun that outranged theirs and could be seen only from the other side. Some of the Rangers left their dug-in positions to help herd the horses to the east end of the ravine, crowding them behind a quickly drawn rope corral. They could not go beyond the ridge without being exposed to a cloud of arrows and a hail of gunfire that was rising steadily from the mass of warriors swirling around.

There was no time for elaborate planning. The heavy slugs were still coming in, and the horses were rearing in panic and trying to bolt. Ingersohl shouted, "We'll have to get out there and kill that bastard!" Then, with hand motions, he signaled in some of his best shots, who immediately rose and ran toward him. "You fellows keep us covered as best you can!" he hollered to Bartlet and Seth.

Everyone was aware of the crisis, and with the increasing light dozens of rifles were trained on the short stretch of ground between the hill and the rock pinnacle. The barrage that quickly developed soon cleared the Indians from the area. But the warriors did not scatter. They settled in the undergrowth about the foot of the pinnacle, and Bartlet and Seth knew that that seemingly open spot had become a death trap.

Ingersohl knew it too, but he led his men into it anyway. It was a proud if unspoken tradition among Ranger captains that they asked no one to do what they were not willing to do themselves.

Once under the pinnacle they turned their guns upward, and whoever was up there was soon hit, for Seth and Bartlet could see an arm flailing in the air as a lone figure lying near the top started to thrash about in pain. But now the price of this daring foray had to be paid. Ingersohl tried to start his men back, but fire from the thicket collapsed him at the foot of the pinnacle. A Ranger who bent to help him went down beside him. Ingersohl waved the others back and from his slumped position began firing to cover their retreat. The Ranger beside him was already dead, and he himself sustained hit after hit till he crumpled under his death blow, still trying to cover for his two remaining men, one mortally wounded, as they straggled back into the Ranger lines.

Seth, Bartlet and the crouching Rangers witnessed this sacrifice stoically. It was a thing that had to be done. Ingersohl had paid the price they might all be paying before this day was out. Their silence expressed it best. Whatever the outcome, this was the fight they had come to fight, without quarter or sentiment. This was a code harsher than any the savages could devise. Shifting back to their positions, the Rangers threw a parting glance at the distant dead bodies and pressed fresh cartridges into their guns.

The action around the tower had brought a pause in the Indians' attack, but now they came on with renewed fury. Bartlet could see the Comanches beginning to bend over the outside of their horses and fire from beneath their mounts' necks. It was a measure of their chilling horsemanship that they could shoot at the Rangers while they themselves almost disappeared from view. But Will Bartlet fought Comanches the way some men fight a lifelong disease. He knew all the antidotes. His order swept around the hillocks like the crack of a whip: "Shoot the goddamn horses!" The sleek attacking ponies started crashing to the ground, throwing their riders, who had to scamper out of range of the Ranger fire. Many were hit, some fatally. It was not only to dismount the riders that Bartlet had given his command; Indians went to war on their most prized steeds, and the loss of these superior animals with their speed, strength and usually long training made some warriors wail in despair.

Then, in spite of the desperate attack on the rock pinnacle, the heavy gun roared out again. This time the bullet went wide and was followed in a moment by another that whined harmlessly overhead. Bartlet and Seth crouched down together at the western end of the redoubt, Bartlet's face furrowed with concern. "Whoever is up there is wounded and can't shoot straight," he said, his eyes following the trim of the rock pinnacle. Seth recalled how urgently Bartlet had wanted to leave the previous day. Now it seemed it was a well-spout of wisdom they should have heeded. Still, there was no recrimination in Bartlet's tone or manner. The captain's craggy face just stared at the pinnacle Seth had missed in the darknenss. "We can't wait much longer for that critter up there to die," he muttered grimly as he rose.

Seth watched him make his determined way around the great circle
of Rangers, measuring at each point how the fight was going, his eyes
constantly searching the sky, where a tarnished sun was trying to
break through. As he returned another slug tore into the earth just
short of the hurriedly pitched rope corral.

"We got to get shut of this place," he said to Seth, kneeling down
beside him. "That critter up there could start shooting straight at
any minute."

Seth stared at him uncertainly. Leaving this fortified place to face
a far superior number of mounted Indians jarred against his instinctive judgment. "Will, if it's that tower that's bedeviling you, maybe
I can take some of the boys and—"

"Maybe you had better just listen," snapped Bartlet, his steel gray
eyes firmly engaging Seth's. Suddenly Seth detected new iron in Bartlet's voice. This was not a council of war. Bartlet was through seeking
advice. The formidable soldier so long masked by his congeniality
was coming to the fore. Now the set of his face said that salvation
lay in discipline and a rapid response to commands. Seth sank back
in silence, realizing that this startling shift measured how desperate
Bartlet reckoned their plight to be.

Bartlet pointed to the distant knob of a hill over a mile further to
the west. "We're going to make for that high spot," he said. "I'll go
first with maybe twenty men and take that hill. They'll be after me,
and when they get me surrounded you bring the rest on and hit them
from the rear." Seth stared at Bartlet's determined face. The captain
left no opening for a response. "You'd better get moving,
Seth . . . warn the men to get ready. Use mostly those from San Antonio. And find Stubbs. Tell him I need to see him."

Within a few minutes men began drawing back from the Ranger
line and settling around Bartlet, among them Tanner, Purdy and
young Prent Salinger. They sat in a circle looking guardedly at one
another as they waited for Stubbs, a man who had come up with
Ingersohl and at times had seemed to be his lieutenant.

When they were huddled together, Bartlet took a look at the distant
hill and said in cool, almost casual language, "We're going to take
that damned hill, and here's how we're going to do it. Stubbs, I want
you and about ten or twelve of your men to stage a mock attempt to
escape from here. You'll leave from the other end of the camp. Don't
go too far out, and turn back as soon as you see them racing to cut
you off. Remember, you're not going out there to fight. Just get them

thinking you've maybe decided the situation is hopeless and are trying to get away."

Stubbs, in spite of his wary look and distant manner, was a Ranger. He nodded without hesitation. "Be ready soon as we can . . . just need to get the horses up. Is there going to be a signal?"

Bartlet thought for a moment. "No, try to leave within the next ten minutes. We'll hear the ruckus you'll cause. That will be all the signal we'll need. Now remember, don't get bogged down out there in a fight, there's still plenty of that ahead."

Stubbs nodded and swung away without a word.

Turning to the others, Bartlet gave his orders in low tones. When Stubbs' men broke from the other end of camp the Indians would be distracted and most of them would start in that direction. At that point the Rangers would leave at a gallop and take that distant hill. "No matter what happens, don't any of you stop till we get there. If you go down, crawl into the brush and watch for the rest of the troop. They'll be coming by directly."

The Rangers all quietly nodded and started checking their guns and stuffing their pockets with ammunition. Prent looked pale but followed the others' cue. Bartlet said to him matter-of-factly, "Son, pay no attention to the noise those redskins figure to be making. Just don't let 'em keep you off that hill."

Prent turned away, a tight mixture of pride and determination in his voice. "Reckon I'll make it."

Seth watched the others preparing to leave, his mind loaded with questions. Then Bartlet pulled the bandage tighter over his shoulder wound and dropped down beside him to answer them.

"Seth, this ain't going to be easy, but I figure it will confuse them enough for us to take that high spot."

Seth shook his head and looked away to the distant hill. To him it seemed as remote and inaccessible as some mountain on the moon. "Will, hadn't I better take them up there? You'll be needed here if—"

"You'd better just do as you're told," snapped Bartlet. Then, catching himself, he continued more softly, "I'm sure we can take that high ground, Seth. Now listen carefully. If my luck does run out, hold that hill till dark, then head west. Stay away from the river, but make sure you camp where you can reach water. Berry knows enough to keep from being ambushed, but keep the group together. Don't go chasing after any small parties, and above all let them do the attacking. Their losses will be higher that way. This isn't their season for war. If you pull them far enough from their camp, they'll soon tire of it."

Seth couldn't hide his confusion. "Shouldn't we be heading south?"

"That's where they expect you to head. Don't ever do anything Indians expect. You've been studying these devils, Seth. They're all steamed up now 'cause they danced themselves into a frenzy. Usually a little steady shootin' helps to settle 'em down."

Seth suspected Bartlet only half believed what he was saying, but the horses had been brought up. "Will, do the men know I'm backing you up?"

Bartlet's wink was meant to instill confidence. "Reckon so. Figure they're counting on it."

As ready as they were, it still came as a shock when Stubbs and his men, leathering their horses for speed, broke out of the east end of the camp. Immediately a chorus of Indian war cries started up and the rising thunder of hooves could be felt through the rocky ground. Bartlet waited a minute to let the Indians commit themselves. Then with a shout, he set out with his men for the run to the hill.

Bartlet's plan to trick the Indians and draw them to the eastern side of the redoubt worked well. It would have worked better had a few of the braves hidden under the pinnacle not seen Bartlet's group leave. The alarm they set up soon had large numbers of warriors circling back to pursue those now fleeing to the west. Seth watched with relief as he saw that Bartlet's men, who were galloping at full tilt, were likely to reach the distant hill first, but already the number of Indians joining in pursuit made it seem impossible to hold. He began shouting to the other Rangers to get ready to leave. Stubbs came by, his horse still heaving from its frantic run. "What now?" he shouted.

"We're taking the whole troop up that hill, hitting the ones attacking Bartlet from the rear. Stay back and see there's no straggling or stopping till we reach him. Any that get hit might best stay in the brush. We'll try for 'em after dark."

Stubbs wheeled his horse away and rushed back to hurry the men mounting their horses at the other end. The gun on the pinnacle had left three horses dead, but Ingersohl and two of his men were gone and their mounts kept the Rangers from having to ride double.

As Seth motioned the troop forward, the Indians, at last overcoming their confusion, were furious at being tricked and began racing along their flanks, releasing arrows and shots in anger well before they were close enough to make them count.

Seth could see that a struggle for the distant hill was developing fast, and he could tell from the way the Indians were beginning to circle that the Rangers had seized the summit. Digging his spurs into Sam, he looked about him. The troop was now covering ground rapidly, but the Indians coming up on both sides, and in ever increasing numbers in his rear, had them surrounded, their screams leaving little doubt how they foresaw this uneven encounter ending.

Bartlet arrived at the hill and glanced back. He knew he'd have a few moments before the pursuing warriors could reach him in force. With his good arm he waved the men to positions behind boulders strewn about the summit. On one side, where a slight depression made the hilltop easier to approach, he placed two of his best guns, Tanner and Purdy, and he hurried Prent with the horses between two large boulders sitting above a deep drop on the off side of the hill. He had not had time to find himself a decent firing position when the first warriors arrived with winded horses but anxious for the honors that would come from striking the enemy first. Two of them raced up the easy access offered by the depression, their lances high in the air. But Bartlet knew how to use his men. In what seemed a single volley, Tanner and Purdy shot both of them through the head. A third, pulling back at this sight, was moments later sprawled lifelessly over his pony's neck. The other Rangers were opening up, and the Indians, never sanguine about frontal attacks, began to circle.

The handful of Rangers fought gamely, but the growing number of Indians inevitably began to tell. Two Rangers were hit but kept fighting. One attempt to get behind their position was thwarted by Bartlet when he cut down a Comanche who had tried to crawl up the hill through undergrowth that had grown close to the summit. Some Kiowa warriors started climbing the steep drop on the off side of the hill, trying to reach the boulders protecting the horses. Prent waited until he could hear their labored breathing, then blew a hole in the first brave's chest and sent him reeling back onto the rocky floor below. The rest quickly slipped down and disappeared. The melee was getting wilder all the time, and now both the Indians and the

Rangers could see and hear the remainder of the troop coming up and the horde of Indians in pursuit.

Watching his troop come up, Bartlet signaled them to positions on the left and right. The few warriors attacking him were scattered as Seth's force thundered into their rear, the few failing to withdraw being blasted from their mounts by the oncoming Rangers. As the main force of Indians achieved the hill, they broke into the traditional surround with warriors trying to ride down the hurriedly dismounting Rangers or themselves dismounting to engage in hand-to-hand combat. Bartlet, standing erect and shouting to his men, saw they were using their six-guns at close quarters with deadly effect, but the Indians had already penetrated the hurriedly forming lines and some of the Rangers were wounded and dying.

Yet Bartlet seemed to have a charmed life. Ignoring their arrows and bullets, he began to get his left flank, stretching back to the large boulders behind, in fighting order. Indian bodies were piling up before this makeshift formation. Bartlet knew that if Black Wolf and the Kiowa chiefs could have ordered their warriors to wipe his Rangers out at any price, it would have been done. But he had been fighting Comanches long enough to know they would never pay the price for such a charge, even if it brought victory.

Tragically, what he didn't know was that his tall, rugged form, boldly directing his men in this desperate fight, had caught the eye of the Comanche war chief, Ice. Ice's face was painted black except for two red streaks above and below his eyes. A handful of mounted youths started screaming war cries as he raised his lance and spurred his pony forward.

Seth, who was making his way toward Bartlet, having urged the Rangers into a number of defensive positions on the steeper and more easily defended right-hand slope, saw the Comanche chief bearing down on his captain. He shouted, but his voice was lost in the uproar. Forgetting his own jeopardy, he began to race toward Bartlet. Things happened swiftly then. Bartlet turned to find Ice almost on top of him and though in spite of his wound he pumped two bullets into the oncoming chief's body, the attack drew his attention from the real threat, which lay with the three young warriors riding hard behind. Seth, seeing it and close enough finally to fire, shot the first two, who clung to their saddles until the Rangers beyond picked them off. The third, however, got through and drove his feathered lance into Bartlet's chest. All eyes were drawn to Will Bartlet's tall figure crumpling to the earth, while the young brave who had struck him slipped from his horse and grabbed the bear-claw necklace from the dead Ice's body. Then, hanging low from his stirrup and allowing his horse to half drag him, the reckless brave escaped into the brush, where he turned to look back at the Rangers already forming a protective circle around their prostrate leader. He quickly pulled the bear-claw necklace around his neck, giving a weird yell as he did so. After a few moments he stared about until he spotted the high, horned headgear of Black Wolf, who was coming up with the Kiowa chiefs. "I am Blood Hawk!" he shouted to the great warrior leader. "Remember me!" But his raspy voice was lost in the clamor of battle.

The Rangers knew Will Bartlet was dying. His words to Seth, who knelt down to remove the lance and tear at the captain's shirt to stop the flow of blood, came in short gasps. "It's too late, Seth. Don't waste time. Keep the men firing till you drive 'em to cover. Remember what I said afore."

Seth remained kneeling till he had stuffed a thick piece of torn shirt into the wound and strapped it into place with the captain's gun belt. Then he rose to find the Rangers still fighting with cold and resolute expressions. Bartlet was a leader the men respected—even revered— but they knew that he, like Ingersohl, had come on this expedition knowing the risks. There were no requiems for Rangers.

After two fierce but unsuccessful attempts to take the hill, the Indians fell back and began to fire from cover. Seth, trying to think like Bartlet, stayed on the dangerous left-hand slope and sent Stubbs to hold the right. "Tell 'em not to shoot till there's some red skin to shoot at," he shouted at the retreating Stubbs. "Ammunition could be a problem before we're finished."

As the fighting slowly grew desultory, Seth could see Rangers shifting about, tending to their wounds or removing guns and shells from their dead or dying companions. He had no idea what their losses were, but he had already learned that among the Rangers they were never as high as suspected. These men, recruited for their cool heads, were experienced at fighting mounted Indians. A glance at the lower slopes told him that the number of Indian bodies not yet recovered might mean losses high enough to discourage further attacks.

But before noon another element had to be factored into Seth's desperate recalling of Bartlet's final words. An icy breeze had sprung up from the northwest and black clouds had begun to mass overhead, extinguishing the weak, sulfurous sun and leaving the land dark and murmuring under a rising wind. He remembered Bartlet studying the sky that morning. Perhaps Will had sensed another break in the weather. Stubbs came dodging over to tell him that the strengthening and increasingly frigid wind was soon going to be a problem on that exposed hill, and Berry, standing nearby, allowed that he smelled dampness and snow. Some of the Rangers, finding a momentary quiet, were starting little fires to heat coffee or warm their hands.

Stubbs and Berry did not ask, but it was clear they wanted to know what Seth was planning to do. Both acknowledged that Seth was in command, but command was never taken for granted here. These were not conscripts dutifully sworn in and awaiting orders; they were self-armed and self-mounted volunteers held together by confidence in leadership. Their only measures of rank were courage and competence, and they were singularly adept at judging both.

It was clear they could not move now, nor could they easily stay there if a storm broke, but Seth realized that Stubbs and Berry, and beyond them the men, were waiting to hear what could be done and how.

Try as he could, Seth could think of no better advice than that left by their dead captain. They would hold there till dark but leave early in the night, moving westward until they found adequate cover and water. If a storm broke, the Indians might or might not follow them. Seth remembered that Bartlet had predicted that in bad weather they would not stray far from their camps.

Quiet and watchful, Berry listened attentively, and when Seth finished he nodded in agreement. Stubbs had his eyes trained on their right flank and away from Seth as he talked. He grunted once or twice, but Seth heard them as grunts of approval.

As they finished, Stubbs prepared to rise, balancing himself on one knee. "If we're pulling out tonight, we'd better get started on digging and rigging."

"Digging?" responded Seth, bracing to rise with him.

"Right." Stubbs knocked dirt from the seat of his jeans as he started to move back to the opposite slope. "We got some bodies here to bury and some wounded that can't be left behind."

"I'll get moving on both," said Berry quietly, as though the same thought had been hanging in his mind.

No one mentioned the Apache scouts who had managed to disappear the night before. It was not an uncommon or even unexpected occurrence. They had weighed their chances against this overwhelming force of Comanches and Kiowas and had opted to live.

10

Elena María López watched the sun sink beyond the endless sweep of prairie, leaving half a dome of sky ablaze in blue-edged scarlet, lavender and gold. Its beauty and incredible hold on her eyes left her understanding for a moment why primitive people were said to fall to their knees before such awesome sunsets, fearing the sun was dying forever.

In the distance Julio was waving his arms at someone closing the corral gate. She saw him turn toward the house, satisfied his signals were understood, and sighed in relief. She had been waiting for him all day. She peered at herself in the mirror, her warm, dark eyes restless, her glowing black hair sweeping in neat folds below her shoulders. She was vexed almost to tears. She was tired of waiting, weary of this parade of protective males and unimaginably bored. It was a measure of her desperation that she had toyed with letting young Ricardo, the lovesick boy who followed her about, kiss her. Fortunately, sensing Julio's anxieties, she had realized that this could only make her stay on this ridiculously confining and unromantic mule farm more difficult to endure.

She had to get home. She was angry that Ramón or her father had not come for her. The trouble on the border must be very serious for them to have left her here this long. Julio and his family were gracious, even embarrassingly kind, but this wretched existence was unbearable for one used to the gay, exciting life daughters of rich *hacendados* enjoyed in Mexico.

She looked at the little derringer she kept hidden in the soft folds of her skirt. Many young women at her social level carried them when traveling abroad. It was thought better if attacked to kill themselves than to be defiled by some unwashed *bandolero*. Elena, however, had no such intentions. If she were attacked, the derringer's one charge would go into her attacker. What happened afterward, she would leave to the stars. Her pious mother continuously ranted at her for not praying daily to her patron saint for protection, but her patron saint was clearly no match for Yoquito Estavez, this damnable bandit who was plaguing her life. She had glimpsed him only once, but his big burly figure and broad sallow face still danced in her mind. It should have been a handsome officer from the Tamaulipas cavalry plotting to abduct her. That, at least, would have brought some excitement to this drab setting.

Now she was preparing to confront Julio. Whatever the risks, she wanted to go home. Another week of smelling his mules and watching his infatuated son stumbling about would threaten her sanity. She was not in love with Ramón D'Valya, her rich and powerful neighbor outside of Laredo, but she could safely flirt with him even in front of her parents. She knew her father was secretly hoping she would accept Ramón's offer of marriage, but she found Ramón overbearing and irritatingly vain about his military rank, a generalship that should have made him an early hero of the Texas revolt. But to the disappointment of his highborn family and many junior officers condemned to serve under him, General D'Valya's tastes ran to mistresses and rare Spanish wines rather than the rigors and dangers of Santa Anna's fatally flawed campaigns. Her father confessed to a low opinion of Ramón's martial talents, but being the wife of a D'Valya still meant access to immense wealth and power. Elena alone remained unenchanted by her prospects. Although his many uniforms looked dashing enough, there was something arch and dictatorial about Ramón's manner, an imperious posturing that had an annoying resemblance to that of her father. Unlike her frail, forbearing mother, Elena was determined not to end up another subdued, near-invisible wife, replacing her husband with religion and repeated visits to the family chapel.

Now she could hear Julio entering the rear patio and asking the widow who served as a maid for a glass of wine. Still looking into the mirror, she opened her blouse and cupped her hands over her breasts. They were full and gave her body a sensuous roundness. An unarticulated hunger was running through her body, demanding to know what her first intimate embrace by a man would be like.

Smiling paternallly, Julio stepped into the parlor, delicately holding and admiring his family's silver filigreed wineglass. He prided himself on his flair for courtly manners and bowed deeply as he saw Elena poised and expectant in a large chair across the room. He had always felt that extreme courtesy, particularly toward women, was the mark of gentility and superior breeding. "Another beautiful day, eh?" he remarked softly, noticing that Elena's expression signaled she had something pressing to say. Aware that she did not drink, he stood the wineglass gently on a table behind him.

Elena had left the top button of her blouse open and carried a half-folded golden fan she held gracefully against her narrow waist. She looked ravishing. "Señor Spinada," she began. To his annoyance, in spite of their family connection she always addressed him formally. "I am deeply in your debt, and of course my father is grateful beyond measure—but now I *must* go home."

Julio settled onto the brightly draped settee opposite her and crossed his legs in an effort to look reassuring. "Of course, my dear, and so you will."

She raised a single delicate rose-tipped finger and tapped it meaningfully against her chin. "When?"

With some effort Julio extracted a small cigar from his vest pocket and after examining it critically placed it in his mouth. "When it is safe, of course."

"Safe! Surely my father can send enough men to escort his own daughter back to Laredo. Please, you must send him a message and also one to Señor D'Valya. Tell them I have to come home!"

Julio smiled patiently but shook his head. He removed the cigar to appraise it again before lighting it. "It is not that simple a matter, Elena."

"Why isn't it?" Elena's eyes flashed. "Is it because some goatherders say there is trouble on the border? There is always trouble down there."

"You do not understand."

Elena brought herself up abruptly and whipped the tightly folded fan against her thigh. "Señor Spinada, since, as you say, I do not understand, I demand you explain this ridiculous delay to me. I am not a child!"

Julio shifted uncomfortably. If only this luscious young female knew how much he wanted her out of his home and out of his care, she would have been shocked, but his predicament was not easy to explain. Bandits like Yoquito Estavez could go wherever they dared and take their chances. They represented only themselves. But for Elena's father, or even this Señor D'Valya, both high officers in the Mexican army, to send armed men deep into country claimed by Texas was another matter. Serious trouble could break out, and his family was certain to suffer. As he looked into Elena's seductive but demanding eyes, he decided he had better confide in her the plan he had been stewing over for weeks.

"Elena, listen to me. You must be patient. I have given this much thought. We have only to wait for the *rinches* to return to San Antonio. Then my friend Señor Bartlet will help me find some men—for he is the law here—who will escort you to the border. I have already prepared a message for your father. His guards will meet you there. It will be very safe. Trust me, there will be no danger."

Elena looked at him uncertainly, yet hope was edging into her soft, sensual face. "Señor Spinada. You are saying the *rinches*, those half-wild *norteamericanos*, will escort a Mexican lady back to her people?"

"I think so."

"Why do they do this?"

"For money."

"Money? How much money?"

"It does not matter. Your father is a generous man, he will not quibble."

She knew this was true. She could not conceal a budding surge of joy. "You have spoken to these *rinches* already?"

"No. But I will do this as soon as my friend Señor Bartlet returns."

The Rangers grimly lowered Will Bartlet into his shallow but well-concealed grave. It had taken them hours to dig it out of the rocky soil, and he was only one among many. A freezing rain squall had been whipping about them for over an hour, and beneath their wind-tortured slickers they were drenched. Water ran under their collars and sloshed in their boots. Though it was only early afternoon the storm had left it as dark as evening, and from the summit of the hill the world appeared gray and miserable in every direction.

The Indians seemed to have disappeared in the howling downpour, and after looking down the slope Berry reported that their dead bodies—including Ice's—that could be seen earlier were gone. It was his opinion that the warriors had withdrawn and it was time for the Rangers to do the same.

Seth and Stubbs looked at him, their faces reflecting the somber thoughts accumulated burying their dead. "You sure it's not a trap?" queried Stubbs.

"Not sure of anything," returned Berry, his tone discouraging such unanswerable questions. "But we can't stay here. If the weather clears, we won't last a day. We've got to find running water."

"The river?" rejoined Stubbs, trying to read Berry's face.

"No. They'll probably have it scouted already. Besides, the ground there is too flat and open. Remember, they know it a damn sight better than we. Our best bet is to stay back in these hills and work west till we hit a decent stream. There's plenty of 'em running up toward the Red." He looked about him like a wary animal sniffing the wind. "And we'd best keep a patrol between us and the river . . . make sure they don't slip by us and set up an ambush."

Berry's quiet manner was anything but authoritative, but his words rang with hard reason and his logic had a sure touch that some of them sensed rose from his Cherokee blood.

It was midnight before the rain stopped. They stood listening to the water that dripped from the trees and overhanging rocks, making it difficult to hear the chug of a little stream that ran at their feet, forming a pool in the rocky basin into which the horses had crowded to drink.

Seth and Stubbs were waiting to hear from Berry, who had led the patrol watching the river. Two shots had rung out almost an hour before, and neither could guess what they had meant. Berry had agreed not to engage the Indians until he could join the main force. Had he himself been attacked, surely there would have been more firing.

The answer did not come until a half hour later, when Prent Salinger, riding flank for Berry, was hailed in by a sentry posted to watch the hills sloping down toward the river. The weary river patrol plodded into the dark clearing herding three figures whose hands were tied behind them and whose bodies slumped forward in their saddles like half-filled sacks of meal.

In the sodden darkness it was difficult to make out faces, but Berry identified himself at once with his soft voice. "Caught these three coming upriver. They was toting this." In the still-dripping gloom he reached down and settled a long-barreled rifle with a thick heavy stock in Seth's hands.

Stubbs was at his side. "Sure as salvation that's one of them guns that bedeviled us this morning. Got old Ingersohl killed, it did, by Jesus!"

"Likely," muttered Seth, passing the bulky rifle over to Stubbs. "And these?" he gestured to the three slumped figures.

"Claim they don't savvy English," said Berry. "They're Comancheros ... found more trade goods in their packs. Guess they were hightailing it for Mex territory."

"Well, by God, they've got as far as they're ever gonna get!" roared Stubbs. "Somebody fetch a rope!"

"Hold on a minute," said Seth, putting a firm hand on Stubbs' shoulder. "We can't see enough to hang anyone till daylight. Besides, hanging 'em right off tells us nothing. They're bound to know something about these redskins."

Stubbs spat in disgust. "They ain't gettin' away."

"Didn't say they were."

With great effort, a little fire was started and the exhausted Rangers, chilled by a night wind that sought out every inch of soaked clothing, took a few swallows of scalding coffee. No one could sleep, and as they spread out in random clusters to await the dawn, many muttered to themselves in a misery Prent Salinger figured could sour a man quicker on this Ranger life than any dangers he'd seen so far.

Berry, taking hardly any time to rest, was gone before daylight and came back with the first gray of dawn to report no sign of hostiles. "We ought to be heading south," he said as he dismounted, pointedly ignoring the three Mexicans huddled together in abject fear.

"Reckon," said Seth. He had not been idle in Berry's absence. He had circled the Rangers and finally found what he was looking for: a Ranger who could speak passable Spanish and a man who had once been a gunsmith by trade. He already had the first one questioning the prisoners. They made no attempt to deny they had been selling goods, including guns, to the Indians, but they argued that they were only merchants and there was no law against trading with Indians even in Texas.

Stubbs, his impatience mounting, abruptly broke into the conversation. "What the hell are you talking about trading for? This is war!

These bastards have been aiding the enemy!" he said angrily. "We're wasting breath. Let's hang 'em and get moving."

To gain time, Seth turned to the gunsmith, who was examining the heavy rifle. "What do you make of it?"

"One of those long-bore rifles they've been trying to forge with heavier metals back east. Most of 'em blow up. Can't handle the charge. Likely they're trying to fashion a gun to take down buffalo."

Seth scratched his head and turned his back on the others. Something was bothering him, and on impulse he pulled Berry aside. He remembered Will Bartlet's once remarking about Comancheros being Mexican citizens. He knew Berry had been with Bartlet for many years and was the one most likely to answer a question that plagued him now. "What would Bartlet have done with these prisoners?" he half whispered.

Berry's response was too quick to hide his own thinking. "Take 'em back to San Antonio for trial."

Seth nodded and studied the earth for a moment. His instincts told him he was in for trouble. There was an ugly tension in the air, but turning back to the others he shouted, "Saddle up! We're moving south."

A strange silence spread over the camp, several men seeming to freeze into place. Stubbs, a rope draped over one arm, was standing above the prisoners. "What about these polecats?" he demanded.

"They're going to stand trial in San Antonio," answered Seth.

"Trial!" exploded Stubbs. "Christ! We don't need any trial! We caught 'em red-handed!"

"If they deserve hanging, they'll hang just as easily down there as up here."

Stubbs, now joined by several Rangers who shared his sentiments, had the three cringing captives surrounded. It was a dangerous moment. Some of the men were already pulling the Mexicans to their feet. But Stubbs, in spite of his sputtering fury, was still a Ranger. He waved the men back as he turned to Seth. "All right." A cold rasping edge roughened his voice. "Take 'em to San Antonio. Give them any kind of trial fitting this scum. Just remember when you're finished we'll be there with a rope to see justice is done."

It was already dark when Julio saw them coming. Their straggling formation, slow pace and hunched shoulders told him they were cold, hungry and very near to exhaustion. He had hoped to invite Señor Bartlet to his home where the big man could rest, bathe and enjoy a feast with his family, but within minutes he heard that Bartlet was dead. At first the shock left him confused and dismayed. But when he realized Seth Redmond was in command, he saw his plan might still succeed if he could somehow get this forceful blue-eyed Ranger to help him.

He had to wait in the shadow of the trees lining the square, for many of the Rangers who had come back earlier with the wounded were on hand to greet the main company, and apparently were now taking charge of the three prisoners the returning force had brought in.

After much searching, he spotted Seth and Prent Salinger standing alone. He came up bowing and quickly opened his conversation by thanking Seth for his help in retrieving the mules.

Seth, his mind on Isabelle and getting home, had to struggle for a moment to remember Julio. But when he did he abruptly responded, "Wasn't very much to it" and turned away. He and Prent were interested only in getting their horses cared for and finding some grub. Refusing to be ignored, Julio continued talking to hold their attention.

"Señores, perhaps you would do me the honor of coming to my home? It is but a short distance. There you can rest, bathe and perhaps dine with me and my very grateful family. Your horses, I assure you, will be well cared for."

Seth and Prent looked at each other. They were weary beyond belief, covered with trail dust and aching for some warm food. Both mounts were exhausted and needed rest. Starting for the Hondo country before morning was out of the question. The thought of being indoors, warm and clean, and for the first time in months tasting properly cooked food dissolved their resistance like a narcotic.

"That's mighty kind of you," said Seth as Prent nodded gratefully to indicate that Julio's invitation had been accepted.

"No, it is you who are kind, señores," said Julio, bowing again. "Come. It will take but a few moments. I have some excellent wine."

Washed and shaved, their stomachs tingling and slowly warming with Julio's wine, Seth and Prent looked like different men. Julio's modest home seemed blissful comfort after their long, bone-jarring weeks on horseback over wet rocky ground. They also experienced a spell of weakness as the delicious odors of cooking food wafted by. But the heaviest shock took place when Elena entered the parlor to be introduced. Seth, his mind on Isabelle, looked at this beautiful girl and felt only a new and almost painful pang of longing for his wife. But Prent, seeing Elena's body outlined in her blue-and-silver gown, stood in a daze as inexplicable as the sensations that cartwheeled from his head to his loins. Never had he been so struck into silence by a woman's presence. He only smiled, not trusting his voice, as he heard Seth saying, "Good evening, señorita. A great pleasure to meet you. We're sure grateful for your family's hospitality."

"Ah, Señor Redmond," said Elena, lowering her eyes. "You are the one who scared off the big bad bandit, Estavez. No?"

"He didn't take much scaring," said Seth, casually turning to Prent. "This is Prent Salinger, a friend and neighbor of mine."

Julio was watching Seth's reaction to Elena. Seth was clearly showing nothing but his native courtesy to all women. Not so his younger companion Prentiss. This poor young man, Julio could see, was almost hypnotized by Elena's beauty. He had not taken his eyes off her once. That was hardly what Julio had hoped for, but the night was young.

At Julio's direction the maid had laid the table out so that Elena sat next to Seth, who was on Julio's right, and Prent and Ricardo sat across from them. Julio lifted his wineglass and proposed a toast that raised this sudden if lavish dinner to a minor celebration. Without further ado a great dish of lamb and mixed vegetables began to circle the table.

Seth could not conceal his appetite, but Prent, conscious of Ricardo's watching Elena's every motion, soon began picking at his food and wishing he could have sat at Elena's side. Somehow he knew he was bothering Ricardo as much as Ricardo was bothering him. But to the chagrin of both it was Seth who was getting Elena's smiles and rapt attention. Julio, watching all this in growing confusion and mounting concern, filled his wineglass and tried to start a general conversation. He had planned to present his proposition to Seth after dinner, but it would have helped ensure its success if the Ranger had shown some physical response to Elena.

Elena was caught up in a dilemma of her own. Julio had whispered to her that Señor Bartlet was gone and now their hopes hung on this Seth Redmond. At first she flirted distantly, confident she could arouse his interest and secure his support, but sensing no reaction from him she was now subtly allowing herself a few bolder gestures.

Seth, feeling the pressure of her hand on his arm, began to sense her closeness and realized this gorgeous girl was inviting a more familiar touch from him in return. For the first time he noticed Prent and Ricardo across the table tasting their food with indifference and following Elena's every move and word in silence. He decided he would put the matter right at once.

Turning to Elena, he waved off Julio's offer of more wine and said with enthusiasm, "I can't hardly wait to tell my wife how kind you've all been to me. Having been gone for quite a spell, I suspect she'll set up a real homecoming. Got me a son too, bet he'll be a mite bigger than before. I can't hardly wait to get back."

"Me, too," echoed Prent weakly, noticing that some of the warmth had gone out of Elena's expression and grateful that she was at last glancing over toward him.

Julio cleared his throat. Patting Seth on the shoulder, he said with little conviction "*Sí.* It is always good to come home, *amigo*, always good to have a little peace after so much excitement."

But Elena found herself slowly slipping into a strange depression. This powerful, vibrant man beside her with his commanding blue eyes clearly found nothing in her ripening body to quicken his male desire. He had simply mentioned his wife and child, but in the subtleties to which she was attuned the words carried a rude rejection. She had never known herself in the presence of men to feel empty and powerless. She was used to males of high office and imposing rank undressing her with their eyes and fumbling ridiculously to effect some contact with her body. But this rawboned *rinche*, who made no pretense to grandeur—and yet whose formidable bearing had scared off the dangerous Estavez—was clearly umoved by all the feminine warmth she had beamed his way. For the first time in her life she lifted the thin-stemmed wineglass before her and drained its contents.

Julio observed all this with a deepening dread, for it was now obvious that his troubles were greater than ever. Manfully he tried to carry on his dinner, for Prent and Ricardo had started to eat even though Elena had grown mute and barely nodded when others spoke.

The truth, known only to herself, was that Elena was suffering from a revelation. She had always envisioned herself leisurely, even whimsically, choosing the men who would enjoy her attentions. But now instinctively she knew this strange man next to her was beyond any inducement she could offer, even her bed. The beauty that had always had a magnetic, almost hypnotic, effect upon men was failing to arouse even a ripple of emotion in this unresponsive and therefore, for her, unknowable man. She felt herself a simpering fool, unreasonably upset yet undeniably miserable. Feeling Julio's eyes on her, she could only stare at the empty wineglass turning slowly in her hand.

The following morning, Julio, forcing himself to be enterprising in the face of failure, sat with Seth over an early breakfast. He was right in suspecting that his petition to arrange an escort for Elena would get an eager response from young Prent but only an awkward silence from Seth. He was ready with another attempt to enlist this reserved but formidable Ranger's aid and friendship.

"Señor Redmond, you know I sell very excellent mules, your kindness in recovering them for me I never forget. But many people who come to buy mules also want horses. What you say I sell some of your very fine horses for you?"

Seth looked at him and slowly managed a smile. This sounded like a godsend for him. He would soon have many horses to sell, but buyers rarely came as far as the Hondo to buy them. He had been depending upon the meager and infrequent government requisitions. The idea of this successful businessman providing him with a handy market in San Antonio seemed almost too good to be true.

"I'd be right grateful," said Seth, finally responding with interest. "Of course, I couldn't let you do it for nothing."

Julio had no intention of doing it for nothing. He knew it would seem a more serious and promising business deal if he pretended he was looking forward to a small percentage of the profits for himself.

He wasn't wrong. On leaving, Seth promised to get him ten or twelve marketable mounts as soon as possible.

But later, at the hospital, surprisingly Seth found the Rangers looking disgruntled. Thoughtfully he approached Berry. "Something wrong?"

Berry nodded, glancing quickly over at Stubbs, whom Seth now saw standing in a group beyond the water trough. "Seems they dug up a traveling judge last night who told 'em there's no law on the Texas books against trading guns to Indians. Must have told 'em 'bout the game Sam Houston is playing too. Anyway, it 'pears this ain't no time to be hanging Mexican citizens, 'specially if they haven't broken any laws."

Seth gave Berry a small canvas bag of papers he had taken from Bartlet's body. "You'll see I've added some figures and notes of my own," he said, "but this report better be kept hereabouts till some government agent comes by. Don't believe there's any in town now."

Stubbs didn't offer any greeting when he rode over, but Seth decided not to take offense, for it was clear that more than one Ranger thought Stubbs had been right about hanging the Comancheros. Besides, Seth was eager to start back to his ranch. Many of the Rangers had already packed up and left. He thanked the few he could see and even dismounted to shake hands with Stubbs. "No hard feelings, I hope," he said.

"None," said Stubbs taking his hand with an unusually strong grip. "A man's got a right to his own way of thinking even if he's wrong as sin."

Seth smiled. He was too happy to be heading home to sustain any feelings of anger. It would not occur to him until long afterward why Stubbs, resentment still hard in his eyes, was nevertheless smiling back at him.

11

Seth enjoyed the trip back to his ranch. Sam had gotten his fill of oats at Julio's and seemed freshened by his rest in the straw-filled barn. The weather had turned clear, and there was a noticeable warmth in the morning sun. Spring had already come to the Southwest. Sprays of flowers could be seen dotting the roll of prairie and the green of leafing trees had started girdling the hills. He knew the land now well enough not to need trails, and his many shortcuts got him across the Medina just after noon. As he rested while Sam, with saddle removed, rolled in the deep grass, he realized he could cut across country and possibly be home by dark.

With the sight of wild deer and javelinas scattering before him, his mind filled with the joy of seeing Isabelle and Jason again, the land seemed to flow beneath him. Sam's steady pace slowly raised the hilltops to the west, telling him he was closing the distance home. His near-deadly stint with the Rangers appeared to have satisfied something in his gut. He no longer secretly rankled at the thought of Isabelle's shameful ordeal. Now they would have a new start—beginning tonight, he hoped. Suddenly, looking at the increasingly familiar range ahead, he was lonely for her, painfully lonely. Without thinking, he urged Sam into a gallop which, because it was almost dark, brought the horse rushing up to a fence line it had to jump without warning. As he landed roughly on the other side, Seth heard himself being hailed. It was a minute or two before he made out a distant rider and was surprised to discover it was Rick Salinger.

"Well, hello!" he shouted back. "What the devil are you doing out here?"

Rick laughed. "Mending that fence you just jumped. By golly, Seth, I'm working for you now. Hired on a while back with Mrs. Redmond. Sure mighty good to see you again."

Nodding but continuing on toward the house, Seth listened while Rick rode alongside and related how Carlos had been sent off and how Brandy was in the hut now with Inez while he himself, their new hired hand, was in the barn. But Rick dearly wanted to know about Prent. How many redskins had he killed and was he considered a sure-enough Ranger by now?

Seth, not wanting to delay reaching Isabelle, took time only to say that Prent was planning a trip to the border and wouldn't be back for a week or two. Explaining that he had to get to the house, he promised to answer all Rick's questions on the morrow.

Rick laughed agreeably, shouting "Fine" as he watched Seth pushing Sam forward and galloping on ahead.

Isabelle was not expecting him. Somehow she had had a feeling there would be some warning when he came, some hint he was on his way. But that evening she had sat quietly, watching Brandy building up the fire, not knowing Seth was already on their land and coming as fast as the wearying Sam could carry him.

It was Inez who heard the hoofbeats first and, running to the door, peered into the darkness to squeal, "It is Señor Redmond! He comes!" With some effort Isabelle pulled herself to her feet and drew her loose dress closer to her body. But it was useless. Her stomach was too far extended to conceal. She knew it was too late for anything but standing and waiting. With resignation she pushed a few strands of hair back into place. Brandy, abandoning the fire and motioning to Inez to follow him, stepped outside and waited to take the horse. Something told him this was a moment Seth and Isabelle had to live alone.

Seth dismounted, hardly seeing Brandy, so anxious was he to enter the house and embrace his wife. He came through the door and saw her standing in the firelight, his first sight finding her looking shockingly weary but still beautiful. Words began forming on his lips but lost their substance as he saw her swollen stomach. Unformed and unnameable emotions kept his face devoid of expression. He struggled to cover the few steps between them but halted as his eyes fixed on

her face. It was lined with fright and drained by despair. The thought
that she might be dying crossed his mind, and his heart almost refused
to beat. Something was wrong . . . terribly, terribly wrong.

That night as they sat together Seth and Isabelle had to struggle
to hold on to each other, for Isabelle was near fainting and too weak
to do more than lay her fears before Seth. She watched as he forced
his uncomprehending mind to resist her words.

"How do you know it's not ours?" he pleaded.

"I don't, but I have this terrible feeling."

"But if you're wrong then all this is for nothing."

"Seth, I pray to God I'm wrong, but I'm horribly frightened. Carrying Jason was never like this."

Seth looked at her. Like so many men, the power of women to bring
forth life baffled him. Still, he knew that most women had an uncanny
sense about the mysteries of their bodies. By some subconscious cal-
endar they knew the rhythms of their life cycles. Intuition tran-
scended all reasoning. Isabelle did not believe this baby was his. In
his heart he didn't either. She sat there looking back at him, her eyes
begging for warmth and understanding. "What will we do?" she asked
wretchedly.

He pulled her closer and kissed her cheek, but his gaze held to the
coals dying low in the fire. "We'll just have to wait," he replied, unable
to keep the bitterness in his mind from distorting the timbre of his
voice.

The next several weeks were difficult ones for Seth. There was no
relief from the agony of wondering, secret pleading and lying in the
night praying that Isabelle's fears were unfounded.

It was not a thing they could continue to talk about, but neither
could it be ignored. With Brandy and Rick handling the ranch work,
Seth started taking strings of horses in to Julio to sell. When he did
he stayed overnight at the mule merchant's house. Surprisingly, from
his very first trip, Elena found it easier to be with him than she
thought, for she soon discovered that, behind those steady blue eyes,
he was brooding about something and it left his mood closer to hers.
She had the good sense to stop wanting him to respond to her like
some silly fop; he was clearly a married man whose feelings for
women weren't expressed in flattery or trifling attentions.

It was strange the way Seth affected her. His angry stance against his and Isabelle's fate had registered in Elena's eyes like the resolute defiance of a man battling the frontier, fearless in his solitude and dealing with life as coolly as he had stared down the dangerous Estavez. Yet, as their acquaintance deepened, she found him human and honest to the point of vulnerability. The more she saw of him, the more she realized he was unlike anyone she'd ever met. While clearly as brave as any Mexican officer who had ever strutted about her father's courtyard, he had none of their irritating airs of superiority, none of their presumptions to being great lovers women couldn't resist. At first his sincerity was so pronounced she almost mistook it for innocence, but then she realized Seth Redmond was simply more real than the men who populated the world she had been raised in. The few hours they spent together discussing life made her arranged and pointless flirtations with rich, self-indulging wastrels like General D'Valya seem shallow and even childish. She found several chances to be alone with him now and talk to him as she would any human being, no longer depending on her beauty to win his favor. She didn't know it, but Seth had secretly begun to see her in a different light, for unbeknownst to Elena her relationship with this dominant yet vibrant man, who pretended nothing and presumed even less, had changed her.

For Seth's part, she made the evenings he spent at Julio's more relaxing, but only because there was no hint of romance to clash with his deep concern about Isabelle. While Julio waited for Prent to arrange an escort, he watched them from a distance, satisfied that this relationship was not endangering his ward. He was only troubled that Elena, now refusing to allow Ricardo to follow her around, had taken to riding out in the afternoons on days when Seth wasn't there. Estavez was still thought to be around, though there had been no word of him for weeks.

Elena simply wanted time to herself. She had been reviewing her earlier life, and the path her family had laid out for her now seemed void of meaning, built on imagined and sterile notions of social rank, imprinted with those jaded dreams of a society that had built a legend about itself to replace its harsh realities. There was no life for her in Laredo except the life her mother had lived before her and her grandmother before that. A priest and a promise of paradise to justify a sunless existence. Somewhere within her Seth had stirred a first realization of true love, though this only served to sadden her, for something told her it meant loneliness. She kept thinking of that whispered axiom of Mexico's privileged classes, that a man may love many times but marries only once, and a woman may marry many times but loves only once. Had she already met her love? Did this love already belong to someone else?

She was thinking this when she looked up to see two riders a hundred yards in front of her awaiting her approach. Something told her to turn and flee, but that would only confirm her worst dread. Instead she slowed to a walk, but as the distance closed her heart began to thump, for she could see they were Mexicans, heavily armed, and they were smiling at her.

Seth knew the string of horses he was now bringing would be the last for a while. They were good stock, almost all the issue of Kentucky sires and mustang mares. Julio had sold quite a few, and Seth was glad to receive the money, for he was planning to buy more prime breeding stock in east Texas. He was down to two healthy stallions standing in stud at the moment.

When he arrived at Julio's, he found considerable excitement. Elena was missing. She had always come in well before sundown, but now shadows were beginning to creep across the yard and Julio was beginning to panic.

"Where did she go?" asked Seth.

Julio hunched his shoulders helplessly. "She never says . . . *Dios!* What we gonna do?"

Seth tried to look calm, but Julio's fright was contagious. "Where is she likely to go?" he queried, not knowing what else to say.

Julio put his hands over his face. "Santa María! Why does she do this to me?"

"Where?" repeated Seth.

"I dunno, better we ask Ricardo." But Ricardo was nowhere to be found.

Fortunately for Elena, the lovesick Ricardo, though ordered not to bother her, had, like a hurt puppy, followed Elena from a distance, hoping life would give him a chance to prove his manhood. He had dreams of getting the drop on an unsuspecting Estavez and bringing him in as a prisoner while Elena followed with adoring eyes. But when he saw two men taking the reins of her horse and leading her away, to be joined by a third, he realized he was seriously outgunned. He couldn't help Elena by getting himself killed. Even as he lathered his horse and sent it pounding back to the mule farm, he realized they could be getting away and he might never see his beautiful Elena again. In the few moments he had watched them through the trees, his heart in his mouth, he had seen they were taking her south.

As he came into the yard, shouting his frightening news, Seth got back up onto Sam. Julio wanted to get more help to go with them, but Seth waited only until Ricardo threw his saddle onto another horse, for the one he had raced back was blown. Then the two of them kicked their spurs in cruelly as they galloped back out over Ricardo's tracks.

When they arrived at the spot where she had been taken, Seth realized that if they were heading south they were surely trying for the border. But the border was still many miles away. He managed to pick up the tracks of four mounts in the declining light and grimly opened the pursuit. After eight or nine miles it was too dark to track further. Seth had decided to bed down there until dawn, then resume the chase, but peering into the darkness he saw a faint light several miles further on and decided it was worth a look.

It was the stale smell of liquor and the sight of old casks and bottles lying around that made him realize he was approaching another shack peddling booze. It was the sight of the bald-headed man passing by one of its narrow windows that convinced him it was the same one he and the Salingers had chased away from the main trail. Finally Ricardo, studying the horses tethered outside, said the mount Elena had been riding was there.

Seth knew Ricardo was armed, but he wasn't sure how the young man would act under fire. Here he didn't have those gun-savvy Salingers behind him. Six horses stood at the hitching post, revealing that there were five others in there besides Elena. Those were worrisome odds. What Seth feared most was a shooting spree in which Elena might be hit. But he couldn't wait; he had the feeling they had come there to deliver her to someone. God only knew who would show up next.

On a hunch he took Ricardo by the arm. "Give me three seconds after I walk through that door. Then I want you to shoot the rest of that broken window out."

Ricardo's voice sounded tight and strained in the darkness. "Señor, you're going alone?"

"Yes, but I don't want them to think I'm alone. Don't be afraid to shout out here."

Seth could almost hear Ricardo swallowing hard. "What should I shout, señor?"

Seth gripped his arm harder, wanting the words to sink in. "Things like 'Watch that door! Don't let anyone out!' "

After a moment Seth could hear Ricardo pulling up his gun and cocking it. "I am ready, señor."

Seth walked in, gun in hand. The bald man, seeing him first, half shouted, "Well, look—"

A shot rang out, and glass sprayed across the room. The three Mexicans came to their feet, and the yellow-toothed Texan reached for his gun belt, which was hanging on a nearby chair. Seth could see Elena sitting in a far corner, her blouse open and her hair in disarray. At the sight of him her face lit up, but "Seth!" was all she could mouth. She looked mortally frightened.

But Seth knew the most dangerous part of his ruse was at hand. He leveled the gun on the bald man and said, as calmly as he could, "Elena, get outside."

A Mexican rose to block her way, but just at that moment Ricardo shouted, "Keep watching that door! Nobody gets out!" As the Mexican slunk out of the way, the bald man found his tongue. "Goddamn it! Don't shoot my place up again like you did last time!"

Elena passed Seth and made the door. "What were you going to do with that girl?" rasped Seth.

"Mister, I got no part in this. These bastards were getting paid to deliver her to one of the meanest sons of bitches I've ever laid eyes on. He's a big greaser who's been drinking my booze that he don't hardly pay for."

"Estavez?"

"That's him, and if you wait a spell you'll see him yourself . . . supposed to be here any minute. Now, like I say, don't shoot my place up, goddamn it! It's hard enough to do business without this shit!"

Outside, Elena and Ricardo were already mounted. Seth swung up on Sam, but he couldn't believe it was that easy, that they were really free. He kept his eyes on the door and probably saved his life, and perhaps the others'. Light from the inside glinted on a rifle barrel being raised in the half shadow. Seth, gun still in hand, fired instinctively. The glint dropped, and the head of a Mexican lay half in and half out of the pool of light at the foot of the door.

Several miles to the north, Ricardo drew alongside Elena to say, "Well, we sure enough saved you."

Elena, who was urging her mount to keep up with Sam, nodded in the darkness and tried to smile. "Yes, you were wonderful," she sighed several times. But he noticed she kept on looking at Seth.

There were many faces of hope, joy and fear watching the great wedges of migratory birds going north over the greening Hondo valley that season. They knew from their almanac calendars it was late March of 1842, but they did not know a Mexican general named Vásquez had been quietly massing troops in Laredo, a Mexican town claimed by Texas, and was ordering them to march on San Antonio. Though surprise was complete, word of the invasion soon spread like prairie fire throughout the Southwest, and a minor panic developed. Jack Hays was back in the settlement, but many of the Ranger companies mustered in the fall had melted away with the coming of the planting season, and all he could draw from the surrounding areas was a hundred volunteers, not enough to hold the town.

But Hays knew that Vásquez' force, like most Mexican army units, was poorly equipped and supplied, and that the long line of communication back to the border would be a nightmare to protect. His main concern was that Vásquez would start to live off the land. Warnings immediately went out to settlers in all directions that livestock, particularly horses, food and firearms were to be moved beyond the enemy's reach or destroyed. Hays wisely decided to wait these invaders out. Mexican foraging parties he could deal with, and he was sure Vásquez had to reckon that large contingents of Texans would soon be approaching from the east.

Yet one Ranger viewed all this with increasing anger and dismay. Prent Salinger knew that his persistent attempts to interest others in forming an escort to protect Elena to the border were about to bear fruit. It had been an unbelievably difficult task. Berry had turned him down flatly, advising him not to go. "The land between here and the river is flatter than a pancake, Prent. Believe me, Mexican bandits can be slicker to handle than Comanches."

"We'll make it," said Prent defensively.

"Make it?" Berry smiled, but not unkindly. "That's only half of your problem, Prent. You have to get back. With each of you toting two hundred in gold, the danger could be doubled."

"You mean the money? How could they know?"

Berry regarded him patiently, but as he extended his hand in farewell he shook his head in grave warning. "Son, you don't know much about Mexicans, do you? Go home. Don't wait to find out the hard way."

But Prent was not deterred. His fascination with Elena drove him to meet Julio's strict conditions. He had even thought to speak to Stubbs, but a few days after Seth left, word had come in that the three freed Comancheros had been found dead in a gulch southwest of town, their bodies strung up in dead cottonwood trees like Christ and the two thieves. For some reason Stubbs could not be located. But now when Prent had finally gotten three older Rangers to agree to his proposal, the Mexican army was entering San Antonio. Elena María López no longer needed an escort.

Seth, with Rick riding along to help, appeared in Hays' camp. Isabelle did not want to be left alone again, and he was reluctant to go, but an emergency had been declared throughout west Texas and all able-bodied men were expected to muster. Hays had heard that Seth had taken over Bartlet's command and led it safely back; he soon had him commanding a patrol of ten volunteers watching the trails that ran south and west.

Downcast and disgusted as Prent was, he was happy to see Seth and his younger brother, but Seth's face seemed to have hardened since he had last seen him at Julio's. His voice sounded tight, and he spoke now only with reluctance. In a way he was glad that Rick's constant chatter helped cover whatever hidden and clearly increasing strain Seth was under.

Julio, crossing himself, watched Mexican soldiers galloping through San Antonio with fearful misgivings. The Mexican army was not known for its good behavior. There were still informers in the settlement who would readily bring up his support of Texas in the revolt, with all its treasonable implications. He was sure they would seize his property and his mules, and it was no idle speculation that he might be shot. He drank half a bottle of wine while he struggled with his frustrations upon hearing that the Texans would not defend the town. He stopped pacing the house at every bugle call and drum-roll, putting down his wineglass and embracing his sons with the desperation of a man facing the gallows.

Fortunately he could not see Elena, for though she had seemed moody beyond belief in recent days she now gave the impression of having arrived at some deep, firm resolve. The sight of Mexican uniforms meant her exile was over. She dressed herself as attractively as she could and insisted that Ricardo rent a small carriage from a nearby stable and deliver her to General Vásquez' headquarters.

There several Mexican officers, resplendent in their braid and blue-and-gold piping, came to attention and bowed as she stepped down from her carriage. Some of them recognized her as Colonel López' daughter; others were enviously aware she was the favorite of General D'Valya. Elena soon had them all enchanted and with little effort persuaded General Vásquez to spare Julio's farm and deliver a note for her which she explained contained only a farewell.

Julio, astonished at the respect shown him by the junior cavalry officer delivering the note, took the missive gratefully and then, as his eyes raced over its contents, breathed a sigh of relief.

My dear Señor Spinada:

I am truly grateful for your patience and protection. You will please express my thanks to Señor Salinger for his many efforts on my behalf. Please, also, if you see Señor Redmond remember to say that I will never forget his courage and graciousness and that one day I hope to see him again. General Vásquez assures me neither you nor your property will be disturbed. I shall convey your regards to my father.

Elena

It was weeks before Jack Hays was proven right, although messages from Sam Houston left little doubt that this token invasion was to impress the United States more than Texas. Talk of the United States annexing Texas, Houston's cherished dream, was rampant in the East, and Mexico wanted to remind Washington that it had never relinquished its claim to Texas soil.

In spite of an uproar of indignation from some quarters, Hays knew Houston did not want another war, which could only endanger the issue of annexation, so as Vásquez began his retreat, he followed him quietly to the border, content with cutting off and wiping out a small patrol attempting one foray too many.

By late April Vásquez was back across the Rio Grande in nearby Laredo. With him, under a pink parasol and riding in General

D'Valya's ornate carriage, was the stunning but now strangely subdued and pensive Elena López.

Doc Michalrath realized he was getting too old for long spells in
the saddle. Secretly he conceded it would be the last time he tried
to reach the Redmond ranch by horse. But word had been coming to
him of the difficulties Isabelle was having with her pregnancy and,
feeling such a trip might be dangerous for her, he at last decided to
come.

Isabelle got up to welcome him and had Inez prepare coffee and
biscuits while he rested. When he first saw her he had to conceal his
expression, for she looked frightfully wasted and even ill, but as he
talked with her his suspicions that this woeful condition was as much
mental as physical began to grow. An hour later, after an exhaustive
examination, he was sure of it. Apart from the continual discomfort
after eating, sudden painful headaches and an inability to sleep, her
pregnancy seemed physically normal. Yet there was no mistaking the
sheen of suppressed hysteria in her eyes.

The old doctor spoke to her calmly and comfortingly. He had great
respect for the role of emotions in the functioning of the human body.
He believed people could literally worry themselves into illness, if
not death. After a few hours he had Isabelle relaxed and feeling better
as he talked about her long life ahead and how important her health
would be to Jason and Seth in those years. As he left Isabelle took
his large, gentle hands in hers and looked at him. Somehow she
wanted this man beside her throughout her ordeal, and yet it seemed
selfish to ask. "Doctor, you say it will be late summer. Would you
come?"

Michalrath took a moment to look into her pleading eyes. The years
had done little to dim his memories of his dead wife. He had always
been a concerned, loving husband, but like all men who lose the
woman they love after sharing a difficult life, he still harbored regrets
about the things he hadn't done. In particular, he often wondered if
he had been there enough when they had first come west and she was
left frightened and alone. Isabelle knew he was looking at her, but
she could never have imagined he was seeing his dead wife, Carrie,
whom he had laid to rest years before. Still, a secret joy arose in her
when he gripped her hands in return and said, "Isabelle, if the good
Lord spares me I'll be here."

◆ ◆ ◆

Brandy came into the hut nettled and disturbed. Inez, startled he was back so early, went to him and saw that his face was strained as though he were fighting down some mute anger.

With Rick gone helping Seth bring badly needed horses to Hays' camp, Brandy had decided he had better take a quick look at their herds on the distant south range to make sure that Mexican foraging parties were not coming this far west. Secretly he felt that worrying about cattle was a waste of time. There were enough longhorns running wild to satisfy any beef needs the Mexicans had. Besides, the future was in horses, and their horse herd was growing. Seth had stayed convinced that the towns to the east were filling up and a new tide of people lured from the eastern states by talk of annexation would make the market for beef soar.

He was hoping Seth was right when he found himself almost on the main trail leading back to San Antonio. To his surprise, four riders were stopped only a quarter of a mile away, one rising in his stirrups and looking in his direction. They seemed to be waiting for two others he could see a mile or two behind them to the east. Oddly, his mind went to the gun at his hip, but he could see no danger in approaching them since they seemed to be nothing more than ranch or farmhands, common enough in this country. As he rode up, a big, heavyset man with a full black mustache looked at him and then at the fine roan he was riding. There was something mean and antagonistic in his eyes. "Where you from, nigger?" he demanded coarsely.

Brandy could see the suspicion already clouding the faces of the others, but instinct warned him that his real danger lay in showing fear. "You got business askin'?" he said evenly.

"Uppity son of a bitch, ain't he?" glowered the heavy mustache. Brandy didn't know they were volunteers Hays had drawn from the east, where the slave population of Texas was growing, some even arriving by boat at Galveston. The slaves represented no threat to the plantation owners, but a natural antipathy existed between them and the small farmers and landless immigrants.

"That's sure a mighty fine horse for a nigger to be riding," said one of the others.

Brandy stared back at them, but he could see the two riders following them were now getting close. "Wuz you gentlemen looking for sumthin' or sumone 'round here?" he asked, struggling to keep his voice steady.

"What we're looking for is our business," said black mustache. "Sure you ain't a runaway?"

The two other riders were finally coming up, and Brandy was relieved to see that one of them was Todd Bonham.

"Hi, Brandy!" called Todd, moving into the group.

"Howdy, Mistah Bonham," said Brandy, keeping his face from betraying his relief.

"You know him?" said mustache.

"Yeah, that's Seth Redmond's hand, he's all right." Todd looked about him, fixing the position of the sun. "We best be heading south. We got plenty ridin' to do." Moving his horse closer to Brandy's, he said quietly, "You seen Bess Salinger lately?"

Brandy nodded. "Yes'm, Missy Bessie bin 'round a fair amount. Missum Isabelle is s'pecting like you know."

Todd nodded, his young, handsome face giving in to a smile as he said, "Tell Bessie I was asking for her."

"Don't tell us there's a gal foolish enough to take up with you?" called one of the men jokingly.

"Sure is and fixing to come a-courtin' her soon as I have me a few more chances to see the elephant in San Antonio."

They all laughed as they pulled away, Todd shouting back to Brandy, "Say howdy to Isabelle for me. Tell her Seth shouldn't be too long. Don't look like those Mexes have come up here to fight."

Brandy watched him go with a strange bitterness beginning to gnaw at his gut. He wondered what would have happened had not Todd Bonham rode up. "Nigger!" He slapped the saddle horn in anger. "Nigger!" Was he really free? Did he have any business riding Seth's highblooded horses? Maybe the degradations of old Mississippi were coming to Texas. He started back. It was a long, lonely ride as he thought of the many people worried and concerned about Isabelle's pregnancy. Did any of them remember that Inez was pregnant too? Ironically, only Isabelle seemed to care, and she was too troubled herself to share his fears. He saw Dr. Michalrath's horse as he rode into the ranch yard. The doctor had come to visit Isabelle on his own. Did he dare ask him to look at Inez too? No, Inez would never agree. She had bitterly insisted she could take care of her baby both before and after its birth. Brandy did not argue. He remembered the slave quarters he had been raised in. He remembered the women's lack of privacy, the denial of their dignity even in childbirth. He knew that Inez, with her slim hips, would need help, and when the time came he intended to get it for her.

But coming into the hut now he was angry at the world, angry at his treatment by those rough-mouthed volunteers, angry at his helplessness and, at a level too deep for understanding, angry at the color of his skin.

Inez came over to him. She kissed him and hugged him close, saying softly, "Something is wrong?"

"No," he answered in resignation. "Nothin' wrong. Everythin' fine."

12

That summer grew more torrid daily. The heated air simmered over the plains, and green bottle flies droned in the slivers of shade the parched animals sought. By late August the sun had sucked the last moisture from the scorched earth, and in the narrowing creek beds the water was down to a trickle between shallow pools.

When Isabelle's first labor pains struck, Rick left at a gallop for Michalrath's. The doctor, expecting him, had a rig ready and young Jed to drive him. He arrived just before dark and found Seth standing outside with Brandy and Berry, the Ranger guide. Isabelle, attended by Bessie Salinger and old Mrs. MacFee, was lying in her bed with a cool, damp rag over her forehead. She had still not entered deep labor.

There was little conversation. Isabelle attempted to smile when she saw the doctor, but he pressed her hand reassuringly and asked the women to remove some of the bed covers, for he saw that Isabelle was drenched in sweat.

It was a strange night. Seth paced beneath the big cottonwood in front and did not hear Berry say that Hays wanted him back and that Prent was already off alerting other volunteers. Hays had his spies too, and he knew the Mexican army was mustering again at Laredo, preparing for another march on San Antonio. This time General Adrian Woll, a European mercenary but one of Mexico's best generals, was to command. The situation had grown serious.

Seth realized he should have asked Berry to stay the night, but he was too distracted by the sounds coming from the house, and after moving up to the door to listen on one occasion he returned to find Berry gone.

Knowing he couldn't help, Seth sat watching his own doorstep for hours. Bessie Salinger came out near midnight to ask that Brandy bring another lantern from the stable. The doctor needed more light. That was all.

Just before dawn Isabelle gripped the rungs of her bed and with one final contraction of her abdomen gave birth to a five-and-a-half-pound male child. The doctor quickly cut and tied the umbilical cord, but his eyes were on the infant Mrs. MacFee was already cleaning up. In his mind's eye was Jason, Isabelle's first child, with his curly blond hair and blue eyes. According to Isabelle, he had been over nine pounds at birth. With apprehension he saw this infant's body was darker than he had hoped, the few strands of hair were black and straight, and above all the eyes had a slight but unmistakable slant. His medical knowledge could not be ignored. He knew he had just delivered a half-breed. Bessie and Mrs. MacFee said nothing, but they could tell from the doctor's face that he was summoning up composure enough to inform Isabelle and Seth.

Isabelle did not speak, but after studying Michalrath's face for a moment she turned to Mrs. MacFee, who was holding the baby, and whispered, "I know." Bessie came to sit beside her and hold her hands. Mrs. MacFee took the chair drawn up to the bed. The three women remained silent as the doctor, washing and drying his hands, rubbed his tired eyes and walked slowly outside to speak to Seth.

"Well?" said Seth, his tension evident in his unshaven face, which even in the darkness was drawn with fatigue.

"Reckon the Lord has his own way of doing things," began Michalrath.

"What the hell does that mean?" Dread suddenly replaced the tension in Seth's face.

"It means what we've been afraid of has happened."

Seth froze for a moment. "You mean the child isn't mine?"

Michalrath's face betrayed the pain of his task. Drawing in his breath, he murmured, "No, Seth, I don't believe it is."

"God!" gasped Seth. "God almighty, what can I do?"

"Nothing."

Seth's face had turned pale, almost ghastly. "Is Isabelle all right?" he muttered, lifting his hands to his head and fixing his eyes on the ground.

"Yes, but I reckon she needs you."

After a moment Seth started forward as though he were going to enter the house, but then he turned again to confront the doctor. "Where's the baby?"

"With her, I guess."

Seth stopped, his hands back over his face, his body shaking as though beyond control. Then, without speaking again, he turned and, swaying like a man without sight, moved slowly toward the stable.

It was late afternoon of that day when Isabelle awoke to find Bessie standing over her with a tray of food. Shortly after dawn she had asked for Seth and was told he was coming, but Dr. Michalrath, suspecting otherwise and wanting her to get some desperately needed rest, had administered some laudanum, after which she had drifted off to sleep.

Now Bessie helped her to sit up and taste the tea and biscuits. Isabelle looked about and realized the day was far advanced. "Where is Seth?" she asked.

Bessie turned to smoothing the bed covers as she talked. "Seems there's some kind of trouble in San Antonio. Those dreadful Mexicans just won't leave us alone. Jack Hays sent for Seth, believe my brother Prent is gone too. Likely they'll be back shortly. My, I do believe we've been having us another wretchedly hot day."

Isabelle stared at her. Bessie's words hardly registered, for her tone was strained with hidden anxiety and pity. After a long silence Isabelle whispered, "Where is the baby?"

"Mrs. MacFee is sitting with it in Jason's room. She's trying to feed it. Eat something, Isabelle, and try to rest. Don't worry. Everything will be all right."

The weak, muffled wail of an infant could be heard through the thin planking within the house.

Isabelle pulled herself up further in the bed and reached back to straighten her long hair behind her. Bessie bit her lip as she saw her friend looking years older. The freshness that had always been part of Isabelle's beauty was gone.

Isabelle made several attempts to eat, but the heat of the day and the agony in her mind made the effort impossible. Dr. Michalrath, she learned, had had to go back to his sick sister, Phoebe, who had spent the night alone. He had left Isabelle some powders to take if she had trouble sleeping and a note saying he would be back in a week if he had not heard from her before then. Dr. Michalrath must have known that Isabelle's trials were far from over.

Turning in the bed, she felt her breasts swollen with milk. One nipple stayed moist as though it were dripping. In the awkward silence between her and Bessie she could still hear the tiny wail of the infant she had just borne. Bessie, though tense and uncertain, was clearly reading her thoughts. "It might be easier, Isabelle, if you don't. Dr. Michalrath thought you and Seth might want to give it to other folks to raise up."

Isabelle looked toward the open door. In the distance she could see a lonely bird circling a tree and then gliding down to perch. It was odd, she thought, that she had never noticed it before. It must have its nest there.

Nervously slipping about, Bessie had crossed to the window and suddenly caught sight of thunderheads building up to the west. "Thank goodness!" she gasped. "Maybe we'll get some rain to break this heat. Mercy, it's about got us all dried up and ready to blow away."

Isabelle did not answer. She wondered if taking enough of those powders Dr. Michalrath had left her would kill her. Lying there, she could see nothing left of her life. Her mind understood why Seth had gone to San Antonio, but her heart knew only that he was gone. She lay there for a quarter of an hour with her eyes closed. Bessie, thinking she might be asleep, did not disturb her. Beyond, the thunderheads moved slowly toward them. Then a low peal of thunder could be heard in the distance. In the silence that followed, the tiny wail of a hungry infant sounded again.

Isabelle opened her eyes. She and Bessie stared at each other for a long, agonizing moment. Then Isabelle sobbed and said, "Bessie, bring it to me. Bring me my baby."

It was evening when Bessie came looking for Brandy. At her call he went to meet her outside the hut. She stood with her pert little face looking up into his. "Mrs. MacFee says she has to get back to her folks. Would you take my rig and see her home, Brandy?"

"Yes'm, Missy Bessie. Be mighty pleased to."

Bessie was starting to turn away but stopped to look back at him with a brief smile. "You didn't happen to see Todd Bonham again, did you?"

"No, ma'am." Brandy couldn't help smiling in turn. "Reckon he should be comin' by 'fore long, though."

Bessie clicked her tongue but quickly gathered her skirts and fled back into the house.

Few people knew that old Mrs. MacFee was one of Brandy's favorite people. He had gone to her place so often for milk for Jason that he had discovered things about her not many others knew.

It had started early in the spring when he had arrived and seen no one in sight except an old lady down near a small stream that ran behind their house. Incredibly, she had had a long, heavy shovel in her hand. He had removed his hat and walked over to ask for the milk, only to discover she was starting a small vegetable garden. She had always greeted Brandy kindly, but now she seemed out of breath and came up slowly as he approached and with some effort struggled to straighten her back. Brandy remembered the small plots slaves were often allowed to keep around their shacks in Mississippi, and he knew the old lady was spading up the earth for a planting. She'd also marked out a place for flowers. After convincing her to sit down, he picked up her shovel and finished the job. For this she insisted he take home two jars of preserves.

Inez had been delighted with the preserves, but to his surprise she was more excited to hear about Mrs. MacFee's garden, particularly the flowers. She wanted to grow some too. She told him that as a child she had always worked in her family's garden and it had always included some flowers. She would make hers a small one, so Seth and Isabelle would not object.

After mulling it over awhile, Brandy had decided he had best approach Mrs. MacFee first. He had discovered she was a farmer's daughter and along with her milk cow had planned on getting in some chickens and maybe a goat. He sensed from her willingness to spend so much time talking to him that in spite of a husband, two sons and a daughter, she was still a little lonely. She advised him to tell Inez to pick a spot for the flowers near the creek, where she could easily get water, and to start fertilizing as soon as possible. She took the last wrinkles out of his brow when she promised to provide Inez with some seeds to start. She also sent along two budding tomato plants and other vegetables.

It was soon clear Inez didn't need any help. She had a touch with plant life and loved making things grow. Before the spring was over, she had tomatoes, peppers, onions, peas and four kinds of flowers beginning to sprout. Seth and Isabelle saw no reason to object to more fresh vegetables coming to their table, and Isabelle loved the sprays of flowers that brought a little color into the house. The garden plot lay between the creek and the near corral and was easy for Inez to get to, but as the weather turned fair Brandy began to worry about the danger of her being there alone. His one consolation was Scout, who had shot up into a sizable dog and was still growing. The big, rangy Scout was fond of Inez and followed her whenever she went to the garden, but Brandy still feared the dog might be off chasing jackrabbits when he should be standing guard. At last he had had to insist that Inez could go only if she agreed to take a rifle along.

The passing of the afternoon storm had broken the high heat, but it was still warm and sultry as Brandy clucked to the mare drawing Bessie's rig and started to take Mrs. MacFee home. He was secretly blessing this opportunity to be alone with her. "How dat new baby doin'?" he asked with genuine interest.

"The child seems to be doing fine," said Mrs. MacFee, her eyes fixed on some distant point up the road.

"And Missum Isabelle?"

The old lady raised a handkerchief to her mouth. "Goodness knows, Brandy, I really can't say."

Brandy shook his head and was silent for a few minutes. Finally he turned to her as though courtesy demanded an additional effort at speech. "Bet you seen a mess of babies born."

"Certainly have. Delivered my second boy myself. Floods washed out the trails, bridges and all, and the doctor couldn't make it through the mud. Brandy, babies are going to come into this world whether there's another soul around to welcome them or not." The old woman tried to smile, but the mood of the Redmond house was still upon her.

"Reckon," said Brandy, turning thoughtful. "But you know, Missum MacFee, sometimes Ah hear dey needs a little help."

The old woman dropped the handkerchief from her mouth and looked at Brandy, her eyes studying his even profile. Something in his tone made her think of Inez. "By the way, how's your garden coming on? I took notice of some ripe tomatoes in Isabelle's kitchen."

"Jus' fine, jus' fine," responded Brandy quickly. " 'Cept Ah do believe she gettin' too big to be workin' out dere."

Mrs. MacFee's face began to soften with understanding. "How's she feeling?"

"Reckon fine so far." Brandy's expression betrayed how anxious he was to continue the discussion.

The old woman patted him on the forearm. "Don't you start worrying yourself and get to stewing, Brandy. Inez is a healthy young girl. She shouldn't have any trouble."

Brandy looked directly at her, hoping it would bring more impact to his words. "You know, Missum MacFee, she's mighty, mighty slim. Dey's the kind that has trouble."

Mrs. MacFee considered his statement for a moment. "Perhaps, but she'll have help."

Brandy could not hold himself back another moment. "Who? Who's gwine to help her?"

Mrs. MacFee did not need to be told that *mestiza* and Negro women did not have doctors for childbirth. Midwives were their common resort, and while in most cases these served well enough, there was no *mestizo* or Negro community out here in which a midwife could be sought. She was not a particularly religious woman, but the many threats that hung over the frontier kept all of them mindful of their standing with God. She knew Isabelle was fond of Inez, as she was herself, and she had lived long enough to realize that however low her origins, Inez had innate courage and character. Underneath the shy withdrawals and childlike prettiness was a woman other women could like. Besides, she was a talented gardener. That argued well for her worth. The tomatoes in Isabelle's kitchen were superior to her own. She liked it when being a good Christian went along with her other inclinations.

"Brandy," she said, "of course I'll be there and help if I can, and I'm sure there'll be others. You stop worrying. My Lord, one would think there isn't enough misery around by the way you get to dreaming up more."

"Yes'm. Reckon you plum right," said Brandy, smiling for the first time as he snapped the reins and urged Bessie's mare into a trot.

For more than a week Seth had tried to lose himself in the excitement around San Antonio. The crisis had brought men from all directions, gathering in the squares near the San Fernando church and preparing for war. Hays knew that General Woll and his twelve hundred Mexican troops had crossed the Rio Grande and were advancing north. Refugio and Goliad had already been occupied, and San Antonio was now threatened. Many Texans wanted to attack him en route, others swore this time they would successfully defend the town. But Hays was under strict orders from President Houston— who had vetoed a vote by the Texas congress to declare war—to do nothing. Houston was not about to play Mexico's game. He sensed that the real battle was already being joined on the floor of the United States Congress, where opposition to the annexation of Texas rose from Northern abolitionists, who feared Texas coming in as a slave state. The Mexican government, equally fearful of having a young, powerful, anticlerical nation on its northern border, had decided that the northerners might be persuaded to annex a slave state but would never agree if it meant committing their nation to war.

But among Texans dissension was running high and tempers flared as groups of men approached Hays and demanded a fight. Seth had been kept busy leading patrols. At the same time, he brooded over his seemingly cursed life, turning aside often to wince or swear at his self-imposed estrangement from Isabelle. Why he had left that morning, he could not fit into words. He only knew he could not look upon the child Isabelle had borne some lecherous lice-ridden savage. Proof of her violation by this human offal was more than he could stomach.

Coming in from his last scout and having found the enemy still twenty-five miles to the south, he knew no battle was imminent. He knew he belonged at home. He decided to go back.

In town he noticed armed men still roaming the streets, but he was suddenly irritated when he saw old Adam Salinger and his son Prent leaving a raucous crowd of volunteers and heading directly toward him. He did not want to speak to the Salingers. Bessie was sure to have told them that he had left Isabelle to face her pain alone. Whatever her distress—and it would be the measure of his shame—he did not want to hear it from them.

Old Adam, brusque as usual, with pistols strapped to his waist and his shotgun resting on his good arm, came limping over, the strong side of his body dragging along the weak. "Seth!" he boomed. "Reckoned we'd find you here. Is Hays fixin' to fight?"

"Don't know."

"Damned disgrace lettin' these greasers come sashaying up here."

Seth sensed they were staring at him, seeing him in a different and probably demeaning light. He wanted to get away. "Reckon Hays has his orders."

"Orders be damned!" spat Adam. "We ought to be attacking 'em right now!"

Seth tried to nod, but Prent's steady staring triggered a quick stab of exasperation. "Maybe you ought to figure Hays knows his business and keep still till he asks for advice."

The rebuke hit Adam like a blow. Tugging at his bad arm, he squared his body around and confronted Seth like an aroused mastiff. "Look here, young fellow, seeing as you ain't in no hurry to fight, you ought to get to hell home where you belong, where any decent man would be! You don't deserve a good woman! For my part, you don't deserve any friends either!" Adam turned away and, painfully forcing his crippled body forward, started across the square. Prent was still watching Seth with a look of confusion that surely contained a flicker of contempt, but he said nothing, just turned quietly and followed his father.

It was Scout's barking that alerted and frightened Inez. She had wandered out to the garden in the lazy hum of an early September afternoon. There wasn't much to do. She couldn't bend or squat down any longer and so had brought only her rifle and a hoe. She had thought she could rid the garden of a few more weeds and bring some late-ripening tomatoes back for Isabelle. The growing season was over, but she enjoyed looking around and planning for next year. Then she heard Scout barking excitedly. It was not like Scout, who rarely barked. He was over beneath the trees along the creek where the undergrowth blocked her view. He might only have encountered a raccoon or bobcat, but Inez seized her rifle and began to move toward the house. She thought of calling to the dog, but Brandy had warned her that that would only tell possible skulkers where she was. Her pregnancy was too advanced for her to run, but she kept moving until she made the yard. There her confidence returned even though she could still hear Scout. She remembered that Brandy and Rick were in the north pasture bringing in colts to brand.

She decided on the house. Isabelle was probably still sitting or lying down despondently, waiting for Inez to help her with the children. Poor Isabelle. It was all she could do to manage Jason, the new baby and herself. She seemed to have no will to go on. Inez was glad Dr. Michalrath was coming tomorrow. He had said in his note that he would be back in a week, and he was keeping his word. She hoped all this talk of fighting in San Antonio would not keep him away.

In the house she found Isabelle slumped in her one big chair and Jason, who could now walk on his own, standing beside her. The baby was asleep on the bed.

Isabelle saw her coming in with the rifle and straightened up ever so slightly in her chair. "Is something wrong?" she asked in the low, weak voice she now seemed unable to change.

"The dog, señora. He is down by the creek barking. He makes much noise. There is trouble maybe."

Isabelle pulled herself from her chair and with one hand at her throat went to the window. "Where's Brandy?"

"He up in north pasture with Rick. I think they bring colts in to brand."

Isabelle shook her head and sighed. "I'd best get up there and warn them."

"No, señora, that would be dangerous."

Isabelle looked at her, and Inez could see she was already on the verge of tears. "Well, good Lord, what can we do?"

"We wait," said Inez. "They have guns, and Brandy is very smart. Always he watches."

Almost an hour later they heard a whine and Scout scratching at the door. He padded in with his head down and blood drying around a long knife cut that ran across his snout below his left eye. "Mercy!" said Isabelle. "No animal did that."

Inez, bolting the door, worked as fast as she could to load another rifle and place a box of ammunition on the floor beneath the window. Isabelle swept the baby to the room beyond the kitchen and with energy produced by fear settled Jason in a protected corner surrounded by his few toys.

Moving about the house and watching in all directions, they waited another tense hour until they heard a familiar shouting and opened the door to watch Brandy and Rick herding a large crowd of gamboling colts into the stable. Inez went hurriedly to meet them.

Brandy, hearing Inez' anxious words, looked about in alarm. He could see she was not hurt, but the danger he was sure she had narrowly escaped left him trembling inwardly. He knew they couldn't wait until dark to find out who had come along the creek bed and tried to kill Scout. He decided he would have to go down there alone, but Rick wouldn't hear of it. "Brandy, stop treating me like a young'un. By God, I'm a man. I can shoot and ride better than any galoot in Texas."

Brandy finally nodded with reluctance, but secretly he was relieved. It was a job that called for at least two. Why wasn't Seth there?

They left at once while they still had enough light to see, but an hour's search produced only the unshod hoofprints of two Indian ponies. The tracks had reached a point along the creek bed where they could easily have seen Inez in her garden.

With darkness closing in, they turned and rode back, grimly aware that these two trespassers were most likely wolves scouting for a Comanche war party.

With the late summer hunts over, Blood Hawk had watched war party after war party leaving camp, going out for trophies and, above all, honor. They would not take him. In furious desperation he had frequently ranted outside the council lodge, saying he was a great war chief with strong medicine, only to find warriors turning their faces away and women keeping their eyes to the ground. Had he not been insane, he would have been killed, for he said things that infuriated many. Black Wolf and other headmen had smoked on this nuisance, but madness was the work of spirits too dangerous to offend.

Then inevitably Blood Hawk's dementia attracted the predatory attention of Red Knife, a near outcast himself, who saw the bear-claw necklace and decided, as he had so often with the property of others, that it should be his. By Comanche custom Red Knife had long since lost respect among his tribesmen for taking another man's squaw and not making restitution. He had also injured several neighbors in a drunken brawl and killed a captured female, who was not his prisoner, because she kept screaming with pain as he raped her. Had he made restitution for these malicious acts, Red Knife could have recovered his honorable standing in the tribe, for he was a relative of Black Wolf's, but he was a big, powerful, surly and above all treacherous man, an ill-tempered bull who chortled at violence and was viciously resentful of any check on his behavior.

He knew Blood Hawk was mad, but starting with the bear-claw necklace, a number of things had been coming together in his mind. He had heard that a war party led by Blood Hawk's father had been wiped out on the Texas frontier and that some of its warriors had been tracked to a small ranch with magnificent horses and only a few whites to kill or carry off. Somehow that story rang true. Despised as he was, no war party would accept him, so with little effort he found himself in the slowly emptying camp sharing some scorched buffalo meat with the Crazy One. It was almost too simple to get the now frenzied Blood Hawk to go on the warpath with him, and even easier to make the madman's eyes shine when he said he would join in making strong medicine to plunder and destroy the *tejano* ranch. It would be a great coup, and much honor would be theirs when they returned.

A few evenings later they slipped into the hills and built a little fire. Blood Hawk beat a small skin drum and chanted words that had meaning only for his deranged mind. Red Knife danced about and threw some wild herbs and roots onto the fire. A pungent odor arose, and Blood Hawk began grinning to himself, dreaming of his return with *tejano* blood on his hands, his father avenged and many fine horses to show. Red Knife pounded the earth with his feet, craved some white man's whisky and quietly decided on the many falsehoods to be told when he returned to their village alone.

The pony tracks by the creek frightened Isabelle more than ever. Brandy wanted to ride to the MacFees and warn them, particularly the old woman he liked so much, but that would have left only Rick at the ranch, and Rick wanted to rush home as he knew his father was in San Antonio and Bessie was now alone with Kate.

Brandy soon exhausted their few possibilities of help. Both MacFee boys had followed Todd Bonham to serve Hays. Isaac Sawyer had his own women to protect, and while his father would likely have sent him quickly enough, Andy Sawyer was too addleheaded to be of much help. Finally they had to reckon that Brandy going for help meant leaving the women alone, for Rick had ridden off, his young face looking pained under an unfamiliar frown of worry.

It was clear that Brandy and Inez would have to spend the night in the house, while Scout, his wound patched up with some pine salve Isabelle had brought from North Carolina, was let outside again to give what warning he could.

No one had any appetite, but Inez nervously sliced some onions and tomatoes and set the one loaf of bread baked that morning on the table.

Isabelle, too exhausted to sustain her first fear, fed the children and put them to sleep. The baby drowsed off at her breast, and she studied it as she had begun to do more and more lately. Its skin had lightened some in the past two weeks, but it was still darker than Jason's, and its face, though becoming clearer and fuller, was still small and thin and its eyes almost black. Oddly, she could not bring herself to give it a name as though this in some way denied its existence. It was Jason, who came up to look at the baby several times a day, who pointed to it one evening, blubbering "Ta-ta."

"Tata," said Isabelle without thinking. But after that, whenever she had to take Jason from his play to feed the baby, she found herself saying "Let's go see Tata." She was too downcast to give the matter much thought, so the name stuck while she told herself she would find a proper name for it before its christening. In truth she was almost beyond caring. For two weeks there had been no respite for her. Seeing Inez asleep in the big chair and Brandy sprawled on the floor near the door, she lay down on the bed next to the baby and closed her eyes. She still could not face thinking about Seth's leaving. Every attempt brought her back to the maelstrom of dread that she was now alone, fighting to keep a breath of life in her body. Her sleep was often a macabre dreaming from which she awoke with a pall of emptiness that sapped the feeble strength from her limbs. Unknowingly Jason kept her with the living. His little arms clasped her neck tightly, and his big blue eyes stared into hers. She had to stay alive for him, she had to take him back to North Carolina, away from this land of conflict and horror. From the depths of her soul she now hated this wilderness, hated its hardness, hated its loneliness and above all hated its fear. Somewhere deep in her mind another hatred was forming, but she could not face it now. Her mirror told her she had aged dreadfully in recent months, but she could not bring herself to care. Without a man's loving eyes on her, she no longer felt pretty. The skin on her hands and about her mouth seemed hardened. Dispirited at each day's end, she could not summon the will to brush and dress her hair. She stared with apathy, now that her stomach was flat again, at the two scars on her pelvis. They were covered with scar tissue, like two red welts that reached up beyond her pubic hair and felt rough to the touch. It was well she did not have a man to make love to her. Would a man's passion survive the feel of those scars?

She must have dozed off, for she was suddenly aware of a rhythmic pounding and opened her eyes. Inez and Brandy were already awake, looking at each other in suspense, as Brandy said, "Dey's a horse comin' up duh trail."

"I don't hear that dog," said Inez in a high whisper.

"You ain't gonna," said Brandy, staring through a crack in the door. "Scout don't bark at old Sam. It's Seth. Lordy, lordy, Seth done come back."

It was almost midnight when Seth came into the house. He knew at once from the presence of Brandy and Inez and the tension in their faces that there was trouble. When he heard it was Indians, he immediately extinguished the one lamp burning low on the mantel. He smothered his irritation. They seemed unaware that even a faint light made them easy targets from the darkness outside, but he was embarrassed into silence by the awkward deference they were showing him and the knowledge that Isabelle was staring mutely in his direction. He had not really looked at her, and now, with the lamp out, he was thankful they could not see one another. Talk in that dark room was curiously hushed, strained and sporadic, but they managed to decide that Brandy and Inez should return to the hut, both heavily armed. Seth stopped them at the door to warn them dawn was the critical time and to be alert. He could vaguely detect their heads nodding in the darkness as they slipped out.

Isabelle and Seth sat in silence, invisible to each other in the darkness. They could not even hear each other's breathing. No words passed between them for the longest time, neither knowing how to begin. Finally Isabelle, grateful the darkness concealed her, said with a choking voice, "So, you're back." She could not see him, but knew he had turned his head toward her.

"Yes, I'm back. Do you want me . . . do you want me back?"

Another long silence ensued as Isabelle put her hand over her mouth, forcing back her muffled sobs as tears rolled down her cheeks and brought a taste of salt to her lips. Seth felt the seconds slip by, each one telling him the depth of her hurt and weighing into his own measure of guilt. It was a quarter of an hour before Isabelle could speak again, and her words barely reached him across the dark room. "Why did you go?"

She could hear him drawing in his breath. "I don't know," he said hopelessly.

Isabelle stared into the darkness. In some distant part of her she knew why he had gone. She knew because something in herself had left too, something that kept her from mothering the child. Her flesh had been joined with the flesh of some painted savage and a baby was here, a half brother to Jason to keep the terror of that violent defilement alive in their lives. She felt the faintest tinge of sorrow for him and then for herself. This pitiless fate had stricken them both.

She looked up and realized he was standing over her, his hands extended toward her. After a few moments' hesitation, her hands moved up slowly and joined his. Feeling her grasping him, he pulled her up and kissed her, at first tentatively but then with a growing need for her warmth that brought their loins together. A ringing began in her head, for she knew now that he wanted her. She pulled away from him only to move the baby to the big chair. Then she came back to the bed, stripping off her clothes with trembling hands and throwing them to the floor with abandon.

13

Dr. Michalrath looked at his young son Jed and decided he had made the right decision. Since dawn they had been traveling in their rig to the Redmond ranch, now only a few miles away. For some time he had been thinking he belonged in San Antonio, where if fighting broke out he would be needed, but in San Antonio Jed would surely be caught in any struggle for the town. He had already lost one son, Bret, in the Rebellion, and had heard his wife, Carrie, sobbing her lost son's name with her dying breath. As a doctor, he knew his sister Phoebe had but a few months to live. If anything happened to Jed, he'd be facing life alone, an old man with his memories waiting for death.

Yet the problem of Isabelle's newborn had burdened his mind that week. He had heard stories of frontier women being raped by savages and giving birth to half-breeds. Many gave these infants to poor Mexican or pacified Indian families to raise. But there were always problems, and emotional ones were by far the worst. Husbands had been known to allow such children to die of exposure or neglect. Others, faced with wives unwilling to abandon their infants, had left. Rumors of Seth being in San Antonio had reached him, and two days ago crusty old Adam Salinger had called by on his way there, asking if there was something to quell the pain in his wounds. Aware of his daughter's friendship with Isabelle, Doc Michalrath had inquired about matters at the Redmond ranch. Old Adam had just shaken his head and grumbled. The garrulous gray-bearded gunfighter could think of nothing fitting to say.

While the doctor mused quietly, Jed steered the rig up to the ranch house and Brandy came toward them, lifting an arm in welcome. Dr. Michalrath pulled a heavy gold watch from his vest pocket and noted that it was getting near noon.

That morning Isabelle had slipped from bed before dawn and whisked the whimpering baby into the kitchen to feed him. Holding the infant to her breast, she silently opened the kitchen door and stepped out naked into the soft night air. She was so exhilarated she had forgotten the threat of Indians as she watched a pale lanternlike moon on the western horizon and felt the cool night breeze probing her body but making it feel good. Their hours of passion that night had left the skin of her stomach and thighs still tingling, and a deep comfort rose in her breast as she realized Seth had exhausted himself in taking her time after time, and had finally fallen into a soundless sleep. Then, suddenly remembering the threat their ranch was under, she slipped back inside, finished feeding the baby and settled him in Jason's room at the foot of the bed. She tiptoed to a pail of well water, filled a basin and, finding her homemade soap, began to wash. It was only when she felt her scars again that she realized Seth, in his excited handling of her, had said nothing about them.

By the time she finished bathing, dawn was beginning to break and a little light was seeping through the windows. Still nude, she slipped back to the bedside, quietly gathering their clothes from the floor and carrying her mirror and brush into the kitchen. There she groomed and dressed her hair, tying her long golden locks behind her with a big blue ribbon, the way she had worn it when very young and first aware of Seth's love. Quickly she went through her dresses and decided on a blue-and-white gingham she and Bessie had cut from material Seth had brought from San Antonio. As she completed her preparations for awakening Seth, she heard Brandy tapping at the kitchen door. It was quite light out now, and as she partially opened the door she could see his look of surprise at her appearance. "Ah see'd someone in duh kitchen from 'cross duh yard," he said apologetically. "Jest wanted to tell you everythin' 'pears to be quiet. Tell Seth Ah'm only figurin' to use dat closest corral."

Brandy bowed and backed away. Isabelle could not see him smiling to himself as he surmised that her being prettied up at such an hour meant Seth had decided to stay.

◆ ◆ ◆

Several miles to the northwest Blood Hawk and Red Knife sat across from each other at a small fire, feasting on a deer killed the day before. They had been to the *tejanos'* ranch twice, yesterday afternoon seeing a Mexican girl alone in the field when Red Knife had slashed a large dog that had attacked them in the brush, and during the night, when they had crept forward on a small knoll Blood Hawk had used when stalking this very ranch the previous year. In the darkness they had watched a horseman arrive, and saw a faint light they had been crawling toward go out.

Red Knife knew they had left pony tracks along the creek bed, and the sign of others crossing theirs meant they had been discovered. They could not delay here for long, but he had seen the handsome horses and he intended to leave with his share. By now his acquisitiveness went beyond horses. It included the Mexican girl, or at least her scalp. Watching her move slowly, awkwardly, heavy with child, aroused the feral predator in him. She would be easy prey. He had concocted a plan to use Blood Hawk to lure the men from the ranch. Blood Hawk, with his wild eyes and sudden outbursts, had become a serious nuisance and was no longer needed. If the *tejanos* did not kill this crazy one, he would have to dispose of him before he fled north.

After eating, they painted their faces with streaks of vermilion and chanted to their medicine spirits. Red Knife lighted a small pipe and passed it to Blood Hawk, then waited for its return before laying out his plan. Today they would slip up again and watch the ranch. But before sundown Blood Hawk would ride close to the house and fire a shot that should bring its two males out in pursuit. He would lead them to a little gully already scouted, and there Red Knife would ambush them.

"The scalps of the *tejanos* will be ours!" roared Blood Hawk, spittle spraying from his mouth. "Then we will torture and kill their women and burn their houses. It will be as child's play."

Red Knife did not think it would be child's play to deal with their men, for in fact he wasn't planning to be in that gully. These *tejanos* riding their sleek horses should have little trouble running the Crazy One down. By the time they returned, he should have what he wanted and be far away.

When Seth awoke that morning he felt an unaccountable peace, making him reluctant to open his eyes. He lay there reliving the heated excitement of Isabelle's abandoned lovemaking as she had drawn him ever closer with her arms and legs as their bodies joined time after time. The tension in the deep recesses in his body seemed to have vanished. His recent angry, brooding and restless moods made this serenity seem almost alien to his mind. When he looked up she was standing a few paces away, looking very pretty and making his senses reel back to the day when he had first been startled by her beauty and felt the magnetism of her willowy body.

Without speaking, she came to him and he pulled her down, kissing and holding her close again. Isabelle could hardly breathe for happiness, but she knew if his hands moved under her skirts they would be making love again, even though Jason was already awake and out of bed and Brandy and Inez were about. But in a corner of her mind lay a veiled anxiety and uncertainty. There was still the baby Seth had never seen.

A few minutes later she had Seth sitting at the table with coffee and warm bread covered with preserves. She had called Jason in to join them, but the little boy had stared shyly at Seth and kept turning to her. Seth, realizing how much he had been away, started to play with him. It was an awkward beginning, but finally Jason giggled and laughed and Seth settled back to beam at his handsome little son.

Brandy, calling from the front step, brought him back to the harsh realities bordering his life, making him uncomfortable that he was still indoors with the sun up as he went to greet him. He noticed that Brandy had a rifle on his shoulder.

"Mornin', Seth. 'Bout dem colts, you fixin' to brand 'em? Ah bin feedin', but dat stable is mighty crowded." Brandy, seeing that Seth was not fully dressed, looked away, adding quickly, "Mebbe we best wait."

The rifle had brought their Indian scare to Seth's mind. "Any sign of trouble?"

"No. Mighty quiet."

Seth studied the knoll behind Brandy for a moment. Quiet didn't mean much in this country. Those on the frontier had learned to be wary of even silence. "I'll be along directly," he said to Brandy. "Feed the stock as best you can. Make sure there's water in the back trough."

Seth closed the door and shook his head as he moved to the kitchen to wash. Underneath it all, Brandy was an unusual man. He never needed half the instructions he had to listen to, yet he never seemed resentful. Inez had gotten a lot of quality in her mate. Seeing him through the kitchen window heading for the stable, rifle in hand, Seth wondered what Brandy really thought of him. At once he knew that it was the first time such a concern had ever entered his mind.

It was while he was washing that he heard the baby cry. Isabelle whisked behind him and slipped into Jason's room. Within seconds the baby ceased crying, and Seth could hear her murmuring to him as she soothed him into silence. He did not move toward them. Isabelle allowed the door to close behind her and did not reappear.

Seth dried himself, pulled on a clean shirt and tucked it inside his belt. He had watched Jason walking unsteadily from the table to his little room, repeating in a babyish babble, "Ta-ta, Ta-ta, Ta-ta." Suddenly in a hurry, he buckled on his gun belt, grabbed his rifle and went out, quietly closing the door. Halfway to the stable he stopped, winced and pounded the stock of the rifle against the ground. Goddamn it, he was still running away. But he couldn't help it. He never wanted to lay eyes on that child. His mind rose in rebellion at the thought of living with a constant reminder that Isabelle's body had been possessed by another, her feminine parts used, her inner organs receiving and nurturing some heathen degenerate's seed.

Tears of fury filled his eyes as he entered the stable, grateful to find Brandy's back to him as he brushed them away.

It was an eerie morning. Seth and Brandy took the colts out to the near corral, roping and branding them and turning them loose. They raced about, then ended up nuzzling one another nervously over the trough. Brandy kept looking about. The work at the ranch had to go on, but he smelled trouble and was annoyed that Seth seemed too aggrieved in mind to be aware of any danger.

Having seen Isabelle that dawning, he was bewildered by Seth's mood. It was only when the morning was almost spent that they heard Scout barking and came out through the stable to see the big black-and-yellow dog, his back stiff, pointing his still-bandaged muzzle toward the knoll and emitting low, full-throated barks that could mean only one thing. "Whoever slashed dat dog is up on duh hill, sure as gospel," said Brandy, checking the breech on his rifle.

Scanning the knoll, Seth asked slowly, "Why isn't Scout up there attacking right now?"

"Dat's a smart dog," responded Brandy tersely. "He done tried dat once." He turned his worried face toward the hut. "What we gonna do?"

Seth had seen a lot more warring Indians than Brandy had. He had been fighting them for years. He had killed his share. He did not have the rank fear their fierce reputation and bloody record could instill in newcomers. He stood studying the knoll and surrounding hills for a full minute before he said, "Brandy, this doesn't set up like an honest-to-God war party. More than likely a couple of bucks trying to steal horses or pick up a careless scalp. Real war parties don't leave tracks where a buddy can find them."

"Mebbe so, Seth, but Ah's got a mess of worry pesterin' me."

Seth almost smiled, but he patted Brandy on the shoulder while he checked his guns, saying, "Well, I'm going to mosey up that knoll. Tell the women where I've gone, but keep a sharp lookout till I get back. Sometimes Injuns scare easily."

Brandy was ready to protest. If they stayed together, they could fight together. But his eye caught something that he was sure would keep Seth close by. In the distance he could see Dr. Michalrath and his son coming up the trail, their rig leaving a trail of dust that was slow to settle in the noon heat.

Isabelle watched Seth greeting the doctor and young Jed as old Michalrath, smiling in return, gestured at once toward the house. She had wanted Seth to come back that morning and had grown increasingly troubled when he hadn't. Smothering her anxiety, she had busied herself in the kitchen, for Inez was now too heavy to help. She had run to the window only at Scout's barking.

As the men came in, the doctor was drawling pleasantly, "Howdy, Isabelle, how's my favorite patient today?" Isabelle sensed he was affecting a lightness he didn't feel.

"Believe I'm doing fine, Doctor," she answered, her gaze slipping away to Seth.

Michalrath noticed that Isabelle was fetchingly dressed for a busy rancher's wife that time of day. She surely looked better than when he last had seen her, but her eyes strained with uncertainty as they turned away from his to seek Seth's. The doctor felt the tension in the air and decided it would be easier for him than for either of them to broach the subject. "Well, now, about that baby. How is it?"

"All right, I hope," said Isabelle almost timidly. "Shall I bring him in?"

"Please." The doctor cleared his throat as he noticed Seth stepping back toward the door. This was what he had feared. These two young people were being thrown into a crucible that could warp their minds and destroy their love.

Isabelle brought the baby in and laid him between the two pillows on the bed. Seth, his eyes down, remained with his back against the door. The doctor bent over the baby and began a quick examination. He could see that the baby's color had lightened and his features were surely clearer, but the mark of Mongolian blood, his Comanche heritage, still lay about his eyes. The child would grow up with an Asian cast to his European features. But it seemed healthy enough, which meant he had been given adequate care. Isabelle had been nursing the baby, and Michalrath concluded that some bonding, however slight, must have begun.

"What's his name?" he asked casually as he straightened up. It was another point from which he hoped to learn. Unnamed babies were unloved babies.

Isabelle had almost answered "Ta-ta," which would have exposed her emotional quandary, the paralysis of her earlier despair, but with her mouth already formed to say "Ta" she found herself saying "Tate."

"Tate, eh. Taylor," responded Michalrath. It was a common enough name in the West, for Zachary Taylor was already a legendary Indian fighter.

At the name Seth drew in a sharp breath. It was enough to alert Michalrath to the task before him.

He stepped over to the big chair and sat down to study the others, his face becoming hard and his voice resolute. "If you plan to keep the child," he said bluntly, "it's got to be as one of your own. If you figure that's more than you can manage, then the child has got to go and be raised up somewhere else."

Seth stared at him in silence, unable to express the fury of rejection mounting in his mind.

Isabelle folded her hands tightly over her breasts and said in a fading voice, "Where would he go?"

"Oh, there's Mexican families that will take him for the gift of a horse, any kind of horse. My own feeling is there are peaceful Cherokees over to east Texas. He wouldn't have to worry about his Indian blood there. Injuns are always glad to get young ones."

Isabelle held a hand over her mouth as she spoke. "How will we know what's . . . what's happening to him?"

"You won't," said the doctor firmly. "You'll never see him again. It's the only way."

Seth was becoming restless and had pulled away from the door. "You seem mighty worried about that kid, Doctor."

"No!" Michalrath snapped. "I'm worried about you. You can't keep this child less'n you make it one of your own. If you don't, believe me, this child will destroy both of you."

There was a long moment of silence.

"Do we have to decide now?" said Isabelle, her fist clenched against her mouth.

"Damn it! We've already decided!" yelled Seth. "Take it the hell out of here! Take it wherever you want! Don't ever tell us where!"

Michalrath looked at Seth steadily for a moment, then turned away and said gently, "Isabelle?"

"Doctor, can we have a day or two?" she half sobbed. "I'm . . . I'm so confused."

"Goddamn it, a few days isn't going to change anything," said Seth, his voice now strident, piercing, unyielding. "The sooner it happens the better."

The doctor sat for several moments in silence, then moved to Isabelle and put his hand on her shoulders. "If I don't take the baby with me now, you'll have to bring him to me. It's your decision, Isabelle, but every day that passes will only make it harder."

Jed rushed excitedly through the door and cut off the conversation. The young man was flushed and clearly frightened. "Dad," he almost shouted. "There's Injuns 'round here. Been close by for a day or two. We got to borrow a rifle!"

The doctor and his son both carried handguns, though neither had used them very much and were not particularly good shots. The doctor had long since developed a fatalism about Indians. There was no predicting them and hence no point in worrying about them. But concern for Jed immediately registered on his face. "Indians?" he said looking at Seth almost accusingly. "I've heard no talk of Indians!"

Seth's curt answer held more irritation than concern. "We've turned up some tracks, that's all. Doesn't smell like a raid. Likely a buck or two out to steal horses."

Standing by his father, Jed looked pale and uncertain. "What about that dog?"

Seth's head tossed with impatience. "Scout got slashed rushing at some prowler. Any real war party would have killed him."

"Just the same," said the doctor, putting his steadying hand on Jed's arm, "I think we better get to warning folks."

The conversation turned to ways the warning could be spread. The doctor and Jed were going to visit the MacFees on their way home. Old Mrs. MacFee had sent word she was having trouble with her back. With their boys gone, her husband, still spry at sixty, would have to ride to the Salingers', where Rick, if he hadn't already, could alert the Sawyers and Bonhams. In such a way word would spread throughout the region. Often such warnings came too late, but there were times they had saved lives.

Knowing they were anxious to leave, Isabelle hurriedly fed the doctor and Jed, trying at the same time to gather her thoughts. Seth hardly spoke during the meal. The few words voiced were about the Indian threat, but, while Jed babbled nervously between bites, the three older minds were still hard on the baby.

Before he left, the doctor paused on the doorstep and turned to Isabelle. "Isabelle, at my age you've learned no matter how terrible things get life has to go on. Only one or two decisions really matter in life, but everything depends upon them. Whatever you do, you and Seth must do together."

Seth came up, thrusting a rifle at him. "I put some cartridges in the rig," he said, his eyes shifting to Isabelle. "Can't we get this business settled now?"

"Give it a day or two," grunted the doctor, stepping down toward the rig. "Remember, the things we do to flesh and blood ain't the kind that can be undone."

Red Knife watched the two men leaving in their rig and grunted with satisfaction. The fewer *tejanos* to be decoyed away from the ranch, the better. From his aerie far back on the knoll he had been studying the ranch buildings and the adjacent corrals. He was planning when the opportunity came to steal into the stable. He was certain the *tejanos* kept their most valuable horses there. He knew now the Mexican girl was in the hut, and a yellow-haired woman kept appearing before the house. By nightfall their thick, smooth scalps would hang from his belt. *Tejano* women were not Comanche squaws. They were helpless in a fight without their men. But much depended upon the Crazy One—perhaps too much. Red Knife thought about Blood Hawk and scowled. He had tried to borrow his bear-claw necklace, but Blood Hawk had ranted that it was his strongest medicine and no bullet could kill him while he wore it. A faint smile flickered across Red Knife's lips. He knew something about bullets. That necklace would be his yet. He looked up at the sun. In a few hours Blood Hawk would ride up to the range and fire his shot. He laid aside the gun he had plundered from a Mexican family he had murdered the year before and took out his knife. Finding a smooth cutting stone, he began sharpening it. The blade sang against the dark stone. He liked the sound of it. He liked the feel of his knife. Many times it had dripped with his enemy's blood. Soon, he mused, he would have it dripping again.

Isabelle and Seth had spent a tortured afternoon. Seth would not stay while she fed the baby, but he returned more furious than ever.

"Isabelle, I want that thing out of my house!"

"Seth, please." Isabelle held her hands over her face as she half moaned. "It's just that he seems so helpless."

"It won't be helpless for long. You're going to kill everything we've ever had together. Can't you see just watching you near it is driving me insane? I want it out of my home and out of my life. Isabelle, listen to me before it's too late—get it out of my sight!"

Isabelle looked at him. He hadn't said it. He didn't need to. His expression could be read no other way. He was lost to her if she kept the baby. Suddenly she realized her fearful blunder. She had made him measure his love for her against her refusal to surrender this strange-looking child, measure his love against this senseless outrage to his pride, measure it and find it wanting. Her heart began thumping, and her head started reeling and growing light. She came forward to fall into his arms. "All right," she gasped. "All right, the baby goes. He will go."

They were too drained for words. He held her firmly, burying his face in her hair and kissing it. They embraced tightly until her deep trembling stopped. As their breaths quieted again and silence swept in, the tiny wail of an infant could be heard through the thin pine planking of the wall.

Brandy looked at Inez, his faint smile turning dubious. "You sure you've got to have it?"

"*Sí.* For Inez' stomach is veree good."

Early in her pregnancy Inez had been persistently bothered by a queasy stomach that made her remember the pregnant women of her village who treated this routine discomfort with small swallows of wine. Inevitably the long ruby bottles Carlos had left crept into her mind, and though Brandy stood adamant at first she finally wore him down with her promise that only a sip was needed. Discovering this was true, and remarking on its good effect on her, he finally devised an arrangement that seemed both secret and safe. He refused to allow any wine in their hut, where it might be seen, but he discovered a space in the darkest stall of the stable where the bottle could be hidden. There Inez could make her way on days when she felt the need. Holding herself to her promise of only a sip, she had given the first bottle an exceedingly long life. Today she felt that her body was particularly heavy and fatigued. By her reckoning she had only a short month to go, but the stress brought on by talk of Indians, and Isabelle's harried looks at noon, had led to thoughts of a soothing mouthful of wine. By late afternoon her desire had grown to where for the first time she asked Brandy to take her tiny wooden cup and bring her back a few sips from the stable. Brandy shook his head at first, but as he watched her clumsily trying to settle herself on their low bed it was not in his heart to deny her. Taking his rifle, he looked to see if the yard was empty. Then he sauntered down to the stable, doing his best to appear unhurried.

Isabelle had wrapped the baby carefully. Though it was very late in the day, Seth was hoping the doctor was still at the MacFees' or at least not too far east to be caught by the speedy Sam in an hour or two. In his mind he did not care if he was on the trail all night. The festering in his brain had now stopped.

No one on the ranch chose to name it, but it afflicted all, like dampness in the air. Brandy would have accepted it openly as fear, for Scout had been acting strangely for hours, and Isabelle, too troubled to be frightened, still obeyed some instinct and kept Jason indoors. It was a tension that mounted with the fear of being watched, and everyone but Seth glanced at the heavy foliage along the creek or on the knoll and felt that had they looked an instant sooner, they would have caught some figure ducking from view.

Seth watched Brandy walking to the stable and decided to take a quick scout around the range before he left. The sun was already low on the horizon, but there would be light for an hour or two after it set.

Though Brandy had disappeared into the stable, Seth called out to him, his strong, resonant voice starting a distant echo. After a few moments Brandy appeared in the wide stable doors, looking his way. "Bring up the horses!" shouted Seth. "We're going to make a scout."

Brandy had been in the dark stall pouring a splash of wine into Inez' cup. He had placed his rifle in the near corner and left it there as he moved hurriedly at Seth's call. Sneaking those few drops of wine had made him nervous. "Bring up the horses" meant Sam and the big roan. Brandy quickly slipped halters and saddles on them and, leading one with each hand, walked them up to the house. It was Seth coming toward him fully armed that reminded him he had forgotten his rifle. He had just turned to glance back at the stable when a distant shot rang out and a spent slug struck the ground at Seth's feet. The suddenness of it made the horses rear up and shy away as Scout, with a long, menacing growl, leaped forward and sped at full tilt toward a tree-studded slope behind the house.

Seth recovered first and shouted to Isabelle, who had come to the door, to stay inside. Inez, hearing the shot, had struggled outside, holding her rifle awkwardly and looking in puzzlement after Scout, who had already leapt a large clump of brush and was disappearing into a straggling grove of beech.

"Let's go," said Seth, swinging a leg up on Sam. Brandy mounted the roan and spun around, riding over and lifting the rifle from the hands of the still-startled Inez. "Git inside duh house—we come back quick as we can," he shouted as the two horses thundered out of the yard, led on by the fading barks of the now-invisible Scout.

Inez stood for a moment watching them go, wiping an errant trickle of sweat from her face. She needed that wine more than ever now. She looked at the stable. It seemed very close. After all, they were coming right back. Laboriously she made her way through the wide-open doors and then on to the dark stall, where she found some wine already in her cup and stood sipping it, satisfying her long hungering for it. She almost wanted to settle down and rest a bit in the cool dark interior of the stall, but at that moment Red Knife, moving stealthily along the corral fence and keeping the grazing stock between him and the house, reached up and released the single iron latch inside the stable's rear half door.

14

With their strained faces tucked in against the wind they spurred their horses beyond the first low-lying ridge before Seth pulled up shouting, "Hold on, this doesn't make sense." As the winded horses circled each other, their sides heaving, he looked quizzically toward the near dip where Scout's barking had died out. "If they didn't come to fight, why did they shoot? If they're here to fight, why are they running?"

Brandy stared at the dip apprehensively. "I dunno, but dey's only one track here we bin chasin'."

Seth glanced in the direction of the ranch. "Damn it, that's it! We're being pulled away from the house on purpose. Whatever they're after, they're after it now!" He pulled Sam's head up and turned for home. "C'mon!"

Terrified, Inez knew she had heard the unmistakable scrape of the iron latch on the stable door. No animal could have caused that. Someone had entered the stable through its corral port. An icy sensation opened at the back of her neck and flowed down her spine. She realized death could be standing only a few stalls away. Brandy had taken her rifle. Her only hope was to hide. She lowered herself slowly and backed into the nearest straw-filled corner. In the stable's rear she heard movement, a furtive stepping on loose straw coming her way. Desperately she wanted to call out but didn't dare. She wanted to run or crawl away but, hunched against the wooden slats with her swollen stomach, she was helpless as a turtle on its back. She heard the rustling sound again, this time closer. Whoever it was was looking into the next stall. If she had to die, she wanted it to be quick, easy. Then something happened. The baby in her belly began to kick. Some primitive maternal instinct seized her, and suddenly she refused to die here helpless on her back. She would rise and scream, she would summon help, she would scare off this intruder. Even as her frantic mind struggled against this hysteria, she reached out to brace and pull herself up. At that moment she touched it. So intent was she on rising she merely held it for support, but before she could move, its familiar grasp flashed across her brain. It was a rifle, the one Brandy had left when answering Seth's call. She yanked it toward her and it swung down alongside her leg, its barrel burying itself in the straw. With her trembling hand she found the hammer and tripped it back just as Red Knife's crimson-streaked face appeared above the low siding of her stall. He peered at her, his eyes finding her face in the faint light. "Hah!" he grunted, pointing to her with an ugly bone knife. Leering down at her, his face slowly contorted into a grin, making it even more hideous under the bright war paint. He was not hurrying. She heard him quietly chortling to himself as he came into the stall, kneeling down to press the tip of the knife into the bare skin above her ankle. At its touch Inez brought the rifle up, its muzzle lifting from the straw and catching him under the chin. She pulled the trigger before he had a chance to react. In horror she watched his face explode in the roar and the crown of his head disappear.

In the silence that followed the thunderous blast she tried to scream, but could only sob. Dreamlike, she sensed a great gushing of fluid between her legs and the next sob died on her lips, for she realized, even as she sat there dazed, that she was going into labor. Her beautiful baby was coming.

They were less than a quarter of a mile from the ranch when they heard the shot. Brandy was sure it had come from the stable, and his heart skipped a beat. He had told Inez to go into the house, but he knew she wanted that wine. He had also taken her gun. The sight of Isabelle coming out and pointing excitedly to the stable brought his fear to near panic.

Seth was waving Isabelle back into the house as he followed Brandy into the stable. They heard the restless stirring of animals disturbed by the shot, but Brandy ran at once to the dark stall where, gulping at Red Knife's almost headless body, he dropped down to hold Inez in his arms and hear her say over and over again as tears made their way down her face, "Our baby, it comes, it comes!"

Seth helped Brandy carry her into the hut, and Isabelle hurried over from the doorstep. Once in bed, Isabelle wept in relief but still found it impossible to say what had happened.

Brandy was not concerned with what had happened. Inez was alive and about to give birth. He had to fetch Mrs. MacFee. Seth and Isabelle looked at him queerly as he told them he had to leave but would be back as quickly as the Lord allowed. Seth, seeing Isabelle starting to remove Inez' wet skirts, left the hut to stand for long moments watching Brandy disappear at full gallop as he drove the roan down the trail toward the MacFees'. Something told him there were only two Indians in this weird attack. With one now dead the other was probably long gone. Returning, Scout, tired by his long run, had settled down by the stable to sleep.

Old Sara MacFee looked at the liniment Michalrath had left for her sore back and decided she wouldn't use it until bedtime. Her boys, Scott and Tyler, were in San Antonio and her husband, Angus, had left that morning with a wagonload of hides, saying that war or no war, he needed money and Mexican pesos were worth a lot more than the Texas "redbacks" that were backed only by their bankrupt government. Her daughter, Carrie, was on the small porch, silent and brooding as ever, a strange girl lost in a dream world from which she ventured only at startling moments to laugh or cry without apparent reason. At first Dr. Michalrath had taken an interest in her, for his lost wife had been named Carrie, but of late Sara had noticed that his glances at the girl carried a hint of resignation close to regret. Old Sara was achingly lonely. Her grown sons and husband were cut from the same coarse cloth, rough and restive men who drank their share of whisky and grimly rode down the wild cattle from which they stripped the hides and sold them. Hardened by the rigors of their life and preferring their own company, they joined her mainly at mealtimes. After she had demanded that they stop their crude and often cruel teasing of Carrie, they had rarely bothered to make conversation.

Now the doctor had come with word of Indians threatening the Redmond ranch. He had wanted her and Carrie to come with him and Jed to the Salingers', but Sara had refused. She would not leave her home, her cow, her chickens. They were her life, all she could reproduce from her memories of a happy childhood on her father's tiny farm in distant Virginia. Michalrath had finally left, warning her to stop stooping over and working in her garden. She was too old to be shoveling and hoeing the hard Texas earth. She had thanked him, giving him a dozen eggs and sending her warmest wishes for good health to Phoebe. The doctor had sat in the rig and tried to smile at the lonely mother and mentally disturbed daughter as Jed clucked to the mare and drove away.

By sundown the old woman was standing behind the house watching some birds flying so high they looked motionless and part of a deep lavender that followed the fading light. She wondered where they were going and from where they had come. Somehow their boundless freedom skirting the edge of night touched a need in her heart that could not be worked into words.

The sound of Brandy racing up to the house was suddenly joined by squawking chickens scattering before his horse in the front yard and the clap of the front screen door as Carrie left the porch. The urgency in Brandy's voice made Sara come quickly to lead him to her kitchen and pump him a glass of water. "Brandy, Brandy, now you must settle down. Nobody is dying."

"But, Missum MacFee, dat baby is comin'. Inez, she—"

"I know, I know," said Sara. "But I've still got to get there yet. Angus left with the team and wagon. We have no horses. Scott and Tyler took them. Heavens, Brandy, I just can't up and leave my animals."

"Missum MacFee, I'll take you back on my horse, he mighty strong."

Sara saw herself riding on the horse's swaying rump with her sorely wrenched back. "Brandy, I can't go without Carrie. She can't stay here alone."

Anguish mounted on Brandy's face. He almost stuttered, saying, "What we gonna do?"

Sara sat down to think for a moment. Her calm contrasted strangely with Brandy's continuing nervous and excited movements. "Our old buckboard is still back of the stable, believe it might do if your horse can draw it. Don't know if there's any fittin' harness around. Guess you'll have to make do with what you find."

Brandy thought of the big roan being strapped into some rusty harness and winced, but he nodded his head vigorously. "Ah'll git over there right quick."

Sara hardly seemed to hear him as she went over her other concerns. The cow had to be milked and tethered to the barn. Her chickens had to be fed and wired in the roost. Coyotes and other varmints were always lurking. She told Carrie quietly but firmly to change her dress, then, taking her pail and a stool to sit on, she went to milk her cow.

Brandy headed for the stable.

In spite of Carrie's reluctance to help, in a little more than half an hour they were ready to go. The powerful roan stallion snorted, stamped and looked wide-eyed as he was backed into an old-fashioned chest yoke, but Brandy fed him two apples he had found in the MacFee stable and an uneasy truce was struck between them.

With Carrie sitting mutely on the bare backboards, they traveled through the dark Texas night, the buckboard creaking under the pull of the roan. They were grateful when the moon finally lifted above the horizon and brought a pale glow to the land. It was almost full, but no one mentioned that on the frontier a full moon in this season was uneasily known as a "Comanche moon."

It was almost eleven when they pulled noisily into the ranch yard. Brandy had a quick fright when he saw the hut in darkness, but Seth swiftly explained that they had moved Inez into the house. Isabelle needed light to tend to her, and if it attracted hostiles, the house would be easier to defend.

Isabelle was more than relieved to see Mrs. MacFee. Inez was in great pain. As Brandy feared, she was having serious trouble delivering. Sara found her already fully dilated and began to worry that the baby's head could not come through. For hours she had Inez with her legs up and open, pressing her stomach and keeping her conscious to the need to press down with all her might. Inez screamed from time to time and sank back in exhaustion on Isabelle's bed, which was now drenched in sweat. Old Sara learned as she struggled that the baby was almost a month early, and at three-thirty in the morning, after tearing the membrane and just managing to work its head out, she realized its prematurity had saved its life. Had the baby been a fraction larger, it would have died in the womb and Inez would shortly have joined it in death.

When Brandy learned that Inez had brought forth a tiny baby girl, he sank to his knees and unabashedly thanked the Lord, tears of joyous relief streaming down his face. Seth stood back and watched him, wondering how a man could look both proud and brave even when he was shedding a torrent of tears.

At five that morning Todd Bonham galloped into the ranch yard and, seeing Seth coming toward him, pointed meaningfully in the direction from which he had come. "Seth, you better mount up. The Mexicans have taken San Antonio again. Hays sent me here with twenty-five men. They're waiting down on the main trail. He wants you to take them south and set up this side of Laredo. Attack any couriers or supply wagons you see coming north."

"Isn't he going to drive them out of San Antonio?"

"Reckon he's figuring to. Old Houston is finally waking up. Believe there's Texan troops already on their way."

Seth drew a deep breath and studied the other's face. Todd had to steady his heaving horse, but Seth could feel he was being treated with the old respect. "Time for some coffee?"

"Nope. Best be on my way. Prent Salinger is going back with me. Hays will send him down if your orders change." Calling out, "Give my respects to Isabelle," Todd glanced anxiously at the graying sky and took off at a determined gait down the trail.

Seth looked at Isabelle, who had been listening from inside the door that had been left ajar. "Oh, Seth," she sighed, her voice weak and drained by her long, exhausting night.

Seth thought for a moment about what a man could say when life whirled him about like this, but in the end he shrugged resignedly and turned to the stable to get Sam.

Many miles to the northwest Blood Hawk rode into a small canyon. Its steep sandstone sides were streaked with red and pale blue, and a tiny pebbly stream trickled along its floor. It was a place to rest, and he had much to think about. He knew now that Red Knife had tricked him, he knew now that the *tejanos* had not foolishly followed him to the gully, and when he himself had arrived there, Red Knife was nowhere to be found. Red Knife had meant for the *tejanos* to kill Blood Hawk, but instead it was he himself who had died. Creeping back to watch from the knoll, Blood Hawk saw Red Knife's body being dragged from the stable. He fingered his bear-claw necklace. It was indeed strong medicine; it had saved him from Red Knife's trap. He knew now why Red Knife had wanted to take it from him.

With a well-placed shot he killed a young jackrabbit and roasted it over a low fire. When shadows began to gather and darken the narrow canyon, he chanted to his secret spirits in thanks, then curled up and slept. That night, as a full moon hovered over the canyon, bathing its high rim and steep facings in a vague bluish light, Blood Hawk received his great medicine dream. It was to change his life, for it would outweigh even his insanity in importance.

He dreamt that on returning to his village his people had rejected him, driving him out onto the prairie because they thought he had killed Red Knife. His denials were lost on Red Knife's powerful relatives, who wickedly seized this chance to rid the camp of both of them. Blood Hawk left, but he called upon his medicine to punish his people for their injustice and before many moons had passed a great tragedy befell them. When a terrible vengeance had been extracted, they called him back in fear and made him a chief.

He awoke with a start to sit up and look about him. It was still early in the night. The shifting lights raised by moonbeams on the canyon's walls convinced him that his spirits were there watching. He took the bear-claw necklace off and, holding it out to them, trembled with joy as he chanted his thanks to the high orb shining above until dawn.

Along with its independence, Texas' southern border was in dispute. The bitter, bloody struggle for the arid flats and chaparral between the Nueces and the Rio Grande was not a war with internationally sanctioned codes of conduct, but an assault upon each other by two peoples whose treatment of enemy nationals would have shamed the merciless Khans of Asia. At its explosive heart, many thought, was Texas avarice and Mexican pride, but the territorial claims and counterclaims had been deeply and even fatally aggravated by the clash of cultures, neither finding the other worthy of respect. The long-simmering guerrilla-like stand-off finally burst into flames on September 11, 1842, when the European mercenary General Adrian Woll, at the head of twelve hundred Mexican troops, entered and captured San Antonio.

The thought of Anglo Texans, some even prominent members of the district court, being taken prisoner on their own soil and a Mexican flag flying over the San Fernando church soon had alarm and outrage whipping across the countryside. Texas militia from all the western counties started marching toward San Antonio. Woll, seeing the mounting numbers, soon abandoned the town and began his retreat to the border. Hays, organizing some Rangers, harassed him south, but Texas was by now an aroused hornet's nest, its armed citizenry falling on the invaders like enraged wolves. One force caught Woll on the Salado and, using the heavy brush as cover, killed over a hundred of his men. But other, smaller groups foolishly coming up on foot were cut off and virtually slaughtered by the faster-moving Mexican cavalry. The Texans taken prisoner were again brutally treated and finally decimated, one in every ten being shot. But the Mexicans were sowing the whirlwind. It would lead to hideous and unforgettable scenes of bloodshed and deep, lasting scars.

Even Sam Houston knew that Texas could not tolerate another invasion of her territory without some military response, but the residents of San Antonio were beginning to look with growing anxiety at the volunteers, angry and heavily armed, trooping outside their mission walls and settling in their plazas. Violence attracts violent men. Along with the many volunteer militias came a miscellany of freebooters and raw-looking adventurers whose ranks were continually inflated by an ominous salting of gunslingers drifting in from parts north and east.

The Rangers called up by Hays showed their customary discipline, but Houston, having received a danger signal from Hays, had to rush General Somervell west to command the swelling mass of militia and irregular volunteers. When Somervell arrived, he immediately tried to instill some military order into this mob, but the Texas army lacked the junior officers and noncommissioned cadres necessary to control a large fighting force. Instead of finding recruits ready to be tamed by military drill, he was surrounded by aroused, cold-eyed men who had come for and wanted Mexican blood. Outlets for their frustrations quickly appeared. The drinking and gambling that flourished at night were already leading to gunplay, and men were being killed. The general soon agreed with Hays that these men had to be either committed to battle or dispersed. It was with a sense of deliverance that the wary inhabitants of San Antonio watched this consortium of heavily armed "patriots" shoulder their guns and depart south.

Seth soon tired of patrolling the flat, empty plain and was relieved after a week when Prent Salinger came to report that Woll was retreating. Seth was to avoid all further contact with the enemy and return to San Antonio. He was glad to go. He was anxious to hear from Isabelle, anxious to hear that she and Jason were safe. Surely by now the baby would be gone, its degrading intrusion in their lives over. He wondered what he could bring back for Isabelle and if he had enough money for some material from which she could cut a dress. It had never struck him until now how hard this life must be on young, pretty women who never found occasion to dress up. Prent made no mention of matters at the ranch, and Seth, remembering his shameful encounter with Adam on the square, did not want to ask.

But he was in for disappointment. Hays, he discovered, had been made a major in the Texas army, though his elevation had failed to alter his quiet, modest ways. Seth was about to ask for leave to visit his ranch when Hays informed him that by presidential decree the Rangers were now part of the Texas army and that Seth himself now held the temporary rank of captain. He was to take ten men to act as a scouting detail for the army when it moved on Laredo. Hays' low-key manner did not conceal the fact that the government considered itself at war. Martial law had been declared. There were no alternatives to be discussed. Seth was to leave and organize his reconnaissance forced immediately.

Biting back his disappointment, he scribbled a note to Isabelle and left it with the crippled Ranger who managed the stable. It would take some time, but every traveler was a postman in those parts and surely it would get there before he did.

For Isabelle the days after Seth's departure had an air of impending crisis. The very sound of the baby's cries left her flushed and confused, draining her like a secret guilt, making her empty and weakening every resolve.

Inez took only a short while to recover from the birth, and the ecstasy she entered into on seeing her tiny baby girl made her slim, dark face glow till it seemed fixed in an ever-expanding smile. Brandy, who chuckled at every move she made, hugged and kissed her warmly when she shyly announced she would call their daughter Teresa after Inez' long-dead mother.

Isabelle came back from the hut time after time thinking of Inez' happiness only to find Tate—for now it was the baby's accepted name—and feel again the burden of banishing this odd, unwanted child to another world, one she would never know. Only Rick's return, the Indian scare having died away, prompted her to action. Rick had brought a note from Bessie saying she would like to come and spend a day with her. Her father, Adam, was now at home with Kate and the weather was staying fair. Bessie's message finished on a jaunty note: "Heard from Sir Lancelot—must talk to you."

Isabelle could only marvel at the miracle of having Bessie to turn to in this lonely land. The girl sensed that Isabelle needed her. She had read into her father's and brother's words more than they had meant to tell, and she had sent off this note. The reference to Sir Lancelot, whom they both knew was Todd Bonham, was only to suggest that it was Bessie who needed her. It was so like Bessie.

A few days later Brandy was taking the Salinger rig down to the stable and the two young women were once again hugging and greeting each other excitedly on the doorstep.

They laid out teacups with fresh biscuits and preserves as they talked, but in spite of their joyful chatter, before long Bessie realized Isabelle's clawing need to get to the agonizing issue of the child. Abruptly she turned their conversation that way.

"Listen to me, Isabelle, you must try to put an end to this. Let me hear what remains to be done." Her tone was soft, untroubled but firm and full of her usual good sense.

It was hours before Isabelle, reaching nervous exhaustion, accepted the inevitability of Michalrath's offer. They would take the baby to him tomorrow. Realizing that it would be a trying day for both of them, Bessie urged that Jason be left with Inez.

While Isabelle fed and prepared her two young ones for bed, Bessie went down to the hut to see Inez' newborn. When she returned she smiled readily, but her face was lightly drawn with concern. "That child is darling," she said, "but Inez looks awfully thin. I don't believe she has much milk. I watched her feeding. The baby was still sucking and fretful at the end."

"It's so tiny," said Isabelle, now conscious of her own swollen breasts. "Perhaps it doesn't need much."

"Perhaps," said Bessie setting a place for the two of them at the table. "Perhaps."

They were already in bed before the conversation finally turned to Bessie. It was when Isabelle, suddenly feeling selfish and ashamed, remembered the note and blurted out, "Oh, Bessie, forgive me. I've been so lost in myself I clear forgot to ask you what you heard from Todd Bonham."

Bessie smiled good-naturedly and snuggled into her pillow. " 'Twasn't much. Actually, I didn't honestly hear from him. Brother Prent just mentioned he'd heard one of the Rangers in San Antonio asking Todd if he had a girl. Todd said yes."

Isabelle was anxious to hear more, but Bessie's eyes were closed and she seemed to be smiling to herself. "Well," prompted Isabelle, nudging her, "is that all?"

"Oh no, this fellow went on to ask what her name was."

Bessie seemed content to let it lie at that, but Isabelle had raised herself in the bed and was now glaring down at her. "Bessie Salinger, you stop teasing me. What did he say?"

Bessie kept her eyes closed, but her face glowed with suppressed jubilation. "Well . . . it seems he said her name was Bess," she murmured. Turning away gently, she signaled with several deep, pleasurable sighs that she was ready for sleep.

Part Three

VEILED HORIZONS

November 1842

15

The descent of the Texas army to the border that fall kept Seth's scouting detail in the saddle most of the day and part of the night. South of San Antonio they were in country sparsely populated by poor Mexican subsistence farmers, broad flat country with large stretches of sunburnt grass. The Mexican army kept close watch on their progress but did little to protect the few isolated villages and farms from Texas foraging parties. Seth saw family after family grieving at the loss of their pathetically few chickens or pigs, or in tears over the ravaging of tenderly cared for gardens. There was little he could do but complain repeatedly to Hays, who in turn complained to Somervell. The hard-pressed general, secretly briefed by Sam Houston, knew the damage this piracy could be doing to the nation's image at a time when the goodwill of foreign powers was being courted to bring pressure to bear on Mexico. Under the treaty of 1836 these people, though Mexican by birth, were Texas citizens, living on Texas soil. An army marching under the flag of Texas was despoiling its own citizens. He gave stern orders, but the command problem made them impossible to carry out. Only the Rangers and seasoned militiamen could be counted on to obey.

The campaign had gotten off to an inauspicious start. Though quick to leave San Antonio, Somervell had been infuriatingly slow in getting to Laredo. The irregulars had chafed at his harsh discipline and the seemingly never-ending delays. There was a growing suspicion that Somervell didn't want or intend to fight at all, that he had been sent by peace-minded Sam Houston in an empty show of force to pacify the war hawks in his own government. After three weeks desertions occurred daily and respect for authority became a matter of personal whim. By the beginning of December they could muster only slightly more than seven hundred men, but by now they were approaching Laredo and plans for taking the town were being openly discussed.

Laredo was a sleepy adobe town on the south bank of the Rio Grande. It had a small, busy marketplace, two churches, a mission and a ferry port for travelers to the north bank. There was only a handful of Mexican troops deployed to defend it when the Texans attacked, most having slipped away toward old Mier, but the townspeople, who wanted nothing more than to be spared an ordeal in which they could only lose, were to pay a bloody price for Woll's foray onto Texas soil. Once the town was taken, the simmering rebellion by the irregulars in the Texas force exploded out of hand. Their looting led to panic among the inhabitants, for as darkness settled it was followed by a drunken orgy of rape and even murder. Somervell tried to restore order by commanding the Rangers to police the town, but as Hays soberly and bitterly explained, "General, you can't get Texans to shoot Texans over Mexicans. Let's push on to Mier and make 'em fight. That's the only way you'll ever get them out of this town."

But the general lacked Hays' gift for command. His repeated demands that the rioting be halted were ignored, and the setting for more than one tragedy that night was in place.

Isabelle knew there was something wrong when young Jed came up to the rig with tears in his eyes. "Aunt Phoebe is doing poorly," he said. "Pa is in praying with her now. Maybe you ladies wouldn't mind waiting on the porch for a spell. I'll fetch some cool lemonade."

Isabelle and Bessie settled into two large chairs on the porch, Isabelle holding the baby in her lap. She had fed him on the trip, and then he had slept. Now he was awake and looking about. His skin had continued to lighten till it seemed only finely tinged with bronze, and she had grown used to its strange eyes. She tried to keep from dwelling on it, but the baby had become almost pretty with his delicate and smooth features and soft, even serene expressions. He rarely cried, and his mouth at her breast gave her a brief sense of inner release. Bessie, watching her from across the porch, was glad there was no one about to notice her own brows knitting with concern.

The doctor came out apologizing for making them wait, but his face carried a message that was explanation enough. His sister was dying, and that morning he had begun her death watch.

It was clear he could not take the baby, for Phoebe, whom he dare not leave, might linger for days. Bessie, now openly worried, could only suggest that if he would tell them where he had arranged to leave the child they would deliver him themselves.

The doctor hesitated. He knew it would be best if Isabelle never discovered where the child had gone, but he was also aware that the longer she kept the baby, the greater the emotional trauma of losing him would be. Worn out by his nightlong prayerful but futile attention to Phoebe, he finally gave them directions to a Mexican settlement some two to three hours' drive to the south. He noticed that they had a horse tied behind the rig that looked to be too valuable an animal to be giving away, but he understood why it was there. Isabelle had taken it to give to Tate's new parents, feeling it was little enough payment for raising a child.

When they arrived, the settlement proved to be only a single narrow street elbowing its way through a clutter of low adobe shacks. The yard areas were littered with squawking chickens, rooting pigs and near-naked children who ran about screaming, but quickly dropped into silence as they saw strangers approach. Bessie, who had checked her handgun and Isabelle's rifle early in the trip, drove up to three women trimming a large basket with flowers. The women turned away from their colorful basket and regarded the rig curiously. Word of the Texas army's depredations had reached the settlement, which was fortunately too far west to be caught in the line of march; but still the trio looked worried. It was several moments before one of them, in a mixture of English and Spanish, said nervously, "*Buenos días, señoras*. You seek something?"

They had been given the name Juanita Jacaza. Bessie now pronounced it as well as she could and added, "Could you tell us where?"

The women exchanged sly glances, and the one who had spoken pointed to the very furthest reach of the settlement. "*Sí*, it is leetle house, you see big pot in front."

Bessie thanked them and moved on. A gaggle of dirty children began tagging after them. Isabelle held the baby as close as she could, for she had started to smell the odors rising from the sewerage that lay in festering pools along the crude street. Just beyond a string of houses a flock of raucous crows was pecking at the body of a dead puppy.

The house was easy enough to find. It sat nearly isolated on the opposite side of the settlement, a large cast-iron pot dominating its front yard. While still yards away, the rank smell of long-fermented grapes told them Juanita Jacaza had been making wine.

They stopped and sat in the rig in silence, looking at the hut. Somehow the sight of it drove the ugliness of their mission to an unbearable level. But within moments the babble of children brought a heavyset, masculine-looking woman to its door. Isabelle watched her push the door open and stride hurriedly into the yard. Big as she was, she moved with the litheness of a cat. Her eyes fell almost immediately on the baby, "Ah, señoras, you wish to see Juanita, no?"

Bessie looked back at her, saying, "Are you Juanita Jacaza?"

The odor of stale perspiration from the woman's body was already making Isabelle hold her breath. She pressed the baby closer as the woman nodded. "Dr. Michalrath says he has spoken to you," Isabelle offered weakly.

"Ah, yes, Señor Doctor. He comes here. Juanita is good woman for help. I find good home for baby."

Isabelle and Bessie looked at each other. "And where will this home be?" asked Isabelle, helpless to deny herself the question.

"Is not to say . . . Is better," said Juanita, smiling uncomfortably.

Bessie released a long-held breath. "Perhaps we better go inside."

Juanita held her hands up. "You no need worry. Juanita take baby now. Better you go before dark, yes?" Her strong, hirsute face lifted as her eyes traveled to the handsome horse tied to the rear of the rig. "You bring leetle present for Juanita, no?"

Bessie climbed out of the rig and motioned to Isabelle to do the same. "I think we'll come in," she said determinedly. The big woman shifted over to stand in front of them.

"Juanita very sorry but have sick friend in bed. Is bad to make noise, need very much sleep."

Bessie looked annoyed. "How long before you'll find this baby a home?"

Juanita smiled and shrugged her heavy shoulders at the unpredictability of such matters. "To say when, señora, is a thing of great difficulty. Perhaps only a leetle while."

Bessie's face moved closer to hers. "We're not leaving this child till we see where we're leaving it."

Juanita was about to bar their way again, but there was something about the pert little woman staring into her face that warned Juanita that she was close to losing that fine-looking horse. "Very well. We go in for a moment only. Please very quiet, sick friend she sleeps."

Inside the cramped house a blanket of flies arose and landed again as the screen door closed. The odor of garbage and stale tobacco momentarily gagged them. A disheveled young girl lay drunk on the bed, her blouse open and her skirt pulled up on one side to her hip. She might have been pretty, but under a deep anesthesia of wine she looked starkly pale and hardly alive. In one corner a table held some unwashed dishes that were dark with insects, and in another a slop bucket was full and covered with greenish scum. Bessie looked about in open revulsion. "This is dreadful! Sickening!" she said. "You expect to keep a baby here?"

"No, no. Señor Doctor say baby no can stay here."

"Where, then?"

"People here travel always to Mexico. Señor Doctor leave money for to take baby. Baby in Mexico in few days."

"My God, my God," said Isabelle, glancing about her and growing weak.

Juanita hurriedly tried to command the situation again. "No worry for baby. Many good wet nurses here. Mexican ladies love babies. No worry. Juanita fix fine."

Bessie turned to her, agony and irritation sharing her face. "Well? Isabelle?"

Isabelle held the baby up and buried her face in its little soft cotton gown. After a long moment in which Bessie watched her tremble, she lowered the baby and said almost inaudibly, "I can't! I just can't!"

A faint scarlet blush against the night sky warned Seth that a fire was raging somewhere in Laredo. While their main body attacked and took the town, he led a patrol down the river, watching for an enemy crossing. Neither Somervell nor Hays wanted the Mexicans to appear unexpectedly in their rear. But by nightfall he knew Woll's force was staying south of the river. It seemed that the bold thrust into Texas was over.

Seth had taken only four men, but all of them were anxious to get back to the battlefront. They had heard the gunfire, which had been heavy but brief, and knew Laredo had been taken. As they neared the outskirts they found the fire still going and bright enough to light up a portion of the town. Seth sent his men ahead as he searched for the Texas flag that would mark their headquarters, but before he had ridden very far he was surrounded by a group of shouting men, many of them drunk. To his amazement, several were carrying silver candlesticks, clocks and even pieces of furniture. He saw one man dragging tapestries of gold-colored cloth, another drapes of velvet. Stunned, he realized that the town was being sacked. He heard himself hailed several times before he spotted two men waving to him to join them. In the flickering light from the steadily leaping flames he recognized Tanner and Purdy. They were holding up a bottle and laughing. He spurred Sam over to them and swung down. "What the hell is going on here?" he exclaimed.

"Just having a little fun, Seth. It's bin mighty dull work gittin' here." Tanner offered him the bottle. "Have a drink? Compliments of the town."

Seth ignored the gesture. "Where's Hays?"

Tanner's eyes straightened. He shifted sideways and took a step back, aware for the first time of Seth's anger. "Ain't seen him for a couple of hours."

"He and Somervell are upriver a piece," said Purdy, his voice now tamed and consciously held level. It was clear they regretted having run into him. Seth turned to mount again when he noticed a persistent screaming in the street beyond. It rose to piercing shrieks, and he caught sight of two women fleeing in panic into his street, pursued by a crowd of hallooing men. Within moments they were cowering in near hysteria against the sand-colored adobe walls of a patio, pleading in gasps of Spanish to be left alone. The men seized them roughly, and, while two held them helpless, others started tearing the clothes from their bodies. One was a pretty young woman with long, satiny black hair and a generous bust. The other was younger, with the slight build of the early teens. From their close resemblance they were doubtless sisters. Seth forced his way through the swelling crowd of jostling men, many drawn by the women's screams but now watching lustily as the helpless girls were stripped nude and forced down onto the patio floor. Above, on a narrow balcony, an old Mexican appeared. His hair was white and he did not look firm enough to stand without supporting himself against the iron guardrail. He was holding an ancient pistol and pointing it at a squat, full-bearded man who stood over the prostrate young women as he opened his pants. The old man shouted something in Spanish, but it was lost as the men standing saw the old one's pistol and several shots rang out. The old man crumpled over the railing and his body came slowly forward. He fell on his head, hitting the stone patio with a dull thud. The bearded man, his pants hanging open, went over to the old man's corpse, kicked it and swore to himself as he stomped back.

Seth had sensed from the beginning what was happening, but it was not until he saw the woman with the beautiful length of hair being thrust to the ground and her legs held open that the image of the Comanches pressing themselves on Isabelle gripped him. Seized with a rising fury the scene slipped into sharp focus before him as he realized that a stable must have caught fire, for the air was filling with slivers of straw ash and had grown heavy and sour like cordite. "Leave her alone!" he heard himself roaring.

At first no one seemed to hear, but, roughly shoving aside two men standing before him, he moved out onto the patio and shouted even louder. "Leave her alone, you son of a bitch, or I'll kill you!"

Silence swept the patio and quickly spread into the surrounding crowd. It was a silence electric with menace. The bearded man was kneeling between the girl's legs, about to penetrate her. He looked up startled, his eyes aflame. Two others, holding her down, turned from him to Seth, their suspenders stretching over their sweat-stained long johns, the veins in their faces now ugly red streaks from drink and lust. They were wild-eyed, manic, dangerously aroused. They were also heavily armed.

Another bearded man with a wide-brimmed hat was standing over the younger girl, glowering at Seth. His hand slipped to his gun. "What the hell are you trying to pull, Ranger? We'uns don't take no orders no more. Clear out before you find yer'self chinnin' with your great-granddaddy."

"I said leave her alone!" repeated Seth, turning his body until his gun grip reached his hand. The man holding the woman's leg on the far side used the bearded man's body as cover to draw his gun. "Git!" he snarled as the barrel rose to point squarely at Seth. The crowd scattered. Death was in the air. The churlish-looking, half-drunk men who had seized the women were far too many to be buffaloed by a single gun, but killing a Ranger could mean deadly retribution. They hesitated. Seth saw the barrel of the gun coming up and something within rang an alarm, but try as he would he could not contain the rage still consuming him. This gang would never be put off by words. He saw the gun being cocked and dropped to one knee to fire as a bullet smashed into his chest and drove him to the ground. Guns roared and a wide gash ripped across his forehead. Blood began to bathe his paling face. He felt darkness descending and suddenly could no longer move. His gun lay far beyond his outstretched hand on the patio as the air above him started exploding. Shots rang out from every side and began raining in from the street. A few feet away the cringing women were weeping uncontrollably, surrounded by dying men. Coming up, guns still smoking in their hands, were Tanner and Purdy, their faces in shock as they stood over Seth. Tanner knelt down and lifted Seth's limp head to find it covered with blood. He looked up at his young cousin. "He's dead," he said in what was almost a whisper.

It was getting dark when Bessie and Isabelle, trying to reach the main trail running west, saw a lamp being lit in a small farmhouse and headed toward it. They hadn't spoken for hours, and Isabelle was still lost in the wretched quandary that overwhelmed her at Juanita's. The gift horse still trailed behind, but the mare, having pulled the rig all day, was tired and had to be rested. Bessie hoped there was feed for it on this farm. As they drove into the yard the old couple appeared at the door, and, seeing it was two women, the man set his gun down behind him.

They proved to be friendly but lonely people and were glad for company. Yes, they had a little feed for the horse and surely two women who had come such a long distance could use a bit themselves. Isabelle and Bessie had not eaten all day, but they had little appetite and tried to protest. The old woman waved them off and started cooking. "Land sakes," she said. "If you don't eat somethin' you're like to git sick. And you with a baby and all."

It brought a little relief to their spirits to be able to wash the heavy trail dust from their bodies, but it was while washing that they realized how very tired they were. Bessie had been holding the reins for almost twelve hours. She knew from the fatigue now numbing her limbs that traveling any more that night was out of the question. She was also worried about the mare. While they washed, the old man had gone to the stable to care for the horses and come back saying, "That mare of yours is plum done. Ought to rest her some. That's a nice-looking horse you had hitched to your rig."

The couple's name was Caldwell, Zeb and Polly. They had come west two years before with their son, who had reluctantly brought along his new wife and baby. Tragically, the previous year all three young Caldwells had died of cholera and the old couple, still grieving, and discouraged, were set on returning to Tennessee. Probably still mourning their grandchild, they made a fuss over Tate, and Isabelle noticed that they seemed to find nothing strange about his features.

After dinner, weariness had Bessie fighting to keep her eyes open, and the old woman smiled in sympathy and went to fetch some blankets. The house was small, but there was a heavy bear rug before the fireplace in the single main room and the two women bedded down there. For Bessie nothing could stave off sleep, but Isabelle, her mind mired in a deepening abyss as it tried to deal with her feelings for Seth and Tate, watched the dim coals in the darkening grate until far into the night.

When he was not enjoying his secret supply of whisky, the surgeon attached to Somervell's staff was a good doctor. But now as he stood over Seth on the patio he shook his head. "Not much use," he said. "He's lost a lot of blood, there's a slug in his chest and that's a mighty bad head wound."

"We've got to try," said Hays.

The doctor shook his head again. "Well, we can bandage him up, but I can't probe for that slug till morning. By then it's likely to be too late."

Hays looked at the Rangers standing behind him. "Get some bandages," he said quietly. "And find a place to move him. We can't leave him out here."

There was a door under the balcony of the house that opened onto the patio. A Ranger went over and tried it. He kicked it open and found an old leather couch filling a wall of the first room. A few minutes later Seth was lying on it unconscious while the surgeon, still shaking his head, was tying strips of torn shirts and bedsheets over his wounds. He opened one of Seth's eyes and grunted quietly to himself. Then he stepped back to look at his patient. "Time for some prayers," he muttered. His tone suggested he was making a diagnosis, but he was actually thinking about having a drink.

Somervell was outraged at the report of what happened in Laredo. This disgrace to the arms of Texas would bring furious repercussions from Houston. Had he the power he would have court-marshaled every man he could prove had been involved, but the general was wise enough to know that any attempt at a formal military tribunal would only invite disaster. His only gesture was to round up as much loot as possible and return it to its rightful owners, a shaky attempt at law enforcement that in the end ensured the dissolution of the army. About angry women and distressed girls who had been violated, he could do nothing.

The following day Hays watched the surgeon work the bullet out of Seth's chest with a knife and thin metal forceps. The surgeon still looked pessimistic, but he noticed that Seth was having intermittent periods of consciousness, moments when water was held to his lips and he sipped.

He turned to Hays. "Well, he's just holding on. Got the constitution of a crocodile or he wouldn't be here. This chest wound is bad, but his head one could be worse. Something's wrong with his eyes . . . just too soon to tell."

"Can't we send him home?"

The doctor registered surprise. "Heavens, no. You can't move him, Major. Half a mile of jolting in a wagon and he'll bleed to death. No, he's lost a critical amount of blood already. It'll be weeks before he can be moved, if then."

Hays looked perplexed. "I'm afraid we're not going to be here for weeks."

The doctor shrugged.

When the men left an old Mexican woman entered the house from the rear. She moved through its many rooms with a certainty that indicated she was familiar with them. She came into the front room and settled into a corner, from where she watched Seth for almost an hour. The Ranger outside on the patio was not aware of her presence, just as no one had noticed her the night before, when the fire had gone out and the patio lay in sooty darkness, coming for the old Mexican man's body and carrying it away in a small cart with the help of a young boy.

After an hour she left, but within another hour she was back with a bowl of soup. Creeping up to Seth's side, she waited until his eyes flicked open, then held a small spoon to his mouth. Now the Ranger outside noticed her, but seeing that she was only trying to feed Seth decided she could do no harm.

That evening she returned, and again she said nothing. With her was a young woman with striking hair and a slim adolescent girl, the two whose rape had been halted by Seth the night before. Again they brought soup. They whispered to one another as he took a few spoonfuls, and they placed some fresh bandages beside him as they left. The one with the striking hair had brought a basin of water and washed the bloodstains off his face. She was the last to leave, and when she did her soft features were troubled and her mouth tight with anger.

Nothing could mask the erupting wave of insurrection in the Texas force. The long-degenerating situation had turned ugly. Over two hundred men deserted in disgust and went home. The remainder refused to acknowledge Somervell as leader and, when he continued to refuse to march on Mier, shouted charges of cowardice and even betrayal at him. It was mostly the irregulars who rebelled against discipline, but many Rangers also felt they had been misled, handled in bad faith. No one doubted any longer that Somervell had never planned to seek out and punish the Mexicans for their violation of Texas soil. He had turned their punitive expedition into a farcical parade.

Somervell, accepting the futility of continuing any pretense to a serious military operation, declared the campaign over and prepared to march back east. The more than three hundred men who remained quickly elected another leader and rode off for Mier. Among them were many Rangers, including one of Hays' most respected lieutenants, Sam Walker. Major Hays himself, still sobered and chagrined by the plundering of Laredo and in particular the obscene abuse of women, followed Somervell, but no one dared suggest that Hays was running from a fight.

Before he left he had come with the surgeon to visit Seth. The Mexican women were there, and the surgeon, after examining Seth, stated that they were doing as much as could be done. Hays, relieved that Seth was not going to be left alone, introduced himself and found that the old woman was better educated and handled herself with greater dignity than he had expected. Hearing his name, she immediately introduced herself and her two granddaughters. She was Señora Castabella and her granddaughters were Rosita and Nina. Her English, though accented, was near perfect.

"We will care for the señor, he is a very good man," she said.

Hays clumsily attempted to offer them money, but the old woman pushed his hand away. "The señor did not take money to defend my granddaughters."

Hays now understood their willingness to nurse Seth. Tanner and Purdy had briefed him on that night. Still, he was leaving a Texan soldier behind in a Mexican town, one that had been badly ravaged. He could not afford to leave enough Rangers to protect Seth. Embarrassed by what he had to say next, Hays turned his eyes away from the old woman and onto the young ones. "What about your people? How will they feel about it?"

The old woman drew herself up. He was surprised at the strength of feeling in her face. "Do not worry, Señor Major, my poor husband, whom your people have murdered, was a close friend of the *alcalde*. The Castabellas are an old and proud family here. This man protected our young women—we will protect him!"

Little Jason stood at the window by himself for the first time and watched the frightening storm. Along with the hail that swept down and roared like a snare drum on the roof, there were streaks of lightning and claps of thunder that shook the air even inside the house. But it was not until a great bolt hit the knoll in front of his eyes and a peal of thunder cracked above him and came down like a hammer blow that sounded like it would split the house to its foundations that he turned and ran squealing to his mother. Early winter was a time for freakish storms, and they usually preceded by a few days a sharp drop in the temperature and skies that warned of blue northers. Isabelle supposed that when the weather broke Seth would soon return. It was only when Isaac Sawyer came with a letter from him that had been passed on by a traveler coming down the main trail that she discovered he had gone south with the army. There had been smatterings of news about fighting around Laredo, but none of the men who had left for San Antonio had returned as yet and little was known about the Mexican trouble.

Brandy and Inez said nothing when she had returned still holding Tate. Brandy listened to her tell how they had left the gift horse with the Caldwells, who had fed and curried Bessie's mare and given them a basket of food and some oats for the mare on their return journey. Brandy, half smiling, remembered how hard it had been to break that animal and sent his eyes up in relief. "Jes' so dat devil horse don't come back."

After Bessie finally left, the loneliness would have depressed Isabelle had she not been distracted and then alarmed by Inez and her baby. She could see the tiny infant was not filling out, and Bessie's words about Inez not having enough milk were proving disturbingly true. Inez had tried feeding her fresh milk from the MacFees' cow, but the child was throwing it up and beginning to cry for longer and longer periods. One night Isabelle could hear it from her bed. She had fed Tate an hour before, but her breasts still felt full. She lay thinking of Brandy and Inez sitting in their hut anxiously rocking their baby, not wanting to ask for the help they so desperately needed. She sat up in the bed and looked toward the hut. Brandy and Inez needed her, she knew now silently peering into the darkness just how much she needed them. Without noticing it she had come to depend upon Brandy's ever-willing hands, his humble gratitude for her and Seth's friendship, the good feeling he spread with his almost childish joy at Inez' love. The harshness of the land had made Brandy's willing devotion seem like warmth from some inner hearth. Though Inez was still little more than a girl, Isabelle had felt the strength and courage she had shown in fighting her way through a life of abuse, and holding her head up under the prejudices of an alien culture. As she sat there her own burdens didn't seem so great. Somehow the near panic she experienced when thinking of Seth and Tate seemed but one more threat in this wilderness that engulfed them all.

She found herself leaving her bed and wrapping a heavy cloak around her body. Seeing that the children were fast asleep, she slipped out the door and made her way to the hut. She came into the candlelight and saw Brandy and Inez leaning over the baby, whose steady crying sounded weaker and almost beyond its strength.

They looked at her in surprise as she unhesitatingly lifted the baby to her and, opening her cloak and nightgown, guided the baby's mouth to her nipple. Within a moment the baby stopped crying as the warm milk began trickling into its body. Seeing Isabelle's exposed breast, Brandy put his head down and covered his face with his hands, but Inez could not help coming to her with tears in her eyes, suppressing a sob but kissing her on the cheek.

Isabelle would remember that night with the three children, Jason, Tate and now Teresa, all of whom had nursed at her breast. She would remember their helplessness and her wonder at the madness of raising them in this torn land of struggle, pain and above all fear. Not until the years unfolded would she grasp that children are really raised by the earth they spring from, its conflicts becoming their conflicts, its trials calling up their strengths, its challenges their dreams.

Brandy and Inez sat in silence for a long spell, their eyes moist with gratitude, until the baby's fullness began to bring on sleep. Then the spell was broken by a hunting coyote howling plaintively to its mate from the moonlit summit of the near but darkly shrouded knoll.

The following morning Isabelle stood out on the prairie and looked straight up at the sun. She knew her heart had made a decision that her head was weighing with alarm. She knew now that she was going to keep Tate, she knew now that her promise to Seth had to be broken. What that decision might mean she was anxiously struggling to face, but what it could mean terrified her. Had anyone been standing close they would have known she was praying. Isabelle couldn't hold back the tears that nearly blinded her. She was a woman with a woman's instincts, a woman's needs. Now she needed a benevolent God, needed his guidance, his comfort. She had cherished the man he had given her to love. She had followed him into this barren waste with its hideous inhabitants and terrifying storms. She had stuck with him in spite of the horror of a savage violation and a loneliness only those who had lived on this lonely frontier could know. She had followed him because she loved him. She was his woman, his wife. The terrors of Texas could not shake her devotion to this man she had married. She asked God only to make him understand, if he found her too weak to abandon Tate, that God had made her that way and she could do no other.

God must also tell him she was a mother, with a mother's instincts, a mother's ready sacrifices to protect her young. She was a mother whose child had not been conceived in love, a child who now threatened the love that had sustained her since childhood. But mothers must brave the world beside the children they bear. She could not do differently, for God had made her that way. Please God, she prayed, make him understand.

16

Seth would often think back on those first confused semiconscious moments in Laredo, and then he would remember whole days that were fragmented or distorted by deliriums, sudden blackouts or blinding headaches. He would remember that the air hanging over him was foul with odors rising from his wounded body. Worst of all, he would recall his growing awareness of total helplessness.

In some vague way he knew he was being cared for, but the sounds, especially the voices, were unfamiliar and the hands that touched and tended to him, though gentle, at no time clasped his and therefore seemed alien. After a week of slowly increasing consciousness he awoke one morning to find Rosita and her grandmother staring down at him. They had waited for his first signs of strength, then moved him at night to the north side of the river, where he was settled in a small abandoned shack overgrown and almost covered with vines and wild brush. The Castabella women were making the arduous and dangerous trip daily to nurse his body and restore his health.

Rosita was very pretty and very patient with him. She tried to discover his name and where he was from. It was clear the Texans had told them nothing. But struggle as he did, his mind, suffering from severe trauma after his head wound, had become blank, and he could not even remember coming to Laredo. In time the grandmother, a well-known figure about town, stopped appearing. Her arrivals in the carriage were attracting too much attention. Rosita was less well known and, being a skillful rider and looking boyish in some old *vaquero* clothes, she dropped by every day. She helped him eat and bathe. She brought him sandals and white cotton pants and shirts. It was local garb, so he would not look too conspicuous if he wandered out. As time passed and his strength returned, Rosita began spending more and more time wandering about the shack, just visiting with him.

For weeks Rosita had lived in secret awe of this bold, apparently fearless man who had ignored cocked guns to save her and her sister from rape. She was a winsome, spirited, yet loving girl. Young, tender of nature, grateful and hopelessly romantic, her nursing soon flowered into an overpowering attachment that, unchecked by her innocence, soon convinced her she was in love. Seth did not realize the day she squeezed his hand and he, in gratitude, squeezed hers back that Rosita read this as a confirmation of mutual affection. Riding home that evening, her pulse started racing; for the first time in her sheltered life she had met a man she truly wanted. This handsome, mystifying *americano* who had come out of the night to save her had, by returning that squeeze, declared himself. By the grace of God and her patron saint, through an act of near tragedy she had found her love.

Seth would remember the following morning as the worst moment of his long convalescence. Rosita did not come. Her grandmother appeared instead. The old woman looked at him with troubled eyes, the only hint she gave of what proved to be a deep, smoldering anger. "Señor, you are married? Yes? No?"

Surprising himself, he quickly muttered, "Yes." It was the first question about himself he had effortlessly answered. It marked an end to his vexing spells of amnesia.

"Then, señor, you are a wicked man."

"Wicked?"

"Rosita, my poor granddaughter, she is in love with you. She says you are in love with her! Oh, wicked man! What will you do next? Sleep with her? Make her your *puta*?"

Seth's hand went up to the deep scar that ran along his hairline. He could feel the beginning of a gigantic headache, several of which he had already suffered in anguish. His face revealed his amazement and helplessness at the old woman's words. "Señora . . . señora—" he began, but his mind refused to clear and he couldn't go on.

Growing furious, she waved him into silence. "Do not pretend. She is only an innocent child. We thought you a man of honor. Now you must leave. We will bring you a horse and you can go when it is dark. It is very dangerous now. Many soldiers are in town—they have already searched some houses. My family can do no more for you. We leave you in the hands of God." With that she left, and as she disappeared Seth turned slowly to fall down on the bed, unable to separate the physical agony, which made his head feel like it was strapped in tightening metal bands, from an emotional agony that swelled till its torment felt like an icy hand clawing at his chest. Suddenly reality was everywhere stabbing into his consciousness. He was married! He had a wife! Slowly, as though recalling an elusive dream, an image of Isabelle's face formed in his mind. Had he been pretending to love another woman, a woman who had helped save his life but one he surely did not love? In his growing confusion he lost track of the old woman's words about soldiers searching for him. He knew he was still too disabled and too disoriented to be traveling alone, but she had made it clear there was no longer a choice. He reached up and held the headboard to steady his vision, which kept opening and losing focus as he turned his head about. He wondered where he could turn to for help, but nothing came except the old woman's final words. "We leave you in the hands of God . . . We leave you in the hands of God."

While Seth lay trapped in his pain and receding amnesia in the lonely hut in Laredo, a small, swarthy man with a thin mustache and flashing white teeth came into the Casa Colorada. His gaze swept the room cautiously and settled on a lone figure sitting against the back wall. Those who had been there when Seth Redmond had confronted Yoquito Estavez would have recognized him as the knife thrower whom Tanner had wounded and Estavez' men had roughly thrown out. His name was Jesús Torres, and throwing knives was only an ancillary skill, one which remained dormant while his wound healed. He was a tall, slim man with broad shoulders and a heavily scarred face, testimony to a sinister life. Suspected of murder and more in Corpus Christi, he also served secretly as an itinerant assassin and sometime spy for the Mexican authorities. In his pay were a handful of informers in and about San Antonio, one of whom was a stable boy who worked in the stable frequented by Rangers. This quick-witted hustler had heard Rangers discussing a companion who had been left seriously wounded in Laredo. The man seemed important, for he held the rank of captain in the Texas army. Not knowing if such information could be worth money, he reported it to Torres. Torres curled his lip as he tried to decide its possible value. At first it hardly seemed promising, but as he began to reason that no wounded Texan could survive in Laredo without Mexican help, his opinion changed. Torres knew his people well enough to know that like him, many of them could be seduced by a windfall of pesos. Perhaps there was more to this incident than he thought. He left a light chalk mark on the church steps, his signal that he had information to sell. The man who had come into the cantina was a skilled Mexican agent posing as a small *ranchero* outside San Antonio.

This seasoned agent knew Torres only by his code name, El Hacha, "the hatchet," after the manner in which he had effected the removal of a troublesome rebel chief in Sonora. The two men grunted a greeting as the agent sat down. He looked about them carefully and, satisfying himself they were safe, he nodded at Torres. "Well?"

"Four hundred pesos," said Torres with as much force as he could summon. He had given his informer the stable boy twenty-five.

"*Amigo*, you are getting too much sun," the agent responded sourly. He was thin and lightly built, but he was a dangerous man. He secretly disliked Torres and even resented being there. He questioned the wisdom of meeting publicly with this fugitive thug. "If you have something to sell, out with it. We talk pesos later."

Torres tried to get lesser amounts, but the agent firmly shook his head, quickly growing restless and finally pushing his chair back with emphasis. "One minute is all you have left, *amigo*, I am a busy man."

Torres, recognizing defeat, told the agent what he knew about a wounded Texan officer in Laredo. The agent studied him as he talked but did not interrupt. "What's his name?" he queried when Torres finished.

Torres was not sure but said he would find out. Anxious to leave, the agent abruptly laid fifty pesos on the table.

"Fifty pesos!" blurted Torres angrily. "You think I am a sheepherder?"

"If the information is reliable, we give you fifty more, but do not expect to meet me again. Your face is too easy to remember. I suggest you leave San Antonio."

"Leave San Antonio!" Torres tried to laugh, but it came out flat and false.

The agent ignored him and discreetly left the cantina. It took this intense if diminutive man several hours to alert his sources for the bits of information he needed, but they worked efficiently and by sundown several Rangers had innocently supplied details that, put together, gave Torres' story the reality a Mexican military command needed to act.

There was a Colonel Rivera on General D'Valya's staff who had handled all intelligence for the military in Tamaulipas. Having been trained by the French, he had very advanced ideas about his work, insisting all communications be short enough to be remembered by couriers, who had orders to destroy written ones at the slightest risk of capture. To him the agent sent a succinct note.

Report Texas Captain Seth Redmond wounded and possibly hiding in Laredo. Condition unknown. Support by locals suspected. More information as available.

The message carried a postscript.

El Hacha now deemed security risk. Request permission to dispose.

17

The two colonels stood in a stone courtyard overlooking the endless sweep of D'Valya lands. They were whispering together about the dispatch Colonel Rivera held in his hand. His companion was Colonel Armonte López, General D'Valya's father-in-law and commander of the large cavalry forces now patrolling both sides of the river.

As usual, General D'Valya was late, and when he appeared in his unmilitary garb he had with him his young bride, Elena María, who greeted her father, Colonel López, with a brief hug of affection.

"Gentlemen," said D'Valya, who had been more than a little wary of Rivera since his arrival from Mexico City. "You wish to see me?" His expression dispelled any notion that their wish might be reciprocal.

Rivera stepped forward. "We have word there is an enemy officer hiding in Laredo. He is reportedly wounded and getting help from the locals. As you know, this is traitorous business. I am requesting that Colonel López find these people and execute them."

The silent Colonel López looked at D'Valya, keeping his strong face devoid of expression. López carried his distinctive military bearing with remarkable ease and gave no indication of the many irritating thoughts crossing his mind. He could not keep from thinking that this man he had encouraged his daughter to marry was really a supercilious ass who lacked the spine to put Rivera in his place. It was clear to López that Rivera, reportedly head of Santa Anna's highly secret spy operation, had come north to check the loyalty and efficiency of border troops. His own knowledge and grasp of military matters warned him that D'Valya could hardly pass close scrutiny as commander of a critical army, not to mention the shifting fortunes of a serious campaign. Already inexcusable mistakes had been made, mistakes that would have sent less well connected men to the capital in disgrace and doubtless their wives with them. Seeing D'Valya hesitating, López quickly spoke up. "I have already authorized a search, General. If the report is true, we will find him." He hoped his words conveyed to D'Valya that Rivera's request could not be denied.

"You will find whom?" asked D'Valya as though he had not fully followed Rivera's words.

Rivera quietly raised the single page of the dispatch again, but his eyes traveled to Elena. They warned that military dispatches were not for civilian ears. Ramón D'Valya followed Rivera's eyes to his wife, then smiled, clearing his throat. "Do you mind, Elena?"

Elena did not mind. She did not like Rivera's eyes on her. She backed off to a small stretch of garden built into the center of the courtyard. In a moment she was glad she had moved away, though not completely out of earshot, for there was no one close enough to hear her little gasp of surprise as the name "Seth Redmond" faintly reached her ears.

Seth waited through that tension-ridden day knowing the sounds he heard were cavalry units going by, some racing along the track that followed the north bank of the river. He was sure that sooner or later they would stop. He would hear commands and know he was surrounded. But the day crept by with tortured slowness and the afternoon brought a gathering of clouds and the scent of rain. Fear kept mounting in his mind that the Castabellas had forsaken him, or perhaps, in their anger over Rosita, had even betrayed him. When darkness finally came, he was sure something was seriously wrong. He had only pieces of fruit left to eat, and he could feel his stomach beginning to contract with hunger. When the rain began, he lay down on the bed and tried to consider his chances of leaving and making his way north on foot. His head and still-weak body told him that escaping without a horse was impossible and even with one it might prove a test he could not meet.

Some hours after dark the rain became heavy, and the roaring downpour muffled the sound of footsteps entering his room. He looked up to see a slim figure standing beside his bed. Two small, delicate hands closed around his. "It is me, Nina," said a girlish voice. "I have food."

He pulled himself up from the bed. It was Rosita's younger sister. She had a dark cape over her head. He wondered if she was frightened, but he soon discovered otherwise. "Señor, there is much trouble," she whispered, but her voice was steady. "You must leave here. Tomorrow morning before dawn I will come for you. Be ready."

"Where am I going?" he asked, trying to make out her young face in the darkness. "I cannot go far without a horse."

"We know," she said, reaching up to touch the heavy growth of fair hair on his face. "There is a razor and soap with the food. You must shave, your beard is much too light for a Mexican. I will bring you a hat with a big brim to cover your head."

Settling down on the bed again, he found himself repeating, "Where are we going?"

"This we will not know till morning. There are many soldiers about. Señor, *por favor*, be ready. There will not be another chance." With that she bent over and kissed him on the forehead. "That is from Rosita," she said, her mouth coming close to his ear. With that she spun about and quickly disappeared, her footsteps suddenly lost in the drone of the rain.

Doña Carlota was a cousin of Ramón D'Valya and until lately had run his large *hacienda* with its many servants, ruling with her firm and competent hands a stylish and orderly estate. A woman in her late thirties, she was still attractive, though the loss of her one romantic love early in life and the relative poverty on her side of the family had reduced her to the role of housekeeper for this foppish cousin. It was thought that with Ramón's marriage and the arrival of Elena María friction would develop between the two women and Carlota would soon be forced to leave. But just the reverse had happened. The two women had liked each other from the beginning. Elena, seeing what a demanding job running the D'Valya lands was, quickly assured Carlota she would be lost without her. The young bride secretly considered herself blessed to have discovered an older, more worldly woman who commanded the respect of men. Carlota was a welcome replacement for her wimpering, praying mother.

Doña Carlota, for her part, was not sorry to see Ramón married.

She had become increasingly irritated at his long string of mistresses, flaunting their half-naked bodies and appalling cheap tastes. Often in the morning she had found them sprawled in his bed—in positions their drunken lust had left them in.

In truth Carlota was mildly amazed that the beautiful Elena María would consent to marry this dissipated and pretentious fool. She certainly could have gone to Mexico City and had her pick of a raft of wealthy and attractive men, or even to Spain, where she might well have caught the eye of a grandee. But upon reflection she surmised that the wealth and influence of the D'Valya name was too strong a magnet for Elena's family to resist.

Elena herself she found refreshingly young if annoyingly naive. Elena had no airs of superiority and seemed truly grateful for her friendship. Nevertheless, this evening Carlota was shocked into silence when Elena called her aside and made a request she had trouble grasping.

"You must find him for me," said Elena. "He is lying wounded somewhere in the village."

"An enemy officer? Elena, are you mad?"

"No. If he is caught he will be shot the way they shot the Texans captured at Mier. I owe him a great favor, Carlota. He is a wonderful man, we must help him."

Carlota looked at her with an expression that failed to measure how incredible she found this request. "Where would I start?" she half whispered, disbelief and helplessness deflating her words.

"Go to the *alcalde*. He knows you, he likes you. Tell him it's for me . . . he has always treated me with great affection."

Carlota backed under the cover of the staircase. "Elena—do you know what you are doing?"

"Yes."

"Do you know how it will look for Ramón if you are caught?"

Elena was silent for only a moment. "We must help him," she said, now speaking in the same half whisper Carlota's voice had fallen to. "Carlota, please . . . we must . . . I must help him."

Don José, the *alcalde* of Laredo, looked at the woman who had asked to see him at this unseemly hour of the night. She was no stranger. Doña Carlota was well known by the *alcalde* and he was well aware he was playing host to a formidable female. "I do not understand," he said, spreading his hands in a gesture of confusion. He was not unattractive, but his well-trimmed beard brought badly needed strength to his pale, aging face.

"Come, come, Don José, don't waste time. There is very little to spare. Where is he?"

"Where is who?"

"There is a Texan soldier lying wounded somewhere in the village. Do not ask me to believe you are not aware of it."

"Doña Carlota, you offend me."

Carlota stared at him, a faint smile loosening one side of her mouth. "We have shared many secrets, *alcalde*, have we not? We shall share one more."

The mayor knew she was referring to the delicacies he had sold her for Ramón's table, delicacies which among other things he had smuggled up the river. As he received no compensation for his office of *alcalde*, he felt this private source of revenue was morally permissible. However, he was starkly aware that government authorities placed little weight on morality. "This is a dangerous business," he said, releasing a breath he had been holding. "Very dangerous."

"Then we must remove as much danger as possible."

"And how do you propose to do that?"

"He must be gone from Laredo by morning."

"I see. And how is that to be arranged?"

Carlota's restraint gave way to impatience. "Perhaps you are better off not knowing. Come, where is he?"

Don José sighed and rubbed his hands nervously. "Doña Carlota, I cannot betray the confidence of close and trusted friends, they would never—"

"Close and trusted friends," repeated Carlota, her eyes searching his. "Ah, yes, of course, close and trusted friends, to be sure, I should have known. The Castabellas have him."

"I did not say that."

"You shall not be required to. I respect your loyalty." Carlota rose, preparing to leave. The *alcalde* came quickly out of his chair, beckoning her back with both hands.

"One moment, Carlota. You should know that this Colonel Rivera is a dangerous man. I do not like him. He speaks to me as he would to a servant. Beware of him, he is out to destroy Ramón. If he discovers someone from the D'Valya household is aiding a fugitive, the general will be in serious trouble."

"I know that."

"And you are not afraid?"

"Of course I am afraid, but I have great faith in our president. He always shoots the wrong people. As you know, it has been your salvation more than once."

"That is unfair."

"Perhaps, but *alcalde,* you're wasting time. If you have something more you wish to say, out with it. I cannot delay much longer."

Don José shook his head in a combination of despair and admiration. This was surely an unusual woman. He would have liked her for himself. "When the *rinches* left," he began warily, "they left this man's horse, a remarkable animal indeed. It was . . . shall we say . . . presented to me as a token of some people's esteem."

Carlota looked at him ruefully. "A token of esteem that might well get you hanged."

"Crudely put—yet typical of you. I would like to return it now. The man will need his horse."

"That he will."

The *alcalde* came closer to her, taking her hands in his. "Carlota, you will remember what I said about Colonel Rivera. He is an evil man."

She pushed his hands away. "Since he has been reaching for my legs under the table since he arrived, I did not imagine him a saint."

The *alcalde's* expression became wistful. "In any case, we have not had this meeting tonight. The horse will be returned, and I am innocent of any knowledge of this bizarre business."

"How typical of you to want it that way."

"Yes. I have no desire to become one of those, as you say, 'wrong people' the president shoots."

Like brides the world over, Elena had pledged to honor her husband, to accept his defects of character and to regard their union as blessed and everlasting in the eyes of heaven. Dutifully she tried to understand and favor him, but his irresolute nature and insatiable vanity led to frustrations that exhausted her patience and drained her sympathies. At the core of the matter lay the many conceits he held about himself. His manner persistently suggested that his immense inherited wealth was the fruit of personal merit and achievement. He had persuaded himself that he was an inspired leader, mistaking the flattery and fawning showered on him by an inexhaustible army of venal bureaucrats and social parasites for respect and adulation. Strangely enough, and most irritating of all for Elena, since he had never seen combat, was his weakness for military honors, many of which he had been awarded on the most specious grounds. It was a source of profound embarrassment for her, particularly in the presence of subordinates who with redoubtable courage had earned those very decorations on the field of battle.

That her husband was an object of secret ridicule and contempt was distressful enough, but there was another side to their marriage that she had to hide from the world, for in its own way it was more disturbing yet.

Ramón, if nothing else, was an experienced lover. He had taken her virginity with amazing facility, and she could feel his skill at physically exciting her. But she was shocked at his lovemaking. Openly innocent and feeling that married she could refuse him nothing, she lay stunned as he manipulated and ravaged her body, tasting and exploring all her orifices in sessions that seemed each more exhausting than the last. She began to rise from their bouts of lovemaking with her nerves frayed and her mind weirdly preoccupied with the obscene passions of this sensuously driven man with whom she shared a bed. Was this marriage? Thoughts of her prim, religious mother and other staid and dignified women went through her head. Could this really be marriage? First doubts and then fears began to assail her, for with all of Ramón's carnal abuse of her young, yielding body she heard no words of love. In fact, he rarely spoke as he embraced her or moved his mouth over her body. She began to feel that he was not making love to her as much as satiating some dark, bottomless lust.

The passage of days found her becoming visibly morbid and depressed, and Doña Carlota quietly read the desperation in Elena's face, which on some mornings was as drawn and bloodless as one racked with fever. "You should have a room of your own," said Carlota casually, after inspecting a row of freshly polished silver.

"I should have what?" said Elena, unable to imagine what had prompted such a remark.

"Your own room," repeated Carlota evenly. "You need some rest."

For a moment Elena looked confused.

"Ramón is a man of peculiar tastes," continued Carlota, her bitter tone suddenly riveting Elena's attention. "You might as well know that a long string of acrobatic whores have taught him how to indulge them. I was hoping marriage would restore him to decency, to normalcy."

Elena began to blush. "Carlota, what in heaven are you saying?"

"Elena, listen to me. You look terrible. Ramón may be your husband, but he is neither a caring nor a sensitive man. He is too weak and selfish to be concerned about you. Already you look ill. You must start demanding some respect, as would any wife. If he doesn't give it, order him out of your bed."

"Order him out of my bed? Carlota, he would be furious. He would disclaim the marriage." Elena's shoulders rose and then slumped at the hopelessness of the thought.

"No, he will be frightened."

"Frightened?"

"Yes, and then he will start drinking. That will give you some peace."

"Drinking?"

"Yes, he always drinks when he's afraid."

Elena put her hands on her head, then drew them over her face. She felt herself getting frantic. "Carlota, this is terrible."

"Yes, it is. And I can only hope you'll do as I say before it gets worse."

Carlota's advice was too alarming to follow that evening, but it spawned a seed of resistance in Elena. She began to deal with Ramón rather than endure him. Sadly but slowly, she accepted the fact that he was incapable of the slowly maturing love she had hoped for. Resignedly she overcame her revulsion to his flagrant habits and allowed him to excite her to climax once during the night, mutely drawing some passing comfort from this physical release. But it was not a solution that could sustain itself. So mechanical was he that the fragile mystery and excitement of sex was soon spoiled and she found herself more and more repelled by his touch. Then one night, as he sucked on her breasts as he frequently did until his body arched in orgasmic spasms, she suddenly no longer saw him as a man sensually enjoying a woman's flesh but as an infant desperately needing the warmth and security it itself lacked. For the first time she saw him as weak and isolated with his perversions; for the first time she sensed she was stronger emotionally than he. Abruptly she pressed him away and, rising on one arm, stared at him in the darkness. "That is enough, Ramón," she said quietly. "It's time we thought of sleep." In the ensuing silence she sensed his hand nearing her thigh. She reached down and thrust it away. "If I can't sleep here, I shall find another bed."

He shrunk back, his face turning into the pillow. Though neither of them slept that night, not another word passed between them. Carlota was right. Whatever transpired in that strange mind of his, Elena could feel that Ramón in some veiled way was afraid. Taking heart from this experience and beginning to feel a new hold on life, the next day she asked Carlota to prepare a separate bedroom. Secretly she was amazed at Carlota's powers of prophecy, for even before nightfall Ramón, becoming aware of this daring decision, called for some Madeira with white rum and was fast getting drunk.

He was drunk again tonight, but this time his fear was rising from another source. Slurring his words, he complained about Colonel Rivera, and threatened to have him shot. But Elena was used to these empty boasts. Rivera struck her as far too imperious and sure of himself to be worried about Ramón. There was bad trouble starting up there, though she could not concern herself about it this evening. Somewhere Seth Redmond was lying wounded and facing certain death if he was discovered. How she could save him she did not know, but her senses were staying tightly and sharply turned to Carlota's return.

So tense and anxious was she that she did not register her father's tall, rain-soaked figure standing at the wide paneled doors and studying his drunken son-in-law from under his brows, his face tightening just perceptibly.

Ramón was about to rise and visit the sideboard where his rum bottle stood uncorked when he saw Colonel López and spoke first. "Well, Armonte, have you caught that spy yet?"

The colonel moved a few steps further into the room. He was carrying his military hat under his arm. "We are not searching for a spy, Excellency. Our dispatch mentioned only a wounded officer." Elena noticed her father's wry enunciation of the word "Excellency." It was clear he was irritated at finding D'Valya intoxicated.

"Same thing," snapped D'Valya. "Why are you here?"

"There is a problem," said López evenly.

"Always it seems there is a problem," ranted Ramón as he finally made his way to the sideboard. "Where would this command be without me?"

Colonel López looked at his daughter to signal her away from an embarrassing scene, but Elena quickly sensed she might hear something here that would be invaluable in her search for Seth. She looked down at the many-colored rings on her fingers and ignored his cue.

"So what is this problem?" rasped Ramón, drink in hand, settling on the couch again.

López cleared his throat. "It is Colonel Rivera, Your Excellency. He is demanding to take command of the search."

"Demanding?"

"Yes, Excellency. I have advised him that these are my men, members of the Tamaulipas Guard, and I alone command."

D'Valya looked at him steadily for a moment, then slowly put his drink down. Whatever thoughts López' words prompted in his mind, they appeared to have a sobering effect. "We can assume he has not found this response agreeable or you would not be here."

"That is correct, General."

"And about the spy?"

"An informer has advised us that there is a suspicious house on the north bank. We plan to seize it before dawn."

Looking troubled, D'Valya got up and, mumbling to himself, began to pace the floor. Elena could see that the rum had not completely canceled out his fear. That very day he had received a secret message from the capital. She suspected it was why he had started drinking that night. He stopped and faced López. "Is Rivera coming here?"

"I'm sure he's already on his way."

"Damn," said Ramón, retrieving his drink. "Well, it's clear what he's after." He raised and emptied his glass. "Armonte, you must not wait until dawn. Seize that house tonight, find that spy and execute him! Rivera must not be allowed to take credit for capturing him."

"Rivera is helpless without troops, Excellency."

The two men stared at each other, a long gnawing issue suddenly being contested. The eyes of both struggled for control, but it was D'Valya's that fell first. "It would be safest to allow him at least a squad of men," said Ramón gravely.

"I firmly object, Your Excellency."

"You are not the one who will be called to account if this spy escapes. Rivera is already reporting us as flagrantly incompetent. He is slyly but cleverly putting a bad face on matters here. He has the president's ear, and I do not want my lands confiscated or myself sent to Mexico City in chains."

"Excellency, can't you see giving in to this request today will lead to bigger and more serious ones tomorrow whether this *tejano* is caught or not?"

D'Valya went back to the sideboard and poured himself another measure of rum. "Colonel, you are wasting time. Go. Catch this *tejano* spy. Shoot him! We don't want him talking about how long he has hidden in Laredo under our noses. If you discover who has been assisting him, have them executed at once."

"Excellency, we'll find out nothing if we shoot everyone who has knowledge of this crime," replied the colonel bitterly.

"I do not wish to know anything about it except that those who connived at it are dead. Armonte, please do not impose on our relationship. You are dismissed!"

Between the house and the stable a small shelter had been built for grooms holding horses being brought up to the main entrance. There in the darkness Elena and Carlota stood close together, protected from the driving rain now beating like a drumroll on the slate roof. Carlota's eyes were cold with warning as she shook her head slowly from side to side. "Elena, this is madness. You cannot go through the village without being recognized. It is terribly dangerous. There are soldiers everywhere."

Elena's hands rose to grip Carlota's cloak. "Carlota, did you find him?"

"Yes," replied Carlota reluctantly. "He's with the Castabellas, but heaven knows where they're hiding him." Elena's eyes lit up. She knew the Castabellas. She had heard of the Italian nobleman who had come to Mexico in the previous century, married the daughter of a rich merchant and begun a family of traders well known in northern Mexico.

"Good," said Elena. "I will go to them. I know the granddaughter Rosita. We danced together in the pageants when we were little girls."

Carlota took her firmly by the hands. "Elena, stop! Think for a moment. The Castabellas will die of fright when they see you. You are the wife of a general and the daughter of a colonel. They know soldiers are searching the village. Use your head, girl. If they have that poor man, they can't dare let you know."

"I must try," Elena said huskily. "Ramón has ordered him to be killed as soon as he is found. I cannot just stand here pretending I'm helpless and let him die."

"You can do little else," said Carlota, drawing her damp cloak closer. "Elena, you must stop intriguing against your own family. Don't be so discouraged. The Castabellas are not fools, perhaps they will save him yet. By now they will have his horse."

"His horse?"

"Yes, it has been returned to him. My guess is that he will be gone by morning."

"That will be too late!" cried Elena, and only Carlota's hand over her mouth kept her from crying out more. Beyond, a horseman had galloped up to the entrance and dismounted swiftly. Seemingly ignoring the rain, he carried himself with an air of importance, and as he passed the huge lanterns hanging over the doorway they could see it was Colonel Rivera.

The two women held to each other and whispered for a few minutes more, then left the shelter and entered the house by a side door. Flying up the back stairs, they slipped into Carlota's room and, as Elena stripped off her clothes, Carlota began pulling out the pants and shirts she often wore when going out riding alone. She wanted to stop Elena from leaving but had already concluded no amount of pleading was going to prevail. In her wisdom she knew something had arisen between Elena and this unknown man, and it was the thing in life that commanded the human heart far more potently than common sense.

In truth, Elena's riding into the rainy night on this dangerous mission was not at the outset the perilous risk it seemed. She was well mounted on a sleek, dark gelding, a wedding present from her father, and like all members of her class her horsemanship was superb. She had grown up in this country and knew it intimately; if apprehended, her identity alone would be protection enough. It was only as she approached the Castabellas' and drew nearer to Seth that the risks mounted.

Her arrival at the Castabellas' clearly proved that Carlota's powers of prophecy had not failed. The old woman looked at her with suppressed terror in her eyes. "Señora D'Valya, *Madre de dios*, what brings you here on such a night?"

"I've come to help," said Elena, ignoring formal greetings and embracing the old woman. Rosita and Nina appeared in the background, their hands clenched tightly before them as though in prayer.

"To help?" mumbled the old woman, her confusion curiously blunting her fear. "Help for what?"

"For the *tejano*," said Elena. "He must leave Laredo tonight. He must leave now!"

"A *tejano*?" breathed the old woman, her eyes betraying a fear of being trapped.

"Please," said Elena, moving past the grandmother and taking a step toward Rosita. "Rosita, we were children together, you must know me well enough to know I would not be here if I did not want to help. You must know this is a great risk for me."

Rosita stared at her. It was true they had been children together, but Elena López came from a military family whose politics had always been conservative and the governments they served often ruthless and dictatorial. The Castabellas had been linked in the past with more than one liberal movement and even an attempt at agrarian reform. Animosities and dark memories of past injustice and oppression died hard in Mexico. Rosita saw the sincerity in Elena's eyes, but she was still the wife of General D'Valya and to permit her to know what was now being viewed as treasonable activity seemed the height of folly.

"You must be mistaken, señora," said Rosita quietly. "We know of no such person."

"Please, you must believe me!" cried Elena. "He will be killed if he does not leave at once."

The old woman seemed to have gathered her wits. "How do you know this?" she asked, affecting more curiosity than concern.

"I have heard my husband and my father speaking. There is also a Colonel Rivera who is joining the search. They have learned of a house on the north bank, where they believe he is hiding. They are surrounding that whole area tonight."

Elena's mention of a house on the north bank registered on the faces of the three women. *"Jesucristo,"* said the old woman, crossing herself.

Elena realized that they were now beginning to believe her and continued pleading. "I'm told his horse has been returned. Tell me where it is and I'll get it to him. Please, there is no time to lose."

Rosita, pulling herself out of shock, suddenly seemed galvanized into life. "You know this man?" she asked quickly.

"Yes, I've met him."

The women looked at each other in the way females have of communicating to each other a possible conflict in their choice of men. Rosita was now caught up in some of Elena's urgency and pulled a dark heavy cloak about her. "Come, we will go together," she said brusquely. "You will never find this house in the dark. It is vacant. His horse is out back."

The heavy sound of cavalry mounts galloping together rose from the street beyond and then faded away. The search was being pressed and drawing nearer. Elena and Rosita, quenching all the lights in the hall, slipped out into the dark, rain-drenched night, leaving the old woman and Nina to light their candle before the image of Mary and the Christ Child, where generations of Castabellas now dead had knelt to pray.

Even with the rain, Seth could hear the horses coming up slowly to the rear of the shack. They were being led, and the muted sounds of Rosita's whisperings told him that in spite of his daylong doubts she had returned. He had gathered his few possessions together and shaved as Nina had warned, for he was on the verge of leaving himself and had half decided that when the downpour let up he would take his fate in his own hands and start out on foot. After the old woman's and Nina's words, and the mounting military sounds he heard emanating from the village, he knew that to remain in that isolated shack much longer was to court death.

The appearance of two women coming into the room made him think both sisters had come for him, but while Rosita rushed forward to kiss him quickly on the cheek, the other hung back, studying him in the dark.

"We must leave at once," said Rosita. "We have your horse, and here is an old sombrero. Wear it."

Seth took the hat and settled it onto his head. "Where are we going?" he asked, trying to make out the other figure in the room. A strange tension engulfed them in the darkness.

"Away from here," snapped Rosita. "This is Elena. She says you two are acquainted, but please . . . leave that till later. Now we must go, *pronto!*"

Confused, but trailing behind the women, Seth found Sam waiting outside. The powerful chestnut whinnied as he caught Seth's scent, and as he climbed into the saddle Seth marveled that the horse he had been mourning as lost forever was his again.

Rosita, turning her mount quickly, led the way. The women had already discussed the approaching risks, and Elena had convinced her that they should go west. "The soldiers will come over to this side at the lower ford," she said, "and work their way up. They always do." Elena had heard her father saying that bandits trying to escape always ran downriver, where there were many hiding places and busy ports along the gulf to swallow them up.

Elena and Rosita had crossed at the upper ford leading west, sure that the Mexicans were not likely to choose that route. They were also sure that darkness and rain would make the inconspicuous shack hard to find. Tragically they were to find they were wrong on both counts.

Colonel López led his contingent of cavalry across the lower ford. They swept up the north bank and headed almost directly for the abandoned shack. He had not told D'Valya he had immediately followed up the informer's report and had not only located the shack but had discovered that it belonged to the Castabellas. This was information he would use at the appropriate time. His aim now was to seize this *tejano* and execute him before Rivera had a chance to say he had assisted in his capture. As a soldier, he saw little point in shooting a man who might be valuable in other ways, but D'Valya clearly felt that as long as this man remained alive Rivera would find a way to use him against them.

So close did they come to snaring all three figures rushing away that had it not been raining so hard they would have seen them clearly and cut them off with ease as they came out onto the main trail. As it was, the colonel came into the shack only minutes behind them, knowing it had just been vacated. He sniffed the air and caught a vague scent that spoke of the perfumed presence of women. The rain had turned the ground around the shack into a spongy overcoating of mud, but the young officer assisting López was able to determine that two and probably three horses had just left and gone west. López swore to himself, quickly ordered his men to remount and led them off in pursuit.

◆ ◆ ◆

Colonel Rivera, a man well schooled in deception, had left General D'Valya with an order to the officer of the day for twenty-five men. He was leading them now in the direction in which he judged his only hope lay. His instincts told him that López had already discovered the spy's hideout and was heading there. He also knew that López was crossing over at the lower ford, the direction in which the *tejano* was most likely to escape. It was clear he was not going to play any part in capturing this spy if he followed López' tracks, for he suspected that once the *tejano* was taken he would not live to undergo any interrogations. He had just found General Ramón D'Valya scared and trying to drown his fears in drink. The general had good reason to be alarmed. Rivera smiled to himself. One more piece of evidence, and he would see that pompous fraud groveling for clemency before the presidential court. His own reward might well be a general's red insignia on his collar.

He knew his one chance was now the possibility that López had guessed wrong, that the fugitive would not go east but instead try to escape west or even north. Of the two, a wounded man would most likely choose west, for there were far more hiding places to hide and find food along the river than on the arid plains stretching toward the open wastes of Texas.

Across the river, he immediately divided his men to cover the several trails that ran along the bank, some reaching back as much as a mile or two from the river. His orders were to stop all travelers. None were to be released until he had personally questioned them. Those who did not stop were to be challenged once and then shot. Colonel Rivera's tone left little doubt that any breach in these orders that resulted in the spy's escape would be a bloody business to answer for.

It was Rosita who first saw the light up ahead. It was a lantern or a small torch that seemed to flicker about in the rain. It also started blinking, which made them rein up and stare at it in silence.

"What is it?" Elena's voice was tight with anxiety.

"I don't know," replied Rosita. "It shouldn't be there. No one lives on that side."

"It's a lantern," said Seth. "And it seems to be blinking because people are walking in front of it. I'm afraid it's a military barricade. We'd better turn back."

Elena was about to say something when all three became aware at once of the pound of horses' hooves behind them.

"Santa María!" gasped Rosita, suppressing a near scream. "They are right behind us! Come, we must try to get through." She whipped her horse forward, and Elena and Seth followed hard behind. They approached the light at full tilt, their horses' hooves throwing up clots of mud and wet stones. Figures began running out on the trail signaling for them to stop as shouts of *Quién vive?* began to ring out, but Rosita lashed her mount savagely forward, bending over its mane and urging it on.

They were past the light when the shots rang out. At first they seemed to have no effect, but even in the darkness that quickly enveloped them again Seth knew both Rosita and her horse had been hit. He pulled alongside and reached out to steady her in the saddle, but her horse was already beginning to shudder and stumble, turning sideways and reeling back a few steps before collapsing to the ground. By then with his remaining strength increased by desperation he pulled her over to Sam, but from her moans and the blood quickly smearing his hands he knew she was seriously hurt.

"We have to put her down somewhere," said Seth, knowing they could not stop there but realizing that Rosita, the woman who had risked her life for him, was now critically wounded.

"Follow me!" shouted Elena, ignoring the uproar rising behind them. "There's a place nearby. It's our only chance." Elena spurred the sleek gelding ahead, and the powerful Sam carrying Seth and Rosita came on steadily behind.

The place "nearby" was much farther than Seth had hoped, for he could tell from Rosita's breathing and her inability to hold on to him that she was losing consciousness and close to dying. When Elena finally pulled off the trail and onto a tree-lined path, Seth imagined he had entered an abandoned estate. He was not far from right. The estate was not abandoned, but the owners, relatives of the D'Valyas, were in the south and only an old caretaker who lived in a wooden shelter on the far side of the mansion was there. Elena, hoping the caretaker was too old and decrepit to be out in this weather, led Seth around to the stables and dismounted to help him carry Rosita in from the chilling rain and settle her on a bed of straw. They pulled open the cloak to find her dress drenched in blood. Undoing her dress, they discovered that the bullet had entered her side and exited under her breast. A feeling of helplessness gripped them in the darkness as they stripped pieces from her skirt and pressed the folds of cloth against her wounds. But it was no use. Rosita, weak from her appalling loss of blood, was slipping away. Other than the waxen damp of her skin, there was no warning, for death is never what it seems. Her pulse simply faded, sputtered faintly, then failed. Kneeling close, they saw her eyes open in the darkness as one hand came up to pull Seth's face down toward her. It was the girl's last gesture on earth, for as her hand slipped away again, in that dank dark stable, away from all the familiar settings of her life, she closed her eyes and entered the great silence men call death.

The world seemed to stop for a moment before Elena drew in her breath and cried, "My God, my God!" The white knuckles of her fist clamped tightly against her mouth. She did not feel the sudden sweep of tears run down her damp face. "What will we do?"

Seth, gently placing Rosita's arms at her sides, came slowly to his feet. It was not a moment he could meet with words, not right away. Finally he spoke, turning toward the weeping figure beside him. "For her we can do nothing, but, Elena, it's too dangerous for you to stay. You should never have come near me to begin with! You must be mad!"

Somehow the darkness made it easier for her to speak. "Seth, they're coming to kill you!"

"Yes, I know, it's me they're after. You have to leave before they come! They can't be far behind."

"If I leave now, you'll be caught for sure. It would be insane to try hiding around here."

"I'm going to get caught anyway," he said, looking down dismally. The brave girl lying dead at his feet had nursed him back from the brink of death, had thought they were going to share a love together, then had lost her short life trying to save him. There was nothing he could do about Rosita now, but he could mount up, ride away and remove the hazard of his presence from Elena, who was recklessly running the same deadly risk. He had decided to do just that when she stepped closer to him and grabbed him by the arm. "Listen," she hissed. Seth lifted his head and tilted it toward the road. At once he picked up the low rumble of many hooves coming up to the front of the estate. There was an unaccountable lull in the stomping for a moment or two, and he was sure the soldiers were spreading out to comb the estate, but then the thumping started again and, as they stood together barely breathing, they heard the heavy pounding moving away to finally die out further down the trail to the west.

Colonel López was a man tormented by a quandary. By some damnable luck Rivera had come across the upper ford and had almost captured the three fugitives he himself had flushed. The dead horse they had found on the trail meant two of the three sought were riding double, which gave his pursuit an advantage. But there were staggering, even ominous, implications surrounding the *tejano*'s incredible escape. Weighing them sobered and actually subdued his initial fury. The fugitive could not have survived these many months without important help. He surely could not have known he had to leave tonight and in this unlikely direction without receiving highly guarded information. The dead horse might be traced to the Castabellas, but their family members living in Laredo were an old grandmother and two young women, hardly likely suspects for this kind of subterfuge. Still, it was no secret they were a family of revolutionary tendencies, often at serious and even violent odds with corrupt or oppressive regimes ruling the country. But if they had undertaken such an exploit, how were they receiving their information and from whom?

Of all the unsettling bits and pieces of this puzzle swirling around Colonel López' mind, none kept emerging with more persistency than his first moments in the abandoned fugitive's shack. That faint waft of perfume had a vague familiarity he could not immediately place. Why it kept occurring to him he did not know, but somehow he could not put the evocative scent out of his mind.

López knew that when Rivera officially reported this incident his own lucky guess that the fugitive would escape to the west would be made to seem like calculated brilliance, while his and Ramón's efforts would be pictured as bumbling attempts by incompetent commanders.

Leaving Rivera behind, he led his men down the road, trying to reason where his quarry was heading. The rain made tracking in the dark an almost impossible task, but there were only a limited number of places reachable in a night's ride, particularly with a mount carrying two. Still, whatever the effort, it must be made, for there would be no salvation for either him or D'Valya if this man escaped.

◆ ◆ ◆

When it occurred to him he was not sure, but the human mind is a strange organ, with functions that escape detection yet subtly guide one's thoughts. López was trying to recall what lay along this trail. It had been months since he had followed it this far and then only to escort Elena on a visit to the D'Valya family before her marriage. They kept an estate here, a *hacienda* Ramón had promised would one day be hers. López knew that in this season it would be inhabited only by an ancient caretaker. How the thought of escorting Elena out here led to another, stranger thought he did not know but the memory of that thin fragrance in the shack was still working on his mind. Then suddenly an incredible suspicion touched the edge of his consciousness, so incredible he suppressed it hurriedly and turned his irritation to the slow pace at which they had been moving.

It was only after he had ordered his men to press forward at a gallop and they began to approach the estate that the reasoning behind this suspicion began to bore its way into his brain, reasoning that refused to be dismissed, reasoning that only grew in strength as he tried to deny it. Who could have known his plans? The familiar scent was beginning to find a place in the catalogue of his mind and the memory of Elena visiting this estate joined it to form a frightening possibility. So shaken was he at the dire picture that he almost forgot to order a halt as they came abreast of the estate. The junior officer, seeing his signal, gave the command but waited until the body of men had stopped before approaching the colonel and saluting. *"Sí, Coronel?"*

López realized that if his suspicions carried even a hint of reality they must never be known. A monstrous weight had gathered in his chest. His own daughter and Ramón's wife concealing and assisting an enemy officer, perhaps even a spy—treason at the very heart of a high military command! This was the stuff of which courts-martial and firing squads were made.

López returned the officer's salute. "You will follow this trail for another hour," he instructed the subordinate. "If the fugitives are not apprehended, return here. Post two men every few miles to watch for signs. The search will resume at dawn."

The young officer looked puzzled at the sudden shift in command, but López spoke quickly to dispel any momentary confusion. "I am going to question the caretaker of this estate. He once worked for me.

Perhaps he has seen or heard something. Pass me one of those lanterns." López' voice carried the need for urgency. "Remember, this fugitive must be taken at all costs."

The young officer saluted and, calling out a sharp command, led the troop off at a run, never noticing that the colonel, with some relief, was belatedly returning his salute.

Left alone, López entered the estate. He knew there was no point in arousing the caretaker. If his suspicions were correct, the old man was indoors avoiding the rain and probably deaf to what was transpiring around him. His instincts led him in the direction of the stables, and finding his horse was stepping on turf, he dismounted and lit his lantern. He then moved slowly between the stable and the house with the lantern tilted downward, watching tensely for fresh tracks. The steady drone of rain seemed to testify to the emptiness of the place, but López carefully made a complete circle of the stables and as he drew near his starting point he was suddenly rewarded. Coming from the darkness before him was the stamp of a hoof and the whinny of a horse. It had not come from his own mount, which he was holding by the bridle, but as he raised his lantern he could see the dim outline of two mounts hitched to the outer rail of the stable and now only a few yards away.

In other circumstances Colonel López would never have stood in the lamplight while searching the darkness for a desperate man wanted by the law, but his mind was captured by another fear that only paralyzed him more as he approached the horses and discovered that one was the sleek gray gelding he had given his daughter only a few months before at her marriage.

Seth and Elena huddled in the darkness and watched the lantern circling the stable. Elena hoped it was the caretaker, but something told her it was not. They had no gun. The derringer Elena normally carried when out by herself she had left with her wide skirts in Carlota's room. Their only hope was to escape detection. Seth, fearing whoever was carrying that lantern would circle the stables until their horses were found, wanted to make a run for it. But Elena whispered frantically that they could not leave Rosita's body here. It might lead to the death or imprisonment of her sister and grandmother. A moment later it was too late for any movement at all. The lantern was already approaching their mounts, and as it drew to within a few paces it stopped. Elena and Seth held their breaths as the lantern came on again, but now it was shining onto the horses and whoever was holding it was remaining deathly silent. For a second the lantern was raised up high as though the holder were glancing about quickly. Then it was lowered and put out. Seth, trying not to move, turned to Elena, who had given an almost imperceptible gasp. He did not know that, as the lantern came down past the holder's face, she had recognized her father.

Colonel López left the estate with dread gripping his heart. This plight was too chilling, too unbelievable for ready acceptance. The terrible possibilities arising from what he had just discovered froze his mind. His own daughter! Ramón's wife! His duty was to arrest her, shoot this *gringo* she was protecting and place her in custody to be tried for treason. If Elena were to be caught, nothing short of that would save him or Ramón. Rivera would use her blatant and undeniable guilt to destroy them. Adding to his distraction was the realization that if she were not caught and this *tejano* escaped, he and D'Valya would surely be charged with incompetence, perhaps collusion.

His first impulse was to go back and talk to his daughter, but that might be used later as evidence that he had been aware of her involvement in the plot. As it stood, no one knew of this but himself. He sat on his horse in the rain looking into the night, knowing he could hope to salvage his career and his future only by risking his daughter's reputation and perhaps even her life. But the thought of his beautiful, spirited child being subjected to the degradations of a Mexican prison, where ravaging and sexual abuse of female inmates was commonplace, soon clinched his decision. But immediately another quandary fell like a pall over his heart. Should he return to Ramón and warn him or follow his command and give Elena time to get safely away from this area and back to the sanctity of her home? His clear duty was to warn his superior, General D'Valya, but something caught in his mind and he stopped again to stare intensely into the night. He had long held strange feelings about this imperious, highborn son-in-law. He knew he could never bring himself to sacrifice his daughter for the sake of his career, but would Ramón be willing to sacrifice his wife? He sat for long moments looking into the darkness, listening to the light rain dripping from the leaves of

the foliage beyond. Finally his mouth tightened in a firm line of resolve, and gathering his reins he turned his mount abruptly and
spurred off at a gallop to join his command.

Elena knew that her father was making it possible for her to escape.
She could only imagine the dreadful repercussions this night could
hold for him, but her mind fought free of a threatening panic as she
grasped how much had to be done before dawn, and by her alone.
Pulling Seth with her, she ran out to the horses. "You must follow
me!" she cried hoarsely. "There is no time to explain."

Seth, still weak but aware he was fighting for his own life and
maybe hers as well, struggled to respond to the energy in her voice.
They mounted, galloped out of the estate and across the dark trail
and went hurtling through the night through rough country that kept
sloping downward, warning Seth that they were approaching the
river. It was still raining and visibility was only a few yards, but
Elena did not hesitate at the water's edge. She moved into the river
with Seth behind her, and after several minutes they had swum their
horses across midchannel. Emerging on the other side, Elena immediately turned west again and, after a long run, turned south into
what seemed a small village. It was close to midnight and the village
appeared to be deserted, but Elena pulled up to a small house behind
a cantina from which one light still showed. She dismounted and
tapped on the door. At first there was no response. She rapped
harder and kicked the door with the toe of her boot. "Pablo!" she
called. Now a bolt could be heard drawing back and the door creaked
open. A short, heavyset man with his hair standing erect and a misshapen face stepped out into the dim light. He took a moment to
examine his visitor. *"Jesucristo!* Señora D'Valya! What are you doing
here?"

"Bringing you a thousand pesos if you will help me."

"A thousand pesos!" Pablo looked at Seth apprehensively. "A thousand pesos. Señora, you want me to kill *el presidente?"*

"No, I want you to hide this man for a day or two."

"This man?" Pablo stared up at Seth in the near darkness. He
seemed to have only one eye and it narrowed slowly, but the sombrero
did not fool him. "A *gringo?"*

"Yes."

Pablo looked like a man trying to catch up to his own thoughts.

He turned and moved closer to Elena. "Señora, *por dios,* are you mad? This is the *tejano* the soldiers are searching for. What will the general say? Señora, *por gracia,* this is very dangerous business."

"That is why I am paying so much."

Pablo stroked his chin, and Seth could now see that one eye was completely shut with a scar crossing over it from forehead to cheek. The squat man shook his head and gripped his visible paunch. "Señora, you know I am very poor man with many troubles."

"You are filthy rich," Elena shot back, "and not one centavo is honestly earned." Seth was startled by her sudden commanding tone. It carried some new and unexpected strength.

"Señora, be reasonable. Your own father will shoot me if I am caught!"

"Then don't get caught!"

"Señora, for such a favor Pablo will need help. This help will not come from lighting candles in church."

"Twelve hundred pesos," said Elena with an air of finality.

Pablo thought for a moment. "*Muy bien,* but do not ask where he is . . . and señora, please remember, if you get caught Pablo cannot say this man found his way here by himself."

In less than an hour Elena was back in Laredo drawing up to the rear of the Castabella home. She found the old woman still up, her face pale and drawn from worry. The news of Rosita's death left her collapsed in a half faint from which she could not be revived until Nina, awakened by Elena's arrival, brought her a glass of strong wine. A nightmarish scene was about to break; Elena could feel the hate and resentment that was building up in the old woman as her senses returned. She herself could think of no fitting words of consolation, and she was helpless to do more than to plead with her to allow Nina and herself to go back and retrieve Rosita's body.

But the old woman thrust away Elena's arm and began to rage. "You and your wretched family, we do not need you to bring us our dead! *Madre de dios!* But for you Rosita would be alive and that miserable *tejano* before a firing squad. God will punish him for betraying her and you for abusing our good faith. Get out of this house! Go back to your colonels and generals. They are used to killing people. One day you and yours will pay for your sins. Remember that each night as you go to sleep. Remember well! For the Castabellas will never forget!"

With young Nina's help, Elena backed out the rear door to avoid being struck by the hysterical woman, but the sound of galloping hooves nearby warned her to get away from the town center and work her way along the back roads until she could make a break for home. It was beginning to feel like the last night of her life.

After another glass of wine the old woman sank to the floor and cried in the bitter realization of how her life had been destroyed within a few months. Her husband had been killed, and now her beautiful granddaughter was gone. Nina, trying to calm her, was starting to tremble with fear, for she was convinced her grandmother was deranged and perhaps turning dangerous. But the old woman was slowly regaining her faculties, slowly realizing that Rosita's body, if found in that stable, could bring tragedy and perhaps even death to this girl trying now to console her, this shy frightened Nina who was all she had left. A rising desperation slowly brought her to her knees and then to a nearby chair. Rubbing the tears from her face, she took Nina by the arms, her fingers gripping into the young girl's flesh. "Nina, you must go to Father Vincente, tell him he must come. Tell him the Castabellas need him. Go on foot and hide at the first sound of horses. God will protect you, child. Now please, go quickly!"

The turbulent Mexican government was well on its way to removing the rich and powerful church from its councils. Yet cardinals and bishops still lived like potentates and exercised an immense de facto political power. But the government, had it studied its own history, had no need to worry about the church's leadership, a conservative, even reactionary body dedicated to preserving its privileges. It was in the lowly ranks of the rural priesthood where revolutions were bred. It was in the minds of these rude, rustic but selfless servants of God who lived with the *campesinos* and *peones*, suffering their misery and exploitation, that violence against ruthless or indifferent regimes was ignited. Because of their calling they often carried their causes under the holy cross that gave the fighting its peculiarly bloody and merciless nature.

The Castabellas, being a wealthy but liberal family, had secretly supported many local attempts to defend the outcast *indios* against their own government. Laredo's smallest church, Saint Augustine's, which had several *indios* in its congregation, survived only through the family's munificence. Father Vincente, whom they had brought from the south where he had already fomented more trouble than was safe, was now the priest of Saint Augustine's. Though unprepossessing in appearance, he was an unusual man in many ways. Dedicated to God, but still a sharp judge of mankind, he had a self-educated mind that easily made him the greatest scholar in unschooled Laredo. His knowledge of history was prodigious, but like many men with a mission, he pretended to only a modest mentality. In truth he was the most dangerous type a government plagued with instability could find among its masses, a man who had a goal greater than himself and who had learned that all human power structures were temporary.

Nina found him asleep, but he was up and wide awake before she had finished her message. He dressed quickly, and they left his poor quarters and made their way swiftly through the darkened streets to the Castabellas'. Here he listened to the old woman, knelt beside her to pray and then advised her to trust in God, who in his omniscience knew where lay the greater good.

Turning businesslike and borrowing a Castabella horse, he was soon off to a low-lying shed by the river. Here, after a huddled conversation with two figures in the dark, he left with a tall, spare man who carried on his mount a blanket and several pieces of rope. Father Vincente did not need to be told where the spare D'Valya estate was, for he had studied that territory as only a man planning a bitter struggle for control of the whole border area could.

They took Rosita's body back to the church and concealed it in the basement. She would have a secret but holy funeral mass, perhaps even be buried in the sanctified walls of the church itself, but even with this Father Vincente was not satisfied. The following morning he called on the Castabellas and found the old woman in bed stricken with grief, but he took time to question Nina closely and learned for the first time how the Castabellas had befriended the wounded *tejano* and paid a terrible price for their charity. It bothered him that they had not come to him in the beginning. Unquestionably it had cost Rosita her life.

Many people, seeing only an unimpressive priest in a shabby cassock going by, would have been more than surprised at Father Vincente's world. It included a secret organization that he rarely used, saving it for more critical purposes. It was an organization that looked upon violence, including assassinations, as an option in the service of God. The motives and even the structure of this organization were known to only a very few, but in one of their rare secret meetings the name of the informer who had betrayed the location of the fugitive to the local military came up, and in consequence some startled fishermen found his body floating in the river the following day.

For the next two days Seth lay in one of the three cubicles beneath the cantina where Pablo's prostitutes took their patrons. He was well fed and given dry clothes, but each day, starting at noon, the noise was incessant. Singing, dancing, brawling and the noises of fornication came through the walls of the cubicle, which were thin as stage scenery. The clamor of squeals and clicking heels lasted till midnight.

After closing time on the third night he was grateful to be moved to a small farmhouse near the river. The farm, he learned, was owned by Pablo but worked by a nephew and his sickly wife. The couple spoke no English and seemed anxious to avoid him. This suited him fine. Since Rosita's death he had been suffering a terrible depression and intermittent headaches assailed him. The following day he heard horses coming into the yard, and for a moment he wondered angrily why Pablo had not left him a gun. But the visitors proved to be Pablo himself along with Elena and another attractive but very troubled-looking woman.

"There," said Pablo, turning to Elena as the three of them crowded into the small bedroom Seth had been confined to. "Now you must pay Pablo. He is very, very poor and in great debt because of many dangerous things he does for you."

Elena looked at him skeptically but handed him a small bag of coins. "Remember," said Elena's strangely concerned companion, fixing Pablo with a withering stare of contempt, "should anyone hear about these 'troubles,' the Sierra Madre will not be big enough to hide you."

"*Por cierto*, señora, but there is no need to worry. Pablo is an honest man."

"Ha!" replied the woman acidly. "And Satan was an altar boy."

Pablo pocketed his purse of coins and made a hurried departure. Elena and her companion, who was introduced as Carlota D'Valya, sat down and looked at Seth earnestly. "How do you feel?" asked Elena.

"I'm all right," said Seth. "Just these damn headaches . . . But I have to get out of here! I've got to get home!"

"You are going home," said Elena. "I've sent a message to Julio. He is sending Ricardo to take you. In the meantime you must rest."

"I don't need rest, and believe me I damn well don't need Ricardo. If you'll give me my horse I can leave tonight."

Elena looked at him firmly. He was aware that something had changed in her. She was no longer the soft, love-struck girl he had met in San Antonio. There was a new, determined streak in her manner and a fresh, almost impaling strength in her eyes. "There will be no horse for you until it's safe to go," she said firmly. "Great sacrifices have been made to save you. Do not let your stubbornness add to them."

Seth had never been spoken to by a woman quite like that before. The fire in her voice and eyes was arresting, even beautiful. "Didn't mean to be ungrateful," he said, sounding like a small boy just chastised. "Reckon I can wait till you figure it's fittin'."

Carlota said, "Come, Elena, we should go now. You two can talk later."

"All right," said Elena, getting up. Then, to Seth, "My father and husband have been ordered to Mexico City. There could be serious trouble. At the moment no one knows, but the soldiers think you have escaped and they are no longer looking for you. Still, that's no reason to take silly chances. I will be back tomorrow."

"Bring me a gun," said Seth impulsively.

"A gun will only make you feel brave. Bravery is the most treacherous fantasy of fools. If Pablo betrayed you I might have killed him, but I would not have considered it bravery. Seth, sometimes it takes courage just to live." Conviction etched lines of fearlessness in her face and he sensed that his own strength, so forcefully conveyed by his complete lack of pretense, had just been equaled.

Carlota, already exiting the room, threw him a knowing glance. "This is armed border country, *amigo*. Rivera has put an attractive price on your head. Guns will hardly get you home from here, but your brain might—use it!"

◆ ◆ ◆

The next few days Seth would remember with more troubling emotions and vague, unsettling regrets than any he had spent in his long captivity. He had time to think about his life, time to think of Isabelle's pale, grieving face and of Jason, who was surely growing into a sturdy little boy. The sights and smells of his distant ranch were becoming real again, along with the voices of Brandy and Inez and even Rick. He wondered where the Rangers were now and why they had left him in this dangerous fix. He could only conclude they had given him up for dead, which, considering his long, helpless ordeal, made sense. But he could not really think about his earlier life without remembering Isabelle's rape and the child of that defilement. Certainly by now the child had been swept from their lives.

But something more was bothering him, something deep and irrational. That child was an alien that had suckled at Isabelle's breast, it had risen in her womb and its heritage could never be denied. That it was not her fault didn't help. He knew that life was merciless, that its senseless batterings could no more be avoided than the elements that tormented the seas and wore the mountains down. Still it rankled, gnawed.

Thankfully Elena, appearing each day in that small bedroom, succeeded in taking him out of himself. Proud and spirited, she would appear before him, reminding him somehow of the wild Texas frontier that a man found dangerous but was drawn to. Elena knew that he was going home to his wife and made no attempt to attract him, but it was not something she could control. She was too distracted to grasp that it wasn't her beauty that was finally arousing him. Certainly there was no way she could have known that it was something in her eyes, in her serene command of his still-dangerous plight, that mystified and enthralled him. She never dreamed that at night, when casting about his bed in search of sleep, he had visions of her still in the room, her radiant spirit infusing her flesh with an iridescence like the edge of fire.

Still, with the passage of days, which soon became a week that saw his strength return, Elena began to sense his desire. As she did, her own secret longing for him quietly returned. At first it confused her. Was he only lonely? Was he finally, after his long separation from a wife he had often mentioned, in need of affection? Was he turning to her in the aftermath of a devastating illness to reaffirm his manhood?

She knew that when he left she might never see him again. She would return to the barren, humiliating role of Señora D'Valya, wife of a lascivious fraud.

But something else was happening. Nature and its generative forces are never truly dormant. When pitted against a mutual danger, a man and woman often find a secret world springing to life between them, a world that suddenly has its own tides of emotion, its own seasons of joy and sadness. Because of the perils they had endured together, Seth and Elena had come to know each other well, their glances now just missing an air of intimacy, their physical closeness increasingly impossible to ignore. They awoke to this realization with a shock, for they had assumed that the constant danger would inhibit all desire, forgetting that the imminence of death is the greatest aphrodisiac of all.

In truth it happened only because Elena was in love. From the beginning she did not resist. He pulled her gently to the bed and undid her blouse. As he began to feel the heat of her bosom and the firming of her nipples, she threw herself into his kisses. If Seth's long period of celibacy increased his ardor, Elena's brief subjection to Ramón's lust had taught her about erotic love. She knew how to excite the male body by using her hands and her own body to return his fire. They made love again and again, bringing each other to trembling heights from which they descended with wild sighs, marking the paroxysms that collapsed them into each other's arms, ready for love again.

Seth was stunned into silence by the wave of passion that engulfed them. Elena's body was smooth and scented and there was a fullness in her breasts and thighs that kept him desiring more. He found a lure in her embrace that no amount of possessing her could exhaust.

Elena was discovering that this, after all, was the only man she had ever loved, this strange, resolute and moody man who belonged to someone else and was going away. Again and again she used the softness of her lips and her yielding body to make them one, deeply aware that the memory of this moment might be her only reward.

Several hours went by before they sank back into the druglike sleep of sexual exhaustion. Only the light footsteps of the couple in the kitchen made them aware that it was growing dark and Elena had yet to make the dangerous trip home. Later, looking back, it seemed best they had parted in the gloom behind that small farmhouse. She kissed him before saying, "I am sending Ricardo for you tonight. Please be ready. Please go with him and do as he says." A terrible surf of emotion roiled about in his mind, and he could not think of anything to say. She spared him by placing a hand over his mouth, knowing in her feminine wisdom that there was nothing he could say. "Now we will all go with God," she whispered and, slipping up onto her gray gelding, was suddenly gone.

Part Four

DRUMBEATS
on the
WIND

April 1846

18

On December 29, 1845, the Republic of Texas was annexed by the United States of America. After a decade of indecision, Sam Houston's dream had become a reality. But the sprawling frontier state, born in conflict and surviving a decade of conflict, remained a battleground, for it was now the van of an expanding and aggressive nation.

If these were historic times, they made little difference to young Jason Redmond, who was anxiously looking for Brandy. The little wagon that Todd Bonham had built for him was not living up to its promise on the short run down the knoll. The run needed to be extended, and Brandy was the man who solved most of Jason's problems. When he first had started to play around the ranch, he would climb the knoll as far as his sturdy little five-year-old legs would propel him, then scamper down. But that had led to a series of bruises and scratches, for the knoll was covered with brush and jutting rocks. Brandy finally cleared and raked smooth a twenty-foot stretch that he could run down safely and when it was wet sit on a barrel top and slide down. Now Jason wanted the run extended so he could enjoy riding his new wagon with a spurt of speed downhill.

Earlier projects had taught Jason that Brandy was a hard man to recruit when he was as busy as he was today. But he had the wits to suborn to his cause little Teresa, for whom he had, in the way of children, invented the name "Taska." Soon the name had stuck. Now the fetching, impish little girl who spirited behind the boys running through the spreading stables of the Redmond ranch was known only as Taska. Jason's younger half brother, Tate, an energetic but quiet, almost pensive boy, was much darker and shorter than he, but Tate patiently followed Jason everywhere, never challenging his leadership. Handsome Jason, blond and blue-eyed as Apollo, was a born explorer and mischief maker. Bright and enterprising, he had already hit upon the surest way to get Brandy to work on his endless projects. The secret was to have little Taska with her big dark eyes and pouty mouth present all his petitions.

As usual, the magic worked. Brandy laughed warmly at his little daughter, looking up and smiling at the way these children got around him, chuckling as he said, "Quick as Ah finish wid dis hay load we gwine to give dat run some study."

Later, when Isabelle saw him up on the knoll, she decided she would have to make sure he didn't make the run too high. She wondered if that wagon with its wooden wheels was safe.

It had been a strange day. Isaac Sawyer had come unexpectedly that morning, bringing word of the annexation. Predictably, for those beyond the settled areas, it caused little excitement, even though old Sawyer said that American troops were already crossing east Texas to reach the Rio Grande. Isabelle made him some coffee and sat down to hear him complain about his son Andy wanting to marry "mad" Carrie MacFee.

In the Pecos country the Indians had been quiet for a spell, but reports from the upper Colorado and Brazos warned that the menace was far from over. War parties traveling to and from Mexico were still being spotted with their captives along the trace. With news of the annexation, many Texans sought comfort in the fact that the United States army was now responsible for peace along the border. The Comanches and Kiowas, they told each other, would soon be subdued and removed from Texas soil. It was only one of many illusions about annexation that the coming seasons would unmercifully shatter.

When Seth had come back from Laredo nearly four years earlier, he was like a man coming back from an alien and illicit life. He felt strangely chastened and burdened by some need to reconcile himself to the world he had left behind. Though his tryst with Elena had seemed compelling and inevitable, as he drew near his ranch the memory of their passion clashed more and more painfully with his loyalty to Isabelle, and even to Jason. It was not simply the act but the feelings behind it that measured the depth of his transgression. He knew now that Elena was not a passing fancy; her memory was too indelible, she was too often astir in his thoughts. Seth, though depressed and confused, had never taken his commitment to marriage lightly, and he could not go on pretending his involvement with Elena hadn't happened. It was not in him to assume innocence to conceal guilt. To remain Seth, the man who lived without pretense, he would have to find a way to tell Isabelle.

This he had promised himself he would do. He intended to honor this commitment to himself just as he would honor his commitment to his wife. A man was only what the truth made him, it was nothing but vanity or arrogance to think he was more. But he had reckoned without knowing about Tate. The abrupt sight of that child turned a dark lingering premonition into brutal fact. At first, seeing the small squirming baby in Isabelle's arms, he could say nothing. He was shaken and only distantly aware that she was talking to him, pleading with him to weigh the harsh alternatives she found she was not equal to, calling upon his Christian conscience to understand what she had felt compelled to do. He simply stared at her, his feelings thrown into such a turmoil that he could only press her away as a sign that he was unable to respond until he had a chance to resolve the emotions that were still welling up in him, still formless but growing bitter as they gained meaning. It ended in a stunned retreat. Seth went down to the creek bed and stared mutely at the sparkling water leaping over the smooth blue-and-coral-streaked stones. Isabelle, her bottom lip clenched between her teeth and equally mute, watched him from the door.

They lived through a long, heart-wrenching week, passing each other in silence, waiting for time to deliver them from an estrangement whose emotional snarl neither could unravel. Isabelle kept praying that he would resign himself to Tate's presence, but Seth could not dissolve the shock of knowing she had accepted the dangerous threat to their love that this half-breed child presented. Not only had she accepted it, she had, incredibly, expected him, after his many warnings, his many pleadings, to do the same.

A torturous month crawled by, and a semblance of life began to resume around a shadowy understanding, a sterile truce, a pretense to normalcy that concealed a vacuum at its middle. Seth never did confess to his intimacy with Elena. He went back to ranching and struggling with the land, taking what solace he could from his memories of Elena's embrace, settling for the knowledge that if Isabelle could not be punished she could be at least be denied what she had denied him, a love for which all else was willingly sacrificed.

Throughout its brief life the Indian policy in the Lone Star Republic had vacillated between peace campaigns and extermination. On balance the efforts at extermination brought more peace than did the sham treaties that neither side could or even intended to honor. Texans could not be kept from moving into Comanche territory, and Comanches, following their long tradition of exterminating their enemies, could not be kept from applying this historically successful solution to these new intruders. But other events entered the scales and affected the struggle.

Blood Hawk had returned to his camp some years before, his mind still filled with his great medicine dream. A day's travel from his village, he began to sing as he rode, making up powerful chants to the spirit helpers that had sent him his dream. Had he not been moving with typical Comanche arrogance deep in his own country and had he not been singing, he would not have drawn the attention of a large Osage war party that was stalking the river basin in search of a Comanche village. By sundown he had led them to his camp, not knowing he had brought death to many of those who greeted him with the customary salute and listened with indifference to his relating of Red Knife's wretched end.

At dawn the black-and-yellow faces of Osage warriors were screaming above the slaughter of whole families they caught asleep and unarmed in their lodges. Furious hand-to-hand fighting broke out in the camp center, and Black Wolf went down under an Osage war club. When the Osage finally withdrew, their belts were heavy with bloody Comanche scalps.

Hurrying in from the brush and outlying tipis, the remaining warriors came together. Before counting their dead they hurriedly sent for help and started a pursuit. Scouts were directed to discover the direction in which the Osage had fled. They were expert trackers and soon found Osage hoofprints heading east at a breakneck pace, but they also found the war party's tracks as they had approached the village. It was not long before they came across Blood Hawk's familiar prints and knew he had led the enemy to their camp.

When the scouts returned, the village was filled with wailing and screeching women, slashing their arms and breasts in mourning. Scalpless bodies of dead Comanches were everywhere being prepared for burial, their horses taken up to be sacrificed at their bier. The next day the warriors gathered to decide on a new chief. Blue Buffalo Hump, a powerful orator, was given the title that would endure as long as did his good fortune, but it would not follow him into adversity. There were no unsuccessful chiefs. But now warriors were taking the floor, enraged at Blood Hawk's stupidity in leading the enemy to their door. That the crafty Osage might well have found the poorly guarded camp on their own did not matter. Their great losses had to be avenged. The Osage were gone, but Blood Hawk was still here walking freely about the camp, passing the empty lodges of relatives hideously slain. His insanity could no longer protect him. He was dragged before the council and accused of harboring evil spirits.

Insane or not, Blood Hawk was frightened, but he had been forewarned by his dream and believed he would live and one day be a chief. He took courage in the face of drawn knives and raised tomahawks and shouted, "I have had a great medicine dream, hear me speak! You wish to blame me for the coming of the Osage. You will try to kill me or drive me away, but if you do a great badness will come upon you and you will suffer much. One day you will know you were wrong and come to seek Blood Hawk's strong medicine. One day you will come to make me a chief."

Many braves scoffed openly, even vulgarly, at his words, one answering, "Did you betray Red Knife to his enemies too?"

"Your spirits are evil, they bring bad feelings to the Comanches," said an old man who had been wounded in the fight.

"Put him to the fire. We will see how strong these spirits he speaks of are," cried a brave whose young wife had been raped and killed by the Osage.

Having nowhere to turn, Blood Hawk held fast to his dream. "Remember!" he shouted. "Great misery will come to this village, your eyes will see only shadows. Powerful spirits have spoken! Blood Hawk will say no more."

Cries for his death were increasing, but Blue Buffalo Hump was a cautious man. Blood Hawk seemed too sure for one bluffing about his prophetic dream. Provoking these secret spirits by slaying him would surely be remembered later and regarded as foolhardy if they, indeed, encountered future trouble.

Late that night warriors, their faces painted black as though bringing death, took him to the edge of the village. There he was told to leave and, on penalty of forfeiting life, never to return. Blood Hawk, knowing he was being given a form of death, faced them stoically. "Remember my words," he said. "When the great spirit turns his face away from you, you will slash your hair and make offerings to me to return. Blood Hawk will wait."

An outcast shunned by neighboring bands, he began a long odyssey that took him north and west out on the Llano Estacado, to the Kwahadis, those strange, wild people who fiercely defended their vast, lonely hunting grounds, treasuring their solitude and showing little desire to mix with others of their own tongue. They did not welcome him but, finding him often demented, tolerated his presence at the fringes of their camps. He was content to rest there, content to sleep in a thin blanket, content to eat scraps. His only worthwhile possession—for his gun had been taken as part of his punishment by his people—was his bear-claw necklace. He occasionally painted his face and chest and wore his necklace, wandering off by himself to look at his reflection in the smooth surface of a stream, remarking to the gaunt boulders about him over and over again, "There is a chief! Oh, yes, you who must die because you will not hear. There is a great chief!"

Late the following spring Blue Buffalo Hump's brother led a war party along the Cimarron. Their scout discovered a wagon halted by a small creek. There was only one man in sight, sitting by the water, with his head down. The war party soon had him surrounded and as they closed in he rose to face them. His attempt to reach his gun was only halfhearted, and the warrior who drove a lance into his heart noticed as he scalped him that the man's face was wet with tears. In the wagon they found a woman and two children, their lifeless bodies covered with quilts and blankets but their faces a mass of pustules, many of which had been scratched open. The stench in the wagon was overwhelming, but the warriors drove their hatchets into the silent heads and stripped the bodies, taking all their clothes and coverings. They found some food and gunpowder in the wagon, but none of the old furniture was of interest to them. The man's body was stripped and dragged into the wagon and a fire was started in the canvas top. Where he had been sitting they found a small bottle of whisky. Grabbing cups left by the dead, they poured it out and gulped it down with grunts of approval.

As the fire engulfed the wagon and burned itself out they made their way back to camp, waving four fresh scalps and jesting far too loudly for a war party stalking prey.

Not two weeks later the camp's three medicine men were being called to more and more tipis. Many children and squaws were running high fevers, kneeling over with crippling pain and weakened by nausea, some sinking into delirium. Throughout the night medicine drums and rattles sounded in vain, sweat baths and cold plunges left sufferers suddenly dead by the water's edge. Braves began watching the red spots that covered their children's and squaws' bodies appearing on their own arms and faces. The living were slowly seized by a paralyzing dread and found it more and more difficult to help the dying. The red spots that itched unmercifully kept rising, forming tiny, ugly blisters that poured forth pus when scratched open. The odor about the camp became unbearable as people lay dead in their own putrefaction. Two of the medicine men succumbed, one dying over his drum. Within a week whole families lay dead in their fetid tipis. The living could no longer muster strength to bury the dead, and panic struck the few still miraculously alive, most of whom ran off howling like rabid wolves, abandoning their village of corpses to the gathering vultures, coyotes and crawling vermin. Though this last desperate act of self-salvation brought on a scene of unimaginable horror, it saved the race. One or two fled to other bands and sometimes spread the lethal pox there, but this scattering of people kept more than one tribe from total oblivion.

A great badness had surely struck the people. Blood Hawk's prophecy would be remembered.

Prent Salinger watched his brother-in-law, Todd Bonham, coming into the yard. Todd was leading a horse carrying the carcass of a deer and a young pronghorn. He and his mount were caked with dried clay, for it was mid-April and the spring rains had left the open range a sea of mud. Prent liked Todd and was glad he and his favorite sister, Bessie, had married. The two ex-Rangers were truly kin. He had more trouble cottoning to shy Jed Michalrath, who had been courting his younger sister, Kate. Jed was pleasant enough, but he was a poor hand with a gun and his language a little too tame and refined for "rail talk" among the boys.

Todd had been hunting with Seth Redmond, whom everybody said seemed restless and uncommonly moody these days, but Prent was anxious to tell Todd what he had learned in San Antonio.

He watched as his brother-in-law carefully lowered the kill beside the porch, put the horses up in the stable and came inside. Todd smiled easily at Prent, his handsome face looking tired under its splotchy coat of mud. "Howdy, Prent, you're back, eh?"

"Sure am," answered Prent, motioning Todd to a chair as he brought the coffeepot from the stove. "I do believe we got us another war brewing."

Todd frowned. "A war?"

"Yep. Old Zack Taylor is down on the border right now and he's recruiting Rangers as scouts. Governor is asking for volunteers. President Polk wants this business with Mexico settled."

Todd rubbed his chin as his eyes reached beyond Prent to the room he shared with Bess and the new baby. "What you fixing to do?"

"Join up, of course. This is the United States army, Todd. We'll get paid."

Todd smiled. Texas was always broke, and rarely did it meet its promises to pay its military, but he had the feeling that Texans fought best when their only reason was defending their home.

Prent was watching him expectantly, tensely awaiting his answer. "Well, what about you?"

Todd hung silent for a moment. Like many men in west Texas, he had a spread of land but little else. There was no money yet in cattle, and large breeding stocks like the Redmonds' were needed to show a profit in horses. Families like his managed only with some subsistence farming and occasional jobs that required horsemanship or a knowledge of the land. In reality they were dirt poor, their women were overworked and their only future lay in land, land that demanded endless labor and continual protection from savages. The two things they had, for their life required them, was mastery of the horse and gun, skills of value only when conflicts had to be resolved. Todd shook his head. "I'll have to speak to Bess," he answered.

"Reckon you can do it today?"

"Reckon so."

◆ ◆ ◆

Isaac Sawyer showed up unexpectedly one morning with a man working for the quartermaster corps of the United States army, a clipped-tongue civilian contractor Isaac spotted wandering along the main trail and steered to the Redmond ranch. The man had a requisition order to purchase as many as sixty-five head of sound saddle stock to be delivered in three weeks to the new United States military installation setting up in Corpus Christi. Seth was amazed at the ease with which this huge deal was settled. He had no experience with civilian contractors handling taxpayers' money or how they swelled their fees. He had asked for a hundred and fifty dollars a horse only as a bargaining point, assuming as always when selling more than one head that some friendly haggling and a reasonable discount would take place. But the man accepted it with alacrity and threw in an extra two hundred and fifty dollars to pay for feed and herding costs till they arrived safely at Corpus Christi. "Remember, when you sign this contract, Mr. Redmond, you've got to deliver those horses as agreed," declared the grinning contractor as he pushed before Seth a long, heavy sheet of paper studded with stamps and containing several paragraphs of suspiciously fine print. Seth, now feeling some confusion, started studying the paper closely, but Isaac Sawyer, leaning over his shoulder and knowing something about bureaucracy, merely grunted and said, "That's just routine stuff, Seth. Best find out how they're planning to pay you."

The contractor answered the question with an eagerness that smelled of secret satisfaction at a profitable day. "I'll be making out a draft against the Treasury of the United States government for the full amount payable in Corpus Christi. It will be honored by any bank there."

Isaac nodded, and Seth signed.

Later, after the contractor had left, Sawyer explained his generosity by saying that the government's usual lack of horse sense permitted contractors to negotiate prices, at the same time agreeing that the more money they spent, the larger their fee.

Reactions around the stunned and excited ranch varied. "Ten thousand dollars!" gasped Isabelle. "Is the man crazy? Has he even looked at the horses? Are you sure he's honest?"

Isaac Sawyer smiled. "Isabelle, you got to learn something about doing business with governments. You're a United States citizen now, and you got to reckon it's your money that gent is spending. That's why he hands it out so freely. Fellows like him wouldn't know a sound horse if one could talk and told him so, and likely he doesn't care. If a dozen scrub ponies show up with that bunch at Corpus Christi, take it from me nothing will ever be said."

"That's disgraceful," said Isabelle, turning her troubled eyes to Seth. "Seth, you play fair with them. If we're going to be citizens of this country, when the children get to learning about patriotism and such I don't want to be looking the other way."

Isaac smiled again, but Isabelle fortunately didn't notice.

"Lordy, lordy, dat's sure a parcel of horses!" exclaimed Brandy, his eyes big in his head. "Be sure you gives 'em dem three devil ones Rick and I can't hardly break."

Seth appeared to listen to everyone, but his mind was already grappling with the problems he saw rising before him. Sixty-five head would seriously cut into his herd, but he had plenty of yearlings and all his brood mares were in foal. With this money he could buy more Thoroughbred stallions and bring in additional Arabian blood from east Texas. Old Sam Houston himself had been importing and raising high-quality horseflesh, and his famous stallion, Copper Bottom, was reported to have several handsome offspring that were for sale.

But getting that many head of spirited horses to Corpus Christi was a task that loomed larger every time he thought of it. He would have to cross notoriously lawless territory, and it would take several men to keep a remuda that large in check. Finally, after exhausting his mind for solutions, he decided he would have to call on his neighbors, not only for aid but—as when he had called on Isaac for counsel—as a sign that he was growing out of his quiet but stubbornly independent ways and sensibly turning to the most salutary tradition of the frontier.

Since their talk lasted until late in the evening, Seth asked Isaac to stay overnight and sent Rick to bring Todd and his brother, Prent, the following morning. It was late afternoon the following day before they showed up, and as it had turned raw with rain threatening, Seth was startled to see Bessie, her two babies and old Adam following them in the rig. As the visitors entered the house and found places before the welcome warmth of the fireplace, Isabelle sent Jason to fetch Inez and put on fresh coffee. Silently she reckoned that she would now have ten people and two babies to feed at dinner.

Bessie took time to hug Isabelle, and Isabelle spent minutes exclaiming over Bessie's babies before Todd, only poorly concealing some brooding concern, began to speak. It was clear that the Bonhams and the Salingers had brought their family discord to the Redmond hearth. "Seth, there's a war setting up with Mexico, and they're recruiting Rangers as scouts. It's good pay and Prent and I figure to join up, but Bessie here won't hear of it. A squatter fellow and his family were wiped out by Comanches a few days ago, and that has got her scared witless." He shifted uncomfortably. " 'Course, she could be right. I sure don't want nothing to happen to her or our little ones, but we need money badly. We've got nothing but debts, and I'm almost bound to go. We come over here to ask if Bessie, the children and old Adam here could stay with you folks while we're gone."

"There's no goddamn room here," growled old Adam, shifting around in his chair. Clearly he had been against the notion from the beginning.

"We didn't really expect you to say yes, knowing you've already got a houseful," said Bessie, hiding her embarrassment under her attempt to give Seth and Isabelle an easy way out. "It's just that I get frantic thinking of that poor man's wife and children."

Isabelle's pulse quickened for a moment at the thought of having Bessie with her, but old Adam was right. There simply wasn't room.

Seth, already planning to hire Todd and Prent to help him deliver the horses to Corpus Christi, suddenly realized that he himself would have to go along, which would leave Isabelle and Jason—his mind excluded Tate—with only Brandy to protect them. Rick, at the first sign of Indian trouble, would leave for the Salingers'.

A strange silence struck the group as Bessie and Todd, avoiding each other's glances, waited for Seth's response. But Prent, seeming the least stressed by his family's troubles, spoke first. "Rick told us about your big sale, Seth. Congratulations. Reckon you'll be shipping in some more blooded stock to breed. Damn if I wouldn't like to get me started breeding some slick horses."

"I don't have a sale, Prent, till I get sixty-five freshly broken head to Corpus Christi."

"Corpus Christi," repeated Prent, his hand going up thoughtfully to cover his chin. "That's where Taylor is mustering his troops, that's where Rangers are signing up. Seth, I could give you a hand takin' 'em down."

Seth rose and regarded him soberly. "Truth is, Prent, I was counting on you and Todd too. I didn't know Bessie would be getting so wrought up about these damned Comanches." He glanced at Bessie, suddenly realizing how his remark sounded, then tried to lighten it up by adding, "Still, can't say as I blame her."

"Nor can I," said Isabelle, looking at Bessie with a warmth that gave Bessie a twinge of hope. Joining her hands firmly before her, Isabelle took a deliberate step toward Seth. "Seth, I hope you're not fixing to go off and leave me and these children alone here again."

Seth turned about silently and moved to throw more wood on the fire. His tone when he spoke was touched with irritation. "Alone? Why alone? You've got Brandy and Rick."

"A man and a boy for a spread this size. Seth, don't talk nonsense. Sooner or later these murdering savages will be after our horses, and we'll be lucky if all they do is run them off."

Isaac Sawyer pushed his chair back to avoid looking like he was taking sides. " 'Fraid she's right," he muttered quietly.

The conversation labored on for most of the afternoon, each side knowing they needed the other, yet neither side seeing how both needs could be met. It was Isaac Sawyer, shunning a conversation he did not feel right sharing, who started roaming casually about the house and who after an hour or two rescued the situation. After quietly slipping outside and circling the house a few times, he came in and stood before the fireplace. From his expression they knew he had something to say, and Isaac was a man the neighbors were always prepared to listen to. They turned to him almost hopefully.

"You know, Seth," he began, "when we helped you build this here house there was only you and Isabelle and Jason. We didn't build no more than was needed, but this place isn't big enough to raise a family. I just been in Jason's room where you've got Tate now. It's so tight in there you got to stick your head out the window to spit. I've been measuring a few things. If you all give me a hand we could add two and a half fair-sized rooms to this house in a week."

There was a quiet moment before Seth took a few steps toward him, his face almost bordering on a smile. "You think we could, Isaac?"

"Sure we could. We'll use plenty of adobe to cut down the chance of fire. I'll bring my tools over in the morning. And let me tell you something else, if it's Indians you're worried about, I'm going to do something for you I've done for my own place. I'm going to bring some metal strips and build you a couple of gun ports."

The rising exclamations of approval were heard by Brandy down in the stable. He had just curried and fed the Salinger mare. He knew that Inez had been called to the house and figured she'd tell him what was happening when she returned. But at the sudden sound he made a prediction that time was to bear out: "Whatever dat ruckus be 'bout, I 'spect it mean mo' work for ole Brandy."

Perhaps because of the frantic activity taking place that week, the days flew by for Isabelle. She and Bessie prepared food, cleaned, tended the children and tried to keep old Adam from worrying about his own place, now lying vacant and unprotected. He was also bothered that young Kate had gone to stay with the Michalraths, even though Jed, the doctor's mild-mannered, even withdrawn son, was always overly shy and respectful toward the young girl, whom he wanted to marry. Secretly Adam was hoping that Kate, like Bessie, would find herself a man like Todd, one who could handle a gun and who never backed off from a fight. Jed struck him as a meek young stripling, permanently suffering from what he called "tenderfootitis."

With the deadline for Corpus Christi closing in, everybody worked from sunup to sundown. Isabelle and Bessie slept in the big bed, with Inez on the floor and Bessie's babies in the open drawers of their new oak bureau. Taska squeezed into the tiny room with the two boys, and their giggling was the last sound heard at night. Todd, Prent and Isaac slept in the hut, and Brandy moved to the stable to bunk below Rick, who was glad for a little company. Brandy, deciding that all this preparation surely meant Indian attacks, rose one day before dawn to dig what he called a "scoopway" between the house and the hut, a precaution that would allow Inez and little Taska to reach the house in case of an attack. Isaac Sawyer didn't find this project as funny as some of the others did, and he showed Brandy how to roof the shallow ditch to keep it from falling in. By crawling fast, Brandy, Inez and their frisky little daughter could reach the house in a little over a minute.

Isaac brought some pieces of lumber he had on hand, and Rick and Prent took a wagon over to their own spread and stripped an old outhouse and one wall of the new smokehouse to bring more. They got mud and rough sand for the adobe from the creek bed, and Isaac mixed it with plain straw and set it in hard wooden frames near low fires to harden. Isaac proved to be a talented builder, making do and improvising with success at every turn. When he installed the gun ports, the house began to resemble a small fort, but now there was room for both families. Todd and Prent made several trips in the wagon to bring over beds, chairs and a second table. But the job seemed endless. Bessie wanted her large cedar chest, and Adam wanted his gun rack. On his last trip Todd declared that there was no end to the things people wanted but they were going to have to make do with what they had, for Seth was itching to start the horses moving south.

The night before they left, Isabelle had trouble sleeping. Seth was leaving again, and her heart told her that his going this time was different from all the others. In the great while that he had been home, they had never again revived that close, binding relationship they once had had. It was now over three years since his return from Laredo, and in spite of her joy and relief on that oft-remembered day, she felt he had come back a stranger and in some elusive way remained one. At first she concluded that his wounds were affecting his mind and triggering his violent or restless moods, but after the first year something in the deep of her warned her it was more than that. She could not understand his refusal to discuss Tate. She had expected his anger, even his demands that another home be sought for the child. But he remained mute, as though something within him denied him the right to complain. When at last he made love to her again after many months, she knew that something was wrong. Something had happened during his long absence in Laredo, something he was hiding from her, and as she squirmed anxiously to return his embrace, her senses, now keyed to his every move, told her that that something was another woman.

Concealing her gnawing fear, she managed to keep herself soft and giving on those rare nights when he desired her, but even when her body, hungering for physical affection, rose to climax, the rapture she had known in the past was gone. There was no outlet for her troubled mind in words, and the mounting tension between them became more and more difficult to hide. Little things grew out of proportion. In one awkward moment of lovemaking he drew back from the two ugly ridges of scar tissue as though silently recalling their origin, and she could not avoid cringing internally. She was nearing exhaustion acting out the emotions each attempt at lovemaking demanded.

Finally, as dreadful as its anticipation came the night when her pretense to passion played out. Feigning physical arousal became impossible. She wanted to cry. A choking sensation overwhelmed her as she felt him go limp, heard his labored breathing die out, watched him shift off her body to stare up into the darkness for long moments before he turned away. She now knew only too well why he had kept silent about Tate, why he seemed lost in a struggle with himself. With her heart beating like thunder she shrank away from the dim shape of his back in the darkness, hugging herself in a vain attempt to halt the draining sensation of defeat.

Trailing the large herd of horses was not an easy task. As they crossed through dry country, the men had to keep them from breaking at the first scent of water. The horses had an annoying tendency to wander out of sight to seek the young grasses in the deeper swales. Seth had wisely brought along a big bay stallion, a six-year-old stud Rick and Brandy had named Sundown from his habit of circling the mares in the breeding pen several times each evening. This powerful, dominant animal at once was the herd leader and kept peace by his very presence. At any scent of wolf or puma he would shepherd the herd together with the energy and determination of a sheepdog.

Having no spare hand to handle a wagon, they did not bother carrying feed. This meant stopping at successive streambeds to graze the horses. At night they took turns keeping watch, and they bought food from occasional settlers whose claims grew sparser as they worked their way south. Their plan was to trail down to the Nueces and follow that stream east to Corpus Christi.

But trouble was soon in the wind. When not watching the horses, their eyes were anxiously combing the horizon, for the bits of information they had garnered from the handful of wary settlers warned that the land ahead was full of menace. The imminence of war had brought a reign of increasing terror along the border, with Mexican patrols working both sides of the river and confiscating all property that fitted their needs. More disturbing still were the reports of large bands of Mexican bandits crossing over into Texas and plundering settlements at every opportunity. These heavily armed marauders were particularly dangerous, for they took no prisoners, not even for ransom, and murdered all those who fell into their hands, including the women they raped.

Seth reckoned they were still a day or two north of the San Miguel when they spotted riders coming up from the south. He and Todd went out to meet them, telling Prent to stay with the horses. The strangers turned out to be an old rancher from just north of San Antonio plus two hired hands. All of them looked haggard and stamped with grief. Their story was grim. They had been trailing twenty head of horses to Corpus Christi, the same destination as Seth, and lost them all to bandits. The rancher's only son had been killed in a running fight, and the desolate old man warned Seth to turn back, telling him he'd never get through. The bandits were sure to spot such a large herd. "Two came up the evening afore, looking to buy a horse," the old man related, his voice carrying the anguish of his loss. "We didn't figure they was checking to see how many guns we had or if more of our outfit were coming up. Should have known that scar-faced greaser and that pig-eyed half-breed were thieving scum. They kilt my boy, and I ain't forgettin'."

"You say there was only two?" asked Todd, looking slightly puzzled.

"Two at first. But they was just a-scoutin'," said the old man. "They run and fetched the main bunch that night and we was hit 'bout noon yesterday. Had to be thirty or forty of 'em, so don't get to thinkin' you can fight 'em off."

Seth thought about trying to hire the two ranch hands to help him get his herd through, but he could see they were already discouraged and exhausted. After Prent provided them with hot coffee, the old rancher rode away, shaking his head sadly.

The following evening, as they came up to the brackish waters of the San Miguel, dust columns to the southwest told them there were riders approaching who would reach their camp well before dark. Seth and Todd trained their eyes on the riders until they determined that there were two of them. "Could be trouble," muttered Todd.

Prent turned to look. "Trouble like that old man talked 'bout, maybe?" His youthful face settled and tightened as his eyes picked up the approaching riders.

When the pair drew nearer, one began to lead the other. And when they reached the camp Seth saw a scar-faced Mexican in front followed closely by an ugly, porcine half-breed. The Mexican was making an effort to smile casually, but Seth had a feeling he had seen the man somewhere before. That scarred face was not easily forgotten.

"*Buenas noches, amigos,*" said the Mexican, doffing his sombrero. With his head uncovered, Seth now remembered him as the knife thrower he had seen in the Casa Colorada the day he had ordered Yoquito Estavez out of town.

"Howdy," said Todd, who was standing closest to them. The visitors looked about as though admiring the horses, but Seth sensed that they were sizing up the three of them. It clearly bothered the tall Mexican that the three had stationed themselves so that Prent was now standing at the newcomers' rear.

"You have some fine horses, señores, perhaps we can buy one, eh?"

"They're not for sale," said Seth. He took a step toward the Mexican, noticing that the half-breed was quietly turning his horse in order to face Prent. "Don't I know you?"

"Me, señor?"

"Yes, you. Aren't you the gent who throws knives and got himself shot up by a ranger in the Casa Colorada?"

A look of uneasy recognition came across the Mexican's face as he stared at Seth. "*Caramba!* Señor, you are the brave *rinche* I watched that day."

"That's right," returned Seth slowly. "And just what might you be doing out here?"

"Ah, señor, me and my *compadre*, we come up from Mexico, is much trouble there. We hope only to buy a good horse for my brother in San Antonio."

Seth and Todd exchanged glances. "Did you happen to see an old rancher with some hired hands trailing about twenty head of stock south?" Todd demanded.

Jesús Torres, the scar-faced assassin, knife handler and sometimes spy, narrowed his cruel face as he appeared to search his memory. "No, señor, you know is very big country, we see no one."

"Funny," said Todd. "We run across him and he claims somebody stole his herd. Gave a description of two of the bastards that doesn't miss you and your friend by much."

Torres and the half-breed now exchanged a quick look that carried a distant hint of alarm. The Mexican replaced his sombrero. "Well, señores, if you have no horses to sell we say *adios*. We have a long way to go."

"You may not have as far to go as you think," Seth said slowly. "Get off that horse." He was turning sideways as his hand swept around and found his gun.

"Señor, we want no trouble. We did not know you were a *rinche*."

"We're all Rangers," said Todd, "and you and that tongue-tied friend of yours better get off those horses before you get blown out of the saddle."

Torres' face stiffened with uncertainty. "Señores, what you gonna do?" There was a thread of panic in his voice.

Seth knew it was time to call the hand. Both these dangerous and increasingly desperate-looking characters were tensing for action. "Maybe take you back to see if that old rancher and his boys recognize you. Likely you know what happens to horse thieves in Texas."

A seizure of fear and fury bunched the ugly contours of the Mexican's face as he jerked his mount up, drew his gun and fired at Seth, his horse's hooves still flailing the air as it plunged out of the circle. In the same instant the half-breed swung around to join him.

Whether it was Seth or Todd who killed the Mexican didn't matter. Both slugs tore into his skull and he was dead before he hit the ground. But as the desperados wheeled their horses back toward Prent, the youth could only manage to wound the half-breed before the sudden roar of gunfire spooked the herd and the horses nearby shied wildly and started to run.

"Go after that bastard and kill him!" Seth shouted to Prent as he raced for his mount. To Todd he simply waved at the herd, signaling that they had to hurry and start turning them in a circle. A stampede here would mean a critical delay in rounding up the stock, and in the back of his mind were the thirty or forty other bandits the half-breed was surely heading for.

Prent mounted and pursued him quickly but had trouble gaining on the wounded bandit for, though bleeding heavily, the man rode with the skill of a Comanche. After two or three miles the half-breed swung into a small coulee. Moments later, Prent heard the crack of a rifle. He felt his horse take the shock of the bullet as it stumbled and went down under him. He rolled away and drew his six-gun, waiting for the man to appear for a second shot. But the man was not trying to kill him; he wanted only to escape. He had deliberately aimed at and brought down Prent's mount. Within moments Prent could hear the distant pounding of horse hooves as the man rode to the far end of the coulee and disappeared. It took him almost an hour to walk back to the camp, aware all the while that the half-breed's escape could mean death for the three of them.

With the horses finally bunched together again and Sundown circling slowly as they started to feed, a troubled-looking Prent, avoiding the others' eyes, threw the heavy saddle he had lugged back onto another mount.

Trying to keep his anger in check, Seth shook his head at Todd and kicked at the earth. "Damn it! I guess we're going to have to drive them back north again."

"If they're coming, Seth, we can't move this herd fast enough to get away," Todd said.

After a moment's silence, Seth came over and stood beside him. Both their eyes were fixed on the horizon. "What then?"

Prent, though standing several feet away, kept his head down as he talked. "Sorry, fellows. I should have killed that bastard. But he sure seemed fair hit, could be he won't make it."

Todd snorted and swore. He turned suddenly to Seth, his hands dropping firmly to his hips. "I say we make a break to the east, along the Atascosa."

Seth remained silent as he studied Todd for several moments. "Think we got any chance of getting there?" Seth's mind was almost visibly reaching for a glimmer of hope.

"Damned if I know, but it's the best bet we got. If we stay north of that basin of water at Choke Canyon they might figure it's too risky up there to follow."

Seth stared in the direction the half-breed had disappeared in. "It means we got to travel night and day." He looked at Prent. "It means we're gambling everything. If they catch us, we can't hold off that many."

"I'm ready," said Prent, anxious to avoid more talk about the escaped half-breed.

"Just pray the sky doesn't cloud up tonight," said Todd, mounting. "A little moonlight would sure help. Horses can be tricky to handle in the dark."

Seth took one more look at the lowering sky that hung over the range beyond where the half-breed had disappeared. "Reckon we'll need more than a little moonlight," he mumbled as he steadied Sam and mounted.

Yoquito Estavez looked suspiciously at the wounded half-breed stretched on the ground before him. The man had barely made it into camp. "You say only three men and so many fine horses?"

"*Sí, tres hombres, señor*," said the half-breed in between his short, ragged breaths.

Yoquito regarded him with more irritation than sympathy. He took a swig of *aguardiente* from a slim bottle. "What did you do? Try to steal the horses yourself? Idiot! Where is Torres?"

"I think he's dead," groaned the half-breed, holding his side where a large wet stain marked his still-bleeding wound.

"Dead!" shouted Yoquito. Pepe and Juan were now standing with him. "A man goes out on a little ride just to look around, and now he is dead!"

"Those men knew him, señor. One of them said he'd seen Torres in Casa Colorada. Señor, *carajo!* They were *rinches.*"

"*Rinches!*" repeated Yoquito, his tone suddenly turning hard and cautious. Pepe and Juan grunted and exchanged glances. Yoquito remained quiet for a moment or two. The scene with the big blue-eyed Ranger and the knife-throwing Torres in the Casa Colorada was coming back.

Pepe shook his head as though increasingly disturbed by his thoughts. "Three *rinches* and so many horses? Yoquito, it is a trap!"

Juan, his face twisting in confusion, wanted more information. He squatted down and questioned the half-breed closely, discovering that the *rinches* had asked about the herd of twenty horses the gang had run off only a day or two before. He rose shaking his head. "Pepe is right, it is a trap!"

Yoquito wasn't so sure. "These horses, how did they look?" he demanded.

"Very fine horses, señor, bring many pesos," croaked the weakened man. "Señor, *por favor,* can someone help me, I am bleeding to death."

Yoquito turned away, signaling to those listening nearby to do what they could for the stricken man. He saw his black cook, Sancho, coming up with a tin of coffee and a long piece of rag. The man was too weak to ride further and would probably be left there to die. It was a merciless code but one that was accepted by these men, who were criminal to the core and the human equivalent of hyenas.

19

Having gotten across a swift-flowing but shallow stretch of the rocky Atascosa, Seth grazed the tired herd for half a day before moving south until the Nueces valley came in on their right. They followed it to Corpus Christi. All of them were still played out from the attack that had never come, a stroke of luck that had left them strongly puzzled. Even Todd, whose idea it had been to race for the Atascosa, kept scratching his stubble of beard and muttering. "Either something I can't figure scared 'em off, or that half-breed didn't make it back," he mused. But Seth was not concerned about explanations. He was secretly relieved that they were drawing closer to Corpus Christi and that columns of United States dragoons and foot soldiers were moving along the river trails beside them.

Their final arrival at the wide, loosely guarded gates of the army encampment was a surprise to them all. Dust was everywhere, and the rows upon rows of tents and wagons serving as shelters were much longer and sprawled out than any of them had imagined. They were just able to see the barren fields beyond, where men were drilling in squads that seemed to be moving about as though one set of muscles controlled every limb. They were told by bystanders that these were some of the best infantry units in the United States army, though neither he nor Todd could see what use that kind of training would be against the Mexican irregulars, who were often as good at guerrilla tactics as Comanches were.

Their biggest surprise came when they found their way into the immense but poorly aired and cluttered quartermaster's tent. A gruff-looking officer, smoking a cigar and casting a faint aroma of whisky, threw them a gesture that passed for a greeting and brusquely demanded their business. Seth stepped forward and showed him the copy of the paper and the bank draft the contractor had given him. The officer drew deeply on his cigar, glanced at the papers and sent a tall, lanky corporal outside to count the horses. Nothing was said about the date on the papers, which indicated that the shipment was one day overdue, nor did this officer seem interested in the condition of the horses. He appeared satisfied to hear there were sixty-five present and quickly stamped the paper, telling Seth that his bank draft, properly countersigned, would be ready in five days.

"Five days," said Seth. "Why five days?"

"Couldn't tell you, mister," said the officer. "But that's how long it takes the provost marshal to sign anything."

Outside, smiling to himself and biting off a chew of tobacco, the lanky corporal pointed out the quickest way to town. Then, seeing that Todd and Seth were nettled about the wait, he tried to explain the five-day delay. "We've had horses run in here as were stolen. Rightful owners would show up a few days later and if they had registered brands the army had to give 'em back. Provost marshal likes to wait till he's reasonably sure you ain't selling somebody else's stock." He looked admiringly at the herd they'd just delivered. "Ah'd say you got some mighty fine horses here, mister."

Young Prent, who had been listening in silence, now showed that he had been busy developing a thought. "Looks like you're satisfied just getting sixty-five head of sound stock," he said to the corporal.

"That's what the order says," allowed the corporal. Clearly he was in no hurry to get back to the officer and that dust-laden litter of supplies inside the tent.

"Reckon I could change this mount I'm riding for one of them?" Prent asked hesitantly, reminding Seth and Todd that the half-breed had killed one of the Salingers' best mares.

The corporal scratched his head and smiled. "Hell, don't see why not. Them dragoons coming in here ain't too slick when it comes to horseflesh. Some of 'em ain't learned to stand snug in the stirrup yet."

While a smiling Prent shifted his saddle and gear over to the snorting and prancing Sundown, Todd was receiving directions to a flat plain west of town where the Rangers were signing up. Seth watched both of them mutely, gripped with the realization of how he would miss these two men he had grown so close to. Something urged him to find a way to hold them, to bind their familiar strengths and loyalties, particularly Todd's, to him. Thinking about the money he would have in a few days, his mind was filled with the ranch and the first excitement of realizable plans. He smiled in spite of himself, thinking back to those beautiful but vague dreams he had held years before in North Carolina which now in this unbelievable and unlikely setting were approaching reality. Yet this reality, stripped of its momentary aura of triumph, still came down to a burden of demanding tasks, most of them fraught with danger and none devoid of risk. The ranch needed a constant acquisition of highbred stallions to strengthen its crossbreeding. This meant traveling to eastern Texas or even Louisiana or Tennessee. What he needed was a big-name sire with a creditable breeding record. There was a growing demand for high-quality saddle horses, and as Prent, happily swapping his mount for Sundown, was evidently aware, a small but rapidly expanding market for stud services. But Seth was still gnawed by the worries that perched like ravens at the edge of his mind. The ranch was poorly protected, and the fence lines, now handled as solitary work, were dangerous to maintain. He had long been in need of additional barn and corral spaces. Too many ailing horses were being lost to cougars and even coyotes. Squatters were beginning to appear on grazing land he wanted and now needed. But even if he acquired the land, how could he and Brandy and Rick protect it? It was dawning on him that this country, its challenges and maybe even its dreams, were too big for one man to conquer alone. On the trip into town he puzzled through and reached two decisions that would one day determine his life and the lives of many others who could not see the darkening road ahead.

Corpus Christi was a small seaport on the Gulf Coast. It had few cobbled streets, but a large number of houses, mostly wood or adobe, were spread out in random clusters from the south shore of its bay. Its air was clear, and a sea breeze brought the smell of its shoreline, which teemed with gulls, terns and sandpipers and rolled to the west in legions of sandy dunes. With the coming of the military camp, the town was crowded with makeshift eating places and bars that never closed. Its single hotel was filled, including the lobby. Lodging could only be found in rooming houses, many hammered together at an abandoned Indian fishing village at the bay's head to meet the demand. Seth was lucky enough to get a large room thrown up against a stable that was clean and surprisingly quiet. A laundress and her daughter who lived across the street gave their clothes a badly needed washing for a dollar.

Seth was amazed at the number of uniforms about, the many military observers from foreign countries, and the undercurrent of excitement that ran through the town night and day. There was open talk of war with Mexico, but there seemed little doubt or even concern about victory. Apart from the aroused citizenry, most surprising of all was the sight of well-dressed and even aristocratic Mexicans slipping self-consciously through the streets. It seemed a foolhardy if not outright dangerous place for them to be, but he noticed they carried themselves with a dignity that kept the few offensive remarks of passing Texans discreetly muted. Later he was to discover that many of these Mexicans owned large tracts of property north of the Rio Grande. Several had immense land grants bestowed on their families the previous century by the Spanish crown. A determination of their legal status, whatever a war brought, would involve the disposition of considerable wealth. No one knew if the annexation of Texas made them United States citizens or if they would be regarded as Mexican subjects, regardless of any holding above the border. Many of these visitors rightly suspected that a *yanqui* victory would turn their property into spoils of war, but since no war had yet been declared, let alone won or lost, their anxious inquiries brought no reliable answers.

Seth spotted a few riding by in covered carriages, but mostly they walked in groups or couples, whispering to each other as they strolled along the sandy cobblestone streets. Watching them pass, Seth did not need to be told why dark-eyed women with smooth, enameled skins and bright shawls awakened in him poignant memories that time had not eroded, memories that brought back indelible scenes of shadowy Laredo, memories that had been isolating him from the world about him like a man in secret exile from a fugitive youth. He did not know that those memories had quietly saddened him, made him lonely with a loneliness he could not keep from others.

But he was aware of the changes in himself, of the changes in his feelings for Isabelle. She was not blameless, after all. Why had she not seen that no man should be asked to live with a symbol of his wife's shame? In choosing the child over the man, she had allowed something to go out of their love, and he was powerless to bring it back. Now something in the deep of him was rising as inexorable as chemistry. Now there was a slowly growing hunger, fueled by the memory of Elena's cool, sensuous body, the lingering taste of her flesh. He had fixed an image of her in his mind, catching the flashes of excitement and passion in her eyes. He would return to Jason and the ranch, he would even return to Isabelle, but part of him would always look back to a shadowy room in Laredo and that vibrant, dazzling girl he could have claimed as his own.

That evening, on impulse, he bought a bottle of whisky. None of them were heavy drinkers, but the occasion was right and once they were comfortable in the room they passed the bottle around and stretched out to spend what Todd and Prent believed would be their last night together.

Seth was slow beginning, but he knew both these men were used to plain language and soon he had them looking at him agape, stunned by his proposals. Both expected to be paid for the arduous and, as it had turned out, perilous task of getting the horses to this faraway post, but neither had expected the five hundred dollars Seth had settled on in his mind. It was a fitting opening for what he was about to propose. With Todd and especially Prent looking at him in astonishment—for both were aware Seth Redmond rarely said things he didn't mean—they heard him offer them, if they joined him instead of the Rangers, ten percent each of his ranch and its future profits. After three years, if the ranch prospered, he would raise it to fifteen percent. There was a long silence as Todd, holding the bottle and staring at Seth, took a healthy swig and passed it on to Prent. Wiping his mouth with the back of his hand, he was the first to speak.

"Are you sure you want to do this, Seth?"

Seth retrieved the bottle from Prent. Lifting it to his mouth, he said, "I've given it a heap of thought, Todd. Yes, I'm set on doing it!" His eyes held theirs. "It's not only that I want you fellows but damn it, think about it, I need you. There's a hell of a lot of work to be done, and trouble is likely to break out everywhere you look. If you don't think you won't be earning your share and more, you better not take it." He drank and passed back the bottle. "That ranch is no safer than we can make it. If the redskins get riled up enough, it's going to take every hand we can muster to keep them from wiping us out. So far we've been lucky. We reckon they've only run off a few head, but the more stock we have around the greater the danger is going to be. Remember, you won't be drawing any pay. You'll be living off a share of the profits, and profits don't pop up every day."

Todd and Prent were silent for a while. Both were recovering from this proposal. At first it had seemed generous, but its demands were becoming clear, and the commitment it involved could shape a man's life. For Todd it was easier. With a wife and two children, a chance to own even a share of a promising horse ranch could not sanely be turned down. The five hundred dollars he was receiving amounted to ten months' pay as a Ranger without any risks and with no opportunity to spend it. Besides, he found himself more worried than he had thought about Bess and his children, and he had fewer regrets than he imagined about giving up the excitement he figured was coming once he rejoined the Rangers. Still, a greater factor than he knew was his liking for Seth. Seth was a strange man in some ways, but Todd saw in him a man still courageous to the core and, though perhaps lacking a sharpness for business, incapable of false dealing. He knew that something was troubling Seth, something that was also affecting Isabelle. Todd had never considered himself a deep man but he could read a lot into little things—things others, like Prent, might let pass.

Young Prent was in a quandary. Like Todd, he liked and admired Seth, but he was still young, unmarried and anxiously looking forward to another spell of adventure with the Rangers. He had also noticed the many sociable females who seemed to have come from all the dance halls in the west to this booming town, and they put him in mind of the good times he had always promised himself. He had heard about the wild doings Todd had enjoyed until his marriage to Bessie and then had been amazed at how soon Bessie had had Todd standing in harness. He reckoned that one day he would love a woman enough to be tamed that way too, but he wasn't ready. Balancing all this was his love of horses and his secret ambition one day to be breeding the finest in the land. At twenty, he was still young. He suspected that Seth had included him in his offer because the long friendship of their families left him no graceful way out. But Prent, if not worldly, was not stupid. He had quietly calculated that in three or four years he and his brother-in-law could be owning thirty percent of a thriving horse ranch. There were surely some risks, but he had the indifference of the young to the possible pitfalls in life. He could almost swear that Todd was going to accept Seth's offer, and he shook his head, knowing that a big part of his excitement at joining the Rangers, just being with Todd, was gone.

He watched Todd and Seth shaking hands and exchanging words of mutual appreciation for what was obviously a deep and long-lasting friendship. He would have liked more time to think things through before committing himself to a deal that might decide his life, determine his future before a chance to see the "elephant." He drained off two sizable swallows of whisky, aware that Seth might not cotton to a man who had trouble making up his mind. He wasn't going to run the risk of a sudden change of heart. Even so, he choked a little before he could bring himself to say, "Believe me, Seth, I sure enough appreciate your offer. If you mean it, I'll sure enough accept it."

The five days were almost up when Seth walked down to the town's general store to buy some rifle ammunition he wanted to keep in reserve. Todd had taken both horses to the smithy to check their shoes for the long trip east. Waiting around had made them restless, and they were anxious to get out of crowded Corpus Christi.

Just when it happened Seth was not sure, but a carriage passed him and then immediately slowed down and stopped. As he approached it, the door on his side opened and a woman stepped out. She looked both strange and familiar, but as he came up to her he recognized with some shock the attractive high cheekbones and regal stance of Carlota D'Valya. He swept his hat off and bowed slightly to accept the white-gloved hand she extended.

"Well, my lord," Carlota said. "Of all people."

"Yes, yes. Quite a surprise," said Seth, wishing now he had shaved and dressed a little more neatly. "How do you happen to be here?"

"Well," answered Carlota, glancing behind her into the carriage. Seth could see a middle-aged man with a well-trimmed beard sitting there. "I'm afraid it would take a little time to explain. Perhaps we could meet."

"I'm leaving tomorrow."

"Tonight, then."

Seth's heart began to beat a little faster. He knew he was going to hear something about Elena, and, try as he would, it was futile to pretend he was not anxious for word of her. "Very well. Where?"

"Right here. I'll come by with the carriage and pick you up. It will give us somewhere to talk. Will eight o'clock be all right?"

"Eight will be fine," he replied as he moved to help her back into the carriage. Having received no introduction, he merely nodded at the mute gentleman and backed off. The carriage started up again and he stood watching it, holding his breath until it had turned and disappeared around the next corner.

It was a night that brought the first hint of spring. The breeze from the gulf, which was usually strong, dropped in the evening until it rippled through the town like a zephyr laden with the musk of the mangrove swamps to the east. Seth saw the carriage coming from a distance as it passed under the solitary lantern posted outside the town's single hotel. The horse broke its canter and slowed as it drew up, and Carlota's white hand appeared at the window to beckon him in. He felt strange settled beside her in the carriage, her dress rustling at every movement and her perfume giving the air a luxurious, even exotic, flavor. But her strong feminine presence only brought Elena to life between them, and he found it impossible to restrain himself. "How is she?" he blurted out, aware of his awkwardness and catching Carlota's brief half smile at some inner satisfaction.

"I thought you would wish to know, señor," she responded quietly.

"Of course I want to know," he almost snapped. "And please don't call me señor. My name is Seth."

She looked away at some quarreling soldiers entering a bar in the street beyond. "Very well, Seth. We are not sure ourselves about Elena, but we are very worried. She is a stubborn woman and would not leave the *hacienda* to come with us. Even her father could not convince her."

"She's in danger?"

"Everyone is in danger. If war breaks out, Colonel López and his troops will move to Matamoros and the *bandidos* and even the poor *peones* will run wild. There has been great trouble around Laredo. Bandits have twice attacked the D'Valya lands, taking our horses and some girls and young women they caught in the fields. The government does not protect us, they are too concerned about you *yanquis*. When Colonel López leaves, we will have only God to turn to."

"Can't the people organize and defend themselves?"

"Ha! Organize, you say? We have no guns, nothing! And there is a revolutionary, a priest, would you believe, a father Vincente who is turning the people against us. We believe he is getting money from the *norteamericanos* to cause trouble."

Seth leaned back in the carriage, watching her face in the light flickering occasionally from the street. "Maybe there'll be no war."

Carlota's voice became droll, nearly sardonic. "Seth, look around you. Do these men look like they've come here to take religious vows? Mexico will pay dearly for her pride, for her refusal to accept what is clearly a judgment of history. Texas is lost. My country will pay for neglecting her subjects, and most of all she will pay for her corruption. We know what you *tejanos* think of us, but my people are as brave as yours. It's only that our government has kept them poor, illiterate, devoid of hope. What can they do?"

Seth listened, taking in this striking woman's strange wisdom, but her words could not fully claim his mind. "And Elena's husband?" he muttered.

"Ramón? Ha! He is back in Mexico City, probably in jail. There is talk he was caught with one of the president's mistresses . . . or was it just some general's? Rely upon it, that pendulum between his legs will hang him yet!"

They talked for a long time before Seth started hinting at the question he found himself afraid to ask. "Has Elena found—" He hesitated, but the expression on his face made Carlota look away.

"Somebody else?" she offered gently.

Seth remained silent.

"There is a young officer on her father's staff. He's very personable and of course very presentable. Like every woman, she needs a man in her life, but I believe her father has made her promise to wait until we see what happens to Ramón. After all, she is still married to him. If he is executed, she will be free. But if he is not, any charges of adultery could endanger her rights to the estate."

"Is she in love with him?"

"That you will have to ask Elena."

Seth shifted about uncomfortably as he wondered about the mute carriage driver sitting above them. The man seemed to know enough to keep the carriage moving and to keep circling the main streets in town. "You are not here alone, are you?" he finally queried, remembering her companion of the afternoon.

"That gentleman you saw today was once the *alcalde* of Laredo. When the revolutionaries started making attempts on his life, he decided to leave. If you are wondering if we are sharing a bed, no, he is just a friend."

As he left her, both knew what Seth wanted, but Carlota again was left to put it into words. "We try to get a messenger through every week. In my next letter to Elena I'll mention meeting you. Is there anything you'd like me to say?"

Seth shook his head. Nothing he could think of matched the deep, disturbed feelings that were welling up in him. He was leaving with Todd tomorrow to go east, and Isabelle and Jason would be waiting for him at the ranch. What his heart urged was impossible. "Just tell her we met," he murmured. "Maybe someday we might meet again."

Carlota nodded and sank back in the shadows. He felt a new and painful sense of emptiness claiming him as he watched the carriage disappear. The next hour he spent wandering along the sandy track that edged the lapping waters of the bay.

When he finally returned to the room, Todd was asleep.

Part Five

June 1846

20

It was a bad time for Seth and Todd to be away. The spring storms that year were the worst Isabelle could remember. They came out of the north and west with massive thunderheads that rose like menacing ramparts, swiftly demolishing the heat and light of the sun with their dark, rolling billows. But within weeks the rains urged the grass forth, and a green mantle surged across the land, bringing strength and stamina to herds of wild grazing animals as it did to the lean Indian ponies being painted with medicine symbols, *puja*, to protect them in war. Isabelle, staring at the horizon, could not shake the nagging fear that assailed her every time Seth left. When Prent returned she learned that Seth had made him and Todd minor partners in the ranch. She knew the dangers and demands of the ranch might one day make it necessary, but Seth's making the decision without consulting her was another measure of their growing estrangement.

She began to awaken each morning with a vague sense of foreboding, yet the presence of so many others, particularly Bessie, was a bulwark against loneliness. It was impossible to withdraw within herself with old Adam and the children continually causing one fuss after the other. Bessie's children were still babies, but Jason was seven and Tate and Taska six. They were all beginning to ride. Tate, though he was the smallest, was a born horseman. Brandy and Rick watched in amazement as he leapt onto ponies bareback and pounded them with his little heels to make them gallop around the corral. Jason and Taska were not far behind him, but Tate had a touch with horse-flesh that wasn't easily matched. He was the first one to work his pony up the run, now almost sixty feet long, and race it down. Isabelle, upon first seeing him, screamed with fright, but Brandy just laughed. "Don't you get to worryin' yourself none, Missum Isabelle, dat little fella could ride a buckin' horse up a cliff."

The days lengthened as the weather warmed and birds coming from the south gathered noisily in the creek bottoms. The Hondo rose with every rain, for the thunderstorms refused to subside, and the children lined up at the window to watch the forks of lightning knifing into the knoll beyond. Isaac Sawyer, visiting one day, said that a great lode of iron or some other metal must be lying beneath the knoll to attract such lightning, but old Adam, who was in a crotchety mood for wet weather bothered his wounds, growled that it was only because it was the highest point about and most likely to get hit.

The boys had clearly lost their initial fear of storms, and only Taska covered her ears when peals of thunder began to rock the house as though artillery shells were falling nearby. Isabelle watched them with their noses pressed to the glass, their eyes fixed on the bare strip of the run that pointed to the top of the knoll. As the bolts of lightning streaked down, the children would start to squeal, hearing the coming thunder that started like paper crinkling in the sky, then gathered volume until it hammered against the roof as though a mighty mallet were smashing through.

Jason, the great adventurer, was also a demon of mischief and possessed an incredible curiosity. Old Adam liked this restless, daring boy and tolerated his endless questions with the patience of the cantankerous old for the spunky young. Jason wanted to know where the geese went when they honked south, where the sun went when it sank in the west, and most of all he wanted to know where the Indians went when they couldn't be seen. Old Adam did his best, occasionally using imagination to supply answers when known facts failed. Still, Jason learned a good deal. One day he came with a question Adam was confident he could make a fair stab at answering. "Where do places get their names from?" demanded Jason. "Who names a river, a mountain, or even a country?"

Chuckling to himself, Adam answered, "Folks who run across't 'em first or folks who can think of a right fittin' name. Others just naturally go along. Your mommy and daddy hit upon calling you Jason. They were the first to see you. Now we all call you that."

Jason looked doubtful. "You mean somebody just figured to call this Texas and that's its name now forever and ever?"

"Reckon."

"How about the creek? Who named it Hondo?"

Adam scratched his head. "Dang if I know. Don't sound like a name a reasonable man would give something."

Bessie, shaking her head and smiling at Isabelle, called from across the room, "Some Spanish nobleman is supposed to have ridden by here a hundred years or so ago and finding the creek pretty deep called it Hondo. Todd says *hondo* is Mexican for deep."

"Just like I said," grunted Adam. "A fair-minded man would have just called it 'Deep.' "

Jason soon put this acquired knowledge and, in his eyes, new power to work. He wanted to name something. He got Taska and Tate to look around for things to name, but he himself first thought of the run. It was after a storm that he hit upon a name he liked, Thunder Run. Isabelle was glad to hear that his pronunciation had gone from 'tunder' to 'thunder,' but she didn't feel that many people would like or use the name. As usual, she was right, but she underestimated her son's persistence. None of the grown-ups seemed to remember this freshly minted name, and nobody used it except Taska and Tate, who were careful to mention it once a day to please him. But Jason was not easily discouraged. One morning he got some old paint from Brandy and, getting his mother to print it out for him, painted the name "Thunder Run" on a large piece of board and posted it at the foot of the knoll where the trail entered the ranch yard. Strangers who happed by for water or directions began going off saying they had come by Thunder Run. Isaac Sawyer laughed when he saw it, but he was quite serious when he said later that a ranch that size, already building a reputation for breeding high-quality horses, should have a name. "The Redmonds' " didn't seem to fit anymore. If Thunder Run was not used around the ranch, it began a slow creep around the neighborhood, and for a time Isabelle wondered if she shouldn't take the sign down. Jason's painful expression at the thought discouraged any action on her part, and she decided to wait for Seth. Jason was already a hard boy to discipline. Her many attempts were dissipating the affection that had once glowed in his eyes, and even with Tate and Taska she was losing her popularity. Instinct told her that Jason was at the stage where a man's heavier hand was needed. She hoped Seth would hurry back. He should be the one to take down Jason's sign.

◆ ◆ ◆

Isabelle gathered that Prent had been having too good a time in Corpus Christi, drinking with Tanner and Purdy and mixing with the brand of women drinking men attract. Apparently Prent had been sent home when Seth and Todd left to seek out some blooded breeding stock in east Texas.

Isabelle sorely wished they would hurry back, for her hidden fears were no longer just uneasy premonitions. For several days she had felt herself seized by a deepening dread. Something was wrong. There were moments when the range around them seemed far too quiet, moments when she caught herself studying the low trim of hills rimming the valley, almost feeling the presence of eyes staring down at her from behind those silent ridges. Worst of all were the moments when she awakened with a start in the night, wanting to scream for Seth to come back. She kept her anxiety to herself until one day she realized she was not alone. She was standing in the garden looking searchingly toward the northwest, where nebulous clouds were drifting streamers across the horizon. Then, turning, she found Inez standing behind her, her eyes fixed on the same strange vista.

The two women stood regarding each other in a curious tension till Isabelle finally said in a half whisper, "You feel something too?"

"Sí, señora." Inez looked away as though ashamed of this admission. "I ask Brandy not to go out alone . . . but he says no worry."

Isaac Sawyer, coming by to help Prent with the stable pump, listened thoughtfully as the two women, at Bessie's urging, haltingly expressed their fears. Unlike Prent, Isaac did not try to reassure them or relieve their minds. He shook his head as he weighed once more his conviction that this horse ranch with its blooded stock was a deadly magnet for Indians, whose total existence, wealth and tribal standing, was built around horseflesh. And these were two women who had suffered the vicious Comanche attack years before. Some said that such a terrifying experience gave women an uncanny sense of when danger threatened again. He decided he'd best get home as there was only addleheaded Andy to protect his wife and daughter.

But the apprehensions that for so long had troubled and frayed Isabelle's nerves turned to a slowly spreading terror on the night Prent decided to sleep in the stable and keep his brother Rick company. Scout's barking around midnight awakened the light-sleeping Brandy, who looked about nervously and slipped from his bed. Something about the way the big dog growled between barks made Brandy think of the time Inez had nearly been murdered in the stable. Scout would bark excitedly when chasing bobcats, raccoons or even coyotes, but ever since he had received the vicious knife cut across his snout, his deep, almost internal, growls meant that some sudden shift of wind carried the scent of Indians.

In spite of his heart-stopping suspicions, Brandy wasn't sure, and a false alarm would only frighten the women and children. Hurrying through the darkness, he entered the stable and warned the Salinger boys. On his return he discovered Inez, who had also heard Scout, already up and placing extra ammunition beside the rifles sitting below the window ledges. She was standing over the sleeping Taska as he came in, looking at him knowingly.

Still he was not ready to awaken and alarm Isabelle and Bessie. But he watched the house and caught old Adam hobbling back from a midnight call to the privy. Quickly he related his suspicions. Old Adam peered into the darkness that surrounded the ranch and, hearing about the dog, nodded his agreement. It was commonly understood that the most dangerous moment was likely to be just before dawn.

The restless Scout was taken to the stable, where Prent and Rick began taking turns at snatches of fitful sleep. At the first hint of dawn the dog sprang up, his back stiff and straight, a low growl starting to rumble through his heavy frame. To Prent and Rick the dog seemed frozen in that posture, his nose pointed toward the rear of the stable, where the half door opened onto the corral close by. Then they heard it; something hit the back of the stable and a blush of light appeared at the half door. Rick raced toward it, his fears mounting as he drew near. He was right. It was a fire arrow. "They're setting us on fire!" he shouted to Prent and jumped through the door. To his left was the horse trough, still almost half filled with water. He grabbed the pail hanging over the pump and scooped up enough water to kill the flame. A cry broke out as another fire arrow hit a few yards beyond. Again he rushed to douse it, but now Prent was yelling from the door and shots were ringing out as rifle slugs smashed into the wooden stable walls and chips flew out around Rick's head. "Come in, you damn fool!" shouted Prent, as he began firing at every flash he could see coming from the outer rail of the far corral. One fire arrow aimed at the thatched roof went over the stable and landed in a mound of dry hay stacked near the front door. Immediately a blaze went up, and now dusky figures could be seen coming toward the front end of the stable. The leading one carried a firebrand. He hurled it into the pile of straw lying before the feed bins. Within seconds the stable, filled with wet mares and colts, broke into an uproar. The blasts of Prent's rifle and the smell of fire had put the animals in a panic, and they were rearing up in their stalls and whinnying with fright.

Inez, who had been awake for hours and had posted herself at the window facing the stable, saw the one with the firebrand rushing toward the stable door. He came into the flood of light thrown out by the burning hay. Without a word she doubled him over with her first shot and turned her sights on the next figure coming into the light. When she fired this one spun around and went down on one knee, her next bullet threw him back like a cloth doll and he lay still. Those behind had turned back, but it was clear from their war whoops that they were circling the stable. Brandy, who came up behind her, failed to get off a shot, but he sensed from their cries that they were now after the house. He posted himself by the hut door, which faced onto the house, and waited. Within seconds two figures carrying firebrands emerged from the far side of the stable and raced toward the kitchen door.

Old Adam hadn't slept that night. After Brandy's warning he had lain down under the gun port facing the stable and decided that if an attack was coming he wasn't going to miss it. Now, with his rifle through the gun port, he heard a growing chorus of war chants rising from the still-dark side of the stable. For a moment he was distracted by the excited voices of Isabelle, Bessie and the children rising behind him, and he missed the two figures suddenly running toward the house with firebrands. Brandy had already opened fire on them from across the yard, but they were still coming on, dangerously close. Taking the rifle from the gun port, Adam reached for a shotgun and pressed it through. The first brand loomed up before him, and his blast lifted the hefty figure carrying it into the air and tossed it backwards, dropping it to the earth again in a helpless heap that covered and smothered the flame. But the other brand was hurled against the kitchen door and fell onto the dry pinewood of the half step before it. Had the Indians come from any other direction, they would have encountered stone or adobe and their firebrands would have fallen harmlessly. But on this side the pine beams that supported the house were still exposed and the plank wall was weathered and stained with grease where it rose behind the great cast iron stove.

Prent and Rick could see the flames beginning their tiny licking at the kitchen door, and together with Brandy they blazed away at the brave who had delivered the brand. But he ducked back to safety and became one with the increasing din in the shadow on the far side of the stable. The warriors, knowing the fire would soon force the whites from cover, began to screech and fire their guns toward the smoldering house.

In spite of their sudden, near-paralyzing fear, Isabelle and Bessie hurried the children into the corners of the great stone fireplace. Bessie took a rifle to the second gun port, but the attackers were deep in the shadows beyond and Adam was wildly shouting that he could see fire outside the kitchen door. Isabelle, rushing to the kitchen, filled a pail with water and, seeing smoke seeping under the door, opened it to try drowning the flame. It was a mistake. The water fell onto the burning wooden half step of the threshold instead of the pine door panels, and the rising light from the fire brought a hail of bullets that knocked the old door off its aging hinges. Immediately the wind created a draft from the outside that swept the fire into the house. Isabelle screamed as she jumped back, and Bessie, coming up behind her, began to pump water into a pot to fight the fire that quickly leaped up along the narrow walls with the heavy draft. Both women screamed for help, and old Adam abandoned his gun port to hobble into the kitchen. There was not room for three of them beside the pump, but he could see that the fire had to be stopped on the outer wall. Smoke was already beginning to sting the women's eyes, and they could no longer speak without choking or coughing violently. Adam tried to get them to wet the wall and keep the fire from advancing on the pump, but in their growing panic they flung the few pots of water down toward the burning door and against the hot draft that was hurrying the flames toward them. After a minute or two the flames began to rise like a thing alive to eat into the grease-stained wall behind the stove and crack the high kitchen window. The heat was becoming unbearable.

Prent and Rick could see the dancing light of the fire coming from the kitchen and knew their father, sister, Isabelle and all the children were doomed if the fire continued to spread.

"We've got to get over there!" shouted Rick.

Prent took him by the shoulders. "Rick, we can't make it, it's too far! They'll kill us for sure!"

"We've got to try!" cried Rick, pulling away.

Prent knew he was right, but they couldn't save their family by dying. The distance was too great, and they'd be running right across the Indians' field of fire. He grabbed his brother again. "Rick, come! We'll try for the hut! It's closer! Then maybe we can get across!"

Rick answered by jerking loose and heading for the hut. Prent was right behind him. Had the Indians not been gleefully watching the fire visible through the burning doorway they would never have made the hut, but by the time the savages caught the two figures racing through the thinning darkness on the far right there was time for only a few random shots before Rick and Prent dove through the door Brandy was holding open for them.

Brandy and Inez had terror imprinted on their faces, for they knew if the house and its people were lost they and little Taska would be next. The arrival of Prent and Rick brought them a brief moment of comfort, but nothing could diminish their horror at the flames slowly licking the kitchen side of the big house.

"I'm heading over there!" ranted Rick.

"You ain't never gonna make it, Rick!" declared Brandy.

"You'll only get yourself killed!" said Prent angrily.

The fire suddenly seemed to explode and leap through the kitchen wall, to be carried by the wind up onto the sloping roof of the main room. The warriors began to scream, knowing now that the whites were trapped. In the hut no one's breath could be heard as all of them realized the main house was doomed. The specter of two babies, two children, two women and a crippled old man falling into Comanche hands to avoid being cremated struck them as an immutable death sentence. Rick had tears in his eyes. "I'm going anyway," he blurted in a half sob, and made for the door. Brandy and Prent grabbed him, for everyone but Rick could see that the light from the burning house now made the passage suicidal. For the terrible moments that Brandy and Prent held Rick the ghastly conflagration rising across the yard silenced every voice.

Then Brandy was screaming, "Duh scoopway! Duh scoopway!"

"Christ! That's right!" roared Prent. "We can get there through the scoopway!"

"Lordy no, we gots to get 'em over here!"

"I'm going!" shouted Rick, who had seen the flames beginning to flicker over the remaining roof of the house. Brandy pulled a chair back from the corner where the opening to the scoopway lay and Rick disappeared in it. Brandy shouted after him, "Hurry! Fetch dem folks back here!"

Rick was already well along the shallow passage that began on the hut side of the scoopway. On his chest and knees he clawed madly with his hands to struggle through the narrow tunnel, praying to himself as he went. "Pa! Sis!" he hissed into the darkness around him. "It's me! I'm coming!"

A mixture of hysteria and panic now filled the house, the women and children joining in each other's frantic screams. The kitchen was ablaze, and the desperate women were trying to beat back the flames with brooms. Old Adam could hear the roar of the fire crossing the roof until it reached and began to crackle above the new addition. He knew the house was lost, and he was trying in the confusion to get the women to take the babies and race across to the hut with the boys. He would take as many guns as he could handle and throw himself in front of the house to open fire on the Indians. Surely Brandy and Inez and likely Prent and Rick would be firing too. There was a chance that he could draw the attackers' fire to himself and the women and children might escape. Isabelle's and Bessie's eyes met his as he shouted to them, but all knew that the fusillade of bullets smashing into the burning house made escape across the yard hopeless. They were ringed by death, and with burning beams beginning to fall on the kitchen side of the house, life for every soul in the room had dwindled down to a matter of minutes.

In that cauldron of terror and confusion, they backed away from the howling fire, in their panic not hearing Jason yelling to them about the scoopway. He started tearing desperately at Isabelle's skirt and pointing to the corner beyond the front door, where, hidden under a hard straw mat, was the opening to the shallow tunnel. Miraculously, everyone seemed to remember it at once. Only later would Isabelle understand why they had failed to think of it sooner as a means of escape. It had been meant for Brandy, Inez and Taska to reach the house; the house, with its supplies and gun ports, was fixed in everyone's mind as the last sanctuary. The ranch could be held only if they held the house. In a crisis no one dreamt of leaving it. But the excited Jason, running to the corner, did not even have to lift the straw mat. It came up by itself, and the dirt-streaked face of a gasping Rick appeared from under it.

There was no time for words. As soon as Rick pulled himself out, Jason and Tate scampered into the hole and disappeared. Rick helped

Bessie in and handed her the baby, motioning for her to move down the scoopway. Bessie seemed smaller as she fell to her knees and squirmed away. Isabelle, glancing at the hole, quickly tore off her heavy skirt and with only a petticoat over her legs slid in. She took the older child but had to struggle to move down the shallow scoopway with her. Rick, frightened and now gagging on the deadly heat and smoke, was shocked to see his father hobbling toward him, his hair and eyebrows singed, his clothes scorched and blackened, but holding three rifles and his shotgun. Seeing burning beams beginning to swing down over the old man, Rick screamed "Dad! Leave the guns! Come on!"

His eyes stinging and nearly blind from the thickening smoke, old Adam hobbled toward the hole. "Son, we need guns! They're still out there!" A perilous life on the southwestern frontier had ingrained in the old man the need for the tools of survival.

Rick took the guns and threw them down the hollow of the scoopway. He reached up to help his father into the hole and saw the heavy beam over the front door veering down toward them. "Pa!" he shouted. "Get down!"

Old Adam tried to swing his body into the hole, but the crippled leg that dragged behind caught in the rough lip of the crude plank opening. Rick tried to pull him down, but the old man only grimaced in pain as the leg twisted up beneath him. Above, the burning beam began scraping along its supports as the flames roared up and above the smoldering door frame. Adam was trying to speak, but Rick sensed from the choking sounds and the half-moaned words that his father was losing consciousness. The heat and smoke were now so intense they were beginning to enter the scoopway. Rick grabbed his father's hanging leg with one hand and reached up to grasp his heavy belt with the other. With all his might he tugged the now-limp figure back. It came with a roar as the heavy beam above tumbled down, smashing Adam's shoulder and breaking the crippled leg until it folded up and followed his now-broken body into the scoopway.

Rick knew his father was dying, knew it but could not accept it. He spoke to him as he dragged the cruelly twisted body with him. "All right, Dad, we're going to make it." His voice could not rise above a whisper, for the effort had him fighting for breath. "We'll be safe in just a bit, Dad." Halfway back he had to stop. His muscles were aching from the strain, but they didn't seem to matter. He tried to speak again, but the reality in the dark oppressive tunnel finally penetrated his mind. His father was dead. He could only lie there in the darkness as the tears welled up in his eyes. "I tried, Dad, honestly I tried," he sobbed.

Brandy and Prent could see the Indians stringing out and leaping in the light of the burning roof on the far side of the house. It was clear that the house was about to collapse in one great conflagration, and they were awaiting attempts by its occupants to escape. Prent, concerned about ammunition, was glad the ever-worried Brandy had kept an ample supply hidden in the hut. Still, now that they were cut off from the house, there would be none to waste.

Bessie was the first to make it through the scoopway. She found it difficult to move with the baby until she remembered how old Liz carried her pups. Placing the infant before her, she gathered both sides of the tiny, thin blanket in her mouth and, lifting the child an inch or two from the ground, crawled to the hut as fast as she could. Isabelle had more trouble, for she was slightly larger than Bessie and had the older child. Finally lying on her back and opening her blouse, she pulled the little one against her chest and buttoned the blouse around her. The frightened child cried but clung to her neck, and now, with her hands and knees free, she worked herself along until she too reached the hut.

Rick, exhausted and choking with grief, almost gave up. It was only his father's final words that kept him going. "They're still out there," he muttered over and over to himself. "They're still out there!"

But the worried faces of those in the hut were already paled and strained when Brandy said he could hear someone coming. He ducked down into the hole to look and immediately his hushed exclamations brought all eyes to his crouching form. Brandy watched Rick appear on his back, forcing himself forward with his legs but dragging behind him something that could only be a body. Rick, his sweating figure and tear-stained face covered with damp clay, was helped from the hole by Brandy, who jumped down again to pull Adam's body to where it could be lifted through the gaping opening.

Bessie and Prent immediately ran to kneel beside their father, startled and aghast at his hideous appearance. His singed and distorted body was no longer a vessel capable of containing life. The blood from his leg and shoulder and the burnt and blackened patches of skin fouling his arms and face could have come from a night of torture at the stake. Prent, his rage supplanting his grief, pulled a blanket from Inez' bed and covered his father up. Isabelle helped Bessie to her feet and guided her onto the stripped bed. Brandy forced his eyes away from the body and back to the fire about to consume the main house. The Indians were now shouting and the coming dawn was beginning to reveal their numbers, telling Brandy and then the others that there were not enough guns in the hut to hold them off. All the adults there fought back their dread of the fate awaiting the children. Bessie's babies, helpless and unfit for rough and rapid travel, would surely be killed. If they lived, Jason, Tate and Taska would be carried off, their lives changed and perhaps stamped with the savages' way forever. Bessie suddenly faced her babies' peril, and rising she shook off her despair and hurried both into a corner, where she pinned their clothes to pillows and thrust them under Taska's bed. "Please, give me a rifle," she gulped over her shoulder, her tone finding a feeble force in her desperation. Isabelle, pressing Jason and Tate to crawl down beside Taska behind Brandy and Inez' low-slung straw-stuffed mattress, answered her frantically.

"Bessie, the guns are in the house . . . we didn't bring them!"

Bessie's agonizing gasp was cut off by Rick's voice. "They're at the end of the scoopway. Poor Pa was trying to bring 'em for you."

"I'll get them," cried Bessie, racing for the scoopway entrance. But Brandy seized her and pushed her back.

"Ah'll fetch 'em," he half shouted. "Remember, Missum Bessie, Ah built dis thing and Ah kin get through it fastest. Truth is, Ah's bin practicin'." He jumped into the hole and disappeared. Brandy wasn't pretending. So great was his fear for his family that he had been working at techniques for getting through the scoopway. The fastest way had proved to be with strokes like a swimmer's arms spread out at sharp angles and feet propelling him along like a frog. Within two or three minutes he was back with two rifles. Prent lifted them from him and gave them to the women. Then, without speaking, Brandy disappeared again. A few minutes later he climbed out of the hole with a third rifle and a shotgun, a bag of shells tied to the trigger guard of the shotgun. Old Adam had thought of everything, and now these guns, salvaged at the cost of his life, could be the margin of survival for his kin. The old man under the blanket would have been satisfied.

As the house collapsed it threw up a shower of sparks. Billows of heavy, dark smoke poured forth as beds, racks of clothes, rugs and stuffed furniture fed the maw of the flames. But its roar could hardly be heard, for the Indians were shouting their frustration and fury that not a single soul had run from the deadly fire. They knew there were whites in that house, even women and children. A brave's torso had been torn open by Adam's fire from the nearest gun port. But instead of fleeing, it seemed these strange whites had stoically endured death by fire. That was strong medicine. It was something that did not fit easily into the Indian mind.

The warriors began looking angrily at the hut. There was no gunfire coming from it, but that was where the two figures running from the stable had disappeared. As they began to retreat to the stable to escape the heat from the burning house, they saw that the squat hut was made of adobe and wouldn't burn. Their war chief, White Antelope, turned to the now-renowned medicine man, Blood Hawk, who had been standing in the rear. "Shall we take the scalps of the white devils in the hut?"

Blood Hawk, his face painted with long streaks of red and black, his greased hair tied in strands, looked at him disapprovingly. White Antelope was a young chief and difficult to control. This raid was really for horses. They had planned to set the stable afire, which would have distracted the whites or brought them out in the open, where they could be killed. But the reckless White Antelope had wanted the scalps of the women in the house, and when the rush on the stable failed, he had turned the attack there. Blood Hawk, though still seized with spells of insanity, had learned to prey on the fears of the tribal chiefs, even if few of them thought much of his wisdom in war. His reputation for having strong medicine, which the Comanches saw in his prophecy of their great devastation, had given him incredible power, which he slyly and skillfully used to bring himself immense wealth and hence a high standing in the tribe. Though there were chiefs who secretly wanted him dead, there were also a few dead or deposed chiefs who had been foolish enough to make such wishes known. His unusual standing in the tribe was unmatched by any other shaman among the wild Koh-eet-senko Comanches. Blood Hawk had become too powerful to protest against and, with his awesome medicine, too dangerous to drive away.

Blood Hawk did not like the whites' failure to come fleeing from the burning house. It was a bad sign. He could only think some new magic was at work. The whites were forever springing up with new magic, the wagon gun that brought down stone walls, the glass that

brought close the faces of distant foes. He did not like it. "Let us take
the horses and go," he counseled. "There is bad medicine here. We've
already lost some braves. The little house with walls of dirt will not
be easily taken." He glanced at the glow that was now rapidly filling
the eastern sky. "Already there is too much light to be making attacks."

White Antelope frowned at these words. Horses could bring him
wealth, but only scalps could heighten his reputation as a war leader.
There were other chiefs in the tribe reaching for the power that came
with large followings. White Antelope knew that many of them were
also out with raiding parties, perhaps returning with long sticks of
scalps, captives, loot and above all tales of brave doings that allowed
a chief to sit and smoke proudly as his people danced and sang of his
prowess in war. He had come with this meddlesome medicine man
only because he had promised to lead them to where the whites had
many fine horses and few guns to guard them. They had scouted this
ranch carefully from the hills to the east and knew there were women
and children in the main house. White Antelope liked captive women,
liked to satiate his lust on them before torturing the life from their
bodies or, if convenient, turning them over to his squaws for years
of drudgery before exhaustion or abuse brought death. He was angry
now that the two he was sure were in the main house had disappeared.
But he remembered in his fury that there was still one left in the hut.
She would not escape.

The attack on the hut was rushed and hence poorly planned, the
fruit of White Antelope's chagrin at the baffling disappearance of
those in the house. Against Blood Hawk's advice, he first tried to
assault the house from the stable side, hoping his warriors could reach
and fire through the open window there. It was a particularly bad
choice since both Rick and Inez were posted at that window. Their
marksmanship soon left a string of dead or badly wounded bodies,
which caused the screaming warriors to break and slink away. It
should have been enough. By Indian standards they already had serious losses. But White Antelope's rage was on the increase.

"I shall show you how a true warrior slays his enemies!" he shouted.
"We shall destroy the wire door with our guns and I will lead you
in!"

The braves' response should have been a warning. Some saw a
frontal assault across the now well-lit yard as a foolish way to fight.
The mystery of the house still troubled them, and the cost of the

rushed assault on the window had brought whines of anguish at this sign of weak medicine. They had not come here to die. Most divisive of all was the knowledge that he had ignored the counsel of Blood Hawk to take the horses and go. This seemed like simple wisdom and more the Comanche way.

But still, at White Antelope's command, many of them slunk down behind every bit of cover they could find and opened a fusillade on the hut door. Bullets smashed against the wooden frame and pinged through the wire screen. Inside, Prent had everyone flat against the walls at right angles to the door. A table, a chair and two shelves of dishes along the back wall were smashed and threw up showers of crockery and wood around the dust-choked room. The screen door rattled back and forth at first, then twisted and rocked against its own hinges. It broke away and with a screeching sound fell in disjointed motions to the floor.

Suddenly White Antelope, mounted and leading a handful of screaming young braves, charged the hut. The maddened war chief and his wildly painted followers began to yell war chants and brandish their hatchets, but they were staying low on their ponies' necks, making difficult if not impossible targets for Brandy and Prent, who were posted at the front window. With Isabelle and Bessie still trying to protect their children and staying as close to the floor as possible, Rick and Inez had trouble shifting around the crowded hut to direct their fire at the oncoming attack. Prent and Brandy kept blazing away, but the thunder of hoofbeats grew louder and shrill war cries began to torment the ear. Then, incredibly, Bessie gasped and began crawling toward the open door. She had realized in tending to her babies that she had left her rifle back on Taska's bed, but her frantic eyes had caught Adam's shotgun standing by the open hole just beyond the door. With a babble that struck Isabelle as a sign of near-madness, Bessie began to rant to herself, "They're coming for my babies! They're coming for my babies!" The roar of Prent's and Brandy's rifles inside the hut drowned her out, but she continued to scream as she struggled forward, now raving to herself between sobs that her babies were not going to die.

The horses behind White Antelope were beginning to shy away as a brave to the left flew off his mount and flopped to the ground. They were almost up to the muzzles of Brandy's and Prent's guns. But in spite of the danger, White Antelope was rising up in the saddle, howling even louder and whirling his hatchet wildly above his head. It was clear he was going to crash through the open doorway and enter the hut. Isabelle, seeing the half-crazed Bessie crawling into that very doorway, moved up behind her to pull her back.

White Antelope was suddenly too close for Prent's and Brandy's guns to bear on him from the window, and the warriors across the yard, seeing their war chief about to gain the hut's entrance, rose from their cover and came rushing forward, their cries swelling the already deafening din. Brandy and Prent started to abandon the window and rush to the door when they saw the mass of warriors rising and racing toward them and dropped down again to open fire on this greatest danger of all. In desperation they yelled for Rick and Inez to cover the door, but Rick and Inez, though now in position, were afraid to fire with Bessie's and now Isabelle's body blocking the way.

Leaping from his horse, White Antelope landed in the archway, shaking the shattered remnants of the door as he came down with a howl of triumph. He was poised to plunge into the hut, strike at the defenders with his hatchet and allow the warriors behind him to flood in. Within moments the scalps of these whites with all their evil magic would be his.

The course of battles, when primitive emotions rise to contest one another, are as unchartable as wind storms at sea. No one really knows what details lead up to the salient events, but often if even one detail is altered the outcome is different. No one in that hut, least of all Bessie herself, knew her mind had been claimed by an instinctual rage. They were not going to kill her babies. Her manic fury was forging weapons of her fingernails, even her teeth. Like a great feral cat, she was ready to savage the Indians' throats and tear out their entrails. She was no longer paralyzed with terror; she was a snarling animal protecting its young to the death. Sprawled in the doorway, she groped over to the shotgun that old Adam always kept loaded. The bag of shells was still tied to the trigger guard, but she ignored it for she was making no attempt to aim the weapon. She simply pulled it to her and pointed it outward. As White Antelope came down on top of her with his ear-splitting cry she looked up to face his broad, muscular stomach with its protruding navel grotesquely adorned with jagged rays of vermilion and blue. Twisting onto her back, she thrust the heavy metal barrel into his navel and pulled the trigger. White Antelope's body rose into the air like that of an acrobat attempting a back flip that lacked the thrust to be completed. The shock of this weird, appalling sight stunned the braves behind him, causing them to hesitate a critical moment while the resumption of fire from Brandy and Prent, joined now by Rick and Inez and even Isabelle, swept through their straggled ranks like deadly hail. It was enough. They broke and ran for the stable.

Blood Hawk's luck had not run out. White Antelope's death and that of several of their war party was blamed on the war chief's refusal to heed Blood Hawk's counsel. Now the medicine man's words went unchallenged. Unfortunately for the Redmond ranch, the Comanches were great horse breeders themselves and knew the value of the many brood mares and powerful stallion studs they found in the stable and the corral. They didn't bother with the colts, many of which were still too young to keep up in long, rugged travel, but they left with thirty of the best breeding stock in west Texas. Had the braves not been busy marking individual animals as their own, they would have remembered Blood Hawk's advice to set the stable on fire as they left. This would have distracted the defenders and delayed any pursuit. But the drive to the north pasture began with a rush, and the last two braves who might have done the deed suddenly realized that one of the whites had left the hut and was firing at them from the front corner of the stable.

As soon as Rick realized the raiders were leaving, he scrambled out of the hut and down to the stable entrance. Brandy and Prent had tried to restrain him, but he tore away, determined to kill one more of these red hellions who had caused his father's death. But as the last one rode out of range he returned to the hut with tears in his eyes. "Reckon they're gone," he muttered miserably, sinking to the floor.

"Yup," sighed Brandy, shaking his head. "And dey took a parcel of our best horseflesh wid 'em."

Prent, who had helped Bessie to the bed and was sitting with his arm around his shaken sister, looked at Isabelle, attempting a smile. "This was a poor day for the ranching business, partner," he quipped, trying to lighten the mood. But Isabelle did not smile back.

21

The war with Mexico for control of the great mountains and deserts of the Southwest did not surprise the Texans, who had endured hostilities on their southern border for over a decade. Nor did it surprise Elena María D'Valya, who had watched her despondent father leaving to join the growing Mexican command in Matamoros. What appalled her was her realization that these *yanquis*, with their well-drilled infantry and their hard-riding, brutally aggressive Ranger force, were failing to bring any semblance of law and order to the borderland they had begun to dominate. Quite the reverse. With the Mexican army in retreat, the country had started falling into the hands of bandits and army deserters turned renegade, who were pretending to be guerrillas harassing the invaders. In the chaos following the breakdown of civil authority the evils of war spread everywhere. Bands of sinister and predatory men came out of the cordilleras to the west to prey upon helpless villages. Travelers were robbed and *rancheros* openly plundered of their livestock. The stronger *haciendas* became veritable fortresses, the weaker bastions of fear. But always in the end it was the Rangers, the *rinches*, who managed again to be the main source of Mexican hatred and terror.

Elena, aware that her staying with her land had put her life into jeopardy, also knew her loyal *vaqueros* and the squad of soldiers her father had left behind would abandon the estate if she left. Her father had come back from his ordeal in Mexico City badly shaken, but with little doubt about their future. His estate and his many holdings along the river were as good as lost. His experience in the capital with his dissolute son-in-law had been sobering enough to mark him for life. Ramón's uncles had procured the wily Rivera a generalship in return for altering his report. Had it not been for sordid incidents of flagrant debauchery, Ramón would have been returned to his command, medals and all. López could see that the Mexican government was too busy with its sinecures and jealousies over its privileges to come to grips with its fatal weaknesses. As a good soldier, he was prepared to fight bravely, but his heart told him his countrymen, peasants and simple farmers, illiterate and cowed by their own organs of authority, were no match for the frontier-hardened, self-confident *yanquis* pouring across the Rio Grande.

He desperately wished Elena had gone with Carlota to Corpus Christi or even back to San Antonio to his cousin Julio, but Elena was stubbornly holding to her land and in some recess of his mind he respected her for it. The kindling, and he prayed, the spread, of spirits like Elena's was Mexico's only hope. But on the day he realized his troops were being outfought and had started their retreat, he left Matamoros along with his gravely ill wife, knowing his daughter would now have to struggle to hold not only her land but her life.

The young lieutenant watched Elena sitting in the candlelight. She was beautiful beyond words, and his body ached to take her in his arms. Yet her head was shaking in refusal at his repeated attempts to convince her to leave.

"No, Luis, I cannot go. This is my home. I must defend it."

"Elena, you're not listening. Matamoros is lost. The army is retreating to Monterrey. I have to join them. I cannot keep these soldiers here to be captured. You must come with me. Your father would have ordered it."

"I have no one and no place to go in Monterrey. If I leave here, this house will be looted and burned. No, Conrado and his men have promised to stay with me." She turned away from him. "Luis, please go and do your duty. Perhaps the fortunes of war will favor us before long."

The young man brought his hands together in exasperation. "Elena . . . I—"

"I know," she said, rising and touching him on the shoulder. "These are dreadful times. Maybe when we consent to give up Texas the *gringos* will leave us in peace."

"Ha! Those *gringos* are after more than Texas!"

Elena picked up the candle and headed for the staircase. Awkwardly he circled her on the short landing and stopped her on the top step. She already sensed why he had impetuously and somewhat daringly come up to her bedroom.

"Elena, we have only tonight left."

She looked at him, taking a step backward. "Luis, please don't start."

"I love you. God knows how I love you. What is wrong with you? Have you no feelings for me?"

"Of course I have feelings for you, but I have a husband."

"Him! That unholy disgrace to the uniform! Please don't pretend you owe him any loyalty."

She started down the stairs. "Luis, come, it is a long ride to Monterrey. You must go. Besides, I have to talk to Conrado."

The young officer stopped her again and, lowering his head to hide his anguish, took her free hand in his. "Elena, what will happen to us? You and I?"

She looked at him, a momentary hint of pity in her eyes. "We are not dying, Luis, we are only going to be separated for a while. Wars often do that to people."

Wiry old Conrado watched the young officer stomping out with an amused smile. The young rooster was still trying to mate with the peacock, eh? The sun-darkened skin of the old *vaquero* brought out the white trim of his beard and his hair showed glints of silver when he removed his sombrero. He held a candle, the only light Elena would allow after dark. There were no bright lanterns to attract marauders, and many of the doors and windows had been boarded up. Conrado wondered if these measures would be enough. Now that the soldiers were leaving, his fifteen men could hardly defend such a large estate. Some bandit gangs, he had heard, numbered over a hundred.

Elena came up to him with an inquiring smile. "Conrado, is there any word?"

Conrado grunted, and his face grew slightly vexed. "Señora, this is dangerous business. Why are you trusting the word of that whoremonger? He would sell his children into slavery for five centavos."

"I'm not trusting him, Conrado. I'm paying him for information."

"And what are we to do with his information?"

Elena turned to stare down the dark hall that led to the barred door. "It will help us decide."

Conrado shook his head resignedly. The D'Valya *hacienda* was living on borrowed time. He had not yet told Elena that her father's estate had been attacked, looted and burned the night before. The D'Valya properties were a much bigger plum and, with the soldiers leaving, an irresistible prize for outlaws. His *vaqueros*, staying only out of loyalty to him, wanted their wives sent south, where there was less danger. Conrado hoped to urge Elena to don some of their coarse leather clothing, darken her face and cut her hair, and slip away with them. But she was not ready. He only hoped she would be in time.

Hours later he led the squat man with the straight-standing hair and the scar slashing down across his eye into their servants' quarters. Elena was waiting for them. She gestured them to keep but one candle burning. Her eyes were holding to the newcomer's expectantly. "Well, Pablo, what have you to tell us?"

"It's very bad, señora."

"Very bad."

"*Sí*. There are very big dangers here. You're making great trouble for poor Pablo."

Elena produced three gold coins from her pocket and deliberately let them clink into his cupped hand. "Pablo, you are the only one I know who gets rich from his troubles. Now, come, please, what can you tell us?"

"Señora, a very bad man is coming here. Very bad. *Dios*, he would steal from a burning church. He has killed many *hombres*. Some of his men come to my cantina, I hear them talk."

"And does this evil son of a bitch have a name?" intruded Conrado.

"They call him Yoquito Estavez. One of my girls says she was carried off and raped by him when she was very young and still a virgin. Her family went to the police, but they said only that she was lucky to be alive. He is very, very bad." He turned to Elena. "You—a beautiful woman—you must not stay here."

"Yoquito Estavez," repeated Elena with an anguished groan. That damnable bastard was still plaguing her life. She had suffered enough at his hands. She looked about her in the dark. Was he going to cost her this fine home too? "Pablo, listen carefully. Find out when he is coming and with how many men. Get us word quickly. I will pay you well."

"Oh, no, señora, I cannot do that. I cannot come here again. Already I think this house is being watched. This man, he kills for nothing."

Conrado cleared his throat and took Pablo by the shoulder. "Are you sure you've told us everything you know?"

"Know? Señor, I know nothing, but a wolf pack does not gather where there is no prey."

"How long?" asked Elena.

Pablo, aware of her meaning, fixed her with his single good eye. "Days, señora. Three maybe . . . maybe just two." They stood in a stillness that hung like another presence in the house. "Maybe even tomorrow . . . *sí* . . . maybe."

Conrado whistled under his breath.

Seth and Todd first heard about it in San Antonio. They met old man MacFee, who had just shifted his smelly load of hides to an eight-mule teamster's wagon.

"Near burnt you out, they did," rose his coarse ranting voice. "Old Adam got hisself killed. Believe they run off a mite of stock. That new sheriff fella has been out to yer place, best see him 'fore you leave."

After being assured that the others at the ranch were alive, Seth and Todd pulled away. They had two stallions and three mares, their firmly arched necks showing their Arabian blood, strung out behind them as they pulled alongside the Ranger stable, where a small office had been set up for the new sheriff.

He was a big, rangy man with a firm handshake and a businesslike manner. "You gents from over to Thunder Run?" he greeted them after a crippled Ranger lounging on the single stuffed chair had advised him they were Seth Redmond and Todd Bonham.

"Thunder Run?" repeated Seth, looking curiously at the sheriff, then at Todd.

The sheriff's expression remained fixed. "Believe it's what you call your spread, ain't it? You're Seth Redmond, ain't you?"

"Right."

"Well, it don't make no matter. Injuns has hit your place pretty hard, got away with some stock. Old Adam Salinger was killed, dang it! Always heard he was a good man. My pa fought with him back in the Choctaw uprising. 'Fraid your house is burnt to the ground. But could have bin plenty worse." He moved back, settling his hip on the rough table that served as a desk. "That's a mighty dangerous stretch of land to be settin' up a horse ranch."

Seth's initial shock was beginning to lessen. "Army going to pursue those stolen horses?" he asked.

"Army's busy fightin' a war."

"How long ago?" asked Todd.

"By now, four or five days. Reckon them redskins is far gone."

Seth looked at Todd and shook his head in grim acceptance. "Reckon they are," he said softly. "Reckon they are." Then, nodding to the sheriff, they turned away.

With the house gone, the big cottonwood tree looked lonely and unfamiliar as they came up the trail. Seth's eyes, seeking for little things he'd grown used to, missed many but caught one that was new. On the low hill behind the blackened foundation of the house was a single cross. He knew it marked old Adam's grave.

Todd, watching for Bessie but anxiously looking around, was the first to see Jason's sign. He pointed to it, grunting to Seth. "Look at that."

Seth looked but had no time to answer, for Rick was hallooing from before the hut and running toward them. Prent and Brandy quickly appeared, hurrying from the stable. The children spotted them and shrieked with joy. The relief on everyone's face at their return momentarily belied the despair that hung over the ranch, despair that Todd felt as he embraced Bessie and that Seth could see in Isabelle's eyes.

It was Todd who, after hearing everyone's rendition of that terrible dawning and studying the skeletal remains of the house, took the bottle of whisky he had bought in San Antonio after hearing the shocking news and poured all the adults a drink. Only Isabelle and Bessie refused, but Brandy, knowing Todd was trying to raise their spirits, came back from the stable with the last two bottles of Carlos' wine. This they consented, with Inez' encouragement, to sip.

Todd was not gifted with words, but he had a way of speaking that sparked faith in others, a raw honesty that never exceeded the simple strengths of truth.

"This is a godawful mess," he started out. "Nobody can say we haven't been hurt bad, and nobody can promise we ain't fixin' to get hurt worse tomorrow. But this ain't country where the law stands at a man's elbow, it ain't where you leave the fighting and holding what's your own to others. This soil is ours, and it will stay ours as long as we got the brisket to fight off thieving Injuns or any other goddamn critters trying to take it from us. I say it's time we started building again, but not with wood." He gestured to the lonely chimney stack

surrounded by the blackened ruins of the house. "This time we'll stick
to stone and adobe. Redskins don't know it, but by burning us out
they taught us some savvy and handed us another chance. I know
you're upset, and you got a right to be, but frettin' about having no
water never dug a well. If we got any future with this spread, it's
gonna have to be fought for. One day, if we win, this sorry fix will be
hard to remember." He cleared his throat. "I'd like to drink to something nobody seems to be remembering. Except for old Adam, who
could have said all this quicker and better than me, y'all are still
breathing. We lost a few horses and a house, but we can breed more
horses and build another house. We can't bring back the dead. Seeing
as we ain't got no church handy, I figure that angel looking out for
us has done won herself a toast."

With that he raised the cup to his lips and emptied it as one by
one the others followed suit. No one noticed that Isabelle was the
last to join in and had to strain to swallow her sip of wine.

Despite the presence of Todd and Prent, the ranch was short of
hands. The heavy loss of breeding stock was serious, but some
mares had been left and miraculously all the colts. Their big
herd of yearlings in the lower pasture had been spared, and some
twenty-odd workable head had been gathered from the breaks and
gullies along the creek. One or two strays were found each morning
for several days. But they were in desperate need of horses and
a large drive for wild mustangs had to be organized. Seth hired
both MacFee boys and Andy Sawyer to help Todd and Prent, who
worked dangerously far to the south and west and were often gone
overnight.

Isaac Sawyer, who came to help lay out the new house, warned
Seth that this time the structure they were describing would require
money. They needed slate for the roof and mortar for the stonework,
glass for the windows and new iron hinges for the doors. Though they
resisted using wood, there was no substitute for it when it came to
doors or window frames, and lumber would be needed for most of
the furniture. But Isaac allowed they could at least nail sheets of tin
to the exterior of every entrance and use cowhides instead of rugs for
the floor. Two squatters were hired to help with the building. Old
man MacFee, now that his sons were working for Seth, hired on with
his smelly wagon to haul materials back from San Antonio. Rick and

Brandy spent half of every day drawing stones and buckets of mud from the creek bed to make adobe.

They cooked outdoors, and the women and children slept in the hut and the men in the stable. Fortunately the summer was almost upon them, and apart from frequent storms the weather was not a problem.

Seth, with ten men working with or for him, was too busy to think about the imminent war, but in the back of his mind, like the scent of a distant fire that tainted the wind, hung his memory of Carlota's words that if war broke out Elena's stubborn refusal to abandon her home might cost her her life.

The work was endless, but Isabelle was glad for this beehive of activity. It served to distract her. In a roundabout way she found she was needed. Seth, constantly plagued by problems, could not keep up with the ranch's growing need for keeping records and seemed unaware of the bills that were steadily mounting as he poured money into the house and paid his hardworking hired hands. From the sum he had received for the horses he had given Todd and Prent a thousand and paid, to her mind, an incredibly high price for the handsome blooded stock he had brought back from Houston. Now he faced a seemingly endless flow of bills for the wagonloads of building materials that old MacFee had been hauling into their yard for weeks. This and meeting a swelling payroll made her aware that by summer's end they would be nearly broke.

At first Seth refused to study the neatly penned pages of addition she laid before him, but Todd, whose eye was on the future, glanced at them and without hesitation sought Seth out in the stable. He found him helping Brandy and Rick preparing new storage bins.

"How many head have we got broke?" he asked, speaking to Seth but looking at Brandy and Rick.

"More'n thirty, maybe 'bout forty," answered Rick, turning to Brandy for agreement.

"Yeah, dat's 'bout right."

"We ought to think of selling 'em," declared Todd.

Seth looked a little uneasy, as though he felt this was not a subject Todd should be bringing up. But Todd was far from discouraged. The money he had earned from Seth had gone to pay his and Bessie's debts. Unlike others, he and Prent had not been drawing any wages.

He still had a family to worry about. "We ain't rounding 'em up to look at 'em, are we?" His tone was too light to sound offensive.

"You got a buyer, maybe?" asked Seth uncomfortably shifting around to face him.

"No, but we ought to be looking for one."

Seth turned back again to the others. "Reckon we will after a spell."

Todd tried hard to smile agreeably, but he could not dismiss the feeling that Seth left the business side too much to chance. "Seth," he said, gripping the top of a nearby stall. "When a man's got something to sell he's always looking for customers."

Seth glanced down and kicked at the dirt floor beneath him. "What is it, Todd? Isabelle been at you? You worried about money?"

"Ain't you?"

Seth rubbed his chin thoughtfully. Why he was so irritated he did not know. He liked Todd, and he had to remember Todd was now a partner. But he was beginning to feel the fetters of having to adjust to the thinking of others, and that he didn't like. With Isabelle he often failed to discuss his decisions, and when he did, he could ignore what resistance she offered. But Todd was not a man he could ignore, not if he wanted him to stay on. And he did. "Reckon we'll give it some thought first chance," he said finally.

"Reckon we should," concluded Todd.

Brandy and Rick exchanged glances. They sensed how much Seth respected Todd, and in some way Brandy at least began to fathom why. Todd was a determined man with strength in his easy stance and confidence in his own judgment, traits that hinted to others of his ability. Brandy felt the ranch could prosper from his counsel. Seth was also a strong-willed man, but in a different way. Seth would meet whatever trials came his way. Todd would attack those that threatened. Todd was aggressive and more single-minded than Seth. There were times when Brandy suspected that this ranch, demanding and consuming as its many problems were, was not the only thing burdening Seth's increasingly troubled mind.

It took the outbreak of war and a strange-looking letter to bring many hanging issues to a head. Old MacFee brought word from San Antonio that Mexican troops had finally attacked Taylor's dragoons on American soil and war had been declared. Two weeks later the old man brought a heavily sealed envelope left at the sheriff's office for forwarding by a uniformed courier riding from Corpus Christi to Austin.

Under Seth's name someone, as an afterthought, had scrawled across the officially stamped envelope *Thunder Run Ranch,* but for all the letter's impressive appearance, the message inside was short and militarily curt.

To Seth Redmond, Esq.

In view of hostilities now being carried out we will require whatever horses you can supply. Please deliver all available stock to Quartermaster General at Corpus Christi, terms in keeping with previous purchase.

J. D. Hadley
Major General U.S. Army

Isabelle and Todd greeted it with some relief, and Prent began to talk eagerly about running another herd south. Secretly Prent was fast tiring of the heavy workload, and his imaginaton swiftly started working on a spree in Corpus Christi. But Seth stared at the brief letter for long moments before he muttered, "This ain't hardly a time for any of us to be leavin'."

Todd turned around and slowly rested his hands on his hips. "If they can't buy our horses, Seth, they'll buy somebody else's. Might even send east for 'em. There's plenty there."

"My God, they pay well enough for them," said Isabelle as Bessie came to stand beside her.

Seth was well aware he had to deliver whatever horses he could to the army. After all, there was a war on. If the need was great enough, the government would simply take them. That's not what had him pondering the prospect of moving a herd south. Somewhere in his mind he wanted to get back to Corpus Christi, back to Carlota, back to where he could find out what he was becoming desperate to know. "Reckon you're right," he mumbled, and strode away.

One of the lighter incidents that would outlive many other memories born of this stressful period was Brandy's "moon room." The presence of the children made it impossible in such cramped quarters for Brandy and Inez to ever be alone. Now, in the warm early summer nights, Brandy found a space down by the garden, where he spread some straw with a few blankets over it. There after dark he and Inez made love whenever their desire became too great to deal with. Bessie, who was quick to notice things and was dying after all this time to get Todd alone, finally maneuvered her willing but somewhat surprised husband down to the moon room. It was a wild and beautiful release for both, and they lived on it and smiled over it for days. Isabelle did not know how to bring the matter up with Seth, who had no inkling the moon room existed, but she did have one other task to carry out. Brandy and Inez were silent lovers. One would never know they were there. But Bessie was passionate to the point of being helpless. She could not hold back her sudden squeals of delight as Todd's hard body pressed into hers. It was Isabelle who had to tell her to stop her squealing as the children were beginning to notice and had started whispering to each other under their blankets.

Addleheaded Andy Sawyer was chosen to go because Todd said he was the least needed of their mustang-trapping crew. Prent went because Seth and Todd knew how badly he wanted to go. They discovered that there was a vast difference between twenty-six head and the earlier herd of sixty-five. And this time they soon learned that the land was clear of bandits. The *bandits* had gone south, where the disruptions caused by the war were offering lush opportunities for looting. By pushing the horses by day and grazing them in the early evening, they covered the roughly hundred and fifty miles in a little over six days and kept the horses in reasonably good shape. But they found the army camp nearly empty, except for garrison troops and some supply companies with their teamsters and mounted guards. The quartermaster's tent was still there, and this time there was no five-day wait. Seth took his bank draft to the nearest bank and collected thirty-nine hundred dollars in freshly printed U.S. bills.

There was no problem finding quarters now, and he left Prent and Andy in a boarding house with strict instructions to guard the money till he returned. A quarter of a mile away he stopped at the general store to get directions to a tiny village where the Mexican civilians had gathered on the quiet coastline just west of town. Once there he had no trouble finding Carlota D'Valya, but several Mexicans watched him warily as he moved along the street. He still had the look and carried the heavy gun belt of the *rinches*.

Carlota answered his knock herself but received him with troubled eyes. From her doorway she led him into a tiny parlor that smelled of cedarwood and incense. A young girl who seemed to hold her breath in his presence served them small glasses of fruit juice slightly tinged with rum.

"You're back," said Carlota tersely. Her tone carried a faint reprimand.

"Was I expected?"

Carlota shook her head. "No. My friends and I expect nothing. This war will end our world."

Seth shifted in his chair awkwardly. "Truth is, I've been wondering if you've heard anything from—"

"From Elena? No, of course not. The last we heard, her father had gone to Matamoros and she is alone. You *yanquis* are winning this wretched war and we . . . we are learning not to hope."

"Are you sure she is still in Laredo?"

"We are sure of nothing, believe me. But where would she go?" Carlota shook her head again. "Nothing could convince that girl to leave. No prayer, no plea, no nothing. What little we can gather from a few destitute and terrified friends who have managed to get here is that she is in great danger."

They had been talking for almost an hour before the man with the well-trimmed beard whom Seth had earlier seen in the carriage with Carlota appeared in the doorway. Seth noticed that he and Carlota exchanged meaningful glances before she said, "Seth, may I present Don José. I don't believe you two have met."

Seth rose out of his chair to accept the man's hand and feel his uncertain handshake. Carlota, now looking anxious, quickly waved Seth back to his seat and turned to the older man. "Well?" Her eyes were glued to Don José's worried face.

"I'm not sure," began Don José, looking at her but nodding toward Seth.

"He is quite safe," said Carlota hurriedly. "What have you heard?"

Don José clasped his hands together as though to keep himself calm. "Well, it could hardly be worse," he started. "The soldiers have left and either the bandits or the revolutionaries are about to take the town."

"And Elena?" Carlota demanded.

"The D'Valya *hacienda* has been attacked twice by some bandit gang. Their leader, some murdering pig with a vile reputation, has sworn to take it. No one expects it to survive. A servant who slipped away by night says Elena is still there."

"*Madre de dios*," rasped Carlota. "I knew it would come to this."

The mention of a bandit chief jolted Seth's memory. "This bandit you mention, does he have a name?" he asked the trembling man.

"Yes, but I cannot remember it. We can ask . . ."

"Was it Estavez?"

"Estavez! Yes, I believe that's it," said Don José, turning to Seth with desperate interest. "You know him?"

"I've met him."

"Ah, yes," said Carlota, pulling herself forward in her chair. "Elena once told me. He's the devil who followed her to San Antonio. *Santa María*, what can we do?"

Seth felt a cold force invading his gut. Somehow his blood seemed to be sinking into his legs, leaving his arms helpless. He fought off the sight of Elena in the hands of that swarthy lecher, but no words rose to register how impotent he felt. There were over a hundred miles between him and Laredo, and what could one man do alone? He steeled himself against the emotions that were rising against his will.

He and Carlota searched each other's eyes for a long moment before she said, "Seth, please, if you love her . . ."

Amazing himself, he returned her grasp. "Love is a powerful word, Carlota, but it won't stop bullets. You've just heard what he said. It may be too late. Considering the odds, it may be impossible." His voice was husky and unnatural.

Carlota raised her hands to his shoulders and held him firmly. "Seth, I'm a woman who has seen much . . . oh, *dios*, believe me, too much of life. We are all lonely, we are all lost. The world is wicked and death is waiting. Listen to me! The only reward God offers for the torment of existence is his gift of love. Don't turn away from it. If you do, you will bear an agony of guilt the rest of your life. Every day will be shadowed with regret."

Seth heard her through a haze as though her voice were only one of many, no longer understanding every word but knowing a terrible truth was clawing its way into his consciousness. Somehow Carlota's words had brought Elena to life in that room. Though he had not seen her for years, he saw her now, her body leaning into the scented air, her eyes beckoning. Something told him he had already passed this moment, already measured this haunting girl against all else in his life. Were memories of her deep, sensuous body exciting him from afar like pollen on the wind? And was this craving for her and her fiery passions really love? Did it matter?

For long moments Carlota kept her eyes on him, aware that words were now pointless, even painful. None came. He hugged her and moved quickly over to and out the door.

"Vaya con dios," she whispered as the *tejano's* horse pounded the earth as he galloped away and she, clutching her hands together, sank to her knees to pray.

Prent Salinger's face was a choleric mixture of resentment and disbelief. He could not resist swearing under his breath as he stood before Seth. "You're telling us to leave afore we've even had a chance for a drink?"

Andy Sawyer was looking on, his features creased with confusion. "We done something wrong, Seth?"

"No, that's not it! Now look, I haven't got time to repeat everything. Get mounted and get going. You didn't come here to drink, and I'm sure as hell not giving you a chance to get into any trouble. Take that money back to the ranch and make sure it gets there. Tell Todd and Isabelle I'll be along in a spell."

"Jesus, Seth, you got to do better than that by us!"

"I don't have to do a damn thing. Now, get riding."

Prent pounded the table with his fist. "And just where the hell are you going?"

Seth stared at him hard. He knew sooner or later his absence would need to be accounted for. What he told Prent had to make sense when he faced Todd and Isabelle. "A friend of mine got hit with some trouble," he said quickly. "Needs help. Something I just have to do." Ignoring them, he pulled his things together, deciding at the last moment to take four hundred dollars of the money with him. He folded it inside his gun belt, knowing that in Mexico it could either save or cost him his life. The other two stared at him as he turned to leave. Prent had more than enough time to grow violently mad.

"This is the goddamnedest thing I've ever heard of, Seth. You're forgetting I'm a partner now!"

"No, you're forgetting you're a partner. Getting that money back to the ranch is a heap more important than boozing up and spreeing around here."

"Well, I'll be gone to hell!" exclaimed Prent, kicking at a chair.

"A fair prediction if you don't get moving," answered Seth as he grabbed his pack and strode away.

After he left, Andy Sawyer stood shaking his head and laughing nervously. "I guess we'd best be headin' for home, Prent. Whatever's itching Seth, he's sure one riled-up son of a bitch. Figure hell might be safer than crossing him now."

The air inside the wreckage-strewn room was rank with the smell of burnt powder and falling plaster. One *vaquero* lay dead in the front hall and two sat on the badly smashed settee having their wounds bound up by Elena. Conrado peered through the boards covering the shattered windows.

"Señora, this is insane! You should have gone with the women. We cannot hold this house any longer. *Por dios*, let us leave tonight!"

Elena was desperately thinking to herself. She had lost her gamble. The terrible consequences of her refusal to leave were finally upon her. Her heart told her that Estavez knew she was there and that he would never allow her to escape. Now she only wanted to save Conrado and his men. She felt in her skirt for her derringer. Against her lifelong resolve to use it only on her attacker, the trapped servant girls caught trying to escape and screaming in terror the night before had convinced her she could not allow herself to be taken alive. Instinct warned her that there was more than rape awaiting her. Greater forces than mere banditry were now at work. The highborn lady of pure Spanish blood, the wife of a general and rich *hacendado*, would know the vengeful and defiling lust of these mongrel men. The terrible scenes she had heard visited upon gentlewomen who had fallen into their hands froze her senses. Females of affluent and landed families had been stripped and humiliated in a thousand obscene ways. They had been forced to perform every perversion these desperados' minds could summon. And one or two, she had heard, were murdered after their ravaged bodies had satisfied Estavez' lust. She, like them, would pay for the sins of generations of haughty and arrogant women who had treated their low-caste male underlings with disdain.

By evening Conrado had devised a plan. They would use the horses they were hiding beneath the servants' quarters. The *vaquero* with the fastest mount would dress in woman's clothing. They would leave in a rush, drawing the bandits away from the house. Elena could either dress as a *vaquero* and ride with them until the decoy separated and made his escape, drawing the bandits away from her, or she could wait until the uproar of their leaving distracted the bandits and depend upon her swift gray gelding to carry her safely to the river and perhaps even across it before dawn.

For reasons of her own, Elena decided on the latter. She had something she wanted to take with her and didn't want it known. Along with the valuables her father had left with her, she had collected the many heirlooms of rare and exquisite jewelry the D'Valyas had acquired over the past century. Their aggregate value was staggering. If she survived, they would be her reward for what the degenerate scion of this family had done to her life. She had them in a pillowcase secreted in an old soot-choked stove corroding in the cramped cellar that held the horses.

As darkness crept in from the east, ropes were cut to act as bindings that would keep the two wounded *vaqueros* in their saddle. The horses were fed and watered, and Conrado made sure that every gun was loaded and extra ammunition was carefully spread among the men. He left Elena a rifle and pistol, though neither could see how she could use them. Elena, surprising the *vaqueros*, had already done her share of fighting, killing two bandits who had scaled the latticework trying to enter the upper windows.

Conrado waited until the bandits started their evening bouts with wine and the casks of liquor they had pillaged from surrounding ranches. Usually they built a fire and roasted stolen chickens and pigs. They made a lot of noise bragging to one another and laughing at one another's jokes. Later there would even be a few guitars. But this bloodthirsty crowd was watching. They had the house surrounded and knew it could not hold out much longer. Conrado did not delude himself: they would surely be expecting an attempt at escape, and they would be watching the heavy wooden doors covering that cellar exit. It wouldn't be easy. He could hear his *vaqueros* praying in hushed voices as he approached Elena for the last time.

"Señora, do not let them take—"

"I know," she said, squeezing his forearm, "I know." The silence in the storage room was like a precursor of death.

They waited a minute or two while Conrado made a final check. Then two *vaqueros* placed their horses flush against the wooden doors and at the snap of Cornado's quirt drove them outward. The *vaqueros* galloped quickly into the night, the one dressed in woman's clothes in the lead. Almost immediately the roar of gunfire broke out and the cries of the bandits and the thunder of their weapons became deafening. Elena tried to get to the stove to retrieve the precious treasure, but the outburst of noise spooked the gray gelding and she had to turn him several times and back him into a corner to steady him. Worse, when she reached the stove she found that someone had shoved it back against the wall and she could not open the heavy door far enough to pull the sack out. The sound of the running fight outside was dying away, and she knew she should be off. She glanced at the gelding. He was snorting and stamping his right front hoof. Eerily, it told her someone was coming. Desperately she strained against the stove, but it wouldn't budge. She needed a stout piece of wood or a bar to pry it from the wall. Remembering a heavy piece of lumber in the near corner, she ran for it and managed to wedge it behind the stove, but now she could hear footsteps. Something in her mind screamed at her to mount the nervous gelding and flee, but she could not resist using the leverage she could feel mounting in the thick board. She did so, and the iron legs of the stove screeched against the stone floor as it moved an inch or two outward, but now a light was coming in through the wide-open doors. It was a small burning brand. A large, bulky figure took form beside it and started moving toward her. It stopped some eight feet away and the small burning brand rose to light up the figure's face. There, for the first time, Elena looked upon the malevolent grinning face of Yoquito Estavez.

22

Seth moved across country, pushing Sam as hard as he dared. Occasionally he saw American patrols, but the land was mostly empty and the weather had turned sultry, the sun drying out the long sweeps of mesquite and salt weed and leaving brittle crusts where in the spring tiny rivulets of water had surfaced over damp earth. He slept only once, in Benavides, but even that rest did not relieve him of his dread that he was too late, and that he was driving himself forward in vain. If by some miracle he was not, what could he do alone against an aroused countryside?

On the third day he struck the river below Laredo. After resting Sam, he crossed it and headed for the town. The few laborers and old women he saw ducked away as he came into view. He began to realize they mistook him for a Ranger, scouting for some nearby force.

As he approached the ancient east plaza of Laredo he had a rude awakening. Though the streets looked nearly deserted, he knew they were not. There were horses standing at hitching posts and a wagon with a restless team drawn up before a long open yard of painted jugs. The silence was as unconvincing as it was ominous. He stopped and sat his horse quietly, waiting for them to make the first move.

It was not long in coming. A shot rang out and a bullet dug into the dirt six feet in front of Sam. The horse shied a little, but Seth patted him on the neck and he quieted down.

"Buenos días," he shouted out.

After a long pause a voice answered him. It was a woman's voice and she spoke in English. "What do you want, *gringo?*"

"I am looking for someone. Can we talk?"

The long, tense silence went unbroken until the female voice rose again. "Are you with the *rinches?*"

"No."

Now he saw faces peering from store windows and from behind buildings. This was one frightened town. He was probably sitting in the sights of dozens of guns. He decided to sit still. Now the feminine voice was back. "Are you Seth Redmond?"

Amazed at the use of his name, he could hardly bring himself to answer "Yes."

He saw someone leaving the cover of a doorway to his right. It was a young woman with a rifle trained on him. She was dressed in boyish garb with two pistol belts making a cross on her waist. As she drew near he could see her familiar features clearly. He was looking at Nina Castabella.

He removed his hat and allowed himself a smile of relief. "Nina, mighty glad it's you."

"Don't be."

"I didn't come to make trouble."

"Trouble!" she almost spat the word. "What would you know about trouble?"

"I've had my share," he answered, realizing with some shock that the innocent girl he had known only two years before had become a hardened woman with the eyes of a killer.

People began to appear now, many approaching them cautiously, trying to hear their words, anxious to know where this would lead.

"I'm trying to find the D'Valya place. Could you tell me how to get there?"

"Ha! That bitch! You have come for her, eh? I think you are too late."

A young man had moved behind Nina and was whispering into her ear. She looked at him doubtfully but then nodded. "You will have to come with us," she said more quietly. "Don't try to run or we will shoot."

In a shed next to the river Seth was marched by Nina and three gun-bearing youths into the presence of an armed priest who was surrounded by a cold-eyed crew with the grim faces of executioners.

After Nina spoke in whispers to the priest, he turned to Seth and smiled. It was not a smile of encouragement. His English was fluent but heavily accented. "So, you have business with the D'Valyas, eh?"

"I've come hoping to help the señora. We've heard she's in trouble."

"*Who* has heard this?"

Instinct warned Seth not to mention the aristocratic Carlota or Don José. He knew he was not talking to bandits. These were far more dangerous: they were the revolutionaries he'd heard about. They were out to destroy the government and the wealthy classes that supported it. "The señora helped me in the past," he attempted to explain. "Figure I'm kind of in her debt."

Father Vincente knew more about how Elena had helped him than he let on, but his concerns proved to be elsewhere. "You are a *rinche*, no?"

"Used to be."

The priest's mouth curved into a smile of warning. "Do not stay here too long, *rinche*, you might be killed."

" 'Spect that's my worry."

"No, señor, it is not. We have seen what you *rinches locos* do when one of you suffers a soldier's fate. Ask the people of Reynosa. We do not need that here. Besides, we are not fighting you *yanquis*. You imperialists will have your day with destiny. Our fight now is with a government that exploits and suppresses its own people."

Seth began to feel annoyed, his face tightening with anger. "I'm only minded to get to the D'Valyas'. If you'll tell me where it is, I'll be off."

Father Vincente studied him long and hard. The priest knew why he could not allow this *gringo* to be killed, though the grim men around him did not. Vincente's revolution was being secretly aided by designing political forces in the United States who wanted the Mexican government disrupted, robbed of public support and its authority undermined. The death of this American in an area he had claimed safe for the revolution would not only be embarrassing, it could be costly. He could not afford the *yanquis'* displeasure.

"*Rinche*," he said finally. "You have heard of Yoquito Estavez?"

"Yes."

"He is one bad *hombre*. He has the D'Valya *hacienda* surrounded. He has many men. If you go there, you will be shot."

"Like I said, it's my choosing."

Vincente shook his head. "Why do you want to die? You will save no one. D'Valya's place will fall by next dawn if not tonight. So you see, *amigo*, it is too late."

"Is someone going to tell me how to get there?"

Vincente shook his head again. This was vexing. The life or virtue of a wealthy, parasitic woman was of no significance to the revolution, but there had to be a way around getting this *gringo* killed. His death might well hurt their cause.

"Nina," he said, using that smile again. "Take the señor somewhere and feed him. The committee must talk. In the meantime he will not be needing his guns or his horse. Relieve him of them."

In a part of the shed that had once been an old harness shop, Seth watched Nina mutely slice bread and put out some preserves. He had no appetite and fumed inwardly at being held against his will, but he began to sense that these arrogant captors might be his salvation. He cleared his throat. "How's your grandmother?"

"Dead."

"I'm sorry."

Nina pushed the food in front of him but made no effort to continue talking. Seth knew silence might only widen the breach between them. He had to keep her engaged. "How did she die?"

"Bandits murdered her."

"Bandits? They were here?"

"In the beginning. Now they wouldn't dare."

"Thank God you were spared."

"I wasn't! They broke into our home and robbed us. Four of them. They drank our wine and got drunk, then they threw me on the floor, stripped me and raped me over and over again. They did terrible things to me. My grandmother tried to stop them and they killed her. Then they got so drunk they fell asleep. Father Vincente and his people were going about the town shooting armed bandits or taking them prisoner. He had our house quietly surrounded and took those four filthy pigs and tied them together with ropes around their necks. They began screaming for help when they heard what he said when he prayed over my grandmother's body. The next morning he made them kneel before the church to be executed for her death. I asked for the pistol and while he held a cross before them upside down, I shot each of them through the head. Since then I have killed three more. No, they will not come here. Like all evil men they are cowards. Father Vincente has the answer to all this madness. A government that is too weak or corrupt to protect its people should be overthrown. Many young people, even some from rich families, have joined him. You

are lucky. He does not give many strangers the good advice he gave
you. Listen to him. He does not say things without a reason."

Seth was stunned by Nina's callous tone and manner. She was
bitter, vengeful and already inured to killing.

One of the well-dressed rifle-brandishing youths appeared and gestured them back to Vincente's presence.

"We are going to send someone to study matters at the D'Valyas',"
began the priest as they settled about him. "We need more information."

"I'll go," said Seth.

Vincente laughed, some of the group joining him. *"Amigo,* you
would not get a chance to dismount. We need someone who can talk
to them and come back. Fortunately we have the very man here." He
nodded to someone hidden behind the curtain hanging before the
door, and old Pablo with his lumpy walk came into the room.

Seth, seeing the slash across the eye and the strange standing hair,
recognized him at once. "Jesus, this man is a criminal, he runs a
brothel," he said louder than he intended.

"That he does," said Vincente, "but the revolution has no time for
moralities, not if one can serve the cause. Pablo can talk to Estavez
and return. You cannot."

Seth was beginning to resent the power of this priest, but he could
see that the man had a strange veiled competence. There was something icy and calculating stirring in him, but in this great rambling
makeshift of a shed he gave off an aura of dedication and conviction
that had ignited unquestioning loyalty in his followers. Only old Pablo
seemed unaffected by him. The ugly, one-eyed conniver moved over
to Seth, his tortured face trying to register hurt and disappointment.
"Señor, I have suffered much trouble for you. Why you call me criminal?"

Seth knew what Pablo was after. By pretending to have trouble
adjusting his belt, he slipped out one of the hundred dollar bills he
had secreted there and concealed it in his hand. But he failed to fool
Father Vincente and he knew it. Still, the priest only smiled that
cryptic smile as Seth unfolded the bill and placed it in Pablo's hand.

"There. Make sure you find out what it is we need to know."

Vincente strolled over and firmly removed the bill from Pablo's
hand. Pablo looked at him aghast. *"Padre, por favor,* poor Pablo must
pay many friends for help. What you ask is very dangerous."

"Pablo, I warned you not to speak of this to anyone. There should be no danger if you talk only to Estavez and only about what I told you. When you come back, this money will be your reward."

"But *Padre,* if poor Pablo does not come back?"

"Then poor Pablo will have no further need of money."

Angry and disgruntled but anxious to get away from this menacing-looking priest, Pablo hobbled back to the door and left.

Seth stood studying Vincente, his eyes revealing his growing uneasiness and grim curiosity. "Am I to know what you're dealing to Estavez?"

"Oh, a simple proposition," said Vincente. "We have a lieutenant of his named Pepe and three of his men in our jail. We were going to execute them, but I am offering to trade them for your woman."

"It won't work."

"Perhaps."

"The lives of his men mean no more to him than yours or mine. I've got to get out of here. I must go to her."

Vincente watched him thoughtfully, absently stroking his chin. "Regrettably, I cannot let you go, *amigo,* but if Pablo fails we will see." He turned away, his mind already elsewhere. "In the meantime, if you have more money in your belt and would like to put it in your pocket, please do. We are proud revolutionaries here, not thieves. If you ever get back, please tell that to your countrymen."

When darkness fell, Pablo knew he had failed. Estavez only laughed at Vincente's offer. "Pepe? *Carajo!* I have waited a long time for this woman. I would not trade her for *el presidente* and ten of his favorite whores."

Pablo tried talking to the bandit's other henchman, Juan, whom he knew had always been close to Pepe and was irked at Yoquito's disregard for a man who had often risked his life in his service. Pablo also knew from the young couple who ran the farm that had been used as a hiding place for Seth that Seth and Señora D'Valya had been lovers, that their trysts had been long and heated, carrying them beyond any awareness that the young couple were back in the house and listening to their audible and seemingly insatiable lovemaking. He made the point to Juan that Seth was her lover and a *rinche,* that he was in Laredo and God only knew how many more *rinches* were racing to join him. Ravishing and killing Elena would surely bring bloody reprisals on them all. Juan, sharing a bottle of wine, listened and, easily picturing himself instead of Pepe in the deadly hands of those revolutionaries, agreed. But he knew Yoquito too well. This woman was like a malevolent drug with him. He would have her, and no threat of consequences, however dire, would deter him.

The wine was long gone before the fighting broke out and men everywhere started running for their horses. It was clear that an attempt to escape was being made at the rear of the house. Pablo did not join them, nor did Juan and some of the others. They were more concerned with what must lie within this rich house that it was so desperately defended, surely more than just a woman. Servants under threat had reported many valuable jewels. It was likely they had been hidden, if not carried off, but if they caught the woman or any of her defenders a little torture might lead to great riches. Juan began to speculate about finding those riches before Yoquito did. Pablo's talk had started him thinking.

Only an alarming report from his spy convinced Vincente to move. His second in command, a tall, angular man called Joachim whose body seemed continually slumped against something and whose face was caught up in a permanent squint, finally got back from their contact just before midnight, relaying word that the D'Valya *hacienda* had fallen and Elena had been taken alive. The priest realized that only by killing him could he keep Seth away now.

"Well, then, we must go," he said resignedly, not noticeably moved by the fury and resentment on Seth's face. "Joachim, how many men do we have?"

"Twenty-five, maybe thirty. *Padre*, we must leave some here."

Vincente frowned. "How many women have you armed?"

"Fourteen besides Nina."

"They can hold things here till we get back."

Seth was beside himself with frustration and an almost blinding hatred for this infuriating priest. As they rushed about, preparing to leave, in defiance of the urgency Seth felt Vincente and Joachim disappeared again, telling Nina they would meet them all at the edge of town.

Seth, angrily buckling on his returned gun belt, muttered to Nina, "If we're too late you'd better be able to run this revolution by yourself."

Nina, who had just begun to show him some warmth, now strode over and pulled him about abruptly. There was real menace in her voice. "We've been filling our churchyard with people for remarks like that. Don't delude yourself. The *padre* is much wiser than you, and he could be much, much harder to kill."

Seth might have agreed he was underestimating Father Vincente had he seen the priest and Joachim at the town's primitive jail. Pepe and the three bandits came to their feet as Vincente entered. Their heavily armed guards rose too, but the priest turned directly to the bound prisoners. He had had them advised he was negotiating for their lives with Estavez, asking only Elena in return. He came now to tell them that Estavez preferred his sexual pleasures more than he valued their lives.

"Son of a whore!" shouted Pepe, who had been sure he at least would be saved. "That stinking pig! That sinful fat bastard! May his soul fry in hell!"

The other prisoners began to groan. Two began to pray openly. The priest now carried out the grim ploy he had been planning on his way there. One of the prisoners he had no intention of releasing. This man had killed two women and a child. Had the deal gone through, he was planning to report this one shot while trying to escape. But now his death was going to serve another end.

Vincente ordered him brought out before the other prisoners and made to kneel. "We must get on with your executions," he said brusquely. "Shoot him, Joachim."

The other prisoners began to scream, *"Padre,* wait, give the man last rites. Let him confess!"

The cleric turned away indifferently. "The church does not perform sacraments for murderers," he snapped. "Joachim, shoot him!"

Joachim put his pistol to the back of the man's head and blew his skull apart. Bits of brain and shattered bone spread over the floor toward the prisoners. Vincente pointed to another one to come forward.

"Dios, dios!" screamed Pepe. "Is there no forgiveness? *Por favor, Padre, por dios,* let us confess our sins. *Padre, Padre,* have mercy!"

Vincente looked at them, his impaling eyes sending fingers of ice around their hearts. Then he pulled at his cassock as if torn by mortal judgments that hovered between bringing and denying salvation. He raised one hand as though he were still struggling with overpowering doubts. Then his stentorian voice filled the room. "Do you repent of your sins?"

The prisoners fell on their knees, the odor of the dead man's brains foul in their nostrils. "*Sí, Padre, sí*, we repent. We are sinners and unworthy of grace, but we repent. *Por favor, Padre*, please save our souls!"

The priest pondered this fearful sight before he said, "Will you serve the Lord as penance for your sins?"

"*Sí, Padre, sí.*"

"Will you help bring this sinner Estavez to suffer the judgment of the Lord?"

"I will kill that fat bastard with my bare hands!" cried Pepe.

The priest seemed to come to his decision only with reluctance and nagging doubts. "Then we will delay your execution until we witness your desire for redemption. But remember, the Lord has heard you. You will not be given a second chance to save your souls."

Tears of gratitude and relief overwhelmed the men as Vincente ordered the guards to rearm them and instructed guards and prisoners alike to get mounted and follow him and Joachim to the edge of town.

Elena had not wanted to be taken alive. That terrible decision had been made and privately sworn to, but the suddenness of her capture thwarted her carrying it out. As Estavez seized her, the two men who came at his shout immediately bound her hands behind her and ushered her into the main room, where candles were already being lit and lanterns brought to bathe the house in light. Estavez had been drinking, but he was not yet drunk. Most of the men started rummaging through the house, looking for loot, but Yoquito just stared at her as though he wanted to savor this moment that had eluded him for so long. Elena, her mind frozen at what she was about to face, paled at the thought of this odious-looking creature touching her, undressing her, raping her. She could not keep her mind off the little derringer hidden in her jacket. She must find a way to reach it before it was discovered.

Yoquito had started drinking again. He held the wine bottle in his hand and gulped at it as he joked with his men, who had begun to gather to see him ravish this highborn señora. Many of them had never seen her before and were startled at her beauty. Usually he gave the women he raped to his men when he was through with them, though all too often they were already near death from his abuse.

At last he approached Elena. Flinging the bottle away, he cut her free, making her easier to undress. First he pulled the ribbons from her hair and her dark locks cascaded down around her shoulders. Then he pulled her jacket off and threw it on the floor. He ran his hands over her breasts and, bending down, tore off her tight-clinging pants, feeling her legs and reaching up beneath her underwear to feel her thighs and buttocks. He forced her legs to open and roughly and lewdly explored her, but he had not found her derringer.

Up close to him Elena could smell his unwashed body and his foul, drunken breath. She could feel herself get nauseous as she saw the half-wild look in his black eyes, telling her he was already dangerously aroused. His face suddenly seemed to turn maniacal and she felt a stab of terror at the realization that he would surely end her ordeal by murdering her. The leering men now crowding about shouted raucously, pleading with him to undress her more so they could see her sensuous body. Without answering them, and as though he were claimed by some inner frenzy of his own, Yoquito ripped off her blouse and the light bodice holding her ample breasts. Her soft, full breasts came forth, her red nipples clear against her white skin. Then he reached for her skimpy cotton underwear and Elena finally stood stark naked, as a chorus of gaping men gasped their lusty admiration, some proposing toasts to her smooth, firm, luscious figure. But Estavez was now beginning to rave. He was losing control. Staring for a moment at her body with animallike excitement, he ended by throwing her down on her own clothes and unbuttoning his pants. Squirming around desperately, trying to evade him, Elena felt the derringer in the jacket pocket pressing into her back. Now, getting her hand behind her, she struggled to get it into the beaded mouth of the pocket. Estavez' hands were already grasping her knees, forcing them open, and she had to turn to him, seeming to give in, to get her hand into the right position. As he started to lower himself, she finally grasped the gun.

Estavez was roaring discordant sounds like an enraged bull as he came down on top of her, his hands grabbing handfuls of her hair and forcing her mouth up to his. It was to be the last violent act in his obscene life, which had so long bordered on and was now surrendering to madness, for Elena's hand appeared with a derringer that went to his temple and she fired its small, smooth bullet into his brain.

◆ ◆ ◆

The sight of lights blazing in the house made them rein up. Vincente, looking about cautiously, whispered to Joachim, who dismounted and ran into the darkness toward the great spread of lawns surrounding the house.

Seth pushed Sam forward, stopping beside the priest. "What are we waiting for?"

"Patience, *amigo*."

"Is that all you preach? Do you think Estavez ever worries about patience? Do you think sitting here being patient will save her?"

The priest looked quietly into the darkness. He could hear sounds coming from the house. To him they sounded like confusion and rancor, but he said to Seth, "*Amigo*, if the bull wishes to kill the toreador he must be bold, but if the toreador wishes to kill the bull he must be patient."

"I guess you didn't hear me. I still want to know why we are waiting."

"For Joachim."

Joachim's running steps could finally be heard in the distance. He came up to Vincente panting. *"Padre*, is very bad . . . over a hundred horses, we cannot win."

"Damn if we're not going to try!" Seth blurted out.

Vincente's arm came over to restrain him. "Do not throw your life away, *amigo*. Dead men win nothing."

"We just can't wait here!" Seth cried. "God knows what they're doing to her!"

"If God knows," the priest crossed himself, "he will understand her pain better than you."

Seth, biting back his anger, did not answer, but after a moment Vincente turned behind him and said quietly, "Everyone dismount and be silent. These arrogant thieves have posted no guards. The Almighty in his infinite grace has opened a door."

Inside, very few of the men heard the light pop of the derringer. So engrossed were they in Yoquito's savage violation of Elena that when he slumped down and Elena, continuing to twist and turn, rolled free of his body, they thought he had simply gotten too drunk to fornicate. It was Juan who rolled him over and saw the thin trickle of blood at his temple and turned to Elena, now standing nude with the empty derringer in her hand.

A mixture of emotions swept the men as they grasped this incredible scene, but not one of these emotions was grief. The sinister and secretly hated bandit chief, Estavez, was dead and this beautiful naked female was theirs, just when their lust was at a boiling point. Like slavering dogs they began closing around her, reaching for her breasts and sinking down to grab her legs. It was Juan's shouting that halted and then backed them up. "Wait!" he yelled. "Use your head instead of that sausage between your legs. Before you all had your turn, you stupid studs, she would be dead. Dead, she cannot tell us where this rich family's valuable jewels are hidden."

A few of the older bandits muttered agreement. "*Sí.* There are plenty of women," said one. "Let's us get the jewels. We have not been fighting the stubborn bastards who ran off for days for only a few moments of pleasure."

More of the men began to cry their assent. "The jewels!" they shouted. "Make her give us the jewels!"

Elena wanted desperately to cover her body, but Juan held her firmly by the wrist and his knife suddenly appeared close to her belly. "So, señora, where are the jewels?"

Elena, fighting back her panic, sensed that surrendering the jewels would not save her life, much less her virtue, but they were her only bargaining point.

"If you will give me my clothes and horse and let me go, I will tell you where they are."

Juan laughed. "So you will tell us they are hidden in a cellar wall and you will leave. How do we know you tell the truth?"

"I will," she said tremulously, knowing her voice was far too shaken to be convincing.

"Ah, no," rasped Juan, putting his knife under her chin and bringing her head up. "Señora, you are not talking to fools. Better you give us the jewels first, eh?"

Elena could not help trying to cover herself with her free hand. Standing there naked before these smirking men was draining her ability to think. "I can't . . . I am afraid you will not let me go."

"That is too bad," said Juan. "But I think some things you will be more afraid of than giving up the jewels." At first he thought of using his knife, but the knife was sharp and he had been drinking. Using it might start her bleeding too much too soon. He had to find a way to wear her down. He knew, for he had seen it with a hundred other captives, that once he broke her spirit she would surrender the jewels. Few captives could stand the torment of slowly increasing torture. After looking again at her nude body, he smiled at the heated faces around him and twisted Elena's wrist to bring her closer to him. "Señora, you are going to make love to a hundred men, starting with me. When we have tired of every hole in your body, we will start over. Sooner or later you will tell us where the jewels are hidden and we will let you go."

The blood drained from her face. Elena knew she was helpless. Why hadn't she killed herself instead of Estavez? The thought of her body being penetrated in grotesque ways by these monsters turned her stomach and she felt herself becoming ill. She knew that the pistol and the rifle Conrado had left for her were still lying on a ledge in the storage cellar. They could not save her, but if she could get that pistol for only a moment she could kill herself and end this hell. She was about to tell them that she would lead them to the jewels in order to get close to the pistol when she saw Pablo hobbling toward her and speaking to Juan.

"You are a foolish man," said Pablo. "Have I not told you a *rinche* is in love with this woman? Have I not told you he will track you down?" He turned toward the others. "He and his friends will track you all down."

The men stirred a little, but few paid attention and none were willing to take their eyes off Elena's body.

"*Rinches!*" sneered Juan. "What can they do? We have a hundred men!"

Pablo shook his head. "That is a lot of men to have to die for just one woman." Pablo knew he was bluffing, but he was sure now they would never let Elena leave alive, certain she would be gang-raped as soon as they had her jewels. But he had to face that frightening priest again as well as that dangerous-looking Seth Redmond, not to mention Elena's father, who could easily come back and have him shot, if not today, then tomorrow. He wanted to be able to say he had done everything he could to save her.

"If you wish to stay here, Pablo, you better shut up!" shouted Juan, who had noticed that Pablo's words were making some of the men restless. "There is no law here, no *policía* to worry about."

Pablo looked at him with his weird-looking eye. "Who speaks of *policía, amigo?* If you steal a man's mule or his money, that man will go to the *policía*. If you burn a man's house down, that man will go to the *policía* and pray to God to punish you. But if you take the woman a man loves and force her to make love to you, that man will come himself to kill you. Who speaks of *policía?*"

Elena pulled her wrist out of Juan's hand and reached down for her clothes. She did not want her dead body lying nude. "All right," she said in almost a whisper. "Come, I will show you where I have hidden the jewels."

Father Vincente stood close to Pepe, whose clothes were ripped in a dozen places and whose face was smeared with dirt. He was to pretend he had just made his escape. "Don't forget," said the priest, "you have only time to shout twice *'Los soldados* are coming!' before we shoot. If you can, throw that woman to the floor and keep her there. Do not waste time on Estavez. We want the woman first."

"*Sí, Padre,*" said Pepe, bowing his head. "I shall wait to deliver the judgment of God to Yoquito. A man with so many sins to confess must be given a long time to die. He must be shown that charity." He glanced at Vincente, afraid he was doing a poor job of concealing his secret craving for revenge. His vision of Estavez with stomach slit, staked out in the *despoblado,* would hardly fit the *padre*'s notion of a repentant sinner.

Vincente stared at him coldly for a few seconds, then turned to his other "converts." "You will circle the house, finding their horses. As soon as you hear us shoot, you will rush in shouting, 'Everyone out! We must save the horses! Hurry or we are lost!' "

"*Entendido, Padre,*" the anxious men assured him, gratitude still straining their faces. "And they will believe us," said one. "We know the signal the band uses for big trouble."

The men slipped away, swallowed up by darkness.

The bandits' failure to post guards enabled the priest to get within twenty feet of the house. Vincente's men were lying on the ground outside the main room. His orders were that they should fire into the house but keep their rifles up so they would hit only the ceiling. Seth reasoned at once that it was to keep from hitting Elena, but Vincente's real motive was to create as much terror as possible in the minds of the bandits. Badly outnumbered, he needed terror. It was one of the tenets of a true revolutionary.

Everyone held his breath as Pepe ran to the front of the house, scaled the few steps and entered. There was a pause such as precedes a mighty crash of thunder before he could be heard shouting at the top of his lungs, *"Los soldados* are coming!" Then a roar like heavy surf rose from the house. Vincente bit his lip and counted slowly to four before he yelled "Fire!" A volley of rifle bullets smashed into the ceiling of the main room, causing several square yards of plaster to crumble and rain down onto the startled bandits. The air became a thick curtain of choking dust, and two lanterns were knocked over and shattered, one setting a shapeless pile of drapes and bric-a-brac on fire. The men running in from two directions shouting that the horses were about to be lost could hardly be heard by the panicking bandits. They climbed over one another trying to escape, many tripping on Yoquito's body, which still lay in the center of the room. Not one thought of rushing to the windows to return the fire.

Pepe had struggled into the room howling his warning as loudly as he could. The shock of seeing him froze the crowd for a moment, giving Pepe a fleeting glimpse of two sights that registered on his brain. One was Estavez' body lying on the floor, drunk or dead, and the other was Elena being kept from covering her nude body by Juan, who was leading her roughly out of the room. Remembering Vincente's orders, he darted toward Elena, but before he had gone far the fusillade from outside smashed into the ceiling and he was blinded by dust and knocked about by scrambling men.

But Elena did not need him now. She was thrown to the floor by Juan himself, who refused to join the stampede breaking out among his men. He wanted those jewels, and with his knife against her ribs he shouted in her ear, "The jewels or you die!" Elena, forgetting her clothes, struggled to her feet and led him staggering through the servants' quarters and into the storage cellar. She pointed to the stove. "In there!" she gasped as she sank back against the ledge holding the guns. Juan pulled the door open and, using his muscular body, pushed the stove farther from the wall. Then he reached in and seized the soft pillowcase that held the treasure. He opened it and thrust his hand in to grasp one of its gold-mounted gems. So excited was he

that his lust disappeared. He would now vanish and leave this cringing woman grateful for her life. But when he looked up, Elena was
holding a large pistol trained on his chest.

"Señora!" he gulped. "*Por dios*, Juan keeps his word! You are free!
What are you doing?"

"This!" she screamed as she fired. His body was hurled back several
feet by the force of the bullet, and the heavy bag of jewels dropped
with a tinkle and a thud to the floor.

It was over. But for Seth another more fateful drama had begun.
His few turbulent days in Laredo had masked a resolve that was
building up in him. There was no denying what his coming here
meant. Though he had traveled only a few hundred miles from his
embattled ranch on the Hondo, he knew, holding Elena and watching
flames from the burning mansion throwing up serpents of light that
coiled and darted into the night, that he had just made a fatal march
across the terrain of life, had followed a secret hunger for this mystifying and magnetic girl beyond borders as dangerous as those di-
viding nations at war. The insurgent temper that had driven him
from the pastoral life of North Carolina to the bloody, disputed wastes
of western Texas was astir again, driving him from the tormenting
judgments of Isabelle to the spirited and sensuous figure of this girl
whose unabashed femininity, even in humiliation, rose to the heroic.
He had found her nude, having slain her captor, a smoking gun in
her hand. Whatever peculiar chemistry fired her, it was an allure that
fed and fulfilled his gnawing need for a world away from what he
now saw as his tarnished past, away from the memories Tate's black
eyes kept alive, away from the awkward and enervating ashes of
Isabelle's love.

He knew he would still have to return to the ranch, face its demanding days, work toward its desperate and still-distant promise,
but he also knew a part of him would never go back. Like that of
many men before him, his world had inexorably split in two, each
half centering about a woman. Life in one meant exile from the other,
life in both threatened exile from his son.

They could not remain long in torn and disputed Laredo. Vincente
wanted them gone. Elena, concealing her jewels, left on her gray
gelding with Seth riding Sam and steering a cautious route north of
the river. They had to stop often to study the land, for danger threat-

ened from all quarters. The river valley was a cauldron of violence and terror. Menacing gangs of desperados were everywhere, looting and killing. Any cloud of dust could well be a harbinger of death. It was two days before they felt safe, for by then they were approaching the plain before Corpus Christi. That night, before they entered town, under a lantern moon, they made wild, lasting love. It was a joining that not only locked their lives together but reached beyond the heated rapture of the moment to shape the destinies of many in the fateful years ahead.

Isabelle listened quietly as Prent and Andy related Seth's abrupt but insistent demand that they return to the ranch, never bothering to explain his own disappearance. Prent still rankled, saying he didn't intend to hold still for that kind of treatment again. Neither he nor Andy could offer any inkling as to where Seth had gone. The hurried mention of a friend in trouble told nothing.

The two young men stood together, their clothes covered with trail dust, their angry expressions fixed on Todd, who was shaking his head, weighing their words, finally dismissing their importance. He, like Bessie, was sure it would all be easily explained when Seth returned. Only Isabelle, hours later in the silence of her room, sensed this incident's faint but fatal menace, its vague warning of another's presence in what she knew was an increasingly inaccessible side of Seth's life. Transfixed by this realization, she sat staring out at the long reaches of mesquite range, the familiar drift of hills, the curving green depression that marked the way of the creek. The amber of late afternoon was over the land, whispering that the day, like the land itself, was aging. Turning to her mirror, she caught the legacy of this country's burnished sun and everlasting winds. Her once bright golden hair and clear ivory skin had taken on the land's amber hue. There were thin lines tinged with white about her mouth and forehead where the skin had folded in against the elements. She was aging. Her eyes looked weary as from some inner but futile searching. Somewhere in her depths she knew the morning of life was over, the blush of hopeful new beginnings gone. She was changing, hardening. These harsh years on this unanointed soil had drained her; the land had offered only its own kind of strength, the strength to struggle and survive. She needed that kind of strength now. Emotions that so long had ruled her heart, that made her cling to Seth, to Tate, and then mistakenly to both, had left her helpless. Those sentiments belonged to that near-forgotten world of crinolines and laughter, the world of Carolina woodlands and the thrills of emerging love and womanhood. Now she sat staring out at a grimmer and grayer world. She and Seth had become strangers, and she steeled herself for the slow creep of shadows falling across the lonely way ahead.

Part Six

MILLS
of the
GODS

May 1859

23

The great migration westward that had started with the "Forty-niners" opened the nation to distances that made men helpless without dependable horseflesh. Losing one's horse was often equivalent to losing one's life on the lonely plains. Marauding Indians swarmed the land, but even white faces were not always friendly. The frontier had become a haven for every man dodging the military, a woman or a rope. Visitors to Thunder Run were given close scrutiny by Todd, and hired hands had to have a convincing story if they came from parts unknown.

But business was booming. A Redmond horse was already a source of pride in the Southwest, famed for endurance in the semiarid stretches of mesquite and piñon country, easily outlasting eastern breeds. Seth was proud of his spread with its endless corrals, farrier shed, smokehouses and the huge, airy stable that could hold up to a hundred head. Bunkhouses for hired hands sat along the wagon road to the main trail. Though intermittent troubles kept the ranch house looking like a small fort, it was roomy and spacious inside, cool in the summer and warm in the winter. He had bought up much of the surrounding property, finally getting the MacFee place when old Mrs. MacFee died and, after "mad" Carrie married Andy Sawyer, the heavy-drinking Angus and his sons drank themselves into debt.

Seth, though no longer young, had aged well. He wore a heavy brush mustache tinged with a silver that became more pronounced as one's eye rose to his temples or followed around his full head of hair. He was still known for his determination and his way with horses, and he had retained much of his commanding air, but unlike Todd, he was not popular in the political sense. Something of that secluded inner world in which he chose to live still remained. He had long since made an uneasy peace with those at Thunder Run. He was still the principal owner of the ranch, even though Isabelle and Bessie refused to deal with him directly and Inez, loyal to Isabelle, no longer approached him. His separation from Isabelle at first had caused wide comment, but a frontier looking back on years of tragic deaths could not linger long on a sundered marriage. Seth had only a few intimate friends, none of whom showed a difference in their feelings for him, but he knew that Isabelle was the recipient of most of the public sympathy and support. Elena's Mexican roots made it easy for local Texans to direct their sentiments at her, but surprisingly she also had her champions, and inevitably her beauty and bearing won acceptance in many circles of prominent men. For a year or two Seth and Elena resided in San Antonio, renting a spacious house near Julio's farm. Carlota and Don José, coming up to live with them, insisted on filling in as servants even though Elena regarded them as family. Yet Seth was restless and ill content there. He was too far from his ranch, too far from its challenges, its unexpected trials, its daily decisions. Todd was a competent manager, but Seth wanted to be part of its now-visible growth. In time he took to staying at the old MacFee place, which made it easier to be on hand every morning, but this soon created problems with Elena, problems that were never to be totally resolved.

The levels of society, both Mexican and Texan, that Elena hoped to enjoy in San Antonio saw no problem with her living with Seth, providing it was to be dignified one day by marriage. Still, Elena did not press him on this; she was too happy to be selfish and too sensible to be demanding. She had come too close to tragedy to take this interlude of bliss lightly. But gradually Seth, after word of Ramón's death arrived, appeared to want marriage, quietly assuring himself he would build a relationship with Jason that Isabelle, even if embittered by divorce, would not resent. But when Seth consulted a lawyer, his eyes were opened to a complication he had never suspected. Divorce meant property sharing. Divorce meant giving Isabelle half his equity in Thunder Run. That together with the equity the Salingers now commanded would give her and Todd control of the ranch.

A sober Seth reluctantly explained this to a puzzled Elena, but she knew how much the ranch meant to him and did not raise the subject again. But married or not, Elena wanted to be with Seth and Seth was spending more and more days around the Hondo. Sometimes he was gone for a week. Inevitably the thought of her moving into the old MacFee place surfaced. It had many drawbacks and the idea was never warmly received by Carlota or Don José, who considered the old farmhouse far too lonely and isolated and, unlike Thunder Run, not built to repel Indians. Less discussed or even mentioned, but equally discouraging, was its nearness to Isabelle. Elena had never met this woman Seth had once loved, but she easily understood how any woman would resent a rival taking up residence eight short miles away. For a time she put it out of her mind.

But the following spring when the range was filling with a slew of gangling foals that had to be gathered and protected against wolves, packs of coyotes and even bears or mountain lions, Seth was gone for almost two weeks. Elena resignedly made the trip out, for she knew in her heart that Seth would never abandon his ranch. Deep instinct warned her not to insist on his staying in San Antonio; the woman who wanted Seth must never allow him to feel there were limits to her love. Had Isabelle mistakenly done this?

Before she left again she had completed plans to enlarge and decorate the old MacFee farmhouse. With some colorful tapestries, lamps and the right furnishings it could be made quite comfortable. She knew Carlota and Don José were far from convinced, but they would realize in time that her happiness was necessary to theirs.

The following month Seth brought Isaac Sawyer and a hired carpenter to study and make many valuable additions to Elena's plans. Within a week, with Elena already deciding to expand the barn into a suitable stable and become part of Seth's life by breeding a few horses herself, the first steps in the beautifying process began that would remove the last traces of the lonely and ill-starred farm the MacFee family had settled.

Because unending military forays into their winter range were depriving the tribes of any power to raid, the valley of the Hondo finally entered a few peaceful, even memorable years. The young ones at Thunder Run—Jason now eighteen, Taska and Tate now almost seventeen—having spent their childhood facing a lonely land together, were inseparable. All three could ride like demons, but agile Tate could do things with a horse that halted the breath and made the heart skip a beat. He could stand on one foot and whip a horse around the corral at top speed. He could do a handstand on the horse's back as it leaped a three-foot rail. By grabbing the stirrups he could swing himself under a horse's belly and come up on the other side. By his early teens he was able to break and train horses faster than any experienced hand they hired. Seth often watched him with grudging admiration but made no attempt, as did Todd, to compliment or encourage him. Tate was also quietly becoming an expert tracker, with an uncanny nose for the hideouts of the occasional Indian raiding parties. He was not going to be as tall as Jason, but his muscular body promised strength and the suppleness of a puma. Yet he was a quiet, moody boy who worshiped Jason, was content to be with Taska but, if often seeking out his mother, showed no interest in other adults. Seth he had taken to watching guardedly from a distance but never approached. Todd confidently prophesied that someday Tate would be "pulling the weight of two men and pulling it better."

Golden-haired Jason was growing into a handsome young man. He was easygoing, almost always smiling and nearly impossible to dislike. His disposition made him popular around the ranch. Tate and Taska were devoted to him, even if there were differences everyone noticed. Jason was as good a hunter as Tate, but he lacked Tate's intensity and ability to read sign. He had the ready warmth of Taska, but he lacked her air of excitement. Seth, thinking he was something of a dreamer, kept looking for ways to "toughen him up." He had noticed as they approached puberty that Jason and Taska were drawing closer together. Already the sap was rising in his son and Taska's body was beginning to round out and match the sensuality that glowed from her mischievously darting eyes. He was not surprised, but it was then that he decided to send Jason east to a military school. Before his son started committing himself in life it might be best he found out that west Texas and one handy girl were not the world.

Sooner or later, men who work around horses are bound to become obsessed with their speed. Horse racing's popularity in the Anglo-Texan neighborhoods of San Antonio near rivaled that of fiestas in their Mexican counterparts. Fleet-footed champions were brought from the East and matched against local steeds; betting was often heavy, often reckless. On national holidays, such as the Fourth of July or fair days, the three-quarter circuit of flatland on the outskirts of town was crowded with stands and betting booths as the public came to see a spectacle that by evening usually impoverished substantial numbers. The papers had been full of stories about the unbeaten Georgia Boy, owned by a wealthy plantation owner near Galveston. He was coming to race Gold Nickel, a local gelding owned by the mayor, a sleek dun-colored horse whose blinding speed on his one outing had made it impossible to find competitors. It was known that a five-thousand-dollar bet had been arranged between the owners.

Seth had lost his youthful interest in breeding fast horses, speed could be bred only at the cost of stamina, and mounts without "bottom" had proved to be of limited value in the West. But, like any other youth, Jason had an interest in excitement. With Todd's approval he managed some selective breeding and had been training, with rising hopes, a long-legged colt Taska had christened Blue Dancer. Seth concluded his son was entering a dream world when he heard of plans to take Blue Dancer in to race against Georgia Boy and Gold Nickel. He took Todd to task with a touch of irritation. "Why are you letting him waste time like that?"

"Letting a young man try something he thinks he can do isn't wasting time."

"You don't think he has a chance of winning, do you? Don't you read the papers?"

"Seth, this is a horse race. What the papers say doesn't matter. Horses don't read the papers."

"You going?"

"Wouldn't miss it for the world. Fourth of July only comes once a year."

Seth was to discover that Elena had no intention of missing it either. She had been looking forward to going into town for this holiday for a month. She was dying to do some shopping and visit a few friends. Carlota and Don José were also coming, having been invited to stay at Julio's with Seth and Elena.

Seth found himself paying for five seats in the stands, secretly getting caught up in the excitement and unable to suppress a little pride that Thunder Run had an entry in the race. There were five horses parading around the infield, and Seth examined them with an eye that had served a lifetime of judging horses. The superb Georgia Boy had the best lines for speed, while Gold Nickel, he decided, should be second. A Mexican entry simply called Laredo made Elena smile. "I should bet it just on a hunch," she laughed. "It has romantic eyes."

"Save your money," cautioned Seth. "I don't believe that oat burner could run to the barn." He looked with greater interest at a big roan some Cherokees had brought down from their reservation. The horse's size was impressive; if there was going to be an upset this might be the animal to do it. He was listed on the program as Smoke. A nearby betting booth had Smoke listed at five to one.

Blue Dancer hardly looked as though he belonged. He was long-legged enough and held his head well, but he seemed fractious and a thin line of foam streaked down his arched neck. Seth noticed his odds were fifteen to one at several betting booths. All things considered, those were pretty fair odds.

In the distance he could see Isabelle and Bessie being joined by Taska, Todd and Jason. They had apparently gotten seats at the finish line. For a moment he stared at them. It seemed strange that a woman with whom he had spent a large part of his life was now only another head in the crowd. He could see from time to time that she was glancing toward him, perhaps wanting a glimpse of Elena, who with her dark tresses over a bright yellow blouse and sequined green skirt could only be partially seen at that distance. But hearing Elena coming up with Carlota and Don José, he could not keep staring. He turned away, just catching Jason settling himself beside his mother. But why wasn't Jason with his horse? It took him a minute or two of studying the horses milling about the infield to sight Tate standing with Blue Dancer, speaking with the judges and horse handlers. Tate was stripped to the waist and carried no quirt.

Something was being announced to the riders, and Seth could see from the judges' gestures that they were being told to line up behind a heavy rope lying across the track. Above them a long stretch of wire had been strung up to mark the end. Apparently their positions had been decided by lot. A hush began to settle over the crowd as a flurry of betting took place just before the start. Seth was hardly surprised when he saw Georgia Boy going off at four to five and Gold Nickel at eight to five. He could hear bookies now hawking Blue Dancer at twenty to one. Only two jockeys, Tate and the squat Indian on Smoke, were riding bareback. Each horse had the number of its position chalked on its forehead. Blue Dancer's number was five.

The start came with everyone standing as a judge on either side of the track dropped the rope and a pistol fired. Georgia Boy, showing his careful training, was off in a flash, three others went pounding after him. Only Laredo seemed to have trouble getting away and reaching stride. Gold Nickel was soon only a length behind Georgia Boy and his jockey was whipping him madly for speed. The race was twice around a three-quarter-mile track, and as they passed the first time Georgia Boy was in command with Gold Nickel finally reaching him and matching him stride for stride. Smoke had settled down in third, Blue Dancer was fourth and Laredo trailed. As the horses swept by shouts of encouragement rose from the crowd. But soon shouts were not enough. Male spectators along the rail began slapping it with rolls of newspaper, several women excitedly folded parasols to join them. People betting the favorites screamed at them to hold the lead, those on long shots beseeched their animals for more speed. Many in the crowd noticed that Tate had not settled on his horse's back like the other riders but was crouched over his mount's neck, his head almost even with Blue Dancer's. Seth could see that his weight was being held forward on the horse's shoulders, and that Tate was keeping a powerful hold on his mount. To his amazement he could see that Blue Dancer, though staying with the torrid pace, was far from being extended. As they came around the final turn Seth began to suspect that Georgia Boy and Gold Nickel were racing each other into defeat; the battle for the lead for over a mile was going to leave both with little for the finishing stretch. As though to fulfill his prediction, Smoke began to close ground on the outside as Laredo came up to join Blue Dancer. Then all of them started to gain on the leaders. The cries of the crowd became deafening as the horses turned into the last quarter mile.

Curiously, Seth had an almost sickening sensation as he realized that Tate was riding the way Comanches did when they swung down to fire under their horse's neck. Yet incredibly, in spite of this, young Tate had Blue Dancer coming on in a determined bid behind Smoke, bringing the now-fired-up Laredo with him. Georgia Boy and Gold Nickel still had their noses out in front, but the field was closing around them and they were beaten. Smoke was the first to snatch the lead as his jockey's quirt beat a vicious tattoo on his flank. But now Tate was setting Blue Dancer down and urging him forward for all he was worth. Game Laredo refused to quit, he held on at Blue Dancer's side, his jockey whipping him savagely in a last futile effort before the wire. But it was not enough; Blue Dancer, with his ears pinned back and driving flat out, kept his head in front. The horses swept under the wire. For a moment the crowd was stunned. Then the judges started signaling Blue Dancer as the winner, Laredo second, Smoke a close third and Georgia Boy outlasting Gold Nickel for fourth.

Cheers from the Thunder Run crowd could be heard across the field. Tate returned slowly and dismounted to the hugs of Taska, Jason and Isabelle. Whether it was from shyness or a reluctance to deal with strangers wasn't clear, but Tate refused to go up to receive the winner's trophy, and after some confusion Jason went up instead.

There was some excitement around Seth too. Neither Julio nor Don José was a betting man, and they had given their five dollars to Elena and Carlota to wager for them. The women had decided out of patriotism to stick with the Mexican horse, even though Seth had said it couldn't win. "I just had a feeling," said Elena. "After all, we fell in love in Laredo."

Carlota had smiled. "You romantics, you're going to cost me money. But remember, you were his second love. Why don't we bet that poor sentimental animal for second? If that lonely-looking *jaca* really has a chance to win, those sly-looking gentlemen in the booths would not be offering us eighteen to one." They bet the horse for second.

Laredo paid nine to one for place and all but Seth had forty-five dollars for their five-dollar investment. Elena couldn't resist teasing him. "They tell me Laredo made it to the barn," she said, looking about. "Did anyone see what happened to Georgia Boy?"

Seth shrugged, tearing up the slip that represented his twenty-five-dollar investment on the favorite. "That's one thing about horse racing," he muttered. "The biggest dummy in the world only has to win a race to look like a pillar of wisdom."

Elena shoved him playfully. "Why don't you go over and congratulate that young boy? He gave a magnificent ride."

Seth stared at the crowd still milling about where the Thunder Run people were examining Tate's trophy. Somehow he didn't want to. Somehow it rankled him that only Tate's awesome skill with horses could have brought Blue Dancer home a victor.

A few hours later, when he was leaving the race grounds, he ran into Todd. Todd had clearly been celebrating and was still elated. "Did you see the hell of a ride he gave that horse? He was as good as any goddamn Comanche!" Seth almost said, Why shouldn't he be, you forget he's half Comanche. But something in Todd's expression stopped him. It was only later that he found himself bothered by the uncomfortable feeling that what he had seen in Todd's face might have been pity, pity he couldn't share in Thunder Run's victory.

When the easily smiling Jason, with his military haircut and his relief at finishing a year of disciplining and military tactics at the Citadel, returned, he found the ranch in a state of shock and confusion. Two of their most valuable stallions had disappeared. Blue Dancer and his progeny had been fun and racing had supplied a little excitement to relieve the unending routine of ranch work, but the two missing stallions, High Clover and Midnight, were the real source of the ranch's profits. Without them the quality of their breeding operation, built up over years, would suffer crippling losses. The horses had been put out to pasture, as was normal practice after a period of stud, and the following morning they had been gone. After a summary inspection of the ground Todd decided that the thieves had been Indians who had driven the horses west. Seth, studying the unshod hoofmarks, agreed.

Though there was no panic, the concern was real. Those stud horses represented considerable wealth, and prime mares from all over the western counties were being sent to Thunder Run for their services. Seth and Todd knew their only hope of seeing them returned lay in discovering the identity of the thieves.

Jason offered to go after the thieves and Todd, after trying to estimate the probable dangers, decided Tate had better accompany him. They were warned to simply find the horses. If recovering them required a fight, they were to wait until Todd and Seth could get there with a dozen or more ranch hands.

The silent hills to the west were still dangerous. Small Comanche war parties, headed for Mexico, still traveled along the trace, and from time to time outlaw bands coming to or from their haunts around Santa Fe or Taos could be encountered along the few waterways. But Tate made his way swiftly out to and beyond the Sabinal. Here the fading tracks turned northward, but Tate had already decided it was not Indians they were tracking. These were whites riding unshod ponies, hoping perhaps to make pursuers think they were natives. But no Indian would have driven horses as poorly as these amateurs, nor would they have wasted so much energy riding around, seemingly uncertain of their way.

Jason had learned to accept Tate's judgment about such things.

Tate did not always have reasons for what he said, but Jason had long been convinced Tate could sense things that weren't apparent to others for hours or even days. But this new fact surely increased their danger. White men planned further ahead than Indians and usually had far more resources to cover their crimes than nomadic tribesmen. What's more, there was something strange about this theft. With unlimited stock to pick from, Indians would have been far more likely to choose younger horses they could train as well as breed. But if it hadn't been Indians it was rustlers, and more than likely they were aware they might be pursued. Tate was beginning to suspect that they were dealing with more than two.

As usual Tate was right.

The faint tracks they were following were suddenly joined by four others, all shod. Jason watched Tate stare at these new tracks for long moments, finally reminding him they were sitting out there in the open, with only God knowing who was close by and maybe watching. But Tate mumbled that these new tracks were several hours old, and as they began to follow them he added that whoever had made them was anxious to get somewhere fast, for they had left at a run.

Moving carefully, it took them until that evening to reach three long-deserted hogans, in back of which they could see a rough corral formed by piles of sagebrush. In this makeshift pen, heads down, munching on the sparse blades of grass, were High Clover and Midnight. Outside the farthest but biggest hogan were three large wagons, and in the same pen as the stallions were several horses includng some heavy stock to pull the wagons. A Mexican herder tended the crowded corral, and nearby two men were squatting over a small fire, sharing a bottle. Before dark they saw the other four riders coming in, bringing what proved to be food and additional bottles.

Tate had already detected that the men driving the horses were arguing among themselves. As they ate and drank, two of them sat quietly with the herder, while three others sat apart. He had noticed that one had left almost immediately, continuing north on the trail toward distant Santa Fe. With darkness Tate crept close enough to hear the three speaking in Spanish. Anger had raised their voices, and wine or whisky was making them repetitious. In time his familiarity with Spanish, a legacy of border life, enabled him to grasp that they were complaining about risking their necks on this long ride to Taos for what they considered meager pay. Horse thieves, no matter what their story, were summarily hanged in these parts.

Tate silently watched the fires go out in the rustlers' camp and for a time studied the two sitting with the herder, quietly smoking in the dark. Slowly but inevitably the three who had been drinking began to roll up in their blankets and were soon emitting a rhythm of drunken snores. Finally, glancing uneasily at the sky, Tate began whispering to Jason. In spite of the odds they would have to try for the horses before dawn; too many things could happen by dawn, all of them bad. He was particularly worried that the rider who had left would return with more men. Right now they had only the two with the herder to worry about. The others were dead drunk.

But Jason could only shake his head when he heard Tate's daring plan for reclaiming the horses. It sounded suicidal. He wanted Jason to follow him into the camp and by sheer surprise overcome those who had remained sober before the others had a chance to react. Jason objected by leaning closer, his face, even in the darkness, nettled with concern and doubt. Tate, understanding, stared back at him without complaint and offered to go alone. Realizing his brother meant it, Jason could only sit back and sigh. Whatever other people, including his father, thought, Jason loved his strange half brother, this proud, brooding rebel he knew would have made any sacrifice for him. He was not going to let him go alone. Taking only the moment it required for the two young men to embrace and wish each other luck, Jason followed Tate into the camp.

He watched Tate slip ahead like a dusky ghost, silently circling the group of loud snoring men and coming to the entrance to the hogan, where three figures lay like dark clumps on the ground. Tate awakened the herder with a hand over his mouth. The man froze with fright, and Tate, warning him by driving the muzzle of his gun into his side, heaved him over to Jason, who pressed his face against the earth. But the bodies were too close together. The other two men were suddenly awake, and Tate had to club one into silence with his gun while trying to throttle the other by pulling his blanket over his head. But the blanket wasn't enough. The startled man managed to get off a panicky shout, and at once the element of surprise was lost. The drunks started coming out of their stupor. One had reached for his gun and was firing wildly from a lying position. Jason released the herder and drew his own gun. Tate lunged across the yard like a springing tiger, and aiming for the orange flashes, he kicked the upraised gun from the outlaw's hand. Then he dropped down beside them. "If you want to die, just move!" he shouted. Jason grabbed the man struggling out of the blanket and, pulling the gun from his holster, hurled him to the ground.

While the men were still stunned, Tate quickly collected their guns. Then he ordered them to build a fire. The men, some of them still groggy, not having shaken off their drunken haze, started to grumble. What the hell did he want? Jason marveled at the cool, even menacing way Tate was ordering them about, for these were dangerous-looking men. Some of them still had knives, and one or two were watching him and Tate for a careless move. Jason wanted to find the stallions and clear out, but Tate was now standing boldly in the fire light, commanding them to take off their boots. Reluctantly they complied. When they did he strung the boots on a piece of canvas line and hung them from the nearest wagon. Then he turned to Jason. "Take that herder and get a halter on our horses . . . bring them out here."

Jason looked at him uncertainly. If he left, Tate would have to cover five of these increasingly desperate and threatening men himself. "You sure this is going to be all right?" he said hoarsely.

"Get the horses," repeated Tate.

Jason hurried the herder to the back of the hogan, where the trembling man finally sought out two halters. Because the Mexican was so scared, they were some time finding High Clover and Midnight in the darkness and fixing halters on them. They had almost finished when shots broke out behind them.

Suspecting the worst, Jason pulled the herder in front of him and started around the hogan to where he could see the fire. Tate was still standing there, but as Jason forced the Mexican forward to get a view of the hogan's entrance he saw two forms on the ground and the three remaining outlaws on their knees. Whatever had happened had convinced the three to follow Tate's every word.

Tate, seeing that Jason was back, ordered the men to open the corral. He signaled Jason to bring up their own horses as the corral was emptied of its now nervous and restless animals. Tate tied the string of boots to the back of a skittish mare before using the captured guns to spook the herd and send them stampeding out over the dark plain.

Then the two left at a run, each leading a stallion. When they finally pulled up to walk their mounts, Jason called out to Tate in the dark. "Tate, did you kill those two men?"

"What two men?"

"Those we left lying on the ground."

"Oh, those."

A long silence ensued and finally Jason had to repeat his question. "Well, did you kill them?"

Tate raised up in the saddle and peered into the darkness ahead. He seemed to be studying the dim outline of hills traced by the spray of stars over the far horizon, but as he put the horses into a run again Jason could just hear him muttering, "Maybe."

In the morning Isabelle started demanding that Todd go after "her boys."

"They're men now, they can take care of themselves" was his response, but his tone was enough to warn her that he was worried. "Can't go, anyway," he said, "Mr. Curtis will be here any moment."

Isabelle stood with her hands on her hips. "Curtis? Reed Curtis? What the devil is he coming here for now?"

"He wants to buy some of our prime stallions but didn't want the ones we offered. Now we've lost two of our best, and he's back."

"What's he been offering?" inquired Bessie.

"Three, maybe four thousand . . . that is, if we let him have his pick."

"And what was his pick?"

Todd smiled meaningfully. "He was after High Clover. Seth wouldn't hear of it."

"Huh," muttered Isabelle, her face still drawn with concern. "Well, we better be hearing something from my boys right soon or somebody has got to go after them."

"Give it till tonight," placated Todd. "Now excuse me, that's Curtis I see coming in the yard."

Reed Curtis was a surprisingly active man considering his sizable paunch and his considerable wealth. He belonged to that breed of men who seek first money, then notoriety, then power. Todd didn't much care for him as a man, but he had learned that the first rule of business is that customers have only one failing—not paying their bills. Everything else is overlooked. Seth was less tolerant; people with exaggerated notions of their own importance bothered him. Curtis had been trying to take over a settlement south of Castroville for some time to build a community he could control. He was a man of enormous ego and occasionally given to dubious means of getting his way. His type was not uncommon in the West, laxity of law and a continuing tide of desperate settlers providing a ready market for them. Today Curtis came alone, but often he brought his henchmen, an uneasy array of drifters, shady figures with furtive expressions or rough misfits with callous ways and vulgar tongues.

He had first tried to buy Thunder Run, making several offers, but Seth had ignored him. Still, Curtis was not a man many people ignored and he'd been trying to buy it in bits and pieces ever since. Todd received him in the large front room of the ranch house. Curtis always expected coffee when he came in the morning or bourbon if he came in the afternoon. But now he seemed under some stress and, rubbing his face with a large silk handkerchief, turned immediately to business. "Going to sell me that stallion?"

"Nope. Couldn't if I wanted to, he's been run off."

"Run off?" roared Curtis. "Who the hell would steal a horse around here?"

"We're going to find out."

"How?"

Todd stared at him for a moment. In spite of the cool interior of the room, Curtis was perspiring. Todd ignored his last question. "He isn't up for sale. Did you want a drink?"

Curtis shifted uncomfortably in his chair and rubbed his open fingers across his mouth. "Haven't got much time today. Maybe we can talk about some of your mares. I've taken a fancy to several."

Todd settled back in his seat. "Reed, we got plenty of horses to sell, but we don't usually sell our breeding stock. Thought you understood that."

"Hell, Todd, everything is for sale, you know damn well it is, providing the price is right."

"Not everything."

"Well, if you don't want to do business, I guess I'm just wasting time. Best be on my way."

"Up to you, Reed. You're welcome to set a spell. Sorry we can't accommodate you."

"Seems to me selling them is better than having them stolen, but reckon a man plays it the way he sees it."

"Reckon that's right."

After Curtis left, Todd, now strangely bothered, went out to the yard and beckoned to Seth, who was coming out of the stable.

"We better get out there," Todd began. "I got a feeling something is wrong, Reed Curtis is trying to buy some of our brood mares, and he's sweating like a whore on Judgment Day."

"Nothing that sidewinder could dream up would surprise me," answered Seth. "We taking some of the boys with us?"

"Not this time. Work has still got to go on around here. I just figure to run down Jason and Tate. By now they might know something."

"Fine. I'll have one of the hands get word to Elena. Shouldn't take us no more than a day or two."

Isabelle looked relieved to hear they were going after her sons. But Bessie, whose daughters were away at school in Louisiana, never liked Todd leaving. "Don't go getting into any gunplay over those damn horses. Thought we were finally going to have some peace around here."

Todd kissed her. He gave no indication that Curtis' visit had him worried or that the boys' delay in returning might mean trouble. When they left he had thought they were trailing a small party of Comanches. Now he wasn't so sure.

They followed the boys' tracks, and just before noon they sighted Jason and Tate coming back, the stallions in tow. Soberly they listened as Jason described the rustlers and how he and Tate had managed to recover High Clover and Midnight. Seth and Todd exchanged glances; they knew now that the situation was far more serious than the boys thought. It took money and organization to move horses from Hondo to Taos; it took something more sinister to make it look like the work of Indians. That they had survived the encounter was amazing. But Jason made it clear that it was Tate who had tamed the outlaws and made it possible to reclaim the stallions.

This incident was to precipitate an unexpected but noticeable shift in Seth's perspective on things, making everyone at Thunder Run stop and breathe a sigh of relief. Tate had already won something of a reputation with his ride on Blue Dancer. For although the mayor had fired the jockey on Gold Nickel for coming in last, the plantation owner from Galveston had offered Tate a hundred dollars a race to ride for him. "That boy is worth twenty lengths to a horse. If he'd been riding Georgia Boy, there'd been room for a buffalo stampede between him and the rest."

Still, nothing could induce Tate to consider the offer.

But privately Seth was finding it harder and harder to ignore him. He was beginning to feel petty, niggardly, as though reluctant to give another man his just due. Hearing how the stallions were recovered, he decided he would look ridiculous not commenting on this display of mettle.

The following day, for the first time in his memory, Tate watched Seth deliberately coming up to speak to him. Puzzled, he stood listening while intentionally gazing the other way.

"Understand you showed real guts getting those horses back." Tate made no effort to turn to face him, and Seth, though embarrassed, had to force himself to go on. "Five-to-one odds is sure a damn rough and sorry picture for a man to have to face."

When Tate finally looked around, his eyes had a distant but hard spark of flint against granite. "I've faced worse!" he snapped, and with a hitch at his belt he swung away.

But worse was coming. Two days later an attempt was made to steal some brood mares from the north pasture. Two ranch hands riding the fence line rode up in time to stop it, but a gunfight broke out and one of the hands was wounded. Seth and Todd had had enough. When Tate came back to say that the hoofprints left behind by the rustlers matched some of those he had seen while trailing the stallions, all work was put aside. Tate was sent back to pick up the tracks and see where they led. To no one's surprise, he followed them to the Curtis spread.

That evening Seth and Todd sat stolidly cleaning their guns as Prent came to report that the ranch hands were ready. All had handguns, and only two or three needed rifles. Seth pointed to the row of rifles mounted on both sides of the fireplace. Rick came in wearing two bone-handled pistols, but his expression said that he had lost some of his boyish craving for action. He sat down quietly beside Jason and watched Tate lean against the rock facing of the mantel, looking into the fire.

It was Isabelle and Bessie who were doing the talking, and both were grim and upset at what they saw coming. "What are you planning to do—kill them all?" Bessie was bending over Todd, her mouth inches from his ear. "Don't you think some of you might be killed or badly maimed? Todd, for God's sake, use your head. This man and his ruffians can surely be handled some other way."

"What other way?"

"Why don't you go to the law?" demanded Isabelle.

Todd shook his head in mute irritation. "The law? Can't you women see, this man is beyond the law."

"Nobody is beyond the law," said Jason.

Seth held up his pistol to check the barrel. "Son, you've been away to school for a while. This isn't South Carolina. The law here is a sheriff and a half-wit deputy in San Antonio . . . not sure he even has any authority in Castroville. But Curtis would laugh him off anyway . . . probably worry more about some mosquito bite."

"Why don't you send them a warning?" insisted Bessie.

"We're planning to," responded Seth. "By morning he'll know exactly how we feel about his rustling our stock."

Isabelle was secretly furious. Was there no end to violence in this godforsaken country? First Indians and now this evil in their own kind. She didn't want her sons killed because these two ex-Rangers thought that talking like reasonable men was backing down. She was about to take the floor, demanding that Curtis be warned before any shooting started, when unexpectedly Isaac Sawyer came through the door and immediately everyone's attention focused on him.

"Evenin'," said Isaac, looking slowly around the room, taking in and nodding at the abundance of guns. "Suspect you're headed for the Curtis place."

"Reckon that's right," said Todd. "We're a little late paying our respects, but we figure to make up for it."

"Then maybe I got here in time."

"What do you mean?" muttered Seth.

"Listen to me. That critter is dangerous as hell. He's done this before. When he wants something, like I hear he wants your ranch, he keeps making it more and more dangerous to hang on to it till folks get scared and let him have the damn thing—usually at his price! He's just starting with you."

Seth grunted, "And we're about to finish with him."

"You won't without a bloody fight."

Todd tried to keep from smiling. "With that riffraff he's hired?"

" 'Tain't all riffraff now. That's what I wanted to warn you about. He's got Sam Cheek, who's already gunned down a heap of men in Louisiana where they got a rope awaiting him, and that scoundrel Aleppo . . . the one from the border with a reputation not fittin' for Christian ears. Curtis knows y'all are fighting men, but he figures you won't pay the price."

"He figured wrong," declared Seth.

"Well, we're going to talk first!" declared Isabelle. "Could be he'll find out fighting us might just be too costly for him."

Isaac stared at her for a moment. "Could make some sense," he allowed. "But be careful. That son of a bitch has got a record for dirty dealing that ain't likely to be beat."

That night was spent in agonizing argument. Isabelle and Bessie discovered that there was no way to keep Seth and Todd from going after Curtis; both had killed men for less. But by midnight it was clear that the women would not give in without a concession, and reluctantly the men finally gave them one. Though hardly anyone believed it would help, they agreed that someone would try to talk to Curtis first.

Jason, catching his mother's eye, volunteered to go. Isabelle and Bessie quickly exchanged looks of relief. They had secretly been hoping for this. Jason was not a firebrand, he was reasonable and if, as some thought, a little too easygoing, he was not a man who took readily to violence or who looked for the bad in people.

"Is he going alone?" asked Todd, still irritated by the decision.

"No, he's not," said Tate, who had been standing quietly in the background.

There was a time when Tate would never have spoken up, or if he had would have been stared down by Seth, but that day was past. The quiet acceptance of this remark, which subtly qualified the decision, made Jason look down and smile.

They left shortly after dawn and spoke very little as they made their way to the Medina crossing and then turned south. Jason seemed thoughtful, and openly unsure of how best to deal with a man of Curtis' ilk. Tate could think of no way to help him except by saying, "Don't worry about working out any deal. What he wants, you haven't got to give. Only thing you can do is warn him. Maybe best if we don't go inside."

Jason nodded, but he wondered how he could manage peace on those terms.

Alerted by his guards, Curtis saw them coming and came out to wait for them on his porch. "Howdy, gentlemen," he began as they rode up. "Why don't you come in and settle yourselves. You're just in time for fresh coffee."

Jason dismounted but stayed by his horse. "Came to talk to you," he said. "Shouldn't take long."

"Well, at least come in."

"Best we stay out here."

Curtis' smiling face rearranged itself into a frown. "All right! What is it you've got to say?"

"Just that if you don't stay away from our ranch there's going to be bloodshed. What you're doing is against the law. Now we don't want any trouble, and we'll forget about the horses you tried to steal, but from now on keep your men off our range. Is that clear?"

Curtis' features moved about uncertainly for a moment but ended up on the verge of a sneer. Tate noticed that men had appeared and were now standing behind them, guns in hand.

"What's clear, my friend, is that you people don't seem to understand. I offered to buy you out at a fair price. Believe me, all of you could end up dearly wishing you had taken my offer."

"The ranch isn't for sale."

"Sure it is. Everything is for sale, son. Who's this?" he nodded at Tate.

"He's my brother."

"Brother?" Curtis hesitated until he suddenly recalled the Redmond woman had a half-breed son. "Oh, yes. Your brother. Well." He looked at Tate. "Brother, you go back to your ranch and tell Seth Redmond he's selling me the two stallions, High Clover and Midnight. I'm even going to be good enough to give him a thousand apiece for them. Make sure he sends along a bill of sale. In the meantime your brother can set here a spell with us, sort of get acquainted. When the horses come we'll turn him loose."

Tate looked around. They were surrounded by a crowd of seedy-looking toughs. One had hair and eyes light enough to make him an albino. He decided, from the description Isaac had offered, that this was surely Sam Cheek. A dark-skinned pocked-face runt, leaning against the back porch, he recognized from a hundred wanted posters as Aleppo. The others were very much like the ones who had rustled the horses: coarse figures, rejects and shiftless troublemakers, dirty and dangerous, moving about with that ugly flux of rodents.

Jason turned to look at Tate, but both knew they were helpless. However this worked out—and it was clear only guns could settle it now—they had no choice. Tate pulled his horse around and, nodding quickly to Curtis, said as nonchalantly as he could, "I'll tell 'em what you want, Mr. Curtis."

"Do that, and tell them if they don't accept my first offer there may not be a second." By then Tate had his horse at a gallop and, pounding it for greater and greater speed, never looked back.

Thunder Run was a cauldron of anger and excitement. Isabelle and Bessie were both in tears. Todd was incensed, but Seth was enraged. "Of all the stupid notions . . . *talking* to that swill-eating bastard . . . now look where we are!"

"What are we going to do?" intruded Prent.

"Give them the horses . . . what *can* we do?" said Tate quietly.

"Give them the horses?" Prent pounded the stock of his rifle. "Why?"

"Because they have Jason. We want him back. They won't keep those horses for long." Tate was loading a cartridge belt as he talked, and no one seemed to notice his final words.

But Seth, stepping closer, addressed him directly. "How many guns they got?"

Tate answered without taking his eyes off the cartridge belt. "Twenty, maybe twenty-five."

Seth looked to Todd for support. "Jess says he can still shoot, so that gives us sixteen. Should be enough."

Todd couldn't keep the grimness out of his voice. "We can't move till we get Jason back. Better get that bill of sale ready."

Isabelle was nervously preparing it. Rick slipped out to bring the stallions up. An air of defeat hung over them all as Tate said, "I'll go back alone. We can figure what to do when Jason is safe."

Outside, Taska was waiting for him. She took his hands in hers and squeezed them as her eyes held his. "Bring him back, Tate, please. Bring him back to me."

Tate would always remember that trip back to the Curtis place as the first time he was able to measure his loneliness. He measured it in the pall that had spread over the ranch because Jason was in danger. Would it have been so had it been him? It was in Taska's eyes, which had pleaded with him to bring back Jason, her love, her life. It was in the new way many people were looking at him, particularly Seth, now that he was a man, a man who had learned as a boy that life was not so precious, that life in a world of rejection was worth little or nothing at all. He knew because of his handling of the rustlers that Jason, and because of Jason the others, thought he was braver than his brother. But Jason didn't have his death wish, Jason had reasons to hold on to life, Jason was loved, Jason had Taska's arms and a ranch awaiting him. Above all, Jason had a sense of belonging; Jason wasn't a mongrel stabled with thoroughbreds. Tate couldn't help his bitterness. He knew that Jason, Taska and his mother understood how he felt, understood it and perhaps because of it, if not in spite of it, loved him. So now Jason had to be rescued, and it couldn't be done in a fight. As he led the stallions up to the Curtis spread, his mind was still wrestling with the problem. Why was it always another's problem that had to be solved; why was it never his?

Jason was less frightened than outraged when he found himself a prisoner of Reed Curtis. But he was levelheaded enough to try to turn this situation into an opportunity to reason with this dangerously unscrupulous man. "You can't win, Mr. Curtis. My father and Todd Salinger are ex-Rangers. Find out something about them before you go any further."

"Son, I know all about them. They're not dealing with wild Indians now. Hey, why don't you try looking on the bright side? I've got big plans for this country, probably could use a bright young fellow like you."

Jason shook his head. "You really think everything is for sale, don't you, Mr. Curtis?"

"It is, son. Look around you, everything from gun hands to ranches can be bought. Keep that in mind. Someday it might make you governor of Texas."

Jason was appalled at the man's conceit. Did he really think men, old rawhiders like his father and Todd, would knuckle under to the likes of him? A strange heaviness settled around his heart as he saw Tate approaching with the stallions. Smiling and rubbing his hands in satisfaction, Curtis went out to meet him.

Tate left the ranch knowing every man at Thunder Run was riding a short distance behind him. The showdown was coming. As soon as Jason was released, their desperate attack would begin. But Tate had seen the numbers Curtis had mustered. This was beginning to look like a costly, maybe impossible business. Isaac Sawyer was right: it was going to take bloodshed and more to save Thunder Run.

He came up to the big man prepared to turn over the stallions and leave with Jason, but something Curtis said struck him strangely. "Glad to see they're coming to their senses over there," he exclaimed as he reached up to run his hand down High Clover's sleek neck. "This is sure prime horseflesh. Did you bring that bill of sale, boy?" Tate gave him the sheet and watched him study it. Finally Curtis looked up and smiled. "You handled this little piece of business right handily, fellow. Could be you'd fit into a mighty big job some day. A man like me could use a handy fellow like you."

Tate stared at him without expression. "I got a job."

"Suit yourself. But think about it . . . got to figure you ain't got much to look forward to, Seth not being your pa and all."

Tate couldn't ever remember hating a man as much as he did this one. That remark touched something inside of him and his mind went fatally forward to a thought, one that became a compulsion when he saw Jason descending the porch. Jason's horse was being brought up as Cheek and Aleppo, with a miscellany of toughs, watched from the door. As Jason mounted, Tate suddenly bent down and whispered to the waiting Curtis, "Maybe we could talk?"

Curtis looked at him curiously for a moment, but when Tate nodded at Jason he turned and smiled. "Yeah, sure. Let your brother get on his way, then we'uns can visit a little."

Jason was quietly startled, even shocked, when he realized Tate was not leaving with him. But something in Tate's manner told him not to object. He had no way of knowing what instructions Tate might have received at Thunder Run.

Tensely, Tate watched Jason ride off, knowing above all that he had to keep his nerve. Everything hung on his getting Curtis alone and striking quickly. Cheek and Aleppo watched him as he followed Curtis into the house, but once inside Tate realized they were only a few steps behind. Curtis, smiling, gestured to a chair. "Want a drink?"

"Not at the moment," answered Tate, eyeing Cheek. "I was hoping we could talk alone."

"These boys are all right," Curtis assured him, falling into a feigned cordial tone. "Could be you're beginning to hanker to work for me?" He pursed his lips and leaned back comfortably. "Not surprised. It's a mighty big opportunity."

Tate shifted in his chair and moved his holster forward on his leg, the heavy cartridge belt feeling firm about his waist. He felt Cheek's eyes on him. Slapping his knee, he turned to Curtis, his voice beginning to tighten. "As you can easily figure, I've got plenty at stake here. I'd prefer to talk alone."

Curtis looked puzzled but quietly grunted to himself before he stood up. Tate thought he was going to send Cheek and Aleppo out of the room, but instead he beckoned Tate to follow him and they moved to an adjoining room, a small, crowded parlor without windows. Curtis closed the door behind Tate and turned to him with a twinge of impatience. "Well, what is it?"

Tate couldn't and didn't wait. He grabbed Curtis by the wrist and spun him around, knocking the breath out of him as he slammed him to the floor. Curtis was stout, but he was husky. He grabbed at Tate's legs, but Tate, using the great power in his shoulders and biceps, twisted Curtis' right arm around till he wrenched it against its socket and, bringing his knee down with all his weight, broke it. The sudden clamor had Cheek breaking through the door, gun in hand, but there was hardly any light and as Cheek peered ahead, trying to make out faces on the two figures clumped together, Tate shot him through the head. Tate knew speed was his only hope. Curtis was rocking the room with bellows of pain as Tate twisted his other arm up behind him and started him through the parlor door. Aleppo was frantically alerting the gunmen outside, and Tate could hear them racing up the porch and trying to enter the house. Aleppo, standing on a chair, kept shouting, "Shoot! Shoot!" But Tate kept Curtis in front of him while Curtis shouted, "Jesus! Don't shoot! Don't shoot till I get away from this maniac!" Tate knew that to hesitate could be fatal. He slid his back along the wall, struggling desperately for the door. Aleppo was trying to get an open shot at him, but Tate kept bobbing his head and rocking the bawling Curtis back and forth. With his free hand he had to shoot at two men standing in the doorway to clear it, but the sight of them falling wounded cowed the others. They were not all Cheeks and Aleppos. On the porch bullets began to whistle by. One cut across Curtis' thick left thigh, and he roared like a bull. "Goddamn it! Stop shooting! You're gonna kill me!"

With the firing stopped Tate got him down and up on his own horse, making him use his good arm to hold on to the saddle horn. Bareback, he jumped on Midnight, who was still standing with High Clover, and reached over for the reins of his mount. He started racing away with Curtis screaming, "Stop him! Stop this son of a bitch!" He noticed only belatedly that High Clover was galloping beside Midnight. It was then he remembered that coming back he had tethered them together. Glancing behind him, he could see Aleppo leading the men in a race for their horses, and long before he managed to get out of sight he could hear them shouting and coming in pursuit.

Not more than ten minutes after Tate left Thunder Run, fourteen men had ridden out to follow him at a distance. The issue was as tragic as it was clear-cut. As soon as Jason was safe, Curtis' hand was going to be called. This was a scene imprinted on the West, law-respecting men with no instruments of law to turn to, men who could live only by a code they had forged. Some of these ranch hands had nothing to gain from this lethal encounter except a makeshift grave, yet to a man they saddled up and came. There was little or no talking, little or no planning. Prent, on the point, did not look back until they were only half a mile from the Curtis spread. Then he signaled by pointing to a long stand of high brush that he felt was the place to wait. A few started to roll smokes; others sat in silence.

Jason soon appeared through the heavy growth, not pressing his mount but continually looking behind him. To their amazement they discovered he was hoping to see Tate, who had not left with him. Seth was confused and concerned. "What the devil kept him there?"

Jason shook his head. "Don't know."

Suddenly shots could be heard in the distance, and everyone realized they were rising from the Curtis place. Prent rode out to where he could get a clearer view in that direction. In a moment he was back. "They're coming this way! I believe it's Tate in front! Get behind that brush; they're heading right for us!"

Tate didn't think they could overtake him, but Curtis, whose mount he had galloping alongside, was holding on only to avoid the torment of falling on his broken arm, but might decide to risk it at any moment. They were going through a field of prairie dog holes, and any of the horses could step into one and go down. Tate tried to watch Curtis and the ground ahead at once and almost missed Prent signaling him to swing in behind them. He went fifty yards too far, but it was enough to make his pursuers think he was going to make a stand, and they slowed up right before the guns of the Thunder Run men.

Aleppo, riding in front, was too easily recognized. He died in his saddle, never knowing what had killed him. The fusillade from the brush so decimated the ranks of the others that a mad scramble to escape caused collisions that threw men to the ground, where they crumbled before the point-blank fire of the continually flashing guns. It was over in less than a minute. The handful that were still able to gallop away disappeared in several directions, their hoofbeats dying out until there was only silence, a silence in which Tate led Curtis back to a hurried and excited circle forming around Seth and Todd.

Curtis, as appalled as he was panicked by the slaughter of his men, was physically frozen as his mind tried to collect itself to save his skin. Not only Prent but others had long since passed judgment on this robber baron. Prent had taken a coil of rope from his saddle and, standing before him, was fixing a noose on one end. "What's that for?" squealed Curtis.

"For you!" spat Prent. "You know the kind of hands rustlers get dealt in Texas."

"Can't we make a deal?" Curtis looked pleadingly to the others. "Somebody help me get free! I'll pay anything you ask!"

"Freedom around here isn't for sale either, Mr. Curtis," said Jason bitterly.

Prent was looking about him for a tree. "Come on, Seth," he said finally, "let's get it over with."

Seth might have been staring at Reed Curtis, but his mind was reaching back over twenty years to Jerkins' Corner and the lynch mob he had left his prisoners with. He remembered the aftermath of that sordid scene, remembered how it had changed people when they looked back. He had felt different when he heard those Comancheros were hanged. He had tried to turn them over to the law, he had done the only thing he could do to help bring justice to this raw land. Now as he stood there he realized if Jason was ever to live at Thunder Run under the protection of the law, men like himself had to do away with the long shadow of the vigilante rope and the ready guns of personal vengeance.

He signaled Prent to him. The firmness of hard decision was in his tone. Curtis would be taken to San Antonio, along with the bodies of Sam Cheek and Aleppo. Curtis would be charged with rustling and harboring criminals wanted by the law. If what Isaac said was true, he was surely wanted elsewhere. All reward money would be shared among the men. Then sixteen men from Thunder Run would sign statements declaring that they would be willing to testify against

Curtis. Prent, though disgruntled, was given charge of the escort. Jason and Rick, quietly relieved, offered to go along.

"Now let's get back," Seth said to the rest of them. "We've still got a ranch to run."

Isabelle, Bessie and particularly Elena were secretly proud of the way Seth had ended this. Was he finally beginning to understand that fighting wasn't the only way?

After they returned to the ranch Isabelle couldn't help noticing Seth, trying to look casual, pouring and serving Tate a drink. For her it was even more surprising to see Tate, who rarely touched liquor, drinking it slowly, his eyes quietly following Seth about the room. Distantly she began to hope what, God willing, this might mean.

All portents pointed to peace and finally even some harmony for Thunder Run, but the following year Brandy, who was beginning to suffer from rheumatism, ran across Seth fussing with a newspaper that had just arrived from San Antonio. "Somethin' in dat paper givin' you misery, Seth?"

Seth grimaced and ran his hand through his hair. "Yeah, and they call him Abe Lincoln."

"Who dat?"

"He didn't get a single goddamn vote in Texas, but he's going to be President of the United States."

Brandy looked confused. "What dat mean?"

Seth put the paper down and stared for long moments out toward the western horizon. It was a day when clouds seemed to be darkening and piling up, a day when the weather was heralding an ominous change. But as Seth turned and headed for the house his mouth visibly hardened with the answer he half whispered. "War, I reckon."

Part Seven

BLOOD
on the
MOON

March 1864

24

Seth and Jason reined in their lathered mounts on the last rise of the wagon road to gaze upon the lonely cluster of buildings that was Thunder Run. For Seth, who had seen it rise from wilderness, it was a distressing sight. From the few colts grazing in its empty corrals to the Confederate flag lifting listlessly in the evening breeze, its desolation matched that of Texas itself. Drained of manpower and its once vast herds of horses, sequestered by Southern armies trying to stave off defeat, it looked abandoned and, for this once again imperiled frontier, dangerously isolated.

Their faces were worn and their beards matted, their tunics encased in dust. It had taken them a week to come from Tennessee, and they were weary beyond belief. Seth had meant to continue along the trail to the turnoff for the old MacFee place. He was anxious to see Elena again, but the big black cavalry horse he was riding had thrown a shoe and he had to get it to the farrier shed at Thunder Run before it went lame. For two years they had fought with their fellow Texans in Hood's famous brigade, but the days when fiery Texans had broken the Union lines at Gaines' Mill were gone. In the disastrous rout at Nashville, Jason's company had been lost and Seth's cavalry unit shattered. They had been given leave only because of continual reports of a frontier reign of terror as Comanche war parties, emboldened by the lack of resistance, burned out and massacred whole settlements along the Brazos and Colorado.

The almost threadbare insignia on their tattered uniforms still showed Seth to be a major and Jason a captain, though in the exhausted Confederate army both had taken commands where needed. Both knew the war was lost, both knew that the many gallant and pathetic sacrifices of blood and wealth had been in vain, both were returning hoping something was left of a world they had left behind. In truth, they were increasingly disturbed. They hadn't seen a soul since crossing the Medina. In San Antonio they had heard government decrees warning citizens to pull back from the frontier, for bloody depredations were being reported every day and the state militia, mostly young boys and wounded veterans, was helpless against the onslaughts of the swiftly striking Comanche and Kiowa war parties. In some places the frontier had been driven back nearly two hundred miles.

The squat square structure of the Thunder Run ranch house, with its gun ports, adobe walls and slate roof, looked formidable from a distance. It reminded Seth of the frail structure housing Elena. His anxieties had been soaring like a fever since hearing from Julio, coming through San Antonio, that her *vaqueros* and her few servants, fearing for their lives, had disappeared by night almost a week ago.

As they moved down into the yard, Brandy, seeing them, dropped the pile of old harness he was carrying to the stable, and came hobbling over. "Lordy, lordy! Seth! Jason! You done come back! Well, hallelujah! Dem ladies gonna be mighty pleased, yes'm, mighty pleased." He was laughing and shaking with an irrepressible sense of relief. "Sure bin powerful worrisome hereabouts for a spell."

Seth dismounted to shake hands with Brandy, while Jason stared with troubled eyes about the empty yard. "Where are the women?" he asked.

"Dey's inside," responded Brandy, his face still aglow with a wide grin. "Ah's sure glad y'all come back. Ain't bin nothin' but trouble and fussin' 'bout Injuns 'round here."

Seth gave Brandy his horse's reins, asking him to replace the shoe. Jason was about to inquire about Tate when the air was suddenly filled with squeals of surprise and screams of excitement as Isabelle, Bessie and Kate came hurrying from the house.

Tate had quickly spotted the fleet mare racing along the rocky edge of the creek. He knew it was Taska and where she was coming from. Sudden anger brought faint lines along his nostrils. Would that girl never learn? He pulled his sweating mount up and rode out to where she would see him.

To many Tate was a puzzling figure. His horsemanship was legendary by now; and experienced ranchers agreed they had yet to see the horse he couldn't break and train to perfection. Many women found him handsome, with his strong shoulders, strange black eyes and dark, soft flowing hair. His facial features were heavy and prominent but they bespoke determination. Still, it was not his looks but his moodiness that continued to shape most people's impressions. He was a withdrawn man, rarely comfortable with strangers. Bessie often remarked that Tate sulked through life "like an outcast neighbor stumbling into a party looking proud, but bitter he wasn't invited."

Yet, if Tate was silent and reclusive, he was far from harmless. There had been occasions when remarks about "dirty half-breeds" from coarse drifters hanging about the stables in San Antonio had led to gunplay. Never drawing first had kept him from trouble with the law, but more than once he had made work for the undertaker. Witnesses claimed nothing local could match his speed with a six-gun and troublemaking strangers were warned not to try.

He frowned as Taska approached him with that graceful swift-riding style her lithe body easily fell into. In spite of the six-gun in her belt and the rifle stock peering from her saddle scabbard, she looked fetchingly feminine. With some effort he forced away the melting effect her soft, tawny beauty always had on him. He had long been aware of her passion for Jason and it kept his physical desires in check, but for Tate what others believed to be a strangely distorted personality was in reality a great loneliness, eased at times by his love for his mother but made bearable only by his fantasies about Taska, whom he worshiped.

"Must you go down there . . . to that woman?" he started with an anger that barely concealed the alarm he was trying to suppress.

Taska had always found her smiles effective with Tate, but now she saw that her warm grin did little to lighten his accusing look. "Tate," she said, reaching over to touch his hand. "If you're fixin' to fuss me out, I'm not telling you my secret."

For once her soft hand grasping his had no effect. It frightened her. "What's the matter?" she murmured, suddenly aware of the worry in his eyes, the dust caking his clothes, the sweat soaking his horse.

He looked behind him before answering. "Red Claw is on the Nueces," he muttered, his voice still tight with anger. "We're going to have to clear out." Red Claw was the sobriquet Anglo Texans had given the notorious Malo Alano, a half-breed Comanche chief who carried an eagle talon stained with vermilion around his neck.

"Clear out! You mean leave Thunder Run?" Tension and fright suddenly edged her voice. "When?"

Tate motioned for them to start toward the ranch. In spite of his mount's near-exhaustion, it responded readily to his touch and began to move forward. Taska, moving the mare up quickly to stay beside him, was now sounding breathless. "When? Please, Tate, when must we . . . clear out?"

"Now! Today, goddamn it! If we had any sense, we'd have left long ago!"

"We can't leave today," replied Taska, confusion joining a growing anxiety in her eyes. "Jason is coming, and so is Seth."

Tate pulled up and stared at her. "You found that out *down there?*"

"Yes. Is that wrong?"

He shook his head, his temper visibly increasing. "Mother had a right to know first."

Taska didn't answer, but she followed him home at a gallop and at the ranch took the reins he threw at her and led his mount to the stable. He had never treated her so roughly before. Grimly she realized it was a measure of how shaken he was. She quickly cared for the horses, which Brandy would move that evening to the cellar for safekeeping, but she mentioned nothing, even to Inez, about the package she had carried back from "down there," which contained a frock Elena D'Valya had allowed her to pick from her own wardrobe to wear for Jason's homecoming.

Bessie had been sitting before the broad stone fireplace that nearly filled one wall of the large oak-beamed living room, reading a letter from her remaining daughter in Louisiana. Both girls had gone east to school, both had married well into rich plantation families around Baton Rouge. But the war had dragged them into misery and want, and one had died of the strange river fever. Both sons-in-law had been wounded. One, like her poor husband, Todd, lay sick and likely dying in a Yankee prison camp. Seeing Isabelle entering the room, she folded the letter and tucked it away. "Is Tate back yet?" she asked lightly, trying to hide her sadness.

"No," murmured Isabelle, running her hand through her wispy blond hair, now streaked through its tightly drawn part with hints of gray. "Neither is Taska." Her eyes suddenly flashed with suppressed irritation. "Wherever is that girl?"

Bessie settled back in the wide cowhide-covered chair with a shrug. "Brandy's been talking of taking the buckboard over to that state depot in Castroville . . . see if any supplies are left. Tate, of course, has got to go with him. But, mercy! I don't see why they're going at all—things being what they are."

Too tense to sit, Isabelle went to stand by the window. "Tate is worried about cartridges . . . says we need gun oil. Doesn't 'pear to me anything's likely to be left."

Bessie sighed. "Simply don't like it with the men away."

Kate, whose husband, young Doc Michalrath, had been killed tending the wounded at Chicamauga, came in silently from the bedroom and settled near her sister. Kate was still pretty but pale now, and shockingly thin from her long grieving over Jed's death. She sat staring at a little flower she had picked behind the house.

Isabelle's hand rose, her knuckles coming hard against her mouth. "If only this wretched war would stop! Those poor boys are dying for nothing."

"Dying for nothing!" Bessie, wincing at Kate, sat up in her chair. "Isabelle, you want some damn Yankees or likely a mess of Negroes tellin' you what to do?"

"Bessie! Please! Stop that rubbish! I've always thought slavery a horrid business, and you know it! Women up north are surely as sick of this war as I am."

Bessie didn't answer. It was a subject that led to much bitterness and discord. They sat in silence for long moments before Isabelle let out a gasp. "Bessie! Kate! Lord have mercy!" She choked before she could go on. "Jason and Seth!" She turned around and almost screamed, "They're back!"

Turning at the farrier shed, Brandy had watched the women hugging Jason warmly, then shifting over awkwardly to offer their cheeks to Seth. It was as though even the trauma of war could not erase the bitter legacy of the past. "Ain't dey a sight frumpin' up like dat to ole Seth?" Brandy mumbled to himself. Through all the business with the Mexican woman coming to the old MacFee place, Brandy had never lost his respect, even affection, for Seth. He felt he understood him in ways others did not.

At the moment, he was deeply troubled and fervently hoping the arrival of Seth and Jason would be the blessing he had been praying for. He agreed with Tate that they should have fled long ago. They were in mortal danger here, and the thought of Inez and his beautiful daughter, Taska, falling into Comanche hands sickened him. He had even thought of leaving with them, but Inez had shaken her head. A Negro traveling alone with a *mestiza* wife and half-breed daughter in a South seething with rebellion and wary of a slave uprising could prove an equal danger. She was right, of course.

Settling the horse down, he bent over to look at its hoof. His rheumatism had made it more difficult to get about, but he still rode out every day looking for tracks, and he quietly kept guns loaded and handy in the hut. Like Tate, he was worried about cartridges. The desperate military demanded everything. Only the militia was allowed a paltry and uneven supply. He wondered at their chance of getting some at the depot.

With his shoulder against the big black, he discovered a bruise and a slight crack in the unshod hoof. He would have to treat it before replacing the shoe, and Seth would have to let the poor horse rest a spell.

In spite of the excitement of their arrival, Jason could not hold back questions even as he returned the women's tight embraces. Why were they still here? Had they seen any signs of Indians? Where was Tate?

Isabelle and Bessie, each enfolded in one of Jason's arms, looked at each other, then quickly drew Jason toward the house, Kate and Seth following. Inside, Isabelle settled him on the sofa and struggled against tears to find the words that described their plight. So far they had seen only small roving bands, likely raiding for horses. Brandy had transferred their few remaining saddle stock from the stable to the deep cellar for safekeeping. But Isaac Sawyer's carefully built house and its surrounding works, the efforts of a lifetime, had been burned down the day after the Sawyer family had left. "Thank God, for some reason they've left us alone, but they'll burn everything to the ground soon as we leave. Heaven help us, Jason, this ranch . . . this home is all we have left. The war has left us in poverty. We've talked of leaving for San Antonio, but there's a shortage of everything and talk of cholera there. Remember, we have to take Inez and Taska. Brandy is black, and Tate is so . . . so quick-tempered. Who's going to make do for a bunch of penniless females? You must have seen what it's like in San Antonio, though there's hardly any place safe now. Folks say those devilish Regulators are as bad as Yankees."

Jason listened, secretly becoming more disturbed and finally angry at his mother's rambling. This was madness. Heartbreaking or not, they simply had to abandon the ranch. He was sure the house had been spared only because scouting warriors had seen its stout defenses. But it took no military savvy to see that the place could never withstand a determined or prolonged attack.

He was glad when Bessie and Isabelle insisted they get to the kitchen and prepare some food. He turned to catch Seth shaking his head knowingly, the menace hanging over this lonely spread stark in his eyes. But strange emotions began filling Jason as he stared at Seth. Perhaps it was his own exhaustion, but never before had he seen his father looking so aged and worn with fatigue. His beard was a messy mottle of gray speared through with white, his skin was parched and crinkled into coarse lines where it gathered about his eyes. Clearly Seth's weary mind was racked with worry while he waited for Brandy to shoe his horse, for if fortified Thunder Run was vulnerable to attack the MacFee place was a death trap. It was something of a miracle it hadn't been burnt out long ago. Jason looked in puzzlement toward the wide front windows. Could it be that the two women, Isabelle and Elena, rivals for his father, were stupidly, even fatally, waiting each other out?

When the men had eaten, Isabelle urged Jason to bathe and even shave. One look in the mirror convinced him of her reasons, but Seth made no attempt to join him. After a few swallows of venison, hard bread and bitter coffee, he started glancing nervously out the window toward the farrier shed. Though he said nothing, his quandary was apparent in his quick, fitful movements. He had to get to Elena.

Bracing himself against the window ledge, he watched the slow-moving shadows of clouds crossing distant hills. The land's very stillness was ominous.

Isabelle was quietly aware that Seth wanted to go. She had looked at him closely only once and had been shocked at his ravaged appearance. The war had been hard on him. He looked ashen with age, his eyes hinting at fatigue too deep to be dissolved by sleep alone. She sensed moments when he was looking toward her, but she refused to return his gaze. When she did look, she saw him at the window, anxious to go. Could she ever forgive him for bringing his paramour to the doorstep of her ranch? How had it come to this?

"Well, I just can't wait," Seth declared to Brandy, shaking his head as he looked at the black's hoof. "You're going to have to lend me a horse . . . I'll be back for this one."

"Dey's a buckskin in da cellar . . . likely he'll do. Give this big rascal just a bit o' rest . . . he be fine."

Thanking Brandy, Seth lugged his saddle, guns and gear around to the deep cellar. He was there throwing his saddle on the buckskin when Tate, still leading Taska, galloped into the yard. Brandy shouted to them excitedly that Seth and Jason had arrived, but they merely nodded to him. They already knew.

When Seth returned leading the buckskin, he caught sight of Taska disappearing into the adobe hut and Brandy standing, his arms akimbo, looking deeply troubled toward the house. He waited for Brandy to notice him. "Something wrong?"

"Reckon dere is," answered Brandy. "Tate, he back . . . lookin' mighty upset . . . best we go and see."

Jason and Tate could not conceal their joy at seeing each other again. Though they grasped each other warmly, both sensed that this was a poor setting for a reunion. Jason was immediately alert to the stress in Tate's face.

Tate was the southwest militia's best scout. He had just raced back from a meeting with Little Cloud, the Wichita boy he had befriended years before and kept from starving over the last winter. Like all scouts, he needed small, unsuspected sources of information to cover the vast stretches he was expected to patrol. Little Cloud lived in the remnants of a rundown hogan along the Sabinal, but he was far enough west to see reflections in the night sky of great fires blazing in war camps along the Nueces. It was he who had warned Tate about Red Claw's presence, promising more information after some risky scouting of his own. "They're coming down the trace and gathering at that rocky bend in the river," finished Tate. "From what we can figure, could be over a hundred."

Jason was first to respond. "That bend in the Nueces—it's got to be over fifty miles from here." His tone underlined the point.

"Fifty miles ain't much when it comes to Comanches," warned Tate. "They move like the wind."

◆   ◆   ◆

Distraught but finally resigned to leaving, Isabelle and Bessie began to plead about things to be taken along. "We can't live without a stitch of clothing or a pan to cook with," insisted Isabelle.

"Heaven knows we'll need that old silver setting and some things to sell," anguished Bessie. "We haven't a blessed cent to our names."

"Would make a damned sight more sense to fetch some cartridges," broke in Tate. "We'd have trouble holding off more than a small party now."

An hour's discussion led to a hasty plan. It was too late to start that evening, but the wagon could be brought up and loaded, the women packing what had to be taken. At dawn Brandy and Tate would take the buckboard to the militia depot at Castroville, a small settlement above the Medina ford. They hoped there would be some cartridges, gun oil and maybe a few supplies there. Jason offered to go along. The presence of an army officer might help.

Rubbing his hands together, Jason looked about this house he had known all his life, forcing away the ugly thought that it would soon be leveled, its adjoining buildings lying in ashes around it. He put his arm comfortingly about his mother and hugged her as he whispered, "Believe some of us could use a drink." Though the room was hardly quiet, everyone heard his words, and Seth, who had been intently following their plans, for he was hastily forming plans of his own, lifted his head. In spite of the exhaustion draining his face, he almost smiled.

What made Seth proceed to throw down such large gulps of Isabelle's raw corn whisky only a man totally spent by exertion, his nerves frayed by anxiety, would know, but it dissolved his resistance to sleep. Seth soon lay sprawled in a chair well away from the fireplace, erupting rough, uneven snores as Isabelle placed a blanket over him and tiptoed away.

Jason himself was feeling somewhat drowsy, for the drink had eased his tension and led his mind to the girl he both wanted and yet hesitated to see. His first trip through the cotton country of the deep South had left him stunned at the abyss between the races. Slave markets and whipping posts said plainly that the whites' debasement of blacks had approached the fanaticism of a primitive religion. Yet he was hardly innocent, having noticed and admired the delicate beauty of southern belles. As a young, handsome officer he had been entertained by many attractive war widows, rich landed gentry whom he escorted into the drawing rooms of Richmond and Roanoke, drawing rooms where Taska, the daughter of an ex-slave, would never be received. Inevitably it had started a troubling conflict in him, one he had suppressed for long periods and must suppress now. He must never offend this girl who had given herself to him and whose passions had so thrilled him in his youth. He must keep it a vague wondering in his eyes, a curious complication that perhaps tomorrow would resolve. Secretly it had burdened his awareness since that first summer he had returned from school, but life had seemed to go on without anyone sensing his quandary. For no one really did except a woman who knew all too well life's built-in tragedies for the unanointed: Inez.

As darkness crept across the land, Taska finished her bath and quietly slipped into the colorful frock Elena and Carlota had helped her choose. Inez watched her in silence, trying to conceal the fears she felt for her daughter, fears she never shared with Brandy, who could only chuckle over his pretty offspring's ways. For the impish little girl with the coy, winsome smiles and wide, expectant eyes had grown into a breathless beauty as wild and willful as the country around her. And her varied heritage had yielded exotic fruit. With her light, lemony skin and deep mauve eyes, she had a bewitching motion that affected men in ways she had only recently come to understand and muse over. But she was hopelessly in love with Jason. Growing up on the lonely range, the handsome boy with the golden hair and the dark, dazzling, ever-tantalizing girl, whose body had ripened early with the mysteries of womanhood, could not be kept apart. By their teens desire was beyond containing, and on a summer's evening, in the now-vacant loft where the lonely Brandy had cherished her mother years ago and she herself had been conceived, Taska and Jason had become lovers. Tate, aware of this fated tryst, rode out to the dark hills to wander most of the night, finding in the loneliness of endless space and faint starlight something akin to the pall that now claimed his world.

Stepping lightly, Taska crossed the yard to find Kate standing before the house watching the last of daylight fade from the western sky. Having been told by Brandy of their plans for leaving on the morrow, she expected the women, like her mother, to be busy hurrying together whatever could be taken. It surprised her to find Kate standing there alone, this poor girl who had never recovered from her husband's death, word of which had not reached her until weeks after he was killed. This not knowing, in many ways, was the cruelest part of the war. Prent, like Tanner and Purdy, had joined Terry's Rangers and none had been heard from in years. They had only gotten rumors that Rick had been wounded around Galveston, where the local garrison was desperately holding off the Union navy. The mails had long since disappeared, and travelers were rare along this dangerous frontier.

Kate's tense face seemed to find release in a smile as she noticed the bright frock. "My, Taska, you look so . . . so pretty."

Taska smiled back and hugged her with genuine warmth. "Someday I might get to be as pretty as you, Kate."

Kate stood in the darkness holding Taska's hands, grateful this warm, affectionate girl was always there with her comforting words and embraces. Yet, being a woman, Kate knew why Taska had come and sensed at once how she could return some of her many kindnesses. "Why don't you wait here, Taska," she said softly. "I'll send Jason out."

Taska couldn't help a little laugh. "Oh, would you?"

"Certainly. A girl shouldn't have to greet a man in the midst of all that fussin' in there."

After Kate's quick whisper to him Jason waited only a few thoughtful moments before rising, straightening his tunic and excusing himself.

Outside, even in the dim light from the window, he was stunned anew by Taska's beauty. Her body seemed slightly more rounded, but her face still had those perfect features and that mixture of innocence and sensuality that melted his will like a drug. But Taska's cheeks were like fire. They clasped hands for a moment before she came into his arms, the warmth and scent of her starting his heart pounding. Even as her mouth, soft and yielding, came to receive his, she began drawing him beneath the great cottonwood tree before the house, her body pressing into his, fighting for closeness, eager for him to envelop her. For long moments they held together tightly as quickening surges of desire began to mount, for Taska was squeezing breathless words of greeting between the long, violent kisses till Jason, responding to her ardor, brought his hand up to slide beneath her frock and cup the fullness of her breast. The need to make their bodies one was impossible to resist. Still embracing, they drifted out through the darkness, guiding each other toward the straw-softened loft of the dark, vacant stable.

Inez knew her daughter was in Jason's arms. She had known of their wild passion ever since the night Taska had given her virginity in the flush and ecstasy of young love. No one had told Inez. No one had needed to. She had read the new tensions, the new tremors in her daughter's nubile body like dark print. Her fears were not ill founded. She knew the ways of the world, and though she liked, even admired, Jason, she was suspicious of the white Texan male's cultic notions about race. Mexican and even Indian girls were useful for the sexual rites that lead to manhood, but marriage sat best with their "own kind." The two women in his father's life etched the point. The white Texan Isabelle was and remained his wife, the Mexican Elena, waiting "down there," his mistress. She had to pray quietly so Brandy would not hear, for it was long after midnight when Taska slipped into the hut and started rustling out of her clothes. Inez gripped and kissed the cross she kept beneath her pillow, once again pleading with her patron saint to keep Taska from child.

Isabelle, the "white Texan wife," had been up a number of times during the night and found Seth snoring heavily and sunk in deep sleep. She knew Jason was with Taska and viewed it with equally troubling emotions. She was no bigot. She loved Taska. But she was all too aware of the penance the world placed on mixed blood and wondered if their love would not bring tragedy to these two young people. Like so much of her life, however, like the loss of this home for which she had sacrificed so much, it was now beyond her control.

Her hands came together in gratitude as she heard Jason come in and stumble to his bed. His very presence in the house made her sigh quietly with relief, for in her mind that stable was not safe. On this treacherous frontier people were murdered in lonely, abandoned stables. Inez had once almost suffered such a fate.

Starved for rest herself, she finally dozed off, but when she shook herself awake again well before dawn, Seth was gone.

Elena had been pacing before her cold fireplace most of the night. She could not escape the premonition that Seth's failure to arrive boded ill. Sleep was impossible. She had resisted Carlota's and Don José's pleading to leave for San Antonio, secretly clinging to the hope that her carefully refurnished farmhouse, made beautiful by its many imported rugs and tapestries, would be spared. Word from her kinsmen, Julio and Ricardo, that Seth and Jason were in San Antonio swelled her hopes. But Carlota, now with shining silver streaks in her dark hair, and the pure white Don José were beyond caring about possessions and near-frantic with worry. At the disappearance of their few domestic and stable hands they had felt a threat so imminent that even the howl of distant wolves or the screech of passing owls caused their breaths to hesitate, their hands to grip their sides in fear.

Carlota had just abandoned her nightlong effort to snatch moments of sleep, and appeared beside the fireplace before dawn carrying two cups of coffee. There were no words exchanged until she, settling down beside Elena, sighed fretfully, half to herself. "Well?"

Elena raised her coffee to her lips and sipped at it. "He will come," she uttered stoically.

"And if he does not?"

Elena stared at her in the sooty darkness. "He will come," she repeated with effort.

Long moments passed. Then suddenly, as though in answer to her words, the faint pounding of a horse's hooves could be heard in the distance. Elena, her face coming alive with excitement and relief, rose and hurried to the door. Carlota, turning to the fireplace, lifted a rifle from their gun rack and took up a position behind her.

It was still too dark to see clearly, but she knew from his voice it was Seth. Running quickly for his embrace, she felt the unkempt roughness of his beard and sensed the desperate tension in the tight clasp of his arms. She tried to speak, but his kisses silenced her.

When he held her away from him to look at her, she saw the gauntness in his face. And when he spoke, his voice was strained, hurried. "You've got to get out of here!" he rasped. "Why didn't you leave long ago? There isn't a soul left this side of the Medina!"

"I was waiting for you!" she half cried, pressing apart his now-restraining arms to work herself closer. "Seth, must we go? Give up our home?"

"Elena! For Christ's sake! Stop talking nonsense! There are war camps little more than a day's ride from here. You have to leave! Now! Hurry!"

Don José had gotten up, and he and Carlota were listening to Seth in the dawn, nodding in fervent agreement at his words. With the increasing light, Elena could see Seth's haggard features and fearful fatigue more distinctly. She searched for something to say. "Then if we must—we'll go! But first, Seth, you must rest, eat something. You look terrible. Are you ill?"

He had not finished the food offered him the day before and realized he was growing weak from hunger. He shook his head in partial answer to her question but, unable to deny his exhaustion any longer, slumped into a chair.

He had already cursed himself for falling asleep at the ranch, awakening with a cold shaft of guilt impaling his breast. The ride over had added to his frustration. The buckskin was not a sound horse. It winded quickly and jumped poorly. He had to get that black back. In this country a man had to be strongly mounted.

He accepted a mug of coffee while he calculated how much time he had to get the three to San Antonio. Julio would surely offer them shelter there. He had made it clear there would be no wagons. Whatever Elena and her people wanted could be carried in backpacks, none big enough to inhibit fast riding. But even these, he knew, watching her run about nervously, would take time to prepare. He was ready to wait patiently until Don José, stripping weapons from the gun rack, shocked him by saying, "I hope you have brought some cartridges, señor. All we have is what's in these guns."

Seth turned on Elena, alarm claiming his face. "Is that true?"

"Seth, they're impossible to get out here. We have only a handful Julio sent us a month ago. Of course we asked always for more but nothing has come. This government . . . this war takes everything. We are left with nothing." Tears were mounting in her eyes as she looked about, bitterly calculating what little could be saved from her soon-to-be-abandoned home. Even her closets of bright clothing would have to be left behind.

Seth was on his feet again. Their plight was far graver than he thought. No ammunition meant that they would be helpless against even chance encounters. He forced his mind to weigh the odds for and against every possible move but kept returning to one. He had to return to Thunder Run. They were also low on cartridges, but he had heard they were going to the depot for more. Surely they would spare him a few dozen rounds. Besides, he wanted to retrieve that black. Figuring finally that he could get back before noon and that they could be across the Medina by sundown, he made his decision.

"Get yourselves ready," he said gulping down the remainder of his coffee and moving toward the door. "I'll be back in an hour or two. And get the horses ready . . . we'll be leaving at once."

Tate and Brandy appeared at first light. Isabelle faced them with a finger to her lips. She hadn't had the heart to wake Jason. He was straddled across the bed in the same position he had collapsed in the night before and his breathing rose like the bellows of a forge. She told them they'd best go without him. Taska, up and about and strangely beaming, offered to go along. They were glad to have her. She could handle the team or a six-gun as well as any man. Brandy had their fastest team hitched to the buckboard and, with Taska astride her sleek mare, they followed Tate at a brisk pace down the wagon road.

25

The coming collapse of the Confederacy threw ominous shadows before it. The fears that accompany surrender to an angry, vengeful enemy were gathering over west Texas. There was fear of neighbors with pro-Union sentiments, fear of bandits running loose in a countryside drained of its rightful defenders, fear of frontier renegades plotting with savages to rob and kill defenseless settlers, even a fear of that chilling nightmare, endemic to the South, a bloody slave uprising. Whether any or all of these fears were reasonably founded hardly mattered. That they preyed upon and distorted people's minds did.

As defeated rebels, agents of the Houston government were losing their legitimacy, and with the slow dissolution of the law, bands of vigilantes had risen like bats from some subterranean cavern. Many were simply raw-handed men who preferred six-gun justice to chaos. But the lure of power had also attracted other, more sinister faces that surfaced quietly, relying on the spread of hysteria to mask their intent. These self-appointed protectors of the public weal called themselves "Regulators," but to a war-weary populace they were a crown of thorns.

Two Regulators who had achieved some notoriety were Riff Connors and Caleb Sutton. Riff was a bully who punched out whores to avoid payment after they had serviced him. He stole from helpless unarmed Mexicans and assaulted itinerant merchants on lonely trails by night. Riff usually avoided retribution by smearing his victims' names. Whores were trying to lure him into alleyways where accomplices waited to rob him. Mexicans were secret informers for the Union. Itinerant merchants were profiteering at the expense of war widows or the lonely wives of soldiers. Few believed him, but people shrugged. Such crimes were common enough. With the threatened Yankee invasion and occupation of their homeland, most people were looking out for themselves. Even neighbors became suspicious of one another's visits, sleeping close to their guns and trusting no one. In such an atmosphere the Regulators thrived.

Caleb, who had just joined Riff Connors, was a drunken preacher, fanatically obsessed with the "sacred right" of southern whites to rule over blacks. Forced out of Louisiana for swindling his own church, he had arrived in west Texas where he expanded this "biblically ordained right to rule" to include Mexicans, Comanches and finally Unionists. Now the main theme of his hysterical harangues was the coming mass rape of our "pure and mostly virginal womanhood" by the "monkey men of Africa," the "mongrel races of Mexico" and "those flesh-eating savages even now spilling blood on our borders and abducting our females to enslave and defile." His hat was frequently passed to choruses of "Amen."

Riff was meeting Caleb in the shadowy bar of a cantina to advise him that a government clerk who had helped him fraudulently appropriate a few but highly valuable supplies from a Confederate warehouse had just sent word of some lingering stock at a state depot in Castroville. Counterfeit papers were being gotten up, and Riff was arranging for two toughs and a wagon to accompany them on the four-hour ride to Castroville. "Get there early," his accomplice had advised. "There's an Indian scare out that way and the agent might just shut down and leave."

So it happened that these two unlikely protectors of the public weal, departing in the middle of the night, had arrived shortly after dawn and were angrily confronting the aged but irate depot agent when a buckboard driven by an old Negro and two outriders, one a strikingly beautiful girl, the other a wary-looking half-breed, appeared hurrying down the trail from the west.

A sudden clap of thunder awoke Jason. He raised his head and saw through the unlatched window a small but quickly moving storm sweeping in from the west, long streamers of moisture hanging from its dark crown. It was only a passing spring downpour, with sunlight visible to the north and south where blue sky peeked through. It swept across the ranch, drumming against the roof and the window, but lasted only while he pulled on his clothes and made his way to the kitchen. Then it stopped.

The house seemed weirdly quiet, almost abandoned. He discovered Isabelle, Bessie and Kate standing outside around a pile of items stacked under a long eave of roof. They were waiting for the rain to let up before stowing the articles in a wagon hitched out front. There was a nervous tension in the air, even as Isabelle and Bessie came to embrace him and as they led him into the kitchen to offer the only breakfast available, corn bread dipped in bacon fat and bitter coffee. He showed little surprise at hearing that Seth had disappeared before dawn, but he grimaced when he heard Tate, Brandy and Taska had gone off to Castroville without him.

With the rain soon followed by a warming sun, he helped move the heavier items into the wagon, then walked around to the cellar with a feeling of uselessness coming over him. On an impulse sired by this mood, he decided to make a quick scout of the nearby ranges he knew so well. Tate's words of the night before had placed a menacing shadow over these familiar if now lonely sweeps of mesquite, but they would offer at least a moment or two of solitude.

Finally in the saddle and coming across the yard, he found Inez struggling to pile up a few of her belongings before the hut. He dismounted and went to embrace her, but she backed away and ended up regarding him sideways.

"Inez, good to see you," he called out, but her pained face made his attempt at affection seem awkward.

"So. You back, eh?"

"Yes—it's been a long spell. Didn't realize how bad things were here."

"Things bad here for a long time."

He knew the issue of Taska was alive between them as they strained to force out words unrelated to their thoughts. Clearly she wanted to get away from him, and now, briskly completing her turn toward the hut, she muttered, "I have much to get ready. Better I finish."

He watched her go, then resignedly mounted again. As he crossed the creek and rode westward his thoughts began gathering about some lonely peak in his mind. The war, the coming devastation of defeat, the crumbling of the illusions that had made the South's cause heroic, even hallowed, all weighed on him, and yet last night he had found in the fierce abandon and wild intensity of Taska's love his first relief from the troubling emotions that had gnawed at him for so long. That ravishing, spirited girl with her passionate yet yielding body had stunned him with the animal energy of her desire. Long into the night he had felt the regenerative force, the visceral warmth her womanhood restored to him.

But that night had also brought its rude awakening. Her adoration of him and her innocence of the vital role she now played jolted him into an awareness of what a fool he had been. The pale cultured women of Richmond and their fragile beauty seemed far away, pallid figures of an alien world. Here where his roots lay, here in this ravaged borderland with its harsh grandeur and endless menace, here was the mate who could match the daunting years ahead. He was not a religious man and surprised himself when he saw in the gift of this dazzling and determined girl the favor of God. In the deep calculus of life these tragic, pain-filled years of conflict that had destroyed so many men's dreams had also produced this woman, and something in the keep of his heart whispered that she had the strength to prevail.

So absorbed was he by this reverie and the revelations it was thrusting into his consciousness that though he was instinctively watching the land about him he was still startled by the appearance before him of a great and familiar rock formation rising from the plain like some lonely castle guarding a mystical realm. It warned him that he was already more than two miles west of the Hondo and should be turning back. Yet its sight sparked a touch of nostalgia, for he and Tate and even Taska had often climbed its prominences as children. Its surprising height provided a clear view in all directions. He decided this towering formation would end his scout, for the creep of urgency began to offset his sudden pull of memory. Reaching the great outcropping would take him a mile further, but as he approached he decided not to climb its summit but instead simply to circle its base while his mind recalled the many childhood scenes its pinnacles and caves revived. It was only when he rounded its western limit that he yanked his mount up sharply and held his breath.

Hoofprints of at least a dozen ponies were spread over a few hundred square feet of ground. He stared at them, aghast. Jason never had been the talented scout Tate, or even Seth, was, but he was no novice. Water filled the potholes around the formation, yet the hoofprints were dry. They had been made since the rain. Rising in his stirrups, he could see the unshod tracks leading off and swiftly disappearing into the rolling land to the west. Immediately he swung his mount about and, laying into it with quirt and spurs, forced it into a wild gallop as he raced headlong back toward the ranch.

Taska had been keeping her quick-stepping mount alongside the buckboard while watching Brandy drive. Her mind was on Jason, her thoughts stirred by the lingering warmth in her thighs. Now as they approached the depot, which proved to be only a small barn with a narrow loading platform before it, she saw Tate ride on ahead and dismount beside the long hitching post that flanked the depot on its near side. Following him with her eyes, she saw two men standing on the platform talking to an elderly clerk in a black vest. She gathered from their wild gestures that they were arguing.

As she and Brandy came closer, a faint apprehension swept over her. She did not like the looks of these men. Suddenly she realized that two others were sprawled in a heavy wagon below the platform, watching her curiously as she rode up. Expecting to see Jason again when she returned she was wearing her best jeans and a colorful yellow blouse that contoured smoothly about her breasts. Her ebony hair, soft and full, was tied into the short ponytail Elena had combed out and shaped for her. She noticed that Brandy was keeping the wagon back behind the hitching post. He too was studying the men on the platform.

"You got salt and coffee and even some barrels of molasses," Riff was shouting at the old man. "We got papers for that stuff, right and proper."

"I don't give a damn what papers you've got," returned the depot agent, poking his face into Riff's like a bantam rooster. "You ain't no militia, and if you want anything here, by God, you're gonna have to pay for it!"

"Ever hear of the Regulators?" snapped Caleb.

"Regulators?" The old man turned to spit. "I might have known I was dealing with trash." He stepped back to stare at the taller man. "You're that Riff Connors, ain't you?"

"That's me," replied Riff, his hand dropping to cover his gun, "and we've wasted enough time talkin'." He turned to the two toughs resting below. "Boys, put all that stuff in the wagon."

"Hold on a moment," said Tate, strolling over. "Those stores belong to the state. You can't take them unless that agent says so."

One of the toughs on the wagon, who slept off his drunks in the stables around San Antonio, recognized Tate. Normally he wouldn't have dared open his mouth, but now they had this sullen, surly half-breed outgunned four to one. "Well, I'll be damned," he exclaimed, spitting a glob of tobacco juice over the side of the wagon, "if it ain't that squint-eyed half-breed from Thunder Run. Riff, you got yourself a sure-enough Injun telling you what to do."

"Just advisin' y'all on how the law reads," said Tate quietly, but there was a cold tremor in his voice that Brandy and Taska knew was the only warning.

"Now hear that!" mocked Riff. "How the law reads! Ha!" He was smirking at the tight-lipped Tate. "Ain't you heard yet, Injun? We're the law 'round here."

"Not by a damn sight!" shouted the old man fearlessly.

Neither Riff Connors nor Caleb Sutton had expected a fight. For a moment Riff was silent. This was not his style. This half-breed looked like he could handle a gun, and behind him they could see a Negro sitting in a wagon with a rifle across his knee. A strikingly attractive girl was sitting on a sleek-looking mare beside him, and from the honey hue of her rich, lemony skin, Riff decided she was a high yellow. He turned to the men below. "Like I said, boys, put the stuff in the wagon." But his hand was no longer near his gun.

"I wouldn't do that," said Tate slowly.

The tough who had recognized Tate jumped to the ground and turned to his companion. "Come along, Zeke, if this damn breed horns in again, we'll blow him back to where the hell he belongs!"

The two reached and braced themselves against the edge of the platform.

"That's far enough," said Tate.

"I'll be go to hell," snarled the first tough, twisting and going for his gun as the one named Zeke spun around with him. But without flinching Tate drew and fired two shots, so close together they sounded like one, then calmly slid his gun back into its holster. The first tough was down and the one called Zeke was holding his arm, his gun on the ground.

"You murdering bastard!" cried Caleb. Riff jumped off the platform and bent over the man sprawled on the ground. He put his hand on his chest, holding it there for a few moments. "He's dead! By Christ, he's dead!" he yowled. He turned his furious eyes on Tate. "You'll pay for this, Injun!" he spat.

"He was only defending state property!" shouted the old man.

"That's every citizen's duty under the law. By jiminy, was I a mite younger I'd take a six-gun to you buzzards myself. Now clear out!"

Brandy, holding his breath, could see that this old man refused to scare. Here were the raw guts he hadn't seen since old Adam Salinger had died. But the danger was far from over. He didn't like the looks of the one called Connors or the way he kept glancing at Taska. He decided to get his daughter back to the ranch as soon as possible. Maybe they could get along without any supplies.

But Tate watched the others put the dead man's body in the wagon and drive away. Before he left, Caleb stared up at the old man and Tate. "You two best be making your peace with God. Neither of you trash is long for this world."

Tate showed the agent a well-worn piece of paper that identified him as a member of the border patrol, part of the state militia. The agent, grateful for his aid, offered to give him the few boxes of shells left for nothing, but Tate said they were for his family's private use and insisted on paying for them. The man responded by throwing in the last half can of gun oil in the depot.

When the small items, along with some coffee and molasses, had been settled in the wagon, Tate gripped the old man's arm in warning. "Really don't think you should be staying here alone, mister. Them polecats is likely to come back."

"Might be," said the gray-haired agent without concern. "But I ain't runnin'." He stood watching Brandy turn the buckboard around, then called out to them, "What's this I hear about Injuns in these parts?"

"It's true," said Tate. "Wouldn't plan on staying here much longer was I you. Where's your diggin's?"

The old man nodded to a path across the trail. "A mile or two up yonder. Finally got my two sons back yesterday from that holy mess at Vicksburg."

"Why don't you mosey up there . . . least for today."

"No siree. I ain't runnin'. Never did before . . . too damn old to start."

Tate jumped down and came over to the buckboard. Brandy looked at him, worry and impatience tightening his face. "Let's git movin', Tate. Ah doan like dis. Ain't no tellin' what dem devils done gone down de road is up to."

"You start back," said Tate. "I'm going to run up and get this stubborn old goat's sons to come fetch him. He shouldn't be here alone."

"We'll be all right," said Taska, quickly tying her prancing mare to the rear of the buckboard and climbing in beside her father. "Just hurry."

"I will!" he shouted behind him as he pulled his mount about and left at a run.

When the wagon carrying the dead tough's body made its first turn in the trail, Riff pulled up and swore under his breath. "By God, we was just plain buffaloed by that damn half-breed. We ought to go back and put some lead in that old bastard's mouth. We should have taken that stuff before the other bunch showed up. Damnation!"

But the right reverend Caleb Sutton was sputtering with his own wrath. He had been mortally disturbed and outraged by the Negro who held the rifle. He was unaware that Brandy was only dealing with his own rampant fears. All he saw was a Negro holding a gun on whites. This was surely the first sign of the apocalyptic collapse he had predicted. To add to his fury and increasingly dark convictions, both the murderer and the girl accompanying the Negro were of mixed blood. Clearly here was the foul freshet before the flood, God's scourge for their lack of vigilance, the mongrelization of the race.

But Riff's frustration had turned to the girl. In spite of the tension and violence they had just experienced, her stirring, tawny beauty had him dangerously aroused. In his debauched mind he was already ravishing her, forcing her to fornicate, sodomizing her body till his lust was satisfied.

He turned to the waiting Zeke, who, with the wagon stopped, was nervously binding his arm. "Just set here a spell," he muttered slipping off his horse.

"What you fixin' to do?" demanded Caleb.

"See what that bunch back there does, now they've got to figurin' we'uns is gone."

The sun had mounted the sky and was fast heating the earth when Seth got the sulky buckskin back to Thunder Run. He wanted to question Brandy about the big black but, hearing from Inez that he was gone, started quietly making his way to the rear cellar. On the way he found Bessie stacking tools alongside the loaded wagon. There were two shovels, a pitchfork, an ax and a two-handled saw, items impossible to replace in the metal-starved Confederacy. Glancing up at him, she said, "Didn't 'spect you'd bother comin' back." Her tone did not encourage a reply.

He stopped, feeling awkward about collapsing and falling asleep the night before. "Just hopin' to borrow a few cartridges," he half mumbled. "We're plumb out."

She straightened up, studying him, her hands on her hips. "Don't believe we've any to spare," she replied coolly. "One would think with smugglers in her family she'd have plenty of what the rest of us are getting by without."

Bessie's long resentment of Elena had never been more apparent. Here she was lumping her with Julio and Ricardo and their illicit traffic across the border. Seth knew there was no other source of these supplies, so desperately needed in blockaded Texas. Contraband goods crossing that long, lonely border were as unstoppable as sundown. Sam Houston had passed laws to control the smuggling, but a populace wanting and needing the necessities of life saw little reason to uphold them.

"Where's Jason?" he asked, seeing nothing to be gained in arguing the point with her.

Bessie threw a look behind her, her eyes taking in the far bank of the creek. "Reckon he'll be back soon . . . not likely he'll go far . . . time like this." She turned and without a closing word or gesture made her way back to the house.

Seth entered the cellar, quickly appraising the horses stabled there. Other than the black, they were hardly choice stock. He couldn't help wondering what fate had befallen the herds of finely bred horses his ranch had once produced. Likely their bones were spread over a hundred battlefields.

He threw his saddle onto the black, which the short rest had seem to cure, and tightened the cinches. Jason would come soon and give him every shell that could be spared. Yet would that be enough? His mind was feverishly at work. Secretly he wanted to get Elena and her people on the trail in time to join those from Thunder Run. There would be some safety in numbers. With Jason, Tate and Brandy, there would be three armed men, and all the women could handle guns, some of them superbly. But as he led the black out into the yard, the

bued with this wild nomadic life, bloodstained as it was, few willingly returned to civilization.

Red Claw, his body squat like that of most Comanches, with outsized arms and bowed legs, his badly pocked face pinched tightly around tiny obsidian eyes, was only half listening to the Kiowa chief, Black Horn. Black Horn held the scalp of the Wichita boy whom a dying shepherd had revealed under torture to be helping the whites. The youth, seeing them coming, had fled his hogan, but they had run him down before he could reach a ranch where they discovered a large adobe-and-slate house like a small fort.

Blood Hawk, who was standing beside them, grunted in recognition as Black Horn described Thunder Run. "It is where my father met his death in the dark moons before my great medicine came." He struck his chest for emphasis. "Let Red Claw capture and torture the life from these *tejanos*, but their scalps belong to me."

Red Claw turned his dark, crabbed face toward the now aging but still-feared medicine man, who had garishly painted himself with a medicine sign that he had received in one of his spells and which, he had told the warriors, would ward off enemy bullets. The watchful and wily Red Claw, though he had painted the medicine sign on one arm, had yet to reveal his real reason for bringing the noisy and demanding Blood Hawk along.

In contrast, the fierce, haughty Black Horn, a Koh-eet-senko, one of the ten greatest warriors in the Kiowa nation, openly held Blood Hawk in contempt and pointedly ignored him. He had long considered this half-mad Comanche and his farcical claims to great medicine a nuisance if not a dangerous fraud. Why the crafty Red Claw had allowed this faker into his camp was baffling. He himself refused to paint Blood Hawk's sign on his body, and scowled in annoyance when many of his warriors did.

Red Claw, though listening intently, showed little concern at the description of Thunder Run as being a small fortress, for he saw no need to attack it. Reports of a wagon stationed before it meant its inhabitants were preparing to flee. On the trail they would be far easier prey. Red Claw's reputation as a torturer tended to obscure the fact that he was also a shrewd, calculating and, because of long training as a guerrilla, formidable war leader. He had taught himself to fight the way the white Rangers did, exploiting every enemy weakness and not expecting bravery or superstition to substitute for firepower or strategic advantage.

He had already correctly judged the thinking of these whites who sought to evade him and had sent his warriors before dawn to cut the trail east of the ranch. He knew a buckboard had slipped out that morning, but it would surely be back, for there were still many women left among these doomed *tejanos*. He was not expecting much of a fight and certainly not a great victory, but he had long since devised special tortures for *tejano* women. His warriors would not go unrewarded.

Riff Connors had climbed a small mound of boulders at the curve of the trail and watched Tate riding off as the buckboard carrying Brandy and Taska turned back up the trail. By the time he had made his way again to the others, his mind had hit upon a promising scheme. His man Zeke would continue to San Antonio with the wagon. They would need that dead body later. He and Caleb would circle back through the brush behind the depot and cut the wagon off further up the trail. He was going to get that girl.

This being Caleb's first assignment, Connors had taken the precaution of bringing a pint of whisky. He produced it now and extended it to Caleb. "Let's quit frettin'. This could work out smoother than spit." His voice had regained its gruff assurance. "We got Clem's body here to prove we wuz attacked. Ain't no one gonna take that half-breed's word over ours."

Caleb, his face still florid with stifled rage, looked at Riff grimly but managed a formidable swallow of the whiskey. He rubbed his mouth with the back of his hand, a gesture from which his lips emerged in a fine, hard line. "What you fixin' to do about that old coot? Folks is bound to lissen to him."

Riff's talent for incriminating his victims had never been sharper. "After we deal with that nigger and the gal we take their wagon back to the depot, shoot that old son of a bitch with the nigger's gun and leave those goddamned fake papers on the nigger's body. Folks will just naturally think they kilt each other in a fight over the stores. We can say we just happened by and poor old Clem here got hisself kilt a-tryin' to help that poor agent out."

Caleb's response was to take a second swig from the bottle. Zeke, sitting in the wagon holding his arm, shook his head in doubt and disbelief. "Riff, you're forgettin' that son of a bitchin' breed . . . anybody goes up against him with a gun is crazy."

"Don't stew on it, Zeke. We gonna set up a little ambush for that big-mouth Injun . . . won't know what's a-happenin' to him till he's wolf bait."

Sending the shaken but grateful Zeke on his way to San Antonio, Riff joined Caleb in another turn at the bottle before they rode into the brush and began to race along a line parallel to the trail. In less than ten minutes Riff caught glimpses of the wagon they were stalking and began to look for a likely spot on the trail to cut it off. His eyes found a stretch ahead where a high shoulder of rock at a turn narrowed the trail on one side. It would be harder to turn the wagon there or even to leave the trail. Signaling to Caleb to head for the far end of the turn, he galloped on ahead.

Brandy was hurrying the team as fast as he could. The fear that assailed him at the depot still hovered in his mind. Somehow movement didn't help. The menace of that encounter was still with him. Taska tried to make light of it, but she sounded more confident than she felt. She too sensed an impending threat and was silently praying that they would reach the ranch quickly or that Tate would come up before any of her fears were realized.

As they started a long turn following a low palisade of rock on one side, they saw two horsemen coming out across the trail and knew at once who they were. Brandy halted the wagon. The sight was chilling. His mind told him that whatever else they were after, they had come for Taska. He himself no longer counted. Fear for his daughter put firmness in his voice. "Taska, git on dat horse and ride. No way dey ever gonna catch you."

Taska looked at her fleet mare reined alongside the wagon. She was certain she could easily outride the two heavy men on the poor-quality horses she had seen at the depot, but she wasn't going to leave her father. "Daddy," she said, gripping his arm. "There's only two of them. Give me the rifle!"

"No, child, you go!" Brandy took up the rifle and threw the reins around the whip socket. Taska tried to reach back for the rifle in her saddle scabbard, but it was too far. She was about to jump down when the sound of horses approaching brought her attention forward again. She felt for the gun in her belt, but it was tucked back between her hip and the wagon seat.

Riff, seeing the wagon stop, at once suspected that the girl might try to escape on that fleet-looking mount. Quickly he motioned to Caleb to draw his gun, and they closed on the wagon.

As they came up, Riff was holding his pistol on Taska and Caleb was covering Brandy. Brandy still held the rifle, but it was pointed at Riff.

"What do you want?" asked Taska, fighting to keep her voice from trembling.

Riff, figuring that the issue was settled and the old nigger's threat with the rifle was a bluff, almost smiled. "Well, missy, all we wants is a little funnin'." He had moved his horse to where he could reach Taska on the wagon. He glanced over at Brandy. "Tell that old nigger to put the gun down before my partner blows his head off."

Brandy, eyeing Caleb, whose pistol was trained on him only a wagon's length away, lowered the muzzle of the rifle an inch or two but kept it fixed on Riff.

"What do you want?" repeated Taska, now watching Riff's hand come up to grab her knee.

Brandy's hands tightened on the rifle. "Ah doan got but one warnin', mistah. Keep yo' hands off her."

"You keep your mouth shut, nigger!" shouted Caleb. "You gonna find we got ways of dealing with sinful trash like you." He thumbed back the hammer on his pistol.

Riff's hand started moving up Taska's leg and was between her thighs when his eyes caught her smooth, well-rounded breasts. He was reaching for them, thinking she was only shying away as her hand clawed behind her for her gun, but he never knew the calamity this move had triggered, for Brandy's rifle blew him out of the saddle and landed him on the ground, his chest shattered and his hard gray eyes turning to dull glass. But Caleb's gun also roared, and Brandy slumped suddenly as the bullet smashed his ribs and entered his chest. Taska, her gun finally freed, fired twice at Caleb, putting two neat holes in his forehead; he was dead before his body crumpled to the ground. His own mount, startled, nervously kicked his corpse before it shied away.

Before she could lower Brandy's body down onto the narrow seat, blood began streaking from his mouth and nostrils. She wanted to scream, but the sight of blood trickling down his face froze her with dread. The bullet had torn deep into his chest, and there was no way she could halt the bleeding. She tried to get him to the back of the buckboard so she could hurry on to the ranch, but he was too heavy for her. As she choked back her screams and struggled with her helpless father, the distant sound of hooves made her look up. It was Tate. Hearing the shots, he had pressed his horse into a frenzied gallop. Riding up to the buckboard, he jumped down to grip Taska's outstretched hands.

"Tate! Help me!" she screamed. "Daddy is hurt! We have to find a doctor!"

Tate looked at Brandy's wound, then back at Taska. There was no doctor this side of San Antonio, and both of them knew it. Brandy was dying. Hearing their voices, he opened his eyes. His voice was weak, but they leaned in above his lips.

"Take me home, child," he whispered. Tears spread in lines of anguish beneath the blood on his face. "Ah wants to die dere . . . wid Inez."

They lifted him to the back of the buckboard, where Taska cradled his head in her arms. Tate, tying his mount opposite Taska's, leaped on the bloodstained seat and whipped the team forward. There was no way he could keep the buckboard from bouncing, but he skillfully kept it to the smooth ground in the center of the trail. Listening to Taska's sobbing and praying and feeling his own heart pound, he could not shake the feeling that this tragedy was only the beginning.

If their years on the frontier had schooled them against panic, it had also given them a knowledge of just how fatal miscalculations could be. Seth and Jason, war-hardened and no strangers to death, faced each other, appalled at the message in the unshod pony tracks, at its threat to their women. Seth, knowing he had to get back to Elena as fast as the black could carry him, felt a sinking sensation even as he heard Jason's retort to his request for cartridges. "Bullets won't help either of us now. We've got to get out of here!"

"What about Tate and Brandy and Taska?" pleaded Isabelle. "Mercy! Shouldn't they be warned?"

"How!" shouted Jason, his glance fixed on the shocked women. "Look . . . fetch your horses. Forget that wagon. We've got to get runnin'. We'll meet the others on the trail . . . they'll be coming this way."

Seth had to resist crying out *Christ? Can't you wait for us? We'll never make it alone!* But they couldn't wait, and he knew it. It served no purpose. Their dying would not save Elena and her people. They were down to the frontier's bedrock rules of survival.

Though they had all started to move, they were frozen in their tracks by the near-frantic Inez, who was rising on her toes and peering down the wagon road, her voice verging on a scream. "They come! See . . . they come fast . . . very fast . . . ay, *por dios* . . . is trouble, no?"

They turned as one to see the buckboard coming toward them at breakneck speed, Tate driving and laying into the foaming team with a high-cracking whip that clearly shouted trouble.

Not a word was spoken, but as the buckboard swung into the yard everyone could see Taska in the back holding her father. At the sight of her bloodstained blouse and the inert form of Brandy in her arms, Inez started to cry out. Seth and Jason rushed to lift Brandy down, both knowing at once that he had only minutes to live. Isabelle wanted him taken into the house, but Inez, choking and speechless with horror and shock, tugged at Seth's arm and pointed to the hut. There was no point in delaying. They took him in and laid him on the low bed. Bessie saw how it was with Inez and motioned the others away.

Alone with Brandy, Inez hugged him in desperation, weeping hysterically. "Brandy, Brandy, don't go!" she pleaded.

With a great effort he managed to open his eyes a fraction. He had lost the strength to speak and could only whisper. "Lord bin good to ole Brandy," he wheezed. "He bring me you."

Inez could only cling to him more tightly, sobbing uncontrollably. Moments passed and her sheltered world of love and devotion, which had blossomed in the meager confines of this hut, was slipping away. When she looked at his face again, the warm, caring Brandy, who had brought his smile into an uncaring world and who had loved her for herself alone, was gone.

Outside, the others were shaken but were striving to follow Tate's words as he tried to relate the fatal encounter and its violent ending in Castroville. Seth and Jason, with the doggedness of veteran soldiers, quietly struggled with the new threat now hanging over them. Without admitting it even to himself, Seth wanted Tate's opinion on how they could save themselves.

When Tate heard about the tracks at the rocky outcropping, his already aroused features visibly tightened and his body became tense as he turned to stare uneasily in that direction. He did not speak until he had stepped over, pulled his mount from the buckboard and leapt into the saddle. "Get ready to leave!" he shouted. "I'll be right back!"

With that he spurred his horse in a wild gallop across the stream.

Seth mounted the black and glanced grimly at the sun, realizing he had been here far longer than he had planned. Surely Elena, Carlota and Don José would be ready. His big black, rested and again seemingly fit, began to fly down the wagon road toward the trail.

From his saddle Tate stared down at the tracks now hardened in the sun-dried clay, knowing Jason was right. It was a large scouting party, and they had scaled these rocks to sight toward the ranch. He wondered how close their main force was. They could still be many miles to the west. With a steady nerve, Tate began to move guardedly in that direction, studying their tracks. This was dangerous work, but he knew every hillock and coulee in that stretch of country from which danger could spring. His eyes roamed back and forth over the ground before him like a hawk soaring low over a meadow. He knew from these tracks that the party was moving quickly, which usually meant they had a distance to go, but that was by no means certain. The range seemed abandoned, and an eerie quiet hovered over the land. But the silence meant nothing. Red Claw was coming; that much he knew.

Elena paced the room again, convinced that Seth had run into trouble. He was hours overdue. It was now near noon. As visibly upset as he had been that morning and as anxious as he had been to get them to San Antonio, nothing else explained his absence.

"Why are we waiting?" demanded Don José. "Why don't we start for San Antonio ourselves? *Dios*, we are not children."

Carlota was poised at the window, where she had been nervously watching the long sweep of land running to the southwest since late morning. "We can't just sit here worrying forever, Elena. I have a terrible feeling something is wrong. Look at that sky."

Elena came up behind her. Another storm was approaching, its dark billows advancing behind ramparts of copper-colored clouds. The sun was still shining, but the clouds were deflecting its rays and causing an eerie lighting over the prairie. Elena turned back to Don José, now so perplexed he was drumming his fingers noisily on the table top. "All right, then, just a few minutes longer. Then we'll go." She was gripping her throat tightly, silently praying Seth would come. She had a stark premonition that their trip to San Antonio was going to be a frightening one.

Don José kept muttering to himself and shaking his head. "The horses have been ready for a long time," he said, his impatience swelling to irritation and anger. "If we don't go soon, they will have to be fed and watered again."

A brittle silence settled between them, abruptly broken by Carlota's gasping, "*Madre de dios!* Come! Hurry! There's something out there!"

Elena turned to her, moving quickly to the window with Don José. "Out where?" she asked breathlessly.

"Out there, behind that little rise of land."

"I see nothing," said Don José.

"It was there only a moment ago."

"What did it look like?" Elena rose onto her toes, trying to see further.

"I thought it was an animal, a stray longhorn or even a buffalo maybe. But no, now I'm sure it was a horned headpiece."

"*Jesucristo!* Comanches!" moaned Don José. "We are lost! *Dios*, why did we wait?"

Carlota was clasping her hands together to keep them from shaking, but her eyes were on Elena.

Throwing a scarf about her head, Elena headed for the door. In the distance thunder rumbled. "Take the guns, we'll leave now. Surely we'll meet Seth before we reach the trail."

Don José, who had earlier smashed all their liquor bottles—an unspoken commandment of the frontier when Indians threatened—could not help thinking that a glass of strong *aguardiente* would steady his nerves. "We are lost!" he kept mumbling to himself. "Lost!" Putting his arm through the strap on his rifle, he tugged at his large, uncomfortable backpack. "Let's pray there is room for fools in heaven. It's our only hope."

But once outside, they heard the pound of distant hooves coming down the wagon road leading from the trail. Through the trees they could see Seth coming at full gallop, the big black carrying him toward them at a furious pace.

Seth came up to the porch to find Elena and Carlota holding rifles and Don José with a large pack strapped to his back. "You ready?" he half shouted, not dismounting.

"Seth?" Elena cried excitedly. "Did you see anything coming here?"

He wiped perspiration from his forehead, as he jutted his head toward her in open concern. "Why?"

"Carlota thinks she saw something near that low hill out back."

Seth motioned them to their horses, hoping Carlota's fears had influenced her imagination or distorted her senses. But his voice had the tightness of suppressed alarm as he turned to lead them off. "Now stay together . . . talk as little as possible. If you see or hear anything, don't shout . . . just pull up. With any luck we'll be over the Medina well before sundown."

They moved along the deeply worn wagon tracks, Seth hurrying ahead, followed by the two women and finally Don José. Thunder was now sounding along the darkening western horizon, but sunlight was still weirdly flooding the plain. Nothing happened until the wagon tracks made their wide swing eastward to join the trail. Then Seth's eyes caught a dim flashing somewhere to the east. Saying nothing, he quickly led the others into a small stand of scrub pines that filled the long thin triangle between the wagon track and the trail. There he jumped from the saddle.

"*Qué pasa?*" inquired Don José, anxiously coming up.

" 'Bout to find out," said Seth. But a curious constraint in his voice hinted that he already knew.

He slipped over to crouch down at the trail's edge looking east. A half mile further on, where the long wagon road that led to Thunder Run fed into the opposite side of the trail, he could see the figures of several braves moving on foot around a high stand of brush, and one or two leading horses across the trail. "Christ almighty," he breathed to himself. They had Thunder Run cut off. Yet the full menace of his own predicament only became clear when he caught the sudden flashing again. A mile beyond the braves was a small rise in the trail. From it a mirror was blinking as it reflected the lingering light of the sun. They had blocked the trail to the east and were signaling to what was surely their main force on some nearby ridge to the west.

Perspiration started to streak down his face, and for a moment his breath was labored. They would have to double back and try to make it through the brush. His eyes shut hard at the lunacy of trying to outrun Comanches through rough country. The ghastly alternatives began piercing his mind, coming on with the slow, penetrating sting of ice. The women could not be taken alive, and yet he could not hold these savages off. Turning back, hopeless as it seemed, was their only option to death. They had only moments to decide. Clearly the Indians knew they were there. He swung back to the others, his face as pale as chalk. "They've cut the trail . . . we can't make it this way." The others' expressions tightened. "They're fixin' to trap us—can't stay here."

"Oh, *Santo Dios, por favor*," moaned Don José.

Elena's hand came up to grip Seth's arm. "What then?"

"There isn't much choosin'," he muttered, seeing the desperate pleas in their eyes.

"You're saying we must go back." Carlota's flat voice concealed the anguish in her words.

Even as she spoke, Seth was grasping at thoughts of making a stand in that defenseless farmhouse, and he instinctively glanced in its direction. But then, beyond a far-distant stand of trees, he saw it, a glowing cherry-red flare against the darkening sky. The house was afire. That last desperate option was gone. Warriors with faces already painted for death were behind them. His startled peering in that direction caused the others to turn toward it.

"Mercy!" cried Carlota. "Our home . . . all our things!"

"Keep your mind on staying alive," returned Seth, the ring of command reviving in his voice. The sun had disappeared, and a sudden loud crackling leapt from forks of lightning spidering across the underbelly of the massing clouds. They joined to explode in a shaft of blazing light that plunged and knifed into the earth in the direction of Thunder Run.

A deafening peal of thunder rolled across the prairie, shaking the earth beneath them. They had to act. Seth, in spite of his exhaustion and frustration, was too seasoned a fighter to succumb to the mute paralysis bred by fear. Desperation actually made his resolve easier. He motioned them to their horses, warning them in a low but resolute voice not to mount but to lead their horses and follow him. Don José, too shaken to remain silent, gulped, "What are we gonna do?"

"Run for it . . . it's our only chance." Seth glanced at the dark, roaring curtain of rain sweeping down upon them. "This storm will help, but it won't last."

"*Por gracia, por dios*, I cannot run with this pack."

"Drop it!"

Don José loosened the straps, and the hefty pack fell from his back. Elena watched her precious collection of valuables slip to the ground, not caring or even remembering Carlota's insistence that they wear the few remaining D'Valya jewels. Both women quickly ran a hand over the slit in their blouse where a derringer, the instruments cynically referred to by Mexican ladies as "last rites," were concealed. They did not know of Red Claw's hideous and diabolical treatment of captives, but they had heard enough of the horrors in store for women to vow not to be taken alive.

After many long minutes of dodging through the brush along the trail, blinded and thoroughly soaked by the driving rain, they began to approach the stretch where Seth had spotted the Comanches. He could see no sign of them now but was sure they were squatting back in the brush. The storm would not reduce their vigilance, but it would limit the distance in which they could see clearly. He moved up cautiously as close as he dared, then turned, motioning the others to move up and huddle around him. His voice edged above the roar of the rain. "We have to count on surprise . . . speed . . . we'll need both. We'll cross the trail here and make for that wide bend in the creek . . . there's cover there. Don't try to stay together, it will slow you up. And no matter what, *don't stop*. If one of us is hit, the others can't help. If you catch a slug or your horse goes down, don't wait for them to finish the job. Comanches can make you wish you hadn't."

There was a moment of silence before Elena, thinking their only hope was to continue up the trail, said with a throaty whisper, "Bend of the creek? Seth, there's no hope for us there!"

"No, but if we get that far we'll make it the rest of the way."

"Make it? Where?"

"To Thunder Run."

Elena's eyes widened as she and Carlota exchanged glances. As Seth turned his horse into the pounding rain and mounted, they followed him, their lips moving in silent prayer.

Except for Taska and the suffering, inconsolable Inez, those at Thunder Run could have headed down the wagon road far sooner. But as the women rushed to gather the few things they could carry and Jason saddled and brought up the many mounts, Taska came weeping from the hut, too distraught even to speak and able only to motion Jason to her. In the hut Inez, still prostrate on the bed and wailing her grief, was clinging to Brandy's body.

Jason came over to take Taska in his arms, seeing her eyes were now a swollen, feverish red. She was trembling and still too overcome to speak. With Jason holding her close, she finally found her voice. "Daddy is dead," she sobbed in anguish.

"Yes, I know," he murmured.

"He died trying to protect me," she choked bitterly, her face burrowing into his shoulder.

"He died like a man," Jason comforted her. " 'Twas the way he would have wanted it." Jason put his mouth close to her ear and whispered, "You must get your mother ready, Taska. We have to leave." To the south and west clouds had been quickly massing, and now thunder began to rumble. Jason could smell the wet saltweed musk that spiced the air during spring storms.

Taska lifted her head to stare strangely at him. "We can't leave till we bury Daddy. We can't leave his body here for them. We can't."

Jason fought an urge to shout, *Girl, there's no time for burying! We're in mortal danger here! Death is its own sanctuary. Brandy is beyond pain from human hands, even those of savages.* But looking into her grief-stricken face, the words wouldn't come.

The storm was ready to break when Tate, his horse in a lather, came rushing in. Astonished, he saw Jason busy digging near Adam's grave. He pulled up where the horses were saddled and looked around to find Bessie frantically waving him over to help carry Brandy's blanket-wrapped body from the hut. He did it, his face a mask of confusion. Whose insanity was this? With the threat of attack rising about them, every moment counted. Fortunately Jason, helped by Kate, who had pulled the second shovel from the wagon, had the shallow grave ready. As Tate helped Bessie and Taska lower the body into its resting place, Jason, his exhausted arms around the shovel, looked up and recited the Twenty-third Psalm from memory. Almost at once Isabelle and Bessie began pulling Inez and Taska from the graveside and down to where the horses waited. Jason took only a moment to throw some heavy branches over Brandy's grave and fling the little wooden cross that marked Adam's plot into the brush. Every borderer knew that the Comanche code of warfare included digging up and defiling their enemies' remains.

As they returned to the yard, lightning began striking about them and sharp claps of thunder jolted them as they mounted their horses. For a few of them there was suddenly something wrong about leaving Thunder Run. Tate, knowing how seriously they had misjudged the approach of the hostiles, already wondered at the wisdom of it. The possibility of being trapped on the trail loomed in his mind. Ominously, it fitted all too well what he had heard about Red Claw's way of fighting, but the knuckles of his hand came against his chin as he accepted the futility of even thinking about it. Whatever else, under the massive attacks he was sure were coming, Thunder Run could not be held. Salvation lay on the other side of the Medina.

It might easily have been missed with the lightning streaking down and thunder rumbling about them, but Tate was too alert. He knew that the quick flashes he caught sight of far down the wagon road were not lightning and the sharp, staccato reports like a distant shattering of rock were not thunder. A gunfight had broken out close to the trail. In his heart he knew it could be the first footfall of death.

Seth knew that waiting would only risk losing what little cover the storm afforded, for it was beginning to abate. He was planning to race across the trail, using the heavy growth on the other side to protect them until they reached the shallow ford that served the trail over the Hondo, still a hundred perilous yards away. But the danger would mount as they swung north to follow the far edge of the creek to the wide bend just visible through the mist a quarter mile further on. From there, with luck, they might reach the wagon road. If these warriors were here only to stalk the road where it joined the trail and ensure that no party leaving Thunder Run could return, it might work. The hard truth was that they were already trapped. The many stupidities that had led to this disaster appalled him. The idea of all these women falling into Comanche hands provoked thoughts so horrible his mind refused to let them form. Elena and Carlota might stick to their rarely mentioned but well-known oaths to cheat the savages of their humiliating orgies, but there were also those at Thunder Run, who he feared would fight until they were overcome.

With his large army Colt in one hand, his reins in the other, he kicked the black forward and heard the women's quirts whipping hard against their horses' flanks as they all broke from cover and raced across the trail.

At first their hoofbeats were muffled by the rain-soaked earth and there was only the sound of rain pelting down on the thick brush, but Seth knew that when the iron-shod hooves began striking the rocky bottom of the stream and its wide sloping banks, their presence would surely draw deadly fire. Miraculously, they made it across the thin ripple of water and were turning north before Seth heard the whoosh of an arrow pass over him like a swooping nighthawk, followed by orange flashes flaring up from the heavy growth on his right. War cries rose immediately, joining the gunfire and drowning out the pound of galloping hooves. Seth could see figures leaping toward them through the drizzle. Digging his spurs into the black, he managed a glance behind him. The women were keeping up, but Don José was twisting in his saddle like a man having trouble with his mount, and a dangerous gap had opened up. There was nothing Seth could do. Their only hope was speed. The Indians kept up a heavy fire, but Seth used his revolver only twice. It was a waste of bullets. Neither side could see well enough to make their shots count, and Seth suddenly realized they might be in for a desperate stand at the bend.

Don José's frantic shouts of alarm rose to match the war cries. Coming last, he had ridden straight into the random hail of lead spit forth by the flashing guns from the undergrowth and his horse had been hit. The game pony was trying to keep up, but the effort was beyond its strength. Don José, an experienced horseman, felt the pony could still make it to the bend even if increasingly trailing the others, but its falling back caused the warriors to concentrate on him, and a steady stream of bullets started whining by and the low whistle of arrows in flight pierced the air on either side. Praying loudly to God, he bent forward in the saddle and urged his struggling animal on. The pony was destined to make it, but Don José was not. An arrow with a jagged iron tip came out of the mist and plunged into his back. The old man fell to the ground, cringing and helpless. Looking up, he made out grotesque forms coming toward him, his eyes finally focusing to shape them into painted savages with raised hatchets growing larger and larger in the mist. His last thoughts, stirring faintly behind the rise of a paralyzing terror, were of that heavy pack, abandoned moments before, that would have stopped the arrow and saved his life.

Tate's sudden halt to stare down the wagon road had those behind him pulling up and peering ahead. One by one they caught the faint orange flashes flickering in the gray blanket of mist over the distant trail. The crackling of gunfire echoed dully toward them like a sinister tocsin, freezing them into silence. Only Inez kept gazing vacantly at the diagonal sweeps of rain, her mind refusing to register the crisis overtaking this race for life. She no longer cared.

Jason moved up beside Tate, saying nothing. Mutely the two sat together, staring down the heavy tracks that marked the road, both knowing the futility of words. For one rare moment the half brothers stayed there, strangers in many ways but held by childhood bonds, forged in that lonely and forbidding land.

Both had learned long ago that fear was the mother of wisdom in this treacherous country, but the icy realization welling up in them now was far more traumatizing than fear. The land was deserted. That gunfire could mean only one thing: Seth was being attacked by hostiles in command of the trail. He was trying to fight his way to Thunder Run. Shocked and sobered, neither could bring himself to voice the obvious. Their judgment had been fatally flawed. The women behind them, including their mother and the girl they both loved, would pay a hellish price. Their only real chance of survival was receding before their eyes. A final flash of lightning plunging into the knoll before the house brought on an explosion of thunder that cried to them to act. The disaster that for two days had hovered in their minds like the darkening approach of death had just descended.

Both felt the terrible imperatives that dispelled any words. They had to help Seth. They had to ensure what little time the defenses of Thunder Run could buy. Tate took up his reins. "I'll go!" He threw a grim glance at Jason as he spun to the others and waved toward the house. "Fort up! There isn't much time!" He left, shouting behind him, "Get that wagon into the cellar . . . don't get too far from the house . . . they're awfully damn close!"

Seth kept the black fully extended and pounding ahead. He had heard the women choking back shrieks of horror as they realized that the savage howling behind them was rising over the prostrate body of Don José. Ahead he could see that the bend of the creek was clear. They would make it to the wagon road, but their respite would be short. Red Claw's trap was snapping shut. Don José's fate was only the beginning.

Elena, clinging to her horse, was too stunned to notice that they were racing by the creek bend, not stopping but turning into the heavy growth that straggled between the sharp bend and the rough wagon road. It was only when they emerged on the road itself she realized they were covering a stretch of ground she had often thought of but had never seen. She was approaching the domain of her lover's wife, Isabelle Redmond. She was riding into those formidable shadows of Thunder Run where her own name was never spoken. She could see Carlota, her head bending over her mount's mane, raindrops or tears streaking down her sobbing face. It reminded her that she too was crying at the shock of losing Don José. But she mustn't cry here, now. She pulled herself up and ran the sleeve of her velvet jacket across her cheeks. She could see Seth looking back and pointing up the road. Someone was coming. Within a minute or two they made out the form of Tate racing toward them. She watched the tall dark youth galloping up to exchange words with Seth. She was taken aback by the sharpness and briskness of his tone and found herself shifting awkwardly as he threw a troubled look at Carlota and herself. Feeling challenged, she stared back at him, but he avoided her eyes.

As the men turned, Seth gestured to her to follow them up the road. Carlota, who had straightened up in the saddle and was holding a handkerchief to her face, looked at Elena and shook her head slowly. Words couldn't match what both sensed. Whatever horrors were now to be endured, they had come to a most ironic setting for death.

At the ranch Taska and Bessie had hurriedly helped Jason hitch up a team and move the wagon and the many horses into the cellar. Kate was sent indoors to strip the molded cowhide covers from the gun ports. Isabelle guided the dazed Inez into the house, allowing her to sink onto the heavy rug before the fireplace. The knowledge that they had been handed a death sentence was slowly gripping them. Isabelle found herself mumbling prayers as she grabbed a broom and swept the uncovered gun ports, now fouled with dust and cobwebs after years of disuse.

Taska's nervous cry that riders were visible on the wagon road took Isabelle outdoors again to see four mounts move rapidly toward her. With a strange feeling in her stomach, she suddenly knew who they were. Peculiar emotions started claiming her as the oncoming riders closed the ground between them, led by the familiar figures of Tate and Seth. But Isabelle, now frozen in her tracks, kept her eyes beyond Seth to the two women coming behind, one of whom was already regarding her with the same tense, fearful curiosity she herself felt. The woman was dark, her features soft, smooth and delicately formed.

Though no longer young, she was still beautiful. Here was the face that had replaced hers on Seth's pillow, the seductive wraith who long had hovered in the far reaches of her mind and cast such a fateful shadow on their life.

But if she expected to see guilt, shame or victory in this woman's face, she was disappointed. Elena confronted her with eyes as frank and steady as she herself could manage. In spite of the tension about them there was something open, even compassionate, in this woman's voice when she said, "I know I've come at a dreadful time—I hope you understand."

Warmth sprang up along Isabelle's cheeks, staining them pink, and she heard herself saying, "Of course I understand. Please, come inside, quickly."

Bessie and Taska moved forward to gather their horses and led them back to the cellar with Tate and Seth following along. None of them spoke even when the cellar doors were closed and barred. Tate quickly jumped to the top of the wagon and broke open the trapdoor above. Pulling himself into the vacant space, he turned and began taking the excess guns, tools and other items Jason was already handing up from the loaded wagon. Seth watched as he pulled his gear from the black, knowing this had to be done but aware it offered little hope. Nothing inside Thunder Run could help them now. Their silence said as much. Still, a defense had to be attempted. The younger ones—Jason, Tate, Taska and even Kate—would fight for life as long as they could. In spite of the cold estrangement he felt surrounding him, he sensed that this besieged band of humans, all of them dealing with fear in his or her own way, was now looking to him for deliverance.

27

The rain had stopped, and the heavy cloud cover had drifted east. To the west fringes of wine-colored sky embroidered the horizon in the first hint of sunset. Red Claw stood on the knoll above the creek, staring down at the ranch house where the *tejanos* had taken cover. He had hoped to avoid attacking this fortified place, yet it made little difference. He had learned how to wear down and destroy stronger outposts than this. He frowned at the mass of impatient warriors milling below him. They were riding about boldly in full view of the trapped whites, making threatening gestures with their weapons, anxious to take the house and its scalps before sundown. They had grown sullen waiting and maneuvering through this long, rain-soaked day. With their overwhelming strength, they saw little need to stalk their prey. Now, believing that Blood Hawk's medicine would protect them from bullets, many were shouting to assault the ranch frontally. At first Red Claw met their boastful talk with words of caution, but important honors went with the first taking of scalps, and a warrior's prestige rose with every conspicuous defiance of danger. In spite of his reputation and successes, leading his people was never easy. Addicted to violence, they were as intent on life-risking acts of courage as they were vain about their battle dress and superstitious about the way they fought. His small eyes narrowed in annoyance at the approaching Black Horn.

Red Claw tersely declared that even with their numbers, assaulting this fortified house was foolhardy. Those gun ports would pour forth

death. Black Horn stolidly agreed with him. The tall Kiowa, pointing
to the wooden panels of the great front door and the latticework
spreading out on both sides, allowed his finger to continue on to the
long, wood-framed windows that ran to the left of the door. "Fire will
open the way for our warriors," he rumbled in his deep, sonorous
voice. "It will leave only quick work for our war clubs!"

Red Claw nodded in assent, but secretly he questioned even this.
He had attacked similar structures on the Kansas border and in the
river valleys to the north. Fire had rarely been the answer. He had
learned the hard way and at the cost of many braves that the secret
weakness of these slate-and-adobe bastions was that almost flat roof.
Once up there, warriors could not be fired on and their war hatchets
could smash through the thin slates, making the stout walls useless
and placing those inside at their mercy. He was quietly conceiving a
plan to achieve this when a group of warriors appeared below him,
mounted and singing a Comanche war chant calling for bravery. Red
Claw gestured some braves to his side. His plan might easily succeed
while these whites were under fire, their minds and senses distracted
by the furor of the attack. These trapped *tejanos* were not newcomers.
Blood Hawk had said that they had been in this country for many
years. They would know the Comanche way.

Somewhere a shot rang out. A warrior had ridden up to the house
and driven a scalp-laden lance into the ground before the front window. It was an act of defiance and disdain and signaled the long-
awaited attack. War cries broke out in a demonic chorus rising on
all sides to shake the air.

Inside the house a chilling calm had replaced the crippling tension
that had risen as the Indians in war regalia, chanting in throaty
unison and brandishing their weapons in grisly gestures, came up to
surround the house. Every suggestion for defense had to fight its way
around a conviction that no defense was possible against such a horde.

Seth came up from the cellar knowing the gun ports had to be
manned swiftly. He and Jason had to defend the front of the house,
protecting that wide oak door and the long stretch of windows. This
vulnerable spot would never be missed. The other three sides were
each protected by two gun ports, yet the ones covering the kitchen
and storeroom would still be difficult to hold. If savages mounted the
roof of the nearby farrier shed, they could fire behind the defenders

with devastating effect. Taska and Tate, both dead shots, were chosen to take up positions there. The most isolated side of the house, where the bedrooms lay opposite the kitchen, faced open ground, clear except for a woodpile that could provide cover for the attackers. Bessie and Kate, both Salingers and both with that Salinger knack for handling guns, took up the gun ports there. Seth warned them to watch for redskins crawling below the window line and rising up without warning to crash into the house. They nodded grimly, Bessie stooping to grasp a hatchet from among the many tools strewn on the floor.

Seeing all this, Elena and Carlota started at Seth expectantly. They were not going to stand idle or huddle beside the weeping Inez while others fought for survival. Seth, needing every gun he could muster, did not discourage them. He led them to the back of the house, feeling that this quarter would be easiest to defend. Here the gun ports were elevated several feet above the rear cellar door. He warned them to keep a close watch on that cellar door. If even an attempt were made to break in, they were to cry for help. If the cellar were taken, the house was lost.

Isabelle he wanted free to carry ammunition, water and, if needed, food to the others. Her several startled and questioning looks were met with brusque explanations. She knew the house better than anyone, could fetch what was needed fastest, would be there to aid any wounded or help if any positions were breached. She did not argue. She knew that Seth, Jason and perhaps even Tate were all pretending these desperate measures could save them, while hiding fears that the house and all in it were doomed. Hearing the screams of the warriors outside, she realized in icy dread that she had a decision to make. Facing it made her eyes harden, her mouth drawn thin and bitter. Yet her decision had already been made on this very spot a quarter of a century before. The Comanches had taken her alive once. Her body was never going to suffer that hideous defilement again.

For an hour the Texans had watched the grotesquely painted faces staring at them from beneath gruesome horned headdresses or caught the slicks of buffalo fat smeared on scarred bodies, flashing behind raised weapons and shields. Slowly the warriors had started circling the house, falling into a silence even more frightening than their chants. Expertly, they kneed their ponies closer, looking under the stark hues of their regalia like a garishly colored snake contracting about its prey. Less than a hundred feet from the house a warrior rose and hurled his spear at the front door. It landed with a thud, embedding itself in the heavy oak. Another rode up to the house and drove a scalp-laden lance into the ground. Shrill war cries needled the air on all sides, igniting a deafening roar as the attack began.

Seth and Jason were struck with a hailstorm of shattered glass as the first volley swept away the front windows and splintered and vibrated the oak door. Flecks of blood appeared on their faces and arms as tiny shards of glass showered the room. They started firing back from either end of the empty window slot, but the savages charged so close that both men were soon emptying their revolvers at point-blank range. The fanatical belief that Blood Hawk's medicine would protect them from bullets had some warriors coming up to strike at the door and the long window ledge with war hatchets, some even trying to climb through. It was impossible to miss them, and a line of dead and wounded began to jolt the attackers into screams of fury that Blood Hawk's powerful medicine was not warding off this lethal rain of lead. On such emotions hangs the balance of battle. It traumatized them to see vigorous warriors, war cries on their lips, mounting the window ledge only to be hammered back mute and wide-eyed in death. One warrior mumbled over the dead body of his father, drove his war club against the earth and wailed in rage, *"Blood Hawk's medicine has failed!"* Others, hearing this, began hanging back, some attempting to pull the dead and wounded with them.

On the kitchen side the attack had brought an immediate crisis. Taska and Tate shot the first warriors coming up from their saddles, but large numbers dismounted and came up against the kitchen door with war clubs. Guns appeared atop the farrier shed, and slugs began to sing around their heads and smash into the wall behind. Tate, who held the storeroom gun port, knew he had to protect the kitchen door or they were lost. The rifle was not fast enough, so, pulling loose his six-guns, he shouted to Taska to fire at the farrier roof while he left his gun port to defend the door. Taska, pressing shells into her rifle as fast as she could, kept blazing away. She could see two heads breaking the line of the farrier roof, and she brought her rifle down on them. She squeezed off a shot and saw one head move. Immediately she fired again and the head rose up and started to turn as her eye caught a body tumbling off the roof. The second head seemed to drop down lower, but something in her mind stayed conscious of it even as she turned her gun onto the figures now coming up flush against her gun port. Two warriors depending on Blood Hawk's medicine fell to their deaths as Tate opened up with his six-guns; Taska's shot penetrated the head of a black-streaked brave brandishing a stocky shotgun.

The air, laden with gun smoke, began to sting the eyes and burn the lungs. The fearsome din made speech impossible. Each side of the house fought its desperate battle unaware of the perils facing the others, any of which could bring its own doom. Bessie and Kate, catching a swarm of warriors coming up behind an immense brave whose body and face were painted vermilion with Blood Hawk's medicine sign smeared in black across his chest, fired at him at the same instant, their combined bullets lifting the brave from the saddle and flinging him like a straw man on top of the woodpile. It had a palling effect upon those following, who sprang from their ponies to kneel or hurry behind the woodpile and open fire on the house. But the gun ports had been made for just this sort of attack, and after blasting out the bedroom windows and peppering the house with a steadily decreasing fire, the Indians settled down to a low, deadly sniping or ducked off to join the riders still screaming and circling the house.

Still, disaster hovered where it was least expected.

Elena and Carlota saw the Indians circling the rear of the house and returned their heavy but random fire. They did not see, for it was below their line of sight, that three braves were silently riding in close to the house. One had his arm outstretched and held a length of rope that ended in a twisted piece of metal shaped like a grappling hook. Above them the roof, which from a distance had looked flat, had a slight incline to allow rainwater to run off. It sloped from back to front, where a rusting drain guided moisture to a cast iron barrel. Running along the back of the roof was a slight ridge that would hold a grapple. Red Claw's strategy was about to bear fruit.

They had no warning, but Elena saw a rope fly upward and immediately sensed danger. She couldn't lower the rifle far enough to shoot the braves, but in a sudden panic she grabbed the heavy pistol lying beside her and thrust it through the gun port. By forcing her head against the top of the barrel slot she could see white war paint on the face of a brave who was looking up. She held the pistol up to her hairline and fired. The powder flash almost blinded her, but the bullet hit the shoulder of the brave, who was about to swing onto the hanging rope, and the rope spurted from his hand as he yowled in pain and his horse shied away.

Of the three ropes hurled upward, only one had taken hold on the roof ridge, but a brave was already scaling his way up. Elena cried to Carlota, "Watch out! They're climbing up!"

Carlota, shaken by the roar of rifles going off inside the house and shocked by Elena's shrieked warning, was unable to visualize savages climbing vertical walls, and could only breathlessly plead, "Where?"

"Right in front of you!" screamed Elena.

Carlota strained to see over her rifle barrel but saw nothing. Then a hand came up to grab the protruding barrel. Desperately she tugged with all her might and the gun jerked free. Quickly she stood up, lowered the rifle barrel as far as she could and fired. The bullet cut a furrow across the top of the climbing warrior's head and he fell, unconscious and sliding into death. The remaining warrior, realizing that the element of surprise was gone, abandoned the now freely hanging rope and sped away.

Suddenly and without warning the firing stopped and everywhere Indians were withdrawing, taking some of the wounded back to cover. Seth, Jason and the grim-faced Tate knew that the fighting was far from over. Glass and splinters of wood covered every room, and the air was heavy with smoke and the acrid smell of burnt powder. As Isabelle rushed about calling out names, they discovered in amazement that though many had been cut with flying glass, no one had been wounded. Seth, hearing that the Indians had attempted to reach the roof, swallowed hard and swore under his breath.

"If they get up there, we're finished!" he moaned.

The realization they had survived the onslaught stunned some of them momentarily. Others, feeling a break in the strain, felt heady. Seeing Carlota so unnerved by her encounter with the climbing brave that she had to steady herself as she entered the main room, Jason lowered his head to whisper to Seth, "We'd best get Bessie or Kate back here."

Carlota was only coming for water from the kitchen pump, but she caught the men staring at her and saw the doubt in their eyes. "I'm staying with Elena!" she cried in defiance, then turned to grim humor to reassure them. "This fighting is like a virgin making love. At first a girl looks awkward, but a woman with Spanish blood learns fast." No one laughed, but Seth, knowing that Jason's eyes were still on him, nodded.

Even though they had beaten back the attack, the gravity of their position had increased. With eight guns blazing, they had exhausted a tragic amount of ammunition. Seth knew that counting or conserving bullets was futile. They could never win this fight. They had only one hope, faint and distant as it now seemed, help from San Antonio. But San Antonio was two days away. Not one of them believed that two days stood between them and oblivion.

Incongruously, or in fatal symbolism, a brilliant sunset was ending the day, the blood red sky working strange hues into the spears of light still penetrating the house. Seth and Jason tried to conceal the wave of resignation that was sapping what little firmness was left in their eyes, but the options before them were numbing, brutal—hopeless.

Though Seth cautioned every side to keep a close watch, the women had started taking turns at slipping into the kitchen for water. Tate moved grimly over to join Seth and Jason. The three sat for long moments in silence before Jason, looking at the fading sunset and the clouds turning purple as their low billows were drained of the fiery red, finally half muttered, "We're gonna have to try."

"Try" was the only word possible if he was thinking of running the murderous gauntlet that lay between this lonely ranch and San Antonio. Seth reckoned the odds to be so high that his mind balked at the prospect. Yet he also shrank from picturing the alternative. Everyone who mattered in his life was surely going to die an ugly, merciless death. There were tales from the north country of surrounded and exhausted parties shooting their womenfolk to spare them the horrors awaiting female captives. But killing one's loved ones to keep them from the hands of savages seemed humane only until a man faced the task. Yet how long could they hope to hold this house? For the first time in his life he was secretly calling on God to make decisions for him. For the first time he felt unequal to giving orders that meant life and death to others. This was not northern Virginia, these were not victorious Yankees surrounding them, men like himself fighting for different causes. Honorable surrender was unthinkable here. This was a primeval conflict for survival. Torture and death were the only terms imaginable. "We have to try," repeated Jason. A tiny voice in Seth's mind told him that his son was right; they had to try. Suicidal as it seemed, it offered the only way to bring a dim but vital ingredient into this bitter and heart-wrenching plight. It was a thing he had learned human beings could not long survive without—hope.

◆ ◆ ◆

Beyond the knoll, where the creek ran south toward the wide bend, a fire had been built and Red Claw stood with his yellow robe about his waist, watching his angry warriors gather. The foul looks they threw at Blood Hawk and the menacing gestures aimed in his direction warned of a dangerous fury seething in their ranks. Belief in Blood Hawk's medicine had brought death to more than one young warrior, his spirit sign promising protection luring them into a foolish bravery. Even now, many wounded were still being helped in and the sight of their blood was convincing these pagan minds that this loud-talking shaman was a fraud. Black Horn nodded his head and grunted in satisfaction, for he had long frowned at this fool's pretenses to power. Now he was openly annoyed to find Blood Hawk's eyes focusing on him as the braves waited for Red Claw to speak.

It was not Red Claw's way to hold a council of war. The failure of this hurried attack to take the house did not bother him. Already Blood Hawk's weak medicine was being blamed for that. Actually, he had brought Blood Hawk along for reasons of his own, and this damage to the medicine man's prestige might even serve his purpose. Power, the only meaningful asset in a primitive society, was the hidden issue. Blood Hawk was wielding more and more power derived from his claims of magic. And Blood Hawk's "magic" was bringing him wealth in the form of gifts of robes and horses, wealth which had enabled him to buy a young, fleshy Mexican girl with large breasts and well-rounded hips, a ripening, lusty female whom Red Claw wanted for his own. Many chiefs with Red Claw's following might have quietly shot this arrogant nuisance during the attack, but Red Claw knew that medicine men, particularly those who lay claim to prophetic powers, could be dangerous. If such an action were to get out and harsh times again fell upon the people, it would be quickly remembered how this half-mad prophet who had once forewarned his tribe about its threatening future had died. Red Claw would have to find a safer way. Now, hearing the agitated braves venting their anger, he sensed one coming. That Mexican girl was already half in his blanket.

The ominous silence that had settled over the great array of braves, who were visibly smoldering at the loss of what they had thought would be an easy victory, warned Red Claw that they were in no mood for long oratory. Wisely, he simply pounded the earth with his rifle stock as he began. "The enemy strikes and rages at the walls of our trap like the great bear in the pit!" he shouted. "But by the next sun *tejano* scalps will decorate our victory sticks!"

The expected war whoops and pounding of weapons in approval did not arise. Instead, a wounded warrior sat up and pointed his lance at Blood Hawk. The silence was now numbing. "What of this medicine that would protect us from our enemies' bullets?" he cried defiantly. "Let us see if this medicine protects *Blood Hawk* from *our* bullets."

Blood Hawk, having watched several braves falling at the onset of the attack, was already alerted to his danger and had shrunk back as he heard the increasingly lethal threats mounting about him. He had been desperately trying to think of reasons why his medicine had failed, something or someone he could blame for breaking the spell of his magic. Such ruses often worked. The need for a convincing response to their deadly charges had Blood Hawk reluctantly coming to his feet, but in his rising desperation he committed a calamitous error. In sweeping across the sea of vengeful faces his eyes at first hesitated over and then returned to settle on Black Horn.

If Blood Hawk's years as a shaman had taught him nothing else, it had taught him the value of dramatic posturing. As he rose above the squatting braves, behind him glowed a brilliant sunset, red streamers bursting up from a blazing orange disc, approaching and dissolving in the great, descending curtain of blue. He raised his hands to the sky and held them in supplication for many moments before he spoke. "My brothers," he began, "the spirits talk with me but they are very angry. They have journeyed to this place where my father sleeps. They have brought a sign that would protect us against the bullets of the *tejanos*. But they know there is one here who has spurned their sign, a chieftain who refused to wear it in battle and at this they are very angry. He has broken the spell."

It took several heartbeats before the full import of Blood Hawk's words dawned on Black Horn. He was being blamed for the failure of this farcical medicine. The dark lines rising to narrow his yellow-painted face should have been warning enough, but a war club decorated with scalps also appeared in his hand as he started toward Blood Hawk. "Blood Hawk has said his father sleeps here," he started ranting as a cold fury gripped him. "If more false words fall from his cowardly mouth, his father will not sleep alone!"

As murmurs and gasps ripped through their ranks, the braves

started rising, some putting their hands over their mouths in disbelief as the furious Black Horn strode toward Blood Hawk. But Red Claw could not allow a medicine man to be slain here. It was an adage with the strength of a commandment that if any member of a war party killed another, that war party would end in tragedy. Stepping between them, he put a restraining hand on Black Horn's chest. "Wait," he said firmly. "Let Blood Hawk prove his medicine is true. Let him go against these *tejanos* alone. If their bullets do not harm him, we will know he has great power."

Luckily Black Horn caught the knowing look in Red Claw's eyes and realized he was hearing wisdom. Why risk possible reproach at killing this *pujakut* if a safer way to destroy him clearly beckoned? "This coward is as weak as his medicine!" he taunted.

Blood Hawk, though nearly paralyzed with fear, knew he must speak. He must reaffirm his power to make medicine, or he was lost. One way or the other Red Claw's words could mean his death. His only hope—a slim one at best—was to play for time. "I will show you the strength of my medicine," he said hoarsely, forcing what volume he could into his voice. "Only I must have time to pray to my spirit helpers. They are angry, their faces are turned away. They will not speak again until tomorrow's sun stands high in the sky."

"By then there will be no *tejanos* to fight!" rasped Black Horn in contempt. "We do not need your spirits, faker! At dawn I will show you how a real warrior destroys his enemies."

Red Claw looked at him quizzically. Black Horn was a formidable fighter. Red Claw liked him and needed him to hold the Kiowa braves together, but Black Horn lacked the subtlety required to outwit these resourceful whites. Black Horn still believed in fire. Well, Red Claw could wait. Fire would not destroy that adobe-and-slate stronghold, but Red Claw now knew how it could be done.

Red Claw's secret strength had always been his ability to reason as his enemies did. He was sure these *tejanos* knew they could not hold the house. Surely they knew that their only hope was help from the outside, help that must come soon. Whatever the risks, they would have to try to get a messenger out, and they would have to try tonight. He turned to the braves who, after hearing Black Horn's angry charges and Blood Hawk's tremulous responses, were muttering in confusion among themselves.

"Hear me!" he shouted, pulling their eyes to him. "These *tejanos* are already ours. They cannot hold out for long. Their only hope is to bring others here to save them. This must not happen. Tonight we must guard every side of this house as a warrior guards his *puja*. No one is to escape. Those trying must be taken and their heads staked where they can greet their friends at the first light of dawn.''

Inside the house there were no discussions, no judgments expressed or strategy weighed. History and an intimate knowledge of one another's strengths resolved the matter without words. Had it meant only one death, Jason, even Taska, might have volunteered. But individual risk was not the issue. This risk was to be shared by all. Success meant a flickering promise of life, failure the horrors of collective death. If there existed a soul in that frail fortress with the animal savvy to escape this trap and reach San Antonio in time to effect their salvation, that soul could only be Tate. He knew it, they knew it, and the realization was marked by a strange happening, destined to be remembered even in this night of indelible moments. Kate came over and, embracing him, kissed him full on the mouth. "We will pray for you," she said in a whisper that was heard throughout the room. "Come back . . . we love you." Darkness hid the startled looks that spread in response, and in the hushed moments that followed concealed the strain of some emotion contorting Tate's face before he bent down to bury it in the softness of Kate's hair.

Moments later it was Bessie squeezing her sister's hand and pulling her aside to say "Why?" who alone heard the half-whispered, half-choked words.

"He has to know he's one of us . . . that he matters . . ."

"What a thing to say. You know nothing about him."

"Bessie, please, he's lonely . . . always has been. A lonely woman doesn't need to know more."

Isabelle, standing back, heard Seth's voice sounding strangely tight and measured, yet because of the morbid stillness in the house reaching like a spirit echo into every room. He was telling Tate to take the big black and go north through the hills before turning for the Medina. Though she could not see them, she knew from Tate's silence that he was nettled at this advice. It was Tate's superior knowledge of the terrain and his acknowledged skill at scouting it that had thrown this fateful task upon him.

But Isabelle remained silent. In truth, she was shaken. She had heard Kate's words to Tate, had fought back tears, for it reminded her again how hard it had always been to love Tate. Even when he had been a child, her feelings for him had never risen with that joyous flush so often brought to life by Jason. Standing alone in the darkness, she realized that her life had been shaped—or misshaped—by this embittered black-eyed youth, so different from others, so disposed to solitude, so defiant, so difficult to know. She was aware now that it had been Tate, not Elena, who had cost her Seth. Yet Tate, like herself, was blameless. Heir to a tragedy that had preceded his birth, he had grown up accepting the alienation awaiting those who, burdened with the knowledge they were not lovingly conceived, find the world loveless.

Several minutes had passed since Carlota returned to the back of the house, and now another softly stepping but unmistakable figure was coming forth. Isabelle felt this strange presence approaching and for a moment wanted to recoil back into the darkness, but the imminence of death was throwing both her pain and her long, lonely years into perspective. Her emotions warned her that important truths were threatening to surface. Even in this darkness Elena D'Valya had an air about her, a gracious, lofty humility which added to her dignity. Isabelle remembered seeing the dark Spanish eyes as she had ridden up and only now realized what it was she had seen in them that had dissolved her own anxieties. She was beginning to sense that, as mankind measures life, fate had not been kind to this woman. Elena was trapped here facing death in her rival's home. She had the embrace but not the name of the man she loved. She was childless. Had she, like Isabelle, spent her years wanting something from Seth that his restive and rebellious spirit was not free to give?

They had hoped to wait until night settled, but Tate saw an almost indiscernible glow in the east and knew it was the moon waiting behind the dark trim of hills. Delaying matters could only heighten his already monstrous risk. His moment and its grim tribute to his talents had come. He approached his mother and Taska and awkwardly, almost apologetically, hugged them. Then, within moments, he was slipping down to lead the big black to the cellar door. He had chosen to ride bareback. Every ounce this horse did not have to carry would add to its speed and endurance. Jason was reaching cautiously to pull back the cellar door when this tense moment between them struck both as likely to be their last. Pausing, they were suddenly gripped by something stronger than intuition. Here alone, away from their women, with reality in command of their reason again, they knew that only a miracle could get Tate through to bring help from San Antonio in time. They grasped each other's hands in a gesture more meaningful than any embrace. Tate could find no words to match his emotions, and Jason was seized by feelings he was not sure could ever be expressed. His voice choked as he said, "Just remember, brother . . . we'll live or die with you . . . tonight you're more important than any of us."

Because of a natural depression, a thin well of darkness lay outside the cellar door. It concealed Tate as he stood staring into the night, holding the black's muzzle to keep it from snorting. His eyes quickly spotted the protruding corner of the farrier shed, the stunted outhouse and the distant slope beyond that he had to reach. But his eyes did not detect the menace his ears readily confirmed was there. The normal noises of night were missing. A pall lay over the land. Silence in a country of nocturnal fauna told its own story. Had he had the time, he would have crouched where he was until some movement or muted signal in the darkness told him how near or far their attackers were. But a sliver of the moon's disk had edged into the inky horizon. Bending over and moving with one hand, almost touching the earth, he led the black to the right of the outhouse and settled there beside a small boulder. He would have liked to mount and make a run for it, but that was what they were expecting. His only hope was to get as far up that rise as he could, giving them as little time as possible to cut him off. It was a tactic fraught with a thousand uncertainties, not the least of which was the survival of his horse. Even a minor injury would keep it from swiftly covering those crucial miles to San Antonio. If only he could smell out where they were waiting; but surely they were everywhere, forming a massive, impenetrable cordon. Expecting anything less was a dangerous delusion. But he had to move. He kept himself close to the ground, but the horse stepping behind him was upright and beginning to prance sideways as his own tense, jerky movements began to make it fractious. He stopped at the foot of a large rock facing, not more than a hundred yards from the house.

Suddenly, from the top of the rock's long incline, two measured hoots of a hunting owl pierced the night and were answered quickly, far too quickly, by two behind. They had gotten between him and the house. Jesus! Was he trapped already? He squatted down close to the rock ledge, discovering that the incline of the rock was so slight he could see the moon peeping up behind its top. He began to count his heartbeats, afraid to move. They had him surrounded, but they could not have seen him for they were not shooting. He couldn't go higher on the rise—they were above him. He couldn't go back—they were behind him. He couldn't stay where he was, for in moments he would be spotted. If they opened fire, they were sure to hit the horse.

Fighting the cold realization that his mission could well be over before it had begun, his eye caught a movement above him where a head and a gun barrel broke the thin symmetry of the rising moon. Without thinking, but instinctively knowing that the gun was about to be aimed, he drew his revolver and fired. The head vanished with a groan, and the ring of a metal gun barrel sliding over rock could be heard as his shot shattered the stillness, instantly replaced by the terrifying roar of warriors, their hideous screaming sounding as feral as that of wolverines closing in on a cornered, helpless prey.

He sprang up onto the black and pointed it up the slope, missing a hail of lead and whirling arrows that smacked into the ground he had just left. The powerful black began to sweep him up to where he knew they were waiting. There was no escape down the wagon road, where they were encamped, and they had blocked the one direction that held any hope of crossing the big corrals beyond the stable and racing for the hills to the north. He was far too experienced to believe anything obvious would work. Suicidal as it seemed, he had to turn toward the wagon road. Knowing the terrible gamble he was taking, he swung the black to the right and dug into it with his heels. The horse responded with tremendous strength, and he found himself almost flying over the ground.

But the Indians were now around him on every side. His riding into obvious peril momentarily confused them, but he could tell by their cries that they had shifted direction and were swinging about to close in on him again. Shots kept ringing out, now coming from every side, and the Indians' risk of shooting one another was mounting.

He crossed the wagon road at a gallop and headed for the creek.

Suddenly they were too close to even shoot. An Indian pony appeared and began to race beside his black, its rider trying to strike at Tate with a war hatchet. Tate, guiding his mount with his knees, caused it to swerve into the smaller Indian mustang and the pony lost stride and fell, tumbling its rider into the darkness. The shouting around him had become deafening. The black turned into the creek bed and plunged across to the opposite bank. Here he swung to the right again, knowing from the thrashing in the creek that they were trying to cross ahead of him. He was finally discovering the immense power of Seth's horse. Speedy as it was, many of the Indian ponies were stubbornly hanging on. But the enormous strides of the big black told Tate, who had no rival at judging horses, that this animal had to be a superior jumper. It was then that a hope of escape slipped up and found a foothold in his mind.

He had known from the beginning that his only chance was to lose them in the darkness, get far enough ahead for a shift in direction they couldn't detect. Fast as the black was, it could not be done with speed alone. But his scouting savvy told him that he held a crucial advantage, particularly in the dark. He knew the ground along this creekbed intimately, and they did not. Up ahead was a wide gully, a washout Seth had often talked about filling, for its steep drop made it a menace to both horses and cattle. Several times they had tried, but the spring rains had kept it open and each year erosion had dug it deeper. If the black could jump that gully and the Indian ponies could not, it would open a gap between them. He knew it was a life-staking gamble. The gully could easily be too much for the black, but desperation was reinforcing resolve. Sensing he was trying to work north, the war party flocked across the creek to narrow his escape route and their ghastly screaming drew suddenly closer. It was too late for half measures. Death was in the lists. He hit the stretch of level ground he knew led up to the gully, only some fifty yards in length. Here he set the black down, urging it on for all it was worth. The black's ears were back as its hoofs ate up the ground at an awesome pace. Tate, high on its shoulders, his sinuous body picking up the horse's rhythm, came up to the lip of the gully and with a deep breath lifted him as skillfully as he could. The black sailed through the air, and for a fraction of a second Tate's heart stopped. The gully was wider than he had thought, and though the black's front hoofs caught the opposite edge its hind legs slammed into the bank below. Yet without urging the black gave another surge upward and, clearing the rim and steadying itself on the level turf, gamely galloped on.

It was the rough, reckless jostling of their ponies as the pursuing braves fought to overtake him that fatefully distracted them, for the moon was giving enough light to see the black jump had they been peering carefully ahead. As it was, when the lead pony shied off at the deep drop, it was too late. The onrush of horses carried the leader over the brink. Howls turned into screams, and a melee of confusion exploded into the night. The piercing cries of pain arising from the gully began to draw the warriors toward it. No one could see clearly what had happened to bring on this uproar, but none could ignore it. Tate knew the next few moments had to count. He kept the black at a full gallop until he saw a heavy stand of brush around a grove of closely grouped trees. It marked an eastward loop of the creek where the first rising ground hinted at the dark hills to the north. He pulled his mount back into the water and hurried on to the next clump of thick brush, where some trees back from the bank were throwing dark silhouettes of branches upward to be lost in the night. There he stopped, dismounted, quickly gripped his horse's mane and, holding its muzzle, stood still.

The silence that settled over the house when Tate left was like a trance. No one dared speak; all minds were on Tate moving through the darkness. They all felt that even speaking in whispers might somehow betray his presence. All of them knew that their lives now hung on him. Seth and Jason, knowing the odds he was facing, were not as shocked as the women when shots broke out and a hellish screaming rent the night. It broke out on the slope to the rear of the house, but then, filling them with horror, swung toward the wagon road. Had Tate found his plight so hopeless he was resigned to riding into death? But the wild screaming continued, and after a few moments they realized he had crossed the wagon road and was heading for the creek. As long as that maniacal clamor kept up and kept moving, they could reason that he had not been taken. Within moments it was clear that he was running along the opposite bank of the creek and heading north. It was hard not to hope. The shouting seemed to be getting fainter, fading away. Perhaps he had made it, gotten through, beaten the terrible odds. God was with them. Inez, suddenly sitting up and listening, crossed herself. They were just about to hug one

another and cry in relief when a sudden increase in the screaming
told them something had happened—something that caused a cres-
cendo of shouting and even a few more wild shots. But after that,
silence rose like a mourning shroud over the house, and all they could
see, looking out, was the empty yard and the dark forms of the other
ranch buildings, just visible under the pale light of the moon.

Part Eight

BESIDE
the
STILL WATERS

April 1864

28

Several hours later, Tate crossed the Medina. He could tell by the stars that it was only an hour or two until dawn. As he worked his way through the dark, rolling hills, swinging steadily eastward, he had been forced to push the black more than was wise. Though he had shaken the Comanches, they surely knew where he was headed, and Red Claw was crafty enough to send scouts to stalk the Medina crossings, hoping to cut him off. Even across this wide, meandering stream he might not be safe. He kept turning over in his mind the many threats that still hung over Thunder Run. One had even increased. Red Claw would know he was racing for help, and the dawning would see a determined effort to destroy the house before it arrived. After the almost nightlong effort, the black was visibly tiring. His life and that of everyone at Thunder Run were riding on this plucky animal. It would soon have to be rested. Secretly he hoped he might see a light as he peered to the east of the soft, murmuring flow of water, but the moon was down again behind a murky horizon and in every direction the ground lay in darkness.

Somewhere around midnight Seth got his first inkling of Tate's fate, but it made the women gasp in awe and alarm. It started with a little flare behind the stable that soon sprang up and bathed the great yard in leaping light. The Indians were putting the ranch buildings to the torch. As flames swept through the spacious stable, the conflagration rose up with a roar, and fire leapt across the gaps to the smokehouse and on to the farrier shed, even reaching the storage bins along the inner corral. Only the house and the adobe hut were spared. But the heat was so intense that the warriors now riding by and firing into the house had to steer clear of the smoke and flying cinders that were making the horses dangerously rank and unruly as they galloped near the flames. But the vicious shouting hinted at a smoldering rage that lay behind this wanton destruction, which could only be meant to frighten these whites. Seth felt an inexplicable relief. These redskins were angry with the kind of anger that might erupt if Tate had escaped.

It was another hour before the fires completely burned down, the smell of charred wood filling the air, the thick, palpable silence slowly returning. Isabelle and Bessie stood hugging each other in the darkness, knowing that the familiar shadows of the stable and its adjoining sheds were gone forever, taking with them years of sacrifice, cherished hopes and memories. Though not affecting its defense, the vacant yard made the house seem more vulnerable, exposed—isolated.

Jason, his features indistinguishable in the dark, was wielding the ax mutely, splitting the pine and cedar furniture to provide the wood needed to bar the windows. Taska helped Seth knock two doors from their hinges, then cut them into slats with the large-tooth saw. Few words were exchanged. Their minds were elsewhere. Their small supply of nails was nearly exhausted by the time they had barricaded the windows sufficiently to keep them from being easily or quickly entered. They kept listening for further sounds, hoping to find a reason for the shouting from the distant stretch of creek, but they heard only a few muffled screams and an occasional wild shot that left them anxiously muttering to each other in half whispers or peering futilely into the dark.

An hour went by. Anxiety and uncertainty sought relief in words. The irrepressible question tumbled forth in a dozen different forms. Had he gotten through? Did those curious sounds from afar have any meaning? If so, what? The questions seemed undirected, nervously voiced into the darkness, but Seth knew they were meant for him. His responses brought little comfort, for in his heart lay the fear that they would have their answer by morning. If the Comanches had taken Tate, they would make sure the defenders knew in some macabre way that he was dead and with him their last hope.

In the wake of the fire and the shrill attack, the women started drifting into the main room, as much to find strength in one another's company as from an instinctive knowledge that the Indians wouldn't return until dawn. Seth and Jason, trying to bolster the others' spirits, related Seth's feeling that the attack could be a good sign and mentioned that the savages in their frustration had foolishly burnt down the farrier shed, which had given them a vantage point for attacking the house. But their words lacked any impact on women suffering from the bitter resolve created by this long night of terror. Perhaps it was the cruel anticipation of seeing the ranch's charred remains at dawn, together with their persistent distressing doubts about Tate, that ignited strange emotions among them. Seth felt it beginning in Elena, in what seemed a clutch of spiritual exasperation. She was saying to Carlota, "If it's God's will we are to die, then we shall die! But how long must we go on standing here trembling in the dark?"

There was no answer, but Elena's words hung in the air, finally prompting Isabelle to say what every woman there—including, surely, Elena, already knew. It was not death at the will of a merciful God they dreaded, but she was only able to utter "It's the wickedness of those savages" before she was cut off by further hurried assurances from Seth and Jason.

Bessie, staring at Elena in the dark with a hint of respect, snapped at Seth, "Stop talking nonsense—we're not children."

Incredibly, it was Inez, suddenly off the floor and leaning against the fireplace, who with her broken speech managed at last to voice Isabelle's thought. "Inez is a weak woman . . . always 'fraid of men . . . only Brandy good to Inez." She turned her head to where Seth and Jason were standing in the gloom. "You think yes . . . but sometimes you not understand . . . *los indios* come . . . man 'fraid to die . . . but woman 'fraid to live . . . for woman hell is helpless body shamed by bad men . . . but even death no stop hatchet . . . knife."

So the ugly fear was named, expressed, disgorged, the sickening degrading fate in store for their bodies, dead or alive, humiliations that would defile every heroic effort or valiant death. But there was something incendiary in this pained admission. Insidiously, a mental state was coming over them that brought its own terror. As women cast in the Christian mold, they couldn't fight off the fact or long endure the thought of this grotesque ending, but something primeval was coming to life in them.

Seth and Jason wanted to speak out, to bring normalcy to this unsettling moment, but they were awed by the mood they felt filling the room. These women, confronted by the hideous menace surrounding them, were not retreating into hysteria but descending to an emotional level far more ominous. Seth, baffled and quietly alarmed, was relieved to hear Carlota requesting that they pray. It gave him a semblance of comfort to hear the rustling of their clothes as one by one they sank to their knees. There was a deathly silence before Carlota started the Lord's prayer, she, Elena and Inez praying in Spanish, Isabelle, Bessie and Kate in English. Taska, unnoticed, began in Spanish and finished in English. The languages were different, but the cadence was the same, and as he listened in the dark of that unbelievable night a weird sensation started along his spine, for it was not with supplicating tones that they were praying together in the darkness, but with an increasingly heavy beat that resembled a chant. What startled him most—in truth stunned him—was that as they finished he found himself thinking with a shudder that there was something in that prayer, or the way it had been rendered, that was akin to the baleful war chant of Comanche braves preparing for battle and death.

The sun was well up in the sky when Tate made it into San Antonio. A few curious people watched him ride by, and a couple of teamsters, guiding their wagons over the mud-and-cobblestone streets, seeing the dust-caked black and his own exhausted expression, nodded uncertain greetings. But he didn't stop until he approached the sheriff's office next to the broad stable entrance.

Here, instead of the quick response to his urgent need he had hoped for, he encountered a nightmare. Zeke was standing before the sheriff's office, hands on hips, watching Tate approach. Around him was a coarse collection of faces, several with that unmistakable scruffy, malevolent look of Regulators. Before the stable stood the wagon carrying the body of the man he had shot at the state depot in Castroville.

"Damn—if it ain't that Injun! That son-of-a-bitchin' murdering Injun!" squalled Zeke. There was a tall one-armed man standing beside him. He was not the sheriff, but he had a commanding air that set him apart. He turned from Zeke and stood studying Tate for a moment. When he spoke his voice was not overbearing but carried authority. "Better get off that horse, fella. You're being accused of murder."

Though Tate could have vomited from worry and fatigue, the irony of this scene infuriated him to the brink of madness. He gripped the black's neck hard, as if getting a grip on his own soul. "Got no time to settle with that trash now." His eyes, which had been fixed on Zeke, shifted to the one-armed man. "Thunder Run bin hit by Injuns. They've got the ranch surrounded and 'less they get some help, nine people, seven of 'em women, are fixin' to die."

"Listen at him!" roared Zeke. "Talkin' 'bout Injuns like he wasn't one hisself."

"Injuns?" replied the tall man. Then, as though suspecting he was being distracted, added dryly, "Don't worry. You'll get a fair trial." His manner was assured, and his missing arm did not reduce his noticeably military bearing.

Biting back his rage, Tate dismounted and tied the black to the hitching post before the stable. In spite of the hour, a crowd was gathering and tension was mounting. His reputation, which clearly this one-armed man was not aware of, kept anyone from approaching him.

"Trial?" Clem was sputtering. "What d'hell you mean 'trial'? We done hold court a'ready. He's guilty as hell. We got the body right here to prove it!"

The tall man ignored Zeke and took a step toward Tate. "I'll have to put you under arrest," he said calmly. He had a gun at his belt with the holster tilted for a cross draw.

"Nobody is putting me under arrest," snarled Tate. "Why in hell's name aren't you raising men to rescue my people?"

Had not this one-armed ex–cavalry captain been appointed marshal and sent by Sam Houston to investigate claims of vigilantism and rumors of state powers being usurped by politically suspicious groups, Tate might have died before this array of guns his desperation was forcing him to defy. But the tall man was not fully convinced by Zeke's story and was impressed with Tate's exhausted appearance and the urgency in his voice. Besides, this grim, determined-looking youth, whom he noticed the crowd was cautiously backing away from, was plainly not going to hold still for any simple arrest. Yet murder was a crime that could not be tolerated, even on the frontier. To give himself a chance to think, he decided on another tack. "Did you shoot this man?" he gestured to the body lying in the wagon.

"I sure as hell did!" shouted Tate. "And there are two more thieving bastards making buzzards happy out on the trail." He nodded toward

Zeke. "And if that lying polecat doesn't get out of my sight, could be I ain't finished!"

At Tate's words, a ripple of confusion, quickly changing to consternation, swept the hard set of Zeke's eyes. Was this half-breed saying he'd gunned down Riff and Caleb on the trail? Was he, Zeke, now alone with this dead body, with this story? He whispered tensely to two straggle-bearded men standing close to him. Something warned him that sooner or later this marshal was going to get to the truth. As though this thought carried a sinister touch of prophecy, a creaky voice arose from the crowd. "Let that boy go! He was no more'n defending state property!" The determined voice of the old depot agent rose from behind the crowd, where he and his two sons had started pressing toward the front.

Zeke felt a touch of panic. Without Riff's shifty mind and criminal guile he was only a bungling lackey, a jackal abandoned by its pack. His animal instinct to survive suddenly triggered a cold sweat. He had to escape this trap, but his doltish brain could offer only one solution, his gun. Incredibly, he imagined that killing this half-breed could still settle the issue. In the teeth of swelling evidence to the contrary, he still felt that the Regulators were surrogates for law in this town. That he could still have made a prudent withdrawal with little lost except an already seedy reputation was beyond his power to conceive. "Git him, boys!" he shouted to the two toughs closest to him and went for his gun.

Had the marshal not been watching Tate, he never would have believed it. As it was, it took two dead men and one mortally wounded one to convince him that he had seen a killing machine at work, and secretly to feel some relief that he had let discretion guide him in his handling of this strange, stark-eyed youth.

The crowd scattered as gunshots punctuated the morning air, many diving for the ground. Only the old agent and his sons were left to stare down at the bodies of Zeke and his two companions, one of whom was still waving a feeble hand in the air. The old agent soon absolved Tate with quick remarks about events at the depot. But Tate had no time for talk about himself. He kept pleading with the marshal to raise help for Thunder Run. Seeing some townspeople leaning over the wounded man and a passing priest kneeling by the dead ones, the marshal directed them into the vacant sheriff's office. Here his face grew more and more sober as the grim facts of the crisis fell from Tate's lips. This ranch was a day's or a night's ride away. It sounded as though as many as a hundred Indians might be in the attacking force. It brought to his mind the battle at Plum Creek, when a wave of Comanches coming from the same border area had demolished whole towns and terrorized ports on the gulf coast. He kept wondering why so many women had let themselves be trapped there. The government had warned civilians months before to withdraw from the frontier and had even sent special messengers with orders to abandon isolated areas.

He shook his head. This was another little-known but tragic side of this damnable war. The Texans who should have been here to protect their homes and womenfolk were fighting or filling casualty lists in Virginia or the Mississippi valley. There was only a handful of able-bodied men left in San Antonio, which was still a predominantly Mexican town, and Mexicans, except for the bandits, were unarmed and not likely to risk their lives for the long-hated *gringos*.

"There may be some troops at Austin or Gonzales," he began, but Tate, who was too wrought up to sit down, was suddenly leaning over him, rapping his knuckles on the sheriff's desk.

"Austin? Gonzales? Christ! You're talking about days! We have to take who we can get and leave now!"

"Figure you'll surely get plenty of help when folks hear there's women caught out there," declared the old agent, his sons quickly nodding agreement.

"Yes, you'll get help, but how much?" The marshal, perplexed by his own question, put force into this words. "Anything less than fifty or sixty men and you're courting suicide."

"We'll raise 'em," said the old man.

The marshal shook his head again, stood up and kicked his chair back against the wall. "Very well, start raising them. I'll do everything I can. Make sure whoever comes is mounted and armed. We'll muster here in two hours."

Tate turned to stare out at the morning sun turning the drying clay streets to a faded yellow that ran along the white adobe walls toward a gentle bend, where a mission rose to mark the beginning of the plaza. *Morning in Thunder Run.* His eyes were fixed on the distant crucifix atop the mission, and as the others were still pondering the marshal's last words no one noticed that his thin, pale lips were moving.

Morning at Thunder Run began with the first gray hint of dawn. In the beginning they heard only a muffled shifting about as the air filled with a sense of impending storm. Seth was strangely aware that the long, brittle silence was about to be broken but could think of only one word to whisper to the others. It carried like a moan of wind throughout the house.

"Ready!" A piercing war cry broke out, followed immediately by a pounding of hooves that swelled in volume until it seemed that a thousand drums were descending on the house from all directions. Warriors assaulted the house on every side and fired through the barred windows. The clamor was deafening, and the roar of gunfire drowned out any other sensation. Seth and Jason worked frantically in the poor light to make their bullets count. The women had been warned not to fire blindly, to wait for sure targets, to remember that every cartridge spent reduced their failing supply. But targets were everywhere. The painted faces howling in the misty dawn were coming up to within a few feet of the gun ports and windows. The women, their fears now dissolved in a bile of rancor and cauterized by rage, drove them back with screams of defiance, but their guardian spirit had vanished. An arrow with a cruelly barbed head tore Carlota's shoulder open, and Bessie, trying to fight from both gun port and window, took a bullet in her thigh. Yet their fiery defense was all for naught. The attack was only a cover for Black Horn and five of his Kiowa braves, who rode in from the rear, swept along the front of the house and hurled bundles of pine faggots against the heavy front door and the latticework surrounding it. Jason saw fire arrows streaking toward him like live coals from the murky yard. Almost immediately a faint glow could be seen as a tiny flame began licking upward against the oak door. "Hurry! Water!" cried Seth to Isabelle, who had seized a gun and was trying to level her sights on the riders galloping by. She flew to the kitchen and grabbed one of the pails Jason, in anticipation of fire, had set out filled and ready. Returning, she found Jason pulling back the big iron bolt that secured the door. To reach the fire, the door had to be opened. Seth, coming over to grab the knob, shouted to Jason to stand back as he pulled the door ajar just enough to allow water to reach the flames without exposing himself. But it was a near-impossible task; slugs and arrows were hitting the door like hail and the fire was spreading dangerously to the latticework beyond the frame. The first pail doused the center flame, but the dry pine faggots, combustible as straw, were still smoldering on either side, some heaped against the latticework. Their persistent attempts kept the fire from creeping up the door, but the outer frame and the latticework were both beyond reach. The fire began to roar as it spread into the distant piles of faggots, igniting tiny flames that licked at the far edge. To clear these faggots and douse this flame, Jason would have to reach outside. He and Seth exchanged a helpless but meaningful glance. The door had begun to splinter from the torrent of bullets directed against it and the rising flames would make him an easy target, but that fire, if unchecked, would eat through the door frame, collapsing the door and spreading into the house.

By now the warriors were circling farther out, gathering to watch the fire gain strength, some still sending burning arrows into the faggots that already had tongues of small flames eating toward the upper part of the door. Seth, knowing Jason was going to risk the fusillade coming against the entrance to get at the fire, was shouting for Bessie and Taska to come to the front. Taska hurried in while Bessie, bleeding but grimly propping herself behind a gun port, sent Kate. Isabelle seized her rifle again, and Seth signaled the two women to take positions at the front windows. The were to fire at the horde of braves gathering beyond, hoping to scatter them and thus give Jason, who had picked up the pitchfork, a chance to knock the burning faggots away without facing a gauntlet of lead.

Jason knew that the fire against the door could be a death sentence to anyone reaching outside, but there was no choice. He must open the door, push the burning sticks away from the woodwork and pull back as quickly as possible. He saw what his father was trying to do, and as Seth and the three women opened fire he cracked open the smoking door and thrust the pitchfork out. Miraculously, he knocked away the nearest bundle with his first try, but the burning sticks leaning against the far edge of the frame were beyond his reach. Twice he grappled with the pitchfork, but to no avail. Then the heavy firing from the front window seemed to bring about a lull in the returning fire. He could see the flames mounting beyond. They were beginning to lick at the far frame; the moment to save the door was passing. Grimly he decided he had to risk it, for in a minute or two it would be too late. Pushing the door open he extended himself enough to push away the burning faggots, all but one. He should have let it go; it was asking too much, more than half of his body was already exposed. But his mind said that one burning stick was as bad as twenty. He couldn't see the flashes of gunpowder lightening up the dark reaches of the yard, but he winced and stiffened as the whining slugs tore open his shoulder and punctured his side. Aware only that he was being hurled against the door, he collapsed. The door was standing open, and instinctively he had tried to fall inward. Throwing caution to the wind, Taska raced to the opening, reached out for a hand hold on his belt and pulled him back over the threshold. Seth helped her work him clear while Kate closed the door. Blood covered his shirt as shock and pain rose into his eyes.

Isabelle ripped desperately at her skirt and petticoats, tearing them into strips to bind his wounds, but Seth, looking down, knew that, though binding might stop the flow of blood from his shoulder, the wound in his side, from which a string of ugly matter had started to ooze, was the forward paw of death. His son was dying. The last living hope of Thunder Run, that softspoken, ever-smiling boy, whom spirits as different as Tate and Taska openly loved and whose brief life had been blighted by family conflicts and calamitous years of war, was going. A cold stab of grief impaled his father. Only the impending crisis contained it and forced it back. Without Jason the end was suddenly closer and more certain. Seth looked at the women bending over the body writhing in pain, their strained words fighting to sustain hope, not yet accepting what the signs said had to be. Strangely, he felt no need to console them, to tell them that his years of fighting savages had taught him that death was not the worst alternative to be faced. Since that haunting prayer, which still taxed his mind, he felt they had accepted all that, that they were ready for what was waiting beyond the fire that was now blazing up beyond the door.

Tate and the old agent and his sons had spread out through the town, announcing in bars and on street corners that volunteers were needed to save the women of Thunder Run. Normally every Anglo-Texan male would have hurried forward, as ready to protect their womenfolk as Islamic fanatics to defend the Koran. But these were not normal times. The whole South was under siege. The war was reaching a bitter end. Rumors of Yankee occupation had people anxious about not only their own but their families' fates. Stories of looting, drumhead trials, executions and even rapes were rampant. Not a few, remembering the government's repeated warnings, questioned why so many women had allowed themselves to be caught there. Finally, the size of the Comanche force inevitably got out and experienced fighters knew that the rescue was going to be a dangerous and costly affair. After two hours, only sixteen men had appeared armed and mounted before the stable. They watched the marshal coming up, viewing them and shaking his head. "I was afraid of this. We wouldn't stand a chance," he declared solemnly. "We've got to wait for more help."

"If we wait, my people have no chance at all!" snapped Tate.

"Son, I can't ask men to risk their lives trying to do what can't be done. Bravery isn't the question. Odds like these only lead to dead heroes—reckon our people have enough of 'em already."

Tate, grimacing and gripping his sides, stared up at the sky. It was nearing noon. How long could the ranch hold out? His mind was having trouble functioning. He had to force away thoughts of his mother or Taska in Comanche hands. Even the first inklings of such scenes threatened his sanity. Yet, relentlessly, time was running out. Every hour, every minute gnawed away at hope, bringing the nightmare closer, exhausting the ranch's frail means to resist those final moments of terror that would leave all those he loved grotesque in death.

Smoke was swirling into the house and nearly blinding them as the great door broke from its burning frame and fell in. The screeching and shouting of Indians, watching with menacing glee and firing their weapons against the red dawn, made Isabelle think of demons rising from hell. Seth had pushed the furniture into a line across the center of the room and, knowing the Indians would now concentrate here, had brought the women forward to crouch behind it. Pieces of the burning door had broken off as it fell and were smoldering in different parts of the room. Seth used the pitchfork stained with Jason's blood to lift them and hurl them out through the opening. The heavy firing had stopped as the Indians waited for the flames to render these *tejanos* helpless. But in the end the adobe and slate did not burn and the fire, consuming only the wood that formed the entrance, petered out, leaving behind a great opening through which the women could see the sunlight pouring down on the yard and through which the Indians could now attack in numbers impossible to stop.

But suddenly a strange quiet reigned and only a few braves could be seen watching from a distance. Seth knew that the Comanches, now confident, were taking time to powwow, to make speeches and savor the coming victory, but the onslaught could not be delayed for long. He made a count of their remaining bullets. There were forty-five rifle shells left. For their pistols he counted only sixteen. Speaking hoarsely, he issued orders that of themselves told of their desperation. Only he, Taska, Inez, Bessie and Kate were to shoot at the attackers. It was too late to depend on lucky shots. Dead Comanches were their only hope. Isabelle, Elena and Carlota were given the pistols and told to shoot only if the Indians broke into the house. Isabelle, bending over the inert form of Jason, who had been moved into the kitchen, listened mutely, her eyes rising to Elena's to find this curiously courageous woman offering her a look that carried the compassion of a psalm. Like Taska, some of the women had dressed in jeans to travel, while the rest wore skirts full enough to cover their legs while riding. But now their clothes were disappearing. Carlota had torn off her blouse and stood in her bodice as Elena tied a strip of cloth around her torn shoulder. Bessie had slipped off her skirts and petticoats to get at the wound in her thigh. Elena and Taska, in the heat of the fire, had thrown off their cumbersome blouses and camisoles, and had only a slim piece of cloth around their chests to hold and cover their ample breasts. But the women's faces, even those of the wounded, remained stoic. Seth, watching them hurrying about seemingly indifferent to their growing nakedness, was again quietly stunned at how much these women resembled Comanche warriors, determinedly stripping themselves down and preparing for battle.

Seth was right. The Indians were parlaying. But it was not to make speeches or gloat over these doomed whites. Black Horn, his countenance fierce with wrath, was demanding that Blood Hawk be the first to charge the now-vulnerable house. Blood Hawk, desperate to escape the dark threats of the day before, had foolishly shouted that it was his medicine and not Black Horn's brave sortie that had brought the fire that had opened a hole in this enemy's stronghold. "Come!" roared Black Horn. "If your great medicine brought that fire, then let it now turn back the bullets of these cowering whites!" Most of the Kiowas were up, shouting and pounding their weapons to show that they shared their chief's anger.

Red Claw stared at Blood Hawk. He was sure now that the medicine man could be disposed of without risk. But his sharp eyes had picked up a complication. Blood Hawk was a Comanche, and there were Comanches in the band who, though bitter at the failure of the medicine man's powers, did not care for these high-handed Kiowas mocking him and demanding his death. Red Claw was too canny a leader to risk dissension in his ranks, for now his mind had turned to more important matters than the disgraced medicine man. This ranch had still not been taken, and the rider who had escaped the night before was surely going for help. Red Claw did not think help would come anytime soon. Like other Comanche leaders, he was well aware that the white soldiers had disappeared from the frontier, and that more and more forays against the settlements were going unpunished. Yet he was taking no chances. He had sent scouts to watch the Medina crossings. If a sizable force appeared, his band could easily disappear into the vast empty reaches that swept westward to the Nueces. Still, to leave without a single white scalp, leaving innumerable dead braves behind . . .

Now Red Claw rose to speak. Out of respect the Kiowas settled down. "Black Horn does well to share his anger with his brothers, but let us hear the spirits speak. Blood Hawk said his medicine will be strong again when the sun is high in the sky, for it is then that the spirits will turn to him again. When the sun stands overhead, Blood Hawk will go against the *tejanos*, and if he speaks truth, and if his medicine protects him, we will know his spirits are no longer angry. Black Horn must know that great wisdom lies in these words."

Black Horn wanted to say *Bah! Stop protecting that coward, or I will rip his scalp off before your eyes!* But Black Horn was seasoned enough to understand the wisdom of Red Claw's words. The minds of these wild young warriors, many from the barren Llano Estacado, were still dangerously primitive. Obsessed with magic and enslaved by superstition, any mention of angry spirits disturbed them, sapped their fighting edge, made them wary of their leaders. But Black Horn, for all that, could not quite contain his fury. He raised his war club with its many-colored scalps, which was the only medicine he believed in, and shouted, "I will not wait for that coward! The time to attack is now! A great victory is ours. Come, a Koh-eet-senko will show you how he destroys his enemies."

It was the sheriff returning that noon who started a strange process in Tate's mind. Fatigued, his nerves wrought up and his heart beating with an uncertain rhythm, he felt himself torn between a desire to race off with whoever was willing to go and at least share the fate of those at Thunder Run or, by some miracle, turn up enough guns to save them.

The arriving sheriff looked drawn and dejected as he nodded to the marshal and slumped resignedly into his chair. It was clear that he had just returned from an overnight mission that had failed.

"You sure look beat!" said the marshal.

"I am," replied the sheriff. He rubbed a darkly weathered hand over his face. "Should have more sense than trying to catch smugglers when half the country is in cahoots with them!"

"Shouldn't you be working with a posse?" inquired the marshal, his mouth firming with concern as he spoke. "Sounds like dangerous doings."

"Oh, I ain't looking for a fight, that ain't the answer. Remember, some of 'em are pretty tough *hombres*, most of them wanted by the law on one side of the border or t'other and all of them armed to the teeth. I don't honestly believe they want a fight either, might bring in troops and 'twouldn't be good for business. I'm just trying to find out how the goddamn stuff gets into town and who's ramrodding their outfit."

The marshal grunted. He had heard about this widespread smuggling problem while in Houston and knew that the government had unofficially thrown up its hands. "As long as folks are willing to pay top prices for those goods," he muttered, "there's no way in hell you're going to stop 'em."

"Reckon so," mumbled the sheriff.

Tate left as the marshal started relating the crisis at Thunder Run. He was too tense for talk and his mind was spinning as he worked to pull some wild and seemingly irreconcilable thoughts together. He had again mounted the black, which, in spite of his frustrating morning, he had rapidly rubbed down, fed and partially rested. He was now heading for the Mexican part of town. He had never been in the Casa Colorada but had heard it had once been an unsavory saloon, a haunt for outlaws and drifters dodging the law. Now it seemed the Mexican community had turned it into a social club, or so it was claimed, though many neighbors scratched their heads in doubt.

Tate had never found it easy to think about Elena D'Valya, whom he resented as he resented Seth. They were two people who had hurt his mother, two people who had selfishly put their sinful, sensuous lives before, as he saw it, duty and even pride. But he also knew that there were many, like Taska, who liked her and many among the townspeople who admired her. He also suspected that there were few men who at one time or another had not relished the thought of making love to her. The sheriff's talk of smugglers had brought to his mind what was common knowledge to many at Thunder Run. Elena's kinsmen, aided by powerful contacts below the border, had been smuggling for some time. What hung in Tate's mind was the sheriff saying these smugglers were well armed. What disturbed him was that most of them were wanted by the law. He didn't know what could come of these unexpected, hurriedly assembled bits of information, but he was desperate enough to pursue every hope.

The Casa Colorada had not changed much over the years, except that Julio Spinada, whose hair was now pure white and who had once been afraid to enter the premises, sat in a large comfortable chair arranged in a far corner where he could view events in the main room. There was still liquor to be had, but unruly behavior was not allowed. The "club" was simply a friendly place where townsmen, wishing to get out of the sun for a companionable glass of wine, could gather.

Tate's arrival put an end to several conversations taking place in groups around the big room. The man behind the counter, who had been resting on a high stool, came to his feet. He took an uncertain step toward the end of the bar that Tate was approaching, but his eyes swept to the corner where Julio was seated. A short, squat man who was standing beside Julio nudged Julio's arm.

Tate realized they recognized him. Few people in town didn't, but their eyes were full of suspicion when there should have been only curiosity. The bartender deliberately remained a few feet from the bar.

"*Sí*, señor, you wish something?"

Tate looked about, unsure how to start. Somehow he had to reach Elena's kinsmen. They were the only ones likely to listen. His most pressing hope was that they would have some authority. Without much thought he said, "I have a message."

In the silence that followed the bartender repeated, "A message?"

"Yes."

"For whom?" requested the bartender. Now he showed a trace of interest and had slowly moved up to place both his hands on the bar. Tate was sure that a shotgun was lying somewhere behind that bar, but he held his breath as he said, "It's from Señora D'Valya."

There was a quick shuffling in a distant part of the room and Tate

made out an old man with snow-white hair tapping the floor with
his cane as he made his way toward him. The man moved with effort,
but his expression was not unfriendly.

"*Buenos días,*" said the old one as he came up. "You are Tate
Redmond, yes?"

"Reckon you know who I am," returned Tate. Although they had
never met, Tate knew he was talking to Julio Spinada and that Elena
and Julio were in some way related, and that her kinsmen were surely
involved in smuggling.

"What is this message?" asked Julio, not missing the tightness and
urgency in Tate's expression.

"The señora and her friend Carlota are trapped at Thunder Run."
Suddenly Tate found himself remembering that Seth and this Julio
were known to be longtime friends. "Seth Redmond, his son, and
seven women are trying to hold off a flock of Comanches, but they
aren't going to make it without help."

Julio abruptly drew himself up like a man trying to deal with a
shock. For a moment he seemed speechless, but then, turning to the
far end of the bar where a door led into some hidden rooms, he called
out, "Ricardo! *Ven acá!*"

A tall, handsome man appeared at the door and, seeing Julio standing next to Tate, came hurriedly to his side. "*Qué pasa*, Papa?"

"Elena, Carlota, Señor Redmond, they are all trapped by *los indios!*
What can we do?"

Ricardo looked puzzled. "*Indios?* How many?"

"Too many to give them any chance without help," said Tate.
"They've been fighting them off for a day now . . . they've got to get
help, and soon!"

Julio and Ricardo stared at each other. In different ways both of
them truly loved Elena and treasured their long friendship with Seth,
but was this not asking the impossible? Even riding fast, Thunder
Run was at least six or seven hours away. To gather a force big enough
to count would take time. And what kind of force could they mount?
Bandits, gunmen and a tough bunch of ex-*vaqueros* that made up
their smuggling organization. Julio realized that such problems could
not be discussed in front of Tate, so, openly showing he was seriously
concerned, he took him by the arm. "Believe me, friend, we will try
to help. But you must go now, we will send word."

"Send word?" Tate, aware of every passing moment, looked ready
to collapse.

"Yes. Where will you be?"

Tate could only cling to hope. "At the stable near the sheriff's office."

Mention of the sheriff widened Julio's eyes. "I see." He bit his lip, mumbling to himself, *"Dios . . .* always such difficulties." Then, louder, "But, please, now you must go."

"I'm going," said Tate. "But for Christ's sake, remember we have to hurry!"

Julio, signaling Ricardo to follow him, turned away and, with his cane rapping a quick beat on the plank floor, led the way to the hidden rooms.

29

Jason died in Isabelle's arms with Taska kneeling beside him, her voice breaking with anguish as she pleaded with him to live. The man who had been her lover but hours before could now only grip her hand feebly with the desperate uncertainty of the blind. The stabbing heartbreak of the moment froze every face in the room. There were no words to fit the horror of watching the once-handsome Jason, his tunic soaked in blood, his wretched attempts to mouth words thwarted by the dark froth rising to his lips. It was impossible not to feel his suffering as one's own, as those watching saw death slowly drain the agony from his eyes and raise its seal to his lips. Only Seth, who had immediately understood that his son had taken his death wound, found words to break the long empty silence. "May the Lord take him to rest in peace," he murmured. Some of the women mumbled prayers to themselves. But death had joined them, Jason's still-open but vacant eyes a reminder of its stark finality. No matter how often their grimly subdued prayers were repeated, they no longer brought consolation.

The low thunder coming from along the creek bottom was their only warning. Black Horn and his Kiowas, pressing to the front, were singing, but many Comanches, crowding forward to share in the kill, were adding to the roar. Seth knew the crisis had come. With all the other buildings burnt to the ground, the big tree in front of the house now seemed immense. Some of its lower branches, he noticed, almost reached the eaves of the house. He called to Bessie, whom they had moved into the main room and fixed in a defending position. Though being helped by Kate, she was still holding the hatchet along with her gun. Seth warned both Salinger girls to watch the tree, for he suddenly sensed that it made the house more vulnerable.

Black Horn, born to war and holding high rank in a nation of warriors, had drawn three black stripes across the mask of vermilion paint that had already removed all humanity from his face. Seth, seeing him and realizing that here was a Kiowa war chief about to lead the attack, tried to shoot him from the saddle, but Black Horn was suddenly on the ground and running forward to drop behind the body of a dead horse. Other warriors were slipping from their ponies and crawling up. Now Seth knew they were getting close enough to reach the wide opening left by the fire in one deadly rush. About him guns began to roar. Inez killed a warrior who was trying to reach the rock base of the forge left in the burnt-out farrier shed. Bessie killed another who was trying to slither up behind the great tree. Seth shouted at them to hold their fire until they were rushed. Every rifle report in the house subtracted from their meager supply of shells. But the women had quickly grasped the coming threat, and Elena, Carlota and Isabelle, still shaking but grimly leaving Jason's body, moved up behind the others with cocked pistols. The rush would bring this howling enemy into point-blank range. Seth, glancing behind him, decided they were ready, whatever the odds.

Black Horn, though merciless to his enemies, was if nothing else a brave man. Though only a handful of his warriors squirmed into position, he did not hesitate. With a great war cry he rose and started forward. Immediately he was joined by others, some coming from far back. Again the screams rose until they were deafening, and garishly painted faces turned men into hideous gargoyles. There was a split second when all in the house seemed to draw in their breaths before Seth shouted, "Now!" The uproar of so many guns going off indoors at once nearly ruptured their eardrums, and the smoke of burning powder stung their eyes to tears. But the volley lifted running warriors from their feet and killed others in midstride. Yet Black Horn, his rifle and war club held high, had reached the opening. Bessie, who could not move, failed to duck away and took another bullet from him, this one through her arm. Other warriors were struggling to force their way in beside him, but the women, fighting down a brief flash of panic, were now shooting with icy precision. The attackers, though increasing in numbers, were coming straight into their guns, and the bodies of wounded braves had started collecting before the opening, an ominous warning to those still coming up. But Black Horn, shouting his rage, was only beginning to fight. Having emptied his gun at Bessie, he was turning to use his scalp-covered war club on Kate. Elena, coming up behind them, shot him in the back and he went to his knees. Two other braves were now fighting inside, one grabbing Taska by her long hair before Inez raised her rifle muzzle to his ear and fired. The other, shooting wildly, put a bullet through Carlota's leg before Seth shot him down and drove him backwards with his foot, making him fall outside. More warriors were coming up, stumbling over the unburned heavy base logs but finally gaining the room. Yet the women would not yield, and when Bessie, finding Black Horn on his knees before her, screamed and used her hatchet on the back of his head, and Kate and Taska, who had been saved by her mother just moments before, each killed a brave, Seth was hit with a wild hope that they might survive. What was saving them was the fact that no Indian could fight until he reached the room. Even so, they were punishing the defenders. Seth, Isabelle and Kate had all suffered flesh wounds, and Elena had taken a bullet through her hand. Seeing Black Horn's head in a pool of blood at Bessie's feet, Seth bent over, swept up his sacred war club and flung it as hard as he could through the opening. Covered with dyed scalps, it sailed through the air, drawing the eyes of the approaching warriors and bringing a strange hush over the fighting. To the primitive mind, that scalp-laden war club flung into their midst by the enemy's hand could only mean that Black Horn, their proud war chief, one of the suicidally brave Koh-eet-senko and one of the few warriors who could not be replaced, had fallen.

Had the Indians truly been soldiers, their attack might still have succeeded, for they would have fought together for a common end. But at heart the Plains Indians were gladiators and each fought in his own way, always mindful of his own glory. Without the rallying cry of a fighting leader urging them on, the attack slackened. Braves had started kneeling outside the house and firing into the opening. The three left fighting inside were already wounded, one managing to stab Inez before Taska killed him. The other two, stumbling over Black Horn's body and falling onto Bessie, wounded her again as she tried to fend them off. Seth and Kate, caught reloading, could not shoot fast enough to save her. Elena, switching her pistol to her good hand, coolly killed them both before they could rise again.

Not waiting for Seth, Taska had started shooting at the braves kneeling before the house, but Seth suddenly shouted to them to hold their fire and signaled everyone to the floor. He was down to three shells. They had to stop shooting at once, or in a moment or two they would be helpless. But the wild abandon with which Black Horn had opened the attack was gone. The warriors were beginning to hesitate, then withdraw across the yard, some stopping to fire a vengeful shot at the opening, none of them realizing the implications when their fire was not returned—none, that is, but the watching Red Claw and the sorely distressed medicine man, Blood Hawk.

Ricardo looked anxiously at his father's distressed face. He knew what was coming. He circled the desk and started speaking as he closed the door. "Papa, stop looking like that. It's hopeless! We can do nothing."

"We must try!"

"How are we going to try? Who of our people will help us to save *gringos?*"

Julio leaned forward and rapped the desk with his cane. "Who will help us? Every unwashed pig on our payroll—that's who! Every whoring wagon driver and those expensive and always thirsty guards will help us! *Dios*, for years they and their hungry relatives have basked in the sun of my generosity. If they refuse I will go to my *compadres* below the border and explain the need for another arrangement."

"You would do that?"

"*Sí!* I will do worse! I will remember those who don't help. They will no longer drink wine and smoke expensive cigars in my club. They will soon have to head for the border . . . and keep riding."

Ricardo shook his head, his face drawn tight with worry bordering on fear. "Papa, it's not that simple. Too many of these men are wanted by the law. They can't show up in town carrying guns, not without chancing trouble and maybe worse with the sheriff. Our contacts report that even a marshal is in town now."

There was a moment of silence. The old man pursed his lips up in thought. "I will take care of the law."

Ricardo leaned across the desk. "Papa, if you say anything they will know who is behind these armed men, who is running the club."

"Ha!" Julio's face lifted in scorn. "Every bartender and whore in town knows. If the stupid sheriff would ask one of them, instead of riding 'round the *condado* all night long talking to himself, he would know too. I think he is too dumb to catch me."

Ricardo sat back, closing his eyes and taking his head in his hands. "Papa—what if it's already too late?"

Julio came to his feet, clasping his side and pointing his cane at his son. "It will be too late if we keep talking. Now, Ricardo, listen to me! Get all the runners out! I want every man they can reach by sundown! And whoever says they will not come—tell them old Julio is collecting names!"

The tension in the sheriff's office that afternoon had the marshal wondering if Tate wasn't edging into madness. He greeted the news that help from Austin would be arriving in "a day or two" by pounding his fist on the wall and shouting that that was as good as giving those at Thunder Run up for lost. He wanted to take the sixteen volunteers and go himself but discovered that a few, upon hearing the marshal explaining the numbers they faced, were having second thoughts. The sheriff reckoned that three or four of them, bothered by the delay, had already drifted away. Tate, thinking his trip to the Casa Colorada had been a failure, was ready to leave alone when a buggy pulled up before the sheriff's office and Julio stepped out. Seeing the star over the sheriff's office, the young Mexican driving him was anxious to leave, but Julio patted him on the knee and told him to wait.

The sheriff immediately recognized old Julio at the entrance and rose to his feet. "Well, I'll be damned! What in the creation brings you here?" His tone was a mixture of faint suspicion and open curiosity.

Leaning on his cane, Julio swept off his hat and bowed benignly. "Señores," he addressed both the sheriff and the marshal, "Julio comes as a good citizen to offer his services to the law."

The sheriff could not help looking a little startled. "Services? What services?" No one noticed the marshal's eyes widening slightly as he saw Tate stepping over to stand beside Julio.

Julio smiled at Tate. "This young man tells me there is much trouble at Thunder Run. Many of my friends would like to help."

The sheriff still had a puzzled look. "Your friends?" He knew Julio had unmistakable power in the Mexican community, but that didn't explain what he was hearing. "And why would your friends want to help us?"

"Señor, we are an emotional people. A close relative of mine, Señora D'Valya, is at Thunder Run, and of course Señor Redmond is a *compadre* of many, many years." His hand rose to his heart. "Their deaths would be a very grievous loss to my people. That is why I ask you to let us help."

The sheriff was still confused but answered, "Well, hell, yes, we could sure use more help. How many men are you talking about?"

Julio put a hand over his eyes while he counted to himself. "We are trying hard," he muttered with a tinge of uncertainty, "but we hope to have eighty . . . maybe ninety men here by sundown."

"Sundown," repeated Tate, his breath sounding short, the word almost hissed. "We'll have to ride all night to be there by morning."

"*Amigo,* we are aware of this," said Julio as though he wished he could say more. His hand took a comforting grip on Tate's shoulder.

The sheriff and the marshal exchanged glances. "Don't reckon there'll be any need to deputize them all," said the sheriff. "This is an emergency. They're citizen volunteers."

The word "deputize" brought a curious expression to Julio's face. He bowed to the lawmen once again. "There is just one more thing, señores. A few of my friends . . . as I said, we are very emotional people . . . have had in the past . . . shall we say . . . little differences with the law. Surely you will be gracious enough to put such trifling matters aside till our friends are rescued, eh?"

There was an awkward silence as the sheriff and the marshal again exchanged glances. This time it caused a shift in both their expressions. It was the marshal who spoke first. "Trifling matters? Trifling matters? Tell me, señor, what might some of these trifling matters be?"

"Does it matter?" said Tate.

"Son, we're the law here . . . differences with us are never trifling. We owe it to peaceful citizens to see that criminals are punished for any crimes."

Tate was growing tense again, and his eyes were suddenly fixed on the two lawmen. "And what do you figure you owe the people at Thunder Run?"

The sheriff did not like the way Tate was standing; he had seen that stance before. It sent a tingle down his spine. "We know what we owe them, son. Don't worry, we aren't letting our hands be tied by any stupid regulations. But there's one question that's got to be answered." He turned to Julio. "Have any of those 'friends' of yours ever killed a lawman?"

Julio thought for a moment, then slowly shook his head. "No, señor, none of my friends have killed a lawman in this country."

The marshal, still eyeing Tate, elected not to ask about Mexico. "That's good," he said, " 'cause the penalty for killing a lawman around here is death by hanging. The law permits no exceptions." To the sheriff's relief, Tate had relaxed his stance.

But he had an eerie feeling his hunch was right when he heard Tate saying, "Funny, I was just calculating what that penalty might be myself."

It was Taska, peering through the kitchen window, who first saw what she thought were riderless horses. They were coming at a full gallop, heading for the house. She screamed to Seth, "Horses are coming!"

Seth knew at a glance that they were not riderless. Displaying their incredible horsemanship, Comanche warriors were hanging down the offside of their mounts, making themselves invisible to the house. In a flash he saw what they were after. "They're making for the tree!" he shouted. "Taska, Hurry!"

Sweeping under the tree, the Comanches leapt for the heavy bottom branches and swung themselves upward. With the agility of monkeys, the young warriors scrambled into the higher limbs, working to keep the thick trunk between themselves and the two rifles firing from the front opening. Quick as they were, two were not quick enough. Seth dropped one before he could swing his leg up onto the lowest branch, and Taska blasted another trying to take hold of an upper limb. But then two more shots were wasted as the Indians were suddenly too high to see or were safely behind the massive trunk. Seth didn't know how many had succeeded in escaping their fire, but it was surely four or five. That was certainly enough. Now there was no way to keep them from attacking the roof.

Surely it was only delaying the inevitable, but Seth, driven by the resolute expressions of the women, had to try. There was only one point from which the roof could now be fired on, the adobe hut. No one needed to be reminded of the scoopway. It was now part of the family legend. But leaving the house and fighting from the hut forced racking decisions. Seth looked at the seven rifle shells they had left. Elena, seeing his quandary, urged him to take them all, saying that if the Indians broke through the roof the pistols would serve better.

No one mentioned that there were only eight cartridges left for the pistols.

"I'd best go with you," said Taska hurriedly. "There's a door and two windows at the back of the hut. They'll know you're there as soon as you fire. You'll need someone to protect you from behind."

Inez swiftly pulled her daughter back and took her place beside Seth. "No, I go! Is better Taska stay here, she shoots with pistol best." No one denied it. Frontier logic ignored all sentiment and pride. Survival depended on any and all concessions needed for defense. "I take only three bullets," finished Inez, picking up a pistol.

Seth looked at her stolidly, but his voice was hoarse and strained. "Shouldn't you take one more . . . in case . . ."

Inez looked through the opening at the little adobe hut where she and Brandy had spent so many happy years. "No," she said. "I am *católica*. Only God says how Inez dies."

The frightening sounds of warriors who had tied ropes to the upper limbs and were swinging over the roof and dropping onto it warned Seth to hurry. He thought of kissing Elena and even Isabelle good-bye, but the setting and the complications of many painful years made it impossible. He slipped into the scoopway and, with the already wounded but still undaunted Inez hard behind him, made his way to the hut.

From the south and east they came, mostly in twos and threes, riding slowly, guardedly watching figures coming toward them on every street they entered. Some had come from the hovels and wine-smelling slums beyond the San Francisco mission, some from the way stations or dark, windowless cantinas that dot the trail where it bends down toward Laredo. Some were night traffickers from the Mexican barrios of San Antonio, men who seldom saw daylight and seemed uncomfortable on sunlit streets. For the most part they were hard-bitten, heavily mustached *mestizos*, though a few were almost hairless, grossly tattooed and of mysterious lineage. Many carried bandoliers or machetes tied to their belts. All were heavily armed. They were as swarthy and evil-looking a band as many passing Anglo Texans had ever seen, and more than one citizen stopped to stroke his chin with mounting concern as they passed. They ran from scarred, evil-looking border types to shady, dandified sharpsters expecting easy pickings at a fiesta. One had a guitar strapped onto his back beside his rifle.

They gathered along the river, on the same stretch over which Julio had once followed Seth, Tanner and Purdy through the mud. Now broad cobblestones lined and contained the flow of the river and Julio sat on the Casa Colorada's weathered porch, his hands on his cane, his head erect but resting on his hands. He talked sternly to the runners as they came up and kept reminding Ricardo to keep count.

Many had long distances to come, and Ricardo was getting annoyed as his father sounded more and more impatient. "Papa, they cannot fly!"

"Let these *cochinos* come as fast as they come for my money," spat Julio.

Not surprisingly, in view of Julio's threat, there had so far been no refusals except for one man, whose wife had screamed that it was impossible. Drunk for three days, he could not sit on his horse. Yet at sundown only half the alerted and expected men had arrived, and Julio, seeing Tate coming excitedly through the slowly swelling crowd, could only take a futile grip on his beard and sigh.

By the time Seth got into position in the hut the braves had torn the slates up and were hacking at the narrow beam which, when broken, would leave a hole large enough for them to shoot through or even drop through to the floor below. One was already pointing a rifle downward when Seth opened fire. The first brave, hit in the back, threw up his hands and tumbled to the edge of the roof, where the badly rusted cast iron drain caught his loincloth and held him for a moment before the weight of his body tore the cloth loose and he dropped to the ground. The surprise that struck the others caused wild confusion. Exposed on the roof, they were helpless. Seth shot another, and two others, running a step or two, jumped desperately to the ground, rolling to freedom as Taska, forced to conserve her meager supply of cartridges, could not shoot. Only one had the presence of mind to strike again at the beam, making the hole wider, and without hesitation he leapt down to the floor below. Taska shattered his skull with her first shot, and the other women, who moments before had been tensely watching their ceiling being chipped open to let in the sky, shouted in frenzied relief.

But the stratagem brought the consequences Taska had predicted.

Red Claw now knew a *tejano* had somehow gotten into the hut. Though he grimaced and stamped his foot in anger, both sides knew that whoever was in that hut was isolated and as good as lost.

The shock and discord this surprise caused was soon over. Angry braves surrounded the hut and began to move closer. There was no way the rear could be protected. Inez lay down along the wall that reached out to form the alcove. Seth, seeing the roof of the house clear of Indians, turned to help her. He could see the rear door, but the window facing the burnt-out stable was cut off by a screen standing behind the bed. Shots began to raise powder from the wall behind Inez. She did not fire back until a painted body rose to fill the window. Then without waiting she blazed away. The body fell back but was swiftly replaced by another. Again she fired, but now a warrior was standing in the rear door, holding a spear which he hurled at Inez. Seth killed him but he could see the heavy spear sticking up, still vibrating, where Inez was lying. Two more braves came up to the rear door, but Seth winged one and both figures dropped out of sight. Suddenly there was silence. Seth could hear Inez choking as though on her own gorge. He wanted to call out to her, but something told him that an Indian, who had slipped in through the second window, was crouching behind the screen. Suddenly two figures appeared at the corner of the porch. He had to swing the rifle to the front again and press in another shell. He had only three left. There was no point waiting. The Indians were hugging the adobe wall and stealthily approaching the front entrance. He thrust the rifle out of the window, turned it flush against the wall, and fired. The agonizing yelp that went up told him he had hit living flesh. Knowing there were two, he was bracing to reach out for a second shot but Inez' pistol went off behind him. He spun around to see a brave, his hand still holding a scalping grip on her hair, slumping dead beside her. She had killed him with her last bullet.

From the house the shooting around the hut was watched in agony. No one spoke, but all were counting the shots, knowing their ammunition was running out. Taska's pistol couldn't help from this distance, and when silence finally came a pall settled over the staring faces, for it was impossible not to think that Seth and Inez were either mortally wounded or dead.

But in the hut Seth was holding his breath. Mysteriously, the Indians had pulled back. Minutes ticked by as he listened to the faint moans and strange gulpings from Inez. He called to her in a low voice but got no answer. Slowly he raised himself up until he glimpsed her lying on her back, one hand against the wall. The hand was covered with blood, as was the near side of her face. He sensed that she was either dead or dying but couldn't risk the noise of moving toward her. He settled back again. After several minutes he thought he heard her muttering weakly in Spanish. After that there was only silence. When he could not resist easing up for another glance, he could tell from the arch of her neck that she was dead.

The next hour saw a morbid mood spread through the house. Bessie, blood seeping from her many wounds, was losing consciousness. Taska, standing on the table and trying to board up the hole in the ceiling, only managed to loosen another beam that finally swung down of its own accord, making the hole larger. Now they could see a wide expanse of sky, cottony clouds drifting across a dome of cobalt blue. But unexpectedly the mood lifted again when Isabelle and Elena made almost simultaneous discoveries. Isabelle, who had left Bessie's bedside choking with grief, was tearfully covering Jason's body when her hand, passing over his shirt pocket, felt the hard forms of four rifle shells. They seemed meaningless till Elena, who had never taken her eyes off the hut, gasped and exclaimed, "Seth! I can see Seth! He's just inside that front window!"

All eyes were now riveted on the hut, and Taska, always thinking ahead, reached for the rifle shells. "I'll take them to him. He must need them desperately by now."

Taska was already heading for the scoopway, but Elena was too fast for her. "No. I'll go. You must stay here. You're the only one who never misses with that pistol. We can't afford to lose you."

Taska studied her for a moment. "My mother is over there," she said. But Elena's answer told her she was putting sentiment before the code of survival.

"That's the reason I must go."

Taska handed her the shells.

In the Indian camp, a furious Red Claw was facing the unpredictability of the primitive mind, a constant and dangerous factor in Plains warfare, for it could appear at critical times, causing defeat and occasionally disaster. Here, however, Red Claw sensed that his troubles were being fanned by a wily old medicine man he should have killed hours ago.

There were several braves who knew that the hut had been empty when they had first attacked. How two armed *tejanos* had reached there without being seen jolted their notions of natural law, especially when Blood Hawk made it known that only powerful medicine could have brought such a thing about. But Blood Hawk was only desperately trying to save his own life. Like Red Claw, he saw signs that the *tejanos* were running out of ammunition. But he also sensed that many of the braves were growing disgruntled at this long, costly siege. A feeling that the spirits were not with them was beginning to simmer in their eyes. More than one warrior returned from the battle pounding the earth with his war club or rifle. It was not hard to plant a fear that the enemy possessed a dangerous magic. Red Claw was looking at the sky. Instinct told him that the unexpected and, for the warriors, mystifying gunfire from the hut had opened a fissure of doubt. It would take careful handling to see that it did not spread. He would not ask the braves to attempt reaching the now-gaping hole in the roof until the *tejanos* in the hut were dead. It would work out, and these *tejanos* would pay for the pain they were causing him. Beyond, he could see Blood Hawk chanting to the sun. Many of the braves, even some Kiowas, were watching him. How his people thirsted for magic! Promise them strong medicine, and they would spread their robes before a prairie fire and confidently fall asleep. Well, his scouts had reported no signs of trouble. He could wait. What he needed for the moment was a distraction for these warriors and a way to silence that desperate and designing Blood Hawk.

Elena emerged from the scoopway spotted with dirt. Seth, stunned to see her, immediately waved her to the floor. His bearded face seemed almost cruel with incredulity. What was she doing there? Was she insane?

Elena held out the four shells. Seth took them, appearing to be grateful but secretly unable to believe they could change matters. Though they could see no Indians, they spoke in whispers. Elena could not help herself. He looked so pathetically old and worn that she reached out and hugged him. Awkwardly he returned her embrace. They stared at each other until she had to escape the hopelessness in his eyes and asked, "Where is Inez?"

He gestured to the rear of the hut, his voice barely audible. "She's dead." Elena, unable to see Inez as the body of an Indian was lying near her and shielding her slight figure, crawled toward her. Coming closer, she could see something on the white adobe wall rising next to Inez' head. Her breath caught in her throat as she realized it was crude, misshapen words written in blood; *Enterreme con Brandy*. She could not keep a tear form trickling down her cheek.

Seth, seeing her, was too spent to deal with emotion. He called to her lightly, "You must go back."

Crawling to him again, she begged quietly, "Come with me."

Seth had already thought of retreating through the scoopway, but what was the use? The Indians had already broken through the roof. Only the threat of his gun was keeping them from attacking there in force.

As long as he held this position, they had to hesitate. Besides, if he left, they were sure to enter the hut and find the scoopway. There would be no returning. All he could do was buy a little time, time that was telling him something his mind could no longer deny—that somehow Tate had failed and they were doomed.

Elena wanted to say something as they sat together, her hand on his, aware now that Seth was convinced their death was certain. But all she could summon up was a thought that had seized her when first she had sensed there could be no escape. "Seth, when two people have loved each other they've lived the only part of life that matters. Death can't change that."

He stared at her, amazed that even in this grotesque setting, in this hopeless moment, he could still feel her strength. Strangely, he could not resign himself to the thought of her dying. "Elena, please, you must fight to live, you mustn't die."

"Fight to live?" She gave him a wan smile. "Life without you, Seth? What am I to do with such a life?"

Seth could only stare at her. He sat there, a man already accepting death, drained of every dream and denied even the will to change his destiny. Exhausted, his mind kept trying to pull together the stray ends of his life. But he was lost, very lost. Was forgiveness a thing a man could offer or even receive? He knew life forgave no one and nothing. It canceled out no memories. They burdened one to the grave. Death, he decided, was surrendering that hunger for the exalted visions of youth which men discover not even a second start at life restores.

He could only turn to her now, feeling that somehow she had always perceived and understood the unspoken and unresolvable conflict that had paupered his spirit and corrupted his years. But beyond that he could not choose. He had to utter the words that had lain so long in the now-distant shadow of the event that had sundered his life. "Be kind to Isabelle," he whispered. "I once loved her very much."

The shadows slipped in from the plaza and the sun's rays lifted to highlight the eastern sky. The marshal watched the sheriff returning from dinner, a toothpick hanging from his mouth. The sheriff nodded as he pulled out the pick. "Anything new?"

"Reckon they'll be coming soon." The marshal spoke casually but looked preoccupied, as though bothered by matters beyond talk.

"That kid's got his share of grit," allowed the sheriff, using his pick, "gettin' those greasers to help him like that. That Julio must sure set a store by that Redmond bunch."

The marshal grunted.

"When do you 'spect we'll start?"

"Soon as he gets back. How much do you know about that fellow?"

"Tate? Enough to wish he'd move to another town." The sheriff turned to study the other man. "You got some notions 'bout him?"

"Only that he and the law are bound to have it out one day."

" 'Spect so." The sheriff was now sucking his teeth. "Who's gonna win?"

"Nobody. But somebody is going to die."

The sound of running horses made them both glance toward the plaza. Tate, followed by Ricardo, was coming toward them at a brisk clip.

Tate was on the ground as the black pulled up. "We're leaving down the Buena Vista in an hour. They're still coming in, but we can't wait."

Ricardo nodded to the two lawmen. "My father sends his regards."

The marshal nodded back. "Just remember, I'm commanding this relief force. How many men do you have?"

"Ninety . . . maybe a few more. I'll be riding with you."

The marshal smiled cryptically, "Know what you're getting into, mister?"

"Reckon so . . . I once wanted to be a Ranger."

Shadows were also creeping across Thunder Run. Drums were sounding in the Indian camp as Red Claw, knowing the time for careful handling was over, watched Blood Hawk finish his spirit dance. Blood Hawk had been holding his bear-claw necklace, which everyone knew was his most powerful medicine, up to the setting sun as he gave his chant.

Blood Hawk knew he had to prove that the spirits had given him real power or he was doomed. And he knew, without looking at the menacing Red Claw, what his test would be. His one hope was that the *tejanos* were out of ammunition, but of this he had to be sure. In desperation he thought of Ice, that long-dead war chief who had offered the bear-claw necklace to the youth who could kill the Ranger captain. He remembered how he had won that necklace and how it had long been looked upon as great medicine. Now, as he finished his spirit dance, he called to a group of young warriors he had already singled out. "Here! See this great necklace! It is strong medicine, it has great power. It will go to the brave who brings Blood Hawk a *tejano* scalp from the house. The spirits will make this young brave a great warrior!"

The young warriors started muttering excitedly to one another, but Blood Hawk could see them eyeing the necklace, seized by every young warrior's dream of achieving high rank as a warrior, of proving himself worthy to be a war leader one day. The necklace and the bravery that would be attached to winning it would be an important beginning. As he turned to see Red Claw smiling grimly at him from the deepening shadows, he knew that for the moment he had won. But as the young braves began to huddle together in twos and threes, the air was split by the wild cry of a sentry who was standing on a rise along the creek. Immediately the warriors ran for their horses, a confused and scowling Red Claw among them.

Seth lay alone in the hut trying to cling to sanity. There was no way out of this death trap. Why the Indians were waiting, he did not know, but surely they had sentries out. If help came they would know about it hours before . . . and by watching their movements, so would he. It was two full days since Tate had left. There could only be one explanation why they were all dying here, abandoned. Tate was lost. A lump formed in his throat as he realized he had once wished for that boy's death. Was the fulfillment of that wish now to be his punishment? He could only think of the silent, brooding, close-lipped young fighter, bitter and lonely like something deep within himself— something, he sensed, that made that dark, restive youth more his spiritual son than easygoing Jason. As evening drew near he could stand it no longer. The sound of flies gathering over the dead bodies behind him began to sicken him. His one glance at them left him near-nauseous. He could see insects crawling over the hardened blood on Inez' face. Suddenly he asked himself what he was waiting for. Death? Soon he would be lying there like Inez, his eyes open but sightless, unable to see the vermin coming to burrow into his body and feast on its corruption.

He shifted around quickly, for he had seen something moving in the overgrown garden plot. After a minute's study he knew it was a horse, a pinto, one of those left running loose when the warriors had leapt into the tree. He began to think about reaching it, of escaping, of trying even at this late hour to reach help. Scant as the chance was, it was still a chance and he'd at least be out there trying, not crouching here losing his sanity. Feeling slightly dizzy from the hot, fetid air of the hut, he could not fight back a sense of being old and weak. To firm up his resolve he had to think about the women again. Any risk that offered a glimmer of hope had to be taken. What encouraged him was the quick spread of lengthy shadows that promised a slim chance of approaching the pony unseen. He decided not to take the rifle. It would be awkward to use on horseback, and if he were caught a few shells would not save him. Habit more than reason made him feel he should still have some sort of weapon. After a brief glimpse behind him he decided on a war hatchet he saw in the belt of the dead brave. Keeping his eyes off Inez' body, he pulled it out.

Miraculously, he slipped out of the rear door of the hut and into the long growth of the deserted garden patch without creating a stir. He could hear a drum in the Indian camp. Perhaps their attention was being held by some ceremony. But surely they had sentries watching the creek and the ground beyond. Moving on all fours through the heavy weeds, he finally reached the pinto. The horse raised its head and fixed him with a nervous eye; its tail, which had been flicking the green bottle flies vigorously, became still and hung down straight. Seth knew the horse had been feeding on something green and lush, for it did not move. Patiently he waited, keeping his eyes down and ignoring the animal until its appetite for the foliage mounted again and it lowered its head to munch. He timed it perfectly. With one slow step toward the horse, he bounded as lightly as he could onto its back and, grabbing the single rein, swung its head toward the creek. Almost immediately the sound of horse's hooves brought a figure up from the thick undergrowth that lined the water. Seth was heading directly toward him. He pulled the war hatchet from his belt, hoping the brave would not have time to sound an alarm. But it was no use. The sentry, unable to get his gun up, let loose a great shout just before the war hatchet cut through the bridge of his nose, reached into his brain and killed him.

Seth knew stealth was worthless now. He had to get away from the ranch and attempt to hide, but the pinto, though doing its best, surprisingly had only a short sprint of speed and as Seth crossed the creek he knew he would need a miracle to escape. As he raced along the far bank, he saw they had already reached the creek and were starting over to cut him off. He found himself racing along the same hard, flat stretch on which Tate had approached the gully. He did not need to be told that the gully was there. He had thought about having it filled several times. He thought for a moment that if he could jump it, precious ground would be gained, but the laboring pinto's limited strides warned him that that was impossible. They were on both sides of him now and gaining. As he sped along the embankment a realization gripped him that any choice he might have had to cut away from the creek's edge was gone. He had to jump the gully, or he was lost. Seth had always been an outstanding horseman, with undisputed talent and a lifetime of experience. Desperately he called on all of it now. He gathered the galloping pinto up, preparing for the jump, and the gallant little horse responded with everything it had, willingly sailing into the air. But this was not the powerful black, the long-legged stallion with the spirit of Pegasus in its limbs. This was an Indian pony of sound but accidental breeding. The helpless animal slammed into the opposite bank with such force it broke its neck, and Seth was jolted free to sprawl stunned and just as helpless on the bank. It was there, shaking his head to clear it and looking up, that he realized Red Claw was standing over him.

30

Even the insidious drug of fatigue could not dull the new fear that arose with darkness. The scream of the sentry and the clamor of running and yelling braves had them all straining to look northward along the creek. It was the same uproar they had heard the night Tate had slipped away. What did it mean? Only Elena, who could no longer catch glimpses of Seth peering from the hut, suspected the terrible truth.

They could hear the excited yips and the high, piercing tones of victory chants as the braves returned to their camp, and almost at once large fires threw angry yellow pennants up against the night. For the first time shrill cries began to sound and a heavy persistent beat from the taut buffalo-hide drums began to vibrate through the house.

Poor Bessie kept drifting in and out of consciousness, one moment conscious and even sipping water and the next dropping off again. She was burning up with fever. Kate, like the others, exhausted, lay down beside her sister from time to time, secretly vowing that if the savages broke in they would not take Bessie alive.

Taska understood when Kate asked for two of the cartridges. Mutely she handed them over. She loaded the remaining half dozen into a six-gun that she slipped into Jason's holster, now hanging from her side. Taska and Isabelle had stood watching the Indian camp. They could see the firelight and hear the drums, but it was only because an Indian occasionally leapt high into the air that they knew they were dancing. No one could bring herself to say how terrifying these signs were. No one mentioned Seth. No one would admit to the suspicion that was devastating them all. An hour went by and the uproar seemed to lessen. Kate came out of the bedroom, her face creased and drawn by the stress of caring for her stricken sister. Bessie was awake again but in terrible pain. Kate had suddenly remembered that she had left packed in the wagon a small bag her doctor husband had left with her. She thought it might contain some laudanum they could give Bessie. There were also some salves that might help their flesh wounds. She wanted to fetch it from the wagon, but Isabelle said no. Kate should stay and comfort Bessie. She and the young, agile Taska would go down to the cellar and search for the bag. No one said anything, but clearly they would need a lantern to see in the dark cellar, and the threat of attack never left their minds. Elena and Carlota watched Taska place the six-gun on the smashed table. They knew it was for them to guard the front opening. The two women grasped each other's hands in the darkness as Elena helped the wounded Carlota to the same chair that Bessie had occupied. Outside they could see the pale light of an almost-full moon softening the night.

With Isabelle carrying the dimmed lantern behind her, Taska led the way down the steep ladder to the rear cellar. As the dark hulk of the wagon loomed before them, Isabelle turned the lantern up. Without hesitating, Taska climbed into the wagon. At that very moment they heard a terrible scream from above.

Kate had settled down beside Bessie again. There was just enough light from the rising moon to see the dim outlines of the room. Their eyes, adjusted to the dark, picked out each other's features and Kate could see Bessie's mouth twisting in agony. She had to keep the pistol near her, and she had laid it on the bed between them. She was not afraid to die. Life without Jed was unbearably lonely. There was never a morning she greeted with joy. She wished it were her and not her beloved sister lying there dying. Then, as she reached for a wet cloth for Bessie's feverish head, it happened.

Two braves swung their rifle stocks against the bottom slats that barred the windows. The lightly nailed pieces of wood loosened, and a second blow sent them flying across the room. Before Kate could get to her feet one had climbed into the room, the other hard behind him. Kate jumped up in such shock she forgot the gun. They grabbed her, one seizing her hands, the other stripping the few clothes from her body. Bessie, looking up, heard her sister's screams as two figures started forcing her to the floor. Kate, fighting desperately to reach the gun, had pulled them almost to the bedside. Though they had torn her clothes off, what they had really come for was her scalp. Panic brought Bessie's head up as her hand groped for the gun and found it. Lifting it, she saw a figure before her that was too large to be Kate and fired. The brave toppled over, but the other, realizing the danger from the bed, turned and smashed his rifle stock downward. Instinctively Bessie fired again, killing him, but his blow landed, crushing her forehead, and she never heard the screams breaking out in the front room.

Carlota was the first to hear it. A rustling at the far end of the burnt-out wall told her that someone had stepped on unburned pine twigs. She hissed to Elena, "Someone's there!" A split second before Kate's scream rose from the bedroom, three braves came out of the night and rushed through the front opening. Immediately they seized the wounded Carlota and started to drag her outside. Elena would have gone for the six-gun, but it was still across the dark room and Carlota was screaming for help. In spite of her wounds, the aging woman battled them as best she could, biting one brave on the arm until he yelped in pain. But already Carlota must have known it was useless. She could not escape three savage youths intent on her life. She did the only thing she could to avenge her death. Elena, coming fearlessly after her, heard the low crack of Carlota's derringer and saw one of the braves slump to the ground. Elena did not need Carlota's example. She already had her own derringer out. As she finally reached her dying friend, the brave who aimed a hatchet at her head felt a small metal barrel pressed into his chest and its low crack was the last thing he heard before entering oblivion. But the third brave was now dragging Carlota's helpless body away as Elena heard screaming and shouting behind her. Taska and Isabelle, calling frantically, had come up from the cellar to find Kate standing nude in the bedroom doorway, sobbing that Bessie was dead. But Taska, hearing Elena still pleading for help, raced outside with the six-gun. As she appeared, Elena was already starting in the direction into which Carlota had been dragged. Taska hurriedly caught up and followed her into the dark. With the moon bathing the landscape in a now-ghoulish light, they stared ahead to see, a few feet beyond, a pale body lying on the ground with three dark figures bending over it. As they moved toward it, Taska scattered the dusky figures with a shot. But coming up, Elena could not help letting out a short, choking scream. Even in the meager light the sight was hideous. Carlota had been stripped, even her bandages torn off. The sadistic need of these savages to strip their victims never stopped. The ragged-edged white top of her head showed that she had been brutally scalped.

The shock of seeing her almost swept their own mortal danger from their minds. Warriors were slipping through the darkness on both sides of them. Taska suddenly pulled Elena up and shouted at her to run. But now the braves were running too. Two of them were close to cutting them off. Taska gauged them as best she could in the darkness and fired. Each one stumbled and fell in turn. But others were appearing out of the dark, and as they neared the front opening she had to run and fire point-blank into the night to drive them off. In the back of her mind she knew the fighting was over—for the last time she pulled the trigger she heard only an empty click.

It was well after ten o'clock when Tate, livid with rage, finally mounted the black and led them out of town. They had lost an hour or two listening to the marshal foolishly trying to get this motley mass of men, with no military training, into some sort of military order. To complicate matters, everything the marshal said had to be translated into Spanish by Ricardo, who, because of their numbers, had to shout at the top of his lungs. The sheriff had arranged for some old men and boys to stand around with torches, but there was far from enough light. Faces flickered in and out of the shadows. The sheriff, sitting astride his horse with the depot agent's sons, saw many profiles he wanted to remember and a few he would have taken into custody if the temporary amnesty hadn't tied his hands. Not a small amount of time was lost answering questions shouted back at the marshal, the darkness giving the questioners welcome anonymity. This time Ricardo had to translate into English. How long would this mission take? How well were *los indios* armed? Where were all the brave *gringos?* The marshal dismissed all such questions with the obscure and visibly disturbing assurance that they would be answered in time. More difficult to deal with were the complaints that several of them had just ridden long distances, at a forced pace, and their horses needed feed and rest. This stumped the marshal and kept him puzzling to himself until Tate came close to demanding he start moving at gunpoint. Fortunately Julio, who had foreseen this problem, appeared driving twenty fresh horses his henchmen had been rounding up all day.

The marshal figured he could guess, after viewing this maverick bunch, why Mexico had lost so many wars. He only hoped that if they wouldn't follow orders they would at least fight when confronted with armed Comanches.

His signal to Tate, who was fuming and regarding him with a grimace that combined menace and disgust, said it was finally time for him to take the point and lead off.

By now Tate was pounding the saddle horn in frustration. He desperately wanted to be at the ranch before dawn. If the ranch were still holding out, dawn would certainly see Red Claw making an overwhelming attack. He hurried the black along, cursing to himself. Dawn! He glanced at the stars and at the angle of the rising moon. He wondered what the coming day held in store for the family he had left besieged. If they were still alive, he was finally coming, having done all that flesh and blood could do, but it would take more than luck to get him there by dawn.

Something more deadly than exhaustion now crept through the darkness of the house. With Bessie's and Carlota's deaths, the spark of hope their presence had helped keep going slowly flickered out. Isabelle, helping Kate cover Bessie's body, knew that she could stand no more. Jason, her son, and Bessie, her best friend, were dead. In her heart she knew that Seth was too. This horror must end. She saw Taska resignedly putting down the empty pistol. Their last shred of defense was gone. There was nothing to save them from the savages' hands now, nothing to spare their bodies the nightmares the next assault would bring. It was the tired voice of Kate, who was kneeling and praying for her dead sister, that caused something to snap in Isabelle's brain, something that carried her overwrought mind over the brink. At Kate's mention of God she screeched hysterically, her face and limbs going out of control, "No! No! Don't you call on God! There is no God! And if there is, he has forgotten us! Forgotten us as he has this whole filthy, evil land where he has created nothing but fear and loneliness and painted heathens who disgrace your body and eat your flesh! We will die here! Do you hear that? We will die here! Forgotten! He has forgotten us!"

Elena rushed in to grasp her and hold her as tenderly as she could.

Isabelle, surrendering to her embrace, sank onto the bed beside Bessie's body with her, sobbing in indescribable pain. Taska watched them breathlessly, but quickly stooped, pulled up Kate and hugged her too. The women stayed like that, clinging closely to one another for long minutes, till finally Elena said, "Isabelle, when all those we love are dead it can be no great tragedy to die. But please, let us try to go as they did, fighting . . . fighting for whatever we have left of life." She paused and guided Isabelle's head to her shoulder. "In spite of what you are thinking, I'm very frightened, but if I am to die I want to face death as bravely as dear Carlota did."

In spite of her pain, Isabelle could not help thinking of Bessie, ill and dying, forcing herself to lift that pistol and fire to save Kate. Taska thought of her mother insisting on taking her place in the hut to protect Seth, and of Elena relating to her the words her mother had scrawled on the wall with her own blood. Surely kind, devoted Brandy had ignored death only a few feet away to protect her from Riff Connors, and Jason, that ever-searching, ever-lost boy who she had loved since childhood and who, in last night's passion, had finally become hers, had died trying to save them all.

Kate, looking at Bessie, had already decided that she was ready for death, but she was a Salinger, and remembered her father, old Adam, telling her that Salingers never died willingly. In her heart a small but growing anger over Bessie's death was spawning a hope that as she left this lonely world she would take at least one more Comanche with her.

Dawn found them just across the Medina. There was no way to keep such a large company from straggling, bunching up, and slowing one another down. At the marshal's insistence they halted several times to close dangerous gaps between those who were close up and able to stay behind Tate and those further back, who were unable to see him in the dark.

Tate could wait no longer. Knowing that the sheriff could now lead them to the ranch, he announced that he, Ricardo, the agent's two sons and some of the volunteers were going to race ahead. He thought they could reach the ranch in a little over an hour. The marshal, figuring that Tate was going no matter what was said, made him agree that if the Indians were still there he was not to attack until the main body came up.

Tate knew that if the Indians were still there his prayers would have been answered.

Remembering Isabelle's outburst, they did not pray during the long hours of what could only be their final night. The women sat together grimly. Not even the iron clamp of fatigue could induce them to sleep. They saw no signs of Indians. Only once during the night did they hear feet approaching and moving about some twenty feet before the front opening. But then there was nothing but silence. It was only with the first light of dawn that Elena realized that something had been placed out there. She called to Isabelle, and together they stared into the darkness. They were there for several minutes as the dawn brightened and a distant shifting of low banked clouds suddenly increased the light. Then they saw it—saw it in all its horror, saw it and knew a freezing tightness in their breasts that no emotion could release. A spear had been struck into the ground like a stake, and at its top was Seth's ghastly burnt head, his face staring at them in an agony even death had not ended.

Neither screamed, nor did Taska or Kate, who came up behind them and stood paralyzed with shock. It was many moments before anyone could speak. Then it was Isabelle, her face ugly with revulsion but hard as granite. "Devils!" she rasped. "Devils!"

Elena had to keep her eyes from focusing. She could not connect this heinous sight to the man she loved. She had to screen it out, protect her memories from it. It was too obscene even for death. It belonged to a stygian world of deformed, demented ghouls, a world beyond the human conception of evil.

It was Taska who saw something coming from the Indian camp, a figure walking alone, moving warily but coming toward them. Silently they stood there, watching it come closer. Only when it reached the tree did they shift slowly back into the room.

It was Blood Hawk. His face was painted red with black circles drawn about his eyes and down the rim of his jaw. A strange medicine sign rose in yellow strokes across his chest. His hair had been dressed with little bones and hung down into two large braids that reached beyond his shoulders. He carried a rifle with Carlota's scalp hanging from its barrel. Even in the poor light they could see the vivid streaks of silver standing out in her dark hair. He seemed uncertain. He had planned to walk through the front opening, gambling they were out of ammunition. He had deliberately approached in the open and very slowly, giving them a chance to shoot while he was still at a distance, but no shots sounded. Yet going through that front opening was dangerous. If they had only one shell left, they could not miss. Better to drop down through that gaping hole in the roof, take them by surprise. He would have his rifle ready. Behind him the cold eyes of Red Claw and his many warriors were watching. Now they must see that his medicine was still strong.

Grabbing one of the ropes still hanging from the tree, he boosted himself up to the lower limbs. From there he grasped a higher hanging rope and with ease swung himself onto the roof.

The women heard his feet landing above them. No words passed between them, but Isabelle picked up the ax. Elena, after a moment's study of the room, pulled the pitchfork from a corner. Kate now held Bessie's hatchet, and Taska had picked up a stout piece of wood that had once been a table leg.

They stood about, looking up at the wide gap in the roof, staring at the brightening sky. In silence they heard Blood Hawk's footsteps approaching the hole, but none flinched when his body came plunging through it.

Remarkably, he landed on his feet and was already bringing the rifle up when Elena, standing behind him, drove the pitchfork into his back with every ounce of strength she had left. Its sharp prongs penetrated through his chest as he collapsed onto the floor. He fell turning his head, trying to look up or behind him, but Isabelle swung the ax with fury and almost severed his twisted head from his body. Still holding it was some flesh, muscle and cartilage, but Kate, flailing away with the hatchet, soon severed it completely. Taska dropped her club and, grabbing the two long braids, swung the head around, covering them all with blood, and flung it back up through the hole to the roof. It sailed into the air, landed and rolled to the edge where it tumbled over, the long braids catching on the rusted iron drain as the gruesomely painted head dropped a foot or two and hung there, twisting gently, finally stopping to look squarely at Seth's, just twenty feet away.

It was enough for the warriors. Too much had gone wrong here. There were evil spirits in that house. This was a bad place to die.

Red Claw could only smile grimly as scouts rushed up to tell him that riders were coming but were still an hour's ride away and no threat. He was a practical man. He was, after all, not without consolations. He had killed some *tejanos,* tortured one to death and gotten rid of Blood Hawk. He had not been defeated, and there would be another day. Best of all, when they returned to their village, that fleshy Mexican girl would be his.

Inside the house everyone stood as though frozen, hardly breathing, waiting tensely for the final assault. They heard a few low shouts and then the rumble of hooves going away from them. What seemed a last muted signal from some distant scout faded, and then came a silence so deep it seemed that death had descended onto the plains beyond. Minutes crawled by at an agonizing pace, each seeming like hours. Surely the savages were grouping for the last fatal attack. Above, through the great hole in the roof, they could see the deep scarlet of dawn giving way to a faint flush of fuchsia spreading before an edge of pale blue. A fresh breeze sprung up, and the great tree in front could be heard gathering its branches to meet it. Another time it would have been only a subtle warning that the weather was changing, but now in the silence that followed Elena slowly straightened up, relaxing her death grip on the pitchfork. Not only Blood Hawk's blood but leakage from her own wounded hand had made the handle sticky. She cast it from her and it clanged to the floor, its tines ringing almost musically for a second or two. She turned to Isabelle and their eyes met in an understanding that could not be measured in words. Somewhere a distant bird began chirping, and the great tree, bending with the wind again, groaned. None dared to whisper, but all of them knew it was over.

Isabelle put down the ax, unconsciously wiping her hands on her bare side and thigh. She reached out to Elena with first one hand, then the other. Together they started to move slowly through the front opening to stand among the dead bodies and the lance holding Seth's head. Taska and Kate followed, and as feeding birds began to flash about the desolate yard, the women stood holding one another and staring up at the sky.

Tate, pushing the black for all it was worth, willing to kill the great horse if that was necessary to reach Thunder Run, had far outstripped the rest of the party. As he galloped up the wagon road toward the ranch, he could see four naked figures striped with paint standing before the house. With a cold clutch seizing his heart he immediately thought they were Indians, that he was too late, that the nauseating scenes of carnage were over—that he had failed. But then through the tears of his rising anguish he glimpsed what he knew was their skin. They were women, almost naked, and they were white. What he had thought was paint was blood, and they were holding one another and looking up at the sky. He stopped a distance away, and now he made out Taska, Kate and Elena, who held his mother in a close embrace. They simply stood there; nothing moved except the great tree above them, which kept swelling with the rising wind. The weather was changing; to the west clouds were piling up in enormous billows that the rising sun had dappled in gold, golden billows soaring up like mighty ramparts as high as the mind could dream.

Suddenly he caught light filtering through the tree, forming an aurora around them. Amazingly, he saw something he had missed in the bitterness and brutality of these hellish days. It was these women, and many like them, following their men and enduring the frontier, who were the real conquerors. It was their strength and devotion that would finally overcome this wilderness. Men returning to the frontier would surely force peace again upon these fierce tribesmen, yet sow into every treaty the seeds of future strife. But the women, defying death and defeat with their gift of life, would bring forth a new breed of natives—children who, forsaking their parents' roots, would call themselves Texans. They would look upon this war-torn country as native soil. In spite of trials and perils, they would come to cherish and defend this awesome land. They would finally bring peace to its cruel, war-weary frontiers. And wasn't he, Tate Redmond, one of that new breed?

He would always remember the women standing there, staring up at that sky, their eyes revealing that whatever they had suffered through, they must go on. He would always see them clinging together on the land they had fought for, the land that had defeated their men, the land that had nurtured their hopes and shattered their dreams. In his mind they would always be there, with their wounds and their memories and their lonely fears for the future, and he would always treasure that sight of them, bloodstained, their arms about one another, facing the coming day, bearing their secret heartaches of grief and pain but looking upward in victory.